The Gaia Collection

The Gaia Effect, Book 1

The Gaia Project, Book 2

The Gaia Solution, Book 3

Claire Buss

Published by CB Visions in 2020

First Edition

www.cbvisions.weebly.com

Cover artwork by Ian Bristow

Other works by Claire Buss:

The Gaia Collection
The Gaia Effect
The Gaia Project
The Gaia Solution

The Roshaven Books
The Rose Thief
The Interspecies Poker Tournament – The Roshaven Case Files No. 27
Ye Olde Magick Shoppe

Poetry
Little Book of Verse, Book 1 of the Little Book Series
Little Book of Spring, Book 2 of the Little Book Series
Little Book of Summer, Book 3 of the Little Book Series
Spooky Little Book, Book 4 of the Little Book Series
Little Book of Winter, Book 5 of the Little Book Series
Someone, Mrs Latimer Had a Fat Cat, Cozy Cat Press

Short Story Collections
Tales from Suburbia
Tales from the Seaside
The Blue Serpent & other tales
Flashing Here and There

Anthologies
Underground Scratchings, Tales from the Underground anthology
Patient Data, The Quantum Soul anthology
A Badger Christmas Carol, The Sparkly Badgers' Christmas Anthology
Haunted, the Sparkly Badgers' Anthology

The Gaia Effect

The Gaia Collection, Book 1

For Kevin

Chapter One

CORPCHAT: *Corporation's 150th Anniversary Lottery winners receive Collection today - what would you choose? Join the virtual conversation in social hub beta throughout the day.*

The light-alarm filled the square bedroom with a warm yellow glow that grew brighter and brighter. Kira Jenkins snuggled deeper into the sheets, reluctant to move. Suddenly she sat up, brown eyes wide open, her short brown hair sticking out at odd angles.

'It's today, it's today,' she squealed, turning to shake her husband. 'Jed. Wake up! It's today!'

Jed grunted, still half asleep. 'Synth-caf?' he asked as he opened one pale grey eye.

Ten minutes later they were both air washed and dressed in standard Corporation tunic and trousers, dark blue for Jed and a mix of forest green and cream for his wife. They stood in the tiny kitchen area of their open plan living space, glancing at each other in excitement as they tried to do normal things like eat breakfast and drink their stimulants. Kira fished out her handheld from her tunic pocket.

'Hey, Jed, look - we made top sweep.'

She held the touchscreen up for Jed to see, then began flicking through her dailies and saw one from her friend Ruth.

MADSR: *Luck K, you'll be a great Mum - so proud xx*

Kira saved the message. Her friends, Ruth and Martha firmly supported the unusual choice she'd made to parent naturally. Most of their family and work colleagues thought it was peculiar. Putting the handheld back in her pocket, Kira picked up her cup and held it in both hands, sipping the hot drink looking up at her husband over the rim.

'You're not likely to get pulled into work tomorrow afternoon, are you?'

'No, should be fine love.' Jed picked up his breakfast bowl. 'Who's coming again?'

Kira rolled her eyes at him in mock exasperation as she ticked the guests off her fingers.

'Our parents, your sister, Pete obviously, Martha and Ruth and her latest fledgling, some of my work colleagues, some of yours – oh, and your cousins. Did you know they're studying at The Academy?'

Jed nodded; his mouth full of food. Before he could speak the vidcom on the wall in the lounge area chimed. Kira walked over and touched the illuminated panel to accept the call.

'Hi Mum.'

'Oh my goodness.' Jean Bishop's smiling round face and twinkly brown eyes appeared on screen. 'I'm so excited for you. Are you ready? Do you think she'll have brown hair like you or will she be darker like Jed? It's so exciting. Did you think about getting the neural jack like I told you? I don't know why you want to be so natural, it's not normal honey. Did I tell you about that girl over on Fifth? Terrible time she had, just terrible and that was all because she didn't want the NanNan...'

Jed watched in amusement as his wife tried to get a word in edgeways. He kissed her on the cheek, motioning that he had to leave for work, but she stopped him by waving at the vidcom link. It was flashing blue. Another call was coming through, this time audio only.

Jed answered the call on his ear comm, the implanted chip that allowed the user to receive and make audio calls. 'Hello?'

'Good, I got you before work. Your father and I have been talking, Jeddidah, and we agree. It's not the right time. Don't you think you should wait? Early Collection never goes well. You recently became the youngest detective on Force and raising children is hard work - do you really think you should be splitting your focus now? At least choose the early years option, it's a wonderful time saver…'

Jed rolled his eyes at Kira as he left, taking the call with him. He walked down the corridor to the lift, descended four floors into the foyer of their apartment building and out through the double doors, murmuring in all the right places until he reached the public skimmer stop.

'Mother, I have to go to work now. We will send an update out later, I promise.'

Jed grinned to himself as he cut her off mid-sentence – parents. The grin slipped, soon that would be him.

__MADSR:__ Bridget Mahoney reads excerpts from 21st century top literature.
Tonight @ Community Hub Four. No virtuality!
This is a sit in event hosted by HistoryNow - click to register.

Sitting on the floor and not bothering to look up, Ruth Maddocks called out through the thick mane of light brown hair hanging around her face.

'Dina? Share my latest. I need to sweep it.'

A younger woman sat on the teacher's chair. She was pixie like – petite with short cropped blonde hair and baby blue eyes. With a small sigh Dina Grey picked up her hand-held and began scrolling.

'The one about boycotting the 150th Anniversary celebrations?'

'No – but do that one too,' Ruth said, trying to tuck her unruly hair out of the way and looking up at her PhD student. 'Bridget's lit reading – she thinks that because it's not virtual more people will come.'

Dina kept scrolling, looking for the right sweep.

'Who knows - they might.'

'Are you going?' Ruth arched her eyebrow at Dina.

'Well... no... I... you see.' Dina started making excuses before she realised Ruth was teasing. 'I'm going to work on my thesis tonight.'

'Dina,' Ruth let out a heavy sigh. 'You can have fun you know. You should come outside with us tonight.'

'Outside?'

Ruth stood up and went to the open door. She poked her head out and looked up and down the corridor to make sure no-one was about before keying the classroom door shut and walking back to Dina with a mischievous glint in her brown eyes.

'We're going to the beach.'

'Beyond the forcefield? Is that allowed?'

Ruth coloured slightly and chose not to answer, instead she began to pack her bag.

'What about the radiation levels?' Dina asked in concern as she gathered her own notes.

'I've being going out of the city for years and I'm okay,' Ruth said, spreading her arms out, bangles clattering. 'There is no toxicity – people need to get a life.'

Dina shrugged, tucking her hair behind her ear.

'Shouldn't you be teaching me good Corporation values?'

'Just because I teach history at Academy, doesn't make me an old Corp fossil you know,' Ruth retorted and started to shut down all her classroom connections.

'I know, I'm sorry,' Dina said in a small voice. She went to the door and re-opened it.

'Relax.' Ruth picked up her bag and followed Dina out of the classroom. 'Are you still coming to the party tomorrow?'

'If it's okay?'

'Yeah sure. I've told K you wanna ask questions.'

'I do.' Dina nodded, relieved at the change of topic. 'Do you think she'll have time?'

The two women continued chatting down the corridor, Dina worrying and Ruth reassuring.

Jed passed through security, looking up at the silver star shaped shield depicting the scales of justice and the sword of truth crested high up on the wall. The office was buzzing as he walked towards his desk.

'What's going on?' Jed nodded a greeting to his partner, Pete Barnes.

'We've got a top priority case meeting with the Chief,' Pete replied as he stood. 'Lucky us.'

Jed followed his partner into Chief Tony Minkov's office, surprised to see a Corporation Medical Agent standing by the side of Chief Minkov's desk. Usually you only saw them at autopsy.

'Sit down, Detectives.' Minkov's gruff voice sounded strained.

The two men sat down in chairs opposite the desk as the Chief, a short man with thinning grey hair and a thick moustache looked worried and shuffled his notes, unwilling to begin.

'Usual disclaimers, no interviews, no family involvement – this is highly classified. We find this bastard and we deal out justice.'

Chief Minkov gestured for the Corporation Medical Agent to address Jenkins and Barnes. Wearing standard black Corporation uniform, the young man held up a touchscreen and began to read.

'At three forty-five this morning a young woman was brought to

Corporation Medical by her parents. It appears she was attacked, whilst out walking, by an unknown male assailant and was violated sexually.'

The two detectives both leaned forward, intent on the details of the attack.

'The Corporation frowns severely upon such activity and wants to promote a clear message of harsh action. It has been approved that the assailant be terminated.'

Pete sat back in his chair and raised his hand to ask a question, but the Corporation Medical Agent ignored him and continued to read.

'Corporation will be recirculating the 'Why Walk?' Campaign throughout media sweeps.' He paused to pick up two info jacks from the Chief's desk and leaning forward, handed one to Pete, the other to Jed. 'Here are your info jacks with all the case details so far. Corporation is confident Force will catch this offender.'

With a nod towards the detectives, the agent turned, shook hands with Chief Minkov and left the now silent room. Pete bounced the jack in his hand before looking up at his boss.

'Who's the Vic, Chief?'

Minkov shuffled his papers again.

'At this time, it's classified.' He stroked his moustache, avoiding the gaze of the two detectives.

'How are we supposed to work the case if we don't know whose been attacked?'

'Review what you've been given,' replied the Chief. 'Get an ID on the perp. That's your priority. Dismissed.'

As they left the office Pete looked at Jed.

'Jenks, you believe this frag?'

Jed shook his head as they returned to their desks to plug in the info jacks. They were non-neural and slotted into the side of their consoles. Once loaded, there wasn't much information. The only real addition were hours and hours and hours of Drone TV covering the approximate area where the attack happened. Jed programmed the ident system to look for two people in the park at the same time and sat back to wait for the results.

ANTIC: *In celebration of the relaunch of the Why Walk? Campaign, Anti-Corp are holding a peaceful stroll through City Forty-Two. Stretch your legs and your rights, sign up now!*

'I see AC are already on the Why Walk? Bandwagon,' Pete remarked, checking the sweeps on his handheld as Jed stood up to leave.

'They don't miss a trick, do they?' Jed bent down slightly to check his console. 'The matrix is still running Pete, but I've got to go – you okay handling this for now?'

Pete gave his partner a mock salute as he continued to scroll the dailies.

Jed shoved his jacket on, trying to clear his head. It was such an odd case and it bothered him that he didn't know who the victim was. But he had other important things to think about right now. Hurrying past security Jed nodded at the guard on the desk. He had to make it to Collection on time, so he decided against taking the public skimmer.

City Forty-Two had a square layout with forcefield generators at each corner. Corporation buildings filled the bulk of the west side with Archive and Academy in the centre and residential flats beyond. The far east of the city was officially abandoned however some people did live there, the ones who couldn't or wouldn't conform to Corporation rule. Force Headquarters were located in the Upper North West, sectors First and Second, looking out over the city - set apart from Corporation yet protecting the citizens.

Checking his wristplant, Jed figured he could make it on time if he cut through Third, the advantage of using his own feet rather than following a skimmer rail. As he set off down the pavement a beautiful woman, with skin that glowed blue, brushed his hand as she walked past him. He jerked it away in surprise. Looking back over his shoulder Jed realised she had stopped and was staring straight at him with eyes sparkling like a thousand stars. He began apologising when a bee, an actual bee, zoomed across his face, taking his attention away.

'Did you see that?' Jed asked, turning back, but the woman had gone. Jed blinked in confusion. Must have been a new kind of advert he thought. The Corporation was always thinking up new ways to insinuate itself into your subconscious. But why a bee? The wristplant beeped a reminder for his appointment. Jed jogged through Third, checking the sweeps as he went – nothing about a bee. As he approached Fourth Sector and the blue-tinged, smart-glass fronted skyscraper - known as Collection Towers, Jed could see Kira waiting for him inside the large open plan lobby.

***PEBAR**: Good luck Jenks*

***CORP:** 150th Anniversary Celebrations continue with VR parade at 4pm – just jack in to join in, bring a friend and experience all the excitement inside your home. Remember the fallen, relive the final victory and rejoice with the founding of Corporation.*

'Hi, sorry, hon.' Jed hugged his wife. 'I got here quick as I could.'

'It's fine, they haven't called us yet.'

They stood to one side of the front desk while Kira rummaged in her bag for the necessary paperwork. Behind the reception desk a woman with immaculate black hair and wearing a crisp black Corp Medical uniform, waved them forward.

'Here for Collection?'

Kira and Jed nodded.

'Okay, I need your credentials. That means photo, biometric and employment plus evidence of good credits for increased living costs, as well as your references.'

The woman held out her hand, fingers grasping at the empty air whilst Jed found his ident and chip and passed it to Kira, her paperwork already in her hand. The woman scanned each item individually, pressed a few buttons on the screen in front of her, and sniffed.

'Lottery winners – the Jenkins?' Again, they nodded. 'I need proof of entry. This isn't enough.'

Kira looked at Jed, biting the corner of her lower lip.

'I didn't bring it,' she said in a small voice.

Jed grinned and took out the winning card from his back pocket.

They hadn't even entered the Anniversary Lottery, thinking it was too small a chance to actually win. Someone had pushed the card through their door on the eve of the Anniversary celebrations. Jed thought it was Kira's mother, but despite being asked numerous times, she was not admitting it. The woman behind the desk swiped the card and passed it back.

'Your references are Miss Martha Hamble and Mr Pete Barnes. Neither one related to either of you, correct?'

They nodded.

'Hmm, seems to be in order. Do you want standard manuals, neural jacks or the full package which…' The woman looked down.

'You're not covered for, so it'll be extra.'

'Standard,' Kira said, a touch defiantly. Both wanted to try the less popular natural route. They could always change their minds later, and besides, this was how their ancestors had done it. Kira had been researching the archives, something her position as junior city archivist allowed. It had been a different world back then, but the way women had looked after their babies personally had resonated deep within her.

The woman sniffed again.

'Suit yourself. I'm guessing you want the VR experience? Nine months of pregnancy in nine minutes?' Not waiting for a reply, she went on. 'We're all out so you'll have to contact your local agent.'

'Its fine,' Kira murmured, secretly relieved.

'Top floor.'

And with that the woman dismissed them from her desk.

Listening to the quiet hum of machinery, Kira could feel the pitter patter of butterfly wings in her stomach and her mouth felt dry. Jed cleared his throat and squeezed his wife's hand. Finally, the elevator stopped, and the doors slid open onto a pristine white corridor. The door at the end was marked Collections. As the young couple walked towards the door, Jed couldn't get the bee he'd seen out of his mind.

'Hey, guess what?' he said.

Kira looked up at him.

'I saw a bee on the way here. Can you believe that? That's gotta be a good sign, right? I mean, I never thought I'd see a live one.'

Kira shrugged, too nervous to speak and Jed softly kissed the top of her head as they stopped in front of an illuminated wall panel.

'Name' it chimed.

'Kira & Jed Jenkins.'

The door swooshed open.

The square white room was empty, devoid of any decoration and lit with harsh, bright white strips. The couple glanced at each other, was this the right place? Another chime sounded, and a soft blue light illuminated a small recess towards the back of the room. As they walked towards it, they became aware of other niches where multiple choice screens hung ready. This was the hard part of Collection, not knowing what your choices would be and trying hard not to hope – any choice could be life changing. Anything at all. They sat on the thin bench provided, looking up at the screen which read 'Baby Jenkins multiple choice, tap when ready.'

Jed turned to look at Kira, 'Ready?'

She couldn't speak, she could only nod. Together they tapped.

Choice 1
Blue eyes & greater academic aptitude
OR
Brown eyes & improved reaction times

Choice 2*
Predisposition to cancer
OR
Predisposition to heart disease

**note – Corp Medical reminds you that genetic predisposition has yet to be eradicated however consequences can be neutralised provided you maintain regular health checks.*

Choice 3
Boy, assigned name Kai
OR
Girl, assigned name Grace

'Three choices, what do you think?' Kira whispered to Jed.

'I don't mind, hon, what do you want?' Jed knew his wife had been thinking about this moment for a long time and he wanted her to be happy. She fidgeted on the bench next to him. Kira had been hoping for the girl/boy choice – not everyone had it. She had been so desperate for a girl she had even prepped the nursery cube for one, despite being told she was silly to have such hope.

'I'd like girl, blue and heart.'

'As you wish.'

He pressed the screen. It blanked then read *Processing.... Please Wait.*

Jed's ear comm pinged. It was the Force control room.

'Jenkins. You're wanted in a security level six briefing; a hover is on its way to pick you up. Be ready in sixty seconds.'

'I've got to go in.' He stood slowly, not wanting to leave.

Kira looked at him in dismay, *how could he leave when they were so close to Collection?* She was about to protest when there was a hum from the screen in front of them. It slid upwards and a small hatch opened. Inside was their collection. A baby girl, freshly grown in the lab womb and ready to be taken home.

Chapter Two

ANTIC: *Why is baby allocation so tightly controlled? Join the discussion in social hub gamma – are you still waiting for your child? Post your Collection experiences now.*

CORPCHAT: *Collection Q&A session today at 4pm, join us in social hub beta.*

Martha Hamble lay still, her head facing the door. She felt nothing. Numb. Oblivious to the young nurse bustling around, checking her vitals and updating the med log. Unaware of her clothes tagged in an evidence bag on the floor. Not seeing her father through the slim window in the door gesturing angrily outside. Her eyes were unfocused, and a tear rolled down her cheek.

The door banged open making her flinch. A tall, broad shouldered man stepped through the doorway, his bald head narrowly missing the top of the door frame.

'Out,' barked Martha's father at the frightened nurse, who immediately put down the med log and swiftly left the room. Roger Hamble breathed heavily through his bulbous nose as he placed a bag of clothes on the floor, by the end of the hospital bed. Unable to look at his daughter he addressed the wall above her head.

'I've made sure your file is redacted. This doesn't go any further. As soon as you're fit to leave, you'll come home, and we'll forget this ugly mess.'

When Martha didn't respond he nodded. 'Good. I have a meeting at Force HQ.'

He moved forward half a step, hesitated and nodded again before leaving. Martha watched the door close before touching her ear comm.

'Kira,' she whispered.

'You can't just leave. How am I supposed to get back by myself?'

Anger had flushed Kira's cheeks as she stared at Jed who shrugged helplessly.

'It's not my call. I've no choice. You know I'd rather...' he trailed off looking at the sleeping baby in Kira's arms.

'It's not fair,' Kira said softly, gazing down at the perfect bundle. 'You haven't even held her yet.'

'I will, we're a family now.'

Jed kissed them both and with a last look back he was gone. Kira took a moment to compose her thoughts.

'Right,' she said. 'We can do this Grace.'

Bending slightly, she picked up the user manual care pack and her bag. Luckily everything else was being delivered, all she had to do was get back to the apartment. But she didn't have the stroller and couldn't use a public skimmer. She had no way of getting home with the baby. They had planned to all walk back together but Kira was feeling too nervous to walk by herself. What if Grace was too hot or too cold or started crying or wanted feeding or she fell out of Kira's arms or… her ear comm pinged.

'Kira?'

'Martha? Is that you?'

There was a long pause.

'Yes, I...'

'Hon, I can't talk right now.'

'NO, wait! May I come over? Please? It's… I... something happened.' Her voice broke and she was unable to continue.

'What happened?' Kira asked, brow furrowed in concerned.

'I... I just...'

'Yes. Yes. Come over. Use your fob if I'm not there. I won't be far behind you.'

Kira cancelled the call and gently stroked the cheek of the peaceful, sleeping baby in her arms.

'I wonder what that's all about,' she pondered aloud before making her outgoing call.

'I need a hover lift from Corp Medical to Apartment Forty-Seven, Upper North please. Mother and child. No luggage.'

As she began to walk towards the door, thinking about the long corridor and elevator journey down to the large foyer below, Kira felt suddenly small and extremely isolated. She paused before pressing the elevator's call button not knowing if she could do this alone.

Let's just get home, she thought. *And then we can figure this out.*

Kira pressed the button and made sure she had a tight hold of her new baby.

ANON45: *Images of Detective Jed Jenkins leaving wife alone at Collection*

JMBISH: *Congratulations to KJ42 & JENKS. Can't wait to meet my granddaughter.*

INJEN: *In honour of my new niece, here are Corp Tech's latest baby-tech deals.*

The starter pack was waiting when they got in. Kira gently placed the still sleeping Grace in her cube then stood by her for a moment, unwilling to leave the baby alone. Eventually she began looking through the pack with high hopes. They were soon dashed - despite their request for the least invasive option, there seemed to be a lot of gadgets.

The WBW strip (What Baby Wants) which told you whether the baby was hungry, tired or needed a nappy change. The self-feeding hover bottle that could be programmed for regular feeds and didn't require holding. Mother scent stickers for Kira to rub on her body and then place around the baby and, worst of all, the baby neural jack. Filled with nursery rhymes and early years education.

'As if I'm going to shove that into a new-born,' thought Kira. She closed the box and pushed it to one side. Her Academy dissertation had been on how much childcare had changed since The Event. She wished it had been taken more seriously when she presented her findings. Using technology to program a baby just didn't feel right. Kira was sure that the touch of one person to another was a far more fulfilling experience. She stroked Grace's soft and wispy fair hair and smiled. If this was motherhood it was very easy so far. Kira started checking her sweeps on her handheld while she waited for Martha.

MSCHILD: *We are submitting our 27th request for Collection.*

Support our cause and sweep it out across the city.

Martha ignored the nurse flapping around her as she dressed in the spare clothes her father had left. If she could just get out of here, she'd feel so much better. But not home, not yet. She needed the one person who understood her completely. She needed to talk about what had happened. She scrubbed her eyes angrily, tears threatening to spill down her face as she turned to face the nurse.

'I'm leaving. My personal locater will inform Force where to find me. You can't keep me here against my will.'

She pushed past the young women trying to keep her in her room.

***MED4AC:** Hamble seen at Med Centre – No Comment status issued.*

Pete glanced across the hover car at his partner.

'I'm sorry Jenks, if it were up to me...'

'It's alright, it's not your fault.' Jed looked out the window as they passed the gleaming blue Collection Towers. 'I don't like leaving Kira on her own and I didn't even get to hold the baby. I mean, it's Collection Day!' Jed hit the front of the hover car in anger. 'Do you even know what we're being pulled in for?'

Pete shook his head.

'Sync me, probably just some tech-head sticking his nose in.' Pete began fiddling with the onboard sweep feed. After a few moments, he cleared his throat. 'Speaking of Corpers, is your sister coming to the baby homecoming?'

Jed knew Pete liked his sister Ingrid, although he wasn't sure why, she hadn't expressed any interest in Pete. All she cared about was her career at Corp Tech and climbing the career ladder as quickly as possible. She didn't talk to Jed often and was absolutely horrified to learn that he and Kira were planning to follow the long out of fashion natural approach to raising their baby.

'Yep. Don't get too excited though.'

'Why not?' Pete turned slightly to look at Jed.

'Unless you're the latest piece of Tech to hit the market I doubt she'll show much interest.'

'Don't you worry about that Jenks, I have a plan,' Pete said.

They landed at Force HQ and walked through the hover bay.

Security waved them onwards to meeting room one.

Chief Minkov stopped talking mid-sentence and Roger Hamble looked up as the two detectives entered the room.

'Good,' Hamble nodded. 'You're here. Sorry to pull you away Jenkins, big day and all but I've got… well... this needs to be sorted and sorted out quick.' He nodded again.

Pete and Jed looked at each other in confusion.

'Sit down, detectives,' said Minkov. 'As of now, you two are the only ones cleared to work the rape case.'

Pete perched on the edge of his chair.

'Do we know who the victim is yet, Sir?'

'The rape victim was, er...' Minkov cleared his throat and looked up at Mr Hamble who was now pacing by the door.

'The victim was Martha Hamble.'

Jed frowned in surprise. He knew Martha. She was Kira's best friend. He had wondered this morning when working through the rape case details why the victim was nameless, now he understood. The daughter of the Marketing Director of fragging Corporation. And not just an assigned daughter, she was an actual made to order. Obvious when you met her - red hair and green eyes were only available to those with the right connections, couple that with the creamy skin and freckles and it literally set her apart from everyone else. Babies weren't grown like that for Collection. It was extremely rare to grow your own these days but when you were on the Board, strings could be pulled. He was going to have to think of something to tell Kira before she got herself involved.

Hamble cleared his throat.

'Her medical file has been redacted, I want nothing on official record,' he said, not looking at either detective. 'You do your job and you find the bastard, and that's the end of it. Keep in contact, I want regular updates and I want a fast resolution, Jenkins. I'm counting on you. See this through and Corporation will look after you.' He glanced at Pete. 'Both of you.'

Mr Hamble checked his wristplant, nodded and left the meeting room.

The detectives stared at the Chief who was frowning.

'I don't need to tell you the firestorm we'll be in if anything, and I mean *anything*, goes wrong on this case.' The chief jabbed his finger at each man. 'Barnes, Jenkins – you get to the bottom of this if it kills you and you do it fast. You have full unit resources, but nothing leaves HQ and you're not to bring anyone else in unless I authorise it, you hear? Get to work.'

Before either detective had chance to react, Minkov got up and walked out of the room.

'Frag. You know her, right? She's one of Kira's friends, isn't she? What, I mean, how do you process… are you good?'

Jed nodded tightly.

'Face it, Pete, this just got personal and I want to close this case fast.'

They began to set themselves up in the meeting room moving furniture and setting up the internal monitors. Pete called up the case file and checked the progress made on the Drone TV. About half the footage had been screened, no leads. Both detectives sat down and focused on the monitors in front of them, determined to be the one who caught sight of the perpetrator.

ANTIC: *Security lock down at Force – do you know what's happening? Upload now and keep the sweeps active, we need your input.*

The door chimed and Kira called out *open*. Grace stirred and whimpered.

'Shhhh my darling,' Kira whispered, bending over the baby cube as Martha came in. Looking up with a smile to greet her friend Kira began frowning instead.

'Oh sweetie! What happened?'

Martha's face was streaked with dried tears, eyes red and puffy. She looked broken. Kira moved forward to hug her friend and Martha jerked back with a small cry. In her cube Grace started making snuffling noises, moving her head from side to side, small whimpers escaping as she grew more distressed.

'Oh, oh, oh, look at that.' Martha caught sight of the baby. 'Oh no. It was today, today was Collection. Oh, I am so, so sorry. I will leave you alone.'

Kira grabbed her friends' hand and despite Martha's stiffening, held on and drew her forward, guiding her to sit on the couch.

'Sit. Breathe. I'll make us all some drinks.'

Martha just looked blankly at her friend. Kira raised her voice slightly, 'I'm going to get Grace's bottle and make us some synth-caf – okay?'

Martha looked towards the kitchen and seemed to realise what her friend was going to do. Kira squeezed Martha's hand, threw a slightly panicked look at the baby cube then hurried over to the kitchen area.

Grace cried louder and louder, sharp shrill wails that seemed to pierce Kira's heart.

'Where is it? Where is it?' she muttered to herself.

Kira opened two cupboards before remembering she'd put the baby formula in with the mugs and glasses. She flipped the drinks machine on and grabbed mugs, a bottle and the formula. When she opened the fridge, she saw the pre-made bottles.

'Idiot.'

Scooping a bottle up, Kira flicked on the auto-warmer button whilst choosing the strong synth-caf option for herself and Martha.

Martha was fluttering her hands, looking worriedly at the crying baby in the cube next to her and half rose out of her seat.

'Should I do something?' she asked.

'No, no I got it. It's her first feed. Loud, isn't she?' Kira's voice trembled as her hands shook to finish as quickly as possible. She could feel her scalp prickling as she got hotter.

'I'm coming, I'm coming,' Kira called. Everything binged at once, so she took Martha her synth-caf and picked up her red-faced baby.

'Shhhh, shhhh.' Kira began to bob the baby up and down as she went back to the kitchen for the milk.

'Here, here, here. It's here.' She put the bottle near Grace's face and the loud wailing cut off suddenly. Both women exhaled.

'Phew – that was intense. Poor little thing, I got you, I got you. You were hungry, weren't you? It's okay, it's okay.'

Kira sat down with Martha. Both women watched the tiny baby drink hungrily. After a few moments Kira looked up at her friend.

'What happened, honey?'

Martha's hands began shaking, sloshing the synth-caf. She gasped as the hot liquid spilled. Quickly she put the mug down on the floor beside her and scrubbed her hands on her trousers, wiping them dry. Martha tried to marshal her thoughts and without looking at her friend began speaking in a low monotone.

'I was walking home from work, through the park on fourth. It's so tranquil and I imagine what the trees will look like when, if, they ever grow back. It was a normal day at work. The same routine. I did... there was a bee. I wondered if I was imagining things. But it was definitely there. You do believe me Kira?' Martha begged, peering up at her friend with a note of desperation in her voice, eyebrows drawn together, eyes pleading for a positive response.

Kira nodded. She was sure Jed had mentioned a bee at Collection.

'I'm not sure what happened... there was a sound… a man... he grabbed me...' Martha started to breathe quicker and quicker, tears rolled down her face. 'I can't Kira, I just... please don't force me.'

'Shhhhh, shhhh it's alright Ma, it's alright.' Kira didn't know what to say, she looked down at Grace, who had stopped feeding and was once again blissfully asleep. 'Just let me put her down.'

Martha had drawn her legs up to meet her body and was hugging her knees, rocking backwards and forwards saying *no, no, no, no, no* under her breath. Kira didn't know what to do but she couldn't leave her friend in such a state, so she touched her ear comm.

'Forty-seven? I need a cocoon for visitor M2 please.'

The apartment lights took on a soft glow as a sedation patch appeared on the arm of the couch next to Martha, who continued to rock. The patch attached itself to Martha's arm and a sedative was released. Martha's movements slowed until she was still, and her breathing returned to normal, then became deeper and calmer.

Kira reluctantly placed the baby back in her cube. She had wanted to enjoy their first moments together, but she felt tense and uneasy, sick with worry as she pulled the cocoon fabric from the top of the couch over her friend. Nothing was turning out the way she thought it would today, and she needed to clear her head before she rang Jed.

She walked over to the small altar in the corner of the room and a sense of calm came over her. She lit a candle, sat down and took a couple of cleansing breaths. Kira imagined herself surrounded by a ball of blue light. With each breath she took in, she drew energy from the earth far beneath her, and with each exhale she visualised all her stress and anxiety leaving the top of her head. When she felt completely calm, Kira thought hard about the light around her and attempted to extend the protective energy from herself to her new daughter and her best friend. Kira was beginning to feel in control of herself again when the door chimed.

'IGA,' an efficient voice announced.

Frag it thought Kira, they weren't supposed to come till tomorrow.

She got up and went to the door. As she opened it, Jed and Pete walked up the corridor and stopped behind the officious looking woman.

'Timing,' muttered Jed as the three of them entered the apartment.

Chapter Three

CORP: *SALE SALE SALE*

We are celebrating successful Collection with 25% off the newest child jack. Updated with the latest spatial awareness problem solving and educational entertainment system, version twelve as standard. Order yours now through your local Corporation Rep.

'What are you two doing here?' Kira whispered as Jed and Pete followed the Infant Growth Assessor lady into the apartment and closed the door behind them. Pete pursed his lips and Jed frowned as they both saw the activated cocoon. The IGA ignored it and pulled out a touchscreen.

'Later,' Jed murmured.

'Good afternoon, I'm your IGA,' announced the woman. 'Who are the parents?'

'We are.' Jed pointed at his wife and put on his best smile as he ushered the IGA into the kitchen area and offered her a beverage. Pete looked at the cocoon again. Kira nibbled her fingernails, turning towards the cube when Grace began to cry. She teetered, not knowing whether to go to her or speak with the IGA. In the end the plaintive noise decided her, and she scooped the baby up, rocking Grace gently, and humming as she walked over to the others.

'I'm here to carry out an infant suitability assessment not drink synth-caf, but I suppose one would be nice. It's not often we get time to indulge while at work. I'm surprised you even have the drinks machine given your requests.'

Jed and Kira looked at each other in confusion.

'Requests?' Kira asked.

'Ah, sorry, we thought you'd be non-conformers you see, because of the no technology request. I mean almost all parents have a NanNan these days and we just thought... well, you know.' The IGA coloured slightly as she sipped her synth-caf. 'No offence.'

'None taken,' Kira said smiling. 'We're not pure naturals but we wanted to try the natural approach with the baby. After my studies I was curious...'

The IGA interrupted.

'Oh, I see, hobbyists then. Each to their own. I'll leave the paperwork for the NanNan as well as our latest brochure and then when you want to order, everything will be there for you.'

'If,' whispered Kira under her breath.

The agent frowned as she walked around the lounge area.

'What's that?' she asked, pointing at the lit candle in the corner of the room.

'Oh. Mm, that's mine. I was just meditating before you arrived.'

'Meditating?'

'Yes. You never heard of it?'

'No. I mean not in real life.' The IGA patted her neat bun. 'I read history at Higher Academy you know; I remember some of the strange customs.' She moved closer peering at the candle on the small table. 'So, what do you do with it?'

'Well,' Kira had followed the IGA into the lounge and she sat down with Grace. 'I believe in balance, so sometimes when I feel stressed or out of sorts I like to try and focus my energy on releasing the things that made me *feel* out of balance. It's easier to think of it in terms of light and colour, moving from dark to bright,' Kira paused, searching for something else to say. 'Controlled breathing helps...'

The IGA interrupted again and pointed at the small blue statue.

'And who is that?'

'That's Gaia. She is the spirit of the Earth, dedicated to keeping the life force of the planet in balance. She can be used as a focus point.' Kira could see the IGA was looking troubled. 'I work in the Archives, so I have approved access.'

'Ah, well I guess that makes sense. Not sure how I would write this up anyway. Probably best not to mention it to anyone. I expect it's quite a personal thing and let's face it we don't tell everyone about everything we do behind closed doors, do we?'

The IGA glanced at the cocoon before turning to look at Kira and smiling, not realising how offensive she sounded. Kira agreed, in disbelief yet relief that the topic would be dropped. The IGA finished her drink and fished out her paperwork.

'Right, here's my checklist. Neural jack's in use?'

'No'.

'Nan-Nan installed – no. Scent patches activated?'

'No'.

'Cube ordered?'

'Yes.'

'Type?'

'Standard sleeping, able to move around our apartment.'

'Hmm,' the IGA looked down her list. 'I don't think there's much point in me going through the rest of the options. They are all classified as high-tech and you've clearly decided against that kind of help. I don't think there's anything else I can do for you today.'

'Don't you want to look at the baby?' Kira queried.

'Do you mind a health probe?'

'Is it non-invasive?'

'It can be.'

'Alright then.'

'Pop her into the cube,' directed the IGA.

Kira did so and watched suspiciously while the IGA brought out a handheld, pressed some buttons and then directed the scan towards Grace laying in her cube. Several bleeps later the IGA handed Kira a readout.

'It's all good. Remember to visit your local Med Centre if you have any queries. Do you have a medical handheld?'

Kira shook her head.

'You might want to look into that otherwise how will you know if the baby is okay? Contact your local Agent, they'll have what you need. I'd recommend a health check at six weeks but obviously get in touch beforehand if you have any worries. Babies are tough little things.'

The IGA gathered her things. After a cheery goodbye she left the apartment.

***IGANN:** Outdated practices on the rise – who do you know who is being retro?*

Share your updates and sweep it out to City Forty-Two.

'Well that was a waste of time.' Kira lifted her daughter out of the cube and turned to look at Jed. 'Are you ready to meet Grace?'

She placed their daughter into his arms. He held her away from him until he realised she wasn't going to cry, then he smiled and brought her closer to him. Kira touched his arm, kissing him on the cheek before walking away to the bedroom.

'My daughter,' Jed said. 'Wow. So tiny.'

He gently stroked her cheek and touched her tiny hand. When she curled her fingers around his, his breath caught.

'Pete, look, look - she's holding my finger.'

Pete grinned.

'She's so perfect. I'm a Dad.' It suddenly seemed like a huge responsibility. 'Woah. I'm a Dad.'

'You oka,. Jenks?'

'Yeah, yeah. Do you want to hold her?'

'You sure?'

'Course.' Jed transferred the sleeping baby into Pete's arms. His heart swelled in his chest as he watched his friend hold his tiny daughter. After a few moments the two men looked at each other and Pete cleared his throat meaningfully.

'Huh? Oh yeah.' Jed called through to the nearby bedroom. 'Kira, what is Martha doing here?'

Jed glanced back at Pete standing awkwardly with his daughter.

'She called me earlier, in pieces, asking if she could come around. I wasn't going to tell her no. What's going on?' Kira replied as she returned to the kitchen with a bundle of cloth in her hands. Jed sidestepped his wife's question.

'Why is she cocooned?'

'She was trying to tell me what happened to her. She was so upset; she wouldn't let me touch her. She started hyperventilating.' Kira gestured towards her cocooned friend. 'I didn't know what else to do – I know we installed the apartment protection system to combat any aggressive behaviour, but I figure this way she'd get some rest and maybe feel better. I was just about to call you when the IGA arrived.' She turned to look at her husband. 'What the frag is going on, Jed?'

She unwrapped the cloth and tied it around her body, watching Jed and Pete, waiting for an answer. Pete half shrugged.

'We can't tell you, Kira. It's classified.' He frowned. 'What are you doing?'

Kira looked confused for a moment then realised what he was talking about.

'It's a baby wrap. I discovered them in Archive. Don't distract me, Pete. What do you mean it's classified? What does that mean? Is she in danger? Am *I* in danger?' She took half a step towards Grace.

'No, you're not in danger, hon,' Jed said. 'It's just... out of our hands. I'm sorry, I know she's your friend, but I can't break case confidentiality.'

Kira huffed a little and took the baby from Pete, placing Grace inside the fabric wrap, close to her body.

'I'm sorry, hon.' Jed tried to placate his wife. 'We needed to speak to Martha and when we checked her locator expecting her to be at the med centre, it flashed up here.'

Kira glared at him.

'I have to finish organising the baby homecoming.'

She pushed past him and stormed straight through to the bedroom.

Jed sighed then looked at his partner.

'Have you got your holo-recorder, Pete?'

'Here? Now?'

'How else are we going to get her into questioning without everyone seeing?'

Pete looked at the cocoon then motioned for Jed to lead the way over to the couch.

'Forty-seven? Retract cocoon, please. Administer revival.'

'Affirmative.'

'Pretty techy for you isn't it, Jenks?'

'It was Mum - Ingrid talked her into getting them for the whole family because she gets serious discount. Not that we had much choice. We came home one day, and it had already been installed.'

While Jed was talking the cocoon disengaged, slid up and over the sleeping Martha and returned to a recess at the top of the couch.

After a few moments Martha began to stir. She looked around.

'Wha… Where is Kira? Why are you here? What's going on?'

'It's alright Martha, may I call you Martha? We just want to talk to you about what happened.' Pete tried to sound as non-threatening as possible.

'Oh.'

Jed moved to sit next to Martha on the couch, but she shrank back with a small gasp, so he veered to one side and sat in the armchair.

'Your father made sure we'd get the case,' Jed said. 'No-one else in Force has any details. Nor will they. But we need to take your statement.' He paused. 'I understand how uncomfortable it might be to talk about.'

Martha looked at him. 'I doubt that.'

'We've found the footage of the attack.'

Martha didn't react, she continued to stare at Jed.

'All we need is your statement and we're one step closer to closing the case.'

Martha didn't respond.

Pete placed the holo on the table in front of the couch and activated the recorder.

'Force Case G7753. Detective Jenkins speaking, also present is Detective Barnes. The date is 15th April 2215. Interview being held with Miss Martha Hamble. Could you please state your name for the record.'

There was a long silence.

'Martha Evelyn Hamble.'

Kira could hear Jed's voice from the bedroom and although she couldn't make out the exact words, he sounded firm and in control, interviewing Martha. The homecoming party was pre-organised, all Kira had to do was access the social file and hit confirm. Everyone knew it was tomorrow but at least this way the parentals would be happy with the officialness. Nothing to do now but relax with her new family yet Martha's distressed arrival had stopped that from happening.

Should she go through to the lounge and interrupt a Force matter? Her friend had after all, come to confide in her. Kira looked down at the innocent, sleeping baby peeping out through the folds of the baby wrap and a wave of protectiveness swept over her. Martha had come to Kira for help not the Force. She couldn't leave Martha out there by herself. Kira came into the lounge. Jed and Pete looked at her, but neither man spoke. Kira sat next to Martha, found her hand and squeezed it tight.

'Mrs Kira Jenkins and child have entered the room,' Jed said.

'Tell us in your own words what happened, Martha.' Pete tried to sound encouraging.

Martha bit her lower lip and swallowed, shifting in her seat. It wasn't until Kira squeezed her hand again that she managed to find the words. In a hushed voice, she began to speak.

'I was walking home from work. It was such a beautiful day yesterday; I could imagine birds singing. I was feeling so happy.' Martha paused then looked up at Kira. 'I knew you had Collection. I was so pleased for you.' She shook her head. 'There was a woman. She was blue. And a bee. There was definitely a bee. I think. Why would I have imagined that?' she said half to herself.

Jed stared at Martha. It can't have been the same person. It was a new ad by Corp. A coincidence, surely. Martha stopped talking and looked down at her hands.

'Go on,' Pete said.

Martha looked up at him, her eyes full of tears.

'He hit me. I fell. I don't remember .. my head.' She touched the side of her head. 'Hurt. I couldn't see. But there was someone on top of me and he, and he, he was...' She started sobbing.

'He was... in me. I never. I had not… I didn't want to. I tried to push him, but I had no strength. He was smothering me, and I had no strength.'

She trailed off.

'I was powerless.'

Her shoulders shook as she cried.

Kira looked at Jed horrified, then tried to hug her friend as best as she could but Grace in the baby wrap made her bulky and Kira was frightened of squashing the baby.

Jed motioned for Pete to stop the recorder.

'Kira,' he said. 'You can't breathe a word of this to anyone.'

Kira scowled at him.

'And who exactly am I going to tell?'

Pete spoke to Jed.

'Her statement matches the footage. We've got the medical files - why don't we leave it as is, Jenks? There's no conflicting evidence. Once facial re-cog comes back, we've got him.'

Jed nodded in agreement and the two men stood, Pete packing away the holo recorder.

'You head home, Pete,' Jed said. 'I've got re-cog on my ear comm, I'll let you know when it pings through.'

'No problem. I'll upload the interview and wait to hear.'

They clasped forearms and Pete left. After the door closed Jed sagged slightly, his head planted for a brief moment against the wall.

Kira and Martha were speaking softly on the couch together. Martha stood and headed through a door on the other side of the lounge.

'Is she okay?' Jed asked.

'She's going to shower. I told her she could use our water credit; we've stockpiled a bit and I think she needs to feel clean.'

'Yeah, sure. We've got the physical evidence.' Jed caught his wife's hand and held it tight. 'I'm so sorry this happened.'

'You will catch him, won't you?'

'We will do whatever it takes to catch him, I promise.'

'And then what happens?'

'It's a termination. You'll probably never hear it on the sweeps. Martha being who she is.'

Grace began to stir inside the baby wrap, making small noises as if she was searching for something.

'I guess she wants feeding again,' Kira said. 'Do you want to do it?'

Jed smiled. 'More than anything.' He made himself comfortable on the couch but before Kira could pass Grace over, he suddenly sat bolt upright.

'What's wrong?'

'Oh no, don't worry. It's not a bad thing. I just remembered something. I promised Mother I'd send out an update and I haven't had time to put anything together yet.'

'Oh, I've already prepared one.' Feeling rather pleased with herself she brought it up on the portable touchscreen for Jed to read through. He read it and handed it back with a grin as he took Grace.

'It's great, hon, thank you. Get it sent out and we can finally start being a real family.'

JENHUB: *So excited to have Grace, she's the most beautiful baby I've ever seen.*

CORP: *Latest Collection a success - baby Grace Jenkins joins Detective Jed Jenkins and Junior Archivist Kira Jenkins, the youngest family unit so far.*

INJEN: *Latest model NanNan beta tests are extremely*

favourable. Click through for details on how to pre-order.

A few hours later Jed was scrolling through his dailies, looking at who had read their update, which was in fact everyone they knew. There were several comments from people expressing their congratulations and excitement about meeting Grace at the party tomorrow. Ingrid's response had been typically impersonal, with the usual new tech links inserted at the bottom. Kira's close friend, Ruth, had been the complete opposite, gushing with congratulations and enthusiastic support for their choice of parenting style.

There was one post from someone he didn't recognise - Dina something or other - expressing her sincere delight at coming to the party. She must be a new friend of Kira's, Jed thought. His jaw cracked as he yawned. Checking his wristplant Jed realised if he didn't go to sleep soon, he'd probably end up going without any at all. Re-cog should be through in a couple of hours and with it, Pete and Jed could arrest the bastard behind Martha's attack.

Chapter Four

Kira stared at the sleeping baby in the crib next to her. She was frightened that if she closed her eyes Grace might need her and she'd miss it. Or even that someone would come in and take her - which was ridiculous seeing as the apartment was locked. But Kira couldn't shake the feeling that something awful was going to happen.

The evening had been extremely subdued. Martha had seemed calmer after her shower, even holding Grace for a time, though she hadn't eaten much. None of them had. Kira and Jed hadn't felt like talking either. They hadn't even celebrated the first day of their new family. Today would be difficult too. With all their guests descending for the homecoming, not only would Kira have to defend her natural parenting style, but she had to make sure no-one found out about Martha, especially Ruth. Ruth might sweep it and use the attack as a soap box to complain about Corporation, not thinking about how upsetting that would be for Martha.

Kira turned over and watched Jed as he slept. He looked so peaceful, as if nothing bad could touch him. Then his ear comm began to ping. Kira elbowed him in the ribs. Jed groaned and touched his ear.

'This is facial re-cog with results for Detective Jenkins. Please activate verbal confirmation.'

'Confirmation activated.'

'Positive match for Michael Greenwood. Apartment Six, Lower 7th. Information uploaded to file.'

The call ended and Jed sat up, touching his comm again.

'Lower 7th.'

Kira shushed him pointing at Grace. Jed continued in a quieter tone.

'I need a security lock-down on Apartment Six. No entry or exit except for Detectives Jenkins and Barnes.' He ended the call and looked at Kira, grim-faced.

'We've got him. I've gotta go.'

He quickly got dressed and nodded towards Grace.

'She slept well.'

'She woke up twice for a feed. You slept right through.'

Jed looked a little sheepish.

'Don't worry. You'll be getting your share of night shifts.' Kira grinned at him.

Jed kissed his wife, turned to leave then came back and softly kissed his baby.

'Will you be alright, you know, with Martha?' He jerked his head in the direction of the guest room.

'We'll be fine. I won't say anything to anyone. You won't be late home, will you?'

'I'll do my best, hon. This is a big deal; you know what Mr. Hamble is like.'

'I know. See you later. Love you.'

'Love you.'

Jed left the room quietly. Kira checked the time. Three thirty am. She could doze for a bit. She looked over at Grace, and scooped the baby out of the cube, laying her gently in the bed. Then she curled her body around the tiny shape, closed her eyes, and tried to sleep.

ANTIC: *Rare snake sighted but not caught – did it slither to freedom?*

CORP: *We remind citizens that animal sightings MUST be reported for immediate containment. Wildlife from outside the city will contain harmful contaminants – don't risk contact. Stay safe, stay inside.*

The skimmer hummed as Jed went through the Upper Community Hub, deserted now but with benches for people to meet, sit and chat, play areas for the children and during the day vendors hawked food and other knick knacks. The streets were empty and apartment blocks dark as he went to pick up his partner. Pete lived in the last apartment block in the Upper sector, the one designed for individual dwelling. As Jed drew close, he saw Pete standing on the corner bleary eyed.

'We got him then?' Pete asked climbing into the skimmer.

'Yep'.

'Where are we going?'

'Apartment Six, Lower 7th – one of the student blocks.'

'Lock-down?'

'Yep.'

Pete grunted. 'Where are we going to question him? Is HQ secure?'

'Should be,' Jed said. 'We can use meeting room one. You still got your holo?'

'Yep.'

The two men spent the rest of the journey in silence, engrossed in their own thoughts.

It was all quiet on Lower 7th, every apartment window dark. The lock-down was still in place and the detectives found apartment six easily. Jed touched the security plate on the side of the door.

'Access request for Detectives Jenkins and Barnes.'

'Confirmed.'

The door slid open. Both men entered. Jed motioned for Pete to go left as he went right. Armed with stunners, they separated to explore the apartment.

Michael Greenwood tossed and turned, dreaming of footsteps. He sat up as the door to his bedroom banged open and a Force Detective aimed a stunner right at him.

'Frag!' Greenwood yelled, arms up. 'Don't shoot!'

'Be quiet,' Jed snapped. 'Michael Greenwood, you are bound by Force Law. Anything you say may be used as evidence against you. At this time, you do not have the right to a Defender. You will be escorted for immediate questioning. You may dress but any act of aggression will be dealt with. Do you understand?'

Greenwood nodded.

'What did I do?'

Jed motioned Greenwood towards a pile of clothes on the floor. He slid out of bed, glancing nervously at the armed stunners following his every move and put on the green tunic and trousers he had discarded earlier that night. Within minutes the detectives had bundled their suspect into the waiting skimmer and were traveling in silence to HQ. Greenwood looked at each of the detectives in turn, and then down at his magno-bound hands.

'But I haven't done anything,' he said.

HQ was dark except for a pool of light where the night guard sat on reception. He greeted them sleepily. 'Detectives.'

Jed and Pete took Greenwood into the meeting room, magno-binding him to an interrogation desk. He started to speak but stopped at the fierce look on Jed's face and dropped his gaze to his bound hands. Jed turned to Pete.

'I need a truth patch, a lie catcher and your holo.'

Pete gathered the various items from the corner of the room where all their equipment was piled. He connected the lie catcher into Greenwood's info jack port at the back of his head and stuck the truth patch to his arm. The lie catcher was designed to pick up on unusual brain wave activity, whilst the truth patch released chemicals that made most people eager to share whatever information they knew. Occasionally the truth patch had no effect. There were other, less accepted, methods of gathering intel – usually left as a last resort.

Greenwood swallowed nervously and watched as Pete took a seat behind the lie catcher readout and Jed sat down in front of him, beginning the holo recorder.

'Force Case G7753. Detective Jenkins speaking, also present is Detective Barnes. The date is 16th April 2215. Mr. Michael Greenwood is present for questioning. In use for interrogation are standard issue lie catcher and Corp Tech truth patch, version four.' Jed looked at the prisoner. 'Please confirm your identity for the record.'

'Michael Greenwood.' He leaned forwards. 'Why am I here?'

'I remind you that you are still under caution. You have been bound by Force Law. Anything you say may be used as evidence against you. At this time, you do not have the right to a Defender. Do you understand?'

Greenwood nodded, sat back in his chair then cleared his throat. 'Yes.'

'Where were you between four and six on the afternoon of April fourteenth?'

'Walking home? I think?' Greenwood looked confused.

There was a pause in the questioning as Pete watched the lie catcher trackers. 'Confirmed.'

'What route did you walk home?' Jed asked.

'Through the park in fourth,' Greenwood answered. 'It's beautiful.'

Jed looked at Pete.

'Confirmed.'

'Did you meet anyone?'

'I don't know... maybe,' Greenwood said, trying to remember. 'There was, I can't...'

'Think harder.'

'Yes, there was a lady, a blue lady.'

'Blue?'

Jed was hoping for more information, but Greenwood only nodded.

'Confirmed,' Pete said, looking back at the screen, sounding surprised.

'And...' Greenwood continued. 'There was a bee.' He reached around to touch the side of his neck and felt a slight bump. 'It stung me!'

'Hands down,' Jed barked.

'Med scan?' Pete said, already getting up and searching the pile of equipment in the corner.

'Interrogation calls for medical scan. Results uploaded to file.'

Pete brought back a handheld and scanned Greenwood. After a few moments the scanner beeped.

'Positive for bee venom,' Pete said slowly.

Jed and Pete looked at each other for a moment before Pete sat back down. Jed cleared his throat and turned back to the suspect.

'Did you see anyone else?'

'No, I… no. The next thing I remember is being at home.' Greenwood looked at each Detective in turn, his brow creased, eyes wide. 'Did something happen?'

'Cue the footage,' Jed said to Pete.

The vid-screen on the wall glowed briefly as Drone TV flickered into life. A young woman walks into view. Greenwood shook his head. The woman seemed familiar. The footage blanked out, then resumed. The woman continues walking past a man, walking past Greenwood himself. Confused at what he is watching, Greenwood leans forward, unsure as to what he will see himself do next.

The screen blanks out again. When the footage continues the man on the screen is holding his neck, looking around as if trying to find someone. He spots the woman who is walking away from him. He moves quickly to catch up with her. He grabs her by the arm and spins her around. She loses her balance and falls, hitting the ground hard. She does not move.

Greenwood gasps.

'Keep watching,' Pete menaced.

The man on the screen has his back to the drone camera, yet despite this it becomes clear that he is undoing his trousers. Greenwood watched with increasing horror as the man sexually assaults the prone woman. When he has finished, the man gets up and walks away as if nothing unusual has happened.

'It might look like me, but it wasn't me. I'd never do something like that.' Greenwood's face had turned pale and tears had formed in his eyes. 'You have to believe me. I couldn't... that poor woman... I didn't...' He sniffed, licked his lips and looked up at the two detectives. 'Those footage blackouts. That's unusual, right?' His voice got firmer. 'That sort of thing doesn't happen anymore. Obviously, this is someone's idea of a sick joke, isn't it? The footage must have been tampered with – maybe it's Anti-Corp - I'm being set up, I would never…'

He trailed off as the two detectives looked at him dispassionately. He lowered his head, his words now no more than a disbelieving whisper.

'It wasn't me; it wasn't me.'

Pete turned the vid-screen off. After a brief pause Jed cleared his throat.

'Your DNA was identified and matched after the victim was taken to Medical and scanned. The footage corroborates your presence at the scene of the crime.'

'I didn't do this, I didn't.'

Pete watched the lie catcher readout, his brow furrowed. He leaned over to Jed and spoke to him in a hushed tone.

'According to this he thinks he's telling the truth, but he can't be, can he? Drugs?'

'We'd better run the full spectrum,' Jed whispered back, then watched as Pete got the syringe from the med kit.

'End of interrogation. Drug analysis requested – full spectrum ordered. Results uploaded to file.'

Jed watched Greenwood as he sat behind the desk muttering to himself, head bowed, and shoulders slumped. Something about this didn't feel right. Hamble had declared the culprit would be terminated, and Jed wanted to be one hundred percent sure that Michael Greenwood had knowingly committed this crime and wasn't an unwitting accomplice to someone or something else.

It must have something to do with the blue woman. Greenwood had seen her, Martha too. And the bee. Just like Jed had. That bee had to mean something. Jed supposed Anti Corp could be trying out a new aggressive campaign to destabilise Corporation. But it didn't make sense. Even if the bee was them, Anti-Corp would never advocate rape, and why hadn't the blue woman affected him in the same way when he saw her? Why didn't the bee sting him? If indeed there had even been a bee. Jed's head was beginning to ache.

Pete finished taking the blood samples.

'Where shall we put him?' he asked, nodding towards the suspect.

Jed refocused.

'The isolation cell. No-one will go that way if we lock it down, and we need to keep this off the mainstream.'

'You take him, I'll get these samples over to analysis,' Pete said, agreeing with his partner. He looked at his watch. 'Should be done by nine.'

Greenwood flinched as Jed came over to him. He tried to protest his innocence again, desperately.

'I didn't do this. You have to believe me. I don't remember a thing, it wasn't me, I'd never...'

He was cut off mid-sentence as Jed administered a sedative. The dose was enough to stop the man from talking but not too much that he couldn't walk by himself. Jed released the magno-binders from the table and took the prisoner out of the room, guiding him through the corridor to isolation.

Jed wasn't convinced whether Greenwood was truly guilty or not but the evidence against him was strong. He was hoping the drug sweep would come back positive for something. At least that would make some sort of sense and it might be the only way to keep the man from death. Jed was appalled someone he knew had been raped in broad daylight by a random stranger, but the confusion and horror Greenwood had shown whilst watching the footage made it difficult for Jed to believe that he was putting on an act.

ANTIC: *Early Force birds catch worm. Do you know more? Share & sweep.*

Thunder rolled through the overcast sky as Martha lay on the bed listening to the rain pelting the window. The weather suited her mood. In fact, if a lightning bolt were to somehow hit her right now, she didn't think it would be a bad thing.

She could hear Kira and Grace moving about in the next room. Meeting Grace had been a real comfort last night. She was so pure and innocent.

Holding the baby had washed away some of the badness Martha felt inside. But the shower she had taken last night hadn't done anything to get rid of the dirty feeling. Her skin still crawled, and she didn't think she would ever be able to bear the touch of any man ever again.

Why her? Why had that man, that nobody of a man, why had he attacked her?

Martha was used to hate mail; she was the daughter of the Marketing Director on the Board of Corporation - but she didn't think this was aimed at him. It wouldn't gain Anti Corp anything to have Mr. Hamble's daughter raped. The only person she knew involved with Anti Corp was Ruth and she would never be part of an organisation who would condone sexual assault.

She could ask Ruth later, at the party - that would help set the mood. '*Hi Ruth – were you aware of an Anti-Corp plan to rape me?*'

A loud banging interrupted Martha's thoughts.

Kira held Grace awkwardly in one arm as she opened the front door and then stepped back as Roger Hamble came striding through.

'Kira,' he nodded as a way of greeting. 'Is my daughter here?'

'I am,' Martha said, appearing from the spare room but not looking at her father.

Kira closed the door as Mr. Hamble strode over to where Martha now stood in the middle of the lounge. Kira walked past them both and hovered by her bedroom door, unsure whether she should stay or go.

'Your mother and I were worried when you didn't come home. We spoke with Medical and they said you'd checked out. We thought something might have happened.'

He peered at his daughter under his bushy eyebrows.

'Something else you mean?' Martha said in a small voice.

Her father ran a hand over his bald head.

'Yes, well, no need for all that. I've got something for you.' He fished in his jacket pocket and brought out a vial of clear liquid. 'A Nano tech memory wipe. Designed to remove painful events. Your mother thought it might be useful, you know, so you can put it behind you and get on with… things.'

Martha glared at her father.

'You mean so she doesn't have to talk to me about it.'

'Now, now Martha, that's not fair. Your mother is delicate.'

'Not fair!' Martha shouted. 'Not fair! Can you even hear the words coming out of your mouth? I do not want your frag damn memory wipe and I do not want you pushing me back into my perfect daughter mould.' She took a step toward him. 'He *raped* me, Father. He raped me. He pushed me and hurt me and raped me. And there was nothing I could do about it.' Martha lurched forward into her father's arms, sobbing. 'I am so sorry, Daddy.'

Hamble wrapped his arms around her and stroked her hair.

'There, there. It's alright. Shhhh,' he whispered, his gaze soft.

Kira hesitated a moment before slipping back into her bedroom.

While she waited, Kira stared out of the window watching the rain as it continued to pour down.

'What has upset you so much today?' she asked the darkening sky.

Grace began to snuffle in her arms, looking for milk and then began crying.

'Alright, alright baby. We'll get your bottle.'

Kira stood by the bedroom door, trying to hear whether the coast was clear or not so she could get to the kitchen. Grace's cry was traveling right through her, and Kira's anxiety level was beginning to rise. She poked her head out the door. Martha and her father were sat on the couch, talking.

Kira hurried towards the kitchen, an intruder in her own apartment. Once there, she took a bottle out of the fridge and activated the self-warmer, turning to go straight back to her bedroom, but Martha's father was now on his feet.

'Kira', he said nodding in her direction before letting himself out of the apartment. Once the door had shut behind him, Kira went over to where Martha sat with the memory wipe vial in her hands. Her movements had momentarily quietened Grace.

'You alright, Ma?'

'Yes. No. I have no idea. I am so sorry Kira – have I ruined Grace's party?'

'No, don't be silly,' Kira replied. 'It's all pre-organised, you know what my mum is like.' She paused, not sure what to say. 'Are you sure you want to stay for it? Because I completely understand if you don't want to be around lots of people.'

'Of course I will be here,' Martha said. 'I think I would rather have something to do then be left alone right now. As long as you don't mind me being here?'

'Of course not,' Kira replied, smiling at her friend. 'Party set-up are arriving at ten and the first guest is due early afternoon. I expect the mothers will turn up any time before that, so we'd better get this little one sorted out at least. I can feed her while you help me figure out what to wear.'

Both women stood for a moment looking at the baby in Kira's arms before walking together towards Kira's bedroom discussing party dresses and checking the latest sweeps.

Jed returned to the meeting room where Pete was waiting.

'Hamble's on his way,' Pete said.

'Great.' Jed sighed and sat down.

'What's wrong, Jenks?'

'This case. This whole thing is so odd. First, we have a rape – a rape! I mean, when was the last time you remember hearing about one of those?'

Pete shrugged.

'Then there's this whole blue lady, bee thing. I mean, I thought it was some kind of promotion for something or other, but this guy saw it too and now he's facing termination for a crime he has no memory of committing. I mean, what the frag?'

'You saw a blue lady?'

'Yeah. On the way to Collection. I just thought it was, you know, advertising or something.'

Pete bit the side of his thumb.

'I saw her too, Jenks. I mean, I think I did. I'm not sure. I didn't see a bee, though.' He paused for a moment. 'I saw a snake.'

' A snake!' Jed's eyes widened.

'Fragging thing slithered around the corner from my apartment and when I followed it, I think I saw a blue lady turn into the alley. I checked it out but there was nothing there. Can you imagine how many credits I'd have got for a live snake?'

Snakes were extremely rare but very, very occasionally they

turned up in the city, attracted to the heat given off by the solar power hubs. They were worth a small fortune.

'What is going on, Pete?'

'No idea,' Pete said. 'You should be talking to Kira and her mates. Aren't they meant to be regularly communing with nature or something?'

Before Jed could answer, the door opened and Mr Hamble entered. Both detectives stood and spoke as one, 'Sir.'

'Sit.'

Pete and Jed sat. Hamble remained standing by the door.

'You've got the bastard then?'

'Yes, Sir,' Jed said. 'Although there seems to be some discrepancies in his statement.'

'Discrepancies? Did Drone TV positively identify him?'

'Yes, Sir.'

'Did you get the DNA sample you needed from Corp Medical?'

'Yes, Sir.'

'And it was a positive match?'

'Yes, Sir but...'

'Then I don't see what the problem is. Get the damn statement completed and I'll order Termination to come and finish the job.'

'We've got the statement, Sir, but the lie catcher shows that whilst Greenwood committed the crime, he has absolutely no memory of doing so. We think a new drug might have affected him so we're just waiting for the labs to come back and...'

Hamble cut him off again.

'There's no new drug. I'm calling in Termination and that's the end of it. Good work men.'

He moved forward to shake Pete's hand, then Jed's.

'But, Sir… '

'It's done, Jenkins. You should be pleased. Go home, spend time with your new family. Nothing more important than family. I'll send my man over to seal the files.'

He nodded to himself then moved over to the far side of the room and made the call for Termination.

Pete looked at Jed's worried face.

'Jenks,' he whispered. 'Greenwood is guilty. He committed the assault; we have the corroborating evidence.'

'I know. It just seems wrong.'

'Of course it does. It happened to someone you know. To someone we know for frag sake. Hamble's right – go home, enjoy being a daddy. I'll stay, close the file and wait for the terminators.'

'You sure?'

'Course.' Pete smiled to himself. 'I can work on my amazing chat up lines for later.'

'Good luck with that.'

Pete's infatuation with Jed's sister Ingrid was a great source of amusement for himself and Kira. Ingrid was so Corp that sometimes they wondered whether she even realised Pete was a person and not an A.I. projection. She certainly had no idea that he near worshipped the ground she walked on. It would be interesting to see if she even turned up at the party at all.

Jed gathered his jacket and clapped his partner on the shoulder before following Hamble, who had finished his call, out of the room. He was waiting for Jed in the corridor.

'Martha is staying at yours.'

Jed wasn't sure whether it was a question or a statement and before he could reply Hamble continued.

'Bill me water and energy rates, you've got extra as it is and it's tight all around. We'll send some of her things over. I understand forty-eight's empty, so consider it an extension. Think of it as my gratitude for, well, you know.'

Hamble strode off leaving Jed staring after him in amazement. It had taken them months of waiting on housing to get their apartment and suddenly they'd been handed an extension. Glancing outside, he noticed the bucketing rain. Turning the collar up on his jacket, Jed nodded to the man on security and went to wait for a public skimmer home.

ANTIC: *Hamble seen leaving Force. Info lock down in place. Do you know more? Share & sweep.*

Chapter Five

JENHUB: *Newest member of City Forty-Two celebrates her homecoming today - send your welcome message to Grace Jenkins here.*

Kira flitted around the apartment in her pink dress, carrying out last minute checks to make sure everything was perfect. She had thought about leaving Grace in her cube, but she didn't want anyone and everyone picking her up and passing her around like a little toy doll. Instead the baby was snuggled into her wrap, close to her mummy. Kira paused for a moment looking down at the beautiful baby wondering to herself whether she'd earnt the right to call herself a mum.

'Is everything in order?' Martha broke Kira's reverie as she walked over from the kitchen looking demure in a perfectly tailored white tunic suit.

'I think so.' Kira looked around the apartment. 'We've got food, drink, music and the door barrier set up to our room when Grace is ready to snooze. I turned the soundproof on, didn't I?'

'Yes, you did.' Martha fiddled with the ornate titanium and sapphire ring on her finger. 'Will Ruth be coming?'

'Yep, and she's bringing a young graduate with her. Why – is that a problem?'

Martha shook her head and walked a few steps back over to the kitchen area before turning around again.

'I think I should take the memory wipe. Do you think I should?' Martha took a step towards her friend. 'I don't know what to do for the best.'

Kira walked over to her friend and put her arm around her.

'You have to do what you think is best, sweetie.'

'I can't bear to feel like this. I do not want to remember. I do not want to have to tell anybody about what happened.' Martha looked away. 'Yet if I do take it, I feel like I am giving in. I always thought I was stronger than that.'

'You are strong, Ma. Stronger than me,' Kira said, squeezing her friend's shoulder. 'Stronger than anyone I've ever known. If taking the wipe will help, then take it. At the end of the day you have to do what's best for you. Look, are you sure you can cope with the party?'

Martha didn't answer. She wiped her eyes and sniffed, pulling the memory wipe vial out of her pocket.

'I am going to take it, Kira. When you were getting Grace ready, I sat in your meditation spot to try and clear my head. If I do not take this wipe, I don't think I will ever stop feeling like this.' She paused, turning the vial up and down in her hand, tears in her eyes. 'I can't spend the rest of my life hoping no-one touches me, talks to me or asks me how I am.'

The two women shared a moment of quiet sympathy, broken only by the door pinging to announce visitors on their way.

'Look, I keyed the door barrier to accept you as well, Ma, so if you need to escape the party, you can,' Kira said.

'Thank you.' Martha unscrewed the vial and swallowed the liquid with a bitter grimace as Jed came rushing through the door.

'Everything alright?' he asked not waiting for a reply. 'I pinged the door to give you a bit of warning. Mother is downstairs so I need to ask you not to mention Martha's case - it's classified. We can't discuss it with anyone, okay?' He stared at the two women. 'Promise me?'

They nodded as Jed's mother – a tall, slender woman with elegantly coiffed silvery hair and creamy brown skin - swept into the apartment followed by a shorter, harassed looking yet smartly dressed black man carrying several bags and packages. Martha discreetly put the empty vial in her pocket.

'Darlings! How are you? The place looks,' Mrs Jenkins paused. 'So quaint. You should have let us host darling, we have so much more space and our décor is so tasteful – especially since we had Pierre in to redecorate.' She waved an immaculately manicured hand around the apartment. 'Where is my gorgeous granddaughter? I simply have to see her. Where is she?'

Kira's mouth tightened.

'Right in front of you.'

Mrs Jenkins stared in horror at the wrap over Kira's party dress which did, Kira had to admit, mar the overall effect. She took the baby out of the wrap.

'This,' Kira smiled, 'is Grace.'

Jed leaned in and gave his daughter a soft kiss on the head. 'Back in a parse.'

Mr Jenkins, struggling to keep control of the packages, coughed. 'Gretchen, dear?'

'Oh, for goodness sake Henry, anywhere, anywhere. Can't you see I'm busy?'

Martha came to the rescue helping Mr Jenkins find a place for the various bags and deftly taking his jacket. Mrs Jenkins leaned over the baby.

'Such a darling, darling. But why are you wearing that … thing?' She looked around, a faint frown wrinkling her brow. 'Where is the NanNan?'

'We decided not to get one Gretchen,' Kira explained.

'I know that but …. Ingrid. Well, I won't say anymore. She's on her way. Must visit the powder room.' Mrs Jenkins glided off to the bathroom leaving a waft of floral perfume in her wake.

'One parent down, one to go,' Kira said under her breath.

When Jed reappeared a few more people had arrived. No sign of his sister yet, or Pete. No doubt Pete would somehow manage to time his arrival to coincide with Ingrid. He usually did. Sometimes Jed wished his sister would show an interest in Pete. He was sure that once it happened, his friend would move on and he would stop having to listen to Pete telling him about how perfect Ingrid was.

Jed walked through the sitting room, nodding and smiling at guests when Kira's parents arrived. Jean and Malcolm Bishop were warm hearted and generous. He loved spending time with them and joined his wife at the door in welcome.

'Mum, Dad. Good journey?'

'Hello lovely.' Jean kissed her son in law on the cheek. 'Yes, it was a good run, wasn't it, Malcolm. Not too bad now the skypass has reopened. We parked around the back, son, so as not to take up spaces. You doing alright, love? You look a bit peaky. I bought some things, a bit of this, a bit of that. Just put it out on the counter, dear.'

Kira tried to look in the containers as Jed carried some over to the kitchen.

'Is this her?' Jean asked, peering into the wrap. 'Oh honey, she's so tiny. Hard to believe you were ever that little. I remember going to collect you and being too scared to even pick you up, you were so small. I thought you would break the minute I touched you, I said to your father, I said Malcolm...' and she carried on chattering away.

Once Jean got going, there was little stopping her. She scooped Grace into her arms and settled down in a nearby chair, directing her husband with the odd word and nod to put the various cakes and other sweetments he was holding on the table.

'Mum,' Kira said slightly bemused. 'We catered.'

'Yes well, those caterers don't know everything, my dear. This celebration cake was passed down six generations, six you hear, so it's just the right sort of occasion to bring it out and share it with your friends. I'm sure no-one will mind. Did I tell you about Betty down the street? No? Well, you know she installed a 'feed-me' because she thought it would help her lose weight? Well, you'll never guess what happened. I said to your father, you'll never guess what happened...' and she was off again, hardly pausing for breath.

Kira shook her head and smiled at Jed, who had returned and was nodding and laughing in all the right places - he had hours and hours of time for her parents. She saw Martha chatting quietly with Jed's father. The door opened, and Ruth arrived resplendent in a red top and bright blue skirt that jingled slightly as she moved, completely overshadowing Dina who followed behind her, dressed in pale shades of grey. Kira leant down to retrieve a sleeping Grace from her mother. The baby was completely unaware the room was full of people who had gathered specially to meet her.

***ACAD:** Highest number of new PhD students enrolled. Support your future and get involved, register your interest in placement – VR interview opportunities available.*

Dina looked around with interest at Kira's apartment. She wanted to use Mrs Jenkins as one of her research subjects for her own dissertation - *Natural Vs NanNan: is technology a realistic substitute?* - and was hoping she'd agree.

'K! Hi honey.' Ruth waved. 'Is this the little bundle? Oh, isn't she adorable.' Ruth cooed over Grace before turning to introduce Dina. 'This is my PhD student Dina Grey, I told you about her, didn't I?' She peered over Kira's shoulder, not waiting for a reply. 'Miserable weather, we almost drowned on the way. Oooh is that some of your mum's cake?' She drifted over to the kitchen, leaving Dina standing awkwardly on her own, not knowing what to say.

'Congratulations on Collection.'

'Thank you.' Kira studied Dina for a moment before taking pity on the young girl. 'I understand you want to interview me as part of your studies?'

Dina nodded.

'Give me a couple of weeks to get used to having Grace and then we can plan some time to meet up. You can come to the Archives if you like.'

Dina smiled in relief at Kira.

'That would be amazing. Thank you so much.'

'No problem. Here, come and meet Jed's cousins, they've just finished studying at Academy too.'

Kira manoeuvred the girl towards a small group haphazardly sprawled in the corner of the room, congratulating herself on her hostess skills.

'Who needs auto-pairing,' she thought.

CORP: *Bob Fellows dies, age 105, inventor of original NanNan - his work lives on. New model to be released soon. Pre-order the NanNan 3000 with your local Corporation Rep.*

As Jed had expected, Pete and Ingrid arrived at the same time. It was clear they had however, travelled separately as Pete was chatting to Ingrid about the weather and the state of the skimmer way. Ingrid, looking immaculate in her standard issue pale green tunic suit, had obviously come straight from work and had a large grey Corp Tech box on levitate next to her.

'Jed,' she gestured curtly to her brother as he greeted them. 'This is for you – in honour of Bob Fellows. It's the next gen NanNan 3000. Beta test was highly favourable, but it's not on the market yet so make sure you fulfil the feedback requirements.'

She left Jed with the box and moved through the apartment with purpose towards the wine, and her mother. Jed sighed. Kira would not be impressed. He moved the box over to the side of the doorway and hoped it wouldn't get in the way too much. People could always use it as a drinks table. Jed looked around for Pete, who was standing halfway to the kitchen and staring longingly after Ingrid.

'Everything okay at HQ, Pete?' Jed spoke in a low tone.

'What?' Pete jumped slightly as he turned around. 'Yeah. Terminators arrived and have it scheduled for nine tonight.'

Jed checked his wristplant, it was almost six.

'I figured they didn't need me there twiddling my thumbs, so I went and got my secret weapon.'

'Secret weapon?'

'Watch this.'

Pete walked towards the kitchen rolling up his sleeve, revealing a silver coin shaped device attached to his forearm. Ingrid glanced over, noted the device and her whole demeanour changed. From where Jed was standing it looked as if she was praising Pete, asking him questions, even smiling at him.

***INJEN:** Latest Force tech bio-monitor generating positive results in initial testing.*

Jed put two and two together. Pete had volunteered for the new equipment beta-test at HQ. Ingrid worked in tech development and lived for her career. If anything would work for Pete, this would. Jed grinned as he watched his friend top up his sister's wine glass and guide her to a free couch. Kira came up behind Jed and leant into him.

'What are you looking so pleased about?'

Jed nodded towards Pete and Ingrid.

'That's not the only one,' she said, pointing out Dina and Ben - one of Jed's cousins - heads together, talking intently, oblivious to the room around them. 'It's almost as if we used pheromone spray.'

Jed laughed. 'How do you know I didn't?'

Kira swatted him playfully.

'How's Grace doing love?' Jed said, changing the subject.

Kira looked down at the little lady snuggled in her wrap.

'She is just fine. I expect she'll want a feed in a bit, and then I'll put her down.'

Jed gently stroked the top of his daughter's head.

Kira continued. 'She's been around to everyone, and they all said she is gorgeous. What was in Ingrid's box?'

'Oh, nothing important. We can open it tomorrow.'

CORPCHAT: *Today's hot topic – should Natural Parenting be banned now that NanNan technology is so advanced? New parents, the Jenkins went natural – what would you do? Share your opinion, spread the sweep.*

Kira settled herself on the couch to feed Grace. She was feeling tired at having to explain, for what felt like the hundredth time, their natural parenting choice to her guests as well as answering the same question over and over, - *Why haven't you activated a NanNan?* But now, with her friends grouped around her, Kira didn't think she could feel any happier. Out of the corner of her eye, she watched a dishevelled Dina and Ben attempt to sneak back to the party from the bathroom. Kira chuckled to herself.

'Something amusing, Kira?' Martha asked.

'The audacity of youth.'

'Hey,' protested Ruth. 'You don't have to be young to be audacious you know.'

'Is that a fact, Ruth?' Martha said, not altogether friendly. 'Why, what have you been up to lately?'

Ruth frowned at her tone but carried on talking.

'Don't give me the lecture, Ma. We sneaked out last night. It was awesome and the sunset over the beach was epic.'

'We?' Kira asked.

'Yes, we.' Ruth blushed slightly and began twirling a stray strand of hair around a finger. 'Just a guy, no-one you know. And before you ask, he is an Anti-Corp supporter and no, he is not a terrorist and yes, I am being careful.' She looked pointedly at Martha as she spoke, who raised her hands and shook her head.

'Don't look at me,' Martha said. 'Who you do in your spare time is up to you.'

There was a pause, then the three women started laughing.

'Oh, K. It was amazing,' Ruth continued. 'There was something in the air, it felt so natural to be out there. I almost felt like,' she gestured towards the small blue figurine nestled in the corner of Kira's alter space, 'like Gaia was right there on that beach with us. Marshall reckons he saw a blue lady in the distance but I'm pretty sure that was either the drugs or the alcohol.' She laughed. 'Maybe both.'

Kira raised an eyebrow.

'What? I'm a grown up. It's all legit. I don't do dodgy anymore. Honest.'

'No, it's not that,' Kira clarified. 'The blue lady – did you see her?'

'No,' Ruth shook her head. 'I mean, it felt very spiritual, but I had other things on my mind and some of that was trying to make sure we didn't get caught. Why do you ask?'

'Well, it's just a bit odd. These blue lady sightings.' Kira glanced at the little blue figurine in the corner. 'Jed told me he saw a blue lady yesterday, on the way to Collection. And he saw a bee, or at least that what he says.'

Ruth thought back.

'Well there definitely wasn't a bee. Marshall only said he thought he saw a blue lady, and it was pretty dark out there. I was more interested in... other things.'

Dina had moved closer to them, listening in to their conversation, she tucked her hair behind her ear and coughed nervously.

'Umm, I've seen her too.' Dina blushed under the sudden scrutiny as the three women turned to look at her.

'I mean, I think I have.' Dina ducked her head slightly and tucked her hair behind her ear again. 'It was a couple of days ago. I was sitting outside Academy waiting for Ruth to come out of class. I suddenly realised there was someone sitting next to me. I was surprised, I hadn't notice them arrive, and before I had time to look around properly, they'd already gone.'

Martha interrupted her.

'So how do you even know anyone was there? It sounds like you never saw them in the first place.'

Dina spoke half to herself, half to Martha sounding frustrated.

'Maybe I'm just not explaining it very well.' Dina pushed her hair behind her ear again and spoke up with more determination. 'I saw a blue lady, but when I looked, she'd already gone. But I know I saw her. She touched my hand. That's how I knew someone was sitting next to me.'

Realising she'd spoken up more loudly, Dina shrank back a little, but Ruth leant over and patted her knee.

'I wondered why you seemed so off when I met you that day.' Ruth began tapping the table thoughtfully. 'You know, now that I think about it, I'm pretty sure it was a blue lady who brushed past me when Marshall and I were on our way out of the city.'

Martha snorted. 'You are just saying that because everyone else has seen her.'

Ruth glared at Martha.

'Have you seen her?'

'Actually, yes,' Martha countered. 'She brushed past me in the park when...' She stopped looking confused.

Kira filled the sudden silence.

'I think it's interesting that so many people have seen a blue lady. Do you think it's a new advert?' Kira wanted to divert the focus from Martha. 'Dina, did you feel drawn to making a purchase after your experience?'

Dina shook her head. 'No. I felt sad, but at peace.'

Ruth listened to them but continued to watch Martha with a slight frown on her face.

'Well, you know, it could have been a manifestation of Gaia,' Kira said, raising her voice to be heard above the mock groans from her friends. 'No, I'm serious. The natural planet needs our help, you can't deny that. We destroyed so much, it's only fair we help nature to rebuild as well. If we can't get more in tune with what's left of nature on the outside of City Forty-Two, soon there won't be anything left.'

'Kira, you don't seriously believe an ancient Greek deity is randomly stalking a handful of your friends.' Ruth sounded incredulous. 'What on earth would she want from us?'

Kira didn't know what to say.

MADSR: *Cosmology Expert delivers final lecture before returning to City Fifteen. Dr Marshall Reynolds talks about the slowing of the universe oscillation and what will happen when the reverberations end. Register interest, VR plug-in available.*

'Ruth - am I correct in thinking your Marshall is the Professor delivering the Cosmology lecture tonight?' Martha said, changing the subject, wanting to know more about Ruth's mystery man. 'Are you two serious?'

'He is, and I don't think so,' Ruth replied. The others all looked at her, waiting for more details. 'There's honestly nothing to tell. He's a visiting lecturer. Goes back next week - bit obsessed with looking up at the stars and asking the big question.' She put on a silly voice and waggled her fingers upwards, 'Are we alone in the verse?'

'You sound smitten to me,' Kira teased, gently lifting Grace to burp her.

'Yes, well, smitten or not, he's gone next week so I'm free and clear of all that.'

Martha leaned over to give Ruth a brief hug.

'We all go through bad and come out good the other side. I have to believe that.' She stood up to get more wine.

'What was all that about?' Ruth asked Kira.

Kira shook her head, standing up.

'Not mine to tell, Ruthie.'

Kira called for everyone's attention.

'Hi, everyone – I'd like to thank you all for coming.' She pointed at the sleeping baby on her shoulder. 'Grace is going to bed now but she's so pleased you all came, and she thanks you for the lovely gifts. We will come visit you all soon.'

The guests murmured good night Grace wishes as Kira took the baby into the bedroom.

ANTIC: *More secret meetings at Corp HQ. Join the online discussion in social hub beta – share what you know, don't let Corporation keep you in the dark.*

Sipping her wine, Martha noticed Jed was alone in the kitchen and went to stand with him.

'Anything?'

Without turning to face her, Jed spoke in a low voice. 'We got him Ma. You don't have to worry.'

She nodded slowly.

'What will happen to him?'

Jed felt uncomfortable talking about it but felt that he owed his friend the truth.

'Your father sent the order down. He's to be terminated.' He looked down at his wristplant. 'About now.'

Before he could say anymore there was a huge flash of light from outside the apartment window and a massive peal of thunder. Kira came hurrying out of the bedroom. Another series of flashes illuminated the windows from the outside. 'Lightning storm!' A couple of the younger guests cried.

Ingrid frowned looking down at her expanded wrist monitor.

'We're not scheduled a static storm tonight.'

'I guess tech isn't always a hundred percent,' Pete commented, taking Ingrid's hand.

She smiled, mellowed by the evening's wine. Everyone else continued to watch through the window as the lightning flashed, gradually slowing down in its intensity, the thunder growling above. When the storm stopped rumbling and the sky fell dark, heavy rain could be heard against the pane.

'What a night!' Kira's mother commented. 'I hope the skypass is still clear so we can get home.'

Kira reassured her. The party guests began talking about the weather and how they were planning to travel home. Martha touched Jed's arm tentatively, her face pale.

'Do you think that was caused by...' She trailed off.

'By termination? I don't think so, Ma. Just a fluke.'

'That was no fluke,' Kira said joining the conversation. 'That was Gaia crying out in pain.'

Jed looked at his wife and shook his head ruefully while Martha stared out of the window.

An hour after the storm had passed, people started to leave the apartment. The soundproofing had kept Grace oblivious to the storm raging outside. Martha had gone to lie down in the bedroom and keep an eye on the sleeping baby. Family, friends and parents all left in small groups, many leaving with food parcels and unopened bottles of wine. By the time Kira managed to get her parents out of the door, she felt exhausted.

'Is that it?'

'Yep. Pete left with Ingrid; they were giggling.'

Jed raised his eyebrows at Kira in mock disbelief.

'I expect we'll hear all about that tomorrow,' Kira said.

She looked around the apartment in dismay. There were glasses, cups, bits of food and cake littered all over the place.

'Come on,' she said to Jed. 'Let's make a start on this lot. I decided not to use the clean-up service thinking it wouldn't be that bad. We can at least get the washer on tonight.'

'I guess,' he said, less than enthusiastic. His wristplant beeped as a message from Pete came through

'Thank you, beta test!'

Jed chuckled.

'Well, I think Pete's having a good evening.'

Kira's eyes widened.

'Apparently volunteering for tech trials at HQ is the way to my sister's heart. Who knew?'

'Is that Pete finally making some headway with Ingrid?' Martha asked, coming through from the bedroom as Jed nodded in response. 'I am sorry for missing the end of the party. I came over so tired I needed to lie down for a bit. I checked on Grace before I left the room, she's fine.'

Kira smiled gratefully as Martha looked at the mess in the apartment.

'Do you want some help?'

Jed replied by tossing Martha a recycling sack.

While they got to work Jed told the two women the news about the apartment next door. Kira squealed and jumped up and down like a little girl. She gave Martha a huge hug.

'This is brilliant, Ma! You can move in, right next door - and be our free babysitter.'

Kira trailed off when she realised Martha wasn't matching her enthusiasm.

'Are you sure you don't need the space?' Martha asked.

Jed shook his head.

'Not right now and after everything you've been through, we'd be more than happy if you wanted to stay with us.' He wanted to hug Martha, but he knew it might be too much too soon. Instead he changed the subject. 'Dina seemed nice.'

Both women nodded and Kira gushed, sounding a little like her mother.

'Oh, she is such a lovely young girl. She's just graduated but now she's on Ruth's PhD trail. I mean, poor thing. But you know, she's here all alone. Her parents died and she doesn't have anyone else except for Academy mates, and you know how they usually drift off. I told her she was welcome to come over anytime. In fact, we're actually going to do lunch next week.'

'It will be nice to have a new member in our little group, especially after Ingrid,' Martha added. They all remembered how awkward lunch had been the one and only time Jed's sister had deigned to come outside without her technology.

'She's a complicated person,' Jed said.

CORPCHAT: *Share your best lightning shot for a chance to win extra water rations.*

ANTIC: *Terminators arrive at Force. What crime deserves such punishment?*

ANON6: *Corp just terminated a rapist!*

CORP: *Use of termination is strictly monitored and was sanctioned unanimously by the Board after reviewing a heinous crime. No further action is necessary.*

ADDITIONAL MEETING OF CORPORATION BOARD FOR CITY FORTY-TWO

DATE: 17th April 2215

VIRTUAL PRESENCE: R HAMBLE, J NICKS, Y ASWAD and P BASJERE

AGENDA

1. **UNSANCTIONED USE OF TERMINATORS**
2. **REDUCTION IN NAN-NAN SALES**
3. **INCREASE OF NATURALS**

MINUTES

1. **WHEN QUESTIONED HAMBLE DEFENDED UNSANCTIONED USE OF TERMINATORS IN PROTECTION OF DAUGHTER. IT WAS AGREED NO FURTHER ACTION TO BE TAKEN. HAMBLE WILL SUBMIT FULL REPORT.**

2. **IT WAS AGREED TO PUSH THE NEW NAN-NAN THROUGH THE SWEEPS AND OFFER REDUCED PRICES FOR THOSE UPGRADING FROM OLDER MODELS. ALL PARTS FOR EARLY MODELS TO BE WITHDRAWN FROM SALE. WATER CREDITS TO BE AWARDED TO THOSE WHO SUCCESSFULLY REFER.**

3. **ALL NATURALS TO BE LISTED AND ACTIVITY TAGGED FOR POTENTIAL UNREST. NOTHING TO REPORT SO FAR. BOARD TO CONSIDER REDUCING WATER CREDITS AS LAST RESORT.**

ANY OTHER BUSINESS – NONE.

Chapter Six

***MADSR:** Terminators used in shocking rape case – is anyone safe?*
Join the virtual discussion in social hub beta.

***FORCE:** Unsanctioned public demonstration will not be tolerated. All those involved in today's incident will be formally tagged and charged.*

Someone was crying.

Kira checked on Grace, who was sleeping peacefully. She could hear sobbing coming from the lounge. Creeping out of the bedroom so as not to wake Jed and the baby, Kira went to investigate.

'Ma, what's the matter?'

Martha lifted her tear-stained face and pointed at the news sweeps projected on the wall. Kira read them in silence. The rape case had finally been swept.

'It doesn't mention your name does it?'

'No,' Martha replied in a small voice.

'No-one will find out Ma.' Kira went over to where her friend was sitting on the couch and put an arm around her. 'It's going to be okay.'

Martha blew her nose.

'I took the wipe, but I still know that it happened.' Martha gestured back to the wall. 'It was me. I was the victim everyone is talking about.'

'You know what the sweeps are like though, Ma.' Kira tried to comfort her. 'They would have found out about the Terminators eventually. Now it's been reported, it'll soon die down when Corporation floods the sweeps about something else. No-one will find out.'

Martha looked at Kira and squeezed her hand.

'Thank you.'

'You'll see,' said Kira. 'They'll be talking about the latest tech in no time.'

Jed hurried into the lounge fully dressed.

'Morning hon. Martha. I've got to go into work early,' Jed said, grabbing an auto-brew from the kitchen. 'There's been something on the sweeps about...'

'Yes,' Kira interrupted. 'We know.'

'Martha, I'm so sorry.' Jed kissed his wife on the top of her head. 'I'll let you know what happens Kira, love you.'

'Love you.' She watched him leave the apartment. 'I hope he doesn't get into trouble.'

'I had better speak to my father,' Martha said.

'Why?'

'If this is on the sweeps, he will assume it originated from Pete or Jed.'

Kira bit her lip.

'Don't worry Kira,' Martha continued. 'I will vouch for them both.'

And she hugged her friend before getting up and returning to her new apartment. Kira didn't have time to dwell on anything as Grace began crying for attention and food.

Pete greeted Jed outside Force HQ.

'How's Martha?'

'Upset, but Kira's with her,' Jed replied. 'How did the sweeps get hold of the case details?'

Pete shrugged and followed his partner into the office. There was an instant summons from the chief on both desks. The two detectives went straight to Minkov's door. Pete knocked.

'Yes?'

Opening the door, Pete stuck his head into the room and Minkov beckoned them both in.

'Good, you're here. What the frag happened?' Chief Minkov jabbed his finger in Jed's direction. 'I've got Hamble breathing down my neck and the fragging sweeps are full of a case no-one is supposed to know anything about.'

'It didn't come from us,' Jed said.

'Of course it didn't fragging come from you. You're not complete idiots.' Breathing hard Minkov motioned for the two detectives to sit down. 'Who else was involved?'

'No-one, Sir,' Pete replied. 'We picked up Greenwood ourselves and carried out the questioning in meeting room one.'

'There was just the night guard,' Jed said. 'We didn't see anyone else.'

'Night guard, eh?' Minkov flicked through the screen in front of him then barked through the com to his secretary. 'Get Pearce in my office ASAP.'

Minkov lifted his gaze back to the two detectives. 'Can you think of anyone else?'

'Just the Terminators, Sir,' Jed said.

'And Mr Hamble,' Pete added. 'And his man.'

The chief rubbed his temples.

'Right,' he said. 'Hamble's on his way in, he wants to speak to both of you...' but before the Chief could continue, his office door banged open and Mr Hamble strode in.

'Hmmph.' Hamble surveyed the room. 'Which one of you broke protocol?'

Chief Minkov had stood up when Hamble entered, and his face reddened in anger.

'You have no jurisdiction to barge in here and accuse my detectives.'

'They had no right to speak to the sweeps,' Mr Hamble retorted.

'My detectives don't speak to the sweeps. We have other lines of enquiry to investigate and a full report will be made.'

The two men glared at each other for a few moments.

'I expect instant updates,' Mr Hamble conceded. He turned and left the room without giving either detective a single glance.

Pete exhaled loudly but said nothing as the chief shot him a sharp look.

'That'll be all. For now.' Minkov dismissed the two men from his office.

Jed's wristplant pinged, a message from Kira. *Martha is speaking to her Dad. Hope everything is alright? K x*

Jed told Pete about it as they returned to their desks.

'I hope she tells him we had nothing to do with it,' Pete grumbled.

'I think he knows we didn't. He's just looking for someone to blame.'

Several hours later the night guard Pearce was escorted to holding in magno-binders, watched by a grim-faced Chief Minkov.

There was no formal apology from Mr Hamble to Pete or Jed, but Martha assured them both that he had apologised to her for jumping to conclusions and that their jobs at Force HQ were safe.

CORP: *Our latest candidates for Corporation's Rising Star are:*
Miss Ingrid Jenkins, Corp Tech
Junior Dr Lewis Barnstable, Med Centre
Mr Vladimir Draganov, Science Division

INJEN: *Ecstatic to be nominated for Rising Star.*
I pledge to work even harder for Corporation.

Three weeks had passed since the leak at Force had been dealt with and an excited Ingrid was telling Jed, Kira and Pete over dinner about her nomination for Corporation Rising Star.

'It means I am a top pick for promotion.' Ingrid beamed at the others sat around the table. 'Isn't that exciting?'

Pete matched her smile, while Kira murmured her congratulations.

'Proud of you sis,' Jed said, as he leant over the table and clinked glasses with her.

'I just never thought it would be me,' Ingrid gushed. 'The department has been so busy, and everyone has been working hard, but it just goes to show – Corporation rewards loyalty and dedication.'

'Speaking of Corporation,' Kira said. 'Did you ever find out about the blue lady campaign, Ingrid?'

'I told you before, Kira, there was no such campaign.'

'Are you sure it's not top secret and you'd have to kill us if you told us?' Jed teased his sister, his voice full of amusement.

'It's not anything to do with Corporation at all.'

'So, you admit there was a blue lady then?' Kira said.

'That's not what I mean.' Ingrid started to get red in the face.

'We've all seen her, love. It's okay to admit you have too.' Pete was grinning with Kira and Jed and failed to realise how upset Ingrid was. She pushed her chair away from the table and stood up.

'I've just remembered, I've paperwork to finish at the office. Thank you for dinner, Kira.'

Before anyone could stop her, Ingrid gathered up her coat and left the apartment. The others stared at each other for a moment.

'I'd better go and see if she's alright.' Pete said his goodbyes and followed his girlfriend out of the apartment.

'I'm sorry, Jed,' said Kira. 'I didn't mean to upset her.'

Jed began to clear the dishes from the table.

'Don't worry about it, hon, she's a corper. I'm sure we'll have them both over for dinner again soon.'

A month later and Ingrid was still giving Pete the cold shoulder, despite how well their relationship had been going. Ingrid claimed it was a busy time at work, but Kira knew she'd caused an issue by raising the topic of the blue lady at dinner.

Kira spoke about the Gaia sightings with her other friends as they tried to figure out whether it was an advertising campaign, a nonsensical prank, or whether it could be the manifestation of an ancient goddess.

She was sure Ingrid had seen the blue lady and was desperate to apologise to her but all her efforts had met with a busy tone and Ingrid's sweep feed was full of work-related posts.

INJEN: *Latest development update – neural nets designed for colleagues to interface seamlessly in the workplace and increase efficiency.*

'Are you still pinging Ingrid?' Ruth asked.

'Yes.'

'Don't bother, K. She's so wrapped up in Corp these days, she probably thinks the blue lady is some kind of rival advertising.'

'A rival? To Corporation?' Dina was intrigued.

'I wish,' Ruth said.

Ruth, Dina, Martha and Kira had been meeting up regularly since Grace's homecoming party. The four women found they had a lot in common and enjoyed each other's company. Initially, Dina had been Ruth's shadow, but gradually she had begun to express her own personality and individuality.

'Do you know why Martha wanted to see us all, Kira?' Dina asked as she shook an old-fashioned rattle at Grace.

'I do.'

'Well?'

'I'm not telling,' Kira grinned at Dina. 'Ma will be here soon, you'll just have to wait.'

'I hate waiting,' Dina grumbled.

Martha came through the door five minutes later, a huge box in her hands.

'Oh good, you are all here.'

The others called out hello and Dina pointed at the box.

'Is that for me?'

'Yes, Dina,' Martha said. 'Let me show you what I have brought you.'

She took off her shoes, coat and bag and brought the box over to where the others were sat in the lounge.

'It's awesome you're part of the gang, Dina,' Ruth playfully punched Dina in the arm.

'And it has been wonderful to talk to you about what I do at the Hydroponics Lab,' Martha said.

'I find it fascinating though, Ma.' Dina was beginning to wonder where the conversation was going.

'You and Ben make such a cute couple,' Kira said. 'You're like the little sister I never had.'

'Okay, now you're going to make me cry,' Dina said as she tucked her blonde hair behind her ear.

Ruth and Kira watched as Martha opened the box she had put on the floor beside her. She gently lifted something up and held it out to Dina.

'Is that...' Dina spoke in hushed tones. 'Is that... an actual tree?'

'It is a fern,' Martha replied.

Kira got up and went over to the small altar in the corner of the room. She bent down and retrieved a small pot with a slightly bigger fern growing within it.

'This is George.' Kira looked fondly at her small plant.

'Mine lives in the bathroom,' Ruth said. 'It gets nice and steamy in there.'

The others laughed as Dina took the tiny fern from Martha and stroked the delicate fronds.

'This is amazing,' Dina said. 'It is real – isn't it?'

'Yes,' Martha replied. 'It is my personal project at SCID – I will have several to give away soon, but I wanted you to have one first.'

'Welcome to our family, Dina.' Kira beamed down at the young girl who was still in awe of the small plant in her hands. 'I have something for you as well. Something for all of you.'

Kira put her fern back and picked up a small blue bag. She settled herself back down on the floor. Grace had rolled over to her tummy and was kicking her legs frantically.

'I've got her.' Martha picked the baby up and started bouncing Grace on her knee.

'Okay,' Kira said. 'I know you tease me about her, but with everything that we've seen and now that Dina is part of our extended family, I wanted you all to have one.'

She fished into the bag and pulled out three miniature female figurines, all painted blue – a match for the one on her altar.

'Oh, Kira, thank you.' Dina peered at the statuette. 'She's beautiful.'

Martha and Ruth also looked curiously at the small yet exquisitely painted lady.

'I guess we can't blame the sightings on Corp anymore,' Ruth said.

'It's Gaia,' Kira replied.

'How can you be so sure?' Martha asked.

'The blue lady experiences are too personal for them to be Corporation.' Kira reached over to take Grace from Martha. She was trying to eat the blue lady figurine. 'I don't believe they are adverts. And adverts for what exactly?'

As each of the women put away her tiny goddess, the conversation moved on to where they were headed for lunch that day.

***DING:** Nature is beautiful.*

***SCID** – Scientific success in the hydroponics lab. Real ferns will be available to collect soon. Limited availability so register your interest with **MAHA**.*

Chapter Seven

DING: *So excited - touring Archive today!*

MAHA: *Thank you for the overwhelming response to the ferns. A new batch will be available soon, please register your interest with SCID.*

Kira hummed as she made the morning synth-caf. The past three months had flown by, Grace was growing so fast. Now she was smiling and grabbing fingers, wide-eyed and interested in everything around her. Life as a family had certainly taken some adjusting to, and the sleepless nights had been so difficult they had come close to turning on the Nan-Nan, but Kira was glad they had stuck to their ideals.

But today - today was going to be a good day. Kira was going to meet Dina at Archive for their first official interview, although they'd spent lots of time together since meeting at the party. She would be introducing Grace to her colleagues for the first time and then give Dina the grand tour. Kira enjoyed taking people around Archive. Not only was it a grand building, it housed carefully preserved film, books, scrolls - even Egyptian papyri spanning thousands of years of history. It was awe inspiring to walk through the hallowed corridors of Archive, pointing out items of special interest to visitors and generally breathing in that delicious book smell. Jed used to laugh at Kira when she tried to explain the smell to him. He claimed she was imagining the whole thing, but everyone else who worked in Archive knew exactly what she meant. It was a truly special place.

Glancing at the wall, Kira realised she was going to be late. She hurried to get Grace dressed and assemble all the baby paraphernalia she would need to travel the few blocks down the road. That was the one thing she missed about being a non-parent - the ability to walk out the door on time.

Martha poked her head around the inner door at the end of the apartment.

'Is it safe?'

Kira laughed.

'Of course it is, Ma.'

Since Mr Hamble had organised the addition of the next-door apartment to Kira and Jed's, it had made sense for Martha to move in straight away. Especially as she had no inclination to go back to her parents. Being around her friends and baby Grace had helped her forget some of the awfulness that had happened to her.

'Are you seeing Dina today?'

'Yeah. We're meeting at Archive; I'm taking Grace with me too. Should be good. What about you?'

Martha grimaced.

'I have got a med check. I would rather not attend but if I do not go...'

'I know, sweetie.'

That was the problem when your father was on the Corporation Board. There were good points like being able to live next door to your best friend, but it seemed your life was forever being scrutinised.

'May I cook for you both tonight?' Martha asked. 'I want to thank you again for letting me stay here.'

'Of course you can – especially if you can work your magic with what's in the cupboard.' Kira gave her friend a big hug. 'And we love having you next door.'

Grace began to babble over the wireless baby monitor.

'Time to get going.'

Martha gave Kira a little wave as the two women separated, each one intent on the day ahead.

Dina winced at the pain in her lower back. It had been eight weeks since her last period. She had eventually decided to make an appointment at Corp Medical in case it was the result of something sinister. She would be able to have the treatment straight away and not risk any complications. Usually she made every attempt to avoid Corporation officials, but Martha had been insistent that she have a check-up, the appointment was booked for tomorrow. Dina looked in the mirror and saw how pale and tired she looked.

Nothing a bit of make-up can't improve on she thought. She activated the *truly natural* option on her mirror and closed her eyes whilst the make-up was applied.

Dina was looking forward to today. Not only would she get to spend some time with Kira and Grace, but she was going to be able to record the first part of her interview with Kira and, best of all, she was getting an insiders' tour of Archive. She was sure not even Ruth had been in there. At least not officially, she thought, recalling Ruth's tales about adventures beyond the city walls. Now that she had left the comforting embrace of the Academy, Dina felt lucky to have found such a welcoming group of women who didn't treat her like a small child. It was so interesting to be able to have conversations about how life used to be, even if Kira's devotions to Gaia were a bit on the unusual side.

Dina checked herself in the mirror, turning her face from side to side. Much better. She applied a med-patch to her back; double checked her notes were in her bag and left the apartment.

The skimmer to Archive moved quickly through the airway. Dina struggled to find a comfortable position. She began to feel pain low down, deep inside her, like a hand was squeezing and tightening her womb rhythmically. She bit her lip at an intense cramp and started to worry. It had been a long time since she'd experienced severe period pain like this. She tried in vain to make herself think of something else and was so relieved when she arrived at Archive.

Dina saw Kira standing outside with Grace and hobbled over, hunched up to ease the pain in her abdomen.

'Dina! Are you okay?'

Dina gave a small nod.

'Bathroom?' she asked.

Kira led her through the doors and to the right.

'I'll be outside,' she said. 'Call me if you need me.'

As Dina went through to a cubicle, she gasped in pain and bent double. Half collapsing on the toilet she felt fluid leaving her body, and with some trepidation she wiped herself and looked to see what had happened. There was lots of blood. It wasn't the usual dark period colour, this was brighter, as if something had cut her on the inside. Dina searched frantically in her purse for her period pen hoping that it would be sufficient to stem the flow. After inserting the pen and finishing up, she stood and turned to see into the bowl. There were lots of clots and more blood. No wonder she had felt it leaving her body. She felt sick as she opened the cubicle door, then crunched her body up as the cramps returned.

'Kira,' she called weakly, then managed to repeat it louder.

The door to the bathroom opened, and Kira's face peered in.

'Yes, sweetie?'

Dina couldn't speak, she pointed behind her. As Kira wheeled Grace's pram cube into the bathroom, she wondered what on earth she was going to see. Looking into the cubicle Kira gasped when she saw the blood and looked at Dina.

'This is your period? Tell me that isn't normal?'

Dina shook her head and said 'no' in a small voice before more cramps made her cry out. Kira touched her ear comm.

'I need medic transport for a young female from Archive.'

She continued speaking to the operator, calmly answering questions as she put her arm around Dina. When Kira finished the call, she pulled the young girl in for a hug.

'They'll be here in five minutes, Dina. Do you want me to call anyone?'

'No. There's no-one. Just you and Ruth and Ma. Will you come with me?'

'Of course I will. Can you make it outside to wait for the Med Van?'

Dina shook her head in misery.

'Okay, sweetie, it's okay. We'll just wait here, it's fine.' Kira tried to soothe her friend while they waited anxiously for the medics to arrive.

Martha frowned at the two medical staff having a heated discussion behind the glass. Something must have gone wrong with the body scan but so far, they weren't talking to her. At last they seemed to come to an agreement and an intercom voice told her she could gather her things and go through to the waiting area.

'What about my results?'

The two medical agents looked at each other before one replied.

'If you could just wait next door, we will ask the Senior Consultant to speak with you shortly.'

And they dimmed the partition preventing any further conversation.

Martha huffed, it was probably nothing but because her father was who he was, they had to make a fuss. If they made her wait around much longer, she wouldn't have time to go and gather supplies to cook for Kira and Jed. She walked through to the outer office as the other door opened and an older man walked into the room.

'Miss Hamble?'

'Yes.'

'Hello, I'm Doctor Pevitt. It appears we have a rather unusual set of circumstances. Your medical scan revealed an anomaly, of sorts.'

Dr Pevitt cleared his throat and rubbed his forehead as he struggled to find the right words.

'Am I sick?' Martha asked, suddenly worried.

'That remains to be seen,' Dr Pevitt muttered, then realising he spoke aloud he coughed again and continued. 'To be blunt, you're pregnant.' He raised his hands and shoulders in a slight shrug. 'It's unclear as to how this has happened. Some genetic mutation perhaps. We'll have to run tests and keep you here, private rooms of course.'

'No. I will not be examined.'

Dr Pevitt made sympathetic noises.

'It's quite a lot to take in, my dear. Once your father arrives, I'm sure you'll begin to understand that staying here is the best course of action.'

Martha stood up and stared at him in growing horror.

'You called my father? You had no right...' She broke off as the door banged open and they both turned to look at Mr Hamble entering the room.

'Good, you're still here. What's going on? What's the emergency? Why couldn't I be informed over the phone?'

'I want to know why you were called at all.' Martha berated the doctor. 'Don't you have any concept of patient confidentiality?'

'Martha, what confidentiality? What are you talking about?'

She held her hands to her stomach protectively.

'Apparently, you are going to be a grandfather.'

Dr Pevitt rushed to fill in the details in the surprised silence that followed but trailed off when Mr Hamble held his hand up and looked directly at him.

'Who else knows about this?'

'Me and the two medical staff who carried out the scan.'

'I want them memory wiped, now. And you, you will sign a confidentiality disclosure and have all medical files relating to my daughter redacted immediately.'

'But the medical implications!' Dr Pevitt pleaded.

'I don't care for implications!' Mr Hamble roared making Martha and the doctor jump. 'Do it. Now!'

Dr Pevitt fled the room stammering affirmatives.

Martha sat down, knees drawn up, hugging herself, looking up at her father.

'I suppose you think I am abnormal too.'

'Martha. We need to keep this quiet while we decide what to do.' Mr Hamble began pacing the floor. 'I think you should move back home so I can have our personal medical staff see to you.'

'No, Father. I need to process this in my own space, in my own time. I am not your little girl anymore – you do not control me.'

She stood up, moved past him and left the room.

'Martha!' Mr Hamble took a step after her but stopped when she allowed the door to bang shut behind her.

She walked numbly through the medical centre corridor and became aware of a voice calling her name. She looked around and saw Kira sat outside Emergencies.

'What are you doing here? Is Grace okay?' Martha asked looking around. Spotting the baby, she put her hand to her chest in relief then frowned as she saw how worried Kira looked.

'It's Dina. She didn't feel well, and then there was an awful lot of blood and I didn't know what to do so I brought her here, and now they won't let me see her because I'm not family! I tried to explain to them that her family have passed away and I'm listed as her emergency contact, but they wouldn't listen.'

Kira looked at the closed door and bit her lip, then looking back at Martha realised her friend looked pale as well.

'Are you alright Ma? You look like you've had a shock - sit down, sit down.'

Kira helped Martha to a seat. Martha began to cry as the realisation that her rape three months ago had left such a permanent mark. She felt incredibly vulnerable and lost as to what to do next.

'Kira,' she half whispered. 'I'm pregnant.'

Kira stared at her friend but before she had time to respond, Pete and Jed walked into the lobby.

'Are they here for me?' Martha whispered.

Kira put a protective arm around her friend.

'What's going on?' Kira asked her husband.

'Why are you always in the thick of things, hon?' Jed said, running his hand over his head. 'We got a call from Medical; we came. I don't know anymore, but I'm guessing it has something to do with us?'

Martha clutched Kira's arm tightly while Kira tried to explain.

'They won't let me in to see Dina. Something bad has happened, I told them she didn't have any family. We are her family for frags sake.'

Glancing back at Martha, Kira shook her head slightly as if to say it wasn't about her. Martha felt confused and then stiffened when she saw her father and Dr Pevitt coming down the corridor towards them.

'Do not let them take me, Kira,' she whispered.

Mr Hamble eyed his daughter then spoke to Jed.

'Why are you here, Jenkins?'

Jed was about to speak, but before he could say anything the doctor cut in.

'I called him. We have another... situation. It's nothing Corp Medical can't handle but I thought it would be prudent to involve the Force in case of any difficulties. The young woman in question has no family.'

'We *are* her family,' Kira said in a loud voice. 'I've been trying to tell you people that for the past half an hour!'

Dr Pevitt looked startled at her outburst, but before he could continue Mr Hamble barked at him.

'What do you mean another incident?'

The doctor stared at the angry, confused faces around him.

'Perhaps we should move into one of the relative rooms? We can discuss everything in private there.'

'Very well,' Mr Hamble said. 'But we keep confidentialities already discussed. This has gone far enough as it is.'

They all walked into the side room indicated by the doctor. Grace began to cry. Kira could feel her face getting redder and redder as, all fingers and thumbs, she struggled to get the baby out of the stroller and find her milk. Jed tried to help but she batted his hands away.

'I got this,' she said.

After a few uncomfortable moments, Kira sat down, settled Grace with her milk and motioned for the doctor to begin.

'Well, about half an hour ago, a young woman...'

'Dina Grey.' Kira interrupted again.

Dr Pevitt scowled at her.

'Yes. Miss Grey came to Medical experiencing severe stomach cramps and blood loss,' he paused, looking around the room. 'It appears she had a miscarriage. Whilst these are not unknown to Corp Medical, it has been almost fifty years since our last incident and there are certain protocols we must follow. One of which includes extensive medical testing and isolation of the patient. In order to begin this process, we need family permission. It transpires that Miss Grey has no family,' he raised his voice in order to finish his sentence sensing Kira about to interrupt again. 'So, we called Force for legal witnesses to the process.'

'You can't be serious,' Martha said, pale faced. 'You can't expect a young woman to surrender her freedom so you can prod her and poke her whilst she tries to come to terms with losing a baby she never knew she could have. It is inhuman!' She turned to stare at her father, imploring him. 'Father, you can't let them do this.'

'Yes, well. It's somewhat out of my hands, Martha. Without legal guardianship, I don't see what I can do.'

Martha rounded on him furiously.

'You sweep legislation to one side for me and then expect me to accept my friends being persecuted? I can't believe you will stand idly by and let the Corporation ruin Dina's life!' She leaned forward. 'She is nineteen years old, Father. Nineteen! I won't let her go through this alone. Let her come home with Kira and me. We will make sure sweeps do not get hold of this and we will allow Medical to treat her at home, non-invasively.' She looked up at him with unshed tears in her eyes. 'Father, please?'

Mr Hamble stared at his daughter for a moment.

'I'll have to pull some strings. Let me speak to my man.' Turning to Dr Pevitt, he fixed him with a glare. 'I want this whole incident redacted. No evidence. Turn all files over to these two.' He pointed at Jed and Pete. 'I'll have my man come in and get you to sign a binding confidentiality. I'm sure I don't need to warn you of the consequences should a word of this be breathed to anyone.' He looked around the room glaring. 'Let's get this girl discharged, I want everyone out of here, pronto.'

Pete stood up first.

'I'll get Dina discharged.'

'I'll come with you,' said Martha. She paused as she passed her father, touching his arm. 'Thank you, Daddy.'

Mr Hamble cleared his throat and spoke to Jed.

'I'll send my man over for agreements. I know you are all friends now, but things change, and I don't want to leave anything to chance. You will agree to never discuss this with anyone else, especially anyone with Anti-Corp ties.'

Scowling, he included Kira in his statement.

She flushed, knowing he was talking about Ruth. Although none of them knew the extent of her involvement with Anti-Corp, it was obvious she had some kind of tie.

The doctor coughed reminded them all he was still in the room.

'Yes?' Mr Hamble asked.

'If the detective will follow me, I'll see about getting the memory wipes we discussed organised. I'd prefer to include myself with that course of action otherwise the temptation - you understand this is a double medical anomaly. I don't know that I could trust myself…' he trailed off under the stern gaze of Mr Hamble.

'Very well,' he nodded. 'Good man for volunteering, know your own weaknesses and act. Admirable, admirable.'

Jed gave his wife and daughter a kiss and whispered, 'see you later, hon,' as he escorted the doctor out of the room.

'Right then. I'll have some things sent over and get my man to organise the medical checks. Kira,' Mr Hamble paused as he tried to find the right words. 'My daughter... ahem... it's important...' He trailed off as Kira came up to him and put her hand on his arm.

'It's okay, Mr Hamble. We love Martha very much and we won't let anything bad happen to her. I promise.'

He reddened and nodded, then patted her hand before leaving the room. Kira exhaled loudly and looked down at the little girl happily babbling away in her arms.

MED4AC: *Hamble seen at Med Centre again. No Comment status released - again.*

ANTIC: *The number of authorised memory wipes has risen. What are Corporation trying to hide?*

MAHA: *Healthy and happy – nothing to worry about. More ferns soon.*

Notes from Anti-Corp Meeting at Academy Student Bar, July 30th 2215

Next beach trip planned for early August to celebrate end of finals.

September's drive for new recruits to be headed up by Bobby as usual. We've lost 17 members so it's important to replace and increase.

Successful bugging of Corp Tech achieved – we should be able to find out what new tech is on its way. Corporation can't hide anything from us.

Next on the bugging list is to get into Science Division so bring some ideas to our next meeting. We need to know what new genetics are being planned.

*Concerns raised again about the militant splinter group **42nd Army** who are now holding their own meetings and talking about extreme violent action against Corporation. Our leader, Victor Bianchi, will speak to their leader, Zane, and report back.*

Meet again in a month's time. Bring all your ideas for new rallies – let's keep fighting Corporation!

Think free – be free.

Chapter Eight

CORP: Report suspicious behaviour for the good of your community. Illegal goods hurt Corporation; we care about you so look after us.

Ruth stubbed out her cigarette into an already overflowing ashtray. She didn't have many packets left and it would be several months before the next shipment arrived, but the nicotine kept her feeling calm and in control. The black market thrived with low tech solutions to everyday life, and there was nothing Corporation could do about it.

They had used *The Event* to consolidate their power, and now a hundred years later most people could never imagine life without the omnipresent Corporation telling them what to do. When a younger, more idealistic Ruth had joined Anti-Corp she'd have done anything to effect change but both her and the movement had changed. These days she only passed on details of students who might be interested in joining Anti-Corp - being a lecturer of advanced studies had few perks, and certainly no high credit rewards, but what it did have was access to a steady stream of young, impressionable minds.

Ruth coughed as her lungs rebelled against the effects of the cigarettes and looked down at the short list on the tablet in front of her. At the top of the list was Dina's name. Ruth picked up her stylus and carefully drew a thick line right through it.

Dina has been bought up in City Fifteen, the closest geographic city to Forty-Two. Fifteen was smaller with a lower gross profit margin, meaning Corporation had had no qualms in downgrading the city after the uprising. After they had relocated the orphans. Dina's parents had been extremely vocal against Corporation. Others had listened to them, and it was the Grey's suspicious deaths that had sparked the Fifteen riots. Dina had been too young to understand what had happened at the time, and when Ruth first heard about her background, she thought Dina would've been desperate to join Anti-Corp. So far, she had shown no interest and Ruth didn't want to push the issue.

If she hadn't taken her to Kira's party, Dina would have never met Ben and never been distracted by that handsome face, and she would never have been invited to join the circle. Not that Ruth minded her inclusion. Being friends with Kira and Martha had originally been part of an Anti-Corp objective but after spending so much time with them Ruth had come to care for them both. It was one of the reasons why she was still on the fringe of Anti-Corp, involved with casual recruitment, rather than heading up new protests.

You can't be an activist and be best friends with the daughter of the Marketing Director of the Corporation Board. Victor had encouraged her to use Martha to discover Corporation weaknesses and opportunities for Anti-Corp to cast doubt over Corporation rule, but she had refused. Ruth shifted in her seat as she thought about the latest scheme she'd been involved with - using Pete's infatuation with Ingrid, Jed's sister, to plant a bug in her office at Corp Tech. Ruth hadn't been keen but felt sure Corporation security sweeps would catch the bug and remove it. Pete thought he'd been delivering a cute teddy to his lady. Ruth had no idea what Pete saw in Ingrid. He was a good-looking guy, but Ingrid, she was tall and blonde, with the personality of a stick. The scheme had worked though. Detailed scans of the Corp Tech building had been downloaded by Victor and his team.

It would be the first time Anti-Corp had access to a high security Corporation facility, provided of course they could get past the security measures. Ruth shook her head, not her problem she tried to tell herself. Her ear comm pinged and Kira, sounding stressed, was on the line.

'Ruth? Can you do me a huge favour? Can you swing by Dina's place and pick up some overnight stuff for her? She's going to be staying with us for a little while. I can't talk now but I'll fill you in when you get here. Dina said you still have an access key?'

Ruth nodded, then realising Kira wouldn't be able to see her spoke aloud. 'Yeah, yeah I have. I'll go now. Is she alright? What's happened?'

'Just get over here, Ruthie. It's too much to even try and put into words.' Kira clicked off.

Ruth gathered her things together. Whatever was going on sounded serious, trying to find new recruits could wait.

ANTIC: Calling all Academy Freshers – free drink and VR experience in the Quad today.

Martha held Dina's hand as they sat in the back of the private air car, courtesy of her father. Both women were preoccupied with their own thoughts and said nothing to each other, but each felt reassured at the close contact.

Kira and Jed sat in the seats in front of the two women, behind the driver. Kira looked back at her friends, then leaned over to Jed. In a low tone she spoke his name to get his attention.

'Jed. What are we going to do now?'

Jed glanced up at the driver and whispered in response.

'There's barely any evidence left at the Medical Centre. Pete's on clean up and he won't leave anything behind. I suggest we get home and call a family meeting.'

He smiled at his wife, confident that Dina could be cared for and helped if she stayed with them. In a louder voice he added,

'It'll mean we'll have an extra guest, but luckily we have all the spare space. I say, the more, the merrier.'

Kira leaned even closer towards him.

'Don't you think it's a bit odd, though?'

'How do you mean?'

'Well, first Martha's attack and all the sightings and now … this. A miscarriage for frag sake. They don't just happen Jed. It's clinically improbable. Since *The Event* I mean. We physically can't have children – any of us. So how did Dina get pregnant?'

Jed hushed his wife.

'I don't know love. I'm sure this is an isolated incident. Just like Martha's attack – which is unrelated I might add.' He glanced at the driver who seemed oblivious to their topic of conversation. 'I don't think we need to worry about a sudden population explosion. Anyway, Corporation will investigate and let us know if we need to be concerned.'

'You are joking?'

'As for the sightings. Kira, they were random projections for some product that never made it past initial tests. Ingrid says it happens all the time. It's just a coincidence that so many people we know were test subjects.'

Kira refused to give in.

'What about Mr Hamble then? Don't you think his behaviour is a little strange? I mean I know he loves his daughter but what's with all the secrecy. You have to agree that isn't *normal procedure* is it?'

As the aircar swung into parking for their apartment, Jed replied,

'You'd be surprised at what the Board gets brushed under the mat, love.'

***CORP:** Collect your updated water ration allocation and discover more ways to conserve with Corporation – we care about every drop.*

Ruth arrived at the apartment within half an hour of Kira calling her, laden with two large bags of Dina's clothes and other essentials. As Kira settled Grace on her play mat, Jed offered to make the drinks. Ruth took one look at Martha and Dina's pale faces, eyes red from crying and quietly asked what was going on. Neither answered, so she sat down with them and waited. Kira plonked herself on the floor, within arm's reach of the baby.

'You want to start, Ma?' she asked.

'Firstly, I don't want to hear any wild fantasies about Anti Corp or resistance or any of that nonsense.' She glared at Ruth who held her hands up in mock submission. 'I mean it. We know you have ties with AC but this time you have to be on our side, otherwise you leave now.'

Ruth looked at the three women and saw how serious they all were.

'I'm in,' she said.

Martha looked over at Dina who gave her a slight nod. She continued.

'Dina had a miscarriage this morning, a medical anomaly. And I, well, I'm pregnant.'

Jed chose that particular moment to bring hot drinks over to the women and stopped in amazement at what Martha had said. The sudden scalding pain on his hand alerted him that he was spilling synth-caf everywhere.

'Ah! Frag, that's hot!' he cried, and danced around Grace trying not to lose any more burning liquid, rushing to get rid of the mugs. 'Pregnant? Pregnant! No wonder Mr Hamble is desperate for everyone to sign a disclosure. Oh, my fragging hand.'

Ruth's mouth hung open; her eyes wide - this was huge. This could be the sweep of the century.

'This could ruin Corporation,' Ruth said to herself and glanced quickly at Kira to see if she had heard her.

'But you won't say anything, will you Ruth?' Kira asked.

'I won't tell anyone. I swear.' Ruth began fiddling with her thick hair hanging over her left shoulder. 'But have you thought about the implications? Corporation...'

'We have to decide what to do next,' Kira said, interrupting Ruth and trying to sound far more confident than she felt. 'Dina, sweetie, you can stay here as long as you want. Do you want to call Ben and let him know what's happened?'

Dina shook her head while Ruth glowered at Kira.

'Not yet,' Dina replied in a small voice. 'I'd like to go lie down to be honest.'

'Of course.'

Martha realised her presence was probably acting as a vicious reminder of what Dina had recently lost.

'I am so sorry Dina,' she said.

'I know.' Dina's voice trembled and her lower lip wobbled. 'I just can't talk about it right now.'

Tears began to roll down her cheeks. She put a hand out to stop the others from hugging her.

'Please, don't.'

Getting up from the floor, Kira gestured to Dina to follow her and took her through the adjoining door into the second apartment and found the spare room. She returned a few moments later and scooped baby Grace up for a cuddle, then spoke to the others.

'What the frag is going on?'

Ruth tried to speak but Jed cleared his throat loudly.

'Before anyone says anything else, I have to remind you all this is still a Force investigation. I have to interview Dina and Martha officially because even though Mr Hamble has asked Corp Medical to purge their records, the information on their pregnancies has to go somewhere.'

He looked nervously at Martha as she realised what he was saying.

'You mean my case still exists?'

Jed nodded.

'Case, what case?' Ruth asked, frustrated at not being able to speak. 'Is this about what happened three months ago?'

Kira looked at Martha who was staring into space.

'Yes,' Kira explained. 'Martha was assaulted and Mr Hamble wanted it off permanent record.'

Jed chimed in.

'Only Force doesn't work for Corporation. We uphold the law and part of that law means keeping a record of crimes committed. It has the highest possible clearance attached to it. Only me, Pete and the Chief have access.'

He turned to face Martha.

'No-one will ever see the details, Ma, but you can't let your father know that we kept the case file open. Pete and I nearly lost our jobs over the news sweep leak and if he knew the file still existed, well, I don't think we would come out the other side this time.'

Martha shook her head. 'I won't say anything, Jed.'

'Wait a parse,' exclaimed Ruth. 'You mean Martha was the ra… I mean, sexual assault that was swept? Does that mean you did or didn't catch him? Was the termination a cover too?'

Kira poked Ruth in the arm for being so thoughtless.

'Ow,' she muttered. 'Sorry Ma.' Ruth continued rubbing her arm. 'This is all news to me. Maybe if you'd kept me in the loop a bit more.'

Ruth hadn't known for sure that Martha had been the rape victim. She'd wondered at all the strange behaviour at the time, but feeling protective of her friend, Ruth had never reported those suspicions to Victor.

'Sorry, what?' She realised everyone was looking at her.

Jed repeated himself.

'I said, you can't breathe a word of this to anyone. You might think we are being ridiculous but I'm serious about this. We all know you have links to Anti-Corp, but we choose to believe that you wouldn't put your friends in danger.'

Ruth shifted uncomfortably.

'It wasn't me who told the news sweeps about the rape – I only just found out about it!'

Grace started to fuss, reacting to the raised voices and Kira began to hush her, rocking her from side to side.

'I need to see to Grace,' she said taking the baby into the bedroom.

Neither Martha nor Jed spoke. They watched Ruth until she bowed her head and conceded.

'I'll sign whatever I need to sign.'

Satisfied, Jed stood up.

'I have to go back to the office – see you later, ladies.'

'I have to go too,' said Ruth. 'Give D a hug from me Ma, I'll check in later. Bye, Kira.'

If she hurried, Ruth would have time to delay the feed from her internal recorder and Victor would never learn about the real rape victim or the pregnancy or the miscarriage.

If she hurried.

Kira came out of the bedroom and saw Martha looking rather forlorn on the couch.

'Would you like to hold Grace?'

Martha smiled and nodded.

'I'll get some milk sorted,' Kira said. 'She's ready for a feed. Shall we order in tonight? I don't feel much like cooking, I'm guessing you don't feel much like it either.'

'Sounds like an excellent idea to me. Should we check on Dina? She might want something.'

'No, let's leave her be. She needs to rest. I don't think any of us can do much for her right now. If she wants us, I'm sure she'll come through.'

Dina heard the murmur of voices through the apartment wall. It had sounded heated out there but now it seemed most people had left. She was curled up in a ball on the bed, feeling wrung out. She couldn't stop the tears from rolling down her face. She thought she had wanted to be on her own, but now that she was alone, her thoughts were all over the place.

How had this happened?

Why had it happened?

What did she do so wrong?

Dina tried to think back over the past three months. As far as she could remember, she hadn't been involved in anything detrimental to her health. The aftermath effects of excessive alcohol and drug abuse could be eradicated through regular Corp Medical check-ups, so nearly everyone had tried one substance or other to excess. But since she'd graduated, Dina hadn't seen much of her old friends and had split her time between Ben and Kira's group.

The only odd thing that had happened to her in the last three months had been that weird encounter with the blue lady, if she had even seen her at all. She hadn't seen the bee like the others. But there had been dreams. Dreams of Dina floating in blue light, enveloped in the warm embrace of her mother, watching tears roll down her beautiful face and hearing her whisper *I'm so sorry, so very sorry.* Dina had few memories of her parents and although the image capture she had of her mother didn't match the beautiful face in her dreams - who else could it be?

Her chest constricted and she thought she might not be able to breath with the weight of her grief pressing down upon her. It wasn't in her plan to apply for Collection anytime soon, so why did it hurt so much? Why did the thought of her body rejecting the tiny foetus fill her with such misery? It should never have been possible in the first place.

Dina thought about Kira's belief in Gaia and the concept that the Earth had its own spirit. She wondered at how such a peaceful idea could be responsible for the intense pain and loss she felt. *I need to know more*, she thought, and as soon as the idea began to grow, Dina felt a little bit stronger, filled with a purpose. This would make her feel better. She would get to the bottom of the blue lady, and she would find out why she and Martha had been made to suffer so much. But right now, she needed someone to hold her, breathe with her, stroke her hair and tell her everything was going to be alright.

She touched her ear comm and called for Ben. There was no answer.

***ANTIC:** Splash out and join Anti-Corp in today's protest – free water for all.*

Ruth hurried around the corner to her apartment and apologised as she ran into someone.

'Oh, it's you.'

'Ruthie, baby!' Bobby Travelli, a skinny man with greasy hair blocked the entrance to her apartment. He gestured for her to open the door.

Frag it thought Ruth.

She only had a small window of opportunity to stop the auto-download of the day's conversations, and she wasn't sure yet whether she wanted Anti-Corp to learn about Dina's miscarriage, or that Martha Hamble was the rape case victim.

'What do you want, Bobby?' she snapped.

'Inside,' he replied, and followed her through the doorway.

Bobby sat himself on the only chair in the compact front room, leaving Ruth standing. She glared at him and stood over by the small window, leaning against the wall.

'Well?'

'Victor is very disappointed, Ruthie. You haven't sent any newbies our way for a couple of weeks. We haven't heard any more about the martyr's daughter. Some of us think you've gone soft.'

Bobby smiled and began to clean his fingernails with an old-fashioned pocketknife. He looked more ridiculous than intimidating.

'Get to the point, Bobby.'

'We need someone in at Science Division. Victor has heard interesting things through the wire, and he needs a body. He told me to let you know that your debt would be repaid in full, *if* you can put the right person in place.'

Ruth snorted.

'As if I'd believe that coming from you.'

'Believe or don't believe, darlin', I speak the truth. Victor said and I quote, *Quentin will finally be laid to eternal rest*.'

Bobby watched closely as a flash of pain crossed Ruth's face.

'You've given me your message, now get out!' she hissed.

Bobby frowned at the viciousness of her tone.

'We need them in place as soon as, Ruthie.'

'Out! Now!'

He put an info jack on the table as he stood up.

'All the details are on here. I'm going, I'm going,' he said quickly as she took a step towards him.

After Bobby had left, Ruth sat down heavily. This was it. This was the last job, the job she never thought would come. After this, Anti Corp would finally return Quentin's remains to her and she could lay him to rest, and it would all be over. She smiled, eyes brimming, at the small image capture on the table. Her laughing in the sunshine with a tall, dark haired man with beard and glasses. On their wedding day.

Shortly after that photo, Quentin had disappeared - a bad deal gone worse with Anti Corp. She had never found out what it was. She had been so desperate to lay him to rest she'd stayed with Anti-Corp, working for them in the hope that one day she'd have his remains returned to her. Victor had promised her he would return them when she cleared Quentin's debt. She had to have him back because she wanted to say goodbye.

Feeling sickened by the whole situation, Ruth went into the bathroom, wiped her auto-record chip, and threw up.

Chapter Nine

***CORP:** National Antique Cake Day – visit the VR kitchen experience and receive a free taste-bud sample, just don't try baking at home!*

Ingrid should have been concentrating on the figures in front of her. There was an important presentation coming up and if she wanted to be considered for promotion, she needed to shine in front of the attending Board members. Glancing at the cute teddy bear sitting on the corner of her desk she smiled despite herself and thought of Pete. Her Pete. Pete, Pete, Pete.

He was a pleasant distraction, and if Ingrid could relax enough to go with the moment, she was certain she would enjoy herself. But she had worked so hard to get to where she was, and she didn't have time for a serious relationship – especially if it meant blowing her chances of promotion. Ingrid tried to push her focus back onto the technical specifications she should have memorised, but Pete's saucy grin kept invading her thoughts. In the end, she decided to call him.

'Hello - Pete?'

'Ingrid! Hi, how are you? Is everything alright?'

'I'm fine. I was wondering, are you available at all this weekend?' Ingrid could feel her face getting hotter and hotter. 'I thought maybe we could do something together. If you want? If you're free?'

'This weekend, huh? I'm free, we can go out or stay in, whatever you like.'

'Let's stay in. I'll serve dinner.' Ingrid felt happier than she had expected. 'See you Friday, at eight.'

Pete confirmed the details and clicked off.

'Right woman, time to focus,' she told herself, and bent over the data again.

INJEN: Excellent sales forecast for the next quarter.

The following day, the day of the presentation, Ingrid woke up feeling miserable. It felt like she'd spent the night downing shots and forgotten to take the hangover remover - yet she hadn't touched alcohol in months. She barely had enough energy to get out of bed, let alone complete her usual morning workout, and the thought of food had her running to the bathroom. Inviting Pete over later now seemed like a terrible mistake. Ingrid requested a mini health scan from her apartment, which had the complete health and well-being programming installed.

'Anomaly detected. Referral to nearest medical centre advised.'

'Negative.' Ingrid paced her bedroom floor. 'Expand please.'

'Anomaly detected. Unable to determine exact specifics. Referral to nearest medical centre advised.'

It seemed this wasn't a random bug she could shake off with a health tonic. Ingrid felt a twinge of worry.

'Negative,' she replied looking at her handheld e-diary for the day. If she hurried, she could pop into the on-site medical office at Corp Tech where she worked and still make it for her early morning presentation. Making sure she was impeccably groomed Ingrid left her apartment mulling over in her mind whether or not to cancel Pete's visit.

Half an hour later she sat on a chair in the medical office while a fresh-faced technician stammered apologies for inadequate equipment and alternated with excitement for her unique condition and assurances that a top-level consultant was on his way and would be here soon. Ingrid wasn't listening. She was stunned. This was simply not possible. Not for *her*. Not for *anyone*. Not now, not today, not ever. A green shimmer waved its way across the room. Ingrid watched entranced as she picked out motes of gold and red. Then something warm embraced her deep inside and stretched to the ends of her being.

Before she had a chance to enjoy the feeling, her bosses neural network invaded her head shattering the colours into a myriad of rainbows.

Ingrid, where are you? We are ready to start, and I need that presentation now!

A jolt went through her body. *This is why you didn't call in sick* she thought.

'I have to go. Tell the consultant to make an appointment with me through my e-diary and,' she paused and looked directly at the technician who appeared more shaken than she was. 'I assume this does come under medical discretion?'

'I'm not sure,' the technician replied. 'I have to tell my superior and then I expect they will tell yours – procedure, you understand.'

Ingrid nodded, gathering her things, and left the room. She wasn't sure whether it was a good idea for her bosses to be informed about her medical anomaly yet, but she also knew there was nothing she could do to prevent it.

Right now she had the presentation of her career to sail through, provided she was able to avoid vomiting everywhere.

***ANTIC:** Communication blackout at Force HQ – upload your feed and spread the sweep.*

There was a lull in paperwork at Force, and Pete was whistling.

'You're in a good mood, Pete,' remarked Jed, leaning back in his chair and watching his friend in amusement.

'That I am, Jenks, that I am.'

'Care to elaborate?'

Pete grinned and sat on the corner of his partners desk.

'Ingrid called me,' he said. 'She wants to get together this weekend, just hang out, me and her.'

Jed was surprised, Ingrid never called anyone. Before he could say anything else, Chief Minkov stuck his head around his door.

'Barnes, Jenkins, my office!'

Jed and Pete let out a collective sigh and walked over.

'Sit down,' the chief barked as they entered the doorway. They sat, exchanging glances.

'Now, you would tell me if this was some kind of joke, wouldn't you? I mean one is unusual – two is unheard of but three! Three! And it's your fragging sister this time.'

'Ingrid? What's she supposed to have done?' Jed asked, a little startled whilst Pete half stood.

Minkov shot him a fierce look and Pete sat back down.

'She's only gone and got herself a fragging medical anomaly. The next thing you'll be telling me is that it's something in the water and everybody is going to have one.'

'Have one what, Sir?' Jed asked, frowning in confusion.

'A baby! A fragging naturally conceived bundle of fragging joy. The Board is going to have a fragging field day, and Hamble is breathing down my neck at the two revelations we've got already down at Corp Medical.'

Pete had grabbed Jed's arm whilst the Chief was speaking and appeared to be in shock.

'Pull yourself together, Barnes, it's not the fragging apocalypse. At least not on my watch. Jenkins, you kept the file open on the rape case, didn't you?'

'Yes, Chief.'

'And you added the rape baby and the miscarriage?'

'Those too, Chief.'

'Right, get the fragging paperwork completed for this other one and get to the bottom of this whole fragging debacle. I can't have babies springing out everywhere, there'll be uproar.' Minkov stopped talking, he was breathing hard and red in the face. He glared at both men. 'And if Anti-Corp gets hold of any of this, you two can kiss your shields goodbye. You find out what's going on and you put an end to it. I don't want out of control riots like those last century – too many people died. I won't have it. This ends now.'

Jed responded with a smart 'Yes Chief,' and dragged Pete out the office, through the department, and into the locker rooms. He chose an empty changing pod, and shoved Pete inside.

'Pete! Pete – buddy! Snap out of it.'

Jed clicked his fingers in front of his friends face and was about to resort to slapping him when Pete spoke in a low voice.

'I'm going to be a Dad.'

He raised his eyes to look at Jed and began to laugh.

'I'm going to be a Dad.'

Ingrid trembled as she made her way to the Managing Director's office. It was the first time she'd been officially summoned, and she was desperately thinking back to the presentation to see if she could figure out what mistake she made. That could be the only reason for being summoned – a colossal mistake that would cost her entire career. But she could not think of anything she had said or done out of place. As far as she was concerned everything had gone smoothly and management had listened to her projections with interest.

The light on the outer door glowed, confirming her identity. She tried to remain calm as she pushed the door open. A tall, thin man stood by the window, hands clasped behind him, looking at the city laid out below.

'Do you know why Corporation is so successful, Miss Jenkins?' He spoke without turning.

Before Ingrid could think of a response he continued.

'Because we *create* the demand, and we *supply* the demand.'

He turned to face her and pursed his lips.

'What you appear to have done, Miss Jenkins, is find a niche market. I am not sure whether we can allow that niche to survive.'

Instinctively Ingrid's hand flew to her still flat stomach. She took an involuntary step backwards. The manging director of Corp Tech walked back to his desk, sat down and gestured for Ingrid to do the same. She did so, wondering what he would say next. He stared across the desk at Ingrid for a few moments.

'It appears you have powerful friends in high places, Miss Jenkins. You can thank them for your continued employment here at Corp Tech. You will remain in your current position until it becomes impossible for you to continue. You will submit to any and all medical investigations deemed necessary. You will not speak to the news sweeps. And when it becomes clear that you have a condition your only response will be *No Comment*. Any questions?'

Ingrid shook her head, then remembering where she was, replied, 'No Sir.'

'Good. Dismissed.'

Once Ingrid had reached the outer door, she let out a huge breath and sagged against the wall as the door closed behind her. Clearly, she had Mr Hamble to thank for the intervention, but it looked like her dream of promotion was well and truly over.

'Thanks for nothing,' she said to her midriff, wishing the whole thing would go away. Unwilling to linger outside the Managing Director's office, Ingrid hurried down to her floor, and the relative sanctuary of her office. As she sat down, she wondered whether it would be possible to terminate the child. Having a baby now would be so… inconvenient. She hadn't planned for Collection anytime soon. Looking up at the Employee of the Month awards that lined her office wall, she felt swamped by a surge of helplessness. Pete would never forgive her. Ingrid picked up the teddy bear on her desk and fiddled with the old-fashioned button on its nose. She didn't think she'd be able to forgive herself either. This way at least she could test all the latest baby products first-hand and drive that product area forward – promotion could always come from a different corner.

***INJEN:** Submit your ideas for new baby tech and win the opportunity to tour Corp Tech and learn how new tech is developed.*

Dina held Martha's hair away from her face as she knelt in front of the toilet. Martha groaned and dry heaved again.

'Are you okay, Ma?'

'I think so.'

Martha put a hand up to pat Dina's and moved away from the toilet bowl. The two women sat on the bathroom floor and looked at each other.

'I am so sorry you have to deal with this,' Martha said, with one hand on her chest. 'It is probably the last thing you want to be doing.'

'Don't be silly. I'm happy to help you.' Dina tucked her hair behind her ear. 'Besides, if it happened once – who knows, maybe it will happen again and then I'll need your help.'

'Believe me, Dina, I feel like I am dying. I would not wish this on anyone.'

Dina stood up and offered Martha a hand, helping her to her feet.

'Don't you have a Med Check today?'

'Yes,' Martha said, grimacing. 'I would rather not be poked and prodded by Corporation but if they can remove this morning sickness, then I will live with it.'

'I wish I could do more for you.'

'Oh, Dina – you are already being the best friend I could ask for.'

And Martha leaned over to hug her before the two women went through the adjoining door to Kira and Jed's apartment.

Kira was sat on the floor deep in thought while Grace entertained herself with various rattles and soft toys. Martha and Dina joined her.

'Anything wrong, K?' Dina asked.

'That was Jed,' Kira said, pointing at the vidcom screen. 'He said Pete had huge news and they are all coming around here for dinner. Ingrid included. He's just getting in touch with Ben now.'

Dina gasped and Kira looked at her in concern.

'He said the whole gang needed to be here. I thought you two...'

'It doesn't matter. He can come. I don't mind.'

'You don't suppose Pete is going to... perhaps... propose?' Martha asked.

Kira burst out laughing, then stopped as she realised there was no other reason for them to all get together.

'He can't be, can he? Not after the run around Ingrid gave him.'

Yet the more she thought about it, it seemed the only explanation there could be.

'What about Ruth?' Martha said.

'Jed wants Ruth here too, but he couldn't get through to her. I tried her ear comm just now - it's nothing but static.'

Dina nodded.

'Sounds about right. She's probably off grid.' She stood up. 'I'll go around if you like, I need to speak to her about my placement, anyway.'

'You sure?' Kira asked.

'I've got to keep busy, Kira, otherwise,' and she trailed off, her eyes filling with tears.

Martha reached up and squeezed her hand.

'It's okay. We understand, Dina. Whatever you need.'

Dina took a deep breath and pushed her grief back down.

'I'll be back in time for the big announcement,' she said, blowing kisses at a gurgly Grace as she left.

'Do you think she is alright?' Kira asked.

Martha fiddled with a cushion.

'I think she is finding her own way of coping with the unbelievable. As we all are.'

Kira nodded.

'But she has been spending a lot of time with Ruth talking about the latest approved Anti Corp campaigns.'

'I know. She feels let down, and despite everything we've been doing, I think she feels abandoned. It can't be easy going through what's she going through without her parents.' Then realising what she said, Kira stammered. 'I... I... I... mean - you've got the same, I mean, it's tough and there's a lot going on and,' Kira trailed off as she realised Martha was laughing, then joined in.

'Oh, you know what I mean.'

'Yes, I know what you mean, Kira.' Martha looked down at the happy baby. 'I still can't quite grasp the fact that I am growing one of these all by myself, without a lab.' Martha held her stomach and continued in a softer voice. 'Even if it was not my choice.'

Kira was teasing Grace with one of her soft toys, making her grab for the bunny ears.

'Have you thought any more about your father's offer of medical intervention?'

'Remove the baby? Do you believe that is the course of action I should take?'

'No!' Kira looked up at Martha in shock. 'I'd never suggest that, Ma.'

'It is something I have considered. Taking the memory pain wipe helped but I still know I was raped. I just do not have any emotional feelings attached to what happened. Not knowing who the father of my child is – and the fact that I never asked for it – it makes me feel unclean on the inside. As if this baby is unclean.'

'Oh, Ma,' Kira's eyes filled with tears. 'It's just an innocent baby, it never did anything wrong.' She looked at Grace playing happily. 'You're not... I mean you wouldn't...' Kira choked off, unable to keep talking.

'No, Kira. I am not going to remove it,' Martha said with a distant look on her face.

'That's good, Ma. I know it's the right thing to do,' Kira said, wiping her face dry.

'I do have a Med Check appointment today though,' Martha continued in a faraway voice. 'I have told them to come to the apartment. I do not want to be poked and prodded at Med Centre.'

'Seems fair enough.'

'Yes,' Martha said, refocusing on Kira and Grace in front of her. 'I refuse to be a Corporation pin cushion. Do not misunderstand me, I want to get through this as safely as possible, but women coped with pregnancy for centuries without being hooked up 24/7 to machines. Speaking of which, did you manage to get the materials I asked for from Archive?'

Kira shook her head.

'No, not yet but the request has gone through, so it shouldn't be a problem. We just need to wait for the repro and then you'll have all the texts you could possibly want. It is kinda exciting isn't it?'

Martha nodded, smiling back at her friend whilst at the same time panic butterflies fluttered madly around her chest.

Dina banged on the door again, she could hear faint movement inside. Ruth opened the door a crack.

'It's me. Ruth? What are you doing? Let me in.'

Dina tried to push the door wider.

'Dina, please, this isn't a great time.'

But Dina ignored her and pushed harder on the door. Ruth gave in and let her through.

'What do you want?' Ruth asked, not looking at Dina.

Dina looked around, expecting Ruth to have a visitor but realised no-one was there.

'Why wouldn't you let me in? What's going on?'

'Stuff,' Ruth said.

Dina coloured but carried on talking.

'Jed and Pete have called a family meeting. And they want you there too.'

Ruth looked up and raised her eyebrows.

'Me?'

'Yep. The whole gang. We tried to reach you, but no-one could get through.'

They both looked at the black screen of Ruth's vidcom. It was turned off.

'Why would you disconnect? Are you okay?' Dina asked, concern in her voice.

Ruth's bottom lip began to tremble.

'Hey, it's okay. I'm here.'

Dina gave her friend a hug. Ruth clung to her and began to speak.

'It's all my fault - the news sweep leaks - everything. And I can't tell anyone because then you won't want anything to do with me anymore, and you guys are my only family. I just want him back. I just want him back.'

She choked off, incoherent with sobs.

'Want who back?' Dina asked.

They separated, and Ruth gestured for Dina to join her on the rug.

After a few moments to calm down, Ruth explained about her late husband's dealings with Anti-Corp, and how she had been putting candidates forward to join Anti-Corp and spy for them.

'Candidates?' Dina asked. 'Like me? You wanted me to spy for Anti-Corp? When were you going to ask me about that?'

Ruth wiped her nose on her sleeve.

'They backed me into a corner, Dina, I had to do it. It was the only way to pay Quentin's debt, and get him back.'

Dina said nothing. The two women stared at each other in silence before Dina puffed out her cheeks.

'Frag's sake, Ruth. Why didn't you tell anyone? Jed could've, I don't know, done something.'

Ruth looked back at Dina, her nose running, eyes red and puffy. She sniffed.

'I couldn't at first, I didn't know anyone well enough, and then when I did, I'd already been helping Anti-Corp for a few years.'

'So you kept quiet, hoping it would go away?'

Ruth bristled, then gave in.

'More or less,' she agreed, her voice small.

'Well.' Dina stood. 'We have to get over to Kira's, so go sort yourself out.' She held out her hand to help Ruth up. 'We can hear what Pete and Jed have to say and then we can tell everyone together.'

Ruth's eyes widened.

'I don't think that's a great idea.'

'We're family, Ruth. And family helps each other, even when they make mistakes.'

Ruth still looked unsure, but Dina refused to hear another word. Now that Dina had people she cared for and who cared for her, she wasn't going to let anything bad happen.

To any of them.

By the time Ruth and Dina got back to Kira's, everyone else had arrived.

'Where's Grace?' Dina asked.

'Asleep in the bedroom. No distractions that way,' Kira explained.

Dina went and sat by Ben. Their relationship had cooled, both trying to come to terms with the miscarriage. But they were still friends. Ruth lingered near the front door, unsure where to sit, and not wanting to be there at all. Kira grabbed Ruth by the arm and pulled her into the loose circle that had formed in the centre of the lounge.

'You have the floor, boys,' Kira said, smiling up at her husband.

Jed turned to look at Pete who stood up and took a handheld

scanner from his pocket.

'Before we begin, this is a bug catcher. I'm not saying anyone here can't be trusted but...'

Pete paused and looked at Ruth. Ruth looked down at her hands, avoiding looking at anyone. Kira, Martha and Dina all looked at each other in confusion. This didn't sound like a proposal.

Pete continued.

'Something bigger than us is happening, and I for one want to get to the bottom of it without Corporation breathing down my neck.'

Ingrid frowned, but said nothing. Pete began the scanning with Jed. Kira leant over to Dina.

'What took you so long?'

Before Dina had a chance to reply the scanner beeped at Ingrid who reddened, flustered.

'It's my clearance chip. I forgot,' she said. 'Let me deactivate – sorry.'

She flicked her wrist, opening her internal screen. Despite many of them not wanting the invasiveness of top line Corp technology, everyone watched with interest. It was fascinating to see it in action.

'All done,' Ingrid said.

Pete smiled down at her, then realised the others were waiting and quickly moved on through the group. Ruth was the last to be scanned. Another beep. They all looked at her in surprise.

'I didn't expect you to have tech,' Ingrid commented.

'It's not mine. It's Anti-Corps.'

Pete's face hardened as he put away the scanner

'So, we've found our mole.'

Dina jumped up. 'It's not like that, Pete. Listen to what Ruth has to say.'

'Not until that bug has been removed.'

'Easy partner,' Jed intervened. 'Kira hon, can you get the med kit please?'

Kira scrambled off the floor and went to the kitchen, her head buzzing with a hundred questions, but she kept quiet, got the med kit and passed it to her husband. Jed knelt down beside Ruth and took her left hand.

'Ruthie, this is going to hurt, even with numbing spray.'

Tears rolled down her face.

'Do it,' Pete said fiercely.

Everyone watched as Jed applied a numbing spray to Ruth's wrist and used the medical kit laser to slice open her arm. He deftly plucked the bug out and before her arm had chance to bleed, he had applied a coagulation foam and used invisible stitching to pull the flesh back together. Jed worked quickly; he was used to removing bugs from Anti-Corp activists. As he finished the group let out a collective breath, and Ruth cradled her arm.

'Talk,' Pete demanded.

FORMAL MEETING OF CORPORATION BOARD FOR CITY FORTY-TWO

DATE: 2nd JULY 2215

VIRTUAL PRESENCE: R HAMBLE, J NICKS, Y ASWAD and P BASJERE

AGENDA

1. **UNPLANNED PREGNANCIES**
2. **CONTAINMENT**
3. **CONTROL**
4. **FILE 0**

MINUTES

1. **TWO PREGNANCIES AND ONE MISCARRIAGE HAVE BEEN REPORTED. MEDICAL HAVE NO EXPLANATIONS. SCIENCE DIVISION TO BEGIN INVESTIGATIONS ASAP.**

2. **SWEEPS WILL BE MONITORED. NON-DISCLOSURES WILL BE SENT TO THE FAMILIES INVOLVED. MEMORY WIPES AT MED CENTRE HAVE BEEN ACTIONED.**

3. **R HAMBLE CONFIRMS PREGNANCY A AND MISCARRIAGE ARE CONTAINED. THEY WILL SUBMIT TO MED CHECKS AT HOME AND SAMPLES WILL BE SENT TO SCIENCE DIVISION. MD OF CORP TECH CONFIRMS PREGNANCY B IS CONTAINED AND WILL SUBMIT TO ALL CORP MED REQUIREMENTS.**

4. **IT WAS DECIDED NOT TO DISCUSS FILE 0 AT THIS TIME.**

ANY OTHER BUSINESS – NONE

Chapter Ten

***SCID:** Intern places now open at Science Division. Register your interest, limited places.*

No-one spoke. Dina was holding Ruth's hand and the others were shaken by what Ruth had told them.

'Ruth.' Jed broke the silence. 'Now that your recorder has been removed – can we trust you?'

Ingrid's mouth twisted, but she held her tongue.

'I won't say anything to anyone,' Ruth said. 'But...'

'But what?' Pete demanded.

'But they'll know sooner or later the chip has been removed. So, what do I tell them?'

'We could always arrest you.' Pete smiled grimly.

'Pete!' Kira wasn't impressed.

'No, he's right, love.' Jed pointed at the deactivated bug on the floor. 'That way we'd have a legitimate reason for removing it. We're always doing Anti-Corp sweeps. Ruth can just say she got caught up in one.'

Kira still didn't look too pleased about the idea, but Ruth was nodding. Ben cleared his throat.

'If this wasn't the big reveal, why exactly were we all gathered here?' he said.

Pete and Ingrid looked at each other.

'We're having a baby,' Ingrid said.

Martha gasped, Dina looked shocked, and Kira's mouth simply hung open.

'I'm going to be a Dad!' Pete was grinning from ear to ear.

Ingrid looked less happy about their news and shook off the various attempts at congratulations.

'There are issues,' she said. 'My employer has been quite firm about my compliance with Corp Medical and my silence about the whole affair. But Pete...'

'Pete wanted his friends to know,' Pete said, still beaming.

'There is a more serious side to this as well,' Jed said. 'The Force is unofficially investigating why these pregnancies are happening. Only Pete and I are working the case - we are, after all, uniquely motivated to get answers.'

'That makes perfect sense to me,' Martha said, nodding.

Dina looked pensive. 'So, what's the plan?'

'I think Ruth's confession has actually helped us fill in some of the gaps,' Jed replied looking at Pete for confirmation. Pete reluctantly nodded.

'Ruth,' Jed continued. 'You told us that Anti-Corp wants to place someone in Science Division.' He looked at Dina. 'Do you think you would be up for that?'

'Now wait a minute,' Kira broke in, but Dina hushed her.

'Yes, I mean, I've got the right qualifications,' she said. 'If Ruth can help me get through selection.'

Ruth's face fell.

'Are you sure D?' she said. 'I mean, you'd be answering directly to Anti-Corp and they are definitely getting more and more aggressive.'

Dina lifted her chin slightly. 'I can do this. I want to know why my baby... why I lost... why this thing happened to me. And Martha and Ingrid. We all deserve an answer.'

'Okay Dina,' Jed said. 'Ruth, you organise getting her in at Science.' He paused, realising both women looked worried. 'Don't worry - I'll be your handler at this end. I'll get you set up with some top of the range surveillance gear and we'll plan all possible exit strategies.'

'What's a handler?' Dina asked.

'Exit strategies?' Ben said. 'What kind of danger do you think Dina is going to be in?'

'A handler is just a name for the person on the outside who looks after the people on the inside,' Jed explained. 'It's old world spy slang, but we still use it in field work. As for danger.' Jed glanced at Pete. 'It's hard to say.'

'Hard to say?' Ben exploded. 'What the frag does that mean? Just because Dina lost our baby doesn't make her expendable, you know.'

'Ben! Calm down.' Dina blushed. 'Not here.'

Jed went over to his cousin and put both hands on his shoulders.

'Ben - we're family. I would never willingly put you, or Dina, in a position of danger. That's why we are going to cover every angle. So nothing surprises us. Okay?'

Ben stared at Jed for a few moments, before reluctantly nodding.

'Anyone else got any objections?' When no-one replied Jed moved on. 'Based on Ruth's revelation that Anti-Corp wanted schematics of Corp Tech, Pete and I will put extra surveillance on Ingrid's building in case of terrorist attack. I doubt they'll be able to get through the security on that place, but again, we leave nothing to chance.'

'They know me there,' Pete added. 'It won't look unusual if I drop by more regularly.'

Jed looked at his wristplant.

'We'd better get you processed Ruth, if you want to be out by the morning.'

'Is it really necessary to arrest her?' Kira spoke up again, but Ruth put out an arm, forestalling any more discussion.

'Let's get it done,' she said. 'We don't have long before the recorder will attempt an auto info dump. It'll be okay Kira.'

Kira muttered under her breath and helped her friend get her things together. Before they were all about to leave, Kira hugged her husband and whispered, 'Look after her please.'

'I will,' Jed promised. 'We'll come straight back once it's all over.'

FORCE: *Another successful bug sweep removed illegal software from Anti-Corp sympathisers. We remind citizens that bugs will not be tolerated.*

Ingrid was looking for her coat when Martha decided to try and talk to her.

'Would you like to stay for a while? We could talk.'

'About what?' replied Ingrid, her expression blank.

Martha coloured, a little embarrassed.

'About the babies, our babies.'

'Oh, I haven't had time to think about it, to be honest. I ought to tell my mother first,' said Ingrid.

'Yes of course, I quite understand. If you ever do want to talk about them, I'm more than happy to,' Martha offered. 'Kira is getting some materials from Archives - you could look through them with me if you want.'

'Perhaps,' Ingrid said. 'But Corp Medical are going to be keeping a close eye on me, so I'm sure there will be nothing to concern myself about. Are you going for your regular check-ups?'

'I do not want to be constantly poked, prodded and monitored.'

Ingrid shrugged.

'I'm sure it's no different to normal medicals. Corporation will look after us you know.'

Martha smiled faintly, trying to ignore the look of incredulity she could see out of the corner of her eye on Kira's face.

Dina watched the exchange in silence. She would have avoided Corp Medical like Martha only now it didn't matter. Her tiny miracle no longer existed. She didn't blame Ben for getting upset - they hadn't talked about the loss in any detail. She didn't know what to say. He didn't know what to say either, so they reverted to that safe place in dying relationships where you said nothing.

Ben coughed to get Dina's attention.

'I'm heading out,' he said. 'You want anything?'

Dina shook her head but smiled in thanks.

'Are you leaving too, Ben?' Kira sounded disappointed. 'Are you sure you don't want to stay for dinner? There's plenty.'

'No thank you.'

'You won't say anything about what went on tonight will you, Ben?' Kira said.

Ben had his hand on the door. 'No, I won't,' he assured Kira without turning around.

ANTIC: *Bug lovers rise up and join our ant farm, share and sweep the city.*
'Divided we fall – together we are mighty!'

Kira watched him leave and chewed on her bottom lip.

'It'll be alright, Kira. Ben won't say anything.' Dina stood beside her.

'Huh?'

'Ben. He won't say anything. He doesn't want anyone to know about… well, you know... about... the failure.'

Dina tried not to cry. Kira turned and hugged her tight.

'You are not a failure, sweetie. You're a fighter.'

Martha murmured her agreement and even Ingrid patted Dina on the shoulder.

'Corporation will sort it out,' Ingrid said confidently. 'Things will go back to normal - Collection and control. The way it should be.'

The others stared at her, but Ingrid wasn't watching their faces. Instead she was accessing her mother's social calendar on her wristplant to see if she would be at home.

'I'll come around soon,' she said. 'I promise.' Then she air kissed them all and left.

'What a Corper!' Dina exclaimed. 'I know she's your sister-in-law Kira, but she is such a tech-head.'

Kira nodded her agreement. A faint ding from the kitchen reminded them of dinner.

'Let's eat,' Kira said, leading the others over to the counter as Grace began to cry. 'You serve, Ma. I'll go get the little one.'

CORP: *NEW!! VR Extreme release their latest must-have experiences – drive a car (includes traffic jam simulator) – fly a plane across the desert – ski down a mountain – swim in the ocean. All these action-packed ventures are waiting for you. Order now through your local Corporation Rep.*

The next morning saw a tired yet determined group of friends gather for their first planning meeting. Kira was bleary-eyed after getting up four times in the night with an extremely unhappy baby and feeling resentful at how well-rested Jed looked. Martha and Dina had waited up for Ruth to get back from processing and spent most of the night talking about how to get to the bottom of whatever it was that was happening to them.

'I had a strange dream last night,' Kira said, joining the others in the lounge with a cup of synth-caf in her hands. 'When I finally got to sleep that is.' She looked pointedly at her husband.

Jed, engrossed in the morning's sweeps, carried on eating breakfast unaware the remark was aimed at him.

'What?' he said, finally noticing the silence and speaking through a mouthful of food.

Kira ignored him, addressing Ruth, Martha and Dina.

'Anyway,' she said. 'I saw Gaia.'

'You saw Gaia,' Ruth repeated in disbelief.

'Yes, I did,' Kira replied, feeling defensive. 'She was walking towards me as the entire city around us exploded into a million pieces. As the pieces rained down, they became trees and a lake and beautiful countryside. I couldn't hear her, but I knew she was talking. It was odd because I was trying so hard to catch what she said, but I couldn't hear anything.'

'What did she look like?' Dina asked.

'Oh, she was beautiful. Blue skin and hair that moved around her on its own with flowers and creatures peeking out. Her eyes were like - '

'Eyes that sparkled like a thousand stars?' Jed asked, sitting up in the chair and paying attention.

'Well, yes,' Kira said, a little confused as to how Jed might know such a thing.

'That's who I saw. On Collection Day. In the street. When I saw the bee. You remember?' he said in excitement.

'A bee?' Martha said. 'I saw a bee.'

'Aren't they supposed to be extinct?' Ruth asked, but when no-one answered her, she shrugged. 'I thought they were extinct.'

Dina came to her rescue. 'Ruth's right, they are extinct. They're also familiars of Gaia.'

'What's a familiar?' Jed asked.

'Familiars are animal shaped spirits and bees are associated with Gaia.'

'How do you know that?' Ruth queried.

Dina flushed. 'I've been doing some research, reading ancient texts. I think I've dreamt of Gaia before too. At first, I thought it was my mother, but the woman was more beautiful than I remembered.'

'What happened?' Kira asked, interested to know if Dina's dream could in anyway be connected to her own.

'I could hear her,' Dina said. 'She just kept on apologising. It was around the time I... when I... well, you know…'

The group quietened, sensing Dina's reluctance to talk about her miscarriage.

Jed offered to refresh everyone's drinks and walked away to the drinks machine with a handful of mugs.

'I did not know Jed believed,' Martha said to Kira in his absence.

'I don't think he does Ma, not really. But even he has to admit strange things have happened to us. And the news sweeps aren't reporting any other pregnancies out there.'

'If it was widespread,' Ruth said. 'We'd definitely be hearing it on the sweeps.'

'Why?' Dina asked.

'Because Corporation wouldn't be able to stop every single person from uploading,' Ruth replied, then hesitated. 'Would they?'

'Who knows?' Dina shrugged.

'Speaking of Anti-Corp.' Kira changed the subject. 'Did they accept your arrest, Ruth?'

'Yep. I've gotta report in later. I'm planning to get D up to speed by then, so I can give them their new mole and not get fitted with a new recorder. That's the last thing we need.'

'What's the last thing we need?' Jed asked, returning with fresh synth-caf.

'Ruth to be reactivated,' Kira said.

'Oh right, yeah. Well, it's not actually the *worst* thing that could happen. We've got some new tech that could hijack whatever Ruth transmits, and process it through our server first.' Jed paused, seeing puzzled faces in front of him. 'It means we can remove anything we don't want Anti-Corp hearing.'

'What about me?' Dina asked. 'What will I have?'

Jed fished around in the bag under his stool, and brought out a thin hollowed disc.

'This is what we call a jack-catcher. It'll fit around your neural jack and capture audio and data information.'

'So you can even read encrypted info dumps?' Ruth was fascinated.

'That's right,' Jed said. 'Anti-Corp might think they've got the upper hand over us at Force, but we are constantly evolving new ways to monitor and counter their actions. We don't want a repeat of the mob action we had after The Event.'

Even though no-one there had been alive then, regularly streamed audio and visual recordings of The Event and its aftermath kept the details fresh in people's minds. The recordings were played to provide a reminder of what had been lost, and what had been gained.

'We'd better get on with this then,' Ruth said. 'This is what I'm thinking...'

She outlined her plan to introduce Dina to her contact at Anti-Corp as a recent graduate, with all the right qualifications to be their Science Division insider. The others listened, each hoping that Dina would find out the answers to all their questions.

Later that afternoon Dina sat in Ruth's flat fiddling with her hair, trying to calm her nerves.

'You ready?' Ruth asked, looking at her wristplant to check the time.

'I guess so.'

Both women jumped when the door chimed, and Ruth went to open the door. The meet with Anti-Corp usually happened at the student's own accommodation but seeing as Dina was staying with Kira and company everyone felt meeting at Ruth's would be less suspicious. Bobby filled the doorway. He greeted Ruth then pushed by her, excited to meet his latest recruit.

'Well aren't you a sweet little chip,' Bobby said looking Dina up and down.

The group had decided to try and make Dina look as innocent as possible by dressing her in her University tunic and keeping hair and make-up simple and natural. So far it was working. Bobby ran through a few general queries about Dina's education and her areas of expertise, then sat back with a self-satisfied smile.

'Your credentials check out. You're exactly what we're looking for. I'm sure Ruthie has told you, Dina, we have an interest in Science Division.'

'And what is it you want me to do?' Dina asked, eyes wide.

'We want to know what it is they're cooking up in their placenta bars,' Bobby said, his grin fading as neither woman reacted to his joke. He carried on. 'We want to know which genes are being spliced, what experiments they're working on - how exactly they plan to continue their vice-like hold over the masses. Everything really. That's where you come in.'

Bobby stopped speaking, waiting for Dina to guess.

'You want me to plant bugs?'

'Something like that. We'll start you off small with a couple of re-cons, see how you do. If they go well...'

Bobby noticed Ruth frowning hard at him.

'Now don't worry yourself, Ruthie. We aren't going to get this little chip in any kind of trouble.'

Bobby cleared his throat and stood up. Dina mirrored his movement. He leant over and swiped his wristplant over Dina's.

'I've got your number. We'll send you your first job in a few days. Let's just leave it at that shall we. Ladies.' Grinning to himself he made his own way out of the apartment.

'Ugh,' Ruth shivered. 'That man is slime personified.'

'I think it went well though,' Dina said.

'He was a little bit vague for my liking,' Ruth replied. 'I'd like to know more but if Anti-Corp are planning something big, I guess we'll find out eventually.'

A week after meeting Bobby, Dina stood in the foyer of Science Division gripping her access card, waiting to pass through security. She was wearing the bugged ear comm from Jed as well as carrying several listening devices scattered about her person. Both Jed and Ruth had assured Dina she would pass through security without a hitch, but standing in line waiting to be swept, Dina could feel sweat trickling down the back of her neck.

Thirty seconds later, and it was all over. She wished she didn't feel so clammy but at least the first hurdle had been negotiated. Now all she had to do was memorise the floor plan, find the places Anti-Corp wanted her to plant bugs in, and be the most unmemorable intern - all without getting caught.

An officious looking man came over to where Dina was standing by a moving staircase.

'You the new intern?'

'Yes, I'm Dina Grey,' she said, holding out her hand in greeting.

The man ignored her hand completely, turned and began walking away from her. He called 'Follow me' over his shoulder without even looking to see if she was and proceeded to ascend the moving staircase.

Dina decided against making small talk as she tried to keep up with him. He swept down an ordinary looking corridor with doors marked numerically, until they reached an empty lab. He retrieved a couple of passes from his pocket and passed them to Dina.

'We need you to clean up,' he said. 'The last intern fried the mechanism of our equipment-washer. While we wait for the parts, we've got a bit of a backlog.'

He swung the door open to reveal tray upon tray upon tray of test-tubes and beakers, petri dishes and syringes.

'I thought it was all automated these days,' Dina said, somewhat surprised.

'Head of SD is a dinosaur,' the man said. 'He likes to keep some of the old traditions alive. When you're done, swipe this card and I'll come get you. Have fun.'

Dina surveyed the room in dismay. Was this some sort of initiation test? At least she was unsupervised, and as an added bonus there happened to be a map of the facility on the wall over the sink. It was looking less and less like a waste of time after all.

ANTIC: *Outdated methods at Science Division – should we trust them with our futures? Upload your links and spread the sweep.*

DING: *Newest intern @ SCID – exciting times ahead!*

Notes from Anti-Corp Meeting at Academy Student Bar, July 31st 2215

Well done to everyone who joined us for the beach party attempt. Even though our wall breech was unsuccessful at least it was well swept – the people deserve to know that outside is safe!

We are in favourable talks with Professor Kamir to ensure any students who took part in the wall breech are given additional duties on campus rather than expulsion.

Successful bugging of Science Division achieved – we are monitoring all feeds to find out what new experiments are being worked out and hope to have a full report by the next meeting.

We'd like to remind members that anyone who decides to follow the 42nd Army should leave Anti-Corp – we do not share the same mission statement and cannot condone the use of excessive violence.

Monitoring headquarters were broken into last week. Nothing was taken so we believe it may have been a student prank but if anyone has any information please come forward.

We have located some nearby woodland outside the wall so submit your ideas for the theme of this year's fall ball.

Meet again in a month's time. Bring all your ideas for new rallies – let's keep fighting Corporation! Think free – be free.

Chapter Eleven

__MADSR:__ Failed wall breach by Academy students – Corpers calling for immediate expulsion. What do you think? Voice your opinion in social hub beta and be heard.

__CORP:__ City Forty-Two increases security measures on perimeter wall.
Corporation keeps you safe from highly toxic HER levels. We care.

__ANTIC:__ HER levels are an urban myth.
Post your images from beyond the wall and fight oppression.

After a month into her assignment at Science Division, Dina thought her brain might atrophy from boredom. Her days were spent cleaning all the antiquated, yet still in use, equipment and performing whatever menial task her mentor didn't feel like doing. Some of these little jobs had been quite interesting, taking her to different parts of the building - useful for her double agent status - but mostly she was reduced to filing of one kind or another.

Today was different. Today the head of Science Division had specifically requested all interns to present themselves outside the entrance to Banner Corridor, the highest security clearance corridor in the complex, at 9am sharp. Dina stood with the four other interns wondering what was going to happen. There had been rumours about an intern who mysteriously went missing when working late on this particular floor. But Dina had done a bit of digging and found out that the young man had been caught in a comprising position with a senior lab technician. They had both been quietly, but firmly, asked to leave. Workplace gossip was useful and had helped Dina plant all her bugs, but she hoped this gathering was not cause for another sudden disappearance.

At 9am the automatic doors to Banner opened, and the five interns crossed the threshold. As the doors swung shut, Dr Basjere, Head of Science Division, exited a side room and joined the nervous group.

'Welcome,' he said, smiling at them all.

There were a few nervous thank-yous and foot shuffles.

'If you would all follow me please.' Dr Basjere set off down the corridor. 'Loyalty is a highly coveted trait. One that we look for in our staff. Here at Science Division we need you to be one hundred percent committed to everything we do.'

Dr Basjere glanced over his shoulder to make sure everyone was still with him. He needn't have worried. The interns were hanging off his every word. Dina brought up the rear, wondering what Basjere was going to say next.

'We have decided that one of you will be our new fulltime scientist working on special projects. But before we make our final selection, we have a tricky problem we would like you to take a look at. We welcome any thoughts and suggestions you might have.'

Dr Basjere stopped outside a pair of double doors. 'Please.' He gestured the interns inside. 'Enjoy this chance to look at the future.'

Dina and the other interns entered the room and came to a standstill. They had entered the nerve hub of the entire division - the Idea Generation Room - a nirvana for anyone who wanted to work in Science Division. The place where the magic happened. Even Dina felt a tingle of excitement as she looked at the idea boards, floating mind maps, probability machines and, most wonderfully of all, the computer hive mind that ran everything.

The hive mind sat behind several layers of plexiglass, protected by intricate security levels, but the interns could still look at it through the window. And it was beautiful.

Dr Basjere had been talking to Dina, but she hadn't heard a word.

'Miss Grey, if you could?' he repeated.

Dina heard this time and hurried to follow the other interns into one of the affectionately named *fishbowls* - a workspace that cut you off from all outside interference and modulated its background to whatever most inspired and motivated the individual. It was achieved through state-of-the-art brain scans, and some dizzying computer programming that Science Division hoped to be able to begin beta testing in people's homes in the near future. That much Dina had been able to glean from one of her break-time gossips.

As the fishbowl closed around her, Dina caught a glimpse of a high-energy radiation warning sign from behind the hive computer. That was unexpected. HER weapons had been behind the devastating effects of The Event, and she had been taught the technology – and the means to recreate it - had been destroyed forever. The testing data popped up on the transparency in front of her. The fishbowl tuned into her own personal wavelength creating her optimal work environment, and she no longer had time to think about anything else.

Later that evening, Dina relayed her days' activities to Kira and the others over dinner. The glimpse of the high-energy radiation sign had everyone worried.

'I reckon that's what Anti-Corp is looking for,' said Ruth. 'If they had that kind of fire power, they could destroy Corporation.'

'And the rest of us,' Pete said.

'But why would anyone want to get rid of Corporation?' Ingrid asked, bemused.

Ingrid didn't come to all of the group meetings, but Pete had refused to exclude her from the essence of what they were trying to achieve. For her part, Ingrid had agreed not to divulge anything as long as it wasn't detrimental to Corporation.

'I didn't get a chance to investigate,' Dina said. 'But I think I did well with the testing so there is a possibility I'll get some additional access to Banner Corridor.'

'And what exactly is it that you think you'll be able to do?' Kira asked.

Dina shrugged, and around a mouthful of food she said thickly, 'I don't know. Snoop, improvise, you know, stuff.'

Jed cleared his throat.

'You don't need to do anything dangerous, Dina. We've got enough evidence to keep Anti-Corp tied up in Legal for a few years - thanks to your double-bugging.'

'Just try and get us a visual on the radiation sign,' Pete said. 'Then we can alert Science Division to the potential of an Anti-Corp attack.'

'Don't worry guys,' Dina said. 'I won't do anything stupid.'

Martha had been quiet throughout the exchange. She had been suffering with terrible morning sickness. Ingrid, however, seemed to be sailing through, looking more and more radiant as the days and weeks went by.

'You okay, Ma?' Kira said gently.

'High-energy radiation,' Martha replied. 'It was a specialised HER weapon that caused our forebears sterility.'

The room fell still as everyone stopped talking and looked at her.

'As you may know, grow-your-own was extremely popular before The Event. People donated sperm and eggs for specific genetic modification. I believe during the bio-warfare they managed to modulate a HER to the right frequency to affect the DNA of reproductive gametes.'

'Only the power of the remodulated beams was underestimated,' Kira joined in. 'So before they realised the irreversible damage they'd caused, everyone left had already been affected.'

'Correct. With no viable human gametes available, Corporation began creating their own, hence establishing their strong power base. Of course, that is the short version, it took place over several decades.'

No-one spoke.

'You don't think Corporation are still dosing us, do you?' Dina said finally. 'And somehow us three got immune, or missed a dose, or something?'

The others looked at her, then back at Martha.

'I can't say for certain. My area of expertise is plants, not people.'

'It's not possible,' Ingrid said. 'I know you want to find a bad guy to blame in all this, but I refuse to believe that Corporation, who look after us from cradle to grave, would have anything to do with deliberately enforcing sterility. I mean, what do they stand to gain?'

'Are you for real?' Ruth spluttered.

Ingrid sat up straighter, becoming red in the face at being directly challenged. Before she could reply, Ruth continued.

'Corporation have everything to gain. We are tame sheep herded from one technological marvel to another, never knowing the wonder of self-miracles.'

Ruth was beginning to get angry, and Ingrid shrunk away from her tirade.

'Don't you think that Kira would love to be Grace's biological mother? Don't you think you should be able to decide whether you can grow life within your own body, and not be at the mercy of the decision of some faceless suit in an office?'

Ruth took a breath to continue, but Kira put her hand on her arm and shook her head.

'Not now, Ruthie.'

Ingrid blinked back tears, unused to being the focus of such anger.

'I think I'd like to go now, Pete. I'm feeling tired.'

She rose gracefully, air kissing her brother goodbye and waving slightly at the others. Pete clasped arms with Jed and tipped his hand to the rest as he walked out with Ingrid.

'Sorry, Jed,' Ruth said. 'I know she's your sister but...'

'Don't worry about it, Ruth. My sister is a Corper through and through. If it's any consolation, I agree with you.'

'It's unlike you to be so aggressive though, Ruth,' said Martha.

'Sorry. I dunno know what came over me – I just felt so angry. I had to say something. It's this whole thing, it's got me on edge.'

'I'm glad I've got you in my corner, Ruthie,' said Kira, giving her friend a quick hug.

'Yeah, me too,' said Dina. 'I'd hate to be on the opposite side.'

Ruth nudged her in the ribs, and Dina laughed. Kira checked her wristplant.

'Look at the time – it's getting late. We'd better clear up,' she said, getting to her feet and collecting dishes. The others groaned as they reluctantly got up to help.

CORP: *Visit your nearest Auto-Doc and get your latest health check. Corporation cares.*

ANON88: *Privileged few get lucky again – what about those who've waited years?*

MADSR: *No comment.*

The following morning, Kira woke to a rapidly flashing handheld. She had over forty messages. Glancing across the bed, she saw Jed had even more. Grace was still sleeping, so Kira picked her handheld up, crept out of the bedroom, and went over to check the apartment vidcom and sync up. Fifteen more vid messages were waiting to be viewed. Something huge had happened last night. That, or something awful had happened to one of their parents. Kira quickly scrolled down the com in her hands, and with relief saw a message from her mother. And Jed's. And Martha's. And Martha's father - marked highly urgent - which remained at the top of the list as she continued to scroll. A scream from Martha's apartment startled Kira so much she nearly dropped her handheld. Jed came running out the bedroom, looking around wildly as the connecting door to Martha's apartment banged open and a furious Martha burst through, trailed by a rather ashen faced Dina.

'She has betrayed all of us,' Martha fumed at Kira. 'She is a selfish, self-centred, miserable old hag and I am glad her husband is dead so he does not have to put up with her anymore.'

'What are you talking about, Ma?' Jed asked.

'Have you not seen it? Do you not know what she has done to us? I will fragging kill her!'

Kira's eyes widened as Dina turned the expanded news feed on and let the sweeps fill the holo-projector on the wall of the lounge.

Another Corporation Cover Up but this time it's more than shady water deals. This time it affects every single one of us. The great and powerful Corporation have been trying to hide the facts but Anti-Corp, as always, has fought hard for the truth and we bring you the truth - the most incredible news since The Event.

NATURAL PREGNANCIES

That's right. You heard it here first. Anti-Corp has learnt that four women in our city have become naturally pregnant.

Martha Hamble (Corporation Marketing Director's daughter)
Ingrid Jenson (high flying exec at Corp Tech)
Ruth Maddocks (Corporation Educator)
Dina Grey (Student)

If you know any of these women, we demand that you upload, share and spread the sweep. Urge them to tell their story about how they broke away from the oppression of Corporation. Let them tell you how you too can start building a new life. A free life. A life without Corporation.

There was more but Kira stopped reading.

'Wait. Ruth's pregnant? When did that happen?'

'Never mind that, Kira, look at what she has done. She has betrayed us.' Martha was beginning to sound hysterical, but she carried on. 'I had one hundred and twenty-four messages on my handheld this morning, and my ear comm will not stop ringing. I have barely had time to adjust to this myself, let alone feel ready to explain it to the entire city.'

There was a knock at the apartment door. Jed opened it. Ruth came in.

'You have got a fragging nerve,' Martha shouted at her as she flew towards the door. Kira managed to catch Martha's arm and slow her down, and Jed blocked her path to Ruth.

'It wasn't me,' Ruth implored, desperation in her voice.

Kira looked at Ruth more closely, she could see her eyes were red and puffy with dark shadows, and she was wearing the same clothes as yesterday.

'You didn't know, did you?'

Ruth shook her head slowly. Jed guided Ruth over to the couch and sat her down next to Dina. Martha, calming a little, allowed Kira to do the same with her. Jed's ear comm pinged.

'It's work. I have to go in.'

They all looked at him coolly.

'I think you should all just stay here for now,' he said. 'Let me see what I can find out.'

And he disappeared into the bedroom to get ready for work.

'Don't we have to attend the protest today?' Dina asked. No-one was listening.

'What the frag, Ruth? What did you do?' Martha asked, her fingers curled into talons, as if she wanted to rake Ruth's eyes out.

Kira made shushing noises and gestures, trying to calm Martha down.

'I didn't *do* anything,' Ruth replied. 'I've not been feeling well so I went for a check-up last night. It was just an auto-doc. I never spoke to an actual person. It found an anomaly.'

'An anomaly?' Martha said.

'Yeah. I got a tip to toe check. I did the scan and I saw… ' Ruth faltered looking at Dina. 'I saw the baby. I am so sorry, Dina. It should've been you, not me. I don't understand.'

Jed reappeared from the bedroom with a wide-awake Grace. He passed the baby to Kira and said his quick goodbyes. As the front door closed behind him Martha sniffed loudly.

'Are we supposed to believe you got yourself pregnant and did not know anything about it until last night?' she said, acid dripping from every word.

'Look, I've not felt well,' Ruth said. 'But I thought it was just stress with getting Quentin back, and trying to find out what Anti-Corp are up to.'

Martha gestured to the sweeps still projecting on the wall.

'And all *this* just happens to be a coincidence?'

'Yeah. I don't have my mic chip Ma, and I'm not reporting back to Anti-Corp anymore. We've gotta find out where the info *did* leak from before it gets any worse.'

'How can it possibly get any worse?'

But before Ruth could respond, Grace began to cry, not used to the loud, aggressive voices. Kira scowled at them.

'You've made Gracie cry. Calm down the both of you. Dina, can you help me in the kitchen please sweetie.'

Ruth and Martha settled back into chairs on opposite sides of the lounge, glaring at one another, as Kira, Grace and Dina went into the kitchen to make baby milk and synth-caf.

CORP: *We urge citizens to remain calm. No-one is at risk. Anomalies happen. For more information please visit your nearest Auto-Doc and get your free med check.*

INJEN: *NO COMMENT.*

The apartment door banged open and Ingrid stood in the doorway quivering with rage.

'What have you done?' Ingrid shrieked at Ruth, who leapt up to defend herself.

Kira strode from the kitchen area into the lounge.

'That is enough. I have never, NEVER, seen such displays of rudeness and aggression in my home, and I will not have it. My home is a place of welcome and love, and I will not have you coming in here treating it like garbage. Do you understand?' Her gaze swept over all of them.

Ingrid, Martha and Ruth all remained silent as Kira continued.

'I am making synth-caf. We will sit down and discuss calmly how the sweeps got hold of this information. Mr Hamble has sent me an important message, and Jed has gone to work to find out what he can about the situation. Can you three control yourselves?'

Kira looked in disapproval at the three women, as Dina began to bring cups over to the lounge area. They all nodded mutely.

ANON88: *How much did they pay Corporation? Why weren't we given a chance?*
Protest against privileged pregnancies, sweep it out and join us.

Mr Hamble's message was brief and to the point. Kira settled herself with Grace on the couch and read it aloud.

'Kira. Tell your friends the leak came from Force. It has been locked down. Inform the others that any contact with the sweeps goes against a legal directive from Corporation. I'll send my man over with the details. Yours R. Hamble.'

By the time Kira had finished reading the message, Martha had calmed down enough to check her handheld. She confirmed that she had a near identical message.

'I suppose he knew we would come together over this,' Martha said, clearing her throat, and shifting in her seat. 'Ruth, I am so sorry I lost my temper. It was incredibly wrong of me to jump to conclusions. I know it is no excuse, but I am feeling rather overwhelmed at the moment...'

She couldn't continue and tears spilled down her face. Ruth was crying too, trying to tell Martha it was okay but not doing a very good job. Ingrid watched the two women curiously, feeling no desire to cry whatsoever.

'I hope Jed isn't going to get into trouble,' Dina said, once tears were dried and hugs exchanged. The others looked at her in alarm.

'What do you mean, Dina?' Kira asked.

'Well, if the leak came from Force, it must have come from the case files Jed has been keeping on all of us. I know he said his boss ordered him to do it, but it went against everything Mr Hamble told him to do. And if he finds out... do you remember how mad Mr Hamble was when the details of the attack got leaked?'

'I do,' Ingrid said. 'Pete nearly lost his job. So did Jed.'

'I guess we just have to wait for Jed to come back,' Kira said. 'And then we'll know more.'

A bleak silence settled on the women, each absorbed in their own thoughts. Ingrid stood.

'I'm going to be late for work,' she announced. 'I only came over here to find out what was going on. I have to go.'

'Are you sure it's safe?' Martha asked.

'It's fine. I have a driver. Management requirements now that...'

She pointed towards her stomach. The others said their distracted goodbyes as she left.

'Sometimes I wish it were me and not Ingrid,' Kira spoke wistfully.

Ruth leant over and put her arm around Kira, hugging her gently.

'I hope Jed won't be too cross with us.' Dina broke the silence.

'Why would he be cross with you?' Kira asked.

'We have to go to the water protest today, remember? As part of my cover?'

'Oh – I'd forgotten all about that,' Kira said. 'I don't want to bring Grace to the protest.'

'Neither do I,' Dina said. 'It's okay – Ruth is coming with me.'

Martha was fiddling with her sleeve, listening to the others. 'I will come too.'

'Are you sure, Ma?' Dina asked.

'Yes, I can't stay indoors all day. Not today.'

'What if someone recognises you?'

Martha shrugged. 'We will all have to adjust to our lives changing from now on.'

'I suppose so,' Kira said. 'You don't mind if I don't come, do you?'

The others all reassured Kira that they didn't and began planning their route to the protest.

Somewhere in City Forty-Two...

'Have you seen the sweeps?'

'Yes. Corporation must have let something slip to result in four pregnancies.'

'It's a bit odd that they all know each other isn't it?'

'We didn't come here to talk about them.'

'Right. The meeting has moved to Corp Tech.'

'Are you sure?'

'Yes. The new secretary is ours. She's been waiting six years for Collection and after this morning's sweeps, she is feeling motivated.'

'Did you get the schematics?'

'Yes.'

'Any problems?'

'No. Anti-Corp think it was a student prank.'

'And they won't find the tech?'

'It's hidden well. All their files were downloaded yesterday. We have everything they have.'

'What's the plan?'

'There's a weakness on the south side.'

'Weak enough?'

'Should be.'

'What do we have?'

'Remotely controlled skimmer full of ammonia nitrate and wired with a remote detonation.'

'And it won't be checked?'

'It's already in place.'

Chapter Twelve

ANTIC: *Biggest Corporation cover-up to date*
Martha Hamble – pregnant!
Ruth Maddocks – pregnant!
Ingrid Jenkins – pregnant!
Dina Grey – pregnant!
Who do you know? Upload your links and spread the sweep.

MED4AC: *We can neither confirm nor deny any medical abnormalities at this time.*

MSCHILD: *Four!! How did that happen? It's not fair.*

Jed caught the news sweep on his way to work. He was concerned - how the frag did the sweeps have all the details? And why did the sweep report Dina as pregnant and not a miscarriage? Nothing was making sense and Jed felt uneasy as he walked through the Community Hub and around the side of Force HQ.

When he got into work there was an immediate summons on his desk to the Chief's office. Knocking, then entering, Jed was relieved to see his partner Pete already there. He didn't recognise the other man. He was short and squat, dressed in a non-regulation grey suit, with greasy looking hair and a faint sneer on his face.

'Jenkins, sit down. You too, Barnes. This is Agent Deveraux from Special Investigations. He'd like to know how the frag the sweeps got hold of our classified files.'

The Chief folded his hands on the desk in front of him and waited for a response. Pete and Jed made a point of not looking at each other. Jed felt confident - he knew that neither of them had leaked the information.

'Sir, I have no idea. We followed protocol to the letter.'

'Have you checked all the internal coding for non-Force elements?' Pete asked.

Jed raised his eyebrows in surprise at that. It was not like Pete to think of the techy solution. Ingrid must be rubbing off on him.

'It's alright detectives,' Agent Deveraux said, smiling with no real warmth behind it. 'We know you didn't leak the information. The both of you are so tightly entwined in this mess on a personal level I believe a leak of this nature would be the last course of action either of you would take.'

Agent Deveraux handed Pete and Jed an info jack each.

'This is everything we have on Anti-Corps movements in the past six months. I think you might be surprised at how widespread their little spies are.'

The agent paused as if deciding whether or not to reveal any more details. He thumbed his earlobe whilst moving back to stand at the side of the Chief's desk.

'In fact,' Deveraux said. 'We also know about your own personal infiltration.'

Pete and Jed tried to keep their face neutral.

'Anti-Corp are not the only ones who look to the student body for convenient bug placers gentlemen. Your apartment has been under surveillance for several months now. Audio only – of course.'

Jed's jaw tightened. Chief Minkov interrupted, glaring at the agent.

'What Deveraux is trying to say is that he wants you to continue in your infiltration of Anti-Corp. Find out everything you can because we will not be left on the side lines holding our arses when this thing kicks off.' Minkov breathed heavily through his nose.

Jed addressed Deveraux.

'I assume you'll be removing that bug immediately. Now that we're on the same page.'

The agent shrugged.

'Sure. Just make sure you use the info jacks I've given you to get up to speed and then continue to update us with your progress.'

Jed nodded, then looked at the chief.

'Anything else, Sir?'

'I want you heading up a team for today's protest, Jenkins. I will not allow these fragging activists to get away with anything. If one of them so much as puts a toe out of line you arrest first, ask questions later. That'll be all.'

ANTIC: *No Comment says Corporation in the face of medical miracles – new experiment gone wrong sparks health scares – check your womb today!*

ANON6: *Martha Hamble was the rape victim!!!*

ANON88: *Serves her right – Corpers deserve it.*

JMBISH: *Have some respect you sweep vultures and leave the poor girl alone!*

MAHA: *Thank you for the supportive messages. I am keeping the baby.*

ANTIC: *We support MAHA.*

'What the frag are SI doing bugging your fragging apartment?' Pete asked when the two men were back at their desks, his face red, fists clenched.

Jed ran a hand through his hair as he sat. His head felt like it was fizzing. Everything seemed to be running out of control. Four women falling pregnant. All of them he, and especially Kira, knew. One of them suffering a miscarriage. And now that their little spy stunt had stumbled on the HER source, things were getting more and more serious.

'I think we need to get ourselves up to spec.' Pete waved the info jack at his partner.

'I agree,' Jed said. 'I'll just send Kira a quick message.'

Hi love, it was an internal leak – we're on it. Tell everyone to stay in and stay safe. I'll fill you in when I get home. Love you xx J.

It took several hours to go through the data on the jacks. Jed was surprised, and a little impressed, at how far Anti-Corp had managed to infiltrate. They had people in every division of Corporation, with access to every level. It was clear to Jed they were planning to release the information about HER from Science Division, but there was no indication as to a timeframe.

The protest planned for this afternoon was about water restrictions.

It was being held outside Corporation HQ, about as far from Science Division as you could get.

Anti-Corp were meant to be demonstrating peacefully, but the Chief didn't trust them - especially after the Special Investigation bombshell. He wanted as many Force operatives on site, and that meant riot gear, as per procedure. Since the pregnancies had been leaked over the news sweep that morning, people were becoming restless. Jed had felt it when he'd walked through the Community Hub on his way to work. There had been a lot of muttering and hostility, much of it broadcast through the news feed and aimed towards the pregnant women. Fortunately, Jed knew Martha and Ingrid had enough sense to keep away from the Hubs, but it didn't stop him worrying about them. Especially his sister, who still believed Corporation could do no wrong.

The Corporation kept a tight control over water allowance. It was the most precious resource there was – if the reports that no usable water existed outside the city were true, that is. Jed had always listened with interest to Ruth's descriptions of what she found beyond the city. Most young people made a foray, but Jed had never got around to it. Then he'd made Detective. And then he'd gotten Grace. It was too much to risk for the sake of idle curiosity. Besides, what possible reason could the Corporation have to lie about water? It made no sense to Jed.

Catching up with the others on his riot team, Jed exchanged greetings with them and then went through his own kit check. Just because they weren't expecting trouble didn't mean he shouldn't be prepared. After gearing up he went to find Pete.

***ANTIC:** Fight Corporation for water rights - today at noon.*

Pete was whistling as he grabbed his stuff from his desk.

'Why do you sound so happy?' Jed asked.

'Half day. I'm off for the weekend, so no responsibilities. And best of all I'm spending it all with Ingrid and…'

Pete remembered where he was and stopped speaking, looking around to see if anyone was listening. Jed knew he meant Ingrid and the unborn baby. He was pleased for his friend, especially now Pete would become family, but he was still caught up in everything they'd learnt this morning.

'Don't you think you should stay here?' Jed said. 'Now that we know more about... well, everything.'

A ping came through Pete's wristplant. He glanced down and grunted.

'Guess who's working late. Again. That woman is a workaholic.'

'You could always stay for protest watch.'

'No thanks,' Pete paused. 'I've got...' He looked around again then continued in a quieter tone. 'Little person things to do. And as for the rest of it.' He waved his hand. 'There's nothing we can do right now. They've put extra security measures in place at Science Division and the other girls are all at home today, right?'

Jed agreed with Pete, but he still felt concerned about the rally.

'Alright Pete. Take care out there, who knows what information they'll leak next. I've got to get my team ready. Have a good one.'

Jed clapped his friend on the back before heading out.

Ingrid sat at her desk. A single droplet of sweat trickled down the side of her face.

'Air-con!'

A tinny voice replied. 'Air temperature is at an optimum nineteen degrees Celsius.'

It seemed natural pregnancy came with pitfall after pitfall, even with regular check-ups. Even so, Ingrid didn't want to feel like she was being parboiled from the inside out if she could help it. Perhaps her electronics weren't functioning properly. The med-tech had told her that changes in her magnetic aura due to the pregnancy could affect her implants, and as some of the tech was in beta test, there were still kinks in the software. A cool breeze swept over her as the doors to her office opened. It was her boss.

Ingrid, you look cooked. He projected with his telepathic neural implants - the latest thing being developed. They were full of bugs and blinking out all the time – Ingrid's especially.

A green shimmer waved its way across the room. Ingrid watched, entranced, picking out motes of gold and red. She felt the fire within embrace her and stretch to the ends of her being. There was something. A noise. A noise that didn't belong. It shattered the colours into a myriad of rainbows as her boss's neural network invaded again.

I'm serious – I need those figures stat. Meeting in t-minus 10.

Her boss left the room and a jolt went through Ingrid's body as she remembered what she was supposed to have been working on. *This is why you aren't finishing on time*, she thought to herself.

Ingrid tapped her receiver and bought up the screen, amalgamating sales and losses. The figures looked good. Only a handful of off radars, and those would be picked up by sales agents. A curl of steam wound its way out of her nostril. Butterflies fluttered in her womb as more sweat trickled down her back.

Dina pushed her way to the front of the crowd, looking for Ruth. Despite the morning's sweeps they'd decided it would be prudent if both of them were present at the peaceful protest, but they'd travelled separately. Who knew how many Anti-Corp eyes were watching them, and being seen at a public event should help maintain their cover, bringing Ruth one step closer to her husband's body.

Dina wished Anti Corp would hurry up with whatever it was they wanted from Science Division. She was looking forward to her next session in the fishbowl, and it seemed she was a front runner for permanent selection.

Bobby appeared next to her.

'Hello, my little pregnant chip.'

'I'm not pregnant,' Dina snapped.

'That's not what the sweeps say.'

'Yeah, well, sometimes the sweeps are wrong.'

There was a tense silence as Dina scanned the crowd looking for Ruth and Martha, wishing Bobby would go away. Finally, he spoke.

'Great job on the planting. We've got everything we need.'

Dina turned to look at him.

'So I'm done?'

'For now,' Bobby confirmed. 'Although we can always use more soldiers. Especially as you are so uniquely qualified to fight against Corporation.' He took her wrist and pressed his own wristplant to her tech, transferring new contact details. 'You can reach me anytime.' He smiled down at Dina, his eyes twinkling, full of mischief.

'Thanks,' Dina muttered, as he melted back into the crowd.

'Air-con,' Ingrid asked again, not bothering to hear the reply.

She messaged the office intern for ice, and when the cup appeared on her desk – the contents began to melt. The cold squares quickly ran into liquid as she picked up the cup. A ripple shuddered through the water as tiny bubbles started to form. She put the cup down, noting her melted fingerprints on its surface. It was stifling in her office, there was no air and the *heat*. She began to panic. *I'm with child. I can't be sick. What is wrong?* Ingrid dialled through to the Med Centre and requested a check-up. She sat half panting as they checked her vitals remotely.

'Infant is fine.'

'What about me?'

'Carrier is normal. Keep up the good work.'

She couldn't believe it. Her hair was stuck to her scalp, her tunic was moulded to her body, and steam was rising from the back of her hands. She looked at her reflection in the window by the side of her desk and thought she saw flickers of flame in her eyes. What was happening?

'What was all that about?' asked Ruth breathlessly, as she and Martha pushed past protestors to stand next to Dina.

'Do you think we should all be here?' Dina asked. 'Aren't you worried at being recognised?'

'We can't stay locked away forever,' Martha said. 'Besides, isn't Jed working this protest? I'm sure we'll be safe.'

'Never mind us,' Ruth interrupted. 'What did Bobby say?'

'Well, he congratulated me on my pregnancy,' Dina sniffed. 'And apparently, I'm all done, for now. At Science Division. They've got what they wanted.'

'I hope you told him to frag off,' Ruth said sharply.

Dina looked down at her feet, hunching her shoulders.

'We should let Jed know,' Martha said, reaching for her ear comm.

Dina grabbed her hand.

'Not here. Later.' Dina gestured at the crowd. 'We just need to show our faces briefly and then we can get back to Kira's. We can fill everyone in then.'

Ruth linked one arm through Dina's and one through Martha's, and the three women began to meander through the protestors. As they passed by the Force defenders, Jed raised his eyebrows at them, but the women smiled serenely at him and continued on their slow circuit.

'Asking for trouble,' Jed muttered, scanning the crowd for troublemakers.

There was a commotion to the left. A man and a woman dressed in garish purple with identical cropped heads, were pushing through the throng roughly, trying to get to where Martha and the others were.

'I know who you are,' shouted the woman. 'You're Hamble's daughter – you're one of the affected.'

Jed discreetly called for back-up and began to make his way over to the women.

'Aren't you going to say anything?' The woman sounded slightly hysterical.

'Yes, I am Martha Hamble. My handle is MAHA, and I will post an update later.'

'I don't want some sweeping update. I want answers. Now!'

The woman pushed Martha hard. Martha wind-milled her arms but lost her balance and fell backwards with a jolt. Jed quickly grabbed the aggressive woman and magno-bound her arms behind her back.

'Get off me!' she screamed as she fought the restraints. 'You can't touch me. Filthy Force scum.'

'Martha – are you okay?' Jed called out.

Dina and Ruth were helping Martha back up. She looked pale and shaken.

'We'll take her home and do a Med check,' Ruth said, using her body to block access to Martha's as they forced their way out of the crowd.

Jed jabbed his finger at two nearby Force Officials. 'You two. Go with them, see them safely home.'

The woman who had attacked Martha was still struggling. Jed touched his ear comm.

'I need an offender transport from Corp HQ protest, now.'

The butterflies rippled inside her. Ingrid got up, hot, exhausted, melting, and walked across the floor in a burning daze. The door was open. The corridor felt cooler and she knew that if she got out of the building, she would feel so much better. She could feel heat absorb her, reflect out of her, resonate with her soul and the child within. Suddenly tendrils of flame were licking her skin in bursts of heat. Her electronics fell out, breaking as they hit the ground. It felt like the sun burnt twice as brightly as Ingrid exploded into flames and woke up with a start. She looked around wildly, before realising she was still at her desk and despite feeling a little warm, she certainly wasn't on fire.

Since finding out she was pregnant this wasn't the first time Ingrid had had a dream about catching fire at work, although what it was supposed to mean was beyond her. She had put it down to an odd side effect from changes in her hormone levels, and her reluctance to go into work this morning after a distressing heat dream, was pure laziness. Just because she was growing a life inside her and not in a laboratory like it was supposed to be, didn't mean she had the luxury of laying around all day. Ingrid was under way too much scrutiny to show any sign of weakness, especially today with the information leak to the sweeps.

A ping on Ingrid's console refocused her attention to the figures in front of her. She had to get this done. She had plans. Suddenly her desk started to move as the floor fell away and a gaping chasm opened up beneath her. Ingrid held her stomach as she tumbled down, her last thoughts of Pete.

A boom rang through the air as the ground shook and a plume of smoke appeared across the city. All around Jed urgent instructions could be heard from Force Control.

'Terrorist attack at Corp Tech. Calling all units for immediate scramble. Terrorist attack at Corp Tech. Calling all units for immediate scramble.'

'Frag!'

Jed looked at his wristplant. Ingrid was still at work. Releasing the aggressive protestor, Jed gathered his team. All the Force skimmers were parked nearby, Jed and his team were in the air and on their way within moments of receiving the call.

***ANON76:** Corp Tech explodes – live feed available.*

When he arrived at the scene, Jed looked at the wreckage in dismay. There was nothing left of the building except a pile of smouldering rubble. Dust hung thick on the air. Force operatives donned their breathing gear and a detective organised the safety barrier. Jed quickly found the first on scene operative.

'Was anyone inside?' Jed asked, his voice sounding thick in his ears.

'Most likely, Sir. Apparently, there was a meeting on the upper floors, but we haven't sent teams into the rubble yet.'

'The list? Do you have the list?'

The operative passed over his handheld. Jed frantically scanned the list, checking, checking.

There. Her name. Ingrid Jenkins. Present. She hadn't left yet.

'Frag it. She shouldn't even be there.'

'Sir?'

'I'll head a team up. Let's get moving.' Jed commandeered the handheld and yelled for his unit to fall in behind.

They headed over to the destruction. Drones hovered above making their own scans. Several had stopped above a patch of rubble, beeping, indicating life signs beneath. Quickly, Jed divided his unit into two teams. Heading up one of the teams, he began to shift the rubble aside using pressure blasts where needed.

The second team found a body first. Jed's heart pounded in his chest as he craned his neck to see. It was a brunette. Relief rushed through his body; he didn't even stop to feel guilty – he had to find his sister. One of his operatives uncovered a man's shoe and Jed wanted to scream in frustration but they had to help anyone they found. After shifting a pile of rubble, the man's leg ended abruptly and one of the rescuers threw up behind a broken chair. This was taking too long. Jed blasted some ceiling wreckage into smaller pieces and a pale arm flopped out with the debris.

'Halt,' Jed yelled.

He knew that arm. He knew that hand. It couldn't be. He began to scrabble desperately with his hands at the debris, gradually clearing enough away for the team to help him pull the inert body out of the wreckage.

It was Ingrid.

And she was not breathing.

'Medic!' Jed screamed.

A medic rushed over. Jed cradled his sister's head on his lap, unaware of the tears streaming down his face. The medic ran his scanner over Ingrid's body, then jerked it back in surprise.

'This one's gone,' he said. 'But there's an anomaly.'

Before he could continue his report, Jed finished it for him.

'Her name is Ingrid. And she's pregnant.'

The medic yelled over to his colleagues. 'I need a gurney - stat.' He tried to move Ingrid from Jed's lap, but Jed shoved him away roughly. 'Sir. We may be able to save the baby.'

One of the Force operatives put a hand on the medic's shoulder, bent down and whispered in his ear. The medic looked up in dismay at Jed clinging on to his dead sister's body.

'I had no idea,' he said. 'I'm so sorry for your loss, but we have to act quickly if we hope to save the child.'

It took four of Jed's unit to pull him away from Ingrid's body. Two more medics ran over with the gurney. Jed was still fighting the men holding him as his sister was air lifted away.

'No! That's my sister. She's not... you can't... get off!'

As the med van disappeared, the fight dropped out of Jed. He sagged into the arms of his men. A skimmer flew into the crime scene, and somebody hurtled off at a run. A young operative tried in vain to stop Pete.

'Sir. You can't enter here. It's a cordon.'

Pete carried on. When he saw Jed, he stopped in his tracks. Jed lifted his tear stained face and shook his head as his friend fell to his knees and howled in pain. For a brief moment, everyone stopped to look.

Pete's howl reverberated around the wreckage, as he poured his grief into it. Without warning, he broke off, staggered to his feet and grabbed Jed by the arms.

'The baby? What about the baby? Not the baby?'

Jed couldn't answer. He didn't know. The medic who had organised Ingrid's gurney came cautiously over to the two men.

'We sent the body to Science Division. I'm sure they'll do everything they can to save the baby but,' he hesitated. 'It didn't look good.'

Not waiting to see whether the two men understood what he had told them, the medic hurried over to another body being pulled from the wreckage. Pete and Jed looked dimly at each other, neither one able to comprehend what had happened.

EMERGENCY MEETING OF CORPORATION BOARD FOR CITY FORTY-TWO

DATE: 31st August 2215

VIRTUAL PRESENCE: J NICKS, Y ASWAD and P BASJERE
R HAMBLE INJURED – MINUTES SENT THROUGH

AGENDA

1. **ATTACK ON CORP TECH**
2. **DECISION ON PREGNANCY B**
3. **PUBLIC UNREST**
4. **CONTINGENCY PLAN**

MINUTES

1. **UNWARRANTED ATTACK ON CORP TECH HAS REVEALED SERIOUS SECURITY BREACH - NEW MEASURES TO BE PUT IN PLACE. ALL EFFORTS MUST BE MADE TO RECOVER PROJECT WORK & RE-HOUSE IN SECURE LOCATION. FAMILIES TO BE SENT CONDOLENCES. ORDERS FOR TERMINATION APPROVED ON CULPRITS.**

2. **PREGNANCY B UPDATE – HOST DIED IN ATTACK. BABY WAS VIABLE BUT DECISION MADE TO TERMINATE FOR MEDICAL STUDY.**
3. **LEVEL OF PUBLIC UNREST NOT TO BE TOLERATED. FORCE MUST EXERCISE GREATER CONTROL. CORPORATION TO FILL THE SWEEPS WITH POSITIVE MESSAGES AND TURN FOCUS.**

4. **CONTINGENCY PLAN A READY FOR EXECUTION – BOARD MEMBERS WILL BE ABLE TO LEAVE THE CITY UNTIL SITUATION RECTIFIED.**

ANY OTHER BUSINESS – NONE

Chapter Thirteen

CORP: *Use your locator tech to check on your loved ones. Corporation looks after you.*

ANTIC: *Our leader, Victor Bianchi speaks out against today's violent action.*
"Radicals have used our peaceful movement as a terrorist springboard."

Twenty minutes after being air lifted to the Medical Centre, Ingrid's body lay within a suspension field in the operating theatre. Several medical staff and two senior consultants, one taller than the other, stood around her.

'And you're sure they don't want the foetus to survive?' The taller consultant asked, reluctant to act. 'If we continue to supply oxygen, there's a very good chance it can be saved.'

'The Board want us to carry out an investigation into how this happened. That means autopsy for both mother and child.' His older colleague replied.

'We can't just let the baby die. Surely emphasis should be on saving the child. I mean, it's a medical marvel, think of what might be possible.'

'This is why we have strict directives. Dead mother – dead child.'

Both consultants looked at Ingrid's lifeless body for a moment longer. The older consultant shook his head and gave the signal to turn off life support. If anyone in the room was shocked, they hid it well. The two consultants watched as the rapid heartbeat of the foetus began to slow and become erratic, before fading away altogether. Neither of them noticed the recorder nestled in the corner of the room, it's small red-light flashing, capturing both image and sound.

MED4AC: *Let's ignore the Hippocratic Oath, shall we?*

ANTIC: *!!!INSTANT UPDATE!!!!*
Ingrid Jenkins killed in building terror attack.
Corporation murders baby – watch the unbelievable footage and spread the sweep.
Stand for the people – join Anti-Corp – justice for Baby J.

Kira stared in shock at the news sweep.

Anti-Corp, who had reported her sister-in-law's death, were blaming Corporation for her murder and using Ingrid and the baby as martyrs for their cause.

Kira threw the remote at the wall, cutting off the transmission. Collecting herself she went over to Grace's cube and stroked her baby's cheek gently as she slept.

Her sister in law was dead. And her unborn child. Dead. In a senseless attack by a radical arm of Anti-Corp. How could this have happened? How did they go from being a group of friends – each the inexplicable recipient of an amazing, beautiful gift - to a family ripped apart, shattered by grief?

MED4AC: *Hamble, Marketing Director of Corporation, rebuilding spine at Corp Medical.*

The vid com chimed. Kira answered when she saw who it was.

'Kira? Are you okay? You're not hurt, are you? Is my granddaughter alright?'

'Yes, Mum. I'm okay.'

'I heard what happened, I can't believe it. Your father and I were still getting over the shock of finding out all your friends were pregnant and then, and then, oh Kira – it's just awful. That poor baby. And Ingrid. Oh, my dear, is there anything we can do?'

For once Kira's mother fell silent. Kira looked at her mother's loving, concerned face, and her shoulders shook as the tears fell.

'Oh, my poor sweet girl. We'll be right over.' Before Kira had chance to say otherwise, her mum signed off.

Martha came out of her side of the apartment, face ashen, her hair in disarray.

'Kira, my father... he was in the building when... when the attack happened.'

'Oh no – is he okay?'

'He is alive, but he is in surgery. The med centre said something about a damaged spinal cord. I have to go and see him. Mother is too scared to leave the house. I can't leave him there all alone.'

'I understand sweetie, but do you think it's safe for you to leave the apartment? By yourself I mean.'

'I will not be by myself,' Martha said. 'Jed has assigned us all a Force shadow, did you not know?'

'No. I can't get through to him. I'm so worried, Ma. His sister just died and...'

'Ingrid is dead? What about the baby?'

'You didn't know?' Kira was confused. 'But how did you know about the attack on Corp Tech?'

'I turned the news sweep on and saw the coverage but before I could read anything, I got the call about my father.' She shook her head in disbelief. 'Ingrid is dead? I can't believe it. Where is Pete?'

'I don't know. I can't get through to Jed. I don't know what's happening. I just know that Ingrid and the baby are... Oh Ma... they're gone. They're just gone, Ma. And I don't understand why it happened. The baby... the baby... it never even started. Why? Why would they do this? I can't...'

Kira stopped talking as the tears took over.

'Oh, Kira.' Martha embraced her, stroking her hair as she cried. 'Poor, poor Ingrid,' she whispered. 'And the baby, that poor innocent baby.'

After a few moments, Kira pushed Martha gently away, and both women dried their eyes. Martha held a protective hand over her stomach.

'I can't believe Anti-Corp wanted to kill them. It had to have been a mistake. Not a baby, Kira. What possible threat could it have been? Or Ingrid for that matter.'

Kira shrugged, her face a picture of misery. Grace woke up and began to cry.

Martha took the Force skimmer provided to the Med Centre. She had to make sure her father was alright. She didn't think she could cope with more bad news.

As Martha reached the side wing of the Medical Centre reserved for VIPs, she saw a red-faced medical officer scurrying away from a closed door. Without knocking, she entered the room and looked in dismay at the amount of electronics surrounding her father.

'Hmm. You came then.' Mr Hamble gestured at all the equipment around him. 'Don't worry about all this. I'm re-growing part of my spine - nothing to it. No need to fuss.'

Martha came over and kissed him gently on the head. 'Oh Daddy. What happened?'

'It was those idiotic anarchists. Blowing up a perfectly respectable building for no good reason. The meeting got moved. Shouldn't have fragging been there in the first place.'

'Did you hear about Ingrid? Jed's sister?' Martha asked.

Mr Hamble's bushy eyebrows drew into a frown. 'Bad business. Just terrible. And the loss of the child. Bad business.'

'How did you know about that? Do they project the sweeps in here?'

Mr Hamble looked uncomfortable. He tried to adjust his position on the hospital bed but gave up when he realised he had no control over his lower limbs yet.

'Father?' Martha demanded. 'What do you know?'

Mr Hamble breathed heavily out of his nose. 'It wasn't my call.' He looked uncomfortable. 'They decided not to save the foetus. It was a board decision. The bodies are to be investigated by Science Division to find out what is going wrong.'

'Going wrong,' Martha repeated, feeling nauseous as she considered her own condition and how the Board must be viewing her.

'Not that there's anything wrong with you,' Mr Hamble said hastily looking in concern at his pale faced daughter. 'It's just an anomaly. That's all.'

Martha took a seat on the chair beside the bed. Several uncomfortable minutes passed until Mr Hamble cleared his voice.

'It isn't safe for you to be here. You should be careful, now that everyone knows who you are and what's happened. In fact, I've been thinking.' He began fiddling with one of the wires sticking out of his arm. 'I want you to leave the city. There's a place, a wilderness camp. Away from the city. It's a test base, highly confidential, to see whether we can exist outside the walls. I want you to go there. You and the others.' He paused as if trying to find the right words. 'You are all in danger. We don't know how people are going to react. The attack today, those idiots blowing up that building. I can't risk you. Any of you. You must go.' He looked up at Martha, waiting for her reply.

'A wilderness camp? What about the radiation levels?' Martha asked.

Hamble tried to move again and gave up with a grunt. 'There's no radiation at Camp Eden. It's a safe place.'

Martha put her hand on his arm before replying. 'I will let the others know, but if they decide to stay, I am staying with them. This is happening to all of us, we need to stick together.'

'I suppose that's the best I'm going to get.'

Jed sat with Pete in the interview room, waiting for their debrief to begin. Pete hadn't said a word since breaking down at the scene of Ingrid's murder. The door opened and Chief Minkov came in, followed by Agent Deveraux.

'Detectives,' the chief said.

Agent Deveraux came over and put a hand on Jed's shoulder. 'I'm sorry for your loss,' he said, in a low voice.

Jed stiffened and turned his head to look up at Deveraux, but the agent had already moved over to Pete and was repeating the gesture.

Pete said nothing.

The Chief settled himself behind his desk while Deveraux leant against the wall, off to one side. Jed looked warily from one to the other, bracing himself for the worst.

'I've read your statement, Jenkins,' the Chief began. 'And Deveraux confirms that Special Investigations monitoring did not pick up any chatter from your Anti-Corp infiltration team relating to the attack.'

Jed cast an uneasy eye on Pete, expecting a reaction.

Nothing.

'We know you didn't know. Frag, none of us knew the target was Corp Tech - it was all pointing towards Science Division. I want you to pull your girl out of there and all association with Anti-Corp stops.'

The Chief glared at Jed, expecting him to protest, but Jed nodded.

'We'll provide some additional eyes on you all, keep you safe in the interim,' Deveraux said.

'Safe?'

The Agent looked at the Chief, who nodded. Deveraux walked closer to the desk. 'We moved on your information about finding high-energy radiation signs at Science Division. Miss Hamble's suggestion about its use was right.' Deveraux paused to make sure he had their complete attention. 'Corporation have been deliberately treating the water and forcing us to remain sterile.'

Pete finally reacted.

'Are you saying that my baby was some sort of secret science experiment?' he said, his voice hoarse and thick with emotion.

'No, Detective Barnes. I am saying that the entire population has been a fragging experiment,' Deveraux replied.

'We are the law,' Minkov said, interrupting him. 'We are not Corporation. We are not paid by Corporation and we are going to get to the fragging bottom of this. Barnes, Jenkins, I want you two to take the rest of the week. Grieve. Do what you need to do. This investigation will still be here when you get back.'

'So, we're just supposed to carry on and pretend that we don't know that we've been kept in the dark our entire lives?' Jed shouted. 'What am I supposed to tell my wife? I won't lie to her; she deserves the truth and...'

Agent Deveraux held up a hand to stop Jed's tirade. 'We will be issuing a release – to inform everyone – but first we need all the facts. There is no need to create mass panic.'

'What about Anti-Corp and what happened today?' Jed asked.

'Those responsible will be brought to justice,' Minkov replied.

Pete leapt up, his chair flying backwards. 'Not if I get there first,' he snarled, and left the room.

Jed made to go after him, but the chief stopped him.

'Make sure he doesn't do anything he'll regret, Jenkins.'

'I'll try, Sir.' He followed his friend out of the office.

Chief Minkov turned in his chair to face Deveraux 'What do you think about Barnes?'

'I think he'll solve our problem,' Deveraux replied. 'Shame to lose a good man though.'

Pete was in the skimmer bay by the time Jed caught up with him.

'Where are you going?' Jed asked.

'I'm going to kill them,' Pete said. 'I'm going to kill them all.'

'I need you, Pete. We all need you. Here, now. Please.'

Jed stretched out a hand. Pete began pacing up and down the corridor before spinning and punching the wall with a loud roar. Then he waited a moment, his fist in the wall, his head bowed before looking up at Jed, and giving a small nod.

'Alright,' he said grimly. 'But I will see this through, Jed.'

'I know.'

At the apartment, Jed's parents had arrived. They were sitting in the lounge, shell-shocked, while a puffy-eyed Kira tried and failed to make light conversation. When Jed and Pete entered the apartment, Gretchen - Jed's mother - seemed to grow paler.

'Jeddidiah, my boy. My sweet boy.'

Gretchen held her arms out to her son, and Jed crossed the floor to greet his mother, clasping hands with his father before sitting on the floor besides them both.

Kira came over to Pete standing near the doorway and burrowed herself into his chest. Pete stood a good foot taller than Kira and could hardly make out what she was saying as she sobbed her sympathy and grief into his shirt. He gently hugged her back, fighting against the waves of pain that lashed through him. These five broken people clung to each other, drowning in their personal grief.

It wasn't until Grace began to cry that they moved. Jed's father came over to Pete and pulled him into a bear hug before going into the kitchen area, while Jed stood up and hugged his wife. They went through to the bedroom together to find out what Grace needed. Mrs Jenkins had been left alone so Pete approached her cautiously. They hadn't made much progress in getting to know each other, and he didn't want to upset her further.

Gretchen looked up at Pete and took one of his hands in hers.

'We lost our daughter, Peter. And you, you lost your love. No-one can ever, ever give her back to us.'

She dropped his hand and began crying again, loud racking sobs that shook her whole body. Mr Jenkins returned to the couch and gathered her into his arms. Pete stood awkwardly not knowing what to do. He jumped when Jed touched his shoulder.

'Help me make synth-caf?' Jed asked.

JENHUB: *A private funeral for Ingrid Jenkins and child has been* *held at the request of the family. All messages of condolences to be sent to the link within.*

It was the day after the funeral. Science Division had refused to release the body... bodies. Protestors had thronged outside the End of Days Chapel forcing the agents from Special Investigation to work hard to keep Jed's family and friends safe. Pete had remained impassive throughout. Not reacting to the service, the farewells, Jed's emotional eulogy – nothing. It was as if he simply wasn't there. The men assigned to protect him had reported no unusual behaviour, but Jed was still concerned. Pete's girlfriend had died in a terrorist attack and Corporation had let his baby die. For the good of science. Pete should've been raging.

MED4AC: *Dina Grey miscarried. Now only two pregnancies left.*

DING*: Looking for BEJE – please get in touch.*

The apartment was subdued. Even Grace was quiet.

'Can I get you anything, Jed?' Kira asked from the doorway as he lay in bed.

'No.'

He lay on his side, staring at the wall. Kira closed the door behind her, she didn't know what else to do.

'Anything?' asked Dina.

Kira shook her head.

'He just needs time,' said Martha.

'I know. I just feel so helpless. How are you doing D? Now that everyone knows about...' Kira trailed off.

'I'm okay. It had to come out sooner or later. I just wish I could get hold of Ben.'

'Still incommunicado, huh?'

'Yeah.' Dina tucked her hair behind her ear. 'He wasn't in Corp Tech, I know that much, but I can't find him.'

The mood of the apartment took over the three women, and they stopped talking. Martha fiddled with her Gaia statue while Kira looked off into space, and Dina played with the baby.

It had been three days since the attack.

MED4AC: *Miscarriage Q&A session to be held later today in social hub beta.*
Ask your question now, sweep your friends, join in the discussion.

'Are you speaking at the Q&A session, D?' Kira asked, casting about for something to talk about.

'No way. I don't want to rehash everything with a bunch of strangers.' Dina squished a soft ball in her hands. 'Women won't leave me alone as it is – asking questions about my private life. I wish it would all go away.'

'I am certain it will blow over eventually,' Martha said, leaning over to rescue the toy from Dina's hands.

'Blow over? Have they left you alone yet?'

Martha gave the ball back to Grace. She had received some nasty sweeps regarding the rape but on the whole people had been supportive, especially when they learned she had decided to keep the baby.

'People just want to identify with you,' Martha explained. 'They want to be able to say it could have been me.'

'I wish it *had* been someone else,' Dina said bitterly. 'I wish everything had happened to someone else.'

Kira regarded her young friend. 'Everything?'

Dina coloured, and tucked her hair behind her ear again. 'I just think that if I hadn't agreed to the whole stupid undercover thing, Ingrid would still be with us.' Dina's voice wobbled and she fought not to cry.

'It wasn't your fault, sweetie,' said Kira. 'They would've found someone else.'

It didn't make Dina feel any better. She felt responsible for Ingrid's death no matter how many times Kira tried to convince her otherwise. If Force hadn't been focusing on Science Division, they might have found out about the terrorist attack on Corp Tech in time.

'It is lovely having you stay here with us Dina.' Martha tried to lighten the mood.

'Thanks. I know it's only temporary, but...'

'Temporary? Who said it was temporary?'

'Well, I didn't think you'd want me here when the baby comes.'

'Oh, stop being so soft.' Martha threw a pillow at Dina. 'I would love you to be here – if you still want to stay?'

Dina hugged the pillow, hiding her face. When she looked up, she had tears in her eyes. 'Yes,' she said. 'Yes, I do.'

The bedroom door opened, and Jed came through. His eyes were bloodshot, and he hadn't shaved. Sitting down next to Kira, he put his head on her shoulder.

'Are you alright, sweetie?'

'No,' Jed replied. 'But I will be.' There was a pause. 'Has anyone heard from Ruth?'

'I didn't see her at the funeral,' Dina said. 'Did she have the details, Kira?'

'Yes, but I think maybe she felt she wouldn't be welcome.'

'Is Pete still angry at her?' asked Martha.

Jed ran a hand over his face, considering his words. 'He hasn't forgiven her for her part in staging the building attack.'

'Her part?' Martha said, frowning. 'She had nothing to do with the bombing.'

Jed looked uncomfortable. 'Ruth gave Pete a teddy bear to give to... Ingrid.' Jed swallowed the lump of emotion that threatened to overwhelm him. 'It was found in the wreckage. There was a scanner inside. Force techies think it was used to get schematics of the building.'

'But she didn't know what they were going to do with it – surely?' Dina looked appalled.

'No, she didn't,' Jed admitted. 'Pete thinks she should've known what was going to happen, and that she should've come forward earlier.'

'No wonder she hasn't shown her face,' Kira said. 'I hope she's alright.'

'I'm sure Ruth will be in touch.' Dina looked down at her hand-held and sent Ruth another ping. 'When she's ready.'

ANON88*: I hope it shatters you like my dreams have shattered.*

In the end, it was a brick through the window that decided it for Ruth. Her apartment was in a low-tech high rise, and it didn't have automated security settings. Thanks to the sweeps reporting every last detail about the two remaining pregnant women, Ruth was easy to find, and therefore easy to attack. The people were angry and frightened, and it didn't take much to stir them into action. Ruth finally replied to one of Dina's pings and told her what had been happening.

Ruthie! Are you okay? It's not safe for you to be there. Come to Kira's and be with the rest of us. There are Force Operatives on their way to get you. D x

'I didn't know if I should come,' Ruth said as she was deposited on the doorstep by two Force operatives an hour later.

Jed had answered the door, and he pulled Ruth over the threshold. Once inside he hugged her and whispered, 'It wasn't your fault.'

Soon Ruth had been hugged and welcomed by everyone.

'Where have you been?' Dina asked.

'Anti-Corp released Quentin's remains. They'd already cremated him, so...' Ruth broke off, unable to speak.

'Hey, hey Ruthie.' Kira hugged her friend. 'It's alright. He's at peace now.'

'I'm okay. I'm okay. He bought the remains over himself.'

'He?' Martha asked.

'Victor – the head of Anti-Corp.'

'Oh wow,' Dina said. 'What did he say?'

Jed leaned forward, intent on Ruth's every word.

'He said they would never have kept him that long, if they'd known.' Ruth sniffed.

'Known what?' Jed asked.

Ruth's voice took on a harsher tone. 'That evil pig of a bastard Bobby never told Victor I was Quentin's wife. Bobby used it as his own personal leverage to keep me working for Anti-Corp.' Ruth looked at Jed red-eyed. 'I swear, Jed, if you don't terminate that piece of crap – I will.'

'Ruth!' Kira exclaimed, shocked.

'I'm not sorry K,' Ruth said, tears running down her face. 'He kept my husband away from me all those years.'

Kira whispered to Jed to go make some more drinks while the others tried to comfort Ruth.

Martha and Ruth were comparing their bumps when the door pinged, and Pete entered. His jaw tightened as he noticed Ruth sitting on the couch. He walked over to the kitchen where Jed and Kira were stood and handed a bag of food to Kira.

'Pity meals,' Pete explained. 'I don't want them.'

'Thanks,' Kira said, touching Pete's hand before taking the bag and putting it on the counter.

'Do you want me to pick you up tomorrow?' Jed asked, clapping a hand on his partner's shoulder.

'No.'

'You sure?' Jed said. 'It's our first day back after...'

Pete shot another disapproving glance over towards the rest of the women in the lounge. 'I'm sure.' He turned to leave but Jed put a hand on his friend's arm to hold him back.

'I'm going to tell the others,' Jed said. 'About the water. Will you stay?'

Pete shook him off. 'You do it,' he said. 'I've got something else to do. I'll see you tomorrow.'

Jed watched his partner leave in concern. He felt anxious about telling his wife and friends what he had learnt and wished Pete had stayed. Walking over to the others, he clapped his hands together, getting their attention.

'I have some news. It's about what Dina discovered at Science Division. Corporation have been treating the water deliberately. Making us sterile. And they've been doing it for years.'

CORP: *Safety is our number one priority – upgrade your security now.*

Speak to your local Corporation Representative.

EMERGENCY MEETING OF CORPORATION BOARD FOR CITY FORTY-TWO

DATE: 5th September 2215

VIRTUAL PRESENCE: J NICKS, Y ASWAD and P BASJERE R HAMBLE INJURED – MINUTES SENT THROUGH

AGENDA

1. **ANTI-CORP INVOLVEMENT IN CORP TECH ATTACK**
2. **CONTROL OF REMAINING PREGNANCIES UPDATE**
3. **IMPROVING CORPORATION IMAGE**
4. **FILE 0**

MINUTES

1. **VICTOR BIANCHI, LEADER OF ANTI-CORP HAS SPOKEN TO THE BOARD AND DENIED INVOLVEMENT IN THE ATTACK ON CORP TECH. THE BOARD ACCEPTS HIS STATEMENT AND IS PUSHING FORWARD TERMINATION FOR ALL MEMBERS OF 42nd ARMY.**

2. **PREGNANCY A AND C ARE LIVING AT THE SAME ADDRESS. BOTH HAVE REFUSED MEDICAL AND ARE UNDER FORCE PROTECTION. ONCE PUBLIC UPSET CEASES, GREATER EFFORTS WILL BE MADE TO BRING THEM UNDER CONTROL.**
3. **PR WILL WORK ON A NEW CAMPAIGN TO IMPROVE CORPORATION IMAGE. SPIN IS NEEDED ON FETUS TERMINATION.**

4. **FILE 0 IS REDUNDANT. SPECIAL INVESTIGATIONS KNOWS ABOUT THE WATER TREATMENT. CONTINGENCY PLAN A IS STILL RELEVANT.**

ANY OTHER BUSINESS – NONE

Notes from Anti-Corp Meeting at Academy Student Bar, September 5th 2215

We are still reeling from the Corp Tech attack – Victor has urged everyone to publicly denounce the attack using their personal handles on the sweeps.

Victor has spoken with the Board and they have accepted his statement that the attack was planned and executed by the 42nd Army who have nothing to do with Anti-Corp.

Victor is arranging to speak to the leaders of 42nd Army and ask them to surrender themselves to the authorities.

If anyone has any contact with members of the 42nd Army, they must disconnect now, or risk being added to the list for termination.

All bugs are to be deactivated. All files and records kept on Corporation buildings and members are to be destroyed.

At this time, it is unclear whether Anti-Corp will continue to meet.

Think free – be free.

Chapter Fourteen

***CORP:** We remind citizens that individual safety is a priority. We put you first.*

Everyone began talking at once.

'What do you mean treating the water?'

'Is it safe?'

'Will Grace be okay?'

Ruth and Martha looked at each other, concern mirrored in their faces.

'Will my baby be okay?' They spoke in unison.

'Why doesn't everyone know about it?' Dina asked.

'I don't have all the facts yet,' Jed said, moving to sit down next to Kira. 'Special Investigations are putting together a sweep release and the case is still open, but with the current mood in the city – well, they didn't want to risk any more panic.'

'The water, Jed, is it safe?' Kira asked, clutching at his arm.

'I think so. We are all still here aren't we?' Jed patted her hand, trying not to show his own concern.

'If Science Division have been using High Energy Radiation to treat our water, it must have been a continuous low dosage designed to attack reproductive cells only and prevent them from repairing themselves,' Martha said thoughtfully.

'Corporation have lied to us and stopped us from having children.' Ruth glared at Jed. 'Why would they do that?'

'I'm sorry, Ruth.' Jed ran a hand through his hair. 'I have no idea. I'm back in work tomorrow. As soon as I find out more you will be the first to know. I promise.'

'Can we sweep about it?' Dina asked.

Jed looked at her.

She coloured slightly.

'I guess not.'

The group lapsed into thoughtful silence as Grace burbled happily on her tummy and began to crawl across the floor to where an interesting looking handbag was within easy reach.

'I have more news.' Martha spoke in a low tone.

'Oh no,' Kira said. 'It's your Dad isn't it – is he okay? Was he badly hurt?'

'He is having his spine regrown, but he will be fine. He has a rather odd request of everyone, he wants us to leave the city. He says there is a place we will be safe. Some kind of wilderness camp.'

'Camp Eden?' Ruth interrupted, sounding excited. 'I've heard all sorts of rumours about it - a hidden science base investigating how tech and nature can co-exist. It's a hangover though, right? From before The Event? It's not funded directly by Corp.'

'I don't know I'm afraid.'

Jed jumped in. 'Not funded by Corp? Like Force and Special Investigations? I thought they were the only ones.'

'No, no, no,' Ruth said. 'But they are probably all that's left now.'

'I never heard about this before.' Dina sounded sceptical.

'When Corporation first came into control there were still factions who disagreed with the way governance was heading,' Jed explained. 'They pooled their resources into setting up independent checks, to stop Corporation becoming a ruthless juggernaut.'

'They've done a fragging poor job,' Dina commented.

'Dina!' Kira exclaimed.

'Sorry Kira, but just look at where we are now, and what we've lost.'

Kira and Dina both looked a little embarrassed at their outbursts, but before they could say anything else Grace distracted everyone by pulling the abandoned NanNan box over onto the floor, narrowly missing herself. Kira leapt up in dismay, the conversation forgotten.

ANON33: *No charges brought against those responsible for building attack yet – who's guilty? Share your thoughts and spread the sweep.*

Later that night, Kira and Jed lay in bed looking up at the ceiling, both wrapped up in their own thoughts.

'Jed? Do you think we should leave the city?'

'I don't want anything to happen to you, hon. But I don't know if Camp Eden is the right answer,' Jed replied. 'I think we should wait.'

'Wait for what?' Her anger flared. 'Another building to blow up? Another loved one to die?'

She calmed down when her husband put his arm around her and pulled her close.

'We should wait to find out what Special Investigations have to say. Let me go in to work tomorrow and learn more.'

Kira snuggled into Jed's chest and spoke in a small voice. 'I don't think Anti-Corp will let this go quietly. Once they find out about the water treatment, things are going to escalate quickly.'

Jed stroked his wife's head and made small shushing noises. 'Let's not start panicking yet. You've all got a security detail and the apartment is protected. I won't let anything happen to you or Grace, or anyone. I promise.'

Jed waited for her reply, but Kira's breathing had slowed and become deeper. Feeling safe in his arms she had finally relaxed and let the stress of the last few days leave her body, falling into a deep sleep. Jed continued to stroke her head and stare up at the ceiling.

Dina was checking her dailies. There were a lot of random approaches from people all over the city asking about her miscarriage – some apologetic and supportive, others downright nasty. Still nothing from Ben but she did notice one from Pete. He had never messaged her before, and he'd only been over that afternoon. She clicked through.

Dina. Can you give me your Anti-Corp contact please? Force wants us to start investigating individuals involved with AC and 42nd Army and I think your guy would be a good place to start. Cheers, Pete.

Dina replied instantly, giving him Bobby's name and number, as well as a brief description. She would do anything to help apprehend those responsible for Ingrid's murder.

Jed was surprised to see an empty chair opposite his desk when he got to work. He double checked his messages, certain that Pete had told him to meet at the office.

Several hours later and Jed was starting to worry. Pete wasn't answering his ear comm and hadn't sent any messages to say why he had been delayed. They were due to meet with the chief in five. Jed knocked on Minkov's door.

'Come in!'

Jed poked his head into the office. 'Sir? Have you heard from Barnes?'

Minkov looked up at Jed from his desk monitor. 'Who am I? His mother?'

'No Sir.' Jed came fully into the room. 'He hasn't come in yet.'

The chief was about to answer when Agent Deveraux entered, without knocking.

'We'll update Barnes later,' said Minkov as he glared at Deveraux. 'Take a seat, Jenkins.'

Jed sat down in the only available chair, leaving Deveraux to stand. The agent gazed at the chief for a moment before clearing his throat.

'We're here to discuss how we tell the city about the water treatment – or if indeed, we should.'

'Are you serious?' asked Jed. 'You can't keep something like this a secret.'

'Corporation managed to do it for at least the past fifty years.'

'Corporation is why we are in this mess,' Minkov said. 'Get on it with, Deveraux.'

Deveraux began pacing back and forth. '*If* we tell the public, I think we should release the information slowly.'

'Slowly – as in telling the privileged first you mean.' Jed snorted. 'Because they don't sweep. No, you can't contain this to one sector. It's all or nothing.'

'Jenkins is right,' agreed Minkov. 'We have to beat the rumour mongers on this. What is your recommendation, Detective?'

'Well, Sir. I think a simple sweep with links to more information should work. We put Force operatives out on the street as a precaution and ride out the reaction.'

'Ride out the reaction – that sounds like a solid plan,' Deveraux said sarcastically.

Jed closed his eyes briefly and pinched the bridge of his nose.

'What's your contribution?' the chief asked, pointing a finger at Deveraux.

'I still think the less said the better...'

'The less said the better?' Jed stood up in anger. 'My sister just died thanks to factions fighting with each other – I seriously doubt continuing to lie to my city is the way forward.' He breathed heavily through his nose.

'Detective,' barked Minkov. 'Sit down.'

Jed looked at his boss and shook his head. 'With respect, Sir, I'm going to find my partner.' Jed glared at Deveraux before leaving the room. The agent raised an eyebrow at Minkov.

'And you're just going to let him go like that?'

'It's none of your fragging business how I run my department.' Minkov stood up and held the door open for the agent. 'I'll get public relations to draw something up and send it over.'

Deveraux stared at MInkov in silence for a moment, then shrugged and left, the door banging shut behind him.

After walking out of the chief's office, Jed had gone to find tech support and ask them to activate Pete's tracker. It led him to the East Sector. There had been a series of unexplained deaths in this abandoned sector last year, and Corporation had initially declared it a hazardous, no-go area. Once the buildings had been cleared drifters had moved in, and then refused to move on. It was a low priority problem as far as Corporation were concerned, preferring to have all undesirables in one place.

Jed entered East Sector cautiously. He'd not been here before. There was something odd about it. He realised there were patches of greenery amongst the buildings. Splashes of moss growing on walls, tendrils of ivy winding themselves around abandoned gates, and small clumps of grass and wildflowers dotting the walkways. He slowed the skimmer and brought out the tracker. Pete was two streets away to the left. Suddenly, Jed heard shots fired and men yelling from that direction. He touched his ear comm and demanded back up before skimming over to investigate.

Pete rested, his back against the wall. Just a few moments. Just to catch his breath. He'd surprised everyone. They hadn't stood a chance. And now they were dead. All of them. Yet Pete felt no relief. Instead he felt cold, and alone. A trickle of blood ran over the hand Pete had pressed to his stomach, but he didn't notice. He was thinking about how he'd arrived at this moment. His beautiful Ingrid was dead - their unborn child murdered before it even had a chance. She would have been a wonderful mother.

Despite his best efforts he had not been able to get around Special Investigations' lock down at Science Division, so Pete didn't even know if it had been a boy or a girl. Better to think of his Ingrid as alive and smiling with her blonde hair hanging around her face and her blue eyes twinkling.

Tears ran unnoticed down Pete's face. He was losing the feeling in his legs. He felt so tired it made sense to stay here and rest. He'd get up in a minute. He ought to thank Dina. And speak to Jed. But his hand was wet and sticky. A small, alarmed part of his brain was telling him to keep pressure on the wound, so he left his hand there and thought about the morning's events.

It hadn't taken him long to find Bobby. He'd hacked into the Corporation mainframe using the next gen code Ingrid had shown him, and then he'd been able to pinpoint a five-block radius via Bobby's ear comm digits. He'd had to skim the streets a few times, but finally Bobby had come around the corner, whistling to himself. It had been easy for him to stun Bobby and load him into the skimmer. Once Pete had tied Bobby up and applied a certain amount of persuasive pressure, he had been only too happy to talk.

'I'm a low-level guy,' he'd protested. 'I just pass messages.'

Pete hadn't believed him. So he removed Bobby's left hand. After all, why should he have both his hands, when Pete's Ingrid was gone? It had taken a while for the stump to stop bleeding and for Bobby to stop yelling, but once Pete had threatened to chop the other hand off, things had gone better.

'I wasn't at Corp Tech,' Bobby spluttered. 'I was with some of my girls at the protest.' Pete knew he was lying. A scumbag scrabbling to say anything to save his worthless life. Once Pete had passed electricity through the raw, dripping stump to refocus his prisoner, he'd been forced to administer some revival drugs. All he wanted to know was where to find the ringleaders. Bobby had told him that Victor, leader of Anti-Corp, was meeting the leaders of the 42nd Army, here, in the abandoned eastern sector of the city. Everyone responsible for Ingrid's death would be in the same place. Pete had made certain of that. One shot through Bobby's head and the smoking laser hole had sent the lowlife away permanently. It had been a kindness in the end and Pete had his information.

It seemed to be getting darker in the building. Pete blinked and tried to focus. There was a burnt-out laser gun next to him, no shots left. He'd have to wait until he felt strong enough to get up. It didn't look like anyone else in the room would be getting up anytime soon. He started to laugh but the blood caught in his throat. He began coughing instead.

'Pete!'

Someone was coming, shouting his name. He tried to reply but couldn't stop coughing up blood.

Jed ran up the corridor, noting the bodies by the doorway at the end. They'd been shot through the head. Instant death. He paused to look at his scanner. Only one sign of life. Pete's tracker confirmed he was inside. Somewhere. Jed tried to open the door, but something was blocking it, he pushed hard until it gave way. Behind the door - another dead body. And there were three more in the room. Pete was propped up against the left wall. He didn't look good. Jed rushed over.

'Pete – Pete! Can you hear me?'

Jed ran a quick diagnostic, taking note of the laser shot to the stomach. He applied a vacuum patch and administered pain relief to the side of Pete's neck.

'I got them,' Pete mumbled. 'Did you see? I got them.'

'Easy, brother,' Jed whispered. 'Easy.'

Force sirens wailed through the air as backup arrived and a fully armed unit came dashing into the room, followed by a medic. The medic sent a drone to scan the room as he hurried over to Pete's slumped body.

'Anything administered?'

'Vacuum seal and pain relief,' Jed answered. 'I just got here.'

The drone beeped to confirm the rest of the bodies were dead, and the medic motioned Jed to help him get Pete onto the hover gurney. The team leader, from the Force unit that had entered with the medic, came over to Jed.

'Detective? I'll get the scene bagged and tagged, but we'll need your statement.'

'I need to go with my partner,' Jed replied.

'Of course. Back at HQ?' The team leader clapped a hand on Jed's shoulder before getting back to his unit.

The medic was steering the stretcher out the door as Jed hurried to catch up.

'I'll ride with you.'

***ANON64:** Shots fired in abandoned sector East. What happened? Sweep and share!!*

Jed was pacing up and down in the waiting area as Chief Minkov and Agent Deveraux arrived.

'Anything?' asked Minkov.

'We've only just arrived, Sir.'

Before Jed could say anything else the door to the emergency examination room opened.

'The patient has refused treatment,' said the female medic standing in the doorway. 'There's nothing more we can do. If you want to say goodbye, now is the time.'

The medic gestured towards the open door. Jed looked at it and did not move. Agent Deveraux made to walk towards the open emergency room, but the chief held out an arm and stopped him.

'Chief, with respect, we need to speak to Detective Barnes.'

'I'll do it,' Jed said. 'He's my partner.'

Pete's eyes were shut when Jed walked in. The medical staff had cleaned him up, but his breathing was shallow, and blood seeped out of the dressing on his torso. Pain flitted across his face, and his hand clutched the sheet beneath him.

'Pete?'

Pete opened his eyes and gradually focused.

Jed gazed at his dying partner.

'Why did you do it?'

'I had to,' Pete whispered. 'You understand?' He gripped onto Jed's arm. 'I had nothing left.' Pete let go of Jed's arm, and closed his eyes, his breath rasping in his chest.

'For Ingrid.'

Agent Deveraux collared Jed as he left the room.

'What did he say?'

'He admitted killing them, if that's what you mean.'

Deveraux glanced at the chief, made his excuses and left. Minkov came over to stand by Jed.

'Did you know Barnes was going to do this?'

Jed stared at him for a moment before answering. 'No, but you did. You and Deveraux. You were hoping he'd solve your 42nd Army problem for you. Well, he has. And now he's going to die - and for what?'

'Jenkins...'

Jed turned and started to walk away. Before he'd gone far, he turned and shook his finger towards his boss.

'You shouldn't have let this happen,' he said, walking back and handing in his badge and laser gun.

Minkov watched Jed disappear around the corner before going to sit with his dying detective.

MED4AC: *Force Detective injured in shoot-out.*

Chapter Fifteen

FORCE: ***ALL SWEEPS**IMPORTANT ANNOUNCEMENT**ALL SWEEPS***

Citizen Update: Corporation have been artificially treating the water supply.

We urge citizens not to panic and to continue using water available while city governance formulate a replacement source.

This is a city-wide top priority.

Click through for more details and help desk access.

MSCHILD: *No children and now no water? Are Corporation trying to kill us?*

MADSR: *I have been drinking the water. I do not have a secret water supply!!!*

MED4AC: *We do not have a separate water supply. Please continue to use your water ration as normal. Click through for more information on signs of dehydration.*

ANON88: *This is all part of Corp's plan – we must fight back! Where are 42nd Army?*

Join me and fight back!

CORP: *Extra water rations are available. Your safety is our priority.*

ANON64: *Don't drink the water! There must be a secret supply! Raid your nearest Corporation outlet and share the sweep!*

MED4AC: *Shoot out Detective dies.*

C42N: *Leaders of Anti-Corp and the 42nd Army have been killed. Force Detective responsible has died.*

ANON27: *Mob rules – mob rules – mob rules – mob rules!!*

When Jed walked through the door to the apartment, Kira ran to him in tears, and hugged him tight.

'Jed,' she sobbed. 'Have you seen the sweeps? It looks like everyone has gone mad. And Pete – is Pete?'

Jed buried his head into his wife's shoulder and tried hard not to cry. They stood, holding one another for several minutes before he was able to step back and speak.

'Pete's gone.'

Kira's hand flew to her mouth and she stumbled backwards a little.

'No – oh no, not Pete.' Tears fell down her face. 'What happened?'

'He went after those responsible for …. for Ingrid.' Jed took a deep breath to steady his voice. 'He was... he was... I found him.'

'Oh sweetie.' Kira took her husband in her arms again. 'I am so sorry.'

Jed took a shower and changed while Kira saw to Grace. Neither spoke for a while as they tried to process what had happened. Eventually they found themselves sat on the couch together.

'Are you okay?' Kira asked, leaning forward to kiss her husband on the cheek.

'I honestly don't know.' Jed tried to smile. 'So much has happened in such a short time.' He ran a hand through his hair. 'I quit Force.'

'You quit!'

'I had no choice. They knew what Pete was going to do and they did nothing to stop him.'

Kira looked down at her hands.

'What will we do now?'

Jed shrugged. Seeing that his wife looked so upset, Jed pulled her in for a hug and began to stroke her hair.

'Everything will be alright – you'll see.' He changed the subject. 'Where are the others?'

'Martha and Dina went to Science Division, and Ruth went to help out at Academy.'

'Do they still have their Force escorts?'

'I think so.'

'Good – they'll get back safely then.'

'Jed, I'm scared. Is it safe for them to be out there? The sweeps...'

'Never mind the sweeps,' Jed interrupted. 'I know who's on escort duty, so I'll call them and get them to bring the girls back, okay?'

Kira sniffed.

'It'll be alright, hon,' Jed said. 'I love you.'

'Love you too.'

***MAHA**: I am working with other scientists to find a cure for the water supply.*

'Ma'am?'

Martha looked at the Force Operative who was trying to get her attention. 'Yes?'

'I have orders to bring you back home.'

'But we only just arrived,' Martha protested.

'Sorry, Ma'am. Science Division is now under Force lock-down. It's not going anywhere.'

Grumbling to herself, Martha went to find Dina who was in one of the fishbowls.

'Dina,' Martha called. 'We have to go.'

'But we just got here!'

'I know, but our escort detail have orders and they are locking down the facility.'

Dina grimaced as she left the fishbowl. She hadn't even had time to begin calculations on how long it would take for the water to be clear of radiation.

As the two women walked back down the corridor, the way was blocked by several people watching something. They drew closer and saw Dr Basjere, Head of Science Division and Corporation board member, being led away in magno-binders.

'I wouldn't like to be in his shoes right now,' Dina commented.

Martha watched; her face ashen then reached for her ear comm to call her father.

'Father?'

'Martha.'

'Are you okay?'

'Why – what's happened?' Mr Hamble answered her gruffly.

'I just saw Dr Basjere get arrested... Are you..? Will you..?'

'Spit it out, girl.'

There was a pause as Martha worked up the courage to ask the question she already knew the answer to.

'Are you going to be arrested?'

Silence.

Mr Hamble cleared his throat. 'I have volunteered to come in for questioning once my spine has been regrown. The Force chief and I have an understanding – of sorts.'

Martha felt light-headed and leant on the wall for support.

'Everything will be fine.' Mr Hamble reassured his daughter. 'I've got my man on the case. Are you at home?'

'I am at Science Division but...'

Before Martha could finish, her father bellowed down the connection.

'Get yourself home NOW – it's not safe. I'll talk to you later.' And he terminated the call.

'Ma'am?'

Martha looked up, still feeling a little dazed.

'This way, Ma'am.'

Dina linked Martha's arm, and the two of them followed the operative out of Science Division and into a waiting skimmer.

'You want me to leave now?'

'Yes, Ma'am. This way please, Ma'am.'

'Alright, alright – there's no need to Ma'am me to death.'

Ruth had only just arrived at Academy, but the campus was largely deserted as students had gone to protest at Corp HQ about the water. There wasn't much she could do anyway, so she meekly followed the operative back to the skimmer.

ANON88: *They had to have known – what makes them special? They have to pay!*

C42N: *There have been city-wide attacks on Corporation buildings and one residential apartment block believed to be the home of R. Maddocks – the pregnant anomaly.*

***FORCE:** All violent activity will be penalised harshly. Think for yourself and don't regret your actions.*

'What about Archive?' Kira asked, pacing up and down the bedroom.

'Archive will be fine, hon,' said Jed. 'It's probably the most secure building in the entire city.'

Kira came to sit on the bed beside him.

'It's getting aggressive out there. What are we going to do?'

'I think you should go to Camp Eden.'

'Mr Hamble's suggestion?'

'Yeah. You know Martha got shoved at the protest?' Kira nodded.

'People know who you are and they're angry. I don't want anything bad to happen to you. To any of you.'

Jed gestured at the wall where the news feed display hung.

'You've seen the sweeps. They just looted Ruth's apartment, and she had that brick through the window.'

Jed took Kira's hands in his own.

'It's not safe in the city for any of you. I can't protect you, Kira, and I can't lose anyone else.'

Jed's voice began to break as he fought to keep his emotions in check.

Kira turned and fished a packed bag out from under the bed and looked a little shamefaced at her husband. He took her hand again and gave it a squeeze. This was the right thing to do.

'Martha and Dina will be back soon,' Jed said. 'I've told Ruth's Force escort to bring her here as well. I made some calls when you were changing Grace. There's a private hover on its way over to take you to Camp Eden. You all need to be out of the city for a few days. I'll let you know when it's safe to come back.'

'What about my parents? Your parents? Our other friends? I feel like I'm running away. I should stay here and help, or something.'

'You are at a higher risk than anyone else, hon. Thanks to the sweeps everyone knows you are friends with two of the mother-to-be anomalies. They know you lost another friend in the terrorist attack. And they know about Pete.'

Jed had to stop as the words stuck in his throat. Kira leaned in and hugged him.

'What about you? What are you going to do?'

'I'll look after what's left of our families.'

'Are you going to reply to your boss?'

Jed puffed out his cheeks and fiddled with his wristplant. Chief Minkov had been calling him every hour on the hour. Each call had gone to message.

'I will, I promise.'

There was a happy gurgling sound as Grace crawled off the side of the bed, only to be caught by the surrounding hover field and gently lifted back up. Both parents turned to look.

'Ingrid sent it over,' Kira said. 'It was the last thing she did before...' Kira dashed tears away from her eyes and leant over to scoop up Grace.

'We're going on a trip, Gracie,' she said, and began smooshing her face into her daughter's and kissing the delighted baby.

'Kira? Jed?' Martha called out sharply as she entered the apartment.

'In here,' Kira replied.

Martha came rushing through the doorway to the bedroom looking pale, her eyes red from crying. Dina trailed behind looking shocked.

'What happened?' Kira said as she thrust Grace into Jed's arms and came over to Martha. 'Are you okay?'

Martha clutched at Kira's arms and then, her legs sagging, she pulled them both to the floor and began crying.

'They found him. They just went in and...' Martha gulped for air. 'Oh Kira. They killed him. They killed my daddy.'

Martha collapsed into wails of anguish as Kira looked over her head in disbelief at Dina. Jed leaned over and grabbed his ear comm from the side of the bed. Reattaching himself, he dialled through to Minkov.

'Sir? Detective Jenkins - reporting for duty.'

There was a long silence.

'About fragging time, Detective. Get in here, ASAP.'

Jed dithered about where to put Grace, who was trying to grab his ear comm, when Kira got his attention by waving her hands and pointing to the play cube. Kissing his wife's head and giving Dina a quick hug, Jed left them trying to comfort Martha on the bedroom floor.

Enough was enough. He was going to make sure there was a peaceful end to this uprising, and he was going to make fragging sure no-one else he loved died.

***MED4AC:** Roger Hamble, Marketing Director for Corporation dies from complications.*

***ANON88:** One down, one arrested, two to go! Don't let them get away with poisoning us!!*

***C42N:** Hamble killed at Med Centre – is anyone safe?*

The two remaining Corporation Board members met in secret, in an underground skimmer bay.

'We have to leave.'

'I agree.'

'Where shall we go?'

'It's too risky for us to travel together. Go south. I hear they're pro Corp down south.'

'What about you?'

'I'm going north. I have family in City 15, they'll protect me.'

They parted with a formal handshake, each returning to their private, blacked out skimmers, confident that they could escape the city unscathed. Neither one had stopped to think about whether their drivers watched the sweeps. Neither one checked to see whether their skimmer was on auto pilot. Neither one saw the collision coming.

Neither one survived.

As Jed travelled into work, Ruth returned to the apartment. Martha had gone for a lie down so Kira explained what had happened to Mr Hamble.

'Frag! What the frag? Are we safe here? Did you see what the bastards did to my flat? What are we going to do?'

'We are going to Camp Eden,' Kira announced. 'Pack a bag, you two, essentials only. We've got secure transport out there.'

'But what about everything that's happening?' asked Dina. 'We can't just leave – can we?'

Ruth held one hand over her belly protectively.

'I actually agree with Kira. It's not safe for us here at the moment. Let's give Force time to calm everything down.' Ruth looked down at herself. 'Kira – have you got any clothes I can borrow?'

'I'm sure I'll have something, sweetie,' Kira said, and the two women headed off into Kira's bedroom.

Dina went reluctantly to her side of the expanded apartment, poked her head around the adjoining door and heard soft sobbing coming from the far bedroom. She hesitated, not wanting to intrude. She knocked on Martha's door and opened it.

'Martha? Are you okay?'

Dina winced, realising what she'd said. Of course Martha wasn't okay. Her father had been killed. The sobbing continued. Dina ventured into Martha's bedroom. She spotted Martha sat on the floor in the corner of the room, knees drawn up, head bent down on crossed arms, shoulders shaking as she cried.

'Martha?'

'Go away.'

'We have to pack. We're leaving for Camp Eden,' Dina paused. 'Shall I pack your stuff?'

No answer.

Dina found an empty bag and began gathering things she thought they might need. Not knowing exactly where they were headed made it tricky, but she put together a few changes of clothes for each of them and various small pieces of tech that might come in useful out in the middle of nowhere.

Martha continued to sob.

Dina left her where she was and walked back through the adjoining door, putting her bags down with the others in a pile in Kira and Jed's lounge.

'Kira,' she called. 'I've got our stuff but Martha, she's just... I don't know what to do.'

Before Kira could reply, the door chimed, and two Force operatives entered.

'Ma'am.' One of the operatives greeted Kira. 'We're here to transport you to Camp Eden. It's getting ugly out there, we have to leave immediately.'

Kira smiled bravely, hoping her fear didn't show.

'I'll get Martha. You two take the bags. I'll meet you down there.'

With Grace snuggled close to her in her baby wrap, Kira went through to Martha's room. 'Martha. Get up. It's time to go.'

Martha lifted her tear stained face and looked at Kira.

'To the middle of nowhere? How do you even know we will be safe there?'

Kira held out her hand.

'Because your father told us to go. He loved you, Martha, and he wanted to protect you and his grandchild. Come on, Ma. Do it for your baby.'

Martha looked dully at the proffered hand for a moment, before finally grasping it and pulling herself up off the floor.

'I haven't packed.'

'Don't worry, Dina packed you some stuff. It's going to be okay.'

As the transporter travelled through the city, Kira was glad of the blacked-out windows and additional security.

***C42N:** The number of people hurt in widespread riots has increased. Force are reminding citizens to stay at home and avoid areas of aggression.*

***ANON88:** Who's in the secret skimmer? Who's getting preferential treatment?*

***MED4AC:** We urge non-emergency cases to visit their nearest auto-doc. We DO NOT have a separate water supply. Please consider whether it is medically necessary for you to attend Med Centre.*

***C42N:** Blacked out private skimmer seen travelling through City Forty-Two. Sweep if you know who's inside.*

A brick hit the window, making the women jump.

'It's alright, ladies,' one of the operatives spoke through the intercom. 'This skimmer is equipped with unbreakable windows. You're quite safe.'

Despite the reassurance, a sense of unease lay over all of them, as they continued to travel towards the city limits.

Ruth leant over and patted Kira's hand. 'I'm sure Jed will be fine.'

Kira smiled weakly and looked back out the window. She didn't think anyone in authority would be safe right now. Hopefully, the people would realise they weren't achieving anything by their actions and go home. Until they did, Kira hoped Jed stayed out of harm's way.

The transporter left the rioters behind and the streets got emptier and emptier. The women began to calm down, each of them feeling mentally exhausted by what they'd been through the past few days. One by one, they drifted off to sleep, lulled by the hum of the transporter's engine and the mild sedative the Force operatives had released into the back of the vehicle.

'Feels wrong, drugging them like this,' commented the older of the two operatives.

'Orders are orders. Detective Jenkins didn't want them getting scared,' the other said. 'And we've still got to make it past city limits.'

City Forty-Two was contained within a forcefield, which apart from one or two weak spots, kept the citizens safe from the alleged toxicity of the ravaged world outside. The residual radiation from the HER wars was the reason the human race had been divided up into small cities dotted throughout the continents – in order to save what was left.

As the transporter approached the official city exit, the two Force operatives started scanning the surroundings for any violent activity. Jed had been worried that angry citizens might gather at the city gate demanding to be let out, but fear of what was outside had kept them away. The transporter stopped briefly, and one of the operatives punched in an access code. Gradually a hole in the shimmering forcefield grew large enough to allow the transporter through, then closed behind them as they left the city behind.

Kira leant her head against the now opaque window. She felt relaxed and at peace. The sedative was beginning to wear off, but she no longer felt as scared. The others still slept, and Grace was tucked within the baby wrap, nestled close.

Kira pressed the intercom to allow her to speak to the Force operatives.

'Do you know how much further we have to travel?'

'No, Ma'am – it's a pre-set course. The transporter is on auto cruise.'

'Oh. I see.'

'But I'm sure it won't be long,' reassured one of them.

Kira went back to staring out of the window. Lulled by the hum of the transporter she closed her eyes again, and drifted. She was stood in a meadow - sweet smelling grass and wildflowers all around her. Bees hummed in the air, and Grace played by her feet.

'I'm so glad you came.' A melodious voice spoke to her.

Kira turned in slow motion and was unsurprised to see the beautiful blue lady stood next to her.

'Are you sure you want us here? It's so beautiful,' Kira asked.

'I am not complete without you. All things must balance. It is time. We are here.'

'We're here. Ma'am?' said one of the Force operatives. 'We've arrived.'

Kira looked around blearily, realising that the transporter had stopped and one of the operatives was speaking to her. The others were waking up.

'Are we here?'

'Where is everything?'

'Who's that?'

'We're just the travel detail, Ma'am,' said the Force operative opening the transporter door and looking at Kira. 'If you're ready?'

The operative gestured that they should exit the transport. Kira turned to look at the others.

'Are you ready?'

Dina and Ruth both gave small nods while Martha looked expressionless, eyes still red from crying. She gave a half shrug and allowed herself to be led out the transporter with the others. After their bags had been deposited on the ground next to them, the transporter turned around and left.

There were two large marquees set up on either side of the camp clearing – one looked like it was used for cooking and eating, the other had its flaps down and nothing was visible. A communal area had been set up towards the rear of the clearing and there were several wooden huts down one side, half hidden by the encroaching forest.

A small Indian man waited patiently for them at the camp entrance, dressed in khaki trousers and tunic, his brown feet bare.

'Welcome to Camp Eden,' he said. 'I'm Moham, I'll be your guide – anything you need or want to know about, just ask.'

Dina grabbed her bag and began to walk forward while the others hung back. 'Where is everyone else?' she asked, looking around with interest.

'They will be back later,' Moham said. 'Can I offer you some refreshment?'

He gestured for the women to follow him further into the clearing. Dina fell in behind, while the others looked doubtfully at each other.

After brief hesitation, they picked up their bags and slowly followed. Everything seemed to have been set up to blend in with the scenery as much as possible, making full use of the natural materials available. Moham stopped beneath the canopy at the far end of the clearing. A number of cushions lay scattered around an empty fire pit.

'This is our communal area,' he gestured. 'Sit, make yourselves comfortable, and I will get some tea brewing.'

Moham returned to the open sided marquee at the beginning of the camp, leaving the women alone. They stood motionless for a moment before Martha dropped her bag with a thump. No-one spoke as they sat down. They waited to see what would happen next.

'Hey, we get signal,' Dina said as she checked her handheld for updates.

The others followed her lead, even Martha, checking to see what they'd missed. There was a video message for Martha. From her father. She activated her ear comm to receive the audio file as well, and watched her father speak to her from his hospital bed, tears rolling down her face.

'Martha. I hope that you never get this message. But if you are watching this, then events have got out of hand. I want you to know that your mother and I love you very much. We always have. I am so proud of you. Throughout your life you have thought about what you wanted, and not let me, or Corporation, or anyone else get in your way. I admire that. I want you to do that now – be strong, be yourself. Be Martha Hamble.'

In the recording, Mr Hamble rubbed his eyes quickly and cleared his throat. There was a brief smile to camera, and the video message stopped.

Martha let out a huge breath. The others watched her in concern.

'Are you alright, Ma?' Kira asked.

'I will be. I will be.'

Chapter Sixteen

It had been one day since the girls had left the city limits. One day since Jed had returned to Force. One day of utter madness. Ordinarily peaceful citizens were trashing public buildings and spaces, whilst others looted service points for foodstuffs. No-one was going to work except for Medical and Force personnel. Force might not be under Corporation jurisdiction, but they signified authority, and were therefore a target for the ire of the people.

Jed was exhausted. He'd been on call for twenty-four hours straight and needed a break. Uncontaminated water was the biggest issue. So far, scientists at Science Division had confirmed that now the HER treatment had stopped, the water would return to normal - in time. However, no-one knew how long that might take. Everyone needed water but no-one wanted to use it, and the medical centre emergency service was close to breaking point trying to keep up with the number of dehydration cases.

Jed self-administered a stimulant and waited for the adrenalin to kick in. It was all too easy to fake the body into feeling full of energy, but if he didn't eat something soon, he might become the next emergency patient. The chief poked his head out of his office door, and seeing Jed motioned him to come through.

'Sir,' Jed said, entering the office.

Minkov was slumped in his chair.

'Deveraux believes we might be ready to start opening talks between what's left of the city leadership. Get this whole thing under control.'

Suddenly the room pitched into darkness as the power cut out.

'Initiate the fragging emergency backup system,' Minkov barked at an internal comms panel. A dull glow emanated from the floor as safety lights came on throughout the building.

'Report!'

But the screens remained dark. The Force's interface had insufficient power to run its diagnostic system. Minkov muttered under his breath before getting up. 'Get me a technician in here, now!' he yelled, sticking his head out his door.

The chief came back to his desk and jabbed a finger at the unresponsive screen before pushing it away.

'Jenkins, procedure states that we must facilitate negotiations between the highest city representatives. If I had my way, I'd terminate the whole fragging lot of them. But you need to find them, bring them here, and set up a holding area.' Minkov rummaged through his desk. 'No-one leaves until we get this mess under control.' He found what he was looking for and handed an info jack to Jed. 'This tells you who to round up. With any luck, they'll be tucked up at home. Anyone located in a trouble zone is to be bound and held for punishment. I will not have them destroy my city.'

Minkov held Jed's eye for a moment, before waving him out of the room and stabbing thick fingers at the unresponsive screens in front of him again.

Jed headed for the skimmer bay – they were solar powered so at least they still worked. As he entered, a number of operatives looked up expectantly.

'I need two volunteers.'

'I'll go.' A freckly, fresh-faced young man, bounced eagerly to his feet. 'Operative Griggs, Sir.'

He was followed with a sigh by a larger, heavy set, older man Jed recognised from the Corp Tech disaster site. 'Me too.'

'What's your name?' Jed asked as he handed them both riot gear to put on.

'Ash, Sir. Matthew Ash.'

'Okay men, this is us.' Jed pointed to the closest skimmer and the three of them got on board, Jed taking the front seat. 'Our job is to collect the most senior city representatives and bring them back to Force HQ.'

He whacked the jack into an info port. A list popped up on the display. The first name was Roger Hamble. Jed pinched the bridge of his nose.

Strike one.

An hour later Jed stood in an underground parking lot looking at the crashed skimmers and mangled remains of two more city leaders – who also happened to be Corporation board directors, and the next names on the list. Jed tried calling through to Med Centre for a deceased body pick-up, but his call wouldn't connect. The power was still out, and the general comms grid looked like it was down too.

'Griggs,' Jed called out. 'I need you to go to Med Centre and get a body pick-up organised. We'll seal the scene and move on.'

'Yes, Detective.'

Griggs saluted, and headed out to the Med Centre on foot while Ash took out a black disc from the kit in the back of the skimmer. He placed the disc in front of the crash site and activated the forcefield. It shimmered as it spread up and over the crime scene, sealing in all the evidence and solidifying so that only a member of Force would be able to deactivate it. Jed nodded in approval then climbed back into the Force skimmer and checked the next name on his list. Professor Kamir, Head of Academy.

Hopefully, he was still alive.

Jed manoeuvred the skimmer across the city, dismayed at the level of vandalism and destruction. It seemed the power cut had calmed some people down; they'd returned to their homes and their emergency energy sources. Passing the charred remains of Corp Tech, Jed felt a stab of pain in his chest. But he didn't want to think about his sister and her fledgling family. Or the fact that his partner was gone. And with Kira and Grace out of the city, it felt like there was not much left to fight for. The city's blackness matched his mood. They rounded the corner and Jed stared at the brilliance radiating out from Academy.

'Separate power grid obviously,' Jed muttered as they parked up.

Students milled around all over the grounds, but there was little sign of the violence that had ravaged the rest of the city. Jed checked his riot gear was firmly in place and armed his stunners. The Academy was the birthplace of Anti-Corp. Members of Force might not be welcome.

They left the skimmer and assessed the area. Jed and Operative Ash breathed a sigh of relief. The students looked scared and lost, not angry or violent. No-one said a word or approached them as they walked through the quad into the main building.

'Where can we find Professor Kamir?' Operative Ash asked a frightened looking girl sitting behind the front desk. The girl stared back at him, wide-eyed.

'C'mon, it's this way,' Jed said, turning left, not waiting to see if Ash was following him.

Jed remembered the way from his wife's enthusiastic description of her tour of Academy. He roughly pushed away thoughts of Kira and Grace. Now was not the time to start worrying about his family. He had work to do. Jed stopped outside a blue door engraved with a huge, many branched, old tree – the crest of the Academy. He rapped twice, before entering the room.

'May I help you?'

An older man turned from a bookcase to look at them. He was tall with white hair sweeping across his brow and, despite his age, stood firm, radiating a quiet strength.

'Professor Kamir, I'm Detective Jenkins. This is Operative Ash. We've come to bring you to Force HQ as part of the city leaders' protocol.'

'Ah.' The Professor placed a book back on the shelf. 'May I collect my coat?'

Jed nodded, and watched the elderly yet spry man stride over to retrieve his hat and coat.

'Lead on, Detective.'

Jed touched his ear comm, intending to call through to the chief, but remembered the defunct network.

'Do you have call access?' he asked the professor.

'Yes - we run on a separate grid. In case of student pranks. It seems to have worked rather in our favour today, eh.'

Jed went over to the touchscreen on the Professor's desk and used his Force chip to log in and override the system. The connection was grainy with no picture.

'Ah,' said the Professor, peering over his shoulder. 'You'll probably only get sound working if it's down at that end. No power, see.'

Jed nodded. 'Chief? It's Jenkins.'

'Jenkins?' Minkov's voice sounded tinny and far away. 'Report.'

'We've got one so far, Sir. Fourth on the list.'

'Where the frag are the first three?'

'Dead, Sir.'

'Hmmph. Who's left?'

'Well, you, Sir. And the Surgeon General from Med Centre. We're going there next.' Jed scratched the side of his head. 'Is there anyone else I should round up, Sir?'

'No. Get back here, ASAP.'

'Sir.' Jed clicked off and cleared the screen down. Operative Ash and Professor Kamir followed him out of the office, and back to the skimmer.

At Med Centre it looked like something out of an old disaster movie – harassed medical staff flitted from corridor to corridor, emergency lighting cast an eerie glow over everything with muffled shouts and various machines beeping erratically in the background. People milled about, some groaning, some holding their injuries close, whilst others looked vacant - in shock. They'd all come for answers.

The desk warden leapt to his feet as Jed approached. 'You've bought a squad for us, then?'

'No. Sorry. I'm here for the Surgeon General. Do you know where he is?'

'But we need you here – we can't cope.' The desk warden spluttered. 'People just keep showing up.'

Jed gave a small shrug, then pointed at Operative Ash.

'You can have him. I'll let HQ know you need more bodies. The Surgeon General?'

The desk warden scowled at Jed and pointed to a corridor on the left. 'He's in surgery.'

Jed left Ash in the foyer and headed down to surgery. There were people everywhere. Jed had to fend off several persistent citizens begging him for answers. At this rate, it looked like Jed might have to fight his way out of Med Centre.

Reaching the surgical wards, Jed cast about for a med tech who might be able to point him in the right direction. The consultant he'd seen at Med Centre before came out of a side room, his sandy brown hair looking dishevelled and his medical tunic crumpled.

'Detective,' he said, greeting Jed in the corridor.

'I'm looking for the Surgeon General.'

'Well, you've found him. Your men will just have to wait like everyone else. We're doing this on a first come, first served basis – apart from emergencies, of course.'

'You don't understand. You need to come with me to Force HQ. Now.'

'Well, I can't leave *now,'* the consultant replied, and tried to walk past Jed. But Jed stood his ground. The consultant went red in the face. 'Don't you people realise what's happening out there? It's mass panic. I have a duty of care to look after these idiots whether I like it or not. I don't have time for your emergency.'

The consultant attempted to brush past Jed again who continued to block his way and took out his magno-binders.

'I charge you as a city representative to take part in the protection of the city,' he said. 'I will take you to Force HQ where you will begin the protocols that will end this crisis. We can do it with magnos, or without – your choice.'

The Surgeon General glared at Jed. 'I want a Force unit in place to back up my people.'

Jed tucked the magnos back into their holder. 'I've left one operative in reception and requested back up,' he said. 'We're stretched thin ourselves. It's the best I can do.'

The Surgeon General's shoulders slumped in defeat. 'Can I at least get my jacket?'

Returning to Force HQ with two city representatives had Jed on edge, contemplating what the consequences would be if anything should happen to the skimmer. He scanned the streets ahead for any signs of a mob, but the skimmer made it to Force HQ with only one detour. Jed herded the two men into meeting room one. As he entered, Jed was reminded of the last interview he had conducted in this room. It felt like a hundred years ago.

'Make yourselves comfortable. I'll send in some refreshments.'

'You can't keep us here indefinitely,' the Surgeon General shouted, as Jed left the room to inform the chief he had two city representatives.

'I think you'll find that until city protection protocol is completed – he can,' Professor Kamir said, smiling as he sat down in the most comfortable chair in the room.

Jed secured the door on his way out of the room. Walking over to the chief's office, he snagged a junior recruit and put in a request for a team to go to Med Centre and help keep the peace.

Whatever that meant.

Jed entered the chief's office without knocking. Minkov and Agent Deveraux were waiting for him.

'Any problems?' Deveraux asked.

'Nope.'

'Let's get this fragging thing over and done with then,' Minkov grumbled. 'Jenkins, I need you to bring in the Anti-Corp representative. He's in holding cell four.'

'Sir'

As Jed walked down to holding the power came back on and the corridor was suddenly bathed in light. Reaching the cells, he wondered who was left from Anti-Corp. Pete had been thorough when he hunted down those responsible for Ingrid's death. Who else could there be?

Chapter Seventeen

***ANON88:** What gives Hamble the right to abandon the rest of us? I hope she gets radiation sickness.*

***MAHA:** Yes, I left City 42, but I will be back.*

Kira couldn't see who was speaking. She knew she was asleep, her limbs felt heavy, and although she was seeing light around her, she couldn't see a person or place.

'I'm so glad you came.' The voice made Kira feel warm and safe, protected.

'I'm so glad we came here,' Dina said. 'Wake up, Kira.' Dina poked Kira in the ribs, and once she was sure Kira was awake, she tossed something at her. It was green and round. 'It's an apple, Kira – an actual apple. Grown in soil, taken from a tree. And it's all ready to eat. Try it – it tastes so much better than the synth ones.' Dina's eyes sparkled as she bounced from foot to foot with excitement.

'Where's Grace?'

'She's fine. Martha has her, they're exploring the orchards. That's where apples grow, you know. You can get red ones too. This place is just amazing.'

'Yeah,' Kira muttered, as she pulled on her trousers and went in search of her daughter.

Kira found Grace crawling through the grass, cooing and burbling, as she explored the undergrowth. Martha and Ruth sat nearby, drinking tea.

'Good morning,' Martha said. 'Did you manage to get any sleep?'

Kira bent down to check on Grace before plopping on the floor next to the others. She idly plucked a stem of grass and began turning it around in her hands.

'Eventually. Thanks for getting up with Grace, Ma.'

'My pleasure, after all I need the practice.'

Martha and Kira smiled at each other as Ruth stretched her feet out into the grass.

'Isn't Camp Eden great?' she said. 'So peaceful.'

Kira looked pensive.

'Aren't you worried about what's happening at home? Whether our friends and families are alright?'

'Of course,' replied Ruth. 'But just being here makes me feel better – like everything is going to be alright.'

Kira looked down at Grace, playing happily.

'Everything is going to be alright, Kira.' Martha leaned over and put her hand on Kira's knee. 'Jed will be okay.'

Kira sniffed and nodded.

'The camp does seem lovely. But where exactly are we? What is this place?'

A man's voice came from behind them. 'Why, it's Eden, of course. Birthplace of man, but without the sin.'

Ruth snorted in response, then began coughing as her tea went down the wrong way. A tanned man in his thirties with a shock of dark hair came to sit on the grass with them, gently patting Ruth on the back until she waved away his assistance. Kira eyed him doubtfully.

'I'm Max, lead scientist at Eden,' he said, and he held out his hand for Kira to shake. She took it, then looked around.

'Where's the rest of your team?'

'Resting, I hope. We got back late last night. We heard all about your arrival from Moham. Have you got everything you need?'

Kira nodded, not knowing what to ask for, even if she did need something.

'Now that we're all here,' Dina asked. 'Can you tell us about Eden, Max?'

Max settled himself more comfortably on the ground.

'Okay,' he said. 'Where shall I start? After The Event, much of the Earth was uninhabitable because of the radiation levels. We had created a self-inflicted mass extinction event.' Max paused to pour himself some tea and looked around to make sure he had everyone's attention. 'You all know your history – our predecessors congregated inside specially built cities and barricaded themselves from the harmful effects. There was recycled water, synth food, and of course, the safe embrace of Corporation.'

The women all nodded. Grace tried some grass and decided it wasn't very tasty.

'About fifty years ago a high-ranking official decided it was time to find out what was going on outside, so they sent a team of scientists to these coordinates with orders to report back.' Max shrugged. 'They never returned. The report was logged and archived, and that was that. I found out about it a year ago and sent a petition in to the Board to try again.'

'And you were successful?' Ruth asked in surprise.

'No, not at first. It took a lot of lobbying and a lot of private funding, but we made it. We've been here about six months now.'

'What have you been researching?' Martha said.

'The Gaia Effect, mostly – seeing whether the Earth has managed to adapt and heal itself.'

'The Gaia Effect?' Kira asked intrigued.

'Yes,' Max said, warming to the topic. 'Nature has eventually worked her magic - cleaning the soil, the air and the water. The Earth has tried to rebalance old ecosystems and develop new ones. Some species haven't survived of course, but others have triumphed.' Max swept an arm out across the camp excitedly. 'In some places luscious forests and swelling grasslands cover the ruins of past cities while animals, birds and insects roam free amongst the disappearing debris of man. Plants have recolonised and freshwater lakes and rivers are teeming with fish and other aquatic life.'

As he paused for breath, Dina leant forward to catch his attention.

'Then in a way, moving mankind into self-contained city modules did the Earth a favour,' she said. 'Forcing ourselves to figure out how to recycle our waste and water has given the Earth a chance to heal.'

'That's right,' Max said, taking a large swallow of tea.

'What about the other team – did you find anything?' Kira asked.

'No, just the remains of their camp and the results of the seeds they'd planted.'

'Which is why you have apples,' Dina exclaimed as Max grinned at her.

'The other team – what happened?' Martha looked around for some trace of them.

Max shifted, looking a little uncomfortable, and seemed to gather his thoughts before speaking again. 'Expeditions don't always go to plan,' he said. 'Sometimes there are causalities. Anything could've happened to them. The important thing is, we are here now.'

'Why have you survived when the other team didn't?' Kira asked.

'We have access to clean, fresh water - it may not have been available to them,' Max explained. 'There's no radiation here, which means...' He was interrupted by Dina.

'Which means you can grow and plant and eat and drink and live! Outside, Kira. No more cities. No more Corporation!'

'I think I would still like indoor plumbing,' Martha remarked. Dina shushed her.

'Why doesn't everyone know about this place, Ma?' Kira asked.

'It was classified, one of Father's secrets. I do not think he even told the rest of the board. He was trying to do the right thing Kira. I know he was.'

Martha's eyes brimmed with tears as she fought to hold it together. Max cleared his throat.

'That's right. Mr Hamble was our benefactor and we reported directly to him.' He added then continued more softly. 'We are all terribly sorry for your loss Martha.'

Martha acknowledged him with a nod and wiped her eyes on the back of her hand.

'What happens now?' Kira turned back to Max.

Max puffed out his cheeks. 'I don't know. I'm a bit behind on the sweeps – we've been off campus for a while but we still get access here. I checked this morning and it looks like they're having a city reps meeting to try and diffuse the situation. I'm guessing Camp Eden is still a secret?'

'Yes, my husband – he's a Force Detective – he sent us here for safety, because of the children.'

'Children?' Max asked a little confused, pointing to Grace. 'Don't you mean child?'

Ruth and Martha shared a smile then pointed to their stomachs. Max stared at the women.

'You mean, you two are...'

'Yes, we are,' said Ruth with a smile.

'How? Did they finally come clean then?' Max looked at the two women and seeing them both look confused, he elaborated. 'About the treated water. Corporation I mean.'

'You knew?' Dina demanded.

'It was top level, but Hamble briefed me fully. He said that our work was more important than we knew because of the mistakes Corporation had made. I didn't think they would just stop treating the water and tell everyone.'

'They didn't,' Kira said, amused at Max's confusion.

'So, how... how did you… I mean, I know how, but why...'

Max was getting redder by the second. Kira took pity on him.

'We only just found out about the water supply, us and the rest of the city. That's why we are here. For our own safety. As for how Martha and Ruth got pregnant – I call it divine intervention.'

Max choked on his tea, and after receiving vigorous pats on the back from Dina, he was able to speak again.

'Divine intervention?' he croaked. 'Like God – you actually believe?'

'No, not God. I'm thinking even older,' Kira said, a faint smile on her face. 'It's not something many people remember but you might know about her given your work here – Gaia, the spirit of the Earth.'

Max interrupted excitedly. 'Oh, we believe! She's real. We've all seen her.'

The women looked quickly at each other, then stared at Max in disbelief. Grace broke the silence by clambering up to Kira and demanding to be fed. Everyone started talking at once until Kira raised her voice over the top of them.

'Hey – can I please feed my daughter and then Max, you need to tell us more.'

The women gathered up their things and went back to the communal area where the rest of the science team were beginning to gather. Kira went through to the kitchen area, looking around for their supplies. After hunting for a few minutes, she found Grace's bottle and milk and came out of the tent to join the rest. Max made the introductions.

'This is my team – Dr Gina Ayres, flora and fauna and Dr Mitch Guardis, geology and radiation.' He pointed at two, virtually identical sun-kissed people, dressed in the same khaki shorts and top as the rest of the team. 'You've already met Moham, he looks after us.' He gestured to the group of women. 'Everyone, this is Kira Jenkins, Martha Hamble, Dina Grey and Ruth Maddocks. Oh, and not forgetting, little Gracie.'

The group chuckled as they settled themselves on the various cushions. Kira and her friends faced Max and his team.

'It will be easier to show you,' Max said as he turned on the camp's holo recorder.

The women all watched with interest as a video began to play, showing the science team members helping themselves to food. Suddenly Dr Ayres, who was facing outwards, dropped her cup, the others followed her gaze reacting in similar shock - but the holo recorder didn't show yet what they were looking at.

'Wait for it,' Max said, as the recorder panned slowly around.

It seemed to take an age, but finally the women could see what the science team had seen. It was a big blue blur. Kira's heart sank in disappointment. A blue blur wasn't evidence. But as she continued to watch, the blur began to glow brighter and brighter until the image of a woman revealed itself. The light faded, and a beautiful blue woman stood before them. Her eyes sparkled like a thousand stars and flowers grew out of her hair which hung down her back, touching the floor. The blue woman was naked yet covered in shapes which moved and danced across her skin. Kira realised they were animals and watched delighted as a swarm of bees lifted out of her skin and flew lazily away. Kira glanced over at the others. Dina and Martha were smiling and crying, Ruth looked like she'd seen a ghost. The recording fizzed out.

'She's real,' breathed Kira.

'She came to me in my dreams and told me... told me... she was sorry.' Dina was sobbing.

Martha could only nod, fighting the vague memories of her attack, memories which threatened to overwhelm her.

'I thought it was the drugs,' Ruth murmured, half to herself. 'I didn't know it was real.'

Max turned the feed off. 'It took a while to find the information in Archives, but we ran a full search, and that's when we discovered her name. Like you said Kira - the spirit of the Earth, Gaia.'

'We think she's happy that we came,' broke in Dr Ayres, sounding breathless, as if she still didn't entirely believe it herself.

'We've only seen her the once, but it was as if she was saying I know you're here, and it's okay,' Dr Guardis added.

'We have to tell the city,' Ruth declared.

'Are you mad?' Dina exclaimed loudly.

Grace began to cry, and Kira comforted her, while Dina

apologised.

Ruth continued. 'I'm serious. So much has happened. The pregnancies, the Anti Corp attacks, Corp lying to everyone. Surely Gaia is a message of hope. Surely everyone deserves to hear that.'

'But how do we prove it?' Kira asked. 'One holo recording, which could have been doctored - no offence - and the dreams of a few random women. It's hardly rock-solid evidence.'

'You of all people should know your religious history, Ruth,' Dina added. 'Every time believers of one deity try to sway believers of another, it ends in bloody wars. You can't force faith on people.'

'I'm not talking about forcing faith on people,' Ruth snapped back. 'She's real. We've seen her, the scientists here have seen her, and others deserve to know Gaia is real. They deserve to know that hope exists.'

'I understand what you are trying to say, Ruth,' Martha reassured her. 'But the people are not ready. They are still reeling from the lies of Corporation. What they need is solid leadership and transparency. Belief in the spirit of the Earth may follow. But looking after our basic needs has to come first.'

Martha stopped talking, trying to gauge how the others felt.

'You sound like a politician,' Dina said.

'Well, I am a Hamble.'

Chapter Eighteen

C42N: *Click through for the latest riot images and live feeds.*

MAHA: *Our city needs transparent leadership from those who care.*

ANON88: *What gives MAHA the right to stick her nose in?*

ANON6: *I agree with MAHA. New governance for the people, by the people.*

ANON27: *Everyone should be able to do what they want.*

MADSR: *Now is the time to elect fairly, no more Corp rule.*

Jed walked Ben to the meeting room in silence. With so many questions swirling around in his head, Jed didn't know where to start. As they reached the meeting room door, Ben grabbed his cousin's arm and stopped him.

'It's not what you think,' Ben said. 'I'm the only one left. The only one they could find.'

Jed stared at him for a moment before shaking his arm free and opening the door. When the two men entered the room, the others were already seated. Minkov gestured to the two empty chairs.

'Take a seat. Both of you.'

Jed sat slowly, unsure why he was being included in the meeting. His cousin looked at the remaining chair suspiciously before also sitting, with a glare for the rest of the room.

'Auto-capture on,' Agent Deveraux said, the holo humming as it began to record. '8th September 2215. This meeting calls forward the remaining high-ranking officials in accordance with city breakdown procedure 3.0. In attendance are Chief Tony Minkov from Force. Professor Faisal Kamir, Head of Academy. Surgeon General William Lee from Med Centre. Agent Jack Deveraux, Special Investigations. Representing Anti-Corp is Ben Jenkins, and the public protector, Detective Jed Jenkins.'

Jed looked up in surprise, but Deveraux avoided his gaze and licked his lips before continuing.

'Corporation Board Member, Roger Hamble – unable to attend, deceased. Corporation Board Member, Julia Nicks – unable to attend, deceased. Corporation Board Member, Yassin Aswad – unable to attend, deceased. Corporation Board Member, Patrick Basjere – unable to attend, bound by law.'

A glowing panel appeared on the table in front of each man. Silently, they all pressed their hands down upon the panel and a DNA sample was taken confirming their identity.

'Declaration of truth initiated. Please repeat after me.' And Deveraux led the men through the declaration.

'I understand that from this moment on I represent the best interests of City Forty-Two. When questioned I vow to share all information truthfully. As a city representative I will uphold the law in all decision making. I understand that failure to do so will result in the loss of my freedom and rights. I make this declaration of my own free will.'

Once the declaration had been completed, the illuminated panels faded, and Deveraux called up the procedural guidance for a city representative meeting on the large screen at the back of the room.

As per procedural guidance 3.0

All decisions must be made unanimously and in one session. The recording will then be sealed to prevent tampering and made available for public record.

Step One: Identify the threat to the City
Step Two: Facilitate solution
Step Three: Identify those responsible for threat
Step Four: Action containment
Step Five: Update leadership

Each man took his time reading through the expected steps.

'Seems pretty fragging obvious what the threat is.' Minkov was the first to speak.

'Corporation lies,' Ben said.

'Anti-Corp terrorism more like,' snarled Minkov.

'Arguing semantics won't get us anywhere,' Professor Kamir said. 'The threat is clearly the hysterical masses running amok outside. We need immediate crowd pacification with regular info jack updates on the water crisis. Rumour mongering certainly isn't helping the situation.'

'And you think gassing the populace will?' the Surgeon General, William Lee asked, incredulous.

'I never said gassing,' Professor Kamir replied. 'But that might be the only course of action available if we can't agree on how to calm the people down.'

'The issue is clean, fresh water, supplied freely without any Corporation involvement,' Jed said, trying to refocus the conversation.

Minkov jabbed his finger into the table. 'Yes - but where are we going to get a free uncontaminated water source from?'

'Aren't people working on the filtering system at Science Dept?' Lee asked, looking at Agent Deveraux.

'They are,' Deveraux conceded. 'But we have to wait for the levels of radiation to dissipate. Nothing we can do about that.'

'So we need a miracle,' snorted Lee.

'There's a place, outside the city limits,' Jed said. 'It's called Camp Eden.'

'Camp Eden?' the Professor scoffed. 'Fifty years ago there was an expedition outside, the whole crew died.'

'Another expedition went last year. They are all still alive and well.'

Jed tried to say more but Ben cut across him angrily.

'And how do *you* know that? Another Corporation cover up? Or is this perhaps a Special Investigations top secret hideaway? Replacing one oppressive regime with another.'

'I know because my wife is there,' Jed replied calmly.

'Special Investigations have no involvement with Camp... what do you call it?' Deveraux said, looking flustered as he tapped away furiously on his handheld.

'Camp Eden was financed by Mr Hamble...'

Ben leapt to his feet. 'So it IS a Corporation cover up,' he yelled.

'Will you *stop* interrupting me. Ben? For frag sake man, sit down – I sent my wife and child out there.' Jed coloured a little when he realised everyone was staring at him. 'They have some tech there. We should be able to set up a live link, and you can talk to the people on the ground. I've told you everything I know.'

Minkov rubbed his jaw. 'I'll get a tech team in to set up the link. It might take a short while. Let's pause the holo and reconvene in an hour.'

Deveraux pressed some buttons on the holo, putting it on hold, and was the first to stand. 'I need a synth-caf,' he said to no-one in particular, and rushed out of the room.

The others followed at a slower pace, but the Chief gestured for Jed to hang back.

'What about him?' Jed pointed to Ben leaving the room.

'He has a detail; they won't let him go far.' The Chief huffed. 'This is a fragging mess we're in, Jenkins. This Camp Whatsaface better not be some rich boy's playground.'

Jed swallowed. He hoped it wasn't as well.

***C42N:** City Forty-Two Representatives meet to end crisis. Sweep your view across.*

***ANON88:** Who gave them the power to decide what we want?*

Forty-five minutes later, a live feed was streaming between Force and Camp Eden. An extremely tanned, slightly dishevelled man stood in the main tent with Kira and Martha off to one side.

'Hi, hon. Are you okay? Where's Grace?' Jed spoke to the screen, ignoring the man for the moment.

'Hi. We're fine, we're all fine. Grace is playing in the orchard with Dina and Ruth. Jed – this is Dr Max Carter, he's in charge here.'

The two men nodded at each other.

'Before we begin, Kira, there's something you should know,' Jed said. He stopped talking as the door opened to the meeting room and the city representatives filed back in. Each resumed their seats around the table, turning so they could all see the video link.

'What's Ben doing there?' Kira whispered to Martha, who shrugged in response.

Jed stayed standing and began the introductions.

'Gentlemen, may I introduce Dr Max Carter, head of the Camp Eden project. Also present are my wife, Kira Jenkins, and Martha Hamble, who some of you know I believe.' There were murmured greetings. Jed carried on. 'Max, ladies – this is William Lee Surgeon General of Med Centre, Head of Academy Professor Faisal Kamir, Agent Jack Deveraux from Special Investigations, Force Chief Tony Minkov and you already know Ben.' Jed paused, shooting a glance at his cousin. 'He's the Anti-Corp representative.'

Kira gasped while Martha merely looked on. Max was a little bemused at their reaction but decided to wait and find out what was happening. Jed walked around the table to take his seat.

'How can I help, gentlemen?' Max rubbed his hands together nervously.

'You can start by telling us exactly what you're doing out there,' Professor Kamir said, sounding disgruntled. 'And why Academy has no knowledge of this *expedition*, if it can even be classed as such.'

Max grimaced and ran a hand through his hair. 'Well, you heard of the failed attempt fifty years ago to set up Camp Eden?'

Kamir nodded and gestured for him to get on with it.

'I found out about it, and thought it was fascinating. I spent a year lobbying anyone I could to fund a new expedition. Mr Hamble was the only person of authority who would listen to my bid. Academy officials told me I was wasting my time, so I never got to pitch to you directly.'

'We get a lot of funding bids,' the Professor said. 'There is a process, you know.'

'So Hamble paid you to do what? Watch the grass grow?' Minkov asked gruffly.

Max barked a laugh. 'We came to test the air, soil and water for contaminants. And to see if we could discover what had happened to the original expedition members.'

'And?' Lee leant forward.

'All our testing came back negative.'

There was a collective sigh of disappointment in the room.

'No, no – negative for contaminants. The radiation levels have gone, we have a fresh water supply here. Mother Nature has begun to heal herself.'

'Begun?' asked Ben, frowning.

'We've been scouting further afield, and the bombing sites are still arid. A nearby lake is devoid of life but with a little human engineering we could help things along. We've been working on a new way of...'

'Yes, yes. All very interesting I'm sure,' Professor Kamir interrupted. 'The real question is how do we get your fresh water to the city? If indeed it is clear of contaminants.'

'We'd need to corroborate your findings,' Lee agreed. 'Can you send some samples to us for verification?'

'We can bring them,' Kira said. 'That is, if it's safe for us to come home?'

Jed tried to sound more confident then he felt. 'I'm working on it.'

Kira looked upset. There was a pause in the discussion as everyone in the meeting room tried to think of a suitable solution for transporting the water into the city. Ben cleared his throat. 'I might have a way we can get the water to the city.'

The others looked at him in surprise.

'Anti-Corp uses the ancient sewer system sometimes - to get in and out of the city undetected. With a little hi-tech investment, the tunnel walls could be resealed, and water flow guided to the abandoned water works. Which would also need servicing, but they should still work.'

'We'd need some serious manpower,' Jed said, looking at his boss. 'And I think I know where we can get that from.'

Minkov rubbed his hands together. 'I like your thinking, Jenkins.'

'Care to explain?' Deveraux asked.

'We round up everyone involved in the rioting, and split them into work teams,' Jed said. 'Force operatives can oversee.'

Ben slapped his hands on the table. 'You want to make the people pay for Corporation's cock up? It should be corpers who fix this, not the man on the street.'

'We all need to work together to fix this, Ben. Water shortage is a serious problem – take your head out of your ass and grow up. It's about time the people of City Forty-Two did something for themselves.'

Jed was breathing hard. He glanced at his wife on the video screen and she gave him a discrete thumbs up. His face twitched as he tried not to grin and muttered his apology to Minkov.

'I agree,' said Lee, surprising himself for speaking up. He carried on quickly. 'We face a hole in governance. Rather than allowing miscreants to ruin our city further, we must all come together.'

Professor Kamir was nodding. 'A new, shared governance. Focused on the problems at hand. It is the only way.'

Martha had been listening to the discussion with interest. She waved her hand to get the room's attention. 'Are we going to open the city walls then?'

'I don't see how else we can solve the water issue, unless you have another idea?' Jed said.

'I think it sounds like the right thing to do,' Martha said. 'But I'm just wondering whether this sudden freedom might be too much - for certain people.'

'You mean Anti-Corp radicals running off?' Ben said, thrusting his chin defiantly at the screen. 'Freedom of choice is freedom of choice,' he continued. 'You can't be seriously considering the continuation of Corporation's restrictive regime? We are on the brink of individual personal freedom here.'

'I am not suggesting anything,' Martha said. 'I just think that we need to be careful. We don't want to destroy the healing that has already happened out here by tramping about all over the place.'

Kira chimed in. 'We have to respect the balance of nature and man working together.'

The men in the room digested the women's words.

'So, what's your grand plan then, my dear?' Professor Kamir asked Martha.

'I think new governance should be voted for by the public, with representatives from each echelon of our society. The best way to move forward should be discussed openly, with the public given the opportunity to have their say. This is an opportunity for City Forty-Two to create a new way of life, interacting with the environment around us for the benefit of man and nature. We could then roll out the concept to other cities.'

Agent Deveraux leant back in his chair. 'Miss Hamble has a valid point. This city is the only one we know of free from Corporation. Other cities are more than likely firmly pro-Corp, pro-Tech and probably still consuming treated water.'

'Won't the sweeps have gotten through to them?' Kira asked.

'Ha!' Ben barked. 'The sweeps are the biggest joke of all. They are held within a self-contained data unit, unhackable – believe me, we've tried.'

Jed and Minkov looked at Ben who held his hands up in mock surrender.

'It's true,' Deveraux agreed. 'Whoever designed the sweeps program created a self-contained media platform. We believe each city has one, but they are not linked and efforts to link them so far have proved ineffective.'

'Even more reason for us to get it right the first time,' Martha declared. 'Then we can save the rest of the world.'

'You can't be serious?' Ben asked, looking around at the room at the resolute faces staring back at him. 'You honestly believe that we can affect that much change?'

'And you're the representative that claims to be fighting against the machine?' Kira said flatly.

'Hey, I'm all in. If you think we can do this.'

'We're happy to liaise at this end with our findings,' offered Max.

Minkov and Agent Deveraux glanced at each other, before they both nodded. Jed looked at Lee and the professor. Each man looked slightly stunned but both nodded in agreement.

Deveraux spoke with authority into the holo again. 'Let the record show Steps One and Two have been actioned.' He paused the holo. 'I suggest we regroup after lunch?'

The other men agreed, and filed out of the meeting room, leaving Jed standing in front of the video screen. Max gave a wave and left the tent.

'Can we come home now?' Kira asked.

'Soon hon. Soon,' Jed said. 'Kiss Gracie for me.'

Jed waved goodbye to his wife and Martha before ending the link, then sat down heavily in an empty chair.

FORCE: *We urge citizens to stay at home and avoid areas of violent activity.*

C42N: *Rioting continues across the city. Sweep your experience, stay safe.*

Jed was sat twirling his Force ID in his hands when the others returned from lunch, and the meeting resumed.

'Welcome back, gentlemen,' Deveraux said, turning on the holo. 'Our next step is to identify and neutralise the culprits responsible for this mess.'

'I believe Force already took care of that,' said Jed.

Ben looked at his cousin, but it was Minkov who explained.

'It's true that Detective Barnes took it upon himself to eliminate the high-ranking members of Anti-Corp.' Minkov spared a sympathetic glance for Jed, who was looking down at the table in front of him. 'Detective Barnes was mortally wounded and declined medical attention. He has been dishonourably discharged from Force, and condolences have been sent out to the families of those murdered.'

Jed's hand tightened on the cup of synth-caf in front of him, but he refrained from speaking or looking up at the others.

'Is there anyone else significant left that we should be aware of?' Deveraux asked Ben, who shifted in his chair.

'Not that I'm aware of. You have to understand; I didn't stand very high in the organisation. I was way below Bobby - Roberto Travelli. And he was only in charge of recruiting.'

'What about the people responsible for the bombing of Corp Tech?' Lee asked.

Jed cleared his throat and pushed his chair back from the table. He leaned forward, his head down, hands clasped together. Ben watched him warily for a moment.

'That was a... splinter cell if you like, the 42nd Army. Radicals who felt we didn't do enough.' Ben paused, fidgeting in his chair before continuing. 'You have to understand Anti-Corp was formed as a student body twenty years ago. It has its roots in Academy, and it looks to the student ranks for new members. We aren't – and we never have been - a terrorist organisation. Frag, I didn't even know about that plan.'

Ben scrubbed a hand through his hair and shot another look at Jed.

'And the culprits responsible for killing the remaining Board members?' Lee asked, a touch of worry in his voice.

Deveraux responded a little too smoothly.

'Hamble was the unfortunate victim of an angry mob. The others were driven to their deaths by staff. Pity.'

Jed finally looked up from the table and corrected the agent.

'Hamble's killers are in custody. The drivers are being investigated to make sure they acted alone and weren't paid off by someone in a position of power.'

The two men glared at each other.

'I want a complete list of Anti-Corp members on my desk first thing in the morning,' Minkov said, jabbing his finger at Ben. 'You can work with Intelligence to provide any gaps in contact information. Everyone will be tagged and charged with a work detail.'

'What about the unruly members of the public out there?' Professor Kamir asked.

'Everyone involved in destruction of property and disturbance of the peace will also be tagged and given a work detail accordingly,' Jed explained.

'So you're just going to give everyone a criminal record?' Ben asked in disbelief.

'No. We are going to make them work off their debt to the sensible members of society who stayed at home and refused to descend into madness.'

'Sounds like mass control if you ask me.'

'I don't remember asking your opinion.'

The cousins scowled at each other, barely flinching when Minkov slammed his fist on the desk.

'That's enough,' he bellowed. 'What's done is done. We need bodies to sort out the water crisis – this way we get bodies. Those idiots stupid enough to get themselves involved in public unrest will work off their debts, and if they don't like it, they can rot in a containment cell. Now,' he said, turning his attention to Deveraux. 'What's left?'

'We need to propose interim governance. A new leadership.'

'Yes,' said Professor Kamir. 'We can't carry on like this indefinitely.'

'I don't have time to deal with bureaucratic nonsense,' Lee said heatedly. 'I have a medical centre to run and real people to help.' He began stuttering as everyone turned to stare at him. 'I mean... not that... it's very...'

'We know what you mean,' Jed said.

Lee smiled gratefully at Jed's rescue.

'What about a senior official from Special Investigations?' Deveraux suggested mildly.

'I think anyone with an institutional background will be unpopular with the people,' Professor Kamir countered. 'Perhaps an academic?'

'What about a member of the public voted for by the rest?' Minkov proposed. 'That way they would have the city behind them.'

'But no real idea of what to do,' Ben muttered.

'I would like to put someone forward as an interim governor,' Jed said. 'Martha Hamble.'

There were some loud mutterings from around the table. 'Hamble!' 'A woman?' 'Is he mad?' 'I say, shouldn't it be someone more distinguished?'

'Let me finish.' Jed had to shout over them. 'She has a unique viewpoint on the situation. Being the daughter of the Marketing Director of the Corporation Board in City Forty-Two, she has links with both hard line Corpers and those at the upper end of society. She is a woman affected by the pregnancy anomaly, so has the sympathy and genuine interest of the general public. She has a scientific background, so the people will trust her explanation of the water crisis and the proposed solution.'

'She certainly understands politics,' Professor Kamir mused. 'Top of her class.'

'I have no objections,' said Lee.

Deveraux looked hard at Jed, before nodding and agreeing, followed swiftly by Ben. Minkov stroked his upper lip thoughtfully and added his approval.

'Let the record state that Martha Hamble will be offered the position of interim Governor on her return,' Deveraux announced. 'She will be assisted by those city representatives here present, as and when appropriate.'

Deveraux looked around the room for any objections before stopping the recording and officially sealing the file. 'I believe we are done here, gentlemen. Thank you for your input.'

Deveraux stood, nodded to the others and shook hands with Minkov before leaving. Once Deveraux had left, most of the men hurried back to their own personal empires – full of self-importance and the desire to tell others what had happened here today. Ben was escorted to Force Intelligence by his minders. Only Jed and Minkov remained. A harassed looking Force operative popped his head in the room.

'Sir? You asked for a status report on the riots?'

Minkov gestured for the operative to continue.

'It's over. Tagging the rioters stopped the escalation and we've got positive idents via Drone TV for all those involved.'

'Thank you, Sergeant. That will be all.' Minkov turned to look at

Jed. 'You holding up, Jenkins?'

'Yes. Sir.'

'Long road ahead of us.'

'Sir?'

Minkov looked at his weary detective and held out a hand. As Jed took it in his own, the chief shook it firmly. 'Till tomorrow, Detective.'

Chapter Nineteen

SIF: UPDATE TO FOLLOW
****
UPDATE TO FOLLOW
City Representatives will post meeting outcome later today.
*****************ALL SWEEPS***************

A bee flew into the window, bumbling its way across the pane, trying to find a way out. Its buzzing grew ever more frantic. Jed watched as it bounced off the pane, again and again and again. Finally, he walked over to the window and opened it. The bee buzzed once around his head and was gone.

The vidcom link chimed, it was Camp Eden. Jed accepted the link and waved a greeting to his wife.

'Hi Jed, are you okay? You look tired.'

'I'm fine,' Jed replied, and he flopped into an empty chair.

'How did the meeting go?'

Jed puffed out his cheeks and nodded.

'That good, huh?'

'I'm sending out a unit to come pick you up, they should be there first thing in the morning.'

'Hang on, aren't you going to tell me what happened?'

'I'll get the file sent over to you. Martha needs to watch it. We'll have a sit down about it tomorrow when you get back.'

Kira sniffed as Jed paused, and looked down at his hands for a moment.

'I miss you,' he said.

'I miss you too.'

They said their goodbyes and Kira watched the screen dwindle to blackness. Martha poked her head into the tent.

'Is everything alright?'

'I don't know. Jed's sending over the file from the rest of the meeting – he says you have to watch it.'

Martha came through into the tent.

'Me?'

Kira nodded. 'They're coming to pick us up tomorrow,' she said. 'I'd better tell the others.'

Martha watched her friend walk out of the tent, leaving her alone. Her reverie was broken by an incoming message on the com system. It was addressed to M Hamble. She pulled up a chair and began to download the file.

SIF: *Interim Governor Martha Hamble appointed. City Representative's Meeting available for download.*

FORCE: *All citizens tagged in the recent riots will be given work duty.*

ANON88: *Fight the fascists! Refuse to be tagged. Blame the Corpers.*

C42N: *Hamble proves a popular choice, but will she solve the water crisis?*

The sun had set by the time Martha had finished listening to the meeting. She felt dazed as she walked out into the communal area where everyone had gathered for the evening meal. Dina beckoned her over.

'Hey Ma, come here and try some of this.'

Martha sat down, hugging her knees, refusing the proffered food.

'Are you okay?' Dina asked.

The group quietened to listen to Martha, but she shook her head, struggling to find the right words. Finally, she spoke.

'The city representatives have met and decided on a course of action regarding the water issue.'

'Well that's good isn't it?' Max queried.

'They are tagging everyone involved in the riots and putting them to work duty.'

Ruth scowled at Martha from across the campfire. 'Work duty?

What are we – some kind of fascist state?'

Martha ignored her. 'The workers will clean and seal the old sewer system so the natural water supply can be brought into the city.'

'Solving the problem of the affected water,' Dina said in a pleased voice.

The others made congratulatory noises.

'That is not all,' Martha said, still holding her knees tight and keeping her eyes down.

'Well,' Ruth demanded. 'Spit it out.'

'They have chosen an interim Governor.'

'What poor fool has been roped into that?' Kira asked.

'Me,' Martha said, finally looking up.

There was a stunned silence as everyone processed the information. Ruth was the first to speak. She leant over to pat Martha on the knee.

'It's about time those in charge used their brains instead of their wallets,' she said.

'Oh, wow, Ma,' Dina's voice squeaked. 'This is so exciting. You'll be in charge of everything!'

'I'm so pleased for you, Ma.' Kira squeezed Martha's arm and then looked horrified as tears began to run down Martha's face. 'Oh sweetie, what's wrong?'

'I can't be in charge, can I?' Martha was half sobbing the words. 'I don't have the faintest idea of what to do. I work with plants, not people.'

'It doesn't matter,' Ruth said brusquely. 'You care about what happens to the city, to the people. You have a good head on those shoulders and I'm sure you'll have advisers.'

'But what if I can't do it?'

'We believe in you,' Kira said.

The Camp Eden scientists who had been listening to the conversation added their encouragement.

'I, for one, think you'll make a great leader,' Max said. 'Listening to you the other night talking about putting the needs of the people first - you can't go far wrong thinking like that.'

Martha looked around the circle and saw the approval on everyone's face. She wiped her eyes dry and lifted her chin a little.

'I will do it. At least, I will try. For the city.' Martha looked down at her tummy. 'For my baby. And for my Father.'

'Hear, hear,' toasted the others, before falling back into their individual conversations, leaving the women from City 42 to themselves.

'Will you be there to help me?' Martha asked her friends.

'Of course we will,' Kira said.

'Actually.' Dina looked sheepish. 'I've been speaking with Max, about staying here. The work they do is fascinating. There's nothing waiting for me in the city. So, if it's alright with you guys?'

Kira looked a little surprised, then noticed Max watching from across the fire. Realising Kira was looking at him, he turned quickly, knocking over his drink and cursing to himself.

'No, we understand,' Kira said, looking back at Dina.

Martha and Ruth echoed their acceptance, and the group fell silent for a moment.

'What about me?' Ruth asked. 'Where do I fit in?'

'With us, silly,' Kira replied, but it was Martha who Ruth was asking.

'I have an idea,' Martha said. 'You would be a wonderful advisor for the interim Governor.'

'Are you sure?'

'I am.'

'This calls for another toast,' Kira said, and refilled everyone's cups. 'To us.'

'To us!'

MAHA: *Proud to be chosen to lead City Forty-Two forward. Tackling the water supply will be my first task.*

C42N: *Anon88 has been bound by law for inciting aggressive behaviour.*

Jed watched the scenery roll past him on his way to Camp Eden. Here and there flashes of green interrupted the tangle of abandoned skimmers and ramshackle buildings. Nature was slowly creeping back but there were still massive swathes of burnt, dead land. Harsh reminders of what had come before.

Jed was looking forward to seeing his wife and baby. Although it had only been a few days since he'd seen them, it felt like weeks. The sweeps had announced the outcome of the City Rep meeting and their plan for the immediate future, which had been received well by the public. Everyone involved in the riots had been tagged for work duty, and there had even been some additional volunteers to help with the clean-up of the city. The skimmer slowed down as Camp Eden came into sight.

Kira shifted from leg to leg impatiently. She wanted to see Jed, and she wanted to go home.

'Over here,' she called, waving. 'I didn't know you were coming as well.'

Jed beamed at her as he hurried over, scooping her up for a hug.

'I missed you,' he said, kissing her. 'Where's Grace?'

'It's okay, she's inside sleeping. I didn't want to wake her, she looked so peaceful.'

Jed kissed his wife again, feeling both relieved his daughter was in such good hands, and a little disappointed at not seeing her straight away.

'Are you ready to go?' Jed asked.

'Almost. Do we have to rush off right now?'

Jed didn't answer, instead he checked his wristplant.

'Is Martha nearby?'

'Yeah, come through. Meet everyone.' Kira took her husband's hand and pulled him after her into the camp complex.

Jed looked around with interest. There were plants everywhere, and insects hummed in the air. He could just make out Dina, and the scientist they'd spoken to on the vid-link, over in the far corner of the camp. Kira was chatting away, telling Jed about this and that, but he was only half listening. Martha sat in the communal area, hands wrapped around a cup, looking off into the distance.

'Martha,' Kira called out.

She turned and waved at the approaching couple.

'Hi Martha. You got the file?' Jed asked.

'Yes.'

'And? Do you accept the post?' Jed held his breath in anticipation.

'I do. But I have a few stipulations.'

Jed's breath whooshed out in relief. He sat down next to her. Kira followed.

'I'm sure whatever they are, it will be fine,' Jed said. 'I have to tell you some things first.'

Ruth came out of the sleeping quarters and seeing the others in the communal area hurried over to join them. Jed smiled a greeting, as Ruth sat down.

'Well,' Martha said. 'This is my first requirement. Ruth will be my personal assistant.'

Jed looked at the two women, and then nodded. 'Makes sense. You'll have other members of the city to guide you as well.'

'Will that be the men I saw in the meeting?' Martha asked.

'I expect so, details haven't been finalised, but I'll be part of that guiding team as well.'

Kira congratulated Jed softly, and he continued. 'There will be a medical rep and an academic rep, as well as someone from Special Investigations.'

'Sounds like you've got almost all bases covered,' Ruth said. 'What about a representative of the populace?'

'Public vote,' Jed replied. 'It's one of the first things we need to organise when we get back to the city.'

'What are the others?' Martha asked.

'A Governor's parade, to begin with.'

'A parade?' Martha gasped, her hand over her mouth.

'Is that a good idea?' Kira asked.

'It's procedure. New governor – city gets a parade. That's why we have to leave...' Jed checked his wristplant, '...five minutes ago.' He got up quickly. 'Come on, everyone, let's get going. We can talk about it in the skimmer.'

There was a moment of stunned silence before the three women slowly got up. A few minutes later and the camp was bustling. Bags were loaded into the skimmer, and grateful farewells were being made between the women and the scientists.

Jed found himself face to face with Dina. 'You're staying then.'

'Yes,' Dina looked down at the floor.

Jed put his finger under her chin and lifted her head. 'You can come back anytime, Dina,' he said. 'You'll always have a home with us. You know that, don't you?'

Dina flung herself at Jed and hugged him tightly. Jed patted her on the back and looked at Kira for some help, but she just grinned at him. Dina broke away and kissed him on the cheek, then went to hug Kira and say goodbye to Grace.

Finally, everyone was in the skimmer, calling goodbye, and promising to stay in touch. They watched Camp Eden dwindle in the distance as the skimmer picked up speed. There was a sudden flash in the brush nearby and a flock of birds swooped into the sky following the skimmer, dancing intricate patterns in the air. Kira watched them, taking it as a good sign.

'What happens when we get back to the city?' Martha asked.

'We have another skimmer waiting for you, with armed guards, for your safety,' Jed replied.

Kira looked at her husband in alarm. 'Is that necessary?'

'I don't think we should take any chances,' Jed said. 'We will follow in this skimmer. It's armoured too, so everyone will be safe.' Jed glanced at Grace who was trying her hardest to eat the strap holding her in place in the travel cube. 'There will be a tour of the city. Sweeps went out this morning informing everyone of the route and encouraging people to attend.'

'And what am I supposed to do?' Martha said, sounding panicked.

Jed tried to sound encouraging. 'Smile. Wave. Be Martha Hamble.'

Kira took Martha's hand and squeezed it. 'You'll do fine Ma. We'll be right behind you.'

C42N: *Join us in meeting our new Governor as she returns to City Forty-Two.*
Download the route and pick your spot. This is not a virtual experience.

The rest of the journey was spent in silence as each of them contemplated the changes that lay ahead. In no time at all, they arrived at the city walls. Martha hugged Kira and Ruth, then got out of the skimmer and into the bigger, grander, open topped version that awaited her.

'Back in a parse,' Jed said to Kira, and went over to the other skimmer to greet the security team. 'Everyone know what they're doing?'

'Yes, Sir. The route is pre-programmed. We'll activate the shield once Miss Hamble is settled, and you'll have direct comm link.'

'Good. Carry on.'

Jed gave Martha a small nod of encouragement and re-joined the others.

The two skimmers entered the city. No-one lived on the city outskirts - this close to the wall the streets were empty. Martha shifted in her seat feeling vulnerable and exposed. No-one spoke. She reached out to touch the personal shield that extended two feet around her, reassuring herself that it existed.

'Alright, Ma?'

Jed's voice sounded tinny yet comforting.

Martha swallowed and managed to croak a yes.

As they rounded the corner it seemed to Martha that every single person in City Forty-Two had come out to line the main street. They were all standing silently, watching her skimmer move closer. Someone, somewhere, began to clap. The sound echoed loudly. Then it was joined by another. And another. And another. The crowd began chanting.

'Hamble. Hamble. Hamble.'

Martha raised a hand tentatively and waved. There was an explosion of noise as the people began cheering and shouting and waving. Martha waved more confidently and began smiling at the people, her people. Streamers flew through the air and children sat on shoulders waving enthusiastically. As if in response to the crowd, the baby moved in her stomach and Martha felt it kick for the first time. Tears of happiness began to stream down her face.

This was a new beginning.

A new beginning for them all.

The Gaia Project

The Gaia Collection, Book 2

In a board room, behind closed doors...

'What's the status of City 42?'

'The revolt is over and Anti-Corp have been destroyed yet...'

'Yet what?'

'The city is not in our hands. An independent governance has been set up, headed by Martha Hamble.'

'Hamble? Hamble? I know that name. Isn't she already a director on our Board?'

'That's the father, Ma'am. But he was a victim of the Anti-Corp riots. Martha's his daughter.'

'Well, that's alright then, isn't it? She's one of us, isn't she?'

'Apparently not, Ma'am.'

'Why do I know her name then?'

'She was one of those affected by the anomalous medical condition.'

'Successfully?'

'No, Ma'am. She carried the child to term and completed a natural pregnancy.'

'Ah. What about the others afflicted?'

'Dina Grey successful miscarried while Ruth Maddocks went to term and completed pregnancy.'

'Wasn't there a fourth?'

'Yes, Ma'am. Ingrid Jenkins. She died in the Anti-Corp terrorist attack on Corp Tech. Medical claimed termination.'

'And there haven't been anymore?'

'Not according to our sources, Ma'am.'

'Well that's something, I suppose. What about the baby labs?'

'Permanently closed. The new governor discovered the production and sale and decided to shut down the supply chain. So far, efforts to re-establish the product line have been unsuccessful.'

'But we have someone on the inside?'

'Yes, Ma'am.'

'Is there anything else I need to know?'

'A small cult has formed, Ma'am. Worshipping Gaia, the Spirit of the Earth. There's been some effigy, but I don't think we have anything to worry about.'

'Ah yes, the blue lady phenomenon. When we take back control order repainting where necessary.'

'What about medical and food supplies? Should we reconnect the city?'

'No, not yet. We cannot allow the success of any leadership outside of Corporation. Which reminds me, have the plans for City 15 been carried out?'

'Everything is in hand, Ma'am.'

'Excellent. Keep me informed.'

Chapter 1

C42N: *Retraining courses still available - have you registered?*

ACAD: *Grow Your Own filling up quick. Today is the final sign up for this rotation. Don't miss out!*

ANON17: *Grow your own is poison. They're hoarding food!*

GOVHAM: *Come to the next open taster, click for details. All food grown in Camp Eden is safe to eat. There are no contaminants. We do not have hidden food supplies. Together we're looking after City 42.*

C42N: *Still no news from City 15. Have you heard from a loved one?*

'I'm worried about Jed,' Kira said as she faced the vid-screen in front of her. It was meant to be synth-caf with the girls but lately it was physically difficult for them to all be in the same place at once. As it was, only Dina had linked into the comm. They were still waiting for Ruth and Martha to appear.

'Why? What's happened? Has he been getting into more fights at work?' Dina sounded sincere but she was fiddling with something off camera, her attention not fully on Kira or the conversation.

'Oh no, nothing like that, he's just not himself. And he has a meeting with his boss today. He thinks they're going to force him to get a new partner, but he says he can't think about it, not since...' Kira trailed off.

'Not since losing his sister and Pete.' Dina had stopped whatever she was doing and was looking straight at Kira. 'You've done everything you can for him you know. Grief is a difficult thing for people to process.'

'But it's been months. So much else has happened.' Kira looked at Dina with pleading eyes. 'I need him. I need you, all of you. I feel like I'm always all on my own.'

'I know, I'm sorry. There's so much to do here, I never seem to have a spare five minutes.' Dina looked away from the screen, her attention momentarily elsewhere. 'Huh. Thought I saw a bee.' She turned back to Kira. 'We've got bees here; did I tell you?'

'Yeah. I've been thinking I should come out to Camp Eden. Bring Grace with me. It would be good to see Max again, have a look at what you guys are getting up to out there. Visit the bees and everything.' Kira tried not to sound too desperate, but she wanted a change of scenery. Besides if there were bees at Camp Eden, maybe Kira would see Gaia as well.

'Yes! You should totally come. It would be great to see you.' Dina was grinning widely at the camera. There was a shout behind her, and she whipped her head round, half rising from the chair. 'Oh wow - sorry Kira, I've got to go. They've spotted something in the trees, some kind of cat. It's so exciting. Catch up with you soon.' The connection went dead.

Kira sighed at the blank screen in front of her. So much for synth-caf with the girls. She was about to turn her comm link off when Martha's face blinked into view.

'Sorry I'm late. I can only stay for five minutes but I wanted to drop in and say hi to you all.' She looked puzzled. 'Where is everyone?'

'Hi, Ma. Dina had to go, they found a cat or something. And Ruth, well, Ruth hasn't turned up yet,' Kira replied, glad to see her friend but annoyed that she was already talking about going.

'That's odd. Ruth didn't tell me she had other plans. At least, I don't think she did.' Martha frowned. 'Kira, I am so tired. I don't know whether I'm coming or going half the time. I've got another meeting in a few minutes, more problems with supplies and I have no idea how we're going to sort this one out.'

Kira took pity on her friend. 'You'll figure it out, Ma, you always do.'

'Thanks, Kira. Look I've got to go but let's try and have dinner soon. We should get all the kids together as well. Ruth said Lucas was trying to crawl yesterday. I can't believe how much time has flown by.' Martha gave a little wave and disconnected her feed before Kira even had chance to agree to the dinner plans. It didn't matter anyway; they were always saying they would make plans but somehow never found the time to actually put them in the diary.

Kira realised that Martha had an important job. She was governor of City 42 and since the Anti-Corp rebellion had removed much of the previous administration, Martha had faced a huge job putting in new procedures and finding staff capable of carrying out her orders. They'd managed to fix the water problem with the nearby river supply and the combined effort of the city's inhabitants had repaired the old sewage works so that clean water came in and dirty water was recycled. Thank goodness Archive had all the records on how the system worked. Without the board members of Corporation to provide the passcodes so many of the city's systems were locked out. The food hydrators still worked but processed sachets were running low, as were medical supplies. No-one seemed to know where or how to get more.

Kira waited a few more minutes in front of the blank screen but there was no sign of Ruth. She pinged her comm, no answer. Since having her baby, Ruth had shrunk into herself. She'd stopped teaching full time in order to look after Sarah, and take care of Lucas for Martha, but she was still liaison for Academy which meant attending various government meetings as well. When Kira did occasionally see her, Ruth was quieter, made less of an effort with her appearance and frequently missed catch ups like these. Turning off the screen, Kira decided to go and see Ruth at the apartment she shared with Martha. Make sure she was alright. She needed to talk to someone about Gaia. She hadn't seen any signs of the goddess for months. There was no talk of a blue lady on the sweeps and Kira wanted to know if any of her friends had seen something, anything. It felt strange that their lives had been so influenced by the spirit of the Earth yet now when they needed guidance more than ever before, she was nowhere to be found.

How did you even go about trying to find a spirit or god or whatever she was? The only thing Kira knew for sure was that too many people had seen Gaia for her to only be a figment of imagination. She went to get Grace ready to go out, determined to speak to at least one of her friends, in person.

DING: *Latest species discovered in Camp Eden - Felis silvestris - a beautiful cat. Check out the images at CE's holopage.*

It was lunchtime by the time Kira arrived at Ruth's door. Grace had decided she was hungry, then produced an explosive nappy which had required Kira to change the baby's outfit. She had then rushed to get Grace into her travel cube before she fell asleep. Kira felt harassed as she flashed her ident in order to gain access to Martha and Ruth's apartment block. Since Martha became governor and Dina had moved out to Camp Eden there had been lots of changes in their living arrangements. Kira often felt sad that her friends weren't the other side of the door, like it had been back when they had all shared a flat but, she knew it made sense for Martha to be seen as a person of importance and to live in a secure, elite, apartment block. At least she wasn't alone, she had Ruth with her.

There was no answer when Kira knocked on the door, so she let herself in. Martha had keyed entry to Kira and Dina in case of emergencies.

'Ruth? Ruth - are you here? It's Kira.' There was no answer, but the cry of a baby echoed down the hallway quickly followed by another.

'Oh, for frag sake! You've woken them up!' Ruth yelled then appeared in a doorway holding her baby girl, Sarah and Martha's baby boy, Lucas. They were both screaming.

'I'm sorry. I was worried about you...' But Kira couldn't hear herself think over the screams of the babies, so she hurried to take Lucas and was surprised when Ruth handed her both children. Kira glanced over at Grace to make sure she was still alright, glad she'd remembered to put the soundproofing on the travel cube. She was fast asleep. The babies stopped crying immediately, both children liked Kira and she held them close to her body, rocking herself and shushing to them.

'That never works for me,' Ruth said bitterly, glaring at Kira.

Kira looked at her friend. Ruth's hair looked unbrushed and matted in places. She had dark shadows under her eyes, her skin was pale, and her shoulders slumped in defeat. 'Why didn't you vid me?' Kira asked softly. 'I could've come over, helped out.'

'Unless you can take over completely what's the point? It's the same mind-numbing grind, day in - day out. Half an hour here or there does nothing. I'm supposed to be at this meeting later and...' Ruth stopped talking as sobs started to escape.

Kira looked around for somewhere to put the children and saw a play cube in the living area. She gently placed both babies inside then set up a sensory loop to keep them entertained. Gentle music began to play accompanied by soft lights and shapes that moved across the cube walls. Kira went into the kitchen and made some synth-caf. She put all the dirty crockery into the steam washer and checked the fridge for baby milk. There was nothing prepared so she started a new batch. 'When did you last eat?' she asked Ruth.

Ruth shrugged her shoulders. Kira wondered if her friend even knew what day of the week it was. She looked in the cupboards. There wasn't much in there, but she found a couple of sachets of nutrient rich meals and activated them in the food hydrator. Then she steered her friend towards a chair and put a hot meal and drink in front of her.

'Eat,' Kira said and gestured at the untouched food. Ruth looked at it and shook her head.

'I don't have much of an appetite these days.' But she did as Kira asked, picking up a fork and toying with the food.

'Ruth, I do appreciate how hard it is having a baby, you know. Let me help you, please.'

Ruth stayed quiet.

Kira tried again. 'Look, I know I didn't go through labour like you did but I have had Grace since her birth. I know how tiring the constant crying can be, what sleepless nights feel like, the non-stop merry-go-round of bottle feeding, washing clothes, making more bottles and changing nappies. I do know how you feel.'

Ruth stared at Kira but still didn't speak.

'It feels like it'll never end but it does get easier, I promise.' Kira gave a small laugh. 'Either that or you finally get the hang of it. I know it's hard, believe me I do, but you have to start taking better care of yourself as well.'

Ruth snorted. 'How am I supposed to find the time to do that? Looking after Sarah and Lucas is a lot harder than looking after one, Kira. You have no idea how tired I am. And Martha is at work all the time, I get no help. I'm trying so hard to not rely on technology but it's ridiculous, I get no time for myself at all. Surely it shouldn't be this hard?' She shoved a spoonful of food into her mouth and avoided Kira's gaze.

Kira stayed quiet. She knew it was hard raising a child. Late night feeds and early morning wake up calls took it out of you. But she also knew that Martha had tried to hire night nannies and Ruth had point blank refused to accept what she termed *outside help*. The two friends sat in silence, one screaming silently for help but not knowing how to ask for it, the other wishing she knew what to do to make things better.

'What time is your meeting?' asked Kira once Ruth had finished eating.

'I'm not sure, I was going to feed the children and then take them to the office crèche. I think I've got all the reports I'm supposed to have.'

'Why don't I feed Lucas, you can do Sarah, and I'll walk with you over to Hamble HQ,' offered Kira.

Ruth smiled in thanks and went to get the children.

MSCHILD: *Protest tomorrow in the Main Square. Bring back lab babies. Natural doesn't work!*

ANON17: *Never mind babies. Bring back Corp! Bring back Corp! Bring back Corp!*

ENCRYPTED MESSAGE FROM NEW CORP TO 7421
>>STATUS REPORT DUE - UPDATE ON THE FOLLOWING:
1. FORCE
2. RESUPPLY
3. BABY LABS
4. PROPAGANDA<<

ENCRYPTED MESSAGE FROM 7421 TO NEW CORP
>>1. The new Security Guard measures have been accepted and implemented. The power shift within Force has begun but Minkov has forced a loophole. He's made Jed Jenkins Captain of the City Guard - we will have no jurisdiction over him.
2. Resupply is still blocked. No-one has managed to figure out the required codes. Supplies are low and will soon become critical.
3. Governor Hamble refuses to reinstate the baby labs. They remain inactive.
4. The use of anonymous sweeps is working well, support is wavering.
Additional question - what about City 15?<<

ENCRYPTED MESSAGE FROM NEW CORP TO 7421
>>REPORT RECEIVED.
UNFORTUNATE DEVELOPMENTS AT FORCE BUT THEY WILL BE DEALT WITH. QUESTION NOTED. STAND BY FOR FURTHER INSTRUCTION<<

Chapter 2

C42N: Do we need Security Guards and Force? Crime is down. Do you feel safe? Join the virtual conversation in social hub beta.

SMAC: New Security Guards are local representatives from your community working together with Force. They're here to keep you safe.

ANON17: What about old Force? Who's watching them?

Jed watched the latest squad of security guards walk down the corridor. It was a new initiative from the governor's office. A mixture of security guards and Force operatives would work together to keep the peace, the idea being that the security guards were representatives from the community and therefore more in touch with daily citizen life. At least that's what Sean MacIntyre, aide to the governor, had told everyone on the daily sweeps. It seemed to Jed that the governor's office was trying to complicate a justice system that worked perfectly fine, but he could see how involving citizens was a good idea.

'You wanted to see me, Boss?' Jed asked as he poked his head around the office door of Tony Minkov, Chief of Force. Since losing Pete, Jed had no patience for the other detectives on Force and had come to blows several times. This had earnt him three official warnings and the threat of unpaid leave in order to attend anger management sessions. But Jed didn't think he'd upset anyone recently, so he had no idea why he was being called in.

'Yes, come in, Jenkins. Sit, sit.' The chief fiddled with his handheld and scratched his head before clearing his throat loudly. 'Things are changing here in City 42. It's happening slowly but it won't be long before old timers like me are pushed out the door and Force changes into something else.' He glanced up and saw the incredulous look on Jed's face. 'No, hear me out, Jenkins. I don't like it. My gut is telling me we need to watch our backs. I need someone I can trust and rely on to look after our city as we see these changes through. Someone who takes their civic duty seriously.' Minkov looked Jed directly in eye. 'The thing is, Jenkins, you're no good to me as a Detective.'

'But, Sir!' Jed protested. 'If this is about me not finding a new partner, I will, I promise. I just haven't found anyone yet. It's been... difficult.'

'It's been difficult for all of us, Jenkins,' Minkov spoke gruffly. In their own way, both men still mourned the loss of Detective Pete Barnes. 'But it doesn't change what needs to be done. I have detectives I can use on local crime. You I need on the other side. You are being promoted to Captain of the City Guard and will be in charge of a team of specialist operatives who will look to the safety of our citizens, our city and be responsible for any future exploration.'

'Future exploration? Isn't that Agent Devereaux's department?' asked Jed.

'Devereaux is on assignment in City 15 but his department has been downsized. Part of these new changes. All the agents have been reassigned elsewhere - another reason why I want you to head up this new division. I need someone with a level head, someone who knows the law, who cares about the city. We can't have a hothead in charge.'

'Do we need a city militia, Sir?' Jed was surprised at such an aggressive move; it wasn't the sort of thing he'd come to expect from Martha's governorship.

'It may seem extreme now, Jenkins, but I remember the City 15 riots and the violent backlash from Corporation. If we want to protect our independence, then we need the appropriate defenders and having you in charge puts my mind at ease.'

'You don't think Corporation still have a standing military, do you?' Jed had never considered the possibility before.

'I wouldn't put anything past them. The fact that we haven't heard anything from Corporation makes me nervous.' Chief Minkov tapped his badge. 'Force has always been a separate entity, we've always stood for truth and justice, working with whatever government has been in place yet our hands were tied without us even knowing thanks to Corporation lies. It's our job to protect City 42's freedom, Jenkins.'

'Yes, Sir. Of course, but, but... I'm still Force, aren't I?'

'Yes, but you report directly to Governor Hamble. Think of me as your counterpart on civilian matters.' Minkov watched closely to see how Jed would react. He thought it was a good idea to split Force, while he still had the power to implement change and could choose the right man for the job. Everything was in too much flux to continue with the old methodology. There had to be the capability for a greater show of force and indeed protection in case Corporation retaliated in some way. It was a distinct possibility that they would. The severe repercussions that happened in City 15 when they tried to shake off Corporation rule had been swift and brutal. It might seem quiet here in City 42 now, but it didn't mean things were going to stay that way.

Jed didn't need to think about it, he wanted a change. 'Thank you, Sir. I accept.'

Minkov held out his hand. 'Good man, you've made the right decision.' They shook. 'You need to report to Governor Hamble's office and get your briefing notes. That new fella, Sean Macinwotsit, should have all the details, but don't let him boss you around - you don't work for him and you certainly don't report to him. Did you get that background check in for him?'

Jed fished his handheld out of his pocket and tapped the screen a few times.

'Yes, Sir. Apparently, he spent some time studying in 15 before he and his parents moved here from City 9.' Jed had been surprised by that; he didn't think anyone had ever chosen to come to City 42 from City 9. He continued reading. 'Strong family ties with Corporation that go back several decades but since being here he hasn't shown any loyalty to Corp.' He looked up at the chief. 'Martha says he's fantastic at his job, she doesn't know what she'd do without him. He could be a runaway?'

'Hmm.' Minkov didn't look convinced. 'Keep an eye on him, Jenkins.'

'Yes, Sir. Will I still be based here, Sir? In my new role?'

'Yes, for now. It makes sense to keep all the equipment and men together, but we can hash out the particulars later. I expect there will be some sort of official ceremony, after all this is a new role with more responsibility to take on.'

'Yes, Sir. I have a city meeting up at Hamble HQ now anyway so I can pick up the details while I'm there.'

The chief agreed and dismissed him.

Thinking to himself, Jed walked slowly out of the building. He felt strange, all his career he'd worked towards becoming a detective. Being partnered with Pete had felt like it was always meant to be. Since his friend had died, he had felt lost and adrift, unsure exactly of what his next move would be. He'd even considered leaving Force completely and retraining to do something else. Unusual but not unheard of. Now though, he felt like he had a purpose again. Being in charge of a city militia - it was different, but it felt like something he could get behind. Since cutting ties with Corporation, the city was alone and vulnerable. Jed needed to be in a position to help protect it and now he was. He strode off confidently to Hamble HQ, as the governor offices were affectionately known, to find out what his first assignment would be. He hoped there wouldn't be too much additional paperwork with this new role. That had always been something he had never been too keen on.

It was a short walk from Force to Hamble HQ. After the destruction of Corp Tech and the discontinuation of lab grown babies, Martha had decided to take over Collection Towers and base her government there. She had made sure that a representative from each area of the city had at least an office, if not an entire floor. Jed wove through the protesters who had started to gather in Main Square. It was peaceful at the moment, but he made a mental note to ensure all operatives had their riot gear, just in case.

'ID.' One of the new security guards held out his hand for Jed's ident. It flashed green when scanned and the guard waved him through. Jed didn't recognise him, or the woman stationed further in the foyer. *They must both be new civilian recruits* he thought as he took the stairs up to Martha's offices. He was met by yet more security checks, this time he knew the staff and spent a few moments chatting with them. Everyone had lost someone in the terrorist attack on Corp Tech, so it had created a bond between those who'd worked the disaster site and those who'd come forward to work in the new government.

A quick look at Martha's office showed the door was firmly shut, keyed red for do not disturb so Jed tried his luck next door where Sean MacIntyre, Martha's aide, could usually be found. He was sitting at his desk frowning and looked up in alarm as Jed entered the room. His brow quickly cleared, and he swiped his screen blank.

'Everything alright?' asked Jed, nodding towards the desk.

'What? Oh that, yes, yes, nothing to worry about. What can I do for you, Detective? The city meeting isn't for another half an hour or so.'

'It's Captain now, Sean. I understand you have my briefing notes, for the City Guard?'

'Oh, oh right, I see. They made you, I mean you're the new... huh, I'd never have thought.' Sean scratched his head and then began opening drawers in his desk until he found the info jack he was looking for. 'Everything is on here,' he said passing the jack over. 'Congratulations, I guess. Hmm?'

'You seem surprised, Sean,' said Jed, bemused by the man's reaction.

'Yes! I mean, no. Of course not. It's just, you're a detective. Were a detective. And there were other candidates who were less... reactive. But you don't want to hear about that.' Sean pulled himself together and smiled at Jed. 'It will be great working with you, I'm sure.'

'U huh. What's my first assignment - do you know?'

'No. Well, maybe. I think it's straight in at the deep end to be honest. Governor Hamble will let you know soon, I'm sure. For now, get your team sorted out, be ready for anything, that sort of thing. You've got all the gear and everything. All the details about the City Guard's responsibilities are on that jack. If there's nothing else?' Sean had risen out of his seat and begun to usher Jed out of the office.

'I guess not. Thanks.' Jed looked at Martha's door again on his way past, but it was still closed. It would have been nice to get his new assignment from the governor directly, but he supposed she was busy getting ready for the city meeting. He'd go back to his old desk later and download the information he'd been given. He might even be able to wangle a new desk now. With half an hour to wait before the meeting was due to start, he got out his handheld to tell Kira the good news and noticed the sweeps had already got there. They never missed a trick.

***ANON17:** Who voted on city militia? I didn't!*

FORCE:** ***Official Announcement Detective Jed Jenkins has been promoted to Captain and will run the new City Guard.*

GOVHAM: *Congratulations to Captain Jenkins and the new City Guard. Together we're looking after City 42.*

ANON40: *Security Guards & Force City Guard. Overkill much?*

C42N: *Captain Jenkins is the new face of City 42's safety. Read more online!*

Chapter 3

***C42N:** Government meeting today. What should be the priority? Join the virtual conversation in social hub beta.*

***MSCHILD:** How do we know they're not still selling babies behind our backs? Why won't they bring back Collection?*

***ANON17:** More food! More food!*

***GOVHAM:** We will release a city-wide update later today. Together we're looking after City 42.*

***ANON40**: Bring back the force-field. Make us feel safe again.*

***CORPTECH2:** Why is Corp Tech still closed? We need our jobs! We need our tech!*

Martha's head hurt. The lack of sleep and the general weariness that came with being a new parent plus the brain numbing exhaustion of running City 42 was relentless. Trying to figure out the answers to problems she didn't even know existed until they were dumped on her desk. Like the first chilling discovery they had made after taking over from Corporation. The previous administration had been growing additional babies in the baby lab and selling them, elsewhere. With the collapse of the computer systems, Martha's team had yet to discover where and why the babies were being sold. It had shocked them all and of course the details had been leaked on the sweeps. There had been near riots but somehow Force had managed to contain the citizens anger, funnelling it towards clearing the debris from Corp Tech and establishing the new sewerage system. But finding out

Corporation policies like that only added to her fears that she wasn't helping the people of her city enough, that she was letting them down when they needed her most.

It never stopped. Even when she did manage to get out of the office, her work followed her home, invading her attempts at privacy. Everyone knew where the new governor of City 42 lived. And no-one seemed to have any qualms about passing by to give their opinion on something, or complain about something or more often than not, have a gawp at Lucas, her natural baby.

Martha sifted through the urgent memos on her handheld. She was pleased to see Chief Minkov had made Jed's new role official. A memo reporting no new natural pregnancies caught her eye, despite the contaminated water supply having been replaced, the number of confirmed natural pregnancies had not exploded as expected. She moved that one to her recycle bin. In a way, no pregnancies were a good thing, considering the limitations of the city's food and medical resources. Martha cast an eye over the crop report from Camp Eden. They were growing food, but they couldn't supply the entire city overnight and anyway, she thought ruefully, many citizens distrusted the natural, organic food, preferring to use their food hydrators and dried sachets. Filing that report under Food she felt a twinge of panic, those packets wouldn't last forever, and supplies were running low. They needed to find a solution.

Rhythmic pounding joined the simmering ache in Martha's head. How could they have run so low? When Corporation had been in charge, the citizens of City 42 had never run out of vital medical supplies or food sachets. But there was no-one left to ask about supply and demand. The mob had lynched the Corporation board members six months ago and despite their best efforts to sift through the records left behind it wasn't clear exactly how re-supply occurred. When the board members had attempted to leave the city, they'd set their computer files to self-destruct and because the whole Corporation system was linked it had wiped out Martha's father's files as well. It was a disaster.

Martha's calendar pinged. At least the power was still running strong - everything was solar powered so they shouldn't have any issues with that. It wasn't like the sun was about to fall out of the sky. Martha sighed. She had a meeting with her advisors in five minutes. Among other things, Martha had requested a complete report on medical supplies and any potential issues, as well as ideas on how to solve those problems. After all the facts and the problems were coming from the people working in the medical centres, they should know what they needed as a priority and surely someone would come forward with information on how it was done in the past.

Medicine didn't magically appear, it had to have been delivered one way or another. Martha rubbed her little blue Gaia statue for luck before heading out of the relative safety of her office and into the jaws of yet another meeting. They would get to the bottom of the supply issue, one way or another.

Entering the room Martha was pleased to see everyone was already there - Jed in his new role as Captain of the City Guard and as a representative from Force, Ruth as representative for Academy and supplying notes from Archive, and the Surgeon General of Med Centre, Dr William Lee. The Force chief didn't attend unless there was a vote and Ben Jenkins, the ex-Anti-Corp representative, had been side-lined to work as Martha's unofficial eyes and ears. He was happier reporting to her without an audience. Which meant the only absence was Agent Devereaux who was meant to be on assignment in City 15. Martha took her chair and smiled at Sean, as he handed her a cup of synth-caf. Martha tapped her handheld, ready to start the session but before she could speak the Surgeon General opened the meeting without any preamble.

'We've figured out why we aren't getting resupplied.'

Martha liked him immensely, no nonsense, straight to the point. She gestured for him to continue.

'There's a transporter pod in the basement, bloody alarm has been going off for weeks, but no-one knew what it was for.' He glanced around the table apologetically. 'Turns out this pod is used to move supplies between Corporation cities. All we need to do is enter the authorisation code and input our request.'

'Fantastic,' said Martha, feeling like things were finally going their way.

'Yes, well, it would be - if we knew what the authorisation code is.'

'What do you mean, you don't know? Someone must know it?' Ruth looked as knackered as Martha felt and had apparently forgotten to brush her hair that morning, luckily her unruly curls hid most of the damage.

'Turns out the code changed regularly and was given to the Med-Techs via Dr Basjere's office over in Science Division. We can't ask him because, well, because he's dead. None of the Med-Techs know where the code originated from. We've checked the computers but with no access passes we're completely locked out.'

'How bad are supplies getting?' Martha wasn't sure she wanted to know.

'We've got about another week, for patching up minor injuries. Thankfully no-one requires any kind of surgery at the moment because we are running low on things like plasma.' The Surgeon General looked down at the handheld in front of him to steady his nerves before continuing. 'I think we should turn all the diagnosis pods off. We don't have the necessary drugs to treat every little complaint and we can't cope with hysterical patients demanding treatment for conditions that only have the potential to manifest. It's a waste of what limited resources we do have left.'

'I agree,' said Jed. 'Force has been stretched thin keeping the peace...'

He was interrupted by Sean. 'Surely the Security Guards can help monitor the situation?' He inclined his head at Jed.

'Let's hope so, but we can do without unnecessary disturbances at Medical,' snapped Jed.

'How will you switch off the diagnostic pods without access to the Corporation mainframe?' Ruth narrowed her eyes suspiciously at Dr Lee.

'We have the kill code for the pods. One of the Med-Techs kept scrupulous records, surprisingly this is one code that still works. We tested it in the outlying pods in East Sector.'

Martha nodded. 'Okay, do it. Terminate the diagnostic pods. I'll send out a sweep informing citizens that we're diverting resources elsewhere, hopefully it won't cause too much panic.'

'It should help, but it doesn't solve our main problem,' replied Dr Lee.

'I know but...' Martha was interrupted.

'I'm sorry Ma'am, but I don't think you do. Without a resupply in the next week or so, citizens will potentially start falling ill and I won't be able to do anything about it. Then we will have mass panic to deal with.' Dr Lee looked around the room. 'We've got to do something.'

'Did City 15 respond to any of our communiques yet, Jed?' Martha asked.

'No, we've had nothing back. Agent Devereaux hasn't reported back yet either. We've had no confirmation that the original messages have even got through to them.'

'I think we have to send a full exploration team out there. Not just an emissary from our city but some scientists and an archivist as well, plus security of course.' Martha felt a flicker of worry. She didn't care for Devereaux very much, but she certainly didn't want anything to happen to him, especially when he was meant to be on a fact-finding mission for her government.

'That would be my recommendation as well,' Jed said. 'We don't even know if Devereaux got to City 15 safely, one man travelling on his own... anything could've happened.' He opened a file on his handheld and sent it to the main screen to display the map from City 42 to City 15 to the others. 'If you look at the terrain, we'd have to cross a dead zone but overall it's not far. We know the transporters aren't working between the cities so it could be that the people of 15 are wondering what's happening over here. We might even run into an envoy from them as we head out over there.'

'Do we have the means to get a full exploration team out there?' asked Martha.

Jed nodded. 'We've got the Force skimmers; they'll do the journey alright. I've got a few people in mind for the team. If it's alright with you, we'll leave tomorrow.' He felt excited, this would be his first mission as Captain and although it was concerning that Devereaux had gone incommunicado, he didn't think anything would've happened to the man. He was too annoying to go missing.

'Make sure you're fully prepared for every scenario, Jed. You will need a diplomatic envoy as well as Force operatives. I do think you should take an archivist and scientists as well as a security force. We don't even know whether 15 will let you in. After all they're still Corporation and we're not,' said Martha.

'I don't think that will be much of a problem,' Ruth observed. 'City 15 has always had strong Anti-Corp roots. It's where the first revolution happened.'

'And failed,' muttered Sean under his breath.

'Well, be careful, please.' Martha's headache was receding somewhat but the churning whirlpool of worry in her stomach more than made up for the lack of pounding. 'I don't want anything to happen to anyone. Could you leave the details of your team with me, please Jed?'-

'Will do.'

'What's next on the agenda, Sean?' asked Martha.

'Citizens have been expressing their unease again at the lack of a force-field. There's been a lot of chatter on the sweeps about letting in disease and vermin although of course those are only rumours. We've had no such actual reports.' Sean looked up from his handheld. 'The new security teams seem to be going down well.'

'Good, well done Sean. That was a great idea, to have the public responsible for their own safety gets everyone more invested in the city. If no-one has any objections, I'll get the updates office to re-sweep the batch of notices we used last month, the ones about the safety beyond the city walls.' Martha looked down the table but there were no objections, so she made a note to action that point. It was something Sean could do but Martha liked to keep her hand in with the day-to-day when she could. 'I also think it's time to roll out a new campaign to encourage citizens to try the fresh food that is coming in from Camp Eden - can you put together some sweeps please, Sean?'

Sean nodded and made a note. 'Food sachets are running low as well, Governor Hamble. We do need to come up with a more permanent solution. Perhaps if we reached out to City 9?'

Jed's ears perked up. 'I think we should wait until we've been to City 15 before we go any further afield,' he said. 'They are likely to be a bit more receptive than a Corporation stronghold.'

Sean smiled and shrugged.

'I quite agree, Jed. One step at a time.' Martha glanced outside at the view overlooking Main Square below. She smiled at the bee that bumped into the window before her attention was distracted by the small crowd gathering at the base of the building. 'As you all probably noticed there is a peaceful protest happening this afternoon in the square. I believe it's another demonstration against the closure of the baby labs but let me assure all of you, that decision is final and will not be revoked.'

'But Governor, all the people want is to raise a family. Like you.' Sean looked a picture of innocence. He had been pushing Martha for weeks to re-open the labs. 'Surely you don't want riots like we had when citizens found out about the baby sales?'

'We did not have riots. The people reacted emotionally to a

shocking situation and I will not blame them for that. But my decision is final. Those labs are not opening again until we find out where all the documented babies grown disappeared to, because they certainly aren't here in City 42.' Martha's nostrils were flaring as she tried to keep her anger under control. She had been absolutely horrified to learn that extra babies had been grown out of their reproduction labs. She was more disturbed that they were unable to find out where the babies had been sent thanks to the computer shutdowns. It was something she was desperate to find out. Martha sounded firm yet her brow was creased with worry. 'Dr Lee, do you know why we haven't had more natural pregnancies?'

The Surgeon General huffed a little before answering. 'As we said before, it will take time for each individual reproductive system to recover from the illegal radiation we all experienced. Everyone will be different, it could take months, it could take generations. We have had some miscarriages which, whilst they are sad news for the couples involved, are encouraging. It shows our natural systems are gradually getting back to normal.'

'Is there anything more we can tell the public?' asked Sean.

'Not really, but we can re-sweep our previous messages, if you think that will help.' Dr Lee looked to Martha, rather than Sean and she nodded in agreement before turning her attention to the next item, education.

Professor Kamir had chosen to step down from his position as Head of Academy and consequently his place on Martha's ruling committee. Ruth had been put forward as liaison due to her teaching background and it was agreed by everyone present that she was an excellent replacement, but Martha wasn't sure whether Ruth was coping well with the new role and motherhood. It was tough on both of them.

'Ruth, how are things at Academy?'

But Ruth didn't answer. She was staring off into space, her head cocked as if she were listening to something else. There was a bee crawling around the window frame closest to her. Martha had to say Ruth's name three times before she realised everyone was looking at her, waiting for her to speak.

'Academy. Right.' Ruth tapped her handheld a few times then read out her report woodenly. 'New curriculum implemented. Lots of interest on the new courses, less actual uptake. Postgraduates are filling in staff gaps where possible. Attendance is still good.' She looked up to see whether she could get away with that recap.

There were no objections to the report, so Ruth moved on to the other update she had available. 'Archive has been busy. They are ensuring all citizens have access to relevant information, but all terrorist related items are strictly monitored and still require governor approval before they can be accessed.'

Sean coughed and Martha looked at him. 'Did you have anything to add to the report, Sean?'

'No, no, you go ahead Ma'am.'

'Right, well, I think that's everything on the agenda. Any other business?' Martha cleared her handheld screen, hoping to be able to make a quick getaway for once.

'Um, I have a couple of items - if it's alright?' Sean asked.

'Of course.' Martha concealed her surprise, she thought Sean had raised everything with her in the short briefing they'd had before this meeting.

'There has been a significant social backlash on the issue of Corp Tech.' Jed looked up sharply and Sean raised his hands in defence. 'It's not coming from me. This is actual chatter. I can show you the screen grabs if you like.' He went to activate the main screen in the room, but Martha forestalled him.

'That's not necessary, Sean. I know many citizens feel we should reopen Corp Tech and continue working on the projects we have been able to recover but until we can solve the supplies issue I think we should be focusing on making sure everyone has enough to eat and any medical needs are met.

'But I think...'

'No, Sean. Now is not the time.' Martha's voice came out sharper than she intended making Ruth flinch slightly. She took a calming breath. 'Anything else?'

Sean had reddened at the admonition but still had one more point he wanted to raise. 'The er... matter of the worshippers. They are starting to become a social nuisance. The new security teams have informed me...'

This time it was Jed who interrupted. 'Do you mean the Gaia followers? How are they a social nuisance?'

Sean bristled. 'Well, they insist on communing with nature right out in the open, causing obstructions in public places and there has been effigy.'

Ruth barked a laugh. 'You can't stop people from meeting in public places - they are public, they have every right to meet.'

'Yes but...'

'No, Sean. Ruth is right. If citizens want to meet in public spaces and celebrate nature, I for one am certainly not going to stop them. As for the effigy, leave it. It's a symbol of hope for many people. Art should be treasured, not destroyed.'

'But they're planting flowers? Encouraging bees!' Sean protested.

'And that is a good thing, Sean. Trust me,' replied Martha.

Sean twisted his mouth slightly as he reluctantly nodded and put his handheld down.

There was a moment of silence. Jed stood up to leave. 'We done?'

'I think so, Jed. Can you wait in my office though please? I'd like to sign off on your guard selection and approve all your supplies.'

Jed nodded and the Surgeon General scooped up his papers in relief. Martha turned her attention to him. 'Treat the essentials, as best you can,' she said. Dr Lee nodded and left the room with Jed close on his heels. Sean bustled out shortly afterwards.

The two women left looked at each other, mirroring their exhaustion.

'Are we done for the day?' Ruth asked hopefully.

'Nearly. You head home. I'll see you there, I want to sign off on Jed's expedition team. I want to make sure he has decent medical and scientific support as well as brute force. Plus, there's the Archivist position to fill - do you think Kira would go?'

Ruth screwed up her face, frowning. 'I don't think she'd leave Grace behind.'

'No, you're right. But if this really is a diplomatic mission then there will be plenty of security and there's no reason to think they wouldn't be safe. It's only City 15.'

'Alright, well you'll have to ask her and see what she thinks. Try not to get caught up in anything else. You look tired.'

'Thanks, I thought I'd try and give you some competition.' The two friends smiled at each other wearily before leaving the conference room together. One to head home to worry about the children, the other to worry some more about all the citizens who relied on her to keep them safe.

GOVHAM: *Our monthly meeting report is available to download. Together we're looking after City 42.*

ANON17: *How does shutting down diagnostic pods help look after us? It's a conspiracy! Killing off the undesirable!*

MED4C42: *Diagnostic pods will be temporarily offline. If you have any serious health concerns, visit your nearest med centre.*

GOVHAM: *Re-sharing our Safety Beyond the Wall info jack. Download yours today and discover the wonders outside. Together we're looking after City 42.*

ANON17: *Don't believe a word - it's a toxic wasteland! Bring back the force-field! Bring back the force-field!*

MSCHILD: *Maybe no force-field is the reason why no pregnancies? Open the baby labs! It's not fair.*

MED4C42: *Find out more about the natural pregnancy cycle. Download your info jack & get up to speed. You could be next!*

ANON17: *Rehashing - resharing - same old, same old. Lies, lies, lies, lies!*

CAMPEDEN: *Visit our online tour today. Discover how the hydroponics centre is growing fresh food for you & your family. It's safe - it's healthy - it's delicious!*

ANON40: *I'd rather eat a dry sachet.*

ENCRYPTED MESSAGE FROM 7421 TO NEW CORP

>>1. The new Corp Tech supporters' group is gaining momentum. Previous employees are desperate to start working on the latest tech. Can I leak the new neural implants yet?

2. Shall I have the appointment of Jed Jenkins to Captain of the City Guard invalidated?

3. They've decided to turn off the medical diagnostic pods. Will you be bringing medical supplies? Things are running low.

4. There is continual backlash about the force-field remaining switched off. I have made sure that all the equipment remains intact.

5. You gave me no instructions for City 15 - they are sending another team out there<<

ENCRYPTED MESSAGE FROM CORP TO 7421

>>REPORT RECEIVED.

1. CONTINUE TO SUPPORT THE CORP TECH MOVEMENT. DO NOT LEAK THE NEURAL IMPLANTS YET. WE WILL BRING IT WITH US.

2. CHIEF MINKOV WILL BE DEALT WITH. DO NOTHING TO JEOPARDISE YOUR POSITION. IF JENKINS LEAVES THE CITY, WE WILL DEAL WITH HIM.

3. SUPPLIES WILL BE PROVIDED FOR THOSE LOYAL TO NEW CORP.

4. CONTINUE TO PROTECT THE FORCE-FIELD EQUIPMENT. WE WILL BE SWITCHING IT BACK ON.

5. PLANS FOR CITY 15 ARE IN MOTION.

STAND BY FOR FURTHER INSTRUCTIONS<<

Chapter 4

C42N: *City Guard or enforced control? Have your say, join the virtual conversation in social hub beta.*

GOVHAM: *City Guard's first mission is to City 15. Together we're looking after City 42.*

ANON17: *Why is City Guard going to City 15? Take-over bid? Watch out 15!*

'Who are you taking with you?' asked Kira as she sat with her husband while he gathered his gear together. She was smiling as she watched him, he seemed more like himself since getting the promotion and the mission. Ever since Pete's death, Jed had been more short-tempered. He'd had fights at Force over imagined slurs, refused to work with anyone else and had become withdrawn. He wasn't sharing things with her anymore. She understood it was part of his coping mechanism, but it sometimes made her feel like a stranger in her own marriage.

'Oh, you know, some of the lads from Force - Ash, you've met him. And there will be a couple of others.'

Kira waited for him to elaborate but he didn't. 'Um, won't there be some sort of scientist and medical presence as well? Isn't it a diplomatic mission?'

'Martha wants me to take Max so I was going to speak to him next. Don't worry about the medical though love, we're all trained in first aid. We'll have med kits with us.' He continued stuffing clothes into a bag.

There was a short silence, broken only by Grace's happy babbling from the front room. Kira wrung her hands together, trying to find the right words. She couldn't bring herself to tell him about her involvement, so she changed tack.

'You will, I mean, it's not dangerous is it? You're going to be alright?'

Jed stopped packing and looked at his wife. His heart ached, he loved her so much, but he felt like he couldn't tell her. Things were still so raw and emotional for him. He honestly believed that if he let in his love for Kira then his grief for his sister and Pete would overwhelm him, and right now he needed to keep functioning. One step at a time.

'We are only going to City 15. We'll be fine. There's obviously been some sort of mix-up on the access codes or something, which is why we can't talk to the city anymore.' He turned his attention back to packing.

'But why have they stopped sending their skimmers over? Do you think they will try to attack us?' She winced hoping he hadn't noticed exactly what she'd said.

'I hardly think that's likely, love.' Jed zipped up his bag. 'City 15 have never been staunchly Corporation. I bet they've followed our lead and got rid of their board of directors. They've probably been locked out of their main systems, like we were.'

'You really think that?' Kira was doubtful.

'I'm sure. Everything is going to be fine. I've got to chat to Max over at Eden now. Alright if I use the main vid?' Kira nodded. Jed picked up his bag and left the bedroom, but Kira couldn't get rid of the sinking feeling in the pit of her stomach.

It took a few minutes for the connection to Camp Eden to clear. There was a lot of static on the vid feed and broken sound until finally it resolved into a clear image.

'Hi Jed, sorry about that. We had a loose wire, looks alright our end now.' Max plonked himself down into a camping chair, looking as tanned and laid-back as ever.

'Yep, reading you loud and clear here as well,' Jed replied.

'So, what's going on, how can I help?'

'Yeah, sorry it's not a social call. We, the governor's office I mean, are putting together an expedition to go over to City 15 and I'd like you, and Dina, to come with us,' Jed explained.

'Really? Why do you want us?' Max beckoned to someone off cam and Dina's face appeared.

'Hi Jed! How are you? How's Kira and Grace?'

Jed grinned at Dina's infectious cheerfulness. 'Hi D. We're all fine, but as I was saying, we want you and Max to come on an expedition to City 15 with us.'

'Oh exciting! Are we going?' Dina looked at Max who nodded.

'I guess we are. But, Jed, you still haven't told me why you want us along?'

'Well, we've had no luck making contact with City 15 since Corporation left 42. And we're running low on medical and food supplies, as you know. Governor Hamble wants us to reach out to 15 personally and find out how we can build a working relationship with them. Having you guys there will help us explain what happened with the water supply and the new food we're growing at Camp. Plus...' Jed trailed off and looked to make sure Kira was still occupied and hadn't come into the room. He hunched closer to the vid screen and lowered his voice. 'We haven't had any response, to any of our communiques. And a previous envoy has gone missing. I think there might be something seriously wrong.'

'What do you mean?' Dina frowned. 'Do you think Corp have done something?'

'I don't know. But it's a possibility.'

Max broke the silence. 'Okay Jed, we'll come and help, of course we will. When do you need us?'

'Appreciate it, Max. Tomorrow. I need you at City 42, first thing tomorrow and...' Dina cut across him.

'What do you mean *first thing tomorrow*! We're doing important work here at Eden. We can't drop everything at a moment's notice to travel to a city where they may or may not want to talk to us.' Dina's cheeks were flushed as she finished speaking.

'Easy, Dina. Jed, of course. We'll be at Main Square for 9am don't worry.' Max put a placating hand on Dina's shoulders and shook his head slightly as she opened her mouth to complain some more.

'Thanks, Max. Appreciate it. See you tomorrow.' Jed signed off the vid comm. He was glad he wasn't in Max's shoes right now. He didn't actually need Dina on the team, but Jed would never have got away with only recruiting Max for the mission. If he'd had his way, he wouldn't have recruited any civilians. Much better to only have his operatives and scope out the situation with them. Jed checked over his bag, one more time, to make sure he had everything he needed. Tomorrow was going to be an interesting day.

Kira listened to make sure Jed was still busy and unlikely to disturb her before she vid-commed her mum.

'Kira, honey, how are you my dear? I was just saying to your father we hadn't heard from you today. You sure you're eating enough, love? You look a bit peaky. It's all well and good eating that newfangled earth grown stuff but you ought to get a couple of sachets as well. It's not natural to rely on the real food alone. I was telling Maureen the other day - she's convinced that we'll be running out of sachets soon and everyone will be reduced to eating beetles and bugs.' Jean Bishop laughed loudly. 'Can you imagine? Beetles and bugs!'

'Mum!' Kira cut in urgently. 'Mum, listen, I can't talk for long. But...' She cocked her head to make sure Jed wasn't coming into the bedroom. 'I'm going to City 15 and I'm taking Grace with me.' *And I haven't told Jed yet* she thought to herself.

'Oh, that'll be nice, dear.'

Kira frowned. 'Did you hear what I said?'

'I may be your mother but I'm not past it yet, dear. You said you were going to City 15 and taking Grace with you. Visiting friends are you, love?'

'Er, no Mum. Martha's asked me to go as an Archive advisor. It's part of a diplomatic mission.' Kira scratched her head. 'You do know that we haven't had any contact from 15 for weeks, don't you, Mum?'

'Oh, I'm sure it's a switched off button somewhere, love. It's all a bit above my head. But a trip will do you good. Get some colour in those cheeks, all that fresh air.' Suddenly Jean seemed to realise that City 15 was a fair distance away from City 42 and involved travelling through the countryside that may or may not be safe. 'But you will have protection, won't you? And you're taking Grace? Are you sure that's a good idea, love? I know it's important to you to raise the child as naturally as possible but exposing her to potentially lethal toxins might be taking it a step too far. Although it is important for her to have new experiences that's true. Is Jed going with you? Of course he is, he wouldn't let you go running off on some mad scheme without him. He'll be there to protect and look after you, keep you out of trouble. Aww it'll be nice, a family trip out. Only do watch out for those animals. I hear all sorts of stories about real animals lurking outside the city walls. Waiting around, looking for any excuse to come in and eat us all in our beds. Why I was telling Jackie the other day...'

Kira let her mother's incessant chatter flow over her. It felt normal and safe and calmed her down. She was nervous about going on this mission, but she had argued her case to Martha intelligently. They did need someone with Archival clearance and a working knowledge of City 15 plus she didn't feel comfortable letting Jed go away without her. And anyway, Kira would make sure absolutely nothing bad happened to her daughter.

Chapter 5

GOVHAM: *Join me in wishing our first inter-city mission success. Together we're looking after City 42.*

ANON17: *Together we're wasting resources.*

C42N: *Will City 15 open trade routes with an independent city? What do you think? Join the discussion in social hub beta.*

Martha groaned as her alarm blared. At least it wasn't a baby crying. Then Lucas started wailing. So much for that. She pushed herself to sitting and blinked blearily. Lucas was still asleep in his cube. Must be Sarah crying, poor Ruth. Come to think of it, poor Martha! She crept out of the bedroom, trying not to wake her son and went to put on the synth-caf and bottle warmers. Lucas might not be awake right now, but it wouldn't be long.

Ruth stumbled into the kitchen with Sarah in arms.

'Oh, thank you,' she said as she saw the warmer already on. 'I can't seem to get going this morning. Sorry about the wake-up call.'

Martha smiled. 'It's fine - we've got a big day, might as well start getting ready for it.'

'You finalised the team, then?' Ruth fumbled with the bottle nearly dropping both it and her baby. Martha's quicker reflexes stopped the bottle from falling off the counter. 'Thanks, sorry. Again.' Ruth was flustered.

'Are you alright, Ruth?' Martha touched her friend's arm in concern. 'Why don't you drop the kids in at the office crèche, get some rest - you've more than earned it. I can look in on them.'

'No, it's alright. I can manage.' She forced a smile. 'I'm fine, honestly. I've never been at my best first thing in the morning. Ah, I think that's your noise-bag.'

New cries filled the air as Lucas made it clear that he was awake and would like his breakfast. Now. Martha hurried back to her room to scoop up her son and returned, chatting to him. 'Morning angel-face, let's get you sorted out. Come on, come on, here it is. There, there. It's alright.'

The kitchen was filled with the sound of two contented babies as their mums leant against worktops and considered the day ahead.

'Jed's not going to be happy about this, you know.' Ruth commented finally.

'No, he's not. But she's right, he can be reckless, and we don't need that on a fact-finding mission. At least this way he won't take unnecessary risks.'

'You hope.'

Martha sighed. 'We need to find out what's happening in City 15. We've got to get these supply routes back open. And we need to start talking to Corporation, one way or another.'

Ruth snorted. She didn't agree with that last part. Now that they were free of Corp, she didn't think they should be so quick to extend an olive branch, but Martha felt they could come to some sort of agreement. 'I still think you're making a mistake. If you invite Corp in, they will take over again and who knows what they'll do to you. Don't you think it sends a mixed message kicking them out only to invite them back for synth-caf?'

'It's not that straightforward and you know it, Ruth. We have to get the medical supply chain restarted, it's crucial, but I'm not going to let them lie to us again.'

There was a strained silence between the two women.

'Right, I think these guys have finished. Are you coming with me to see the exploration team off?' Martha asked.

Ruth nodded and rushed to get her bag organised. Martha smiled at her friend, she seemed fine. Kira had pinged her to say she was worried about Ruth, but she seemed the same as always to Martha. Having someone else struggling with being a single parent while working was a blessing. At least she had someone to talk about it with. Setting up the crèche facilities at Hamble HQ for when both of them had to work had been relatively easy but it didn't stop Martha from feeling guilty, like she was letting Lucas down every time she left him there to go to work. But she was governor. She, if nobody else, had to put the citizens of City 42 first.

'You don't have to come with me, you know. We can say goodbye here.' Jed was impatient to leave. The expedition team were meeting up and heading out to City 15 this morning. It felt good to have something proactive to get on with, away from all the memories City 42 held.

'I know, but we are. You ready?' Kira had Grace all bundled up, looking like they were about to begin an expedition instead of Jed. He noticed that their skimmer was also full of bags.

'Are you planning to stay with your mum for a few days, then?' Jed asked.

Kira murmured noncommittally as she buckled Grace into her safety seat and then began piloting the skimmer towards Hamble HQ. Jed looked out the window at the city buildings. Martha taking over Collection Towers for her government offices was working well, so far. The rubble from the destruction of Corp Tech had been cleared but nothing new had been decided on yet. *It will probably end up as a memorial space* Jed reflected. A fitting tribute.

It didn't take long to get to Hamble HQ. It looked like everyone else on the team was already assembled. Even Ruth was there. Jed scrambled out of the skimmer, grabbing his gear on his way, leaving Kira to deal with Grace.

Martha smiled nervously at him as he came over. 'Morning, Jed. Are you ready?'

Jed nodded, eager to get the formalities over with so they could be on their way. His team were already packed into a couple of Force skimmers and Ash discreetly took Jed's gear away, stowing it securely in one of their vehicles.

'I believe you know the science team.' Martha was grinning as both Max and Dina came forward from the small crowd now gathering.

'Good to see you, buddy,' Jed clasped hands with Max firmly and smiled genuinely at him. When Dina had decided to stay out at Camp Eden with Max, initially the group had worried about her, but Max had been there for her and together, their relationship had blossomed. It was good to see them both again. 'I'm not sure there'll be much scientific for you guys to get stuck into but happy to have you on board. Hey, D.'

Dina hugged him. 'You never know what we might find out there, that's the best bit!' She was excited and looked past Jed to wave enthusiastically at Kira and Grace.

'I still think you should take a Med Tech with you.' Martha put up a hand to forestall Jed's arguments for not taking one. 'I know, I know, all the guys from Force have basic first aid but we don't know what we're walking into and I wanted you to have someone who knows intimately what supplies we need urgently.'

'You've given us the list. I'm sure we can figure it out. We've got Max and Dina with us for any science jargon. It'll be fine. We're going to City 15, not the back end of beyond.' Jed didn't want any more civilians on this mission, just in case.

'Hmm.' Martha didn't sound convinced, but she had already given in to Jed's request for no more civilians yesterday when she'd mentioned a med-tech. She knew he wasn't going to like what she had to tell him next. 'As I said yesterday, I want you to take someone from Archive, to document the journey and to gather any pertinent information from City 15 while you're there. I believe you know each other.' Martha waited anxiously for Jed to connect the dots.

He looked, lips pressed into a thin line, eyes narrowed from Martha to Kira who had come to join them. 'I suppose this was all your idea?' he asked his wife. She shrugged self-consciously, aware of everyone else's gaze upon them. 'What about Grace?'

'She's coming as well,' replied Kira.

'What? Do you think that's a sensible idea?'

'I do.' Kira decided against saying anything else with everyone watching, they could discuss it later. She and Martha had talked about it at length last night. They both hoped having his family along would ground Jed somewhat and prevent too much reckless behaviour. And besides, the expedition did need an archivist.

Jed stared at his wife, he was irritated that she went behind his back, but he knew he couldn't show it now, in front of the entire expedition. He was also annoyed to admit to himself that Kira was the most qualified archivist they had so it made sense to bring her along, even though he'd prefer someone else. She had been studying everything Archive held on the other nearby cities, and without full access to their own systems as they travelled, it could be invaluable information. He nodded curtly and waited to see if there were to be any further surprises.

Martha let out a breath she hadn't realised she'd been holding. She turned and addressed the small crowd in front of her.

'I want to thank you all for volunteering for this mission to City 15. We don't know what you will find when you get there but I am confident you have the skills and experience to deal with any situation. Remember, we want to establish a line of communication and more importantly, supply routes.' She paused to look at the people in front of her. 'Corporation are not the enemy.'

There was a lot of muttering and side wise glances from the members of the expedition team. Martha held up her hand.

'Please, let me finish. I'm not saying Corporation are blameless, but the fact of the matter is, we simply do not know their level of influence in other cities. We cannot assume the same blanket control throughout, we must go forward with an open mind and gather all the facts. I look to all of you to be our fact gatherers, our champions and our protectors.'

There was a smattering of applause. Most of the team were serious and resolute, keen to begin their mission. Martha looked at her friends, Kira and Dina were smiling at her at least, Ruth seemed pensive. Martha walked towards them, trying to ignore the knot of worry in her stomach.

'Great speech,' Dina teased.

'You will both be extra careful, won't you?' Martha asked. 'Especially you, Kira. No risk taking. Keep Grace safe.'

'I will.' Kira was feeling nervous now, it had seemed like such a good idea at the time. Was she making a mistake? Was bringing Grace along the most dangerous thing she could do?

The women hugged, eyes glinting yet smiling at each other. Jed whistled to get everyone's attention. His team were ready to leave, all kit stowed and everyone within the vehicles. Kira, Dina and Max hurried to the second skimmer. Once Grace was safely ensconced inside, Kira had a brief panic that she hadn't thought of everything but reminded herself that it was unlikely she'd forgotten anything significant. Being a mother had forced her to be organised, whether she was naturally inclined to be so or not.

Martha watched the skimmers leave the plaza in single file. She hoped she wasn't making a mistake. Ruth came to stand next to her. A bee bumbled along nearby, unnoticed by either of them. Both women too preoccupied with their own thoughts and worries.

'Everything go okay?'

'I think so. Jed took it well, I thought.' Martha tried to sound positive.

'Yeah? Well, I wouldn't like to be in Kira's shoes later.' Ruth linked arms with Martha and the two women started walking away.

'She can hold her own, believe me. Jed will probably come away thinking it was all part of his great idea in the first place.'

Ruth chuckled but like Martha, she couldn't quite shake the feeling of impending doom. Their friends were travelling into the unknown, all they could do now was wait.

Chapter 6

At first the journey was exciting. The small convoy passed close by Max's science base; Camp Eden. Both he and Dina kept Kira amused with anecdotes about their life in the camp and pointed out the interesting flora and fauna as they passed. But soon the vehicles travelled into a burn zone, where nature had yet to conquer the radioactive ravages inflicted upon the planet by man. It was a sobering contrast to the lush young forests that surrounded Camp Eden.

'Do we know why this land hasn't recovered yet, Max?' Kira asked.

'The soil is too acidic. We know there were heavier HER attacks in certain places but without the remains of any landmarks it's difficult to know what was here before. It could've been a military base or a government building of some kind.'

'Will the ground ever recover?'

'It should do, in time,' Max replied. 'All we can do is hope that with enough care and attention, Mother Nature will spread her magic a little further for us.'

'You mean Gaia.' Kira smiled at the sun-kissed scientist.

'Yes, our fabulous blue lady.'

'Any more sightings?' Kira hadn't seen or felt Gaia since the events leading up to the overthrow of Corporation and the beginning of the new governance under Martha's leadership.

'No,' Dina replied sadly. 'Sometimes I wonder whether we imagined it all in the first place but then I remind myself of the recording we have and all our individual experiences. I know she's real but, I suppose she has more important things to do at the moment then come and see us. There have been bee sightings inside the city though, that's exciting.'

'I know, we saw one the other day. There's also a small collection of Gaia followers who have been terrorising Sean,' replied Kira.

'Sean? Isn't he Martha's aide?' asked Max.

'Yeah, that's him.'

'What sort of things have they been doing?' asked Dina, she was intrigued.

Kira laughed. 'Oh, highly inflammatory stuff like meeting in the new parks, planting flowers and I think one of them painted a picture of Gaia on a blank wall.'

'Oh,' Dina sounded disappointed for a moment. 'Was it a good picture?'

'It didn't look much like Her. I don't think they've seen the real thing, like us.' Kira paused, feeling saddened that there hadn't been any new sightings. 'You never know, City 15 might have some blue lady tales for us.'

'Do you think Corporation is still in charge over there?' Dina was doubtful. She was from City 15 originally and although she only had scattered memories of her childhood there, she knew the reason she'd been orphaned and left the city was down to Anti-Corp uprisings.

'I honestly don't know. I'm just hoping we can reconnect the medical supply train.' Kira hadn't told her friends yet but, her Mum needed regular medicine to keep a mutated genetic condition under control. With the disrupted supply chains, the medicine Jean Bishop needed was dwindling fast, despite Kira and her family's efforts to stockpile as much as possible. With no new supplies arriving, they would run out soon and then Kira's mum would swiftly begin to deteriorate and become severely ill. And Kira knew her mum would not be the only one. The reduced medical supplies were a taboo subject as everyone tried to manage their own needs privately. There wasn't much of a community sharing spirit when it came to such a serious situation. Kira couldn't blame them; people were trying to keep their families safe. That was the reason for this expedition after all.

Chapter 7

City 15 was smaller than 42 but laid out in a similar grid pattern. There was a greater Academy presence here; it had been originally designed to be a city of learning. Its Professors would often visit 42 for guest lectures but no-one had been for months, not since City 42 overthrew Corporation.

As the envoy approached, Ash swept the city for its protective force-field.

'Huh.'

'What?' Jed looked at the screen on the dashboard.

'There's no force-field.'

'On alert people.' Jed called back to the rest of his team. 'We don't know what we're going into.' Jed pressed the comm channel to speak to the other transporter. 'Kira? Pick up please.'

'Yes, Jed? We're here.'

'The city force-field is down so we're going in on high alert. I want you to stay inside your vehicle at all times. It's armoured for your protection.'

'Uh... okay.' Kira looked at her fellow passengers in alarm, but Max and Dina seemed relaxed about the news and smiled reassuringly so she tried to push her unease away.

Jed watched the dashboard as Ash ran through all the usual checks. There was no response to their hails. The force-field was down. Comms were unresponsive. Power signatures were negative. It looked like there was no-one there at all.

The two vehicles passed through the open gateway and followed the empty road towards the middle of the city. There were no skimmers, no lights, no people. No signs of life at all.

'Where is everyone?' murmured Ash. Every building scan was coming up empty.

'If we knew that, we wouldn't be here.' Jed felt like they were walking straight into a trap and he'd brought his wife and child along for the ride. He glanced back through the rear-view to reassure himself the second vehicle was still there. It was.

They arrived at the central plaza. Still devoid of life. Jed gave out the orders.

'Alpha Team, I want you to use your rebreathers and fan out. Do a block-by-block check, out to ten blocks then report back. Scan the buildings but don't enter them. Report in if you see anything suspicious. Stay together.'

There were confident assurances from the team. The operatives were used to working together and the four of them left the skimmer eagerly to explore what was happening in City 15.

'Ash, run a diagnostic on what is working here. There has to be some sort of signal somewhere. The rest of Beta Team, with me.' Jed left the skimmer, confident that Ash would check everything that could be checked. He was a solid team member; you could always count on his level-headedness in a crisis.

When Jed got to the second skimmer, Kira popped out to see him straight away.

'I thought I told you to stay in the vehicle at all times.'

'Jed! What's going on? Where is everyone?'

'I don't know, love. We're running scans and checking what we can. I need you to stay here and stay safe, okay?' He kissed her on the cheek then beckoned to Max to move within speaking range.

'Max. I need you and Dina to run some air quality tests. I don't know why we haven't met anyone yet, but just in case I want to make sure the atmosphere isn't toxic.'

'Of course. We'll go find a water sample as well. Best to be on the safe side.'

'Do you have your rebreathers with you?' Jed asked.

'Yeah,' Max fumbled in his bag and drew out a pair. Kira looked on, wide eyed as Dina and Max put on the rebreathers and left the skimmer to begin running their tests.

'I don't have a rebreather, neither does Grace,' she told her husband in a small voice.

'Which is why you are staying in the vehicle.' Jed gave her a quick kiss and pushed her gently back into the skimmer. 'Let us run these initial tests. Make sure everything is safe before you come out.' He closed the skimmer door, leaving Kira to stare after him as he put on his rebreather and led Beta Team across the opposite side of the plaza to start scanning the buildings in that direction.

'Well, I guess that leaves us on our own then, Gracie.' Kira spoke aloud but the little girl didn't stir, the skimmer journey having lulled her to sleep. All Kira could do was watch the two teams of City Guard operatives venture out into the city and her friends standing in the middle of the plaza, scanning the air quality. It didn't take that long before Max took off his rebreather and gave Kira a thumbs up signal. She sighed. She probably ought to stay in the skimmer. Frag it. Grace was fast asleep, and it wasn't like she was going to go far. She carefully opened the door, closed it behind her and escaped into the plaza.

'Air's alright then?' Kira smiled up at Max.

'Yep. Nothing going on that I can tell. There's no insect life though, which is peculiar. We'd expect to register something at least.' He tapped his handheld a few times. 'We need to find a water supply now - any ideas, Kira? You've been to City 15 before, haven't you?'

Kira shook her head. 'No, but I did some research on the city before we left. If this is Central Plaza, then...' She spun round and pointed at a large, imposing building behind them with what looked like marble columns around huge wooden doors. 'That is the Academy Library - there will be a public water supply in there. Let me get Grace and I'll come with you.'

Dina frowned. 'Didn't Jed tell you to stay in the skimmer?'

Kira stared at Dina until she laughed self-consciously and raised her hands in defeat. Kira stalked away. She wasn't some fragile touchscreen; she was more than capable of looking after herself and her child. When she got back to the skimmer, Grace was beginning to stir. By the time Kira had checked her nappy and gathered together all the paraphernalia she needed to take with her, Max and Dina were standing outside, bored expressions on their faces. Kira felt even more irritated. People without children had no idea how long it took to do the simplest of things. Securing Grace into her carrier, Kira slammed the skimmer door shut and began walking towards the Academy Library. Max and Dina scrambled to catch up with her.

'Got everything?' Max asked.

'Yep.'

He took longer strides in order to get in front of Kira. 'I think I ought to go into the building first, you know. Just in case.'

Kira was still feeling annoyed, but she knew he was right. She didn't want to walk headfirst into danger and she certainly didn't want to put Grace in harm's way. Dina linked her arm through Kira's and smiled tentatively. Kira relaxed; she was overreacting. She squeezed arms with Dina and looked ahead to see what the library had to offer.

It was impressive. As Max swung the doors open, the interior gleamed in the light. Obviously, the library wasn't full of actual books, they were kept safe in Archive but, there were rows and rows of info booths with mounted screens and a variety of seating options from percher stools to full on recliners so students could browse the extensive cache of information in comfort. Max swept the general area with his handheld and turned back to the others.

'There doesn't seem to be anything wrong with the atmosphere. No heat signatures either. There's no-one here.'

'No-one?' Dina was surprised. She thought the citizens would've come here for safety from whatever had happened in City 15.

Kira walked over to the nearest touchscreen and tried to activate it. Nothing. The screen remained blank. 'Looks like there's no power here, either. Dead.'

They all jumped as the door banged behind them and Jed strode in with the rest of Beta Team. They took their rebreathers off when they saw the others weren't wearing them.

'I thought I told you to stay in the vehicle?' He ran an anxious glance over Kira and Grace.

'We're fine. Max checked the atmosphere, it's all clear here. No toxins. No people either, apparently.' Kira swept an arm over the interior of the library and pointed to the touchscreens. 'All dead.'

Jed nodded. 'We've found nothing either. All building sweeps are coming up empty. I'm waiting for Alpha Team to check in and then I'll report to Martha.'

Max cleared his throat. 'What's our next step here then?'

'Well, we'll release a couple of drones to do a more thorough sweep of the city, in case our initial once over missed anything. I'll program one to do the perimeter as well, see what we can find. It's up to Governor Hamble what we do after that.'

'Right.' Max nodded thoughtfully but whatever he was going to say was interrupted by the return of Alpha Team.

'Nothing to report, Sir,' said the Alpha Team leader.

'Right, let's head back to the skimmers and set up a makeshift camp. I want a perimeter with lookouts. We still don't know what happened here,' Jed said.

The City Guard operatives nodded and moved with purpose back to their skimmer to unpack the equipment and sleeping pods. Max, Dina and Kira trailed behind. This wasn't turning out to be quite the field trip they had expected.

'Ash, anything to report?' Jed poked his head into the front of the skimmer with the comms system.

'It's not good, Sir. The city mainframe has been locked out, just like ours, so there's no way of communicating with 42 or accessing 15's supply manifest. The best I can do is tell you where their Med Centre is then we can go and see if there's anything left to salvage.'

Jed nodded. 'Can you release a couple of drones on a city-wide sweep, include the city perimeter? I want to make sure we haven't missed anything.'

'Yep, doing it now.'

'And get me a link to the governor's office, will you?' Jed waited while Ash tapped quickly into his console and barely noticed the whine of the drones leaving the skimmer. *Where could an entire city of people go?* he thought. *Why wasn't there anyone here?*

'Here you go, Sir.'

'Thanks, Ash.' Jed looked at the small vid screen in front of him. The connection jumped twice before Martha's face appeared.

'Jed! You made good time. How is City 15? Have you met with the city officials yet?'

'Er no, not exactly.'

'Not exactly? What do you mean? What's happened?' Martha asked anxiously.

'There's no-one here. At least no-one obvious. We did a preliminary scan on approach, the city's forcefield was down. Upon entering we have been unable to establish any contact. There are no signs of life, Martha. Nothing.'

Martha looked blankly at Jed, trying to process the information. He waited for her to say something, but nothing was forthcoming.

'What do you want us to do?' he asked. Still no reply. 'Look, Martha, we're sending out some drones to do a city-wide scan, it might show something we missed. The air is clean so we'll send some teams out to investigate the medical centre, see if we can't find out what's happened.'

Martha fixed her gaze on him, finally coming to. 'Yes, yes, do that. Look for them, Jed. They can't have all disappeared. Not the entire city.'

'We will, Martha. I'll let you know as soon as we find anything. Over and out.' The connection jumped twice again as it disconnected making Jed suspicious. 'Was that a secure line, Ash?'

Ash looked up from his console. 'Secure into the governor's office but anyone with the right clearance could've listened in.'

'Can we try and get a more secure line next time? I don't know what we're going to find here, and the less people involved the better.'

'Yes, Sir,' said Ash.

Jed left him monitoring the drones and went to find the others.

Max was setting up a makeshift camp site for the non-operatives. It was nothing fancy, a few chairs and a small fold-up table. Somewhere for them to sit and wait a bit more comfortably than the inside of a skimmer. Kira had popped up Grace's play cube and the little girl was happily swiping at the walls, playing her interactive games without a care in the world. Dina handed Kira a cup of synth-caf which she took gratefully.

'What do you think has happened here?' Dina asked.

'I have no idea. It's all so...' Kira gestured round at the empty streets. 'So odd. I mean, where does an entire city go?'

They lapsed into silence, sipping their drinks and waiting. No-one sure what else to say.

It took about an hour for the full sweeps to come back. Ash called Jed over to the skimmer console.

'The entire city is empty, Sir. As expected, but see this shape here on the perimeter sweep?'

Jed nodded.

'That's a biomass signature. It's faint but it's large. Hopefully that will give us an idea of what's happened or at least where everyone has gone.'

'How far away is it?' Jed asked.

'About twenty minutes, in that direction.' Ash pointed south. The opposite side to the city from where the expedition team had entered.

'Alpha Team - on me. We're heading out - full gear, two minutes!' Jed barked then lowered his voice to speak to Ash again. 'I want you to stay here, keep monitoring the scans, let me know if anything changes.

Beta Team are on lookout patrol, so you've got fire power if anything happens. We'll radio in every half an hour.' He glanced over to Kira. 'Keep them safe, Ash.'

Ash nodded.

Jed picked up his gear and jogged over to the civilians. 'I'm heading out with Alpha Team, the perimeter sweep picked something up on the south side.' He addressed Max. 'Want to come, Doc?'

'Er, yeah, of course. Let me get my pack.' Max shoved his analyser into a nearby backpack and smiled crookedly at Kira, leaning in to kiss Dina on the head. 'Back soon!'

'What about me?' Dina was put out.

'I need you to stay here, with Kira and Grace. Keep monitoring the atmosphere. Let us know if anything changes but I'm sure we won't be long.' Jed gave Kira a quick hug and ruffled Grace's hair as she played in her cube before heading out with Max and the team of operatives.

'Do you think they'll be alright?' Dina asked watching them leave.

'Any synth-caf left?' asked Kira.

Dina looked at her in surprise then nodded and poured a fresh cup.

'Keep an eye on Grace, would you?' Kira took the cup and marched over to the skimmer where Ash still sat, eyes glued to his console. 'Hey, Ash, want some synth-caf?' Kira beamed at him.

'Er, yeah, sure. Thanks Ma'am.'

'Oh, call me Kira. We know each other well enough now. How are you doing?'

'Good thanks.' Ash smiled back at Kira, wondering why the sudden interest in his welfare.

'Family is important, isn't it, Ash?'

'Yes, yes of course it is. Is everything alright - is Grace okay?' Ash asked in alarm.

'Oh, she's fine, thanks. But it's important to know what our family is up to isn't it? So we can help to keep them safe.'

The penny dropped. 'You want to know where Alpha Team have gone. Here, look.' Ash showed Kira the dark shape on the perimeter of City 15's wall and Kira's stomach tightened in dread.

'Can we get a visual?'

'Um, yeah, I'm sure it will be alright.' Ash pushed a few buttons and Jed's cam feed sprang into life on the dashboard screen. Through a dark screen, it showed the skimmer passing buildings. They were still travelling to the southern side of the city. Ash and Kira watched the screen in silence.

'It's not exciting I'm afraid.'

'That's alright, Ash. This makes me feel like I'm there with him. Do you mind?' Kira gestured to the empty seat next to him and climbed into the skimmer. The passing buildings on screen began slowing down. Alpha Team had arrived at their destination.

Jed's voice sounded tinny as he ordered the operatives out the skimmer and into standard formation, with him in the lead. They passed through the southern wall gateway and Kira cried out in surprise.

Chapter 8

'What the...' Jed looked at the scene in front of him in disbelief. Bodies lay on the ground. Not moving. His eyes darted frantically. There lay an elderly couple, nestled into each other on the brown, stubbly grass. Beyond them, a young couple with a small baby, recipients of recent collection. A group of Academy students were clustered together, handhelds still in their hands but screens wiped black. And over there, a familiar profile. It was Agent Devereaux. Dead with the rest of City 15. It didn't look real. It was as if every citizen had come outside the city walls and lain down to die. There was no blood, no wounds, no immediately obvious signs of distress. Just groups of people.

A crow landed on one of the bodies and walked up to the face where it proceeded to peck at the corpse. The bird raised its head triumphantly, a bloody eyeball hanging from its beak. There was a retching sound to Jed's left as one of the City Guard bent over to empty his stomach.

'Sorry, Sir.'

Jed waved away his apology. He didn't feel too clever either. 'Max, what happened here?'

Max's usual sunny disposition had vanished, he looked pale under his permanent tan and was carefully scanning the area. 'Can you see this grass?'

Jed looked down at his feet in confusion. 'Yeah, there's grass. What of it?'

'What colour is it?'

'It's green, Max. For frag's sake! Don't we have bigger things to worry about than the colour of the grass?'

Max nodded to himself. 'Yes, it's green here but it's brown over there. As if it's been treated with something. Some kind of chemical maybe. But not airborne.' He checked his handheld. 'No, no toxins in the air.' He looked around swiftly. 'No immediate water supply either. So, were they doused from above?' He looked up. 'Possible, possible.'

'Max, what happened here?'

'Hmm?' Max didn't appear to realise he had been thinking out loud. 'I'm sorry, Jed. I don't know. I have a few theories, but I need to gather some samples and its delicate work. Could you go back for Dina for me? She's good in the field. I'll be fine here.'

Jed nodded and moved away reluctantly. He signalled for the Alpha Team Leader. 'Take the skimmer back and collect Dina please. Brief her on the situation and make sure she brings any and all equipment she needs. Take Hudson with you. I don't want his delicate stomach getting in the way. And don't, under any circumstances, bring my wife back with you.'

The operative saluted crisply and barked an order at Hudson. Without delay, the two men piled in the skimmer and sped away.

'The rest of you, I want a droid security perimeter set up outside the city wall. You lot watch inside the city. There may still be survivors,' said Jed.

'Sir, what happened here?'

'That is what we are going to find out. Now, get to work.'

The operatives fanned out, perimeter drones didn't take long to set up and Jed's team knew what they were doing. He was confident they would get on with it without the need for him to oversee them. He went back to Max.

'Max, I mean, have you ever...'

'Seen anything like this? Can't say I have, Jed. The only positives I can give you at the moment is that it looks like no-one suffered. But why they're dead I can't tell you.' Max shook his head. 'Without further tests, it's hard to say. It may be that time of death is fairly recent. I just don't know. I'm sorry.'

Jed nodded and the two men stood in quiet reflection for a moment, watching as more crows began circling the field.

'We need to get a body count. Is it safe?' Jed asked.

'It appears to be. I wouldn't touch anyone for now but walking past, getting a head count, should be fine. Shall I start this end?'

Jed nodded gratefully and strode off to the far side of the bodies. It was eerie. He kept expecting someone to move, kept thinking he saw something in the corner of his eye. But there was nothing. Each and everyone looked like they'd just lain down for a nap. It wasn't long before the two men met in the middle. They took a note of each other's numbers and then continued. When Max returned to the city walls with his final count, the skimmer had returned with Dina.

'I make it four hundred and twenty-eight - you?'

'Same.'

Dina hurried over, pale-faced but determined to do whatever she needed. 'I bought the full sample kit. I wasn't sure what you'd want to test.' Her eyes strayed over to the bodies and she swallowed. 'Do we know anything?'

'Nothing I'd care to share without further investigation. Come on, we've got work to do.' Max gave her a brief hug and then opened up one of the cases she had brought. He extracted protective suits for them both to wear. Dina prepared the sample kits and once they'd both suited up, the two scientists bent to their task. They took samples of skin, hair, sediment from under the fingernails, swatches of cloth, made soil and grass solutions as well as taking samples of any food they could see. They tried to be random with their sampling yet followed a loose grid pattern to ensure they had something to test from across the site. It was getting dark by the time they'd finished.

'Do we need to worry about scavengers, Max?' Jed asked when they returned.

'It's a distinct possibility. I'm surprised we haven't seen anything more than the crows if I'm honest.'

'I'll set up a stasis field, then. Can you do the tests here, or do you need to go back to the other skimmer?'

'I think we should test here. I'd hate to bring back any potential contaminants.' Max looked back at the bodies. 'Whatever it is, it was done deliberately and clearly by someone these citizens trusted. There are no signs of violence whatsoever.'

Jed nodded grimly and left Max with Dina to sort out a quick field lab in order to process their samples. He went to the skimmer and activated the comms.

'Beta Camp. Beta Camp, Operative Ash, are you there?' asked Jed.

'Receiving you loud and clear, Sir.'

'As am I.' Kira's voice sounded strained.

Jed closed his eyes in dismay. He hadn't wanted her to see this.

'Jed, are you still there?' asked Kira.

'Yes, I'm still here.'

'What happened?'

'I don't know, love. We're running tests. Max and Dina will know more soon. Is Grace alright? Are you okay?'

'We're fine. Martha's sent a message. She wants an update.'

'What did you tell her?'

'Nothing, we haven't replied yet.'

'Please keep it that way. I'll report in and give her an update, don't worry. I'll let you know when we find anything out. I need to have a private word with Ash now, is that alright?'

'Yes hon, of course. I'll speak to you later?'

'Yep. Love you.'

'Love you too.'

There was a crackle and a fair amount of static as Kira unplugged herself from the comms system and climbed out of the skimmer, taking Grace with her. The baby began whimpering, she'd been happily playing with the skimmer belts in the back. Kira distracted her with an old-fashioned chew toy she had in her pocket. Grace's teeth were coming in and at least this way she could enjoy gnawing on a brightly coloured toy rather than endure semi-painful injections into her gums. Besides, they weren't even anywhere near a working med centre and there was no-one here to make those injections. Kira felt miserable, her heart aching for all those dead people she'd seen through Jed's cam.

'Ash, try and keep Kira busy. Away from here. I don't know how long this testing will take but I don't want too much traffic between the sites until I know there is no risk of contamination. If something happens out here, I need you to take Kira back to City 42. Understood?'

'Yes, Sir.'

'How much did she see?'

'Er, the bodies, Sir. We both saw the bodies before I cut the feed. Sorry, Sir.'

'It's alright. I need you to send a message to Governor Hamble to contact me on a secure line. In the interim, you're in charge of Beta Team. Make the camp secure, get the pods set up for sleeping and make sure you rotate a night watch.'

'Yes, Sir.'

'Oh, and I need a headcount for City 15 when you get a moment please.'

'I have that, Sir. It's four hundred and twenty-eight according to the Archive log. It's the only thing I've been able to hack so far.'

'Right. Thanks. I'll radio in again at 1900 hours but if you see anything, anything unusual, you get in touch. Understood.'

'Yes, Sir.'

'Over and out.'

Kira and Grace were waiting outside the skimmer when Ash opened the door.

'What did he say?'

'Um, they are staying there to run the analysis. In case of contamination.' Ash replied.

'Okay, so we're meant to stay here and camp in the plaza?'

'That's about the size of it, Ma'am.'

'Don't Ma'am me, Ash. Kira is fine. Can we get a comms link back to City 42? To Martha's office?'

Feeling relieved that Kira wasn't asking about the other campsite, Ash nodded and turned back to establish a connection. He pulled the screen out and round so Kira could see from outside the skimmer. It took longer than expected but eventually he'd managed to open a channel to Martha's office.

'Here you go, it's ready when you are. Can you ask the governor to check her secure messages as well, please? There should be one from us, telling her to contact Captain Jenkins in the field.'

'Yes, of course. Thanks, Ash.'

'Also...'

'You don't want me to mention the bodies, do you?' asked Kira, her voice quiet.

'No Ma'am. We should wait for the Captain to report in.' Ash was relieved she'd mentioned it first. He didn't want to tell Mrs Jenkins what she could and couldn't say.

'It's okay, Ash. I won't tell her what we've seen. I just want to talk to her.' Kira peered through the static as the connection stabilised, she was barely able to make out a desk and a shadowy shape. 'Martha? Are you there?'

'Who is this?' It was a man's voice. Kira couldn't quite place him, but he sounded familiar.

'Kira Jenkins. Who is this? Where's Martha?'

'Ms Hamble is... unavailable for comment.' And the line went dead. Kira blinked in surprise. What was all that about? She turned to look for Ash to tell him what happened, but he was helping the rest of Beta Team make up the sleeping pods for the night. Perhaps Kira had tried at a bad time. She carried Grace over to one of the larger pods and was relieved to see her cube already set up. A good night's sleep. That's what everyone needed. Kira began sorting out her daughter for bed, hoping things would seem clearer in the morning.

ENCRYPTED MESSAGE FROM NEW CORP TO 7421
>>IMPLEMENT OPERATION VNC - CONFIRM<<

ENCRYPTED MESSAGE FROM 7421 TO NEW CORP
>>Absolutely confirmed! You won't be disappointed<<

Chapter 9

***C42N:** No news from City 15. Do you have an update? Sweep what you know.*

***SMAC:** The Governor will release a statement about City 15.*

***ANON17:** What's going on? They should've been there by now! Who's keeping secrets? Together they're telling us lies!*

'Who was that on the comms?' Martha frowned at Sean as she came back into her office. She was sure she'd seen Kira's face on the screen behind him, but the image had been distorted so it was difficult to know for sure.

'No-one, Ma'am. A poor connection with the news feed. Seems we're having static issues.'

'Wonderful,' said Martha. 'I suppose we'd better add that to the long list of things to resolve.'

'Yes, Ma'am.'

'That was meant to be rhetorical, Sean.'

'Yes, Ma'am.'

Martha pinched her nose and closed her eyes briefly. She had never warmed to Sean. He was efficient at his job, invaluable really, but he always seemed to be lurking at the edges of City 42's latest disaster. Ruth was convinced he was going to make a play for power but so far all he'd done was simply be everywhere. Usually before Martha had the chance to respond publicly and often with all the information at his fingertips, before she had even had chance to review the latest reports. With herself and Ruth feeling exhausted all the time Martha supposed it was important to have at least one fully capable team member. Stimulants only went so far and when their effects wore off, she often felt worse than she had before.

'Sean, have we heard from the expedition team at City 15 yet?'

'No, Ma'am.'

'So why did you sweep about the update? Without my authority?'

'There was a lot of negative chatter on the Sweeps, Ma'am. I thought we'd get ahead of it, for once,' Sean replied.

Martha couldn't fault his logic.

'Next time, run it past me first, please. All sweeps from government officials have to be pre-approved, you know that - it was your idea,' she said.

'Yes, Ma'am.' Sean cocked his head to one side as he checked his handheld. 'There is only one more meeting today - about the waste removal system. Why don't you let me deal with that and I'll let you know if the team check in. You look tired.'

Martha bristled slightly. She knew she looked tired, she didn't need to be reminded about it but her sensible side was leaping with joy at the thought of being able to leave the office early or at least on time for once.

'Are you sure you're happy to take that meeting solo? It's fairly routine, so there shouldn't be anything untoward and you can ping me instantly if anything...'

Sean broke in smoothly. 'It will be fine. Go. Relax. I've got everything covered.'

Martha felt like she was being dismissed but chalked it up to being tired and overreacting. She gathered her handheld and her jacket and smiled gratefully at Sean as they both walked to her office door. After all, he was only trying to help. She stopped at the door and turned to him.

'One more thing, Sean. How many babies are left in the growth labs?' asked Martha, hoping that she hadn't already asked him that question today. The earlier meeting had reminded her that there were still a few collections left. She was so tired, she thought if she closed her eyes, she might never wake up again.

'Seven, plus one unclaimed in the lab,' Sean replied.

'Unclaimed? How did that happen? Don't we have a waiting list?' Martha rubbed her temple with one hand, swiping her handheld with the other, trying to find the report.

'I can't speak for my predecessor.' Sean was calm, cool and collected, as always. 'But yes, there is an unclaimed child in the lab.'

He checked his own handheld. 'Looks like mixed race, four months old.' He looked up at Martha. 'I can have it reassigned.'

'It? Boy or girl, Sean?'

'Er, boy.'

Martha felt a pang of sadness. The same age as Pete and Ingrid's baby, if it had survived. And mixed race. She started to feel more awake as she considered the possibility. No. It couldn't be. Could it?

'Can you transfer that file over to my personal handheld please?'

'The orphan? Why?'

'Thank you, Sean. As for the babies left in the growth lab, have they all been assigned?'

The lines around Sean's mouth tightened momentarily before he replied. 'Yes, but we have eight families petitioning for new ones to be grown. They're getting more and more support daily for reopening the labs. Couldn't the orphan could be sent off to one of them?'

'I want to look into where he came from first. Thank you, Sean. Is there anything else?' Martha hoped not.

'No, Ma'am. But we do need to discuss the baby lab reopening...'

'Tomorrow, Sean. Tomorrow.'

He nodded, swiped his handheld and flashed a half grin at Martha as he left her to lock her office behind them.

Checking the time Martha realised that it was already past the end of normal office hours. She pinged her friend.

'Are Lucas and Sarah alright?'

'Yeah, they're fine. You finished already?'

'On way now, just need to check one thing.'

'Don't be too late.'

Martha smiled, feeling lighter. For once she had an earlier finish than usual and time to spend with her son. It was looking like a good evening ahead. As soon as she'd looked into the orphaned boy situation.

MSCHILD: *Governor Hamble consistently refuses to discuss reopening the growth labs. Who does she think she is? Just because she had her baby.*
It's not fair.

Sean smiled at the collection of people around the table. They were what was left of the Corporation supporters in City 42. Those who had held powerful positions before the uprising and had now been left to obscurity. It was true, some had made it onto Governor Hamble's advisory team but in low level positions. He would still have to be wary of them, if they didn't feel like they were being offered something more than they already had they might inform Martha of what was happening here today. And Sean wasn't quite ready for that, yet.

'Gentlemen, Ladies, let's open the discussion, shall we? First item of business - level of confidence in the current administration.'

Chapter 10

C42N: *Do you think we should have an election? Join the conversation in social hub beta.*

ANON17: *GOVHAM can't even attend her own meetings. What can possibly be more important?*

SMAC: *Waste management is at the top of the Governor's agenda.*

Martha pinged Ruth again but there was no reply. That was nothing new. She probably had her hands full with Sarah and Lucas. Martha felt a pang of guilt for not being at home with her baby, but their childcare arrangement was part of their working agreement. Ruth shouldered the bulk of childcare whilst Martha focused on her role as governor of City 42. So far, so good, but it was only a temporary fix. They would have to come up with something more permanent, especially if Martha's hunch was right.

She thanked Gaia that the baby lab was in the same building as her office, she didn't think she could bear to travel half-way across the city to find out whether she was right or not.

Inside the baby lab, the seven infants that were still growing pulsed gently within their synthetic cocoons. Such a peaceful environment thought Martha as she looked for a staff member. There should always be someone on duty but there didn't seem to be anyone here. A low rumbling noise was coming from the left-hand side of the room. Martha went over to investigate.

There, in the large cube, designed for sleeping multiple infants, a grown man lay snoring. A baby was tucked into the crook of his arm and was also peacefully sleeping. It was a surprising scene yet one that tugged Martha's heartstrings. She too wished she could nap so contentedly, with her baby but, she never seemed to have the time. She cleared her throat and the snoozing giant snorted then opened his eyes.

'Don't wake the baby,' he whispered as he extended the crook of his arm, releasing the child from his embrace and snuggling him into a pile of nearby blankets. Then there was a rather inelegant scramble for the man to get up off the floor and out of the cube. He stretched his neck making it crack loudly then peered intently at his visitor. 'Do I know you?'

'I hope so. Governor Hamble.' Martha extended her hand and smiled warmly at the surprised look on the man's face.

He hurriedly wiped his hands on his trousers and then double shook Martha's hand. 'Marty, Miss Hamble. An honour to meet you. Great to see you here. An honour, truly an honour. How can I help you? You don't need another baby, do you? I mean, you already have one, don't you.' He trailed off, realising that what he was saying wasn't coming out quite right. He tried again. 'Governor Hamble, what can I do for you?'

She smiled at him, letting him know that he wasn't in any kind of trouble, then pointed to the child in the cube.

'What can you tell me about this baby?'

Marty looked at the little boy. 'Well, bit of an odd one this. He came to us from Corp Medical, about four months ago. It was around the time of the terrorist attack, so we figured the family who were assigned him had perished in the tragedy.'

'Why wasn't he reported?'

'Ah, well, you see. There was a lot of confusion after the terrorist attack. We lost valuable staff members and then the computer lock-down didn't help. It was tricky to back track the files, find out who this little fella belongs to and then of course your governorship came into being and it all sort of, well...' He trailed off not entirely sure how to explain what had happened.

'This little guy got lost in the system.' Martha's eyes filled with tears. 'Has he been well looked after?'

'Yes, yes, of course. We all cherish him dearly. Mr Sean knows all about him of course. He told us the little lad would be reassigned soon.'

'I see.' Martha's brain whirled. Surely Sean should've bought this information to her sooner. It felt like he had been trying to hide it. But to what end? 'I'd like to take him home with me. What do I need to do?'

'Er, Governor Hamble, um, that's kind of you but, don't you already have a child at home?'

'I do.' Martha waited to see what the man would say next. She wasn't sure she should be doing this, but she needed to take the baby home. She had to know if her hunch was right.

C42N: *GOVHAM leaves Hamble HQ with new baby.*

MSCHILD: *How dare Hamble take that baby! She already has one. Who else is she screwing over? It should've been mine!*

ANON17: *Hamble is a baby-stealer. I bet she's still selling them.*

'Where have you been?' Ruth sounded harassed. The children had been irritable, when one stopped mithering, the other one started. It was as though they had an evil plan. She stopped in her tracks, mouth open in surprise when she saw Martha carrying another baby. 'Is there something you want to tell me?'

'I think this is Ingrid and Pete's child.'

Ruth went pale and dropped to sit in a nearby chair. 'How?'

'I don't know.'

'What the frag happened after I left today?'

'I was wrapping things up with Sean and I was discussing how many babies were left in the baby lab and who was still on the waiting list, when he mentioned an uncollected baby.'

'Uncollected? But that would never happen. I know of at least five families desperate for a child who aren't even on the waiting list.'

Martha clutched the sleeping baby closer to her. 'Is it still that bad?'

'Women aren't falling pregnant, Ma. It was just us, and nobody else since. There's a lot of unhappy people out there. And finding out about the hundreds of babies that were grown and shipped out has horrified everyone.'

'That's not my fault. No-one knew about it, just like the treated water.'

'Yeah, but the discovery was made under your government,' said Ruth. 'People are stupid, Ma. They blame you even though they know you didn't really have anything to do with it.'

'I know, you're right. We are trying to get to the bottom of it. The scientists are doing everything they can to figure out the long-term effects of the irradiated water and as soon as we crack the computers, we'll find out why the city was selling babies.'

'If we crack the computers,' said Ruth.

The women lapsed into silence as they considered one of the biggest threats to Martha's governorship. If she couldn't explain why Corporation had been selling babies without telling anyone and solve the problem of women not falling pregnant soon, then she was going to lose a huge support base.

'A lot of people still think you're doing that,' said Ruth.

'Doing what?' asked Martha.

'Selling babies.'

'And who exactly am I selling all these babies to?'

Ruth shrugged and turned her attention to the baby in Martha's arms. 'What makes you think it's Pete's?' she asked.

'Well, he's mixed race, not unusual I know but that is what their baby would've been. He's the right age, again - it could be a coincidence but when I spoke to the tech in the baby lab it seemed to click into place. The child was bought there shortly after the terrorist attack. The one that Ingrid...'

'But we all saw the footage, thanks to Anti-Corp. On the sweeps. The doctors confirming the termination of mother and child.'

'Yes, but we never actually saw them terminate the child, did we? And they never released the bodies for the funeral. We looked throughout Corp Medical for some kind of sign that those bodies had been kept and found nothing.'

Ruth rolled her eyes. 'Are you suggesting that Ingrid is still alive, as well? Died her hair brown, working in some menial job somewhere, biding her time before taking back her baby?'

'No, of course no. Don't be so melodramatic.'

'Look, I know you feel bad about the baby situation, but you can't latch on to an uncollected child and decide it's Pete and Ingrid's baby. You just can't. You need proof, Ma.'

'I am well aware of that. We are going to run a DNA test.'

'What? Here?' Ruth was incredulous.

'Yes.'

'How?'

Martha smiled grimly and went through to her bedroom. When she returned, a NanNan 3000 was following her.

'Where did you get that from?' Ruth was surprised.

'Kira gave it to me. It was the last present Ingrid ever brought her and Jed. I don't think either of them could bear to get rid of it, but they had no use for it either.'

'And it does DNA testing?'

'Let's find out, shall we?' Martha was still holding the baby in her arms and seemed reluctant to put him down. As if he would disappear if she did. One handed, she opened the medical diagnostics app on the NanNan, scrolling until she found what she was looking for. DNA test.

'Hang on a minute though, Ma. We don't have any of Ingrid or Pete's DNA and there is no central network anymore. How will the NanNan be able to tell us anything useful?' asked Ruth.

'Jed has their personnel files. Backed up into his personal system, which I have emergency access to. Kira told me about it when she caught him looking at their individual data streams.' Martha's voice went soft. 'Apparently it helped him feel connected to them still.'

'So, we're really doing this then? We're going to test this kid to see if it's Ingrid and Pete's?'

Martha nodded resolutely. The NanNan was ready, she hit the button for the scan and watched nervously as the android took a hair sample from the small baby. It took mere moments to process the hair and the results were soon available to download. Saving the data to her handheld, Martha went over to the main screen in the living room and accessed the Jenkins' personal system.

Ruth looked round nervously, knowing that Kira and Jed were miles away in City 15, but still feeling like she was prying into their personal privacy uninvited. 'I don't know about this, Ma.'

'Oh hush.' Martha navigated the system expertly, finding the DNA profiles quickly and then holding up the recent scan from the child.

The two women looked at the patterns in front of them. Despite Ruth being a history teacher and Martha originally a plant biologist by trade, it was clear that the child's DNA had matching bands with his parents. Ingrid Jenkins and Pete Barnes.

Martha looked down at the baby in her arms. 'He is. He's Pete and Ingrid's baby.'

Ruth looked like she'd seen a ghost. 'We have to tell Jed, and Kira. Can we get in contact with them?'

Martha nodded.

'I think so. They took the latest comm units with them so provided they're not in a location with high interference, we should be alright.'

'Do we tell them now?' asked Ruth.

'Yes. What are we waiting for?'

'I don't know but should we wait for them to come back? I mean, isn't this mission, expedition, whatever you want to call it, highly critical? Don't we want them focused on the field and not wanting to rush back home?' Ruth sounded dubious.

Martha was quiet. She wanted to scream it from the rooftops, but Ruth might have a point. It wouldn't do much good to distract Jed while he was on mission. They should wait before telling him. The baby began to fidget in her arms.

'Do we have enough supplies for another one?' Martha asked Ruth, just as Sarah, then Lucas began to cry.

'I guess we'll find out,' sighed Ruth. Being a mum to three babies loomed ahead of her and she didn't think she particularly relished the prospect.

ENCRYPTED MESSAGE FROM 7421 TO NEW CORP
>>*URGENT - Hamble has discovered the child, what do I do?*<<

ENCRYPTED MESSAGE FROM NEW CORP TO 7421
>>EVIDENTLY, YOUR INCOMPETENCE KNOWS NO BOUNDS. THE CHILD SHOULD'VE BEEN DEALT WITH MONTHS AGO<<
>>DO NOTHING. I WILL DEAL WITH IT<<

ENCRYPTED MESSAGE FROM 7421 TO NEW CORP
>>*What about City 15? They've found the bodies. I can't keep it from the Governor for much longer*<<

ENCRYPTED MESSAGE FROM NEW CORP TO 7421
>>DO WE HAVE SUPPORT?<<

ENCRYPTED MESSAGE FROM 7421 TO NEW CORP
>>*Yes, most of the old Corpers are open to the idea of a new leadership. What do you want me to do next?*<<

ENCRYPTED MESSAGE FROM NEW CORP TO 7421
>>HOLD THE VOTE<<

Chapter 11

'I want to do something useful,' announced Kira.

Ash looked up in surprise. He had thought she'd turned in for the night. 'What sort of thing are you thinking?' he asked cautiously.

'I think we should go look for medical supplies. After all, that is one of the reasons we came here in the first place.'

'True, but now is not the best time.'

'No, I don't mean now, this minute. Of course not. It's night-time. But I think first thing in the morning you, me, and a couple of operatives should go to 15's med centre and see what's left.'

'I'll have to get it confirmed with Captain Jenkins, but I can't see any real issue with it.' Ash thought for a moment. 'But doesn't Dina have the list of medicines we need?'

'I have a copy as well. I know what we need to get.' Kira was beaming. She hated feeling like she had nothing to do. This would give her purpose. It would also get them moving around the city which would divert Grace's attention from trying to eat skimmer tread and playing with spare Force riot gear stored in the transporters.

'I'll radio through, let you know.' Ash waited until Kira had gone before setting up the comms link with Alpha Team.

'Alpha Team, Alpha Team. This is Operative Ash, Beta Camp - do you read me? Over.'

'Loud and clear, Ash. This is Captain Jenkins. Switching to visual comms. Over.'

The vid screen in the transporter flickered and Jed's head came slowly into view. The connection wasn't the best but at least they had visual comms.

'How are things there, Ash?'

'Everything's fine, Sir. Perimeter is set, night watch has been organised. The team have eaten, those not on duty are resting. Your wife is fine, she's turned in for the night with your daughter. We don't anticipate any problems.'

'Good, good. Max and Dina are still running analysis here. It will probably take another twelve to fourteen hours. I need you to sit tight for now.'

'Actually, Sir, I was wondering whether Beta Team could visit the Med Centre, see if there are any supplies available. That was our secondary mission after all.'

'It was.' Jed thought for a moment. 'OK, do it. Take Kira and Grace with you, give them a protective detail at all times. I'm not expecting any trouble but that's usually when it hits. Do you have the list of meds we need?'

'Yes, Sir. At least, your wife does, Sir.'

'Ah. Okay.' Jed grinned. 'Try not to let her get you into too much trouble, Ash.'

'Yes, Sir.' Ash grinned back at his commanding officer. They said goodnight and signed off the comms. Nothing to do now but try and sleep peacefully until morning.

No-one slept much in the end and Beta Team broke camp early, packing everything away into one skimmer and emptying out the other one as much as possible. Everyone was feeling optimistic that they would be filling the empty skimmer's containers and storage areas with medical supplies.

'We are going to walk there, aren't we?' Kira asked Ash anxiously. She didn't feel like being cooped up in that vehicle for a minute longer than necessary.

'We can do, Ma'am. We won't all fit in anyway.' Ash smiled then looked down at Grace who was trying her best to pull herself up to standing on a nearby box of dried food pouches. 'What about Grace?'

'Oh, don't worry. I have her stroller. If we waited for her to toddle to the Med Centre, we'd be waiting all day.' In a few deft moves, Kira undid the contraption lying on the floor next to her and with an expert flick of her wrist, a fully functional stroller now stood waiting for its passenger.

'Impressive. They fold up well, don't they?' Ash said.

'Believe me, the first time you try to undo these things, it takes you half an hour but with a little one, you get plenty of practice getting the stroller in and out of skimmers.' Kira scooped up Grace and secured her into the seat. 'Are we ready?'

Ash nodded then called the order to move out. Half of Beta Team were to stay there and guard the camp whilst the rest were to come to the med centre, the empty skimmer following the human crocodile. Kira noticed with a faint smile that the most heavily armed operatives surrounded her and Grace. She didn't mind. This was Jed's way of making sure she was safe. The impending doom feeling she had had yesterday was gone. Kira knew Max and Dina would get to the bottom of what happened to the citizens of 15. Now she felt an odd sort of an excitement. She was on an exploratory mission to find much needed medical supplies and she could think of no reason why the supplies they were looking for wouldn't be there. It felt good to be part of such a positive action.

Two hours later, Kira and Ash sat dejectedly on the benches outside the med centre. It wasn't a particularly big building and it hadn't taken Beta Team long to scout through. It was completely empty. There were beds, tables and chairs but all the electronics had been ripped out and taken away. Every single medical cabinet was cleaned out. Not even a handheld med scanner had been left behind. Kira's mind was spinning. Who had the kind of manpower to empty out a med centre so efficiently? Was it Corporation? Had they somehow expected City 42 to send an envoy and instead of agreeing to meet, they had instead decided to remove anything and everything that could've been helpful? They had even taken small things like child plasters and the holographic stickers they loved so much. All the food hydrators had been shut down and without the city key codes, Ash had been unable to get anything turned back on. Thank goodness someone had considered that eventuality and brought enough supplies with them for the entire expedition.

Ash tapped at his handheld despondently. All his scans had come back negative. There were no harmful elements in the air or anything contaminating the building. It was completely empty.

'I suppose we ought to report into Jed.' Kira spoke at last.

Ash nodded and walked back to the still empty skimmer. So much for thinking they would be able to achieve something positive today.

'Alpha Team. Alpha Team come in please. This is Beta Team. Operative Ash speaking. Over.'

'Beta Team received, this is Captain Jenkins. Switching to visual. Over.'

The vid comm on the dash flickered once more into life and Jed's hopeful face looked out. He was soon frowning.

'The entire place is empty? Actually empty?'

'Yes, Sir. There is some furniture but otherwise nothing is left. No food, no water, no medical supplies and no access to the city's mainframe.'

'Any sign as to who did this?'

'No, Sir. There are no messages left behind or even any real evidence that anyone was here in the first place. Just an empty building.'

'And you're sure there aren't any contaminants?'

'No, Sir. No contaminants.'

There was a pause as Jed digested the information. They had completely failed in their medical re-supply mission and the mysterious deaths of the entire population of City 15 was the absolute worst possible scenario. Trying to explain what they'd found to City 42 wouldn't help Martha's position at all.

'Go back to camp, Ash. Get the skimmers ready to move out. We are on our way back as well. If you can think of anywhere else to investigate before we leave, let me know but I think we've done everything here we can.'

'Yes, Sir. See you back at camp, Sir.'

Chapter 12

'Are the results in?' Jed asked as he poked his head under the tarpaulin Max and Dina had rigged up to keep their testing under some kind of shelter. Not that the weather was bad here in City 15 but more to limit the chances of any kind of contamination. Dina's eyes were rimmed in red as she looked up at Jed and nodded. She didn't speak. She wasn't sure she could. Max squeezed her shoulder as he stood upright, his lanky form towering over both of them.

'They were poisoned. Looks like it came through the city's airways, most likely at some point in the evening which is why we see the grouping we do. Families together, students, work colleagues, that sort of thing,' he explained.

'What about the individual bodies?' asked Jed.

'I'm guessing they were gassed in the street. Anyone who was inside a building would've been affected at the same time,' replied Max.

'Do you think it was a complete city-wide assault? All at once?'

'It looks that way. From what we've been able to determine, time of death is pretty much the same across the board.'

'And they didn't miss a single person,' said Dina quietly. 'Our count matches the city's population. Every single resident was targeted.'

Jed was quiet for a moment then asked the obvious question. 'So why aren't they in their homes or wherever they happened to be when the airborne assault occurred?'

'I think, and this is pure conjecture, that the bodies were removed from the city and placed outside the city walls to be destroyed,' said Max. 'I believe the discolouration in the grass is down to an accelerant, I think we arrived before they were able to complete that task. Whoever they are.'

Jed shook his head in disbelief. He began pacing up and down. 'We interrupted them? Why haven't they finished us off as well? Where are they?'

Dina tapped one of the monitors, bringing up their analysis for Jed. 'It looks like the toxin they used was fast acting and quick to break down. In some of the later samples we collected and tested there were only trace amounts of the poison left. If we hadn't known what to look for, we would have missed it.'

'Are you telling me that they, what, ran out of poison?' Jed sounded annoyed. 'Whoever did this clearly doesn't have an issue with killing people. If we interrupted them, why weren't we attacked? There's not that many of us, they could have wiped all of us out with a few well-placed snipers.'

Max shook his head and gestured to the outer wall. 'I think the poison was released by drone, remotely.'

'Remotely? By whom?' asked Jed.

'I don't know.'

'Okay, so let's say for a moment that's exactly what happened, what about the bodies? How did they get here?' Jed jabbed a finger towards the southern wall that hid the mass genocide of City 15.

'I'm not sure,' Max replied. 'It may be that they were teleported somehow...' But Jed interrupted him.

'Teleported? What, some kind of alien ship came along and moved all our people for no fragging reason?'

Dina caught hold of one of Jed's arms that was gesturing wildly. 'Jed, hey, calm down. Listen to Max's theory. We're trying to help.'

Max had stepped back, a little out of the way, and he hovered protectively behind Dina. 'Look, Jed. I don't have the answers. I don't know what happened here but someone extremely powerful and resourceful gassed an entire city. For whatever reason the tech they used to do this is nowhere to be seen. But I think it's safe to say that they will be back. We should leave. Now.'

Jed stared at Max for a long moment, unable to fully comprehend what he was saying. 'Who would do this... not Corporation, surely?' he murmured.

'We don't know what Corporation is capable of,' Dina retorted. 'But Max is right, we need to pack up and leave. Whoever did this will easily be able to deal with us.'

Jed started nodding and began yelling instructions as he walked away from the makeshift lab. Alpha Team scurried to collect and stow all their gear whilst Max and Dina swiftly packed away all their samples and equipment.

'What about the dead bodies, Max?' Dina asked quietly as they worked quickly.

'Nature will do what nature does.'

Dina rubbed her eyes, trying not to cry. 'It feels so wrong to leave them out there like that.'

'I know but we can't risk the time it would take to dig a grave for them all.'

'We could burn them.' Dina turned her tear-stained face up to him, eyes filled with hope that he would agree.

Max nodded. 'Yes, we could burn them.' He hugged Dina briefly then jogged over to Jed and started gesturing expansively. Dina watched Jed's face as he listened to Max. There was a brief flash of pain and a tight nod. Max came back to Dina.

'He says pack it all up then he'll get his team to, well, do what's necessary.'

Dina nodded and wiped her nose on her sleeve. 'We'll bear witness and send their souls on. Gaia would want that.'

The camp quickly became nothing more than a skimmer and a few scuffs in the ground to show that someone had been there. Max had identified the accelerant as a simple bio liquid, one they themselves used for various things. There was more of it in the skimmer, so Jed ordered Alpha Team to spray the field of dead again. The team stood for a moment, heads bowed, keeping their thoughts to themselves.

Dina whispered a small prayer. 'Honour the earth, honour the sky, honour the water, honour Gaia who watches over us, honour all those we share this planet with. Send these souls to her loving embrace, we will remember you.' Her eyes filled with tears that sprang down her cheeks and fell to the ground, but she didn't care. She was horrified to have witnessed such an atrocity, scared that they might all be in danger and deeply saddened that so many people had lost their lives at the whim of an unknown enemy.

There was a soft whoosh as Jed lit the first fire. Other operatives lit strategic points around the grave site and they all watched for a moment as the flames took hold, licking greedily at the bodies.

'C'mon, we don't need to stay to the end.' Max steered Dina away from the mass cremation and gently manoeuvred her into the skimmer.

Soon they were all travelling away from the southern wall of City 15, back towards Kira and Grace and the rest of the team at Central Plaza.

Jed had tried to report in to Martha using the small comms system he had but there must have been some kind of interference as nothing was going through. He would have to report on the bigger comms array in the other skimmer. But he could do that as they left the city. After Max's revelation he had no desire to hang around and be the next series of victims to the nameless enemy that had destroyed City 15.

Jed was relieved when he saw Kira waving at him as they returned to the first camp site. It looked like Ash had received the brief message telling him to get everything packed up ready to go as there nothing in the plaza apart from the skimmer. He quickly ran over and swept his wife up into a huge hug. She looked a little surprised yet pleased.

'So, what happened?' asked Kira.

'We'll fill you in on the way but we're getting out of here first.' Jed looked back over his shoulder and called for Dina and Max to get in the second skimmer with him, Ash, Kira and of course, Grace. They would take the science supplies and kit bags etc. It meant all the operatives were travelling together but Jed wanted to have a frank conversation with Martha and the fewer ears listening in, the better.

'Roll out,' Jed ordered.

The two skimmers began travelling out of the city. A single spy drone watched them, unnoticed, from the sky above. Its recorder blinking, transmitting data back to its source.

Jed tried to connect his call through to Martha's office, but it wasn't until the skimmer had left the outer walls of City 15 that the connection held. Martha's face swam into view, her eyes looked bruised with dark shadows beneath them and her forehead was wrinkled in a concerned frown.

'Jed! Finally! We've been trying to get hold of you for hours. I need a report for the board. What is the situation in City 15?'

'Martha.' Jed nodded a greeting. He angled the comm screen so he could talk to her directly without either of them being distracted by the passengers in the back of the skimmer. He needn't have worried as Kira was grilling Max and Dina about everything they'd seen at the wall and wasn't paying attention to Jed.

'Obviously I'll file a full report but, I've never seen anything like it, Ma.'

Martha knew it must be serious, Jed rarely shortened her name except in times of crisis. She schooled her face to stillness and listened attentively as Jed began his report, relaying what they had initially found, namely the lack of any life signs.

'No life signs at all?' Martha interrupted then apologised and gestured for Jed to continue.

'Operative Ash discovered an unusual biomass signature outside the southern wall of the city so Alpha Team, including myself, Max and Dina went to investigate. Beta Team, headed up by Operative Ash and Kira, remained behind. They went to investigate the Med Centre but found nothing, it had been completely emptied of all supplies.'

Martha's face paled.

'Alpha Team travelled to the southern exit of the city and discovered the entire population of City 15 outside the city walls.'

Martha breathed a sigh of relief. 'What were they doing out there? They weren't hiding from us, were they?'

Jed shook his head. 'No, Ma. They were all dead.'

There was a long silence.

'Dead?' asked Martha in disbelief.

'Yes. Max and Dina performed a series of experiments to determine the cause of death and discovered it was an airborne poison.'

'But not everyone? Not every single person was dead, surely?' Martha interrupted again.

Jed gave a curt nod and continued with his report. 'Max's theory is that the bodies were removed immediately post-mortem by some kind of transporter technology although we have no proof of that.'

'Did they... were they... had they suffered?' Martha's eyes glinted wetly.

'They looked peaceful. Arranged in their family or friend groupings.'

'What did you do with them?'

'We burnt them.'

Martha blinked rapidly in surprise. And then slowly nodded. She knew he was right; they couldn't leave all those people lying out there. It was disrespectful to their memory. She could barely believe it though, such a huge loss of life. How was she going to tell the citizens of City 42 what happened? Could she keep them safe against a similar attack?

'How long until you get back?' she finally managed to ask.

'I'm not sure to be honest, we left in a hurry. We might regroup at

Camp Eden before heading back into the city - with your permission, of course. Max and Dina want the chance to put together their notes for the official report.'

Martha nodded distractedly, 'Yes, yes, of course.' She knew she had to tell Jed about Pete and Ingrid's baby but now didn't seem to be the moment. One of her aides appeared in the doorway of her office, gesturing frantically, desperately trying to get Martha's attention. She held up one finger to the young woman.

'Jed, I have to go. Is there anything else pertinent I should know before going into this meeting?'

'No, Martha. You have the facts. I am sorry to have been the bearer of such grim news.'

'And you've got no idea who was behind this?'

Jed shook his head. 'I can only guess at Corporation, but I never thought they would be this ruthless. Especially to a city that wasn't in direct uprising. It makes me nervous, Martha. I'm not sure that being in City 42 is particularly safe for anyone now. If they, whoever they are, can do that to City 15 without raising any alarms, it doesn't seem like a big leap to wipe us out as well.'

Martha privately agreed with him but said nothing further, instead she said her goodbyes and signed off. Her aide looked like she was about to faint with relief at finally being able to interrupt her boss.

Chapter 13

C42N: *An emergency board meeting has been called - what happened in City 15? Join the conversation in social hub beta.*

ANON17: *What's gone wrong now?*

SMAC*: Board meetings are normal. We will release the usual update after the meeting.*

CORPTECH2: *Give us back our jobs!*

MSCHILD: *Stop stealing babies! Give us proper leadership!*

ANON40: *Hamble to resign! Hamble to resign!*

'Ma'am? They've called an emergency meeting, Ma'am. Everyone's already there. And... and...'

'Yes, I know,' said Martha. 'The board is meeting as usual this afternoon. I'd hardly call it an emergency, Jess.'

'No, Ma'am, that's not it at all - they're all in there now, talking about you. And Sean is running the meeting. I really think you need to be there.' The young aide's brow was creased with worry.

At hearing that, Martha quickly stood up, gripping her handheld tightly, her thoughts spiralling wildly. She had thought the board were convening a meeting to discuss the results of the expedition out to City 15. But she hadn't submitted her report yet and that meeting was meant to be later this afternoon, not now. This sounded like something else. Martha started to feel cross. Who did Sean think he was, calling an emergency meeting like this without any consultation whatsoever?

Martha entered the board room with as much dignity as she could muster after practically running down the corridor. She slowed her pace in surprise at what she saw. Every seat was full, and Sean was running the meeting from her chair. He looked comfortable and at ease. Her stomach prickled nervously. She tried to make sense of what was happening. Ruth wasn't there, neither was Chief Minkov from Force and Dr Lee refused to look her in the eye.

'Ladies, Gentlemen.' Martha greeted the room then turned to her chair. 'Sean? Is there something I should know?'

'Martha, so good of you to join us.' Sean looked slowly around the room and then faced her with a little smirk and a small shrug of his shoulders. 'There doesn't appear to be a chair for you.'

Martha ignored his comment. 'Why has this meeting been called?'

'Well... we're voting.'

'And what exactly are you voting on?'

'Your fitness to be governor,' replied Sean with a look of satisfaction.

Martha blanched and steadied herself on the back of a chair. That was unexpected. Sean smiled.

'We were totting up the results. Now, where were we?'

An administrative assistant whom Martha recognised but couldn't for the life of her remember who he was, cleared his throat and gave a little nod in Sean's direction. 'On the matter of confidence in the current governor, we have twenty nays, three yays, one non-attendance and no abstainers.'

'I'm sorry Ms Hamble, it appears your government do not think you are fit to run this city. Someone will help you clear out your desk.' Sean gestured to one of the men standing around the outskirts of the room. Martha realised it was a security guard, but he wasn't dressed in Force uniform. His jumpsuit was emblazoned with a large C. Was he a Corporation security guard? Here, in her board room? What the hell was going on? She held up her hand to stop the guard's progress towards her.

'That won't be necessary thank you, Sean. I am perfectly capable of collecting my personal effects by myself.'

'It's not that we don't trust you, but you see, we don't trust you.' Sean jabbed a finger aggressively in her direction while addressing the room. 'Because, not only did Ms Hamble have full knowledge of the additional babies her father sanctioned for creation and sale - elsewhere, not here in City 42 where many families are desperate for children of their own,' he paused for breath. 'She removed a child from the baby lab yesterday, without going through the proper channels.' He turned to face her. 'When exactly are you going to return that child, Ms Hamble? Stealing the next generation from desperate families is one thing but when you already have progeny of your own, well, that's downright cruel.' Sean's eyes glinted maliciously at the sounds of disbelief that came from people sitting around the table.

Martha knew there was no point in defending her father or protesting that she'd known nothing about the sales. The entire city already knew the previous administration had been involved with the additional growth and sale of babies. It was the second horrific discovery her government had made after the water treatment. None of them had had any idea such practices had been occurring. Holding her dignity together, her voice barely shook as she acquiesced.

'Very well, an escort to my office would be acceptable.'

Martha turned and walked slowly back the way she had come, numb with disbelief. She thanked her foresight and the brilliance of Operative Ash that her entire system was backed up onto an independent drive that only she could access, from home. A backup system that she had never shared with Sean. He may think he had removed her from office, but he hadn't locked her out of her city, and she would do everything within her power to get to the bottom of whatever the frag was happening right now.

It took five minutes to empty out her office. She grabbed her fern, her Gaia statue and the few personal effects scattered about the room not even bothering to look at the computer or info grabs that scattered her desk.

The Corporation guard nodded towards the handheld Martha still gripped tightly.

'It's my personal one,' she replied crisply. He shrugged and stood to one side, allowing her to exit.

There was no-one around to watch Martha leave for which she was extremely grateful. She held her head high, carrying her meagre effects, and signalled for a nearby city skimmer to take her home. She'd be damned if she was going to use one of the governor ones. For all she knew it would deliberately crash or whisk her away to prison.

***C42N:** Shocking Update - Martha Hamble deposed!*
Who will run City 42 now?

ANON17: *Clear out the trash, make way for Corporation to return.*

MSCHILD: *What about the baby Hamble stole? Is she going to get away with it?*

SMAC: *I can confirm the removal of Martha Hamble as governor of City 42. More details to follow.*

She knew she was experiencing some kind of detached shock. She couldn't actually feel anything, she felt numb. Her brain was still trying to process the mass murder Jed had reported from City 15 and now, now she had lost her position as City Governor. And no-one knew about the murders. No-one knew about City 15. Or did Sean already know? And was that security guard wearing a Corporation uniform? Was Corp back in City 42? What the hell was going on? As all these thoughts swirled around her head, she considered the possibility that City 15 and the whole expedition out there had been a set up for Jed. Sean could use the massacre as a reason to get rid of the Force militia, those loyal to the city and to her. No-one had any proof of what happened out there. It would be one man's word against another, and Sean clearly had the support of the board plus some serious backing if Corporation truly was back in City 42.

She had always known it would be a possibility that Corporation would try and retake control, but she had hoped she would've had the chance to talk to their representatives and work out some kind of feasible arrangement. She didn't think the changes her government had instigated had been arduous for the city, if anything she had tried to do everything within her power to help each and every citizen.

She was still mulling over her options when she got to the apartment she shared with Ruth. She could hear children crying from outside the front door and she suddenly felt like her son, and the others, were in grave danger. She rushed into the apartment and saw at once all three children were in an expanded play cube. They didn't appear to be harmed in any way, but Martha rushed to soothe them. Lucas soon quietened down after a hug from his mother but Sarah and the as yet, unnamed little one, were harder to pacify. Martha tried calling for Ruth but there was no answer. In desperation she activated the cartoon ring around the cube and quickly all three children were absorbed by the bright colours and shapes, the odd sniff being the only sign that they were ever in distress. Putting Lucas down, Martha checked her room first, but it was empty, so she went through to Ruth's and found her crumpled body on the floor.

Chapter 14

C42N: *Who is fit to take over from Martha Hamble as Governor of City 42? Join the discussion in social hub beta.*

SMAC: *The additional security guards are here to keep you safe. A new Governor will be announced in due course.*

ANON17: *Good riddance to bad rubbish - let's bring Corporation back.*

MED4C42: *Diagnostic pods will remain closed. Supplies are still limited.*

ACAD: *All our courses will continue as normal. Students are expected to attend. Ruth Maddocks has stepped down.*

FORCE: *No comment.*

'Ruth! Ruth - can you hear me? Oh frag, are you okay? What happened?' Martha ran to where her friend lay on the floor, face down, and crouched beside her. Martha shook her shoulder gently but there was no response. She tried to remember her basic medical training, but she couldn't gather her thoughts together coherently. She wasn't sure whether she was doing the right thing or not but she decided to roll Ruth over on her side so she could see her face. Ruth was still breathing but her eyes were closed. She groaned a little at the movement and a small bottle rolled out of her hand.

Martha picked up the bottle and read the label. Sleeping tablets? Why was Ruth taking these? They were out of date judging by the label and as she shook the bottle slightly, Martha realised there were still a few left. These must be left over from Ruth's dabbling in the black market she thought. Before becoming pregnant Ruth had still indulged in the old-fashioned habit of smoking but of course that all changed with the baby. Ruth hadn't wanted to do anything to endanger the miracle.

Was Ruth taking these tablets because of Sarah? Martha knew the baby cried a lot at night, but she couldn't understand why Ruth had taken some now, during the daytime. Then the realisation hit her. Ruth had tried to take her own life. Tears pricked Martha's eyes, she felt awful - how could she have missed her friend's despair? Then Martha felt angry, Ruth could have endangered her son. It wasn't like Ruth to be self-involved; she had always put their babies first and had seemed happy to take on the childcare but clearly the arrangement wasn't working.

Fresh wails came from the children in the front room. Martha grabbed her handheld from her pocket, embarrassed to have only thought of this now.

'Run a basic health scan,' she ordered and then let out a relieved breath when everything came back within normal parameters. It looked like Ruth hadn't taken enough tablets to cause any permanent damage. Instead, she would have a good night's sleep for once.

Hurrying back to the children, Martha rang the only person she could think of who would be able to help at a moment's notice. Kira's mum.

'Thank you so much for coming, Jean.' Martha answered the door with Lucas on one hip and Sarah on the other leaving the third child sniffling in the play cube. She tried to smile but her bottom lip wobbled.

'Oh Martha, my dear. I can see we've got ourselves into a bit of a pickle here. You've got your hands full and no mistake. Not to worry, love. I'm here now and we'll get everything in order. I've brought along Malcolm with some bits and pieces, so I'll stay with you tonight. He can help us with Ruth. Here, give me Sarah.' And she held her arms out for the little girl who went willingly.

Jean took charge, ushering Martha to the sofa and tucking her son into her arms so they could comfort each other. She motioned for them to stay where they were as she went through to check on Ruth, her husband in tow, Sarah still being cuddled.

Martha felt herself calming down, helped by the peaceful slumbering of her son. He had quietened as well, thanks to being held by his mummy. Thinking about that connection bought tears to her eyes as she watched the other little boy in the play cube who would never know his parents.

There were some muffled noises and a loud grunt from Ruth's room then Jean and Malcolm both came back through, Jean pulling the door close so as not to disturb Ruth. She caught Martha's eye and smiled.

'I expect she'd sleep through a fire alarm but just in case. Snoring like a bear she is. It's best she gets her rest.'

Malcolm walked over to Martha and gave her hand a brief squeeze. 'Bad business, love. Try not to worry, we'll get through.'

She struggled to blink away the tears. She'd always liked Kira's dad, but it was when he spoke to her like this that she really missed her own, gruff father. She watched as Jean directed her husband to set up two sleeping cubes in the front room whilst she busied herself making up three bottles and some synth-caf. She somehow managed to entertain Sarah and unpack the bags she'd brought with her at the same time.

There were little packages of dried biscuits, some desiccated fruit, nuts and best of all, a tin with some freshly baked biscuits. Despite the food issues City 42 had been having, somehow Jean never missed the opportunity to bake and bring a little something round when she visited. When it was ready, Jean brought the synth-caf over to Martha and a bottle for Lucas when he woke, then nestled Sarah and two more bottles in the other sofa before going to pick up the new baby.

'So, who's this extra little one then?' she asked as she sat down with a baby either side, deftly feeding them both their milk. She waited patiently for Martha to answer, checking on the children and sipping her synth-caf, seeming to have an extra pair of hands as she dealt with burps, dribbles and managing not to spill her own drink. When they'd finished, Jean snuggled both children sleepily into the opposite corners of the sofa and hemmed them in with cushions, letting them fall sleep.

Martha looked down at her son. She cleared her throat, trying to think of how to tell Jean who the extra child was.

'Oh, Jean. Where to start? The baby - it's Pete and Ingrid's. I don't know how he survived but we ran a DNA test to confirm it. I don't even think he has a name,' Martha said, close to tears. 'And then I found out Ruth has stepped down from Academy, but I didn't know she was struggling, she never said a thing. I came home, found her like that and... and... rang you.'

'Have you told Jed yet? Or his parents?' Jean asked.

Martha shook her head, horrified that she hadn't yet thought about contacting Jed or his parents, Gretchen and Henry Jenkins.

'Right then.' Jean extracted herself out of the sofa and put her cup down. 'I'll talk to Gretchen; she can be a bit prickly at the best of times. Probably best if I break this news rather than you. I see you've had a lot of sweeps today.' Jean waited expectantly for Martha to deny the obvious rumours that were flying over the sweeps but when she didn't speak and looked at Jean in mute appeal, she tutted to herself. 'Well, well, well. They finally took some action. I can't say I'm surprised. I always thought Corporation gave up too easy. That's not to say you haven't done a fine job my dear, a fine job, but they weren't about to loosen their claws from our city. That's for sure. Well, what will be will be I suppose, we'll have to ride it out whichever way it goes. But don't worry, my love, me and Malcolm will make sure nothing happens to you or the children. Do you want me to see to Lucas as well, love?' Jean asked gently.

Martha shook her head to clear the fuzziness. 'No, it's okay. I'll do it. But I think I'll turn in as well. Do you need me to do anything?'

'No dear, it's all under control. But, do you know when Kira and Jed will be back?'

'No, not yet. They're coming back from City 15 now. They should check in when they get back to Camp Eden. Should I stay up for that, do you think?' Martha dithered, not knowing what to do for the best.

Jean pushed her gently in the direction of her room. 'You go get some rest. Take your handheld, that way you'll hear the comms and if it comes in here, I'll come get you. We'll tell him, don't worry, dear.'

Martha nodded gratefully and let herself be ushered into her room. It was blissfully dark and quiet. She lay Lucas in his cube and without bothering to undress, fell into her own bed and was asleep within minutes.

Jean poked her head into Martha's room and nodded with satisfaction. Then she squared her shoulders, about to make a terribly difficult phone call to Jed's mother. She hoped the woman wouldn't ask too many questions because she had no answers to give.

'Gretchen? It's Jean. Jean Bishop.'

'Yes, hello? It's rather late for a social call, isn't it?'

'There's something important you should know.'

'I already do. That silly young girl got herself more than she bargained for and has been voted out of office. Just because she was Hamble's daughter, doesn't mean she was the right person for the job.'

'Hmm, that's not what I wanted to talk to you about.'

'Where are you? Are you at her apartment? Is Jed there? That boy has been avoiding my pings. I don't want him caught up in any kind of scandal.' Gretchen patted her perfectly coiffed hair. 'He does have a career ahead of him, you know.'

'Jed's not here, but I do need to speak to you.'

Gretchen leaned in closer to the vid comm. 'Is it true that Martha stole a baby from the growth lab?'

Jean sighed. 'It's your grandson.'

'I beg your pardon.' Gretchen's face had gone white, her lips pinched, eyes round. 'Is this your idea of some kind of dreadful prank?'

'No.' For once Jean Bishop was at a loss of what to say, so she stayed quiet.

Gretchen's nostrils flared wildly as she controlled her grief and anger, then she abruptly cut the link.

'You'd better put on another pot of synth-caf, love,' Jean said to her husband. 'I think we'll have some visitors soon.'

ANON40: *Lots of people visiting Hamble's apartment - how much longer does she get to stay there?*

C42N: *Both Kira & Jed Jenkins' parents have visited Martha Hamble's apartment. Did something terrible happen in City 15? Sweep what you know!*

Chapter 15

'Can we stop at Camp Eden?' asked Kira. She was still feeling nauseous at the thought of the deaths they had seen and the cremation they'd performed. She wanted to replenish her spirit by spending some time in the lush green of the science camp, revisit the orchards and tune in to nature. If she was lucky enough, she'd get to see Gaia again, too. It seemed like the most obvious place to try. There wasn't much nature to be found in City 42, yet.

'Yes, love. I want to reconnect to the sweeps, get a handle on what's been happening while we were away, before we get back to the city,' Jed replied.

'Why? What did Martha say?'

'It's not what she said, it's how she looked. Something's going on.'

Kira laughed softly. 'Don't forget she's got two babies keeping her awake on top of running an entire city. Do you remember how tired we used to get?'

They both looked fondly at Grace who was staring out of the skimmer window, cooing and gurgling at unseen magic.

It didn't take long to get to Camp Eden. Both skimmers were fully charged, and everyone wanted to get as far away from City 15 as quickly as possible. The camp was, as always, a place of peace and tranquillity. Moham was at hand to greet them all. The operatives sloped off to the mess tent, eager to get a hot meal while the others, including Ash, congregated in the relaxation area. Moham bought over real tea and some fresh fruit for them. Kira felt so relaxed that for a moment, she wished they could forget everything else and live here, in this peace, forever.

'Are those new, Moham?' Kira pointed to the beehives that nestled in the far corner of the camp, near the orchard.

'Yes, we have been fortunate - a queen has taken up residence in the first hive so it shouldn't be long before we have honey to share,' replied Moham, grinning.

'That's wonderful. Any sightings?' She didn't have to be specific, Moham knew she meant Gaia. He shook his head sadly.

'Aha!' exclaimed Ash, making everyone jump. 'Sorry. Finally got connected to the Sweeps.'

They all opened their handhelds and began to check their messages and most importantly the newsfeed. Then everyone started talking at once.

'Martha's been removed from office?'

'She stole a baby? That can't be right.'

'Corporation are back in City 42? What the frag happened in the last two days?'

Kira, Dina and Jed were all trying to talk over each other, shouting louder and louder to make themselves be heard.

'HEY! ENOUGH!' Max's shout startled Grace so much, she began to cry. Kira shot him a wounded look. 'I'm sorry but we won't get to the bottom of anything with you lot shouting over each other. We've all got different top news stories so let's share what we have and try to sift the fact from the fiction. Alright?'

There was a bit of grumbling, but the others knew Max was right.

'Who goes first?' asked Kira.

'Why don't you start? Read your private messages first.' Max replied, then turned to his left. 'Ash, can you keep track of it all please?'

Ash nodded.

'Okay. Personal messages - I've got one from my mum, well several actually. Hoping we're alright, asking about the meds - she's running low.' Kira paused to try and stop tears from overcoming her. 'She says something awful has happened to Ma... wait, and to Ruth. That was her last message.' Kira frantically scrolled. 'I don't have anything from either of those two though.'

Dina shook her head, 'Me either, I've got nothing useful in personal. Jed?'

Jed looked grave. 'I have an emergency message from Martha on a private channel. It's not good news. She's been ousted as governor. Corporation security guards were in place at Hamble HQ and it seems Sean MacIntyre has taken over, in the interim. Nothing about Ruth.'

'What do we do? We should get back there - it has to be some kind of mistake, doesn't it?' Dina pleaded, looking at the others for reassurance.

'We stay put. Martha says to contact her as soon as we can.' Jed turned to Ash. 'You set up her backup system, didn't you? Can you get me access, see if we can't get a decent comms link established? Off the main network?'

'Of course.' Ash nodded and let Max lead him over to the tech centre of the camp. Everything was fairly high-end so it wouldn't be too difficult to establish a secure connection.

'Kira, reply to your Mum. Let her know we're all okay but keep it vague. Ask her to wait before sending anymore messages. We don't want too much chatter on an open channel,' Jed said and Kira began tapping away, trying to sound light and airy in her message when inside she was panicking.

'Dina, what sweeps have you got? Dina!'

Dina jumped; she'd been miles away.

'Um, I don't... what?'

'Sweeps. What are your top sweeps?' asked Jed.

'Right.' Dina looked down at her handheld and started reading.

C42N: *Do we want Sean MacIntyre in charge? Do you think someone else would be a better fit? Do you agree with Hamble's ejection? Join the discussion in social hub beta.*

ANON17: *Don't bother coming back, Jenkins. City 42 needs no protector but Corporation.*

SMAC: *I have the best interests of City 42 at the heart of everything I do. Bringing back Corporation will help everyone. More supplies - more tech - safety.*

ACAD: *We remain open to students. New leadership to be determined.*

ANON17: *GOVHAM stole a baby! Why hasn't she returned him?*

C42N: *Hamble is not returning the baby. Sweep your views.*

ANON40: *When will we actually start getting fresh supplies? So far nothing has changed.*

CORPTECH2: *Finally! With Corp back we will be able to rebuild and bring you the latest tech.*

MSCHILD: *Why hasn't SMAC confirmed the reopening of the baby labs? I want my collection! Tell Hamble to bring back that baby!*

MED4C42: *We still do not have any new medical supplies. We are NOT turning diagnostic pods back on.*

Dina finished reading. 'ANON17 is such a dick, Jed. Ignore him,' she said.

'Don't worry, Dina. I've had worse. Your top sweeps pretty much match what I've got as well. No real difference. None of it makes any sense though,' Jed replied. 'It looks like Sean doesn't have the whole city convinced although there's more Corporation support than I expected. And why would Martha steal a baby from the lab?'

'She must have had a good reason. There's no way Ruth would want another one in their flat,' replied Dina.

'I know what you mean. Has she said anything to you?' Kira asked in concern.

Dina shifted uncomfortably. 'Well... I know she's not been coping too well. Feeling tired, super emotional, like she doesn't know what she's doing or what's the best way to do things. You know, that sort of thing.'

'But she won't ask us for help so what are we supposed to do?' Kira felt sad. Surely, she would have been the perfect person for Ruth to talk to. She'd recently gone through the same thing Ruth was going through. Well, mostly. Apart from the birth. And Ruth had had Martha to support her through that. It had all gone well at the med centre, despite everyone involved having to use centuries old resources from Archive to ensure best practice and the highest level of care. But it had all gone fine. And Sarah was such a lovely baby. As was Lucas.

'Look, I don't know why she hasn't said anything. Have you asked her how she's feeling? Maybe she doesn't want to bother you.' Dina shrugged. 'I thought they were going to get some help, you know, what with Martha working so hard and being away from Lucas - which I know she doesn't enjoy very much either. They were talking about your NanNan.' Dina faltered and looked at Jed.

'It doesn't work,' he replied gruffly and stood up, leaving the two women to their conversation.

'He doesn't mean anything by it, Dina.' Kira watched her husband walk away, feeling once again his pain at having lost his sister and best friend.

'Do you think Ruth and Martha are alright?' asked Dina.

'If I know Ash, we will have a secure comms connection with them soon and we'll be able to find out for ourselves. Let's try not to worry.' Kira turned her attention to her daughter and tried to quieten the feeling of dread building in the pit of her stomach.

Ash hurried over with a larger comms screen than the usual handheld. 'Here, use this portable. It's got a faster uplink.'

'And this will be secure? Martha and no-one else?' asked Jed as he took the device.

'It's as secure as I can manage. Provided no-one suspects Martha of having a backdoor system, we should be fine. If Corporation have only moved back into the city, it will take them a while to sift through everything. Even they don't have unlimited resources.' He paused, considered what he'd witnessed in the past few days. 'Do they?'

Jed said nothing. Instead he pinged Martha. Kira and Dina came to join him, and everyone held their breath waiting to see if she would answer the call.

'Hello? Jed, is that you?'

'Yes, Martha. It's me. Are you alright? Can you talk?'

'Yes, yes I can talk. Let me try and improved the screen resolution.' The vid screen went black then fuzzy and then a clear image swam into view. Martha looked pale, red-eyed yet the sight of seeing her friends, her family, seemed to bolster her. She gave a brief smile in greeting, then began to speak.

'After you checked in with your mission report, Jed, I was alerted to an emergency board meeting that had been called in my absence. At first, I thought it was the meeting I was meant to brief everyone about the results of your expedition however it turned out to be something else entirely. It appears Sean MacIntyre has been building a base of support with those still loyal to Corporation and those dissatisfied with my governance. A call of no-confidence was issued, and I have been removed from office.'

There was silence from the team at Camp Eden as Martha confirmed the sweeps. They all sensed there was more to come.

'I can confirm that a Corporation security officer escorted me from the premises. I do not know how long there has been a Corp presence in the city. It could have been a spare uniform dug out to inspire confidence. I believe Sean and the rest of them are too short-sighted to see how dangerous it is to invite Corporation back into the city without any kind of accord drawn up. I think we have to assume that Sean is a Corper, through and through.'

There was murmured ascent through the group watching.

'Have you seen the sweeps?'

Kira nodded and then realised that Martha might not be able to see her on the edge of the vid comm screen. 'We've seen the sweeps,' she said. 'Or some of them anyway. Martha - they're accusing you of stealing a child.'

'I know.'

'Well... did you?'

'Of course not.' She paused. 'Technically yes, but I had good reason.' Martha turned to focus directly on Jed. 'I found Pete and Ingrid's child.'

The colour drained from Jed's face and he would've dropped the vid comm if Ash hadn't reacted quickly and caught it. There was a scrambled moment of connection as the link dipped and then re-established itself. Kira tried to get Jed's attention to see if he was alright, but he appeared unresponsive. Dina tugged her sleeve.

'Can you believe this?' she whispered.

Kira shook her head in bewilderment. This was huge. The baby survived. Somehow survived. And had been left in the growth lab all this time. Why didn't anybody know?

'How do you know?' Jed's voice sounded wooden, unemotional.

'We opened your NanNan and ran a DNA test. I accessed your personal records. I apologise but I needed to be sure.'

Jed cocked his head to one side, unable to process the information. After a moment he shook his head. 'I just need...' he began to speak but faltered and walked away. Kira took a half step after him but stopped, unsure if she should intrude.

'I'll go with him,' Max said and followed Jed who stumbled a little in his shock. Kira moved closer to the comms screen.

'Who else knows about this, Ma?' she asked.

'Ruth and your mother. I needed some help here.'

'Of course - three children...' but before Kira could finish Martha interrupted her.

'It's not just that. Kira... Ruth... she took an overdose.' Martha's voice broke as she spoke the words.

'She didn't?' whispered Dina.

'Is she... did she...?' Kira couldn't bring herself to ask.

'She's fine. Well, no, she's not fine. She's a mess but she is alive. I want to send her, your parents and the children out to Camp Eden. I need you to stay there, for your safety but also to keep you out of whatever is happening here in the city. It's not safe for us - again. I don't want to put anyone at risk.'

'What about you?' Dina realised Martha hadn't included herself in that plan. 'Are you intending to stay in the city? They're going to crucify you for everything that has gone wrong, is going wrong. That's not fair!'

'They're going to do that anyway, Dina. At least this way I can try and gather some loyal supporters and protect the rights of the citizens of City 42 as best I can.'

'But Martha...'

'It's okay. I'm counting on you to find us the help we need.'

'Me?'

'All of you. Kira, you still have plans for the nearest cities in the area, don't you?' asked Martha.

'Yes. But why...?' Kira frowned then answered her own question. 'Oh, you want us to try and establish contact somewhere else.'

'Yes, I do. And this is where I think you should go,' said Martha as she outlined her plan.

Chapter 16

'Jed, are you alright?'

Kira had gone to find her husband. She smiled gratefully at Max who dipped his head and went back to Dina and the last of the hot tea.

'Jed?' Kira called his name again.

He turned his face to look at her.

'Can you believe it? I mean, it's something I hoped for. I could never accept that the doctors would terminate a new life like that. It felt so wrong. Something that even Corporation couldn't do. And I was right. I was right, Kira. My nephew - he's alive!' Jed smiled crookedly at her. He was obviously still fighting the grief of losing his sister and best friend but now at least he had some family back. He clutched her arm. 'Do you think he can, I mean, would he... should he come and live with us? Do you think?'

Kira shook her head, unsure. 'I don't know, love. I don't know who the legal guardian would be. It might be your mother.'

'Oh, no.' Jed shook his head. 'Oh no, no, no. She can't raise him. She doesn't raise children well.'

'She didn't do such a bad job with you.'

Jed barked a laugh and then went for his handheld. 'I have to talk to her.'

Kira stopped him. 'You can't, love. Not yet. We need you to come back to the conversation, Martha has some ideas. You need to listen.'

Jed looked at her, not understanding at first and then remembering everything that had happened. It was difficult to focus, he still felt giddy at the good news. 'Right. Yes. What happens next. Of course. Come on, then.' He took his wife's hand and together they walked back to the others.

'Jed.' Martha sounded relieved when she saw him. 'Are you alright?'

He nodded. 'Can we see him? My nephew?'

Martha shook her head.

'He's asleep I'm afraid and you probably ought to speak to your mother. She's not happy about the current situation,' Martha said. 'I'm trying to find out the legal standpoint but nothing like this has ever happened before and I only have access to limited resources.'

'I want him with us. With Kira and me and Grace. I'll deal with my mother.' Jed was emphatic.

'Okay. Good. Now, listen. This is what I think we should do. I will send the children, Kira's parents and Ruth out to you guys at Camp Eden. Max, is the camp secure? I mean, do you have the resources to keep the children safe?' Martha asked.

Max ran his hands through his hair. 'Well, we have enough space and we can feed them no problem. But this isn't a military camp, Martha. We don't have weapons or anything like that.'

'No, I didn't think you would have. Jed, I've been in touch with Chief Minkov. He is sending out the rest of your militia team, fully equipped with all their gear and vehicles.'

Kira interrupted. 'Won't that leave the city exposed?'

'Corporation are already here, Kira. Besides the chief feels the rest of the Force operatives he has are still loyal to the shield and will do their best to protect citizen rights. They have their own riot gear and supplies. We will keep the citizens safe.'

'You're definitely not coming?' asked Jed.

'I need to stay here. If nothing else I need to keep attention away from you and try to prevent Corporation dismantling everything we've worked so hard to achieve. I still have friends. I won't be alone.' She leaned into the vidcom. 'Look after Lucas, won't you?'

'Ma! Of course we will and we'll all see each other soon.' Kira replied, eyes shining.

'What's our next move?' Jed asked. 'I assume you are not sending the rest of my team out here to sit on our hands?'

'No. I want you to try and make contact with another city.'

'Which one?' Jed was intrigued.

'As I told the others, I've been thinking about that,' said Martha. 'We should probably split our focus and send one team to City 9 by the coast. I know it's a Corporation stronghold, but they may have access to additional transportation and information about what's beyond our country. If we've started to heal, there's a chance the rest of the world has too. We can then send a second team into the mountains to find City 36. Corporation might not be that far north.'

'What about what happened in City 15?' asked Jed.

'We can't let that stop us from finding out more information. We need to know if Corporation rules everywhere in our country and whether they have a presence abroad. We need to know for sure who was behind City 15. We can't let the death of all those people be in vain. The rest of the cities - if they still exist - have to know that this kind of corruption cannot be allowed to rule our lives, and our children's lives. We have to try.' Martha waited to see what her friends would say.

Jed nodded in agreement. 'I'll wait until the rest of my team gets here and then we'll decide who goes where. Are your comms secure?'

'They are for now. Ash and I set up an enclosed comms ring a while back. It should be untraceable.'

'Who do you have to help you, Martha?' Kira asked in concern.

'Ben is dropping by.'

'Ben? I don't think that's a good idea,' said Jed.

'You may be right, Jed, but at the very least he knows how to stay under the radar and that is something we all need to do. Look, I have to go, the children...' Martha looked away from the console for a moment. 'They'll be with you tomorrow morning. Take good care of them.' And she signed off, not letting anyone respond to her final words.

The group drifted away to chat amongst themselves and digest the news leaving Kira and Jed alone.

'I'd better sort out the operatives. Are you alright with Grace?' Jed asked.

'Yes, I can manage. Come and find me when you're done.' Kira gave him a quick kiss and took Grace back to the cohabitation tent. She had just put Grace down for the night when the others came back and made themselves comfortable on the other side of the sleeping area. Jed's team had decided to make camp on the other side of the clearing and use their pods, so it wasn't too crowded in the tent.

'Kira? You all done?' Jed asked quietly.

She nodded and came with him to sit with the rest of them, casting a quick glance back at Grace's cube. The baby was already fast asleep.

'We need to know about these two cities Martha wants us to try and communicate with. Did you happen to download the details before you left 42?' Jed asked his wife.

'Of course I did. I can forward the full files over to your handhelds, but I can give you a brief outline now if you like.'

'Yes please.'

'City 9 is based on the southern coastline of the country. It's where a lot of trade and travel used to occur, before The Event I mean, so the infrastructure for water transport should still be available.'

'Will there be boats?' Dina's eyes sparkled in excitement.

'I don't know, maybe. But the real problem will be finding someone who knows how to operate them. It's one of the lost skills unfortunately. Anyway, City 9 have, or had, different technology to us, they were originally working on cleaning the seawater - I don't know how badly the HER weapons affected the ocean. Or to what extent marine life was afflicted. The rising sea temperatures have of course changed the entire ecosystem. It's mainly jellyfish in that region, or at least it was.'

'Jellyfish eh, bet they make you feel wobbly,' joked Max.

Dina poked him in the arm as the others rolled their eyes. 'I think they are edible,' she said. 'If prepared correctly. It's something else to try, I guess.' However breezy she sounded Dina didn't look convinced.

'What do we know about the Corporation presence in City 9?' Jed asked.

'It's a Corp controlled city so I expect they will be everywhere. From the reports Archive had, City 9 has more tech than we do but otherwise standard Corporation stuff. I'd be surprised if Corporation didn't have all the coastal regions under their control to be honest. One thing we can hope is that they haven't treated their water supply the way they did in 42. We might see natural reproduction in action.'

There was a brief silence as the group digested the information Kira shared.

'What about 36 then, up in the mountains?' asked Max.

'That is in completely the other direction. If you consider the entire map of our island, the two cities couldn't be further apart. It will take us at least a day and a half to travel up there. Not knowing what the travel routes are like, of course.'

'It seems like it's in the middle of nowhere,' Dina commented as she looked at the map on her handheld. 'Why would they establish a city up there?'

'It sort of is but that could work well in our favour,' replied Kira.

'The citizens of 36 are more likely to be self-reliant and I think there's a greater chance for them to be out from under the rule of Corporation. It would have been difficult to resupply up there initially, so their technology is either state of the art or incredibly basic. They might have rediscovered some of the old trades and industries. It's definitely where I'd go if I was looking for a safe place away from Corporation. I think 9 puts us close to potential trade routes which, let's face it, Corporation will be all over.'

'Oh, I wanted to see the jellyfish,' Dina said wistfully.

'Kira, make sure you send everyone the full reports for both cities, please.' Jed looked around at the group. 'I want everyone to have read them by tomorrow morning. I think the best thing to do is to split into teams and cover both our bases, but I want to make sure we have all the facts before we make any kind of decisions.'

Kira nodded and began tapping out instructions on her handheld. It wouldn't take long to transfer the info parcels to the others.

Later that evening, when everyone was absorbed in reading about cities 9 and 36, Kira discussed Jed's idea with him.

'Do you really think we should split up? After what we saw in 15? Surely safety in numbers is the way to go.'

'I think we need answers and fast,' replied Jed. 'If the chief is sending the rest of my team out here then we will have ample numbers of operatives to run two missions plus extra skimmers and supplies. We ought to try and get as much intel as possible. And splitting up our expertise base makes sense as well.' He smiled at his wife. 'It seems pointless to send an experienced anthropologist such as yourself to a seaport to eat jellyfish and two biologists up to the mountains to carry out research on what may be a tribe of people adapted to a completely different way of life.'

Kira gave him a huge hug. 'Then we are going to 36?'

'More than likely, love. More than likely.' Jed paused. 'Look, if your parents are coming here, will you leave Grace with them so she can stay here, at Camp Eden?'

Kira frowned and glanced at the nearby cube. 'I don't know. We could be gone a week or longer. My gut says she'll be safer if she's with us. And Jed, don't forget, Mum's not well. She can't have much medication left.' Her voice changed, becoming urgent and low. 'We should take her with us, use her condition as a bargaining chip for medication.'

'Yes, but, if it's Corporation medication we're after, she may be better off travelling to 9 with Dina and Max.'

Kira was silent.

'Hey, don't worry, everything will work out - you'll see. We'll find some meds for your mum, and a safe place for the children, and us, to live.' He checked his wristplant. 'It's getting late, we'd better get some rest. Everyone will be here in the morning and I need to report to Martha first thing with our plan.'

Kira nodded, hugged her husband and went to curl up on the camp bed, next to Grace's cube. She didn't think she would be able to sleep a wink but within minutes she had drifted away, imagining what the people of 36 would be like and whether they'd share their way of life with the rest of them.

Jed was pleased. It seemed to him that a workable plan was beginning to come together. It was a shame to have to split everyone up, but it made sense to send the expertise where it could be used effectively. Max and Dina would be alright. If 9 was all Corper, they'd be able to blend in, more or less, and their scientific skills might even gain them access to whatever research or plans Corporation was working on. The more he thought about it, the more Jed realised that they had no idea whether Corporation was a worldwide entity or whether it just held sway on their island. Travelling to a coastal city would more than likely provide that information. Or at least a few clues to what lay beyond the ocean.

Corporation had taught them that there had been fifty cities established around the globe after The Event. Cities where the remains of the human population had been sent to survive and re-establish themselves but after everything that had happened recently, Jed had a hard time believing that to be the whole truth. What if there were competing organisations? What if there were more people, more cities? More soberly, what if there were less? Jed couldn't believe that 42 was it, now that 15 was gone. Half of him hoped that they never came up against the power behind that mass execution whilst the other half was desperate to fight back in retaliation. No-one should have that kind of power or think they had the justification to wipe out a city on a whim. No-one.

Chapter 17

C42N: *What will Hamble do now? Join the conversation in social hub beta.*

FORCE: *We are merging with Corp Security. The safety of City 42 citizens is paramount.*

ANON17: *Why isn't the team back from City 15 yet? What are they trying to hide?*

GJENK: *Hamble did not 'snatch' the baby-lab child. It is my grandson. My son will become legal guardian.*

MSCHILD: *How do we know GJENK is telling the truth? That baby died in Corp Tech tragedy.*

CORPTECH2: *We are thrilled to hear of another survivor.*

SMAC: *The Governor Office can confirm the child in the baby-lab did belong to Ingrid Jenkins and Pete Barnes. We extend our sympathies for the mix-up in placement.*

Martha was trying to pack. She knew that Lucas was going to be in safe hands, but her heart hurt at the thought of sending him away.

'Am I doing the right thing?' She asked Jean as she tried to fold clothes and not bawl her eyes out.

'Martha, my lovely, come on. Don't get yourself into such a state. You don't have to do this you know, love. You could just leave them all to it. There's no reason for you to stay here.' Jean rubbed Martha gently on the back.

'I have to. I promised my Father I would look after the citizens of City 42.' Martha turned to look at Jean. 'I haven't done a very good job so far, have I?'

'You did an excellent job. You uncovered the water treatment and you found us a safe, clean alternative. You sorted out all that mess after Corp Tech was destroyed. You even found the little boy - who we need a name for by the way. We can't keep calling him the boy. Have you had any thoughts?'

'I'm not sure it's my place...'

'Peter, I think we should call him Peter,' Jean interrupted. 'I'll tell Gretchen. I see she swept about it - good of her. I'm surprised she hasn't decided she's coming with us, but her lot are all tied into Corporation and if they're back in town then she'll do well out of it I expect.'

'She knows we're going to Camp Eden?'

'Not as such, but she's knows we're going to go meet Jed, introduce him to his nephew. I had to say something, love. She was hell bent on taking that child, Peter, with her when she left. If I hadn't had my Malcolm to back me up, I dread to think what would've happened.'

Martha couldn't help smiling at that. Jean was a dynamo, a real force of nature, whereas Kira's dad was one of the gentlest, softly spoken men she'd ever come across.

'Now look, you listen to me. I say you come with us. Think about the realities here, Martha. You're a young girl, a young mother for goodness sake. It won't do your Lucas any good to be away from you for an extended period of time. I mean, did you hear about that girl over on 7th? She left her one with the NanNan exclusively so she could carry on gadding about like a mad thing and in the end the child wanted nothing to do with her. They emancipated themselves. Do you remember that? How that girl ever got a baby from the lottery I'll never know but I guess that was Corporation for you.'

Martha hadn't heard that one but there were plenty of stories like it. People who were so ill-equipped for the role of parenthood that they relied too heavily on the available tech and their children were total corpers and tech heads.

It all works in Corporations' favour she thought. She couldn't imagine Lucas growing up without her. Martha picked up a jumpsuit and began refolding it for the tenth time. Should she stay and be the voice for the people? She felt confused, the more she considered Jean's words, the more she realised that her son had to come first.

'Besides, we need you to help Ruth out of this black hole she's got herself into. She'll listen to you,' remarked Jean.

'I'm not sure about that,' replied Martha, guilt flickering in her stomach. 'I didn't even know she was struggling. And she hasn't been told about City 15 yet. How is she going to react to that?'

'I don't know, love. But she needs to be told. She can't keep ignoring Sarah forever, especially now the little one will never meet her father. We've got to surround Ruth with love and help her through whatever it is she's struggling with, that's all there is to it.'

Martha put down the clothes she had been folding and unfolding.

'You're absolutely right, Jean. Lucas needs me and so does Ruth. There's nothing I can do here, apart from become the target practice for everything Corporation want to blame on me. It's clear they intend to take back the city and if all my family have left then I'm only staying to be a martyr.'

'Your father wouldn't have wanted that for you, love. He sent you to Eden before, didn't he?'

Martha nodded, thinking fondly of her father's gruffness. The door pinged, surprising both women.

'Are you expecting anyone, dear?' asked Jean.

'I don't think so... oh, it's probably Ben.' Martha hurried to key open the door. Sure enough, Jed's cousin Ben sauntered into the flat. He grinned widely when he saw Jean, she was his Aunty by marriage and much loved.

'Lo, Auntie. I didn't know you'd be here. I brought these for Kira to pass on to you.' He reached round to the satchel slung across his body and took out a large bag of medical supplies.

Jean held out a hand for the bag and looked inside. For once she was lost for words. She crushed the bag shut and pressed it to her chest, smiling at Ben, eyes shining brightly.

'What is it?' asked Martha.

'Auntie's medicine. Or at least as much as I could find. I figured once you lot get out to Eden the scientists out there might be able to replicate it or something.'

'That's so good of you, Ben. Thank you.'

'Well, I got to look after my family, right? I hear you've been busy, Martha. Stealing babies, upsetting things.'

Martha replied hotly. 'I did NOT steal a baby. I'll have you know that Peter belongs with us and I am only bringing him to his real family.' Then she flushed as she realised Ben was teasing her. 'Do you want to meet him? I think he must be a second cousin or something to you.'

Ben nodded and followed Martha over to the play cube where the three little ones were happily playing together.

'He looks like Pete, don't he?' Ben said softly. 'Except for them eyes, those are Ingrid's eyes.' He sniffed rather loudly then reached into his satchel again pulling out a couple of handhelds. 'These are for you. They're encrypted so they won't show up on Corp's radar but use them sparingly to get in touch with me. I'm being watched.' He jerked a head towards the pile of packed bags. 'You going too?'

Martha nodded. 'Why don't you come with us?'

'To the middle of the jungle with a load of rug-rats? Not my style, Martha. Besides you might need an inside man.'

'You will be careful, won't you?'

'Model citizen I am, they got nothing on me. Besides, working for Chief Minkov now, ain't I? I got a bit of muscle behind me if anything goes wrong.'

That was a surprise to Martha, she had always thought the chief had little or no time for Ben after he had been exposed as an active Anti-Corp member in the wake of the terrorist attack on Corp Tech. Clearly the two men had moved on. However, Force was now out of favour as well.

'Watch out for Corporation, Ben. They're after Minkov too. We'll be in touch; let you know how we get on. You can always come and join us later, if you want to?'

He nodded, looked like he was going to hug her then decided against it. Instead he planted a kiss on his Auntie's cheek and called out a goodbye to everyone.

Martha watched him leave then gave herself a little shake. She needed to pack the rest of her things now, Jean was right. She couldn't do anything here; she'd tried her best. What she needed to do was find a safe place for herself, her child and her friends. She tried to ignore the growing fear that whatever had wiped out City 15 was coming for them next.

Ruth sat motionless in her room. There was hustle and bustle around her as Kira's mum packed up her life for her. She watched dispassionately. There wasn't much here anyway. Mostly baby things and most of those had been Martha getting over excited and buying two of everything. Sarah was in the front room. Ruth knew she should feel a twinge of guilt over abandoning the children's care the other day, but she didn't feel anything. Apart from empty. She couldn't see the point in travelling out to Camp Eden. If Corporation had returned to the city, it wouldn't take them long to travel out to Eden and bring everyone back under control. Living under their regime would be simpler. She could pass Sarah off to a NanNan and get some faceless job somewhere. Jacking in whenever she wanted any kind of distraction and keeping her friends virtual. Then she wouldn't have to hear people whispering or catch their looks of pity.

Anger stirred in the pit of her stomach momentarily, but her apathy took over. There wasn't any point. Ruth realised that Jean was stood in front of her, holding things in her hands.

'Whatever you think is best, Jean. I don't care.' And with that Ruth lay down and rolled over, her back to the room and to the lady who was trying to help. Jean tutted and went to find Martha.

'We need to do something about that girl, Martha. She's not coping well. I think we ought to keep Sarah safely away for now; although maybe that's the worst thing to do. I wonder if we should put the two of them together in a room and see what happens. I can't say I can abide a baby crying at all hours. There's no need for that. Not when we have so many hands available. It costs nothing for a hug, and it does you the world of good.'

Martha let Jean ramble on. She was worried about Ruth and felt intensely guilty that she hadn't noticed the signs prior to Ruth's suicide attempt. A change of scenery might do her some good. Perhaps Gaia would visit her out in Camp Eden. City 42 didn't feel like a very spiritual place at the moment. The sweeps were full of derogatory comments aimed at Martha and the people who had supported her in office, which included Ruth. A lot of those people had also stepped down. What kind of lives would they now live? Martha supposed the most politically agile would hang on to the coat tails of the next rising star, which seemed to be Sean.

Gretchen had at least smoothed over the baby-snatching by sweeping that the child was her grandson and he would be going into care with Kira and Jed. There was surprisingly little commentary on the revelation that the baby belonged to Ingrid, that his apparent death had been the spark that began the revolution. Martha supposed that was because Corporation were extending their influence over the sweeps again. The whole business exhausted her. Now that she'd made the decision to leave, she just wanted to leave.

The door pinged. It was a member of the City Guard, one of Jed's operatives he'd left behind and who would be travelling with them to Camp Eden. 'The skimmer is ready for you, Ma'am er, Ms Hamble.'

'Thank you. We'll be down shortly.' She smiled at the young woman and went to get the children. With Martha carrying Lucas and Sarah, Jean took Peter and Malcolm piled all the bags onto a hover transport to take them down to the skimmer. It just remained to get Ruth moving and out of the door.

Jean had finished packing for Ruth and was busy directing her husband in the best way to stack the various bags. Martha shook Ruth's shoulder as she lay on the bed, facing away from the room.

'It's time to go.'

There was no response.

'Ruth, come on. It's time to leave. You don't have to do anything, just come with us.' Still no response. Martha walked around to the other side of the bed and saw her friend staring off into nothing, breathing but otherwise showing no sign of life whatsoever. 'I know you can hear me. You better get your arse up and out of that bed. We are not leaving you behind no matter how pathetic you think you have become. One day soon you'll realise you're being a complete and utter idiot and then you can apologise, but for now, get up and get out of that door.' Martha ended up shouting which of course upset the two little ones in her arms, but it also made Ruth's eyes widen in surprise as she got up and woodenly walked out of the door.

'Alright, dear?' Jean asked.

'Let's go,' Martha replied tightly, trying to soothe the children she was carrying whilst bristling in anger that Ruth was allowed to give up like that. Not on her watch.

There were two skimmers waiting for them, down at pavement level. It took two trips to bring down all the luggage and equipment. They left the NanNan behind. Martha felt that Kira and Jed wouldn't look too favourably upon the robot being used in Camp Eden and she hoped that all the childcare wouldn't fall firmly on her shoulders. Just because she was no longer governor did not mean she had a burning desire to become governess to four children. Malcolm got in with the luggage while the women and children took the second skimmer. They were both armoured, both had tinted windows, and both had armed guards. Clearly Jed's team were taking no risks. Not that Martha was expecting any trouble. No-one, apart from Ben and Chief Minkov, knew they were leaving the city and she was certain the chief was loyal to the citizens of 42 and had no connections or ties to Corporation whatsoever. He was a good man and reminded her of her late father. She wished she could have spent longer getting to know him or at least had the chance to say goodbye properly.

The skimmers finally left the building and began their journey out of the city. They attracted little attention and without the force-field in place were able to leave freely and travel onwards to Camp Eden. No-one in the skimmers noticed the lone spy drone watching and recording them leaving.

MSCHILD: *Why is Hamble leaving the city? So what if GJENK said she could have the child. Are there no laws?*

ANON17: *Let them go. We don't need them. 42 is better off without them.*

NEWCORP: *Thank you for welcoming New Corporation. City 15 has ceased to operate. New Corporation looks forward to making City 42 great again.*

C42N: *This sweep channel has been deactivated.*

ANON40: *What happened to City 15?*

CORPSECURITY*: We will now replace FORCE for all your safety & security needs. Same location, new team. We will protect & serve City 42.*

FORCE: *This sweep channel has been deactivated.*

ANON40: *Seriously - what happened to City 15?*

ANON40: *This sweep channel has been deactivated.*

SMAC: *The sweeps are experiencing a few technical difficulties. Nothing to worry about.*

ENCRYPTED MESSAGE FROM 7421 TO NEW CORP
>>*They've left the city. Hamble and Maddocks, the children and some ex-Force Operatives loyal to Jenkins. Do you want me to pursue?*<<

ENCRYPTED MESSAGE FROM NEW CORP TO 7421
>>I AM AWARE OF YOUR INCOMPETENCE. WHY DID YOU NOT REACTIVATE THE FORCEFIELD?<<

ENCRYPTED MESSAGE FROM 7421 TO NEW CORP
>>*It was the next item on the list - I'm sorry, I've been dealing with the sweep accounts. And anyway, where would they go? You can track them, can't you? Bring them back.*<<

ENCRYPTED MESSAGE FROM NEW CORP TO 7421
>>WE ARE WATCHING EVERYTHING. I WILL DEAL WITH THE NON-CONFORMERS IN DUE COURSE. REMOVE MINKOV FROM OFFICE. BEGIN ROLLING OUT THE NEURAL IMPLANTS<<

ENCRYPTED MESSAGE FROM 7421 TO NEW CORP
>>*Already? The infrastructure isn't in place for the implants. Corp Tech has still not been properly reformed - maybe we should wait a while, get the medical supply situation under control?*<<

ENCRYPTED MESSAGE FROM NEW CORP TO 7421
>>YOU HAVE YOUR ORDERS. EVERYTHING ELSE WILL BE DEALT WITH<<

Chapter 18

'Ma! You made it. Have you come to see us off?' Dina was delighted to see Martha at Camp Eden.

'No. I'm here to join you,' replied Martha as she watched Kira run to hug her parents.

'Join us? That's amazing! Which city do you want to go to?'

Martha shrugged. She'd been so focused on getting to Camp Eden, she hadn't thought about the new mission to reach out to other cities. After Ben had warned her about using the comms link, she hadn't checked in with Jed, but they could work out the detailed plan of action now everyone was here. She looked down at the little boy in her arms and knew she needed to go and find Jed before she did anything else. Smiling at Dina she wandered further into the camp.

Jed stood with Ash, looking at some maps on the camp's vid screen. The two men were completely absorbed in what they were doing and didn't hear Martha approach. She coughed quietly.

Ash turned and grinned at Martha, made his excuses and left them to it. Jed tutted at Ash breaking his concentration then realised who else was there.

'Is that... Is that him?' His voice sounded hoarse.

'Jed, meet Peter, your nephew.' Martha held out the little boy to his uncle. The child responded by stretching out his little arms and gurgling happily.

Tears pricked Jed's eyes as he took the boy and began talking to him softly. Martha watched for a few moments then quietly left them alone. They needed time to bond and get to know each other.

Dina grabbed her elbow and spun her round.

'Come on, we're all in the communal tent. Moham's making tea.' Dina chattered happily as she led Martha over to where the others had gathered. Jean and Malcolm had bought Lucas and Sarah to the tent and were making a huge fuss over Grace who they hadn't seen for at least three days. Ruth was sitting listlessly to one side. Kira was nowhere to be seen. Dina saw Martha looking around.

'Kira's gone to meet Peter. That's such a great name by the way. Is he a good baby?' Dina asked.

'He's been an angel, so far at least. Considering how much change has happened to him,' replied Martha.

Moham pressed hot tea into Ruth's hands and she looked up at him curiously. Then she seemed to remember who he was and where she was. She took a sip of tea and began to look around, taking in her surroundings. Dina made to go and speak to her, but Martha held her back.

'Not yet, let her have her tea. Come and see the kids with me.'

Dina didn't need much encouragement to go and play. Soon excited gurgles were echoing across the camp.

Kira joined them with young Peter in her arms. 'Isn't he adorable? Don't you think he looks like Pete? With Ingrid's eyes though.'

Martha nodded. 'Where's Jed?'

'He's gone to sort out the operatives. The camp is pretty full now, we don't want to overrun the experiments or destroy any of the natural habitats so Moham is helping him get everything worked out.' Kira watched the children playing together for a moment before continuing. 'He thinks we should talk about next steps when the kids have all gone to bed, what do you think?'

'I think that would be the best idea. Too distracting otherwise,' replied Martha.

The women spent the next few hours happily playing with the children, getting dinner organised and then putting their precious families into bed. They had just sat down to talk about what they were going to do next when one of Jed's operatives came running up.

'Sir? We've got a drone at the edge of camp.'

Jed leapt up. 'A drone? Show me.'

The others followed to see what the commotion was. There hovering on the edge of camp was a spy drone.

'How long has it been there?' asked Jed.

'Hard to tell, Sir. We noticed it about five minutes ago and I came straight to find you and report it.'

Jed frowned. It didn't look like one of theirs, it was more compact and if anything, looked more expensive. Martha pushed through the others and came to stand next to Jed.

'What do you think?' she asked.

But before he had chance to answer a tinny voice issued from the drone.

'Ms Hamble. So good to see you. I had hoped to make your acquaintance in City 42 but alas by the time I arrived, you had already left. I see you have surrounded yourself with an illegal militia, some women and several children. A rather odd selection, don't you think?'

'And who exactly am I talking to?' Martha asked.

'Well now, that's privileged information. If you'd stayed in the city, maybe we could've built a wonderful friendship. Alas, now I must treat you as an enemy of New Corporation.'

Dina and Kira looked at each frowning. Dina mouthed the question 'New Corporation?' but Kira shrugged. She didn't know what it meant either.

'Why am I your enemy?' asked Martha.

'You were instrumental in an illegal takeover, were you not? You put yourself in charge, did you not? I believe all four members of the Board delegated to look after City 42 perished, have they not? Your father amongst them. I am surprised. I never thought a lady such as yourself would have patricide listed amongst her crimes.'

Martha reddened but chose not to answer. She knew she hadn't killed her father. The others came to stand closer to her, trying to offer moral support without saying anything.

'What do you want?' asked Jed.

'Ah, the newly appointed Captain of the Guard. You do realise that your new position is bogus and all the operatives you have with you have been officially listed as deserters.'

'Corporation have no jurisdiction over Force,' replied Jed.

'Times change. We do now. I'm afraid your Chief has stepped down from office. Ill health apparently. He doesn't have long left.'

Kira put a warning hand on Jed's arm, and he swallowed his retort. The drone continued.

'I am here to inform you that you have two choices. You either leave Camp Eden within the next twenty-four hours and try your luck out there in the wilderness or you return to City 42 where you will be tried for your crimes against New Corporation. Make the right decision and we may show mercy. I warn you though, if you attempt to make contact with another New Corporation city you will be arrested. New Corporation does not tolerate activists.'

'Is that why you destroyed City 15?' shouted Dina, overcome with emotion.

Ruth turned pale as she wavered on her feet while Martha cursed inwardly. That was not how she had planned to tell Ruth about what had happened.

'City 15 were warned multiple times. But your fearless leader sealed their fate and accelerated their decimation by attempting to reach out and make contact. We will not tolerate any alternatives to New Corporation rule.'

There was silence. The group had a lot of questions, but no-one felt like talking to the drone any further.

'I see you are taking a moment. Let me help with that. I remind you that you have twenty-four hours to return to City 42 where the children will be confiscated, and you will all be held for questioning. If we are satisfied that you are no longer a threat to New Corporation you will be security tagged, separated and assigned new roles within the city. Your children may or may not be assigned back to you.'

Ruth surprised everyone by interrupting the drone. 'You can't do that! You can't take away my child. She's biologically mine, I grew her - no thanks to your experimentations.'

'Be that as it may, Ms Maddocks. Your recent overdose brings into question your fitness as a parent.'

There was a long silence. The drone remained hovering in place, watching each and every one of them.

'Twenty-four hours,' the tinny voice announced before the drone flew abruptly away.

Stunned, Jed looked for his wife and pulled her into an embrace. Dina was clinging to Max and Ruth had gone to stand with Martha who had a determined look on her face.

'It's time to break camp,' she announced but Ruth blocked her path.

'It's time for you to tell me what happened in City 15,' she said. The others gave the two women a wide berth as Martha quietly explained what had happened to all the people in City 15. Ruth shook her head at first, unable to comprehend the brutality, then as she realised Martha was telling the truth, she began to cry. It was a sombre reminder to everyone else how ruthless New Corporation were.

'It's horrible, Ruth, I still can't believe it happened. Like it should have been a dream,' Dina said, trying to help comfort her friend with a hug as she walked with Ruth and Martha back over to some chairs. Kira came to join them with some hot, sweet tea so Martha used the opportunity to slip away and find Jed. They met in the communal tent.

'How many men do you have, Jed? How many skimmers?' Martha's voice was all business. Internally she was deeply shaken by the casual show of force New Corporation had demonstrated. This was a different kind of Corporation to what she was used to. Yes, the previous regime had been instrumental in treating the water supply and keeping everyone sterile, but she truly believed that had been a result of circumstance rather than malicious intent. What had happened in City 15 didn't feel like the Corporation she had grown up with but, she didn't have time to think about that now. She needed to focus on getting everyone to safety.

'I've got twenty operatives, so I'd split them down the middle. Ten to each mission? I'll head up one team, put Ash in charge of the other,' replied Jed.

'It's a pity we don't have two Ashes - we could do with his tech expertise, especially in maintaining comms between the two teams. If such things are possible,' mused Martha.

'We might not have two Ashes, but Dina is pretty quick on the uptake, she's been watching what Ash has been doing. I reckon he could get her up to speed quickly enough.'

'Okay so... does that mean we split Dina and Max up?'

'You talking about us?' Dina asked in a cheery voice as she joined the conversation, making Martha jump.

'We're trying to organise the two teams,' she said.

'Well, surely you need all of us to chip in, tell you what we think.'

'I'm sorry, Dina. We don't have time for that kind of delegation and discussion. Jed and I are taking charge.'

Dina's face fell. 'Will we at least have a say after you've made the decision for us?'

Martha shook her head. 'It's not up for public debate.' She deliberately turned away from her friend, feeling awful for doing so but knowing that if they waited for everyone to have their say, the twenty-four hours deadline would come and go. Dina stalked away.

'I'd like to stay with Kira,' Jed stated.

'I figured as much. You and Kira can head out to City 36. Take Dina with you.'

'So you are splitting up Dina and Max then? They won't be happy about that.'

Martha put her head in her hands. She could feel the stress weighing down on her. 'Fine.' She looked up. 'Call everyone together, Jed. I assume your team will at least do as they're told?'

Jed nodded and went to round the others up. It didn't take long; they had been hovering nearby.

'Right, this is the situation,' began Martha. 'As you heard, we have less than twenty-four hours to break camp and get out of here. I don't know whether they will try to destroy us like they did City 15, but I am certainly not going to take that risk.'

'Does this mean you've decided to let us decide for ourselves what we want to do?' Dina asked.

Martha felt stung by Dina's words, but she couldn't blame her. 'We will be splitting up into two missions, one to City 9, the other to City 36. We do not know what to expect from either city. We will be at opposite ends of the country and each team will have to deal with any problems they uncover themselves. So, if you volunteer for a particular city, you need to understand that it's not easy to turn around and go somewhere else instead.'

The group were silent.

'Anyone have a preference?' Martha asked.

'I would like to go to City 36,' Kira stated calmly. 'I'll take Grace, Peter and my parents with me.' She did not mention Jed.

'We want to go to City 9,' Dina announced, grabbing Max's hand and speaking with a slight lift to her chin, expecting some kind of disagreement.

'I think the greater Corporation presence will be at City 9. Are you sure you feel confident enough to face that?' Martha asked.

Dina nodded.

'I think Ruth and Sarah should go with you, Kira.' Martha turned to Ruth for her agreement, but she looked back with emotionless eyes. It didn't make any difference to Ruth where she went.

'What about you?' Kira asked. 'If you think City 9 is going to be a strong base for Corporation, I don't think you should go there. You're a wanted woman now. We all are.'

'Exactly why you're going to take Lucas and I'm going to City 9. And Jed is coming with me.'

No-one said anything. Everyone waited to see Jed's reaction. Kira grabbed his hand tightly and he pulled her into a quick embrace. Then he nodded curtly and took over the rest of the discussion.

'Ash, you're headed up to 36,' Jed said. 'Brief Dina on the comms system. Let's try and get a secure connection established now before we head out.' Then he walked off to split his operatives into two teams and oversee the distribution of supplies and vehicles. The team heading out to 36 would need more than those going to 9. Jed knew Martha was right, but he was still disappointed. He didn't want to be apart from his wife now they'd been threatened by New Corp and he'd only just met Peter. But taking the children to 9 was too much of a risk. A small voice in his head wondered whether they were making a mistake by putting all their children together, but Kira seemed certain that 36 was more likely to be out from under Corporation control. There was no tactical advantage for Corporation to have a strong foothold in a city in the middle of a remote mountain range. The people that lived there were likely to be more self-reliant than those in City 42.

They had to try and find somewhere safe, find someone who could teach them the skills they would need to survive. The fight with Corporation wasn't over but they were woefully underprepared if the causal show of force demonstrated by the faceless drone voice was anything to go by.

'Ruth? Ruth?' Jean called out. There was no response. 'I do not know what to do with that girl, Malcolm.'

Her husband patted her arm in sympathy as the two of them tried to chivvy Ruth along.

'Come along, Ruth. You need to stow your gear in the right skimmer. Make sure Sarah has everything she needs.' Jean peered up at the blank faced woman. 'You do care about your daughter, don't you?' Again, no response. Jean threw her hands up in despair and turned to go, then had second thoughts and took Sarah out of Ruth's arms. 'Come along baby girl, let's get you some milk before we have to leave.'

Ruth made no move to stop her. She was still trying to process the fact that Sarah's father and the dozens of other people she knew from City 15 were all dead. Nothing felt real. Cigarette smoke drifted past her face, making her nose twitch. She blinked in surprise and looked beside her. Malcolm had sparked up and was offering her a drag. Ruth took the cigarette with shaky fingers; it had been months since she'd smoked. She inhaled deeply, savouring the hot smoke.

'You know, that little girl needs you,' said Malcolm. Ruth continued to smoke in silence.

'It's just...' she said finally.

'Yep.'

'And I don't know if I can.' Ruth's voice was quiet as she admitted her own fear of not being able to be there for her daughter.

Malcolm ground the cigarette stub into the floor with the heel of his shoe.

'None of us know for sure, love. We have to do the best we can.' Malcolm passed over the half full cigarette carton. 'Come on, we've got to find a place to hide those before Jean kills me.'

Ruth gave a small laugh and followed him back to the tents. While she helped Jean and Martha pack up all the baby bits and pieces, Dina was getting a quick but intense tech lesson from Ash.

'It's pretty simple, these comms are designed to work on a different frequency to the ones Corporation use but that doesn't mean they won't switch. You'll be able to tell if they are by the opening tone, listen.' Ash turned on the comms system and it clicked twice. 'Two clicks and we're okay, any more or less and it's not a safe channel.' He dug around in his pockets for an info jack. 'This has a list of subsequent channels to try should the first one get compromised.'

'What if they all get compromised?' asked Dina nervously.

'We won't use the comms too often,' replied Jed, as he came to join them. 'You happy with how everything works, Dina?'

'Yeah, I think so.'

'Good. Go make sure you've both got everything you need. We need to get moving.' Jed watched as the camp bustled before him. They were leaving the main Camp Eden scientists behind, there wasn't room to take everyone with them and Jed was hoping New Corporation would leave them alone. After all, Camp Eden had originally been a Corporation idea. He beckoned to Max to come with him as he walked by.

'Hey, Max. Can you run through the testing kit with Ash please? I want to make sure he knows how to test the air and water as they're travelling and once they get to City 36.'

'Yeah of course. We've got two kits; it makes sense for them to take one.' Max hurried to get the equipment and was soon taking Ash through the basics. It was simple enough, as long as he sampled correctly the machine would do the rest.

With everything packed, the two teams were ready to go. All that remained was to say goodbye. Jean hugged everyone, regardless of whether they were coming with her or not. No-one minded, it was comforting. Dina and Kira hugged, the children were peppered with kisses and had no idea what was going on. Max shook hands with Ash and wished him luck, Jed finished briefing the team headed out to City 36. Ruth was crying, happy and sad tears mingled together as she hugged Martha tight. Everyone was ready to go; it was just Kira and Jed left to say goodbye.

'Are you going to be alright?' Kira asked him.

Jed laughed softly. 'It should be me asking you that.' He paused. 'Have you got everything? For Grace? And the others?'

'Mm, we should be alright. We've got half the dried food and a treatment system for water. All the milk for the kids. Reusable nappies. I'm confident City 36 will be able to re-supply us.'

Jed gathered his wife in his arms and held her close. He smelled her hair and tried to take comfort in the fact that they were doing the right thing. He hoped. He wasn't going to ask what Kira would do if City 36 didn't exist anymore. His wife was resourceful.

Chapter 19

NEWCORP: *Neural implants are now available from your local med centre. Get hooked in. Be part of New Corp.*

SMAC: *The new Governor for City 42 will be announced later today.*

CORPTECH2: *Plans have been drawn up for the new Tech Towers. Corp Tech will be rebuilt at the same site.*

ACAD: *All retraining and Grow Your Own courses have been cancelled. New pre-approved courses will be available soon.*

Sean looked out of the window at City 42 with pleasure. They'd finally painted over that awful Gaia graffiti on the wall across from Collection. He was going to be in charge now and he would be putting New Corporation rule firmly in place. There was bound to be the odd objection, but the citizens would accept the new neural implants and anything else New Corp implemented.

'Here's your synth-caf, Sean.'

'Thanks, Jon. Is everything ready for the meeting?'

'Yes. Do you think we'll have to have the implants as well?' asked Jon, Sean's aide.

'I don't think so. New Corp know we're loyal to them, it shouldn't be a problem,' Sean replied but he was slightly anxious about the implants. They were designed to dampen down independent thinking and therefore negate any thoughts about disloyalty to New Corp, keep citizens more docile and less likely to question anything. 'They'll want us able to think independently, Jon. After all, we'll be running the city.'

'Are you're going to say yes then, when they offer you the governorship?'

Sean puffed out his chest a little. 'Of course. Hamble made a mess of things, dismantling the HER water treatment plant - telling women they could have children. Look what happened there. Nothing. Just bitter disappointment.' He turned away from the window with a smile. 'With Corp Medical back in firm control, we'll be able to neutralise any embryos created outside the designated population growth lines. People can't be allowed to just create life wantonly.' He gazed at the meeting table, then frowned. 'Shouldn't there be snacks?'

Jon mumbled an affirmative and hurried out to get some organised. Sean checked his wristplant. The New Corp board members should be arriving soon. He was sure appointment to governor after everything he'd done was a mere formality. Subduing the Chief of Force had been more difficult than expected. Minkov inspired terrific loyalty in his team, but they'd managed to remove him from office. Fortunately for Sean, the chief had been too busy promoting Jenkins and creating his ridiculous mini militia to pay full attention to the influx of Corp loyal operatives and the move to becoming Corp Security. Minkov and his handful of loyal detectives had been unable to stand up to that show of force. Ha Force. What a ridiculous name, thought Sean. That would be the first thing to change. Corp Security worked well enough in City 9 it would work fine here.

The door to the conference room swung open. Three men and a woman walked into the room. The woman was thin, her steel-grey hair cut in a smart bob, her face devoid of any warmth. She looked at Sean then cocked a finger. One of the men on her right took out a scanner and walked towards him. Sean raised his hands in the air in submission and took half a step backwards.

'What's this?' he asked.

'Just checking for bugs,' the man replied.

The woman walked around the board room. She wiped her finger across the table and seemed surprised when it came back clean. The scanner beeped once, and the man pocketed the device. She looked at him and he shook his head. The woman sniffed and sat down at the head of the table, gesturing for Sean to join her.

'My name is Clarity Jones,' she said. 'I am the Chief Executive of the Board of Directors for Corporation owned City 42. Tell me, Mr MacIntyre, why was the rebel governor not apprehended?'

'I, uh, well, I didn't think she would leave the city and I thought...'

'That seems to have been your problem.' Ms Jones steepled her fingers. 'I believe your instructions were clear, to initiate the vote of no confidence and dismantle the fake government. It wasn't to allow everyone to leave the city freely and go who knows where. What exactly gave you difficulty?'

'But you sent the drone, to Camp Eden! You already know where they are.' Sean looked at the men who had entered the room with Ms Jones for support, but they remained standing still, blank faced yet alert.

'We did indeed, Mr MacIntyre. It may, however, be a case of too little, too late,' replied Ms Jones calmly.

'It doesn't matter if they don't come back. If they go out into the wild, they'll just die of radiation poisoning. We can harass them with drones and keep them moving, they'll soon run out of supplies.' Sean tried to sound confident.

'You seem to think the resources of New Corp are expressly available to clear up your mess. New Corp Militia is not your private clean-up crew.'

'No, but, but there are resources and, and...' Sean dropped his head and fell silent. This was not how he had expected this meeting to go. The silence dragged. 'Anyway, there's nowhere for them to go. City 9 is New Corp and if they try to go to City 36, they'll die faster. I don't see why you're so worried.' Sean sounded sulky. 'We can always threaten the family they left behind, make them come back.'

Ms Jones tilted her head to one side. 'Left behind?'

Sean warmed to his idea. 'Yes. We can apprehend whoever it is, threaten them or something and then they'll be forced to come back.'

'I see. And what family members does Martha Hamble have left?'

'Her mother.'

Ms Jones nodded. 'Yes, Mrs Hamble is a staunch supporter of New Corp and has funded many of our projects. I understand relationships between her and her daughter are strained at best.'

'Alright, alright, bad example.' Sean started thinking aloud. 'Dina Grey's family was lost in the City 15 riots and Ruth Maddocks lost her only link in the recent sanitation.' He started pacing. 'What about the Jenkins?'

Ms Jones regarded Sean coolly. 'Gretchen Jenkins is to be sworn in as a new board member today. I doubt we will be able to threaten her or something.'

'Okay, okay. We can't threaten Kira Jenkins parents - they left with her... but, there's a cousin!' He faced Ms Jones in triumph. 'We could use him as leverage.'

Ms Jones gestured imperiously for a handheld from one of her attendants. She swiped the screen a few times then read aloud.

'Ben Jenkins, last remaining Anti-Corp activist, cousin to Jed Jenkins. Linked with disrupting sweeps, infiltration at Force and known to be highly skilled in data stream interfacing.' She raised her head to look at Sean. 'Attempts were made to apprehend Mr Jenkins this morning. He has been terminated.'

'He's what? But...' Sean was momentarily dumbfounded but quickly rallied. 'It doesn't matter. They won't come back here, and I doubt very much they will survive out there. I don't see why we need to be so worried.'

'I am concerned, Mr MacIntyre, because these people have left with an idea burning in their little minds. And ideas are dangerous. They lead to free thinking. Corporation was not built on free thinking.'

Sean scoffed a little. 'You don't seriously think anyone will listen to them? Why don't you wipe them out? They're only a bunch of...' Ms Jones cut him off.

'They are a group of well-respected citizens from City 42 who uncovered the sterilisation plot, managed several natural pregnancies and have made alleged contact with the spirit of this planet. Despite our best efforts to keep this information under wraps, it has spread. And even if they don't have all the facts, people will listen.'

'No.' Sean shook his head emphatically. 'They won't. Not once they mention that blue woman nonsense. People will think they're crazy. There's no such thing as spirits of the Earth.'

Ms Jones narrowed her eyes. 'I can see you are perfectly suited for your role as advisor, Mr MacIntyre. Could you organise some synth-caf for the rest of the board members who will be arriving soon? No need to attend. I'm sure you have some important filing to fulfil.' With that she dismissed him from her thoughts, her focus now on the handheld in front of her. One of her personal security caught Sean's eye and jerked his head towards the doorway.

Sean walked woodenly out of the room. This was not what was supposed to have happened. He should be celebrating after being made governor, not dismissed from the meeting room. A small niggle of doubt began to writhe at the back of his mind. Had he done the right thing? His thoughts churned as he began brewing fresh synth-caf for the meeting. It must be some sort of mistake. Ms Jones would soon see he was an invaluable member of the City 42 team. He needed to prove his worth, that was all.

NEWCORP: *For crimes against New Corporation the following individuals are wanted for questioning:*
Martha Hamble
Lucas Hamble
Jed Jenkins
Kira Jenkins
Grace Jenkins
Peter Jenkins
Jean Bishop
Malcolm Bishop
Ruth Maddocks
Sarah Maddocks
Dina Grey
If you see any of these fugitives, your duty to City 42 & New Corporation requires you to report their whereabouts immediately. In addition, there are several people of interest that New Corporation would like to talk to. Download the list, come forward if mentioned. Help to keep your city safe.

Chapter 20

It's not safe. It's not safe. It's not safe. Martha woke up in a cold sweat, the warning ringing in her ears. She tried to remember the dream, but it was fading fast. All she was left with was a vague memory of a blue lady. Gaia had spoken to her, warned her. It's not safe. But what wasn't safe?

Dina began tossing and turning, mumbling in her sleep before sitting up abruptly, wide awake. 'It's not safe!' she shouted.

'Did you see her too?' Martha asked.

Dina nodded and took a shaky breath. 'What did Gaia mean? What isn't safe?'

'I don't know but there was something about that dream. It frightened me, Dina.'

'Me too.' The two women hugged, trying to calm themselves down.

'Are we doing the right thing?' asked Martha.

'We are. We'll be at City 9 tomorrow. We've got to get information so we can decide what to do next. You made the best decision, Ma.'

'Did I? What if they decide to kill all the citizens of another city so they can get to us?'

'They won't,' said Jed. He'd woken up and turned his seat round in the skimmer so he could face them. 'From what we know City 9 is a pro-Corp city. They'll probably know we're there the minute we set foot in the city, but I don't think they'll target us.'

'Won't they arrest us?' asked Dina.

'They could've done that at Camp Eden. They let us go, they must have known we'd head here. I think they're waiting to see what we'll do next,' replied Jed. 'If we keep a low profile and try to blend in as much as possible, I think they'll leave us alone.'

'That doesn't make any sense,' Martha said.

'Yes, it does. Listen. You and Ruth are the first natural parents our city had in decades. Who knows if any of the other cities have had natural pregnancy? You bring hope to so many families wanting children. Plus, Gaia spoke to you. It could be that Corporation are hoping Gaia will show herself again so they can capture her or something.'

Dina scoffed at the idea, but Martha thought Jed might have a point. They spent the rest of the journey in silence. The landscape outside the skimmer window had been flat and featureless except for frequent dead zones of burnt earth. Vegetation had tried to gain purchase here and there, but it was scattered at best. The odd flock of birds swooped through the sky now and then, but they didn't see any larger animals. They hadn't stopped the entire trip, everyone taking turns to navigate and the whole group eating on the move. They'd all felt the urgency to get to City 9 as soon as possible, find out what they could and make a plan for their future.

Leaving the skimmers and all the operatives well outside the city limits; Jed, Max, Dina and Martha entered City 9 on foot. The city force-fields were turned on, but a single gateway allowed visitors through. The security guards didn't seem that interested in their small group. A skimmer had arrived at the same time as them, drawing attention away from the foot traffic so everyone walked through the gateway unobserved, before anyone had chance to change their mind. The city was different to 42 in so many ways, there were no trees or social areas for people to congregate but there were lots of people walking purposefully.

'What do they have on their heads?' asked Max.

'Those are the new neural implants. Ben told me about them,' replied Dina.

Everyone they saw was wearing the new tech which made Martha, Jed and the rest of them stand out for not having them.

'We'll have to get some and mod them. You can do that, can't you, Dina?' asked Jed.

She nodded as they walked further into the city, looking for a nearby shared space. They found an automated building with a free room, so they took it and dumped all their bags, keen to get out and start their mission. Their first step was to upgrade their tech. After leaving the room, they found themselves standing on the edge of a busy plaza.

'New in town?' asked an oily voice. A small man in a scruffy looking grey jumpsuit was standing to one side, his eyes darting left and right as he spoke to them. He looked like the kind of person they needed to avoid but also the type of person who would be able to help them out.

Martha shrank back and let Jed do the talking.

'We need to upgrade - think you can point us in the right direction?'

'Name's Marv and tech upgrades are my speciality. This way.' The shifty man gestured for the group to follow him. He led them off the main street through a side passage which skirted but did not go down any of the tight looking alleys. Martha began to think they might actually get what they needed.

After a few minutes they stopped outside a small shop. A faded auto-ad was flickering in the window, made even harder to see by the layer of grime over both window and door. The man held the door open and everyone filed in. Jed was pleased he'd left the rest of the team outside the city limits with the skimmers. They needed to maintain a low profile here.

The shop looked like nothing special from the outside but inside it was a tech lover's dream. It had everything - the latest wristplant, integrated arm swipes, retina sweeps as well as the one thing they didn't have any of. They latest tech from New Corp. Neural implants.

'So whaddaya need?' The man sensed he was going to make a small fortune and he wasn't wrong. By the time Jed had bought some neural implants and new wristplants for himself, Martha, Dina and Max, the seller's grin was as wide as his face.

'Do you need help fitting them?' The man peered at the side of Jed's head. 'Looks like you've not had one before.'

'Er, no, thank you. We can manage.' Jed handed over the requested tokens and the small group tried to remember how to get back to the lodgings they'd checked into near the entrance to the town. No-one was about as they accessed their shared room. They hadn't felt comfortable splitting up even though it was a tight squeeze, all of them together. Now that they'd made it to City 9, they didn't want to take any risks. Gaia's warning still resonated with Dina and Martha and the men had seen how shaken up they'd been. Everyone knew they needed to be careful in this city.

'Do you think you can deactivate these, Dina?' Jed asked, pointing to the neural implants on the table.

'I think so. If the information Ben sent is correct and these are the same model, it should be straightforward enough. I need a little space.' She shooed everyone away from the small table and set to work. In Ben's last communique he'd explained how New Corp was rolling out the neural implants to every citizen and had outlined the basics of deactivating them. No-one had heard from Ben in a couple of days and Jed had been reluctant to send any unnecessary messages. There was a good chance New Corp knew where they were, so there was no need to be blatant and advertise the fact. And with New Corp cracking down on non-conformers there was no way they could walk around City 9 without the neural implants in evidence. They'd be noticed. It was bad enough their clothing wasn't the same as what everyone else was wearing, but at least they could stick to their story of being travellers. City 9 must have travellers being so close to the coast. Martha still held on to the hope they would find transport away from this island. It would mean waiting for Kira and the rest to finish up in 36 and travel back down the length of the country but it was a small price to pay for escaping Corporation rule. She was excited about going out tomorrow to explore and see what they could find out.

The loudspeaker announcement made them all jump. 'Curfew in ten minutes. Curfew in ten minutes. All outer doors will be locked. All outer doors will be locked.'

'Well, that was unexpected,' Jed commented. 'I'm going to have a shower.' And he locked himself into the bathroom. Dina had her head bent over the components of the neural implants, leaving Martha and Max with nothing to do.

'Shall we see what's on the news sweeps or did you want to order some food?' Max asked.

'Let's find something to eat. There's bound to be something that everyone will like,' replied Martha.

The two of them checked the small screen nestled on the wall next to the synth-caf machine. The options were all the same sorts of instant, dried food variety they used to eat in 42. Martha felt a stab of disappointment. She had thought that with City 9 being by the coast, there might have been some hint of fresh fish available to eat. But then she considered their team hadn't had chance to check out the local area thoroughly. The one thing they had been able to clear was the water supply. It was contaminant free, thank goodness.

Every time a drone passed the window of their room, Martha flinched. She couldn't help it. She knew New Corp would probably have tabs on all of them but if their luck held New Corp might leave them alone while they were here. They couldn't return to 42, where they would stand trial for their crimes. But she didn't know what New Corp would do now they'd travelled to City 9.

Martha let Max order the food. It all tasted the same to her anyway. She made sure the synth-caf machine was fully stocked. She didn't think they'd get much sleep tonight and she wanted to make sure she was as caffeinated as possible.

Two hours later and Dina uttered an exalted 'Yes!' bringing everyone over to her small table.

'I've done it! They won't try to change the neural pathways anymore, but they'll still look like everyone else's. Max, come here.' She beckoned him to come closer and as he bent down towards her, she moved his hair out of the way and fixed the implant in place. 'It has self-adhesive nanos which are separate to the ones that change the neural pathways. These ones don't think for themselves, they just stick,' she explained. 'Give it a shake!'

Max shook his head a little then, feeling braver moved his head around rapidly. The implant stayed in place. 'Well done, D.' He smiled at her.

Dina grinned back at him. 'Come on you two, let's get these fitted then someone can put mine on.' Martha stepped forward first while Jed grabbed some more food from the replicator so they could eat and discuss their next step.

'At least we look a bit more like everyone else now,' he commented once his implant was in place. 'Are we all clear on the plan for tomorrow?'

'Yes, Max is going to try and reach the ocean, we need to see whether it's cordoned off or whether citizens have free access. We also need to find out what condition the water is in,' Martha said.

'Fine with me,' replied Max. 'If I run into any problems, I'll flash my scientist card at them. It usually confuses low level enforcers enough to leave me alone.'

'But you've got your panic button just in case?' asked Jed.

Max nodded. They had all had them installed on the way to City 9, deep in the left armpit so they couldn't be set off by accident.

'Me and Ma are going to see if we can find any fresh food,' said

Dina.

'Plus, two women shopping for food will be less conspicuous then if we send Jed,' teased Martha.

There was a brief chuckle from Jed. 'I'm going to try and do a loop of the city. See how big it is, what other exits and entrances there are, whether there are any obvious weak spots. It will be good to see whether there is Force here or if it's New Corp Security. We need to resupply in case of a quick getaway. Our food sachets are running low.' Everyone nodded in agreement, happy with their assignments.

'I still can't wrap my head around New Corp,' Dina said. 'I mean, I understand they felt they had to retaliate against the uprising in 42. That makes sense to me. But why rebrand?'

'If they rebranded at all.' Martha chipped in. 'They could be another arm of a massive worldwide conglomerate. Or they could be a takeover company, trying to keep things feeling similar so there is less panic. New Corp feel very different to me.' She paused, checking she had everyone's attention. 'We can't forget 15.'

Dina shook her head and reached out for Max's hand to squeeze in comfort. They would never forget City 15.

ENCRYPTED MESSAGE FROM CITY 9 TO CITY 42
>>*Martha Hamble, Dina Grey & Jed Jenkins have entered City 9*<<

ENCRYPTED MESSAGE FROM CITY 42 TO CITY 9
>>FOLLOW THEM AND REPORT BACK<<

ENCRYPTED MESSAGE FROM CITY 9 TO CITY 42
>>*Do you want us to apprehend them for questioning?*<<

ENCRYPTED MESSAGE FROM CITY 42 TO CITY 9
>>NOT YET. LET'S SEE WHAT THEY DO. THEY MIGHT LEAD US TO THE RESISTANCE<<

Chapter 21

Kira smiled. She was suspended in a warm, dark place, gently floating but it didn't feel scary. She felt safe and content. The darkness became lighter as a soft golden glow expanded from everywhere at once. Colours flooded her awareness and Kira realised she was now floating above the Earth, holding hands with her blue lady. She was with Gaia. And she was dreaming.

'We've missed you so much. Why haven't you shown yourself? Guided us? We need you!' exclaimed Kira.

The blue lady smiled sadly, and a tear rolled down her face. She turned to look the other way and Kira saw a deep cut down the side of Gaia's neck, over her shoulder and disappearing down her back. It was black and dull with grey shadows pulsing either side of the gash. Kira put a hand out to help but then faltered.

'You're too weak. You haven't healed enough yet. Can we help in some way?' she asked.

Gaia turned to look at her again and her entire face was transformed by a glowing smile as she nodded. Kira felt excited.

'We're trying to find a new place to live, somewhere free of Corporation where we can raise the children and... and... I don't know, help you heal somehow.'

Gaia put out a hand and touched Kira's face gently before she started to fade, still smiling.

Kira woke slowly, basking in the remnants of her dream, feeling her spirit refreshed.

'You look happy,' commented Ruth. 'Dreaming of Jed?'

'No. It was Gaia, she came to me - oh, Ruth! She hasn't forgotten us. She needs our help to heal herself and us finding somewhere to live is all part of it, I just know it.' Kira's face glowed in excitement, but Ruth was less enthusiastic, and half nodded.

'Well, we're here,' she said.

Kira scrambled out of the skimmer in excitement. But City 36 wasn't so much a city as a collection of huts and by the looks of things, they had all been abandoned some time ago. Kira was so disappointed. She had pinned her hopes on finding a group of people out here, who had learned to be self-sufficient and live off the land with no involvement whatsoever from Corporation. Maybe even be without technology. Instead, all she had were derelict huts that looked like they wouldn't survive the next five minutes let alone a harsh winter. There were even abandoned beehives.

Ash came to join her; he'd finished making his sweeps.

'There's nothing here. I'm sorry Kira. There's no sign of there ever being a force-field or a comms network or any kind of technology that we would recognise. It's also a dead zone for our comms. Are you sure this is the right place?'

'According to the Archives it is.' She surveyed the ruins in dismay. 'Do we have enough supplies to make it back to the others? They will be in City 9 by now. It seems we split up for no reason.'

'We should have, but... something feels odd about this place, don't you think?' Ash shivered. 'I mean think about it. Why have the city listed in the archives if there is absolutely nothing here? And I'm not being funny but these huts, as much as they look like they're about to fall down in disrepair, they also look like they've only just been put together. Out of old wood but... there's something here that's not right.'

'You're very observant, friend.' A new voice startled Kira and Ash who turned to stare a gun barrel in the face. Behind the gun was a gruff looking man, wrapped up against the chill, his moustache bristling as he gestured with the rifle. 'How many of you are there?'

'Why? Who are you?' demanded Ash.

'Name's Tomas.' The man narrowed his eyes. 'I'll ask you again, how many are with you?'

'Fourteen adults. Four children.' Kira held her hands out in supplication, hoping that the mention of children would generate enough sympathy to at least allow them to leave.

'Children?' Tomas seemed surprised. He lowered his weapon. 'You'd better come with me.' He turned and walked away without waiting to see if they were following him. Kira and Ash stared at each other. Should they follow? At the rise of the hill, Tomas turned back and gestured impatiently. Kira shrugged. She'd come all this way to find a new kind of civilisation. It appeared it had found her. She went to the communal skimmer to get Grace and tell the others. She decided they could carry the children, rather than use the strollers, not knowing what the terrain would be like. It meant Ash had to carry Peter, but he didn't seem to mind. In fact, all of the operatives were rather taken with the little fella.

The operatives piled out of their skimmer, wearing minimal gear. It looked unthreatening but in reality, they were well armed to protect the rest of the group.

Tomas had not waited for them at the top of the hill and had begun his descent. The group quickly followed him.

'Are you sure this is a good idea, love? We could be walking into who knows what, do you even know that man's name? And is that a gun he's holding? I'm not sure about this at all, Kira. Think of the children. We can't run headlong into things. You're meant to be being responsible.' Jean was concerned.

'His name is Tomas, Mum, and I know, but we've come all this way. I refuse to believe there is no settlement of any kind here. These people could be our future,' replied Kira.

'Or they could be our end. I think we should leave some of us behind. As a security measure.' Ruth joined the conversation, which surprised everyone.

'We'll be fine. Ruth, remember that vision I told you about? From Gaia? I think this is what she meant. I have to take the first step here. It will be worth it; I can feel it.'

Neither Kira's mum nor Ruth looked convinced. Jean fell back to keep an eye on Ruth who was still withdrawn although she had begun to take a little interest in caring for Sarah and was carrying her at the moment.

Kira dragged her attention back to the direction the strange man had gone and realised he'd disappeared. She faltered and stopped descending. The operatives had fanned out ahead and Ash was staying back with Kira and the others. One of the operatives gave a shout and beckoned the others over. There was a cave opening set into the hill. Tomas reappeared at the mouth of the cave.

'Well, come if you're coming,' he said. And stomped off back the way he had come.

Ash split the operatives up, some in front, some flanking and some in the rear. They were all well trained and knew they had precious cargo to protect as they entered the cave.

It was like nothing Kira had been expecting. The cave felt warm and dry with light brackets spaced out equally along the wall. As they went further in, Kira became aware of a noise, it sounded like people talking. The tunnel opened out into a large cavern, remodelled into a communal area. There were stalls with goods for sale and some long tables where a handful of people were sitting and chatting. Without realising it, they'd all stopped walking. Everyone gaped at the small, underground community.

'Welcome to Hope.' Tomas was smiling, it made him look a lot less formidable. He'd slung the rifle on his shoulder and was standing in front of the marketplace.

'This isn't City 36?' Kira didn't know whether to be impressed or disappointed.

'City 36 hasn't existed for a long time. We don't answer to the Coalition.'

'Coalition?' whispered Jean to Ruth. 'Who are they?

'They were before Corporation - way before,' Ruth whispered back, her background as a history teacher coming to the rescue.

'Come, let me take you to the elders hall. We'll get you some refreshments and you can meet the rest of the council. Then you can tell us where you've come from and why you're here. Come, please.' Tomas was gesturing for them to follow him again. This time he led them to the left and down a passageway to another, smaller cavern where groups of tables and chairs were arranged in both large and small configurations. There were a few groups of people dotted about but more interesting than that were the two tables on the right-hand side, spread with some food and hot drinks.

'Please, help yourself,' he said, and the group moved towards them eagerly, exclaiming in surprise at the sorts of things available. There were dried fruits and nuts, some hard bread and a large tureen of steaming hot chocolate.

'We ought to check the food first before we eat anything, Kira,' warned Ash.

'Okay, how long will that take?'

'It'll be a couple of hours before the results come back - it's harder to detect anomalies in foodstuffs with the small handhelds,' replied Ash.

'Oh, Ash! I'm sure it will be alright. It doesn't look like there's anything wrong with the food and it would be rude not to.' Carried away in her excitement, Kira left Ash to his doubts and went to join her mum and Ruth in trying some of the fare available.

Ash did not eat anything. He ran his tests.

'This is amazing,' Kira said sipping a cup of hot chocolate as she addressed Tomas. 'Where did all this come from? Did you grow it? Make it?'

'Of course we did. Where else would it have come from?' he asked, a slight frown creasing his brow.

'A food replicator?' replied Kira.

'What's a food replicator?'

'Fascinating,' said Kira. 'Where do you grow your food?' Kira was buzzing, she felt like they'd found what they were looking for and she couldn't wait to tell Jed and the others. This was the place; she could feel it.

'Come, sit, eat. We will introduce ourselves to each other and then we can take you on a tour,' said Tomas, avoiding Kira's question.

The group sat down at one of the larger tables. Tomas smiled and nodded, deflecting their questions with ease. Clearly, he was waiting for more senior members of his settlement to arrive. They didn't wait long.

A dark-haired, slim woman in her fifties hurried into the cavern, she slowed as she caught sight of them and approached, patting her hair and smoothing her dress over her legs. Her gaze lingered on the children before finally turning to address Kira who sat closest to Tomas.

'Welcome to Hope. I don't know how you found us but you are welcome here. You and your children. Tell me, who is in command out there? Is it still Coalition?' The lady sat down in a nearby empty chair.

'Um, I don't...' Kira began to speak but Ruth interrupted so she could explain.

'Coalition were the original governing group that formed after The Event. It was made up of what was left of the various countries' government and military across the globe, who came together in a massive effort to build the cities and leave a legacy.' The woman nodded in agreement, so Ruth continued. 'There has been a lot of speculation as to what exactly had happened to them and how Corporation came to be the overriding power, but the Archives are sketchy at best as to what caused the change in power.' She turned to the woman. 'Basically, Coalition don't exist anymore.'

The women paled and then rallied quickly. 'Where are my manners? Please, I am Gloria, one of the council members here at Hope. I see you've already met Tomas. Do you need more time to recover and rest? I have so many questions.'

'No please, ask away. We have questions of our own. Shall we take turns?' Kira was half joking, but she hoped this woman, this Gloria, would take her seriously.

'Sounds wonderful,' Gloria smiled at her.

Both women spoke at the same time, 'So...' then laughed and Gloria gestured to Kira, 'Please, your turn.'

'How long have you been here?' Kira asked.

'Hope was established soon after the fall of the City 36, the city Coalition had created. Their design wasn't the right fit for this part of the country. Don't get me wrong, Coalition worked hard trying to find a solution for everyone but that was part of the problem. You can't put a one size fits all plaster on the type of problem the world faced. There would be communities that didn't fit within that defined social setting. Plus, the HER radiation was highly toxic this far north. There had been a processing plant up here, used for generating new weapons. It was blown up towards the end of the conflict and decimated the land and waters for miles and miles around.'

Kira was absorbed. 'Didn't you have protection from the radiation?'

'From what we've been able to learn, infrastructure was difficult in the early days. We have often wondered why Coalition wanted to bother with an outpost here, so remote from everyone else and so isolated. You can probably tell that we don't have much tech here. Some old communicators but otherwise, we are self-sufficient. My turn. Where are you from?' Gloria turned her attention on the rest of the group.

'We have travelled from City 42, down in the South. The city was under Corporation control, they are the company who came after Coalition,' replied Kira.

'So, Coalition doesn't exist anymore?'

'No, but I wouldn't get too excited,' replied Kira. 'What followed has not been exactly fair to the remaining populace, at least not in our experience.'

Kira went on to explain how City 42 had been run with the deliberate sterility, the baby lottery and the total control of Corporation over every aspect of everybody's life. The others in her party were content to let her speak. Tomas and Gloria drank in every word. When Kira got to the part about Martha, Ruth and Ingrid's natural births, Gloria clapped her hands together. Kira trailed off, made uncertain by her host's reaction.

'Forgive me,' said Gloria. 'Reproduction has always been a difficult aspect to our community. Obviously, we do procreate, yet radiation levels affected everyone so badly. We've suffered with mutations, genetic deformities and other related medical conditions.'

'How have you managed to overcome them?' asked Ash.

'Everyone is required to have at least four offspring and the gene lines are mixed as much as possible. Obviously, we don't have the scientific equipment to check that our DNA pool is as varied as it could be, but we've done our best. Those matches that resulted in high numbers of defects were soon dissolved. It may sound barbaric, but the survival of our colony has always been at the forefront of everything we've tried to achieve here.'

The visitors took a moment to digest this.

'Why have you come here?' Gloria asked, breaking the silence.

'Martha Hamble, the new governor of City 42, was ousted and it appears Corporation have re-entered our city, as New Corporation this time. But they are more ruthless than before. I don't know if it's the same company as before, it feels like they might have evolved again,' Kira explained. 'There's a lot we don't know. Basically, we were threatened with imprisonment and the reassignment of our children if we stayed. We couldn't stay. It was out of the question. Our group split up to see if we could find any communities out here that had also escaped the total control of Corporation.'

'Where did the others go?'

'They went to the coast, to City 9,' replied Kira.

'I think it's highly unlikely that you will ever see them again.'

'I'm sorry?' Ash asked the question, but everyone was concerned.

'The southern coastal city has always been a stronghold for Coalition. It was the only way to interact with the wider world out there. A real place of power and influence. It doesn't matter what they're calling themselves now, I can guarantee that City 9 will not be a safe place for your friends.' Gloria looked at the children who were happily playing on the floor under the watchful eyes of Jean and Malcolm. 'They don't also have children with them, do they?'

Kira shook her head.

'Come, I can see that all these questions are tiring. Would you like to have a look around?' asked Gloria. 'We have some guest quarters which should be ready for you now as well. I can show you our little community and then leave you to settle in. I'm sure you have lots to process.'

'Thank you, that would be very kind.' A sudden thought occurred to Kira. 'What about our vehicles? We left them by the ruins of 36. Will they be safe there?'

'Tomas will help your men move them. We have several axillary caves for large items such as sledges, carts, that sort of thing. I'm sure your vehicles will fit there. They might attract a lot of interested questions though.' Gloria laughed.

Kira smiled in response but found she couldn't relax fully. It was probably the strangeness of everything and the utter and total lack of a Corporation presence that had her on edge.

'Let's have this tour then.' She smiled brightly at Gloria and stood.

Gloria spoke to Tomas, asking him to find space for their vehicles while Ash organised a couple of operatives to go back with the man to the entrance and help secure the skimmers. The rest of the group gathered themselves together and prepared to be led through Hope. By now, the children were relatively sleepy and snuggled themselves comfortably into their individual carriers. Kira wished she too could be picked up and smooshed but she knew it was important that she paid attention to her surroundings. She activated her cam and smiled at Ash as she noticed him doing the same. They should have some footage to share with the others, at some point, when comms connections were re-established.

'Lead on,' Kira said to Gloria and soon the group crocodiled out of the cavern, most of them eager to see what awaited them elsewhere in this underground grotto but as they exited the cavern, Ash grabbed Kira's arm.

Chapter 22

'I don't think we should follow this Gloria woman further into the cave. We haven't had all of the analysis back yet. I don't think you should've eaten that food. I'm not comfortable with this, Kira. For all we know, we could be walking into danger.'

'But, Ash, don't you feel it? This place is where we're meant to be, I know it.'

Kira was trying to convince herself as well as Ash. This felt like it could be the right place for them, but something was niggling at her.

'I really think we should return to the skimmers. Wait for the results.' Ash sounded so determined to go back that Kira decided to concede.

'Uh, Gloria?' asked Kira. 'Look, the offer of a tour is wonderful, but we need to check in with the other team, make sure our vehicles are secure and get the children ready for bed - I'm sure you understand?'

Gloria faltered and looked back at Kira in disbelief. 'You mean, you don't want to do the rest of the tour?'

'Can't we do it tomorrow?' pleaded Kira.

Gloria patted her hair, obviously reluctant to let them go back to their vehicles. 'Well, I'm sure it will be fine. There's nowhere else for you to go, is there?' And she laughed lightly.

All that did was increase the niggle in Kira's stomach and she suddenly felt relieved that she'd listen to Ash.

'What about first thing in the morning?' suggested Gloria. 'We'll come and collect you for breakfast. It'll be lovely, you can meet our children. They're usually at their best first thing in the morning.' Gloria smiled encouragingly.

Kira nodded while her thoughts whirled. At their best? What did that mean? It did answer one question for her - there were children in

Hope.

They turned to go back the way they had come when Kira realised she had no idea what direction she needed to travel in.

'Where is our team please, Gloria?'

'Oh, Greg will show you the way.' Gloria gave a limp wave in their direction at a young man who stood nearby before she turned and left them in the cavern, her shoulders bowed slightly in disappointment.

Kira felt terrible. Was she squandering the opportunity to be part of Gaia's vision for them all? But she had to listen to her team, and she had to listen to her gut. Family came first.

'Ash, do you...' Kira started to speak but Ash motioned her into silence with a curt shake of his head. He hoped she'd get the message. They needed to wait until they got back to the skimmers and could talk in privacy. And get the results of the tests.

They mutely followed Greg through a different set of tunnels to the one they had arrived until he brought them out into a large entrance way. Kira felt relieved to see not only their skimmers but the rest of their team, all together in one place.

Tomas came over to meet them. He pointed to an old-fashioned phone on the wall of the cavern. 'If there's anything you need, just holler on this. One of us will come sort you out.'

'Does this actually work?' Kira asked in wonder.

'Not in the original sense but there'll be someone on the other end who will answer the call, should you need anything.' Tomas waited to see whether they would ask for anything now and when they didn't, he half shrugged and said goodnight, taking Greg with him.

Ash spent a few moments chatting with the operatives who had been sent to get the skimmers. They had nothing to report out of the ordinary. There had been a fair amount of interest in them and their vehicles but that was to be expected. No-one had tried to touch anything or take anything and there had been no sign of any threatening behaviour.

As Jean and Ruth put the children down in their cubes, Ash checked the food and environmental tests he had been running. It was bad news. He went to find Kira.

'Kira, we can't stay here. It isn't safe.'

'What do you mean?' she asked.

'Radiation levels are borderline dangerous. If we stay here any longer than the next twenty-four hours, we run the risk of developing radiation sickness.' He cast a glance in the direction of the children. 'Especially them. I think we ought to dose everyone straight away as a precaution and be on our way by morning.'

'Is it that serious? Should we leave now?'

'It is serious, but I think leaving now, abruptly and in the dark, isn't the best idea. If everyone takes the shot, we're good for twenty-four hours. If we leave in the morning, we can try and get back into signal range with the others and report in. We don't know if they've been successful or not, none of our messages seem to have gone through either. This is a bit of a dead zone.'

Kira nodded. She was bitterly disappointed that Hope wasn't the refuge she had been so sure it would be. But there was no way she was going to risk Grace's health and well-being for the sake of a few fruits and vegetables they'd somehow managed to grow but that were apparently contaminated anyway. Her stomach clenched at the thought of the food they had eaten a short while ago.

'Where are the anti-radiation meds?' she asked Ash. He pointed them out to her, she grabbed a handful and hurried over with them to her parents, Ruth and the kids.

'I have some bad news, I'm afraid,' Kira said.

'There's a surprise,' Ruth commented sourly.

'There are dangerous levels of background radiation here. We can't stay so we'll be leaving in the morning.'

Ruth paled, her eyes darting around the cavern and made to grab Sarah, acting as if she was going to make a run for it. Kira put a hand on her arm.

'It's alright Ruth, we're leaving first thing in the morning. Here, take this shot and give one to Sarah. It will protect you against the radiation.'

'Thank you, love,' said Jean. 'We'll get all the kiddies dosed up and us of course but shouldn't we leave now? I mean we know now this isn't the place, I know you had your heart set on it all and everything, but we don't want to put anyone at risk, do we? And I was saying to your father something didn't feel quite right here. I couldn't quite put my finger on it but obviously it's those people. They are all sick and they want us to stay and get sick with them. It's just, it's not right, Kira dear. Not right at all.'

'No, Mum, I know. And we are leaving but we're safe here in our pods with our meds. Ash will set up a night watch and we'll leave first thing in the morning. Okay?'

Jean looked worried but nodded.

'Don't eat or drink anything else from here either, stick to our ration packs.'

'Yes, dear. Those are running low as well you know. As is my medicine. These things won't last for ever, love.'

'I know, Mum, I know. We will find you some more medicine, I promise. Try not to worry.' Kira finished giving Grace her shot and smiled fondly at the little girl who was busy trying to eat her own foot. This was her world right here, her daughter and Jed. Thinking of him hurt her chest, she missed him so much. She hoped he was safe and that he was having better luck then they were.

'Can you believe our luck?' Gloria was pacing in her rooms, Tomas and a couple of other elders were sitting in various chairs, nursing their drinks. 'This is what we need, a fresh infusion into our gene pool. This could be the answer to all our problems.'

'I think you're simplifying it a bit there, Gloria,' Tomas commented drily.

'What do you mean?'

'You can't expect a group of total strangers to jump in and start having sex with us, just because they're new. They might not even want to stay. And there are a helluva lot more men than women in that group. You can count the old woman out for starters, she isn't going to bear any more children. Which leaves Kira and the sour-faced one. Two women aren't going to help us create lots more children that quickly.'

'No but it's two new women. And all those men can mix their DNA with the viable women we have left. Our sickly children can mate with their strong ones and, and...'

'Gloria, you're talking madness. They might not even want to stay. Staying would put their health at risk. Be realistic. You know that's not a sickly gene that we're fighting here. There's radiation in the air and in the water that is slowly poisoning us.'

'And what am I supposed to do about that? Force everyone to leave their lives behind? Up-sticks and risk their safety out there? We don't know what's out there! Coalition or whatever they're calling themselves these days could be ready to pounce on us as soon as we reveal our position. Another reason why we can't let them leave.'

'I don't think you have the right to force them to stay.'

'Are you going to stand against me on this, Tomas?'

'I am. These people are looking for a fresh start. We would be offering them sickness and death.'

At that Gloria seemed to crumble from within and she half fell into a chair. 'But it's so unfair, they all look so healthy and the children...' She began to cry.

Tomas got up and put his arm around her, pulling her into his embrace. 'I know, but we have to do what's right. We cannot keep them here against their will. It makes us no better than Coalition.'

After she'd finished weeping, Gloria pulled herself together and smiled gratefully at Tomas for his support.

'Do you think they will leave in the night? Without saying goodbye?'

'I think they have more sense than that. But we may have to catch them early in the morning, to wish them well on their journey.'

Gloria nodded and lapsed into silence, disappointed that her hopes of saving their community lay in tatters once more. She didn't want to believe that everyone who lived in Hope was so badly riddled with radiation that there was literally nothing she could do to save any of them. They would all die, gradually peter out as their immune systems gave up trying to fight the radiation sickness. Another group of humanity would be lost.

Chapter 23

'What will happen to all these people here in Hope, Ash?' Kira asked quietly. It looked like everyone in their group was sleeping or at least resting. The children were completely oblivious to any danger they might be in. They had adapted remarkably well to life on the road. It helped that they were still young enough to be easily entertained and not all that mobile. Kira dreaded to think what the journey would've been like with toddlers who wanted to walk and run all the time. It would have been impossible. She was lucky Grace wasn't walking yet but it wouldn't long.

'I'm so sorry, Kira. They're not going to make it. It could be days, weeks, even months but eventually their bodies will succumb to the background radiation levels present and they will die.' Ash hated having to tell Kira this, but he didn't want her thinking there was any way they could stay here.

'And there's nothing we can do?'

'Even if we had stockpiles of our anti-radiation medicine it wouldn't do them any good. Once they stopped taking the meds they'd be right back where they started. They are slowly poisoning themselves with the air they breathe, the water they're drinking and the food they're eating.'

Kira felt so useless. She was now grateful they hadn't taken the tour, met the rest of the community and the children. She didn't think her heart could take meeting children that she knew would be dead before the year was out.

'And we haven't put everyone at risk, have we?' she asked.

'We're lucky. We have the right meds with us, everyone is dosed up. We only ingested a small amount of food and drink and our bodies are actually pretty well equipped to deal with this stuff initially. It's the constant bombardment that becomes lethal. As long as we leave in the morning, take another dose and monitor everyone's vitals, we should be fine.'

'What if we were to take their children with us? Could we save them?'

Ash's heart broke a little as he looked at the hope in Kira's face. He shook his head. He couldn't find the words. He felt like he was letting her down, but he couldn't think about all the lives that would be lost here. This was much, much worse than the casual genocide of City 15. It explained why there had been no attempts by New Corp to investigate this settlement and extend Corp rule. The people who lived here would be dead soon enough. Why waste the resources?

The two of them sat in their misery long into the early hours of the morning, not speaking. There was nothing more either of them could think of to say. They took comfort in each other's presence and tried to focus on the next stage of their journey.

It was still dark when the operatives started to stir. No-one was going to sleep in today. The children were wide awake and full of beans, clamouring for breakfast. Surprisingly, Ruth was taking charge today, it seemed that the brush with danger had invigorated her. She was still rather acerbic with anyone who wasn't a small child, but she had prepared breakfast for all four children and although she looked tired, today she had made an effort and brushed her hair. Kira didn't say anything directly but shared a delighted grin with her mum. They had both been worried about Ruth's general apathy and lack of desire to get involved with looking after her own baby.

There was a commotion in the entrance to the cavern as Gloria, Tomas and few other residents of Hope appeared. They looked resolute and Kira feared they would try to stop them leave.

'Good morning,' she said. 'As you can see, we are getting ready to leave. I wanted to thank you for your hospitality...'

Gloria cut her off. 'There's no need. We can see you are more technologically advanced than we are. You have probably discovered our health issues and I cannot blame you for not wanting to put yourself and your children at risk. I only wish we could have met under more pleasant circumstances.'

Kira held her hands out to the woman, who took them hesitantly. 'So you know, you know what will happen here?'

Gloria couldn't speak but she nodded once, swiftly, eyes bright, smile brittle. Kira squeezed her hands and closed her eyes in sympathy. This was so much harder than she'd thought it would be. A loud bang of a skimmer door shutting made them both jump and Kira looked to see that everyone was ready to leave. She didn't know what else to say so instead she hugged Gloria briefly and held a hand out to Tomas who shook it warmly. Ash, too, came over to formally say goodbye to the leaders of Hope but everyone else stayed in the skimmers.

Kira felt like her skin was crawling, but she knew it was only in her imagination. She'd taken the medicine; she would take the next dose and she would closely monitor her health. Everything would be fine, for them. Turning away, trying not to cry, Kira hurried to her skimmer, followed by Ash. Gloria and Tomas lifted their arms in farewell and watched in sadness as the vehicles drove out of the cavern, able to escape the doom that awaited the people left behind.

No-one spoke for a long time as the group journeyed back the way they had come. Meds were taken and they had short breaks to eat and drink from their dwindling supplies. Even the children seemed to realise that now was not the time to be fractious and they sat quietly or dozed as the countryside swept past them. Eventually the small convoy stopped for the evening and as the operatives began to set up camp, Ash began sweeping for comms messages from the other team. They had made good progress and should be back in range of some sort of comms array. Finally, he found a small, weak signal. It took a while but the message that they had been trying to send to Jed's team eventually went through and a short message from them arrived.

MESSAGE FROM TEAM 9 TO TEAM 36:
We have arrived safely and secured neural implants. We will re-con tomorrow and report back.

MESSAGE FROM TEAM 36 to TEAM 9:
Unfortunately, City 36 is non-viable, there are high levels of radiation. All of team 36 have been dosed with anti-radiation meds. We will begin the journey back down to City 9 unless we hear differently. Hopefully your re-con will be more successful. Looking forward to getting the team back together.

Chapter 24

'Have you seen the message from the others?' Dina called out.

Everyone gathered by the comm and read the details.

'Oh, that's terrible,' said Max. 'I was hoping 36 might be a serious option for us. I thought it would be off Corporation's radar, a safe place for us.'

'No, it's completely radioactive instead. Those poor, poor people. Jed? Will the children be alright?' Martha asked urgently.

'Yes, they should be fine. As long as they took their meds and there's no way Kira would forget to do something like that.' Jed looked up at Martha and took a double take. She'd done her best to disguise her features by chopping all her hair off to a close crop and putting colour filters in her eyes to change them. 'Looks good, Ma.'

Martha flushed and smoothed her clothing apprehensively. She was fairly certain she didn't look like the ex-governor of City 42 anymore. Through the internal room replicator, they'd been able to order the same jumpsuits they'd seen everyone else in the city wearing. Together with their fake neural implants, they were feeling confident that they looked the same as everyone else. It was time to test the theory.

'Everyone clear on their objective?' asked Jed.

'Checking the ocean and nosing around the docks,' replied Max.

'Getting a feel for how the city works, looking for fresh food and keeping out of the way of New Corp security patrols,' replied Dina, moving to stand next to Martha who nodded in agreement.

'Right, and I'll try and get a circuit of the city completed. See if there are any other entries or exits, any places to avoid, anything that points to the people behind City 15.'

'I think all of New Corp are responsible for that,' Dina muttered sourly as they prepared their packs.

'Did you check in with the operatives?' Jed asked her before they left.

'Yes, they are maintaining their position, outside the reach of the scanners, and have hidden their own signals so as not to raise any suspicion. If a drone flies directly over them, we won't be able to do much about it, but they've tried to use their surroundings to camouflage themselves as much as possible. They are maintaining comm silence until we report in this evening.' Dina felt a sense of pride in being able to sound so professional. Who knew she would have gone from student, to field scientist to rebel comms officer in less than a year?

They headed out of their room, trying to look as inconspicuous as possible. The two men went one way and soon split again while the women strolled off in the opposite direction.

'I suppose we should look for some breakfast or something,' suggested Martha.

'Yeah, shall we try one of these?' Dina pointed to a replicator on the corner. It was advertising nutrient enhanced synth-caf, designed to set you up for a busy day ahead. It was popular, a swift moving queue had formed in front, so they joined the line. Martha felt in her pocket for tokens. When they reached the machine both women stared in dismay, it required a retinal scan to issue the drinks.

'Here, allow me.' A man pushed between them and lowered his eye to the scanner, it bleeped and pulsed green. He pressed for three and juggled them away from the dispenser. The two women followed cautiously.

'You're new in town, aren't you?' he asked as he passed the drinks over.

'What makes you say that?' Martha asked casually, trying not to sound alarmed.

'You've clearly never paid for anything here before, otherwise the retinal scan wouldn't have thrown you. And although you've done a good job, those neural implants are fake, they're not connected to the mainframe.' He took a sip of his synth-caf, watching them over the rim of his cup then grimaced at the flavour. 'Look this stuff is awful. You want some real coffee? No strings.' He held his arms out as if to show he was no threat.

Martha looked at Dina who shrugged her shoulders minutely. Both women were armed, knew how to use the stun guns, and they both had internal trackers so Jed would be able to find them if they ran into any kind of trouble. Besides there was something about this man they felt they could trust.

'Okay, lead on,' Martha replied.

'Great. I'll take those.' And he swiped the untouched synth-cafs from their hands, depositing them in the nearest refuse receptacle. With a jerk of his head he motioned for them to follow him down a nearby side street and set off a steady pace which had them scrambling to keep up. They followed the side streets for some time as the man seemed to want to keep a low profile, which was fine with them. Finally, they arrived at his destination. The building was an old red brick with an imposing black door. However, when he pushed the door open, the rich aroma of real coffee wafted out into the street. He grinned and ushered them inside.

It was a short walk down a dimly lit hallway before they came out into a kitchen. A large scarred wooden table dominated the middle of the room with various mismatched chairs arranged around the outside. There were real books, scraps of paper and pens scattered across the tabletop. A saucepan rack hung above their heads with shiny copper pans glinting in the electric lights. An old-fashioned range cooker filled one wall. It was like stepping into a history book. Then Martha noticed the plexiglass surrounding the entire scene. The man had laughter in his eyes as he beckoned them to follow him to the left. A small doorway led them into what looked like a communal restroom. There was a less interesting set up of table and chairs in here but at least they had found the source of the aroma, and it was real coffee.

'Perk of the job,' the man explained as he poured them each a cup. 'This is the city's museum, hence the impressive kitchen. But the replicators here are second to none and designed to provide the average punter with a realistic experience for their entry fee.' Martha put a hand to her pocket for tokens, but the man shook his head. 'No need.' He passed them a cup of coffee each.

Both women wrapped their hands around the hot mugs and inhaled the aroma. It felt wonderful to indulge.

'Do we stand out a lot then?' Martha asked.

'You've done a good job but for those used to looking out for non-conformers, you stick out. You're lucky you ran into me and not a security patrol. They wouldn't be giving you coffee. Where you from?'

'City 42,' Dina announced. Martha blinked at her in surprise.

'Ah. The rebel city. Although that's all finished with now. They executed quite a few dissenters up there, if you believe the sweeps of course.' He passed them a handheld.

NEWCORP: *News from City 42.*
Ben Jenkins has been terminated for crimes against the authority.
Nick Sedgwick has been terminated for crimes against the authority.
Dana Chrystal has been terminated for crimes against the authority.
Zavier Duparre, also known as ANON17, has been terminated for crimes against the authority.

Martha paled and sat down heavily on a nearby chair while Dina stifled a gasp.

'Hey, I'm sure it wasn't your fault.' The man looked worriedly at his guests. 'Look, I'm Zac. I curate the museum and I'm nosy but whatever you're doing here you don't have to worry about me reporting you to Corp Security. I keep my head down and my nose clean. I thought you looked interesting and it broke my heart to think of you drinking that synth-sludge.' He was smiling encouragingly at them.

'Thank you, Zac. I'm Martha and this is Dina. It's true we have come from City 42. We're looking for a way off the island. We had hoped that City 9 would hold the answer.'

Zac's face fell. 'I'm sorry. There's no travel out of here. The docks used to be open and we traded with some of the coastal cities across the water but when New Corp cracked down, everything stopped. We can't even get comms over there anymore. The docks have been dismantled, every boat destroyed, and the water is too poisonous to risk swimming in, although our forefathers used to enjoy a dip in the ocean - can you believe that?'

But Martha and Dina weren't listening. They had pinned their hopes on being able to get a boat and try their luck across the sea. Then Martha recalled something Zac had said.

'You said when New Corp cracked down - when was that?'

'Oof, about six months ago? I think. Things started to change, gradually at first, more in line with all things Corp. I guess we didn't notice at first and then by the time we started to question things a bit, they'd already got all their infrastructure in place and it was too late to do anything about it.' He looked at their worried faces. 'Oh, it's okay.

Toe the line and you're fine. More or less the same as the previous incarnation.'

'Except for the neural implants.' Dina pointed out.

'Well yeah, they suck but there are ways to get around them - as you know.'

Max looked around with interest as he walked towards the docks. City 9 was different from City 42. It had more integrated tech and definitely had less personality. As he grew closer to the ocean, Max realised there was no way he would get to stand on the beach or obtain a sample of seawater. The area bristled with New Corp Security and there were stiff security measures along the entire length. There was also a lack of civilians in the area making him stand out. He tried to make it look as though he were looking for a person rather than access to the seashore and back tracked slightly looking for somewhere to sit and rethink his plan of action.

The food hydrators were out of the question. He'd been more observant than Martha and Dina and noticed people using the retinal scan to pay for their beverages. Instead he looked for a slightly more old-fashioned establishment, somewhere that would still take the tokens he had in his pocket. At last he found one, a small, dingy looking café with a peeling sign in the window announcing tokens still taken. Max headed in and was welcomed with the delicious odour of bread baking. Things were looking up.

It turned out they weren't quite as optimistic as he first thought, the bread aroma was fake, but he was able to buy a synth-caf and a packet of rehydrated oatmeal with his tokens. As he sat by the window Max looked out and considered his options. He hadn't seen any boats in the harbour. There was clearly no citizen access to the beach which was a cordoned off area. One reason could be that New Corp didn't want anyone leaving City 9 via the docks because it wasn't safe to travel on the water or maybe they didn't have the transportation anymore. Alternatively, they just didn't want anyone leaving City 9.

There was no sign of any fresh food available, no dock trade or fishing opportunities. It didn't even smell fishy. Max sipped his synth-caf thinking about what high levels of HER would have done to the ocean.

It may be that the acidity of the water was too much for the material boats are made of and that was why they could not make the journey across the ocean. If high levels of radiation existed within the marine life left in the ocean, they wouldn't be safe to consume so New Corp could be trying to protect their citizens by not letting them fish. It would certainly be counter-productive to allow people to slowly poison themselves.

Realising that he'd finished both his drink and breakfast, Max stood up to leave. Time to go back to the room and wait for the others. He may have disappointing news, but he hoped the rest of them had been more fortunate.

Jed tried to look as inconspicuous as possible as he walked through the city. Luckily it seemed that the citizens in City 9 did still actually walk so at least that behaviour wasn't unusual. However, everyone seemed to be highly motivated with a pre-determined purpose and Jed couldn't help wondering whether he stuck out like a sore thumb. He tried to walk with as much purpose and confidence as he could muster. It didn't help that he was feeling hungry and there didn't seem to be any shops selling food, let alone street vendors. There was the odd replicator on a street corner, but Jed didn't want to give away his ignorance by attempting to use one, especially as they all seemed busy.

City 9 was laid out in much the same grid pattern as 15 and 42 except that one edge ended in a bristling cordon, clearly the ocean lay that way. Jed continued to loop around the city, noting the walls and the power generators for the force-field. The same set up as 42. There seemed to be more a mixture of buildings here than in his city though. Corp buildings intermingled with living accommodations and it was difficult to tell whether there was a dedicated Archive or Academy presence. Jed realised that each block was a self-contained unit. The citizens of 9 lived, worked and learnt all in one area, never needing to travel elsewhere. Clearly, they were still free to walk around the city at the moment, to use the food hydrators for example, but Jed wondered how long that would last for.

The only positive thing he noticed as he walked the city's circuit were evidence of sky skimmers. There were skimmer pads located at regular intervals and some of them appeared to be citizen driven, they weren't all New Corp Security but whether any of them had clearance to leave the force-field or indeed the capability to cross the ocean from this island to the next, he did not know. Somehow, they'd have to try and find out. Hopefully there would be an info point somewhere Dina could hack.

Jed finished his circuit, feeling a little defeated that there was no obvious solution to their problem. He hoped their presence here had gone unnoticed. He had no desire to tangle with the power behind the destruction of City 15. All he wanted to do was find a safe place for himself, his family and his friends. He spotted Max walking towards him and lifted a hand in greeting. Judging by his face, he'd had as much luck as Jed.

Chapter 25

'I think we should have taken the tour,' Dina said as the two of them walked back to their room.

'Maybe, but at least this way we have an excuse to come back with Jed and Max and see if we can get a bit more information out of Zac.'

'You think he's hiding something?' Dina asked.

'I think he knows more than he's letting on and who knows, he might be able to help us in some other way.'

'You don't think he's going to report us to New Corp, do you?'

'No, I think we are safe on that front.' They arrived shortly after Max and Jed. It didn't take long for them each to share their fact-finding missions.

'We found out something else as well,' said Martha. 'It's about Ben. Jed, I'm so sorry but... he's been terminated.'

'What? How do you know that?' Jed darted his gaze between Martha and Dina.

'When we were in the museum, with Zac, he showed us the sweeps from City 42. Apparently, they've rounded up four dissenters and had them all terminated. Ben was on the list. I'm sorry, Jed.' Martha reached out an arm but Jed flinched away from it.

'I can't... this is unreal.' He looked up at Dina in disbelief. 'He said he was going to be careful. He said.'

Dina gave him a hug murmuring words of comfort. Max and Martha looked on uncomfortably until Jed recovered. With a parting squeeze he extracted himself from Dina's arms and cleared his throat loudly.

'We ought to try and let Kira know what we've found out. Dina, can you get another message out to them?' he asked.

'Their comms have been down, but now that we know they're heading back, I should be able to get through to them,' Dina replied.

Martha felt the familiar tug on her heart when they spoke about the other team. She missed Lucas.

'Send the message Dina, but keep it brief,' Jed was back to business. 'Outline the facts - no ships, high level of New Corp presence. Try to break the news about Ben as gently as you can, please.' Then he addressed the others. 'We need to come up with a different plan.'

'What about Zac?' asked Martha.

'Well, if you think he has something to hide, I'm not sure all of us heading down there will encourage him to talk,' Jed replied honestly.

'I don't think he's necessarily hiding a bad thing. I think he might be able to help us,' said Martha.

'He should certainly be able to fill in some of the blanks on the history of this city. He runs a museum for goodness' sake. The closest thing they have to Archive here. All we've found are the sweeps,' commented Max, waving a hand at the vid screen in the room. It was displaying City 9 sweeps only.

'You're both right. Shall we go back tomorrow? Try and find out more?' asked Jed.

'I think that is a great idea.' Martha was pleased, she wanted to talk to Zac again.

There wasn't much to do other than wait for tomorrow to come. Dina had a scrambler channel running on one of their handhelds in case they heard anything from Corp Security about them or anyone matching their description. But there was nothing. And the sweeps were full of City 9 news, the usual new tech sales and gossipy pieces. In the end it lulled Martha to sleep. She was exhausted. She hadn't had any time to herself since everything had happened. She didn't feel like she'd said goodbye to Lucas properly and she missed him. She hoped it wouldn't be long before the two groups could come back together.

The next morning, they all woke early, eager to get out and do something productive. So far, coming to City 9 had only confirmed their fears and not provided them with any new ideas on what to do next.

'Do you think you'll be able to find the museum?' Jed asked.

Dina flashed her handheld at him, she'd downloaded the visitors guide from the museum yesterday. They were going primarily to talk to Zac and try and get a feel for his loyalties but at the same time she was excited to have a proper look around the museum. Kira would be so jealous.

They set off as soon as they could, there was no point in arriving too early and hanging around outside drawing attention to themselves. But when they got there, things were different from how Martha and Dina remembered them. For one the door was boarded up and the entire building had an air of neglect about it. Which not only didn't fit in with the general demeanour of the rest of the city but it certainly wasn't what the building had looked like yesterday.

'Is this the place?' Jed asked.

Martha nodded but something was definitely wrong here. She walked up to the front of the building and felt a slight resistance. She smiled then pushed her body forwards through the glamour shield that had been erected. This was old tech at its best. She supposed that Zac would only want serious visitors to his museum. Obviously, he had lowered the shield yesterday for some other reason. Either way it was ingenious. He wouldn't get bothered with people who weren't all that interested and he knew that anyone who made it through the glamour wanted to view the museum.

The others had been surprised when Martha disappeared, then Dina clapped her hands delightedly and followed before Jed or Max had chance to issue any kind of warning. The two men shrugged and followed suit. They might as well walk into the unknown together.

Past the glamour shield the building looked as it had yesterday, the front door was ajar, and an open sign could just be seen. Martha pushed the door wider and went in eagerly.

'Martha! Dina! Good to see you again.' Zac was there, standing in the atrium, arms wide in welcome. His smile slipped slightly when he clocked Max and Jed but a warm handshake from Max seemed to settle his nerves somewhat. 'I had no idea you'd be back so soon! Welcome to my little museum, guys. Tell me you're going to take the tour this time?'

'We are. Four please,' Dina said, taking charge.

'For you - no fee. Enjoy. I'll see you for coffee on the other side,' replied Zac and with a flourish he whipped back a nearby red curtain and pointed the start of the tour out to the group. With trepidation they walked through the curtain. After all, they could be walking into anything, anything at all.

It turned out to be a harmless museum of twenty-first century styled housing. Martha and Dina marvelled at how households managed with so little technology, Jed was staggered by the huge discrepancy in wages and lifestyles throughout the various echelons of society. Kira had often tried to interest him in things like this but to actually see it so vividly, in this unique setting, was much more interesting. Max walked along contentedly, it wasn't field science so it wasn't quite his thing but Dina was happy, and they seemed to be in no danger so that was his priority right now.

All too soon they came to the end of the tour and a door led them onto a small sitting area where the delicious aroma of coffee was wafting towards them.

'Is that actual coffee?' asked Jed.

Martha and Dina nodded excitedly. They had neglected to tell the others about this particular perk. Soon there was nothing but contented sighs.

'Did you enjoy my little museum, then?' Zac reappeared with a plate of biscuits that he deposited on their table, gesturing for them to help themselves. No-one needed to be asked twice. Good biscuits were like gold dust in the freezedried food supply world.

'Fascinating,' said Jed, spraying crumbs across the table. 'Sorry.'

'Really? I'm glad you think so. You don't think the front door glamour is too much, do you?'

'No, I think it's a brilliant idea - you're showing off old tech and dissuading those who aren't interested in the museum from coming in. I should imagine it's pretty difficult to keep these displays fresh and stop people from vandalising or stealing things,' replied Dina.

'It's not so bad, I have pretty good security here.'

'How much do we owe you for the entry?' asked Max, feeling in his pockets for the remainder of his tokens.

'Oh, the museum is free. They used to be free in the old world, so I figured why not.'

'How do you make any money?' pondered Martha aloud.

'Ha ha! That's easy - the wondrous gift shop. But don't worry I won't make you go in there. I get the impression you came back for more than the museum tour.' Zac's intelligent eyes swept up and down the group as he waited for someone to come clean and tell him why they were really there.

'Okay, fair enough.' Jed put down his mug. 'We want to know if you know a way out of City 9, across the ocean to the other side.'

'What makes you think the other side is better than this one?' asked

Zac carefully.

'We don't. We know we can't stay here, though.'

'Four people can disappear easily enough,' countered Zac.

'There are more than four of us.'

'But you already know that,' said Martha softly. 'You know who we are, don't you? Are you going to report us?'

Zac looked at each of them in turn before slowly shaking his head.

'Yes, I know who you are, but I have no love for New Corp, and I don't agree with what they did to City 15.'

'I had no idea that the citizens here even knew about 15,' Dina commented in surprise.

'It's not common knowledge so don't expect the average drone off the street to know anything about it but there's a small group of us. Disconnected from the neural network. Not loyal to New Corp and just trying to keep our heads above water. We don't have weapons or a way of fighting back but we do have information and we help where we can.'

'You'll help us, then?' Jed wanted to make sure this guy was on the same page. He didn't know why exactly, but he didn't trust Zac yet. There might be an answer to their problems here, there might not.

'You can't leave City 9 by boat. They don't exist anymore. Besides the seawater is too toxic for any kind of material to spend any length of time on there.'

Max nodded to himself, exactly what he had thought.

'You might be able to do it by air. I know someone who runs a private airstrip. He might be convinced to fly you over the water to the nearest safe zone, but it won't be cheap. I hope you have more than tokens to offer.'

Martha looked at Jed, she didn't think they had anything of any value at all to offer but this guy might be their only option.

'We'll get whatever it is he wants,' she replied confidently. 'But we need to get in touch with our other party first.'

'There are more of you, here in the city?' Zac sounded surprised.

'No.' Martha didn't elaborate. She didn't want to put Zac into any further danger by telling him more than he needed to know.

Zac nodded to himself. Trust worked both ways, he was well aware of that. 'Look, I think we should get you out of the city at least. You've been lucky so far, but New Corp Security patrols are getting more and more invasive. It won't take them long to figure out who you are when you fail the retinal ident scan. I'm assuming you haven't registered your irises in the city's mainframe?'

There were faint no's and head shakes.

'Look, it's not all bad. I can take you to an abandoned outpost nearby, you can get in touch with whoever you need to and then when you're ready, get in touch with me. I'll take you to Artem. He'll come up with some mad plan to get you out of here - for a price - everybody wins. What do you say?' Zac looked at them, his face so open and honest that the group couldn't help but trust and believe him.

'Sounds like a plan,' Jed replied.

'Do you have any gear with you?' Zac asked.

'It's in our room,' replied Martha.

'Now that is risky, patrols can search public shared space without regard to whether guests are present or not. It's probably best if I go and collect your things.'

'Now wait a minute, we've done alright so far,' Jed protested.

'Yes, but every time you go out there, your face gets ident scanned hundreds of times from every camera, every model citizen, every food replicator. Believe me, if the powers that be don't know you are here, they will soon.'

'Okay fine, then let me come with you at least. Leave the others here to lie low. I know where everything is that we need. We didn't leave it lying around, you know. We have some common sense.' Jed's pride was a little hurt, this wasn't his first mission, he wasn't a rookie.

Zac nodded. 'Okay, but do me a favour, wear this and try not to look at anything.' He threw a baseball cap at Jed who caught it in surprise.

'Won't this make me stick out even more?'

'Not today, it's games day and everyone will be wearing one, trust me.' Zac stood up. 'Let's get moving, shall we? Game time is the perfect time to get you out of the city without being noticed.'

Jed stood and put the cap on his head, he hoped trusting Zac was the right thing to do. They were putting an awful lot of trust into a stranger's hands. The others helped themselves to more coffee as they waited for Jed and Zac to come back.

The two men were able to stroll through the city unnoticed. Zac had been right; they didn't stick out at all. It seemed like all the citizens of City 9 were out in force, all clad with different coloured baseball hats. It was surreal.

'How is this happening?' asked Jed in a low voice.

'People get attached to the strangest things and no matter how hard Corp or even New Corp tried with their neural implants, they couldn't get rid of the love of the game,' explained Zac.

'Huh.'

Jed entered their room cautiously, but nothing looked out of place. 'I guess Security haven't been by yet.'

'Yeah, you probably got lucky with it being game day. We should hurry. Whilst we don't stick out at the moment, once everyone has gone into the stadium we will.'

Jed nodded and went through the room briskly. Fortunately, they had been neat and consistent with where they had placed their things and it didn't take long to gather everything together. Back on the street they did look slightly out of place carrying three bags each, especially as the crowds were thinning with the game about to start. But they managed to make it back to the museum without incident. They did see one security patrol, but the three guards were so involved in ribbing the fourth man with them on his choice of team, they didn't even see Jed and Zac.

'What's the plan now?' asked Max, once everyone had been reunited.

'We've got about ninety minutes until the end of game time. Everyone will be piling out then, that's the best time to leave the city. You should have something to eat, get some rest. We'll have to move fast once the game finishes. Curfew,' Zac replied.

'Are you coming with us?' asked Martha.

'Well, I'll have to take you past the city wall. You'll need a local in case you run into a patrol. After that, it's up to you but, if you'll take me, I'll come with you.'

The others said nothing. This was an unexpected development. The silence dragged on uncomfortably until Zac coughed and stood.

'I'll, er... let you talk amongst yourselves.' And he left the room.

'What do you think?' Martha asked the others.

'Do you think he's some kind of spy? For New Corp, I mean?' asked Dina.

'I know what you mean. I don't know. He's been truthful with us so far. And let's face it, how long will he survive in a city that clearly only wants biddable, controlled citizens while he's running a museum that celebrates a way of life wiped out two hundred years ago?' Martha felt she would know if Zac were a spy. Just because Sean had completely hoodwinked her back in 42 didn't mean she had lost all judgement. Besides, she rather liked Zac. It would be nice to have another person to talk to.

'I don't think he's a spy for New Corp, but I don't think he's told us everything he knows,' Max volunteered.

'After everything that's happened, I don't know whether we can afford to trust anyone new. And I'm not keen on taking a stranger with us when we go to meet with the others. Those are our children we are potentially putting at risk,' said Jed.

'It doesn't seem fair of us to discount Zac after all the help he's giving us here in City 9. We would have been identified and contained by now for sure.' Martha tried to argue her case.

'Possibly, possibly not. Are you ready to take the risk, Martha?'

'Look, where are we going to lead him? To two skimmers hidden on the outskirts of the city where ten fully armed, fully trained operatives will be on hand to detain him if necessary.'

Jed nodded. He had already executed that plan in his mind. If Zac came with them, he would be swept for bugs, tagged and more than likely magno-bound under armed guard until Jed could prove one way or another whether he was with them or against them.

'We'd better put him out of his misery, otherwise he might decide to defect and alert New Corp to us being here in City 9,' Dina joked weakly.

Martha glared at her as she went to tell Zac the good news.

ENCRYPTED MESSAGE FROM CITY 9 TO CITY 42
>>*Martha Hamble, Dina Grey & Jed Jenkins plus one other have visited the City 9 museum twice. This confirms our suspicions that the museum is linked to the Resistance - why else would they visit it twice?* <<

ENCRYPTED MESSAGE FROM CITY 42 TO CITY 9
>>SEND A STRIKE FORCE IN TO RETRIEVE ANY DATA AND THEN REPURPOSE THE BUILDING. DETAIN FOR QUESTIONING ANY CITIZENS. ANY SIGHTINGS OF KIRA JENKINS OR RUTH MADDOCKS?<<

ENCRYPTED MESSAGE FROM CITY 9 TO CITY 42
>>*No, although a communication was intercepted originating from Hamble's base here in City 9. We have been unable to decode the message but it was tagged for Team 36.*<<

ENCRYPTED MESSAGE FROM CITY 42 TO CITY 9
>>THEY MUST HAVE SPLIT UP AND SENT THE OTHERS UP TO CITY 36. EXCELLENT, RADIATION LEVELS ARE TOXIC IN THE NORTH. SHOULD YOU INTERCEPT ANY MORE COMMUNIQUES, REPORT THEM IMMEDIATELY<<

Chapter 26

Zac led Jed and the others to a disused service hatch. It exited outside the city, unaffected by the force and was unguarded. By the time New Corp Security arrived at Zac's museum, there was no-one there to apprehend. On their journey from the city limits out to camp, Zac's handheld beeped frantically.

'What's that?' asked Dina.

Zac looked at his screen in dismay. 'New Corp have breached the museum. They're trying to download my servers, but they triggered the self-destruct.'

'Will they know where we've gone?' asked Jed.

Zac answered distractedly as he flicked through his handheld. 'No, no, they won't be able to get hold of any of my files. It's fine.' He kept going until he found what he was looking for, then he looked up at the others. 'That's that then. The museum is gone.'

Martha patted his shoulder in commiseration while the others expressed their sorrow. They continued the journey to the skimmers in silence. On arrival, Jed went to check in with the operatives, so Dina, Martha and Max took Zac over to the communal tent. The largest of their temporary structures, it housed the shared food supplies, a travel hydrator and a synth-caf machine. There were no tables, they were too bulky to pack and only a handful of fold away chairs.

'We haven't got much but help yourself to a hot drink, whatever you need. No coffee though, I'm afraid. Will you be alright here for a moment?' asked Martha.

Zac nodded and busied himself making a synth-caf while the others went to find Jed. He was checking the comms system.

'Listen, there's a message from Kira,' Jed said and he read it aloud. 'I didn't think 9 would have what we need, New Corp are too prevalent. I can't believe Ben is gone - Mum is in bits. I dread to think what would have happened to us if we'd stayed. We're about a day away, see you all soon.'

'At least they've made good time,' commented Max. 'It'll be good to have everyone in one place.'

'I can't wait to see Lucas and the other children,' said Martha. 'I hope he's alright.'

'I'm sure he's fine, Ma. But what about Zac? Are we magno-binding him?' asked Dina. 'He just lost his entire livelihood and I can't help but think it's because he was helping us.'

'No, we won't bind him,' replied Jed. 'But he stays away from the armoury and the comms system. And he doesn't leave camp without an escort.'

'Are you talking about me, by any chance?' Zac asked with a smile, which slipped as no-one said anything. 'Um, do you want me to go away?'

'Actually, what can you tell us about this Artem? I assume you managed to make contact?' asked Jed.

'Yes, I sent him a message. He has his own airstrip which is about half a day's journey from here. We should be welcome to stay on his estate for as long as we need to, he enjoys having visitors,' replied Zac.

'And he's definitely not loyal to New Corp?' asked Martha.

'No, definitely not.'

Martha smiled encouragingly and took Zac back with her to the communal tent while the others drifted apart to see to their own errands. Jed felt like he wouldn't be able to relax until he was reunited with Kira, Grace and Peter. He missed them all fiercely and he couldn't wait to get to know Peter better. In order to distract himself, Jed checked on the camp security. He didn't want to be surprised by any New Corp drones.

'I get the impression the others don't trust me very much,' Zac said to Martha as they strolled through the grassy verge next to the road.

'It's not that they don't trust you, they don't know you. I don't know you.' She smiled at him, to show that she didn't mean it in a negative way.

'I'm just me. There's not much to tell.'

'I'm listening.' Martha linked an arm through Zac's and waited patiently. She was desperate for him to open up to her so she could prove the others wrong; that Zac was trustworthy, and they had been right to bring him with them on their journey.

'Well, I was grown in 9. They have a small baby lab, but most children came from 42 until you closed down that operation. My parents are both dead, resisters to various Corp initiatives.'

'Sorry,' whispered Martha, feeling guilty. She hadn't considered the ramifications of their actions before. Not knowing what the other cities nearby were like had made it difficult to consider the possibility that her actions would have negative consequences for others.

'It's okay, it happened a long time ago - way before your coup, but that did lead to a major crackdown by the way. The museum belonged to my parents. Naturally I lived there, so I sort of carried on running the place. It does, did, alright. People, if nothing else, are pretty curious about things that have gone before. I was regularly checked by New Corp Security to make sure I wasn't planning any additional nefarious activity.'

'Bit of a risk to throw everything in with us, then.'

'Yes and no. There is nothing left in 9 for me. My business has been destroyed and apart from wearing a fake neural transmitter there's not much resistance one person can achieve, provided he doesn't want to end up instantly detained.'

'I suppose not.' Martha paused, trying to find the right words. 'But you have helped others, haven't you?'

Zac nodded but said nothing.

'Are you Anti-Corp?'

'What's Anti-Corp?' he asked.

'It's what the organisation was called in City 42 that opposed Corporation. I thought you might have heard of it,' Martha explained.

'No, there's no Anti-Corp.' Zac stopped walking and looked directly into Martha's eyes. 'We're the Resistance.'

A thrill leapt through her body. 'I knew it! I knew you were hiding something.'

'Well, I had to make sure it was safe before I could tell you,' said Zac.

'You had to make sure it was safe before you could tell us?' Martha laughed. 'You do know who we are, right?'

Zac chuckled. 'I know, but you can never be too careful.' He got serious. 'New Corp will be after us both now.'

'And your friend, Artem, he can help us?'

'I hope so.' They lapsed into silence and walked on like that for a few minutes until Zac revived the conversation. 'What about you, anyway - what's your background?'

'Well, my father was on the Board in City 42 so I'm a made to order.'

'Wow, that's rare these days.'

'Yep, that's me. No siblings.'

'Hang on, your father was on the Board? What does he do now? Did he defect as well? Is that how you managed such a successful coup?'

'He was murdered. He was helping us but things got out of hand and he was in the way.' Martha's voice wobbled a little.

'Oh, frag, I'm so sorry.'

'It's alright, I've come to terms with it - more or less. After mob rule got rid of the Corporation Board the city officials made me governor and I did the best I could. It was hard not having access to the Corporation mainframe and their systems. I guess we never considered the amount of behind the scenes organisation that goes into running a city. Plus, there was Lucas.'

'Lucas?'

'Yes, I'm a mum.' Martha waited on tenterhooks to see what kind of reaction Zac would display.

'Huh.' That was all he said. 'Assignment?'

'Nope.'

'Huh.' He looked a little stunned but as he didn't ask any further questions, Martha decided not to volunteer any additional information. She glanced at him, but he wasn't looking in her direction. She tucked her hair behind her ears and checked again. This time he caught her eye and gave her a brief smile.

They lapsed into a comfortable silence, each thinking about what the other had told them. Both had questions but neither was ready to quiz the other yet. It was getting dark when they returned to the communal tent and helped themselves from the dwindling supply of dried rations, joining the others.

'When the other team arrive, we'll pool our supplies, rest for one more evening and then head out to your contact, Zac,' said Jed. 'I assume they will be able to help us out on the supplies front?'

'Shouldn't be a problem but I warn you, Artem doesn't give anything away for free. There will be some kind of price.'

'We have a supply of tokens - would that be enough?' Dina wondered.

Zac's mouth twisted a little. 'It's not normally that kind of price.' He looked up at the others. 'Look, I don't know what he's going to say. He can help us, but... I can't even begin to guess what the fee will be. I'll do everything in my power to keep it reasonable. He's a good guy, he's just a better businessman.'

Jed stewed on this for a while. Besides their dwindling rations which they needed to increase, not give away, they didn't have anything of any value they could trade. This was beginning to look like it could be a problem. At least he had an up to date inventory list now, surely, they would be able to barter something. All he had to do was wait one more day.

ENCRYPTED MESSAGE FROM CITY 42 TO CITY 9
>>DID YOU APPREHEND THEM?<<

ENCRYPTED MESSAGE FROM CITY 9 TO CITY 42
>>*No, they escaped. Hamble and the others have met up with the rest of their group. There was some kind of illegal computer programme running at the museum so we have terminated it.*<<

ENCRYPTED MESSAGE FROM CITY 42 TO CITY 9
>>GOOD. DO YOU KNOW WHERE THEY ARE GOING NOW?<<

ENCRYPTED MESSAGE FROM CITY 9 TO CITY 42
>>*There's only one place they can go. Artem Misner's enclosure is the only populated place left.*<<

ENCRYPTED MESSAGE FROM CITY 42 TO CITY 9
>>DO WE HAVE EYES?<<

ENCRYPTED MESSAGE FROM CITY 9 TO CITY 42
>>*Of course.*<<

ENCRYPTED MESSAGE FROM CITY 42 TO CITY 9
>>CONTINUE TO MONITOR AND REPORT REGULARLY. LET'S GET AS MANY DISSIDENTS AS POSSIBLE IN ONE PLACE BEFORE ORDERING THE STRIKE<<

Chapter 27

Kira was frantic. Grace had started crying in the night and then she'd vomited everywhere. It had been stressful trying to soothe Grace while at the same time strip her off, wash her, get clean clothes, clean up the mess, try not to wake the others, which of course didn't work, and then listen to Grace scream inconsolably as Kira quickly changed and washed herself. She was now sitting upright with her poorly little girl snuggled into her chest. Grace had been sick three times and was running a high fever. She wouldn't take anything except for the tiniest sips of water.

'Why is she so poorly?' Kira asked her mum, but Jean shook her head.

'Children get sick, my lovely. Do you remember burning up with that temperature when you were little? Came out of nowhere, it did. Caught us all by surprise, one minute you were playing happily with your toys, the next you were a droopy, crying little thing. Didn't take you long to throw up everywhere - I never could get the smell out of the old cloth doll you had. Had to throw that away we did, didn't we, Malcolm? Oh, he's asleep. Bless him, he can sleep through most anything. But I wouldn't worry, my love, it'll be a stray sickness bug she's picked up. Could've got it from anywhere. Children do, you know. It's because they're so inquisitive, they love to poke things and prod things and put them in their mouths. It's a wonder any of us make it to adulthood, it really is.' She caught the panicked expression on her daughter's face. 'Honestly, love, she'll be fine - you'll see. It's a twenty-four-hour bug. You gave her some medicine, didn't you? Keep offering her fluids and don't let her temperature get too high and she'll be fine. It's sleep she needs now. That's a great healer.'

'But what if she's really ill? What if she's got radiation poisoning from that stupid cave? I should never have taken her in there. I could've killed her!' Kira was on the verge of tears.

'Now listen to me, young lady. You haven't killed your little girl, she's right there on your knee. Sleeping peacefully and looking like an angel, if I might add. That's silly talk, that is. We all went into the caves and Grace is the only one who is poorly and yes, I know, we are bigger than her, but the other small ones are all fine. It could be anything that has caused this. Anything. She might have been harbouring a bug for a couple of days. It's not your fault. Children get sick. Mark my words, she'll be right as rain tomorrow.'

Kira sniffed, feeling useless but trying to take comfort from her mum's words. She had run the radiation wand over Grace, and the other children, several times and it had never alarmed or even come back with any kind of warning reading. Not even borderline. They hadn't stayed at the caves long enough. But her baby girl was ill. And Kira didn't know why. She gently tucked a curl behind Grace's ear and held her close.

By the time morning arrived, Grace had been sick twice more and Kira was at her wits' end. She wasn't taking in any advice her mum was trying to give and had decided to use the skimmer's inbuilt refuse system to incinerate all the blankets that they'd used to mop up the vomit, so frightened that she was going to infect everyone else. Luckily, they did have a few spare ones, but if Grace continued to be sick, some of the adults would be going cold tonight.

Fortunately, Kira wasn't needed for any kind of driving duty. Instead, she barricaded herself and Grace into the rear of the second skimmer, the one which carried most of the equipment, and only allowed one operative in to drive the vehicle. He was instructed to stay firmly behind the plexiglass window which was not to be lowered under any circumstances. She also ordered Ash to tell Jed what had happened. He wanted to intervene, but Jean told him to let Kira get on with it.

'The poor dear is scared witless. Nothing we say will get through to her. Let her be with her little one and she'll soon see that everything will be alright. Make sure she's got lots of disinfectant in there with her so the bugs don't leap from the child to the grown up and everything will be fine. The last thing we want is for Kira to start vomiting as well.'

Ash left her to it and went to check on Ruth before he sent a message to Jed. He found her with Lucas, Sarah and Peter.

'Are you okay, Ruth? Can I get you anything?'

'A bit more space would be good,' Ruth joked with a smile. She and the children had been squashed into the first skimmer with Kira's parents. Luckily most of the operatives were happy to walk alongside and they'd been able to maintain a steady pace.

Ash nodded and went to make sure they would still make their rendezvous with Jed and the others. Despite Grace's sickness, he didn't want them to be late. The rest of the journey went smoothly, and by the time they reached the other group, Kira was passed out exhausted in her designated sick bay. Little Grace was sleeping off the tail end of her sickness.

Martha rushed to be reunited with Lucas and was hugging Ruth and Sarah, so pleased to see them both again. Dina and Max were entertaining Peter, making him giggle whilst Ash gave Jed a brief report.

'Once we left Hope there were no issues, apart from...' Ash trailed off.

'Thanks, Ash. I'll go see her now.' Jed was concerned by Kira's behaviour and had been worried ever since receiving Ash's message. He gave Peter a quick kiss on the head before he hurried to the skimmer.

The rest of the operatives had gone into Jed's makeshift camp with all the supplies they could carry. They would put all their resources together and get an idea as to whether they had anything worth trading when they went to see Artem. Zac wandered over and started chatting with Ash about tech before Martha brought over Lucas, Ruth and Sarah and the conversation changed to cooing over the children. Whilst Zac and Ruth were chatting, Martha spoke to Jean.

'Ruth seems better,' she said.

'She's come on leaps and bounds, love. It was that scare in those caves that did it, I think. A proper brush with death, if you like. Realised she can't go on without caring about life and the people in it. Knows she needs to be there for her little one, she does. It's difficult times we live in, Martha. Difficult times.'

They both turned their gaze to the skimmer where Kira was.

'Do you think I ought to go see if she's alright?' asked Martha.

'Let Jed see to her, love. You introduce me to this new young man and tell me all about your adventures,' said Jean, taking Martha's mind off her friend.

Jed eased the door to the skimmer open and Kira's eyes flew open in panic. The stale smell of old vomit and unwashed bodies hit Jed in the face, and he had to take a moment before he could continue.

'NO! Don't come in. It's not safe,' Kira cried out.

'Kira, love. It's me. It's Jed.'

'Jed? Did we make it already? Is that you? Oh Jed, Grace is sick. She's really, really sick and I don't know what to do.'

'Alright love, let me take her. Come on. It's alright. I've got her.' Jed reached in and extracted his daughter from Kira's arms. The little girl felt a little warm, but Jed was sure that was from having been held by her mum for hours on end. He used the handheld scanner Max had given him and swept it over their daughter. Kira waited on tenterhooks for the resulting beep.

'Well?' she asked.

'She's fine. No bugs. No radiation. A little dehydrated but we can sort that out. Now let's check you.'

'No, no, I'm fine. I need to be there for her in case, in case...' Kira wilted under Jed's stern gaze. 'Okay, let's do me.'

He ran the scanner again. 'Well, no sign of infection but like Grace you're dehydrated and are suffering from exhaustion.' He grinned at his wife. 'You also stink. I'm sending you to the wash pod.'

Kira looked at him, momentarily overwhelmed by everything that had happened. She began to cry.

'Hey, hey, love. It's alright. It's okay. Grace is okay. You're okay. We're back together and everything is going to be alright. Come on, out you get of the stink mobile.' And Jed helped his wife out of the skimmer, supporting her wobbly legs as she took in the sight of everyone back together again.

'I do stink, don't I?' Kira asked.

'Yes, you do.'

'And Grace is going to be alright?'

'Yes, love. She is.'

Kira allowed herself to be led to the wash pod and hugged her husband gratefully before going inside and getting clean. It was probably the most awkward piece of kit they'd had to carry with them, but easily the most appreciated. Jed went in search of his mother-in-law to put his daughter into safe hands and to find some clean clothes for Kira.

Dina and Max were filling Ruth in on their adventures, while she was trying to simultaneously tell them about everything that had happened to her group. Martha and Zac had taken over the rations check and were trying to put together some sort of meal everyone could share - it was going to be a bit hit and miss but at least they were all together. The two teams of operatives were greeting each other like long lost family and bragging about the things they'd seen. No-one knew what they would be walking into tomorrow when they went to see Artem. Even Zac hadn't been able to offer up much in the way of information, which bothered Jed.

But for now, for tonight, it was about the group being back together; reconnecting and sharing their stories. Jed looked down fondly at Peter and Grace playing together. It was a time for family bonding.

Chapter 28

'So, Zac, where exactly is this compound?' asked Jed, once the evening meal had finished and the children were all in bed.

'I don't exactly know...'

'I thought you said it was some kind of huge mansion or something. It's got a runway - how can you not know where it is?' Dina was incredulous.

Zac shrugged and laughed nervously. 'I've never actually met him.'

'What?' Jed grabbed Zac's arm. 'You've never even met him?' He glared at the man, fighting the urge to punch him. 'Do you work for New Corp?'

'No!' Zac wrenched his arm out of Jed's grip. 'I would never work for them.' He was breathing heavily now, and the two men stood toe to toe, both on the verge of violence.

'Hey, what's going on?' Somehow Kira slid herself between the two of them, forcing them both to back down.

'He doesn't even know this Artem guy. He's never met him. We could be walking into anything.' Jed turned his anger onto his wife. 'Are you ready to risk your family's safety on some random bloke's word?'

'That's not fair, Jed. Calm down.' Kira turned away from her husband, ignoring him for the moment. 'Zac, please explain.'

Zac huffed a little and darted his eyes around, but there was no consolation for him. Everyone was blank faced, watching, waiting to hear what he had to say. He looked at the floor and scuffed his shoes.

'Zac?' Martha's voice was soft yet pleading.

'I have never met Artem, but I have sent others, like you, to him and he helps people. He's on the side of the Resistance but he always has a price. I can't tell you what that will be except that it's not tokens. He doesn't need them.' Zac focused on Martha, she alone seemed sympathetic to him. 'He contacted me through my museum years ago. He was impressed with my collection, even donated some bits over the years.'

'And what did he ask for in return?' asked Jed.

'He has, had, a plug-in to my network port. It was untraceable but it allowed him access to the city's sweeps, so he knows what New Corp is up to. We can trust him,' replied Zac.

'Oh, we can, can we?' Jed didn't sound convinced and walked away, signalling to his operative team leaders. He wanted to review the security protocols again. He was not going to be caught out unawares.

The rest of the group quickly broke up, leaving Martha and Zac on their own.

'Why didn't you tell us you didn't know Artem?' asked Martha.

'I didn't think it was important. I trust the guy; I thought my word would be enough. Obviously not.'

'Don't blame Jed, he's been through a lot recently. We all have. And...' She paused, uncertain how to continue.

'And?'

Martha flushed. 'We don't really know you, Zac. We're putting a lot on faith here. I mean, you're only with us because I vouched for you.'

'Yeah, thanks.' Zac walked away, hands in his pockets. An operative peeled away from camp to follow him while Martha looked on helplessly. Deciding there was nothing more she could say, she went to find the others who were sitting together discussing what would happen tomorrow.

'This Artem guy, have you got a last name?' asked Ruth.

'Yeah, it's Artem Misner I think,' replied Martha, sitting down to join them with a cup of synth-caf. 'Why?'

'Misner... Misner... I think I know him,' mused Ruth.

'Ha! You think you know everyone,' said Kira, making the group laugh.

'Yeah but Misner, that's distinctive isn't it? I'm sure I've heard it somewhere before.' Ruth trailed off.

'Is Zac okay?' Dina asked Martha.

'Yeah I think so. Frustrated that he doesn't know more, I think. He wants to help us. It's not his fault he's never been to the complex before.'

'Aha!' shouted Ruth, making everyone jump. 'I know where I know him from. We were, er... friends, back in the early Anti-Corp days.' She was blushing slightly. 'If it's the same Artem then he's definitely on our side. I didn't realise he'd done so well for himself.'

'Yeah, how does one person end up with their own runway, mansion and secure complex?' asked Dina.

'Luck?' suggested Martha.

'More like a combination of smuggling, connections and other illegal dealings,' replied Jed. 'The sort of person I would usually be locking up not running to for help.' He checked his wristplant. 'It's getting late, we ought to try and get some rest. It's an early start in the morning.'

The others murmured agreement and went off to bed. Kira yawned sleepily as she checked on Grace then sighed heavily, getting into bed with her husband.

'How did we get here, Jed?'

'What do you mean, love?'

'We're fugitives, on the run because the spirit of the Earth showed herself to us and asked for help. We're about to go beg some rogue to grant us passage across the ocean to who knows what and New Corp could probably wipe us all out at any minute. I don't know whether to be excited or scared.'

'I feel the same, but we can't stop now. And we can't go back.'

'I know. I wish we had some reassurances that we were doing the right thing,' said Kira as she snuggled into her husband's arms and drifted into sleep. A bee buzzed lazily around their heads before bumbling out across the camp.

The next morning Zac joined them all for breakfast. 'I've received the coordinates for Artem.' He passed his handheld over to Ash who input them into one of the skimmer's pads that he had with him.

'Hmm, not far. Looks like it will take a couple of hours. I'll go tell the team.' Ash handed it back to Zac and with a nod from Jed walked over to the operatives milling in camp. He began to round them up. It wouldn't take long for them to pack away the makeshift camp and be ready to move out.

'Right, let's get ready to go then.' Jed rubbed his hands together and stood up. The rest of them followed, gathering nearby bits and bobs so nothing was left behind. By the time the children were all strapped into the skimmer, everyone was ready, so the group moved out.

Ash was right. It only took a couple of hours to get to Artem's complex. And when they arrived, they were met with a closed fence, armed guards and vicious looking dogs.

Chapter 29

'Halt! State your business!' shouted one of the security guards.

Jed motioned for Zac to exit the skimmer and come with him to speak to the guard. They walked forward cautiously, Zac eyeing the rifles nervously. As they neared the fence, Jed gave Zac a little nudge of encouragement. He gulped and took half a step forward.

'Er... it's me. Zac, Zac Ridgley. Um, I'm here to see Artem? He sent me the coordinates. He should be expecting me, um, us I mean.'

There was a tense pause as the guard spoke into his wristplant and they all waited for a response.

'Da.' The guard nodded in their direction. '*Otkryt' vorota*!'

Before Jed had chance to ask Zac what that meant the gates started to open. The two men scrambled back to the skimmer as the vehicles then drove into the armed complex.

'This Artem guy is serious, huh?' Dina mused as they looked out the window at the gates closing swiftly behind them.

Nobody responded as the vehicles followed the gravel driveway that led up to an impressive looking house. The entire roof was covered with solar panels and antennae of various shapes and sizes. Huge generators sat on either side of the building and a single figure stood on the steps to greet them. He was a tall, powerfully built man with a buzz cut and chiselled jaw.

'That's Artem,' said Zac as everyone prepared to leave the vehicles. Kira, Martha and Ruth gathered up their children while Dina took Peter. Jed, Ash, Max and Zac went first, leaving Jean and Malcolm bringing up the rear. Jed had already ordered the operatives to stay with the skimmers until they had established their position here.

'Zac!' Artem started to walk down the steps with his arms held wide. 'You made it, my friend. So good to see you.' As he grew closer, he held out his hand and grabbed one of Zac's, pumping it enthusiastically. His gaze roamed across the group, taking in the children and the operatives beyond. Then he did a double take. 'Ruthie?'

Ruth flushed and nodded, shifting Sarah to a more comfortable position on her hip.

'RUTHIE!' Artem roared and tried to crush her in a bear hug. The loud noise and commotion made Sarah cry which caused Lucas and then Grace follow suit. Peter looked on seriously. 'Oh *rebyonochek, rebyonochek.* Hush, hush now, I am sorry little one.' Artem half shrugged apologetically as the mothers soothed the babies. 'Come. Come into house. We will have wine. And talk!' He swung his body round and threw an arm around both Zac and Ruth's shoulders. 'My Zac and my Ruthie! What a day, what a day.' He steered them up the stairs and into his home. The rest of the group followed behind.

On entering, various staff members bustled around them, taking jackets and ushering them sideways into a reception room which had been prepared for them. There were wash bowls and towels, water and fruit juice to drink and an array of snacks - fresh fruit, biscuits, crackers, smoked sausage and even some chocolate. Dina walked forward enthusiastically but Kira held her back from approaching the food. She remembered what had happened in City 36.

Artem had let go of Zac and Ruth and turned to see why no-one was helping themselves. 'What? You no like? You want something different?' A puzzled look upon his face.

'It's not that, it looks lovely, so generous of you. It's just... is it safe? What are your radiation levels like?' asked Kira.

'My radiation levels? Ha! You funny lady. There is no radiation here - this safe place. Please eat, eat!' Artem gestured wildly at the table.

It was all they needed. Jed sent Ash back to the skimmers to tell the operatives to come through and have something to eat. Everyone else hurried forward, chattering excitedly and exclaiming over each new morsel they discovered. Once they satisfied their initial hunger the team relaxed, sitting around the room with plates of food and a drink, waiting to see what would happen next. Ruth went to sit next to Artem, having left Sarah with her Auntie Jean.

'Ruthie. My Ruthie. Life shines on you, eh?' Artem nodded towards the baby.

'Sort of. You know she's natural?'

'I know. I get all sweeps.' Artem spread his arms expansively. 'Corp fart and I know. Hahaha!'

'Why haven't they tried to stop you?' asked Jed.

'I pay. They leave me alone to do what I do, and I pay. Always a greedy man at top. Always wanting something, I get something.' Artem shrugged as if it were no big deal.

'They could wipe you out if they wanted to then,' said Jed, feeling defeated.

'No, no, no, no, no. Is not happening. I have antennae. I get all sweeps. I am network. No-one breathes, I don't know.' Seeing that Jed looked unconvinced Artem started to point the people dotted around the room.

'Her - Dina. Lost family in 15 riots, very sad. Lost baby. Very, very sad. Work in Camp Eden. Now here.' He moved on. 'Him, Dr Max. Him big scientist fella. He discover Earth, she heal. This is good. Good work.' Artem nodded in satisfaction as people began paying attention to what he was saying. 'You. You Jean and Malcolm. You lovely peoples. You look after and you talk. Jabber, jabber, jabber. Hahaha!'

Everyone was smiling but he wasn't finished.

'You. You Ashvin - you big time techie. You come see my system. You learn.' The finger moved on. 'You Martha Hamble, you governor, important lady. Special lady, special baby.' His eyes misted slightly. 'Much loves. And you! You Kira and Jed. Importants people. You are seeing her, blue lady. Gaia.'

He sat back in satisfaction.

'What about me then?' asked Ruth in an amused voice.

'You're my Ruthie. Is enough.'

Zac coughed, feeling a little miffed at being ignored. Artem huffed at him and waved a hand. 'You Zac. Everyone know Zac. Is good.'

Jed put his plate down on the floor. 'Well, you clearly know who we are. Who are you?'

All eyes swivelled back to Artem. He leant back in his chair and began speaking, using his hands expansively.

'Me, I am Artem. I listen and I collect and I pay. Corporation they no see what I do. Some peoples come to me and I help. I have plane. Is enough.'

'So, will you help us?' asked Jed.

There was a tense moment until Artem clapped his hands. 'Of

course! I help you and you show me blue lady. Come. I bring room.'

Kira shared a worried look with Jed. None of them had the power to make Gaia appear. She hadn't seen her in weeks and apart from the one dream, there had hardly been any contact. The group dutifully followed Artem back into the large foyer of his house and began to ascend the grand staircase. He showed them to the guest wing, containing enough bedrooms for them all, including dorm rooms with bunks for all the operatives.

'You rest. Have shower. Take moment. We will talk more at dinner.' And he left them to their own devices.

Jed cleared his throat. 'Well, I guess we'll all take a shower then. Ash, can you organise Alpha and Beta team to get their gear sorted out? I want everyone to take the opportunity for a wash and a rest.' He waited while Ash jogged back to the team to relay the message before turning back to the others. 'See you back here in an hour?'

Everyone nodded and went through to their respective rooms.

'What do you think about Artem?' Kira asked her husband.

'He's certainly a character.'

'Should we be worried that he pays New Corp to leave him alone?'

'It must be a fragging big pay out for them to turn a blind eye to all this.' Jed gestured around. 'The man is an information nexus. He must have something on everyone. I can't believe it's tokens that keep them away.'

'Do you think he will help us?'

'I think if he finds us interesting enough then yes, he'll help us.'

'Well,' said Kira. 'We'd better be extremely interesting at dinner then.' And she hurried off to get freshened up.

When everyone was ready, they reconvened and made their way downstairs, following the delicious aromas to the dining room where Artem was waiting for them. There was one long table for the operatives and a smaller one with four highchairs Artem had produced from somewhere. Everyone sat looking forward to a delicious meal.

As staff served the first course of some kind of vegetable broth, Dina spoke up. 'Where do you get your produce, Artem?'

'I grow and I buy. Is not hard. Always something for something,' he replied.

Everyone tucked in, the children playing with breadsticks.

As the soup bowls were cleared away and a simple roast chicken dinner began to be served, Artem broached the reason they were there.

'So, you want help. For what?'

'We want to find a safe place to live, away from Corporation,' began Jed, but his wife interrupted him.

'Gaia wants us to help her. We need to cross the ocean, spread the news that the planet has begun to heal. Remove the yoke of Corporation. Spread her message of renewal and new life.' She faltered as she realised everyone was gazing at her. 'She told me she needed us.'

'Is not hard to get you over there. I have plane. Will be hard to make point. Lots of space - not lots of people and Corporation have many eyes.' Artem shook his head. 'Will be difficult.'

'Have you been over there?' asked Jed. 'Can you tell us what it's like?'

'No, only flown. But skies are clear.' Artem grinned. 'I know place. I take you.' Then he frowned and steepled his fingers, pursing his lips before speaking again. 'Is not same. Is wilder, bigger, more space and more danger. But the cities, they still there. Not glitter like 9. You been 9?'

Jed, Martha, Dina and Max nodded sadly while Zac grinned then realised he was the only one and hastily took a sip of his drink.

'Does that mean New Corporation is fully in control over there?' asked Martha.

'I think in cities, yes. They should have tech and med and Collection - all things.'

'So where are they getting their babies from?' asked Ruth. 'We shut down the baby lab in 42.'

'Is not only lab, *milaya*.'

'What do you mean, it's not the only lab? There are more?' Kira was aghast. She looked at Jed in horror who half shrugged. He had no idea there were more labs.

'Is big world, yes?' Artem gazed around the table. 'You only met me today. Be more surprises tomorrow.' He chuckled at his own cleverness but when he realised no-one else was laughing, he grew serious once more. 'Listen, when you shut your baby lab you put Corp in panic. These babies sell for high credit. You stop Corp credit. This is very bad. Why they punish 15. So sad.' Artem shook his head. 'Now we have new New Corp and you lady, you pissed them off.' Artem wagged a finger in Martha's direction. 'These new neural implants, this is not what tech should be. All sheeps bleating, baa! Baa! Baa!'

No-one knew what to say but Artem didn't seem to notice. He continued.

'Med labs. That's how they do it.'

'How they do what?' asked Dina.

'Make the babies! They gather all the sperms and all the eggs then it's mix, mix, mix and bingy bangy bongy babies.'

'What in the Med Centres?' Martha was incredulous. 'Are you sure?'

Artem nodded vigorously.

'What about the sterilisation though?' Martha asked.

'Is cocktail. They dose you in water. But you know this - you broke water in 42, yes?' Artem looked back and forth for confirmation.

Dina nodded. 'Yeah, we found out they were treating the water but, are they doing that everywhere?'

'Yes! But they can undo it with sperms and eggs. Sneaky, sneaky, sneaky.' Artem shrugged as if it were a small thing but the others were shocked. This was something that even Martha's father hadn't known about, if he had been telling the truth.

Jed tried changing the subject. 'What about the force behind City 15? Do you know who that was?'

'Is militia.'

'New Corp have a militia?' Jed wanted to know more. 'Do you know where they are based? What their set up is like?'

'Is ghost. No chitter chatter.' Artem looked downcast then grinned again. 'But once they speak, I know.'

'How have they managed to build a militia without anyone noticing?' Martha asked, addressing Jed.

'Well, the chief thought they never disbanded to be honest.'

'Is true,' Artem piped up. 'In beginning Coalition think problem - problem is genes. They no good. Event cause sickness and genes, no good. So, if people have babies, babies no good. This very bad. They make cocktail and sterilise and think we grow little bit and all is fine, all is okay.' He stopped talking and the whole room waited for him to continue.

'And?' prompted Ruth.

'And nothing. Stayed same. Babies grown, is what it is. What you're going to do?' Artem focused on his dinner and for a while no-one said anything while they processed what they'd learnt.

'I have a question.'

Everyone turned to look at Zac in surprise, not expecting him to have anything to add.

'Why don't they have the tech to grow their own babies over there?' he asked Artem.

'Is good question. Power. Power and technology. Is what Corporation have.' He paused to take a long drink. 'Over there is big place. Spread out. Harder to connect than here. Everyone sterile and everyone desperate for baby. Desperate means do anything, pay anything, give anything. And so, Corporation provide. They also destroy.'

'We know,' muttered Ruth.

'You think control here is control. Control there is air.'

'Is there any place for us over there?' Kira asked. 'It sounds like we'd be better off staying here.'

Artem was quiet and he looked at Zac who nodded briefly.

'The Resistance will take you. And I take you to the Resistance.'

'Oh, that's wonderful!' gushed Kira feeling relieved, turning to smile at Martha and the others. Martha started guiltily; she had not mentioned Zac's revelation about the Resistance to anyone else yet.

'For a price. Is business,' said Artem.

Silence fell as everyone turned to look at Artem.

'Yes, there must be price. Artem never does business without price.' But he seemed to be embarrassed and cleared his throat several times before continuing. 'I want to meet Gaia. I want to see mother of Earth. You show me and I fly.' He sat back in his chair, waiting to see what would happen.

Everyone turned to look at Kira this time. She flushed under the scrutiny.

'Um, we can't conjure Gaia up, you know? She is the spirit of the Earth. She only shows herself when she wants to,' Kira said tentatively, unsure as to how Artem would react.

'But you've seen her. You, all seen.' Artem looked around the table.

'Well, yes. But not all at the same time.' Kira's gaze flitted to her friends, looking at them to help her out.

'I saw her in the street but unexpectedly,' offered Jed.

'I saw her in Camp Eden,' said Max.

'And she sat next to me on a bench,' Dina chipped in.

'I saw her in the park,' said Martha softly, a faint tremor in her voice.

'Yes,' said Artem, pleased. 'You all see. You tell her to see me.'

Kira didn't think she had much of a choice. 'I'll see what I can do,' she said faintly.

No-one spoke much after that, eating their dessert in silence and withdrawing to the next room for coffee. It wasn't until they split up into smaller groups that Jed cornered Kira and asked her the obvious question.

'How exactly are you going to get Gaia to appear?'

'I don't know. Try to reach her spiritually, I guess. I'm assuming this place has some kind of natural garden.' Kira glanced around, but it was too dark outside to see. 'I think it's a problem for tomorrow. The children are tired, I'm tired. I think a decent night's sleep would do us all the world of good.'

Kira and Jed made their excuses to the group, taking Peter and Grace with them to their guest room. Kira had no idea how she was going call Gaia forward but the moment her head hit the pillow she was fast asleep.

Chapter 30

Kira awoke to birdsong. Through the open window she could smell fresh grass after rain. The sun peeped through the curtains casting golden rays across the floor. She stirred slowly and realised was not there. The children were gone too. That shocked her into being fully awake. She leapt out of bed and grabbed a nearby jumper, chucking it on over her jumpsuit before hurrying out of the room. As Kira reached the top of the stairs, she heard laughter from the dining room and felt instant relief. On entering she saw she was the last to wake and everyone else, including all of Alpha and Beta team, were already seated and having breakfast. She smiled self-consciously and hurried over to Jed.

'Morning, love.'

'Morning,' she replied, giving him a quick kiss before going to grab a cup of coffee.

'So, today we meet Gaia, yes?' Artem spoke to Kira.

'Um, yes, we can try. Do you have a garden?'

'I have big garden. Herbs, plants and wild space.'

'That would probably be best.' Kira felt too nervous to eat anything. 'Can you take me there? We might as well make a start.'

'Do you want some company?' asked Ruth but Kira shook her head and stood waiting for Artem. He kissed Ruth on the cheek which surprised everyone and then beckoned to Kira to follow him out of the French windows.

The gardens were beautiful, perfectly sculpted and full of heady perfume, but it was towards the bottom that Artem led Kira. He ducked under a hedge bower and stood to one side to let Kira take in the wild garden. It was stunning. Completely overgrown, full of every wildflower imaginable and bees, there were bees buzzing from flower to flower collecting nectar.

'Oh, this is perfect,' exclaimed Kira softly.

Artem stood expectantly, waiting for Kira to work her magic but she didn't know what she should do. She took a deep breath and tried to connect with the environment around her, but Artem's presence was off putting. Kira bent down to take off her socks and let her bare feet connect with the earth beneath her. She took another deep breath and tried to imagine blue energy from the Earth rising through her feet, travelling through her body and leaving the top of her head. At the same time, she visualised all the bad things that she'd been holding onto being swept out of her aura. After a good twenty minutes or so she felt relaxed and at one with the Earth around her, she thought she could sense Gaia and opened her eyes in hope but there was nothing there. Artem had adopted a lotus position on the ground to her right and he looked at her with hope in his eyes.

'I'm so sorry, Artem. I don't know what else to do. We could try lighting some candles and calling out for Gaia to appear, but I thought this would work.'

'Is okay. You tried. You stay and you try. Gaia come, then we go.' He helped her up and started walking back to the dining room while Kira processed what he'd said. If she couldn't summon Gaia, then Artem wasn't going to take them across the ocean. He also wasn't going to let them leave either. Her heart sank at the impossible task before her.

In the dining room everyone had gone except for Ruth. Artem left the two women together shouting over his shoulder that he'd talk to them later as he walked out the room.

'How did it go?' asked Ruth.

'Shouldn't I be asking you that?' countered Kira.

Ruth blushed. 'We're just old friends, reacquainting ourselves, that's all.' She nodded towards the garden. 'I gather it didn't work?'

'Oh, Ruth. I don't even know what to do! She's always sort of appeared before, hasn't she? I tried to connect with the Earth and open myself to her spirit. but nothing happened. And Artem...'

'And Artem what?'

'He said it didn't matter and I could try again, and we would stay until I did it.'

'Okay.'

'No, you're not listening, Ruth. He won't let us go until I've made contact, until Gaia manifests. We could be here forever!'

'I'm sure he didn't mean that,' Ruth replied but she looked worried. 'Let me speak to him.'

'Thank you. We can't stay here indefinitely, can we?'

Ruth shrugged and the women left the dining room in search of their children. They found them playing in a small sandpit around the side of the house.

'How'd it go?' asked Jed but Kira shook her head.

The day passed and there was no sign of Gaia. That evening as they went in to dinner, Kira hurried over to Ruth.

'Did you speak to Artem yet?' she asked, but Ruth shook her head.

Artem displayed the same jovial manner despite the muted response from the rest of them. Only the children were in high spirits earning themselves indulgent smiles and the odd laugh from the grown-ups. Once everyone had eaten and the families had left the dinner table, Kira managed to corner Ruth again.

'Well, are you going to speak to him?'

'Yes, but not right now!' Ruth muttered and turned away from her friend, smiling at Artem who was cooing over Sarah.

As the evening dragged on, Kira grew more and more restless; passing on her irritability to Grace and Peter until even Jed begged her to sit down and relax. She noticed Artem and Ruth whispering in the corner and was hoping her friend was managing to persuade Artem to help them anyway. At one point he shook his head vigorously but somehow Ruth made him smile again. Finally, Artem stood up.

'Goodnight one, goodnight all,' he announced as he left the room whistling. Kira darted over to her friend.

'Well?'

'He's agreed to take us, but he wants to wait until the morning before he announces it. He didn't want to but...'

'You convinced him!' Kira said happily.

'I agreed to stay.'

'You what?' Kira wasn't sure she had heard her friend correctly.

'I agreed to stay. Last night Artem asked if I would like to stay with him, here at his home and I told him I'd think about it. I was going to come with you, Kira, to the ends of the Earth if that's what it took, but this is the price for Artem to take you over the ocean. Me staying.'

'Do you want to stay?' Kira didn't like the idea of her friend being forced to do anything she didn't want to.

Ruth nodded shyly. 'I do. Sarah loves it here and Artem makes her laugh. She's never going to meet her real dad, Kira, and this feels like somewhere I could call home.' Ruth bit her lip pensively and looked at her friend. 'Is it alright with you?' she asked.

Kira could feel the tears springing into her eyes as she hugged her friend. 'Of course it's alright. It's not like we'll never see each other again.' The two women were laughing and hugging so much that Martha, Dina and the others came over to see what all the commotion was.

'Ruth is staying here and Artem is going to take us in his plane, no charge,' explained Kira.

'Are you sure you're alright with that, Ruth?' asked Jed.

'Yes, yes I am. I'll miss you all though.' There was more hugging and exclaiming over what had happened until Martha changed the subject.

'Has anyone seen Zac?' she asked.

'He was at dinner,' replied Jed. 'But he didn't come back in here. I think he wanted some time to himself.'

'Oh, okay,' said Martha, a little disappointed.

It was Jean who finally chivvied everyone to bed, and they were all still chattering happily as they ascended the staircase and went to their respective rooms.

The next morning, Artem was waiting for them in the dining room. He was practically bouncing on his toes in excitement. Once they were all gathered for breakfast he began to speak.

'I have announcement. Gaia came to me. To me! In my garden, she walk, and she touch flowers. Bees buzz. And I see her. I see Gaia! In my garden!'

'Oh, Artem. That's wonderful!' said Kira. 'What did she say?'

'She say nothing. But she came and after I say we go and so I know, we go. Is good to go.'

Everyone began talking at once until Jed banged the table with his cup for a bit of silence.

'Alright, I know you're all excited but listen, now is the time to decide whether you want to come or whether you want to stay. And believe me, it's fine if you want to stay.' He looked around the room to make sure everyone realised he was being honest. 'I'm going,' he said and then he sat down and looked at his wife.

'We're going, Grace and me and Peter.' Kira turned to look at her parents.

'We're staying, love. Artem's been telling me about some new medication he can get for my condition and anyways you don't want us two oldies gadding around with you. No, we'll stay here, won't we, Malcolm? And then when you've finished adventuring you can come back and tell us all about it.' Jean beamed at her daughter who smiled back. It felt like the right decision to Kira as well.

'I'm going!'

'And me,' smiled Max, holding Dina's hand.

The attention of the table fell upon Martha, Ash and Zac.

'Well obviously Lucas and I are coming,' said Martha.

'Yep, I'm in. You'll need a good techy,' said Ash which left Zac.

Zac looked at Artem for a long time before slowly nodding and turning to address Kira and Jed. 'I'll come too.'

'I fly, we all go. Is good.' Artem was smiling hugely and there was an air of festivity about the room.

No-one was thinking about where they were going and what was actually going to happen. It wasn't until later when Kira and Jed were packing up the gear in their room that they began to talk about what it was they were doing.

'Are we going to be alright, Jed?' Kira asked.

'With regards to what, love?'

'Going in a plane with some mad Russian, across the ocean to join some Resistance we've never heard of to try and spread the word of Gaia, an earth spirit that hardly anyone has ever seen and who nobody knows how to contact!' She finally stopped for breath.

He stopped what he was doing to give her a hug. 'I reckon we're about to find out.'

The Gaia Solution

The Gaia Collection, Book 3

Chapter One

'We shouldn't have left them,' muttered Kira as she looked out of the plane window. They were heading for the Resistance base, across the ocean, away from her island. She could make out several drones buzzing around Artem's compound where they had left her parents, Ruth and baby Sarah, and the rest of the Force soldiers. She squinted. It looked like a convoy of skimmers was heading towards the buildings.

'Artem says they will be well protected, hon. He told me about several security measures he has in place. New Corp won't try anything, they don't have the firepower to win.' Jed tried to reassure his wife, but he too felt uneasy. Who really knew what New Corp had at their disposal?

'But my mum is down there. And dad. And Ruth and Sarah. It doesn't feel right.'

'They didn't want to come with us, Kira. And to be honest, I can't blame them. Your mum needs to rest, she needs the medicine Artem has, and as for Ruth, I think it's better for her to stay.' Jed glanced out the plane window. 'You know, we probably should've left the other children there as well. Safer there than here.' At that moment, the plane hit a pocket of turbulence and bounced its passengers around. Jed chuckled nervously as he gripped the arm rests.

Everyone, apart from Zac, was nervous about flying. No-one, apart from Zac, had flown before.

A loud boom made them both jump and look out of the window again.

'NO!' screamed Kira. 'Stop the plane, stop the fragging plane.' She scrabbled with the seat belt, trying to get out of her seat before her fingers had managed to undo the clasp. 'We have to go back! WE HAVE TO GO BACK!'

Her manic response frightened the children, Grace and Peter. They began screaming which woke Lucas who had been sleeping peacefully next to Martha. The three babies fed into each other's dismay, their cries growing louder and louder. Ash unclipped his seatbelt and hurried over to try and soothe Grace and Peter while darting shocked glances out the window.

Jed stared in disbelief at the smoke and flames rising from the ground below. Artem's complex had been destroyed. Jed was frozen, unable to move or speak. In his head he was back in City 42, staring at a pale arm sticking out from the rubble of Corp Tech. His chest constricted and he couldn't breathe. Kira's frantic screams had faded into the background, his ears were deafened by rushing blood. Bile rose up his throat as he shook his head to try and clear his thoughts.

Max was banging on the pilot's door, demanding that they open the cockpit. A confused looking Zac appeared.

'What's wrong, Max?' Zac's eyes darted to the other passengers, frowning in confusion at the screams of anguish coming from Kira and the crying children.

'They've blown the complex up. We have to go back.'

'What?' Zac couldn't comprehend what Max was trying to tell him. He ducked his head to look out of one of the side windows and saw the huge plume of black smoke. He stared blankly for a moment then clenched his jaw before going back into the cockpit, letting the door shut behind him.

Kira had finally managed to undo her seatbelt and rushed over to the door, pushing past Max. She started banging and shouting but there was no answer.

'Everyone, please, return to your seats. We cannot go back. We only go forwards. If New Corp can destroy home, they can shoot down plane. I will get you to Resistance.' The mic crackled as Artem stopped talking.

Kira banged the door a few more times, sobbing before her legs gave way and she crumbled to the floor. Max looked beseechingly at Dina for some help. Together they tried to move her, but she was a dead weight. Dina wrapped her arms around her friend, trying to whisper words of comfort.

Martha, pale-faced and feeling shaky, stood up, her arms tightly wrapped around Lucas as she went to check on Jed. He still hadn't moved and was staring into nothing. She shifted the baby in her arms and put one hand on Jed's shoulder but there was no reaction.

'Jed? Jed, can you hear me?' Martha called to the others. 'I think he's in shock.' Then she dashed to the toilet, making it just in time as she threw up everything she had eaten that day.

At that moment, Zac came out of the cockpit, stopping briefly to make sure Max and Dina were alright before stepping over Kira and hurrying to be with Martha.

'Are you okay?' He put a comforting arm on her back.

'Am I okay? After New Corp just blew up my friend...' Martha's bottom lip wobbled, and a sharp cry escaped. She leaned back into Zac's arms, her shoulders shaking as she wept. The little boy in her arms confused about what was happening.

'Compound report, over.' Artem tried to hail a member of his staff on the plane's radio but there was no reply. Nothing but static. He checked the plane's fuel gauges; they were half full. He could risk banking right and circling around to see what had happened. 'Everyone, hold tight.' Artem's voice came over the intercom as he banked the plane.

Max stumbled in the aisle but managed to flop into an empty chair. Dina and Kira were wedged together in the aisle and Jed had never left his seat, but Martha, Lucas and Zac tipped into the open toilet cubicle.

'Ow!'

'Are you okay?'

'Just get off us.' Martha pushed Zac away. 'What the frag is going on?'

'Artem is circling back to see what happened,' called Max. 'You'd better buckle up. We don't know what we're getting into.'

Martha pushed past Zac, her face red from crying. She clipped herself and Lucas into a seat, ignoring everything else.

Zac frowned at her as he stalked past, going back to the cockpit. He had only been trying to help.

'How's it looking, Artem?' Zac asked as he plugged himself back into the co-pilot controls.

'There is... nothing.'

Zac and Artem looked out the window at rubble and smoke. The entire compound had been destroyed.

'Do you think anyone made it?' Zac was scanning the scene for any signs of life.

'With warning, maybe. I have bunker. But this, this was attack from nowhere. My Ruth and little one... gone.' Artem's hands tightened on the pilot controls turning his knuckles white. 'They will pay for this.' He increased the throttle, sweeping the plane round in a full arc, accelerating away from the attack zone. 'They will pay.'

A second boom filled the skies as Artem's supply of biogas ignited. The plane shuddered, caught in the blast radius but their course held steady. The continual noise and turbulence pulled Jed out of his nonresponsive state.

'What happened? Kira? Where's Kira?' He panicked, the plaintive cries of his children confusing him further.

'She's here,' Max called and waved from the front of the plane to get Jed's attention. 'She's here, on the floor.'

Jed noticed Ash crouched down next to Grace and Peter and clapped one grateful hand on the man's shoulder as he fumbled one-handed, trying to undo his seat belt. Finally free, he hurried over to Max. Dina looked up at him with a tear stained face.

'I heard what they said in the cockpit. There's nothing left.'

But Jed didn't know what to say in response. None of them did.

'Kira? Kira, hon? Can you stand?' Jed reached out for his wife and she grabbed his hand, squeezing it tight. He pulled her upright and guided her back to their seats. She clung onto him, stumbling as she shuffled across the plane's causeway. Grace lifted her arms when she saw her mum, but Kira didn't register her. Ash did his best to distract the confused little girl.

'I'll make some synth-caf, extra sugar, for the shock.' Max didn't know what else to do but he wanted to do something.

'I'll help,' said Dina, looking for anything to take her mind off what they had witnessed.

'What happened, Jed?' Kira's voice was shaky.

'New Corp must have struck Artem's compound.'

'Because they thought we were there?'

'I suppose.' Jed couldn't quite believe it himself.

'So, we killed them. We killed all those people and Ruth and Sarah and my mum and dad. Oh, oh, Jed, we killed my parents! And Sarah, she's not even Grace's age and we killed her. We just left them all to die. How could you? HOW COULD YOU?' Kira was screaming and hitting her husband in rage and grief.

Jed withstood the blows, knowing there was nothing he could say or do right now to help his wife. He held her loosely as the punches began to lose their potency and the sobs became louder. He was struggling to comprehend how the attack had happened let alone the fact that Kira had lost her parents, one of her closest friends and a baby had died. Not to mention all the Force operatives he'd left behind and the soldiers and staff Artem had had at the compound.

Max and Dina handed out the hot drinks. Involuntarily Jed took a sip then winced at the sweetness but dutifully drank the whole cup and it did calm the jitters he had been feeling inside. Martha was holding Lucas tightly, rocking back and forth - more to comfort herself than the child who had no idea what had happened. Dina and Max sat a couple of rows over, ashen faces, hands clasped around their mugs of synth-caf, disbelief etched on their face. Jed looked to his daughter Grace and his nephew Peter. They had both calmed down. The initial turbulence and reaction to the explosion had frightened them both badly but Ash had stepped in and distracted the children with silly faces and biscuits. Jed mouthed a silent thank you at his second-in-command.

Kira had quietened now. She pushed her hair away from her face and wiped her eyes, sniffing loudly. Seeing Ash crouched nearby and entertaining the kids, she half-fell out of her chair in her haste to check on them herself. Her abrupt movements startled the kids, but they didn't cry, just regarded her with big, wide eyes. She knelt in front of them, giving them both a kiss and trying to smile.

'Mum-mum,' gurgled Grace, holding out a small, chubby hand.

'Yes, it's mum-mum, darling.' Kira's voice wavered as she thought about her mum, but she cleared her throat and in a wobbly voice asked them if they wanted to choose something else to eat. Ash stood up and moved out of her way.

'Do you think she's alright?' Jed asked him.

Both of them watched Kira for a moment.

'I don't think any of us are,' replied Ash in a soft voice.

Jed nodded. He had expected the rage and the tears but trying to put a brave face on everything was not like his wife. He was worried. 'Do you know how much longer the flight is?'

'A couple of hours I think, maybe a bit longer after that circling back. The best thing any of us can do now is try and get some rest.' Ash patted Jed on the shoulder. He started opening the overhead lockers looking for blankets and pillows to hand out to everyone.

An odd silence fell over the group. Even the children were quiet.

The friends sat apart, each trying to work through their initial shock and grief.

Once the children were asleep, Kira lay back in her chair, staring blindly out of the plane's window. She'd just lost both her parents and her first reaction was to turn to her mum to figure out how to deal with such grief and every time she thought about doing that, it was like another blow to her body because her mum wasn't there anymore.

'Do you think...?' Kira turned to Jed, to try and ask him whether he thought there was any chance her parents had survived but he had fallen asleep. She watched him sleep, a slight frown in his forehead, the only sign that things weren't as they should be.

Unable to sleep, Kira longed for the flight to end and for the plane to touch down. Eventually there was a crackle on the intercom.

'We have arrived. Please, keep seatbelts on and remain seated until plane has touched down and we are parked in hangar.' Artem's voice lacked its usual vitality, matching the feeling of despair the rest of the passengers were feeling. No-one spoke as the plane came to a standstill or when Zac came out of the cabin to open the doors of the plane and extend the stairs.

'Um. There should be someone to meet us, they'll get the bulk of your belongings brought in so no need to worry about those. Just bring what you need now, the essentials. Are you ready?' His gaze flicked from person to person. He seemed nervous.

Martha was the first to stand. She had her bag slung across her body and Lucas held tightly on one hip. She stalked down the gangway and out into the night air. Zac hurried after her.

'Do you need any help?' Dina asked as she hovered next to Kira's chair.

'Can you take Peter, please?' Kira's voice was unemotional. She moved mechanically, checking they hadn't forgotten anything before taking Grace out of her seat and carrying her own bag.

Dina picked up Peter and shrugged slightly at Max as she followed Kira out of the plane.

'Sir? Are you ready to leave the plane?'

Jed flinched in his seat at hearing Ash's voice.

'Yes. Let's go,' he said, standing up and grabbing his own bag.

Max clapped Ash on the back as the men exited. Hearing someone address him as a superior had given Jed the momentum he needed to get moving. He knew the full force of grief would soon hit them all but for now they needed to keep moving.

Once outside, Jed activated the cube strollers they had brought with them from the island for the children. Martha decided to keep hold of Lucas, but Kira gratefully placed Grace inside and Peter was eager to join his cousin. The children were excited at being off the plane and were cooing with interest.

Artem was the last to leave. There was no point in him flying back to his compound. It didn't exist anymore. He had made sure all the controls had been turned off and closed the exit behind him. The plane looked lonely in the empty hangar bay. He patted the bodywork fondly as he locked up and looked for the others who were gathered uncertainly behind Zac.

Chapter Two

'General Ridgley. Glad to have you back, Sir.' A smartly turned out woman in a khaki jumpsuit saluted Zac as the group walked towards her, stopping by the hangar bay doors. 'What happened? We had reports of an explosion on the island?'

General? mouthed Dina to Max who shrugged. She looked at Artem. 'Did you know?' she whispered.

'Da. Is fine.' The big Russian grinned at them but Dina tutted at him.

'You could have said something,' she hissed at him but was interrupted by Zac speaking.

'Thank you, Colonel Archer. Good to be back.' Zac glanced back briefly at the others but made no explanations. 'Artem's compound was attacked and destroyed.' He let out a breath. 'We were lucky to get out in one piece. What's the latest report here?'

Colonel Archer cast a doubtful eye over the odd group of civilians stood with him.

'It's alright, Colonel. You can speak freely. I vouch for all of them,' said Zac firmly as he started to walk out of the hangar.

Everyone hurried to keep up while at the same time looking around them to see where they were. There wasn't much to see. The airstrip was empty and there were a few buildings in the distance. Archer and Zac led them along a marked path for pedestrians, leading them away from the runway, towards a security fence and the buildings.

'Yes, Sir. We've had three new groups of refugees arrive and have been able to update the cities file accordingly. Together with the information you and Misner were able to provide we have an up to date indication of the strength of New Corp.'

'Anything else?'

'Yes, Sir. There have been some developments in the environmental scans. Humphries is waiting to give you a full debrief.'

'Very good, Colonel. Please escort our guests to the base and see that they are made comfortable.' He nodded at the Russian. 'Artem, please, you are welcome here as well.' Zac finally spoke directly to Martha. 'I'll join you and the others as soon as I can. And I'll explain everything.' He half smiled at her before walking swiftly away from them, towards a waiting skimmer, on the other side of the security fence.

Martha could feel all eyes on her, but she did not know what to say. Colonel Archer came to the rescue.

'Welcome to the Resistance. I'm Colonel Archer and I will escort you to your quarters.'

Nobody replied.

Archer tried again. 'Look, I'm sorry for the circumstances that brought you here, especially if you lost someone. We've all lost people here. But the Resistance will welcome you, if you choose to join us.'

'Are we free to leave?' asked Dina bluntly.

Archer regarded her for a moment before replying. 'There's nowhere to go.' And she walked away.

Artem was already moving and whistling as if nothing had happened. Nobody else knew what to say in response and the rest of the group unwillingly followed as Archer led them through the gate in the security fence. They walked half the length of the airstrip before they arrived at several squat, red brick buildings. A few soldiers were running drills to the right of them and Martha spied the skimmer Zac had taken over to the left. It was parked and empty. She tried to think what was important for her to notice but a blue light caught her attention in the corner of her left eye. She turned her head and stopped walking abruptly. Shimmering in the distance was Gaia.

Dina bumped into her, breaking Martha's line of sight but she grabbed Dina's arm excitedly and pointed.

'Look! Look! Did you see her?'

The others looked confused because there was nothing there. Colonel Archer turned back to find out what the delay was.

'See what?' she asked.

Martha ignored her, turning instead to Kira. 'Did you see her? Gaia? She was just there?'

Kira stared in the direction Martha was pointing but there was nobody there. She shook her head at her friend and started pushing the cube stroller again, closing the gap between her and the colonel.

Dina patted Martha on the arm as she walked by.

'I did see her. I did.' But Martha was talking to no-one. Casting another look in the direction she'd seen the blue lady, she sighed in frustration. 'I did.'

'Wait here,' ordered Archer as she took them through an external door into a small waiting room. She waved her wrist at a security panel and another door swished open for her, closing quickly behind.

'Implants,' explained Artem as he took one of the seats.

'You don't have one?' asked Dina, taking the chair next to him.

'I am not official member of Resistance. I fly plane now and then but always I go back.' He tried to smile at her. 'Now, I don't know.'

Dina smiled back sadly and watched the others. Kira had Peter and Grace in a double cube. Both children were stood up, looking around interestedly and holding onto the cube sides. They wouldn't be able to climb out, but they had a good view of everything. Martha still held Lucas. There was another collapsible cube in her bag, but she hadn't activated it yet preferring instead to hold her son. Dina couldn't blame her. Sarah used to share that cube with Lucas. She grabbed Max's hand as he stood next to her, squeezing it tight.

Max looked down at his girlfriend and gave her a quick smile. He was uneasy. It was taking Colonel Archer an awfully long time to come back from wherever it was she had gone.

The door opened.

A second soldier, dressed in the same khaki jumpsuit, followed Archer out of the doors. He was short with close-cropped hair and thick glasses that he adjusted nervously as everyone stared at him.

'This is Lieutenant Kolwowsky. He'll inject you with one of our security chips then you'll be able to open doors and access the medical and food supplies. It doesn't hurt,' said Archer and she waited for someone to volunteer.

No-one came forward. Kira looked at Jed for reassurance while Max and Dina shrugged at each other. Martha was waiting for someone else to go first while Artem looked on in amusement. But before he could speak Ash stood up.

'Er… I'll go first?' he volunteered, holding out his left arm.

Jed frowned at him for being so quick to comply making Ash falter.

'Is this really necessary?' Jed asked Archer.

'It is if you want access to the base. Everyone here has one,' she replied.

'What about the children?' asked Martha in concern, holding Lucas even closer to her.

'Um...' For the first time Archer looked unsure. She glanced at Kolwowsky for help.

'We don't have any babies here but all our children have a chip so they can get to school, in and out of the mess hall, that sort of thing. It's perfectly safe, I promise.' He smiled encouragingly at them.

Jed nodded once and Ash stepped forward again. Kolwowsky grinned as he moved closer with his med-gun. A quick stab in the arm and the chip was embedded. He turned to Max and Dina who were stood nearby and waited for them to roll up their sleeves.

'Is this so you can keep an eye on us?' asked Martha, eyeing the med-gun doubtfully as Kolwowsky came to administer her chip and one for Lucas. The little boy didn't even murmur at the injection.

'The chip does have tracking capability but that's not such a bad thing when there's nothing but desert outside of our dome, ' replied Archer.

'This place is domed?' Max looked out of the window in surprise, he hadn't noticed the tell-tale shimmer.

'Yep, new tech developed right here,' Kolwowsky replied. 'We aim to find better ways to get things done here.'

'Thank you, Lieutenant. That will be all.' Archer raised an eyebrow at the soldier as he threw her a cheeky grin alongside a salute, going back the way he had come.

'If you will follow me, I'll take you to your barracks. It's not much but you won't be disturbed, and we've put you all together.' She waved her arm at the doors to open them and gestured for the group to proceed her down the corridor.

'I don't like this, Jed. We could be walking into anything,' muttered Kira as they passed by several doors but no signs of other people.

'Let's just wait and see, hon. Wait and see.'

'Artem better have an explanation for how this happened,' Kira said bitterly.

'It wasn't his fault. We couldn't have known New Corp would attack. I think we were lucky to get away.'

Kira glowered at him but said nothing. Her parents were dead.

Ruth and her little girl were dead. There was no luck in any of that.

Archer led them to the end of the corridor and stopped in front of a set of double doors. 'This is you,' she gestured.

Dina went first, feeling silly as she opened the doors with a wave of her arm. The others followed her inside. The doors led into a communal area with a few sofas and a small kitchen. There were more doors on the righthand side. Dina opened the nearest and revealed a small bedroom with two single beds and a small set of drawers for personal items.

Kira opened another to reveal the same layout.

'There's enough space for all of you. I'll leave you to settle in. Someone will be along soon with your belongings. There are some supplies in the cupboards, but we all eat our main meals together in the communal mess hall at the other end of the corridor. Dinner is at 1800 hours. If you need anything, you can reach Lieutenant Kolwowsky on line one.' She tossed a couple of two-way radios onto the table.

'That's a bit old school, isn't it?' commented Max.

'We make the most of everything available to us here at the Resistance.' Archer gave a brief smile before leaving. The doors slid closed behind her.

There was silence as the group looked around them.

'I'll make some synth-caf,' announced Kira, unpacking a pouch she had in her hand luggage and going in search of mugs in the small kitchen.

Martha expanded the cube Grace and Peter were in, turning on its entertainment capabilities and putting Lucas in with the other children. She joined Kira in the kitchen area and soon there were several cups of steaming synth-caf circulating the group.

Chapter Three

Zac stood in his office and scanned the briefing file in front of him, looking up briefly as Colonel Archer arrived. He was aware of her standing to his left but said nothing as he finished looking over the report.

'Not what we'd hoped, Archer.'

'No, Sir. Fewer groups of refugees are arriving. I don't think there will be many more. We can clear cities 24, 30 and 11 from the board. They're not viable.'

Zac glanced at the map on the wall. It was accurate as they had been able to make it. Everyone who arrived was questioned carefully to determine which city they came from, which cities they'd passed and other important environmental information.

'You can take 36 off the map, as well as 15.'

'Were they both destroyed by New Corp?'

'No. 36 is full of radiation, it won't be safe to inhabit for decades to come. Shame really, a stronghold in the mountains would have been a tactical advantage.'

'Not when you read the latest report, Sir.' Archer bit her lip as she waited for her superior to catch up on the results of weeks of investigation. She caught herself tapping her fingers impatiently and held back the urge to speak before he'd finished reading. Finally, Zac put the handheld down and leaned heavily on the desk in front of him.

'The entire country?'

'That's what it looks like, Sir.'

'And the calculations are correct?'

'To the best of our knowledge.' Archer paused. 'Who are the people you brought with you, Sir?'

Zac pushed himself to standing and began ticking names off his fingers. 'Artem you know. From City 42 we have their former rebel leader, Martha Hamble with her son as well as Archivist Kira Jenkins and former Force detective Jed Jenkins with their children. Dr Max Carter and Dina Grey are scientists, originally from Camp Eden, and Ash is one of Jed's men.'

'Perhaps their scientists can independently verify the data for us. It might also make them join our cause, when they know some of the facts.'

'I don't think we need to worry about whether they will join or not. None of them are pro New Corp.'

'How do you know, Sir?'

Zac closed down his info wall.

'New Corp wiped out Artem's complex...'

'Yes, we know that, Sir.' Archer interrupted.

'Kira's parents were there. As was one of the new mothers from City 42. With her child.'

Wide-eyed, Archer paled and took a step back.

'Are they all… dead?'

'Completely annihilated. I don't think we need to be worried about them being motivated to help us. We might have to hold them back.' Zac gestured at the discarded handheld on the table. 'Make sure they get a copy of your latest report. I want them to have all the facts.'

'Not redacted?'

'No, Archer. There's no time for secrets. We need to pull together and find a solution, fast. Dismissed.'

Archer saluted and they went their separate ways. Although he hadn't shown it to Archer, Zac was shaken by what had happened to Artem's compound and all he could think of was finding Martha and making sure she was alright.

Dina was exploring the quarters they had been assigned. There was no sign of previous occupancy and the food supplies were sparse. The info screen on the wall of the communal area began flashing, indicating a new message. Intrigued, Dina walked over and tapped the screen to access the information. She stopped reading after a few minutes.

'Guys! You'd better come and see this. Now!' she called to the others.

Kira and Martha looked up from the play cube where they had

been half-heartedly entertaining the children. Jed, Max and Ash had been chatting in the kitchen area, refreshing their synth-caf. They all came to join Dina at the info screen.

'Read this.' Dina pointed and the screen and scrolled backwards to the beginning.

Field Report to Resistance Headquarters

The recent scientific expedition to our coastline has confirmed initial suspicions. Sea levels are rising, rapidly. Shoreline erosion has increased, and internal waterways are flooding up and down the country. The pre-existing flood works near the coast are now redundant as they reside several metres below water. The recommendation of this report is to find higher ground, fast. We predict that the nearby island currently inhabited by New Corporation and its denizens will be underwater by the end of the year.

Martha stood in front of the screen, blocking the view to the others.

'Do you know what this means?'

Max nodded. 'Everyone we left behind will be drowned before the end of the year unless they can find a safe way off that island. If they've got their facts right, that is.'

'I doubt New Corp are planning to evacuate everyone. I didn't see any sign of any ships, just business as usual in City 9,' commented Jed.

'They must have some kind of plan, there's no way New Corp would allow themselves to perish,' argued Kira.

'You're right. New Corp won't perish. The people in charge left the island several months ago. One final management level remains but I doubt they'll be there long. New Corp control cities 42 and 9 remotely from headquarters we have been unable to find. Yet.' Zac spoke confidently but he scanned the group, looking for signs of friendliness or hostility.

'You knew New Corp had the firepower to destroy Artem's compound, didn't you?' Kira accused Zac.

'Not exactly.'

'What the frag does that mean?' exploded Jed.

Zac raised his arms in surrender. 'It means, we thought they might have the fire power, but we didn't know they were ready to use it.' He looked directly at Kira. 'I had no idea they would attack. I am so, so very sorry for your loss.'

Kira gave a curt nod and turned away, unwilling to share her grief with him.

'And what about you, Zac? Did your parents really own that museum? Was it all a cover? Why were you even there?' Martha was angry.

'My aunt and uncle, who practically raised me so yes, that bit is true. But it was also a convenient cover to spy on New Corp's communication network and try to figure out what their plans were. Being in City 9 was potentially a death sentence for anyone from the Resistance, which is why I was there.' He looked directly into her eyes. 'Sometimes a leader has to lead.'

Martha flushed and looked away, but the group weren't done with Zac yet.

'Why didn't you tell us you were the leader of the Resistance? Why the subterfuge?' Jed demanded. 'What else aren't you telling us?'

'Nothing. I've told Archer to give you full access to everything. Our whole camp, supplies and all our intel.' Zac took a deep breath. 'I need your help.'

Dina barked a laugh. 'What can we possibly help you with?'

Zac nodded towards the info screen. 'As you've read, we are on the verge of massive environmental upheaval, and I was hoping your connection to Gaia would help get us some answers on what to expect next.'

'Is that all?' asked Martha.

'Obviously we could use your scientific expertise and your understanding of anthropology. Your team has some unique skills, a fresh outlook and you're clearly problem solvers. Look at how you dealt with the clean water supply in City 42 - that was inspired thinking. We need your help. Will you stay?' Zac looked hopefully around the room.

It was Ash who spoke up this time.

'We need some time, to process all this. To grieve.'

'Of course. You can reach me on the comm. Anything you need, let my team know.' Zac paused. 'But I need to know your answer by morning. Time is something we don't have a lot of. We'll speak then.' He left them alone. It was a risky move, they could decide they were better off without getting involved in the Resistance, but after what had happened at Artem's, Zac was confident they would join the fight.

He needed them to.

Ash went to the door to make sure Zac had gone and that nobody else was nearby. The corridor was empty. He turned to the others.

'For what it's worth, I think we should pitch in. Helping them helps us,' he said.

'We don't know anything about where we are, who the people are, what's going on...' Dina trailed off.

'Exactly. We have no idea what's going on and he needs us. We have the upper hand here.' Ash looked to the others for confirmation. Martha was nodding but Kira looked pensive.

'How are we supposed to stop a world-wide environmental catastrophe?' she asked.

'You're the Gaia whisperer - ask for help I guess,' suggested Dina.

Kira put her head in her hands and spoke through her fingers. 'It doesn't work like that! It's not like I can just ping Gaia, you know.'

'It worked at Artem's...' Dina faltered. 'Where is Artem?'

'He said he needed some air, went for a walk I think,' replied Max. 'But Dina's right. You and Martha have had the most interaction with Gaia. She obviously feels deeply connected to you two. Maybe she will speak to you again, tell you what's going on. In her unique way.'

'I'd rather she just lay it out in black and white for all of us to understand,' muttered Jed.

'That would be too easy,' replied Kira with a small smile. 'I take it that means we're staying?' She looked at the others for confirmation. There were shared smiles and small nods. 'I know I feel safer here with the children then out there. For now, at least. We can rest here. Recuperate and plan what to do next. How we fight back. But first things first, we need to unpack.'

'Unpack what? Our bags haven't arrived yet!' grumbled Dina.

The door chimed and Kolwowsky appeared with an auto trolley, piled high with their bags. He stopped short at the sight of everyone staring at him and adjusted his glasses.

'Is everything alright?'

Max nodded and strode over. 'Let me help you with that.' He deftly took over the controls and steered the trolley towards the back of the communal area where the bedrooms were located.

'Can I get you anything else? Will you be joining us for dinner?' Kolwowsky asked hopefully.

'Yes. What time and where do we need to go?' asked Jed, he'd forgotten what Archer had told them.

'Dinner is at 1800 hours. Here's a map of the base.' Kolwowsky tapped their info screen as he was talking and pointed to a collection of purple dots. 'This is you. You can change the settings to search for people, but I figured it would more straightforward to show you where you are to start with.' He dragged a finger across the screen to a large area highlighted yellow. 'This is the mess hall.' Looking up, he grinned at Jed. 'I'll see you there. If you need anything else before then, let me know.' He adjusted his glasses again before smiling and leaving.

'Helpful, aren't they?' Martha remarked.

'A little too keen,' said Kira.

'Let's go to dinner and see what the vibe is like. The Resistance might be what we've been looking for.' Dina was looking forward to finding out more.

Chapter Four

They heard the mess hall before they found it. A cacophony that only grew louder as they entered. Long rows of tables with bench seating were laid out parallel to each other. Other people were entering and leaving the mess hall through the doors behind Kira, Jed and the others and at first no-one noticed them, but then Lucas started to cry, frightened by the loud noise.

Instantly heads swivelled at the sound of a child crying. Kira scanned the crowd, there were some young children but none of them were younger than about five or six. There were no other babies. She inched closer to Jed, holding Grace tightly with one arm, and found her husband's free hand, grasping it tightly. Jed held onto Peter with his other arm and squeezed Kira's hand in mutual support.

'Hi! Hey, over here!' It was Kolwowsky waving at them. He'd secured the end of one of the tables with enough seating for them all to sit together.

On closer inspection Kira noticed the food was already on the tables; her stomach rumbled as the smell of what looked like stew hit her nose. She was hungrier than she'd imagined.

As they sat down the conversation levels in the room began to rise again, the topic of discussion almost exclusively the new arrivals. Martha had managed to soothe Lucas enough to stop him crying but he clung to her tightly. She fumbled in her bag for a bottle of milk and smiled gratefully at Dina who came to her rescue. As Martha fed her son, Dina spooned out some of the stew for her and grabbed a hunk of bread. There were carafes of water on the table and empty glasses, so Max poured for everyone.

Kira shared small pieces of bread with Grace while Jed fed Peter. The others tucked in, no-one saying a word as they focused on eating. It was delicious and clearly not rehydrated food sachets.

'We grow everything in our allotments,' said Kolwowsky, grinning at them as everyone enjoyed their food. 'How are you settling in?'

'Okay, thanks,' replied Dina. She'd finished first. 'There isn't much in the fridge though, can we get some more supplies from somewhere?'

'Sure. I'll take you to Stores when you're finished here. You'll have to sign for what you want - the internal AI system monitors who has what preventing hoarding and ensuring there is enough for everyone.'

'Internal AI system?' Ash interrupted. 'Is it interactive? Can I see it in action?'

Kolwowsky laughed. 'It's just a Stores system, but sure, you can see it in action. We call it Frank.'

'Excellent,' replied Ash. He turned to Dina. 'I'll come with you to Stores, if that's alright?'

'Sure.' She was keen to see an AI system working as well.

'I'd like to take a look at your allotment if that's allowed?' asked Max. 'Part of my work at Camp Eden involved increasing crop yields. I might be able to lend a hand.'

Kolwowsky nodded enthusiastically around a mouthful of food. He cleared his throat. 'That would be great, we try and get everyone to pitch in round here and I know they're short handed over there. If you turn left out of here and follow the corridor all the way to the end, you'll reach the allotment. Bennett should be there; she will show you around. She's in charge of Allotment.'

'I will come too. Botany is my field of expertise after all,' said Martha.

Kolwowsky eyed the little boy on her lap who was looking wide-eyed at everything. 'What about him? I'm not sure it's really a safe space for children.'

'Do you actually have any creche facilities?' asked Kira.

'Er no, not really. There's a school for the kids but with today being Saturday there won't be any teachers around till Monday.' He leaned closer to the group. 'There aren't many babies in the Resistance. In fact, I think yours are the youngest children we have here.'

'I can keep hold of Lucas for you if you like, Ma. I'm not really in the mood to explore.' Kira felt tired. They had the play cube and individual sleeping cubes for each child. Being collapsible, the cubes had been easy to pack and there was plenty of space in their quarters for the children to explore safely.

Martha tightened her hold on her little boy. 'No. It's alright. I would rather keep him with me.'

Kira stared at her friend for a moment and then turned her attention to Kolwowsky, feeling a little hurt. 'How many people, families, do you have here?'

'Er... I'm not sure exactly. The internal monitors will give you access to the databank. I think we have about five hundred people here now. We had a new group arrive yesterday, just before you.'

'A new group? From where?' asked Jed.

'We have people coming from all over.' Kolwowsky helped himself to some more stew. 'Cities are becoming unstable all the time and resources are so tightly controlled by New Corp that most of 'em would've starved if they'd stayed where they were.' He seemed completely oblivious to the group's reaction to his words.

'How many cities have you contacted?' Jed was keen to find out exactly how widespread the Resistance was.

'I don't know. It's not my remit. Colonel Archer oversees that side of things. I'm sure she'd be happy to answer any questions you might have though.' Kolwowsky grinned at Jed before stuffing the last of his bread in his mouth.

Jed nodded and turned to speak to Ash in a low voice. 'I'm going to see what I can find out, keep your eyes and ears open as you check out Stores. We need to get a measure of Resistance.'

Ash nodded. They all had questions but the first thing they needed to do was gather as much information as possible.

The doors to the mess hall banged open and an incredibly drunk Russian staggered in, singing at the top of his voice, a bottle clutched tightly in one hand.

'Jed!' hissed Kira. 'Go get him before he causes any more disturbance!' She held an arm out for Peter and managed to balance both children on her knees.

Pushing his chair back, Jed stood and walked over to Artem, who had thankfully stopped singing and was looking around blearily.

'Jed! My comrade! Here, toast me.' Artem shoved the bottle in Jed's face while throwing a heavy arm around the man's shoulders.

Staggering slightly, Jed managed to turn the larger man towards the table where the others were sitting. Ignoring the stares from the rest of the room, he guided Artem over and half-dropped him onto the bench.

'Comrades!' bellowed Artem, looking blearily at them. 'Come! Drink with me.' He snagged the bottle back from Jed, sloshing the contents on the table before pouring large shots in several of the cups on the table. 'For lost ones!' he roared then downed a large shot.

Kira picked her shot up. 'For my parents,' she said before swallowing the liquor with a grimace.

'To Ruth,' said Dina in a small voice while Max echoed her and they both sank their shots.

'For the lost ones.' Ash held on to his dog tags as he drank, toasting his team who had all perished at the compound explosion.

'For the lost ones,' repeated Jed, watching his wife in concern as she tried to hold it together. Putting his cup down, he cleared his throat. 'I'll take him back to our rooms, then go find Archer. Everyone happy?'

There was murmured assent from the group as they prepared to leave the mess hall.

'Come on, big fella. Let's get you back to our rooms.' Jed heaved Artem up to his feet and let the drunk man lean heavily on him. 'Can you manage both?' he asked Kira.

She nodded and hefted the children onto her hips. Luckily it wasn't far to their quarters and the children were more interested in clinging on to Kira than getting down and exploring.

A swipe of his arm opened the doors and Jed staggered through to the communal area, dumping Artem on one of the sofas. At once, the large Russian began snoring gently.

'At least he looks peaceful,' Jed commented to Kira.

She shrugged slightly and put the children in the play cube. Keeping the volume low, she activated the play screen and left them watching educational cartoons. 'What do I do with him if he wakes up?'

'Try and get him into that room at the end. It's where we put his stuff.' Jed regarded the slumbering man. 'Perhaps several cups of synth-caf?'

Kira nodded and leaned into him for a quick hug. 'Be safe?'

'Always. Ping me on my wristplant if anything happens. I'll be as quick as I can. Will you be alright?'

'Yeah. I just need some rest. I'll be fine.' She smiled up at him. 'Go on, see what you can find out from Archer.' She looked over at the internal screen. 'If I get chance, I'll look on their system and see what's on there.'

Jed kissed her on the forehead, said goodbye to the children and left.

Kira looked at the sleeping man and the entertained children and decided to make herself a drink. In the kitchen area, she turned to say something to her mum, then gasped as the full force of her grief hit. Her vision swam and she bit her fist, trying to stop the tears. A low cry escaped her involuntarily and she doubled over. She couldn't stop the tears from coming or the loud sobs from escaping. Kira flinched as thick arms encircled her.

'I am sorry. I am so, so sorry.' It was Artem; he'd left the couch without her noticing and was holding her gently. 'Cry for them. For your mother, your father. For Ruth and little girl. For all innocents caught in fire.' He was talking in a low voice, a continual stream of comforting phrases as he held her in her grief.

Kira cried and cried and cried until she thought she didn't have any tears left. It was almost silent. Tears flooded down her face as she took large gulping breaths, unable to halt the sobs, completely oblivious to everything around her. As her crying subsided, Kira remembered where she was.

'Are the children alright?' She tried to move, to see into the cube but Artem was holding onto her more tightly than she realised. Paying more attention to the man holding her, she realised his shoulders were still shaking. Her grief had unlocked his own, now it was her turn to clumsily hold him.

'It's alright, it wasn't your fault. You couldn't have known what would happen, none of us could.' She tried to comfort him as he'd comforted her and together, they stayed slumped on the kitchen floor until both had finished weeping.

Chapter Five

Dina and Ash followed Kolwowsky down a corridor, not really listening to him as he kept up a running commentary of where they were in the base.

'You alright?' asked Ash quietly.

Dina glanced sidewise at Ash. 'Yeah, you?'

'Not really.' He looked up at Kolwowsky to make sure he wasn't paying them any attention. 'I can't believe what happened. I can't believe we lost so many people at once.'

'I know. First, they wiped out City 15 and then... and then Artem's place. Part of me feels relieved that we got away but then I feel guilty for even thinking that. Like I shouldn't be glad I'm alive when all those people are dead.' Dina blinked hard and cleared her throat. 'And you and Jed, you lost your team, every operative. How do you deal with that?'

Ash glanced at Kolwowsky again, he was still talking. Something about solar panels and renewable energy supplies. 'To be honest, I don't know. They were my friends, people I worked with, people I respected. It's like they're on another mission or something. Like they're not really gone. But I think... I think Jed is having a tougher time with it.'

'Because of Kira's parents?'

'Not just because of them. Did you see how he reacted in the plane? He went into some kind of shock. I think he was reliving the attack on Corp Tech. I heard him whisper Ingrid's name.' Ash looked at Dina to see what she thought.

'I can understand why the destruction of Artem's place would trigger those memories for him. I guess we keep an eye on him, look out for any signs that he's struggling to deal with things. I keep thinking Ruth and Sarah must have survived somehow.' She paused and stopped walking. 'Because... because, how could they? How could New Corp kill a baby?' With a hand to her mouth she started crying.

Kolwowsky stopped walking and turned back in surprise. Ash shook his head at the soldier who made to walk towards Dina and put his own arm around her. From one of his pockets he found a tissue and offered it to her.

'We have to believe they are in a better place now. Hold on to the thought that Sarah is with Ruth, that they are together.' Ash didn't know whether his words were comforting or not. It was how he tried to think about it. Not that Ruth and Sarah had been brutally murdered but that they were together, somewhere else. It seemed to work as Dina stopped crying and took some gulping breaths to try and steady herself.

'Are you okay?' Kolwowsky was concerned. 'Can I take you to medical or something?'

'No, no, I'm okay. It's just... been a tough day.' Dina sniffed and wiped her nose on the rapidly disintegrating tissue before shoving in her pocket. 'Come on, let's carry on.'

'Ah, we're here.' Kolwowsky waved his arm at the nearest door and it swung open to reveal the Stores area and a large screen in front of metal shelving that reached backwards into the warehouse, disappearing into the gloom. There was a pattern on the screen that swirled and pulsed. A pleasant male voice issued from speakers on the side.

Hello, Lieutenant Kolwowsky. It is good to see you. You have seventeen credits left on your account. What would you like to order today?

'Hello, Frank. I don't want to order anything today, thank you.' Kolwowsky grinned at the others. 'May I introduce you to two new members of Resistance. This is Dina and Ash. You should have them on your personnel list. Please confirm.'

The pattern on the screen changed and shifted its focus over to where Dina and Ash were standing.

'Fascinating,' breathed Ash.

Hello, Mr Ash. Hello, Miss Grey. Welcome to the Resistance. You each have fifty credits on your account. What would you like to order today?

'Er...' Dina's mind went blank. What did they need to order?

'Bring up a supplies list please, Frank.' Kolwowsky came to the rescue. The screen changed from its swirly pattern to a list of things available and Kolwowsky explained. 'It's an interactive screen, touch the area that you're interested in and Frank will list everything he has under that subheading. Look.' And he tapped the heading Personal Hygiene. A list of available items appeared including shampoo, toothbrushes and soap.

'Oh, okay, I see.' Dina moved forward eagerly. 'Let's see, we need some baby milk and some more synth-caf, probably some toothpaste and oh look, biscuits. Let's have some of those.' She continued to murmur to herself as she found her way round the system. 'Okay, I think I'm done. Do you want to add anything, Ash?'

He chuckled as he shook his head.

I'm sorry. You have insufficient credits for this order. Please review what you have selected.

Dina's face fell.

'Don't worry. We can sort that out,' Kolwowsky said. He turned to the screen. 'Frank? Please add Operative Ash and Miss Grey's allowance together.'

Confirmed. I'm sorry. You have insufficient credits for this order. Please review what you have selected.

'Uh... Frank? Please add Martha Hamble's allowance to the order?' asked Dina.

I am unable to comply. Individuals must be present in order for their credits to be used. I'm sorry. You have insufficient credits for this order. Please review what you have selected.

'How much are they short please, Frank?' Kolwowsky wanted Ash and Dina to take away everything they'd ordered.

This order requires an additional three credits.

Kolwowsky breathed a sigh of relief. 'Please take three credits from my allowance to complete this order.'

'No, we couldn't!' exclaimed Dina but he waved his hand at her.

'Don't worry, I get a refreshed credit allowance tomorrow. Besides, you need this stuff, biscuits and all.'

Thank you. Your order is complete. Please wait.

There was a whirring sound.

'That's the automated pickers. They will go and get the things off the shelf for you and bring the items here for you to collect. It won't take long.' There was a pause as they waited for the automatons to finish. A receipt churned out from the bottom of Frank's screen.

Kolwowsky picked it up and scanned it. 'Ah. That's where all your credits went. On the baby milk.' He pointed it out as he passed the receipt over to Dina.

'Why is that so expensive?' she asked.

'I guess because your babies are the only ones we have here, and it must be in short supply. The less we have of something, the more credits it costs. It's Frank's way of trying to stop us being wasteful with our resources. It's not easy to replace some of this stuff.'

'Will we be able to get more? I don't think the younger children are old enough to move onto solids yet,' asked Dina.

'Frank will alert Colonel Archer if an item low in stock is being regularly requested and then we see whether we can produce more in-house or...' He trailed off, not sure whether he should continue.

'Or?' prompted Ash.

'Or whether we can get it from outside. But that's really not my remit. Ah, your order.' Relieved that the conversation was interrupted, Kolwowsky opened the hatch and let the items be pushed through by one of the pickers. There were a couple of hover baskets on the ground and he started to fill one up with their items. 'You can use one of these to take your things back to your rooms. Bring it back when you're done. We don't have that many and everyone needs to use Stores.'

Dina and Ash nodded and watched how he activated the basket.

'Pretty neat bit of tech,' commented Ash. 'Is it an in-house build?'

'Yeah, we have a great tech department. If you have the necessary clearance, I can take you over there. They're always looking for new recruits, their gadgets are in high demand.'

'I can imagine,' murmured Dina.

'How do we know what level clearance we have?' asked Ash.

'Oh, right. If you go to your internal screen in your rooms and wave your wrist at the scanner on the bottom, it will load up your clearance, how many credits you have left, your work assignment, that sort of thing.'

'Work assignment?'

'Yeah, we all pitch in around here. The Resistance needs everyone to pull together and everyone to contribute.' Kolwowsky grinned at them before ushering them out of Stores and together with their laden hover basket they walked back to their quarters.

Chapter Six

'Left out of here and down to the end,' commented Max as he held the mess hall door open for Martha. 'Do you want me to carry something?' He looked on as Martha struggled to hoist her son back onto her hip and prevent her bag from falling off her opposite shoulder.

'No, I can manage.'

The bag fell off her shoulder, and as it landed on the floor the clasp undid and things rolled out. Among them the little blue Gaia statue and a holocube picture of Ruth, Martha, Lucas and Sarah. In her haste to snatch the cube up, Martha staggered and nearly fell, half dropping Lucas to the floor. He began crying in surprise at being nearly dropped.

'For frag's sake!' shouted Martha and she dropped to her knees letting go of her son but grabbing the holocube. She put her head in her hands to hide her face.

'Hey, it's alright. It's just a bag.' Max bent down to pick up the various items on the floor and put them back. Then he picked up Lucas, slung the bag over his shoulder and held a hand out to Martha. 'Come on. Let's go get some air.'

She looked up at him, her hair hanging across her face, and considered refusing his helping hand, but realised she was being petulant, so she grabbed it and pulled herself up off the floor. Clutching the holocube tightly she looked at her son.

'I can carry him to the allotment. He's not heavy,' Max offered.

Martha nodded. She desperately wanted to snatch her son back, to keep him safe, to prevent anything bad from happening to him, but she knew she was being irrational. Nothing would happen to Lucas while he was being carried by Max. She looked down at the holocube in her hand and squeezed her eyes shut. Even looking at a picture of her friend was too much. She reached over and tucked the holocube into the side pocket of the bag Max was carrying.

Max started walking slowly down the corridor and Martha soon followed. They didn't speak and she was grateful for the silence. She knew she was experiencing shock at losing her friend and Kira's parents. About fleeing her country and being here at the camp of Resistance. She had a hundred questions for Zac, a thousand really but all she really wanted to do was curl up with her son somewhere safe and warm, miles away from anyone who would try to hurt them.

As they neared the end of the corridor, Martha noticed a set of double doors that led outside the compound.

'This must be it,' she said as she waved her arm in front of the doors to open them. Nothing happened for a moment then the doors swung open ponderously.

Nature assaulted their senses. Martha could smell soil and herbal fragrances with the sour tang of manure underlying everything. Everywhere she looked there were splashes of green and the faintest buzz of insects in the air. She moved forward eagerly to see for herself what the Resistance was growing in their allotments.

'Here, this needs to be spread over bed four.' A short woman pointed to the far corner where a new raised bed was being prepared and tossed a bag of compost at Martha who barely caught it. 'You can press these seeds into bed three. That's half a dozen every half an inch.' She slapped a packet of seeds in Max's spare hand and didn't seem to notice the baby boy clinging to his other side. 'When you've finished, come and see me in greenhouse five. We have a replanting disaster to deal with.' When neither of them moved, the woman clapped her hands loudly. 'Chop, chop! We have lots to do.' She marched away from them, in the apparent direction of the greenhouses.

Max looked to Martha, but she had already started walking over to bed four, intent on carrying out her instructions. He dithered for a moment, but Lucas wasn't that heavy, and he could easily put a couple of seeds into some soil. He found that kneeling worked best as he shuffled along the side of the planter, but after a short while, his arm holding Lucas was burning with the continuous dead weight of the small child. Max craned his neck to look at the boy's face and realised he was asleep. Spying an empty wheelbarrow nearby and some flat hessian sacks, Max made a little nest for the boy and placed the sleeping child inside. He waited a moment to make sure Lucas didn't wake up then bent back to his seeding task.

Martha was tilling the compost gently into the bed. It felt good to feel the soil beneath her fingers, reconnecting herself with nature. She felt the ball of stress inside her ease slightly and started to breathe more regularly. She shied away from any thoughts of Ruth or Sarah, instead focusing intently on the task before her. When she had finished, she turned to see Max had also finished but there was no sign of Lucas.

'What have you done with my son?' Martha shrieked, flying towards Max, clawed hands aiming for his face.

Max deftly caught her wrists and shushed her, tilting his head to the wheelbarrow at the side of him. Martha slumped in his hold and took a shaky breath, dispelling the panic that had threatened to overcome her.

'I am sorry. I just... I panicked when I couldn't see him.' She looked down at the sleeping boy in the wheelbarrow, clenching her hands to stop them from shaking. 'That is an ingenious use for one of those.'

'Is it okay?'

'Yes, he's fine.' Martha looked over towards the greenhouses. 'Shall we?'

Max nodded and began wheeling. Martha started picking the dirt out of her nails as she looked around her at the variety of plants growing. Looking up she couldn't see the tell-tale shimmer of a dome.

'I thought the entire base here was under a dome?'

'That's what they said.'

Martha pointed upwards and Max took in the lack of shimmer.

'Huh,' he said. He looked around. 'Maybe we're at the back end of the base and the dome doesn't stretch that far?'

'It's not exactly secure though, is it?'

They arrived at the greenhouse and Max gently manoeuvred the wheelbarrow inside. It was steamy and smelled loamy. The short woman they'd seen earlier was to their left muttering under her breath as she examined the tomato plants currently sitting in rows.

'Ah, you're here. Right, we have to get these tomatoes replanted into richer soil to increase their yield. The new pots are over there.' She pointed to the bench opposite the tomato plants. 'Come on, no time to waste.'

Max parked the wheelbarrow and started at one end of the bench, while Martha took the middle. The woman finally took a proper look at them.

'You're not my gardeners. Where are you from? Have you been decontaminated?' She peered at them suspiciously.

'We are from, er... we are new, recently arrived and no, we have not been decontaminated. I did not know we were supposed to have been.' Martha had stopped what she was doing, mindful of the delicate plants in front of her.

The woman sniffed. 'You should be alright. Don't stop now, these plants need to be rehomed.' She glared at them for a few moments as they continued repotting. 'Who are you then, anyway?'

Forgetting where he was, Max launched into an introduction. 'I'm Dr Max Carter, I headed up a research station called Camp Eden just outside of City 42. We were investigating how the planet has been recovering from The Event and testing out new strains of edible plants, ones that were more disease resistance, quicker growers, that sort of thing.'

A gleam of interest lit up the woman's eyes. 'Did you bring samples with you? Seeds or seedlings?'

'I... uh... no. Sorry. We left in a bit of a hurry. But I did bring my research files, I'd be happy to share our findings with you.'

'That's something, I suppose. Shame you didn't have better priorities. We could've used a fresh injection of viable plants.' The woman continued working for a few moments before addressing Martha. 'And you, who are you? Another scientist from this camp?'

'No, I am a botanist, or was a botanist. My name is Martha Hamble.'

'Is it now? You're a disgraced governor who lost control of her city, way I heard it. No mention of being a botanist.' She noticed Martha stiffen at her remark. 'Yes, we get the sweeps over here, sometimes. We know what's happening on that little island of yours.' She looked at the row of plants Martha had re-potted. 'But you seem to know what you're doing I'll give you that. There's a place for you, for both of you, here. If you want it. If you haven't had your work assignments yet.'

Max shook his head. 'No, we haven't had those yet.'

'You will. Everyone in the Resistance is assigned somewhere. I'll put a request in, if you like. Colonel Archer knows I need more hands down here.'

'That is very kind,' replied Martha. 'But who exactly are you?'

'I'm Bennett, Lisa Bennett. Head grower and hardest worker in the Resistance.' She caught Max smiling at her statement. 'Oh, you think someone else works harder than me? Plants don't grow themselves you know.' And Bennett stomped off, calling behind her. 'And take your kid out of my wheelbarrow!'

Martha retrieved him swiftly and motioned for Max to follow her out of the greenhouse.

'What an odd woman,' remarked Martha.

'I kinda liked her. I'd be happy to work here, if we do get assigned.'

'I suppose we'll have to wait and see. We'd better get back to the others, let them know what we've found.' Martha kept hold of Lucas this time but seemed happy for Max to carry her bag. Working in the gardens had relaxed her a little and she was intrigued to learn more about Bennett and her allotment.

Chapter Seven

Jed walked confidently down the corridor but in fact he had no idea where he was going. He was hoping he'd come across Archer or Kolwowsky but so far, he had yet to see anyone. After reaching a second dead end, he leant on the wall and sighed heavily.

Voice activation accepted. Hello, Captain Jenkins, how may I assist you?

Jed flinched at the unexpected voice and noticed the flat panel on the wall beside him.

'And who are you?'

My name is Lola. How may I assist you?

'Er... I'm looking for Colonel Archer.'

Colonel Archer is currently in her office. May I direct you?

'Yes, please, Lola.'

Follow the blue line and you will soon reach your destination. Have a pleasant day, Captain Jenkins.

'Er... you too, Lola.' Jed felt a little silly talking to the wall but was impressed at the blue arrows that appeared along the corridor, highlighting the direction he needed to walk in order to find Colonel Archer. Now that he had some guidance, it didn't take him long to get to where he wanted to be.

Waving his arm at the entrance where the arrows ended, Jed expected to be able to go through straight away, but the doors did not open. Nothing happened. He could hear voices talking, so he rapped smartly and waited. The voices stopped talking and the doors slid open as Colonel Archer stood in the doorway.

She blinked in surprise. 'Jenkins. Can I help you?'

Jed pushed past her and was satisfied to see Zac was also in the room.

'Yes. You can start by answering my questions,' he said.

Archer exchanged a glance with Zac before gesturing to the table and chairs on the far side of the room. 'Maybe we should sit down.'

'I'm fine, thanks,' replied Jed stiffly and watched them both take a seat before continuing. 'Look, Zac, you led us to believe you were a museum owner's son, biding his time in City 9. Then Artem's complex gets destroyed, my entire team is massacred, and you fly us over here where for some insane reason you are apparently in charge of the whole fragging Resistance. You owe me an explanation.' Jed was breathing hard by the time he'd finished talking. It had taken all his self-control not to grab hold of Zac and physically shake him.

'How dare you speak to the General like that! If it wasn't for him, you and your family would never have made it here.' Archer leapt to Zac's defence.

'Archer, it's fine.' Zac waved a hand at his second-in-command. 'You're right, Jed. You do deserve an explanation. Please, sit down.'

Jed scowled at Zac but took a seat. He leant back and crossed his arms, waiting for the excuses to begin.

'Firstly, my aunt and uncle did own that museum but yes, I was using it as a cover for my work with the Resistance.' He paused and smiled briefly at Archer. 'I have only recently been promoted to General.'

'Okay, well…' Jed was thrown, he hadn't expected Zac to start explaining things straight away. 'Look, I can understand not coming right out and telling us you were Resistance, that's common sense. But what about my team, my in-laws, Ruth and...' Jed trailed off.

'I had no idea New Corp would make a move like that. If I had had the slightest clue, I would have made sure everyone left the complex, together. I honestly thought your team, and everyone else, would be perfectly safe. Artem was planning on flying straight back to continue our intelligence monitoring. Obviously, that is no longer the case.'

'So now you're flying blind.'

'Not entirely but yes, we don't have the same information coverage we did have. But New Corp are predictable; free thinkers are not exactly encouraged,' replied Zac.

Archer coughed gently and flicked her glaze to the open handheld on Zac's desk.

'We are in the middle of planning a memorial service. For the people you lost. We want to show you that the Resistance is deeply sorry you were targeted. We lost some people at Artem's place too.' A shadow fell across Zac's face.

'I appreciate that, we all will. It's important to say goodbye, even when there's nothing to say goodbye to.' Jed pushed away the memory of his sister, keeping his emotions in check. He changed subject brusquely. 'Where did you get all your tech from? Kolwowsky was talking about an AI in Stores, I met Lola on my way here - how is that the case?'

This time Archer replied. 'It's true we are the Resistance but we're also all that's left. We have the best minds here and have scavenged much of our material from abandoned cities.'

Jed interrupted. 'What do you mean, you're all that's left. All that's left of what?'

'The human race. There are small settlements in zones one and two, we're all that's left of zone three and we haven't been able to make contact with zone four.'

Jed burst out laughing, waiting for Zac and Archer to stop their charade and join in. When he realised they weren't, his laughter died.

'Are you serious?'

Zac nodded and went to the info screen. He tapped a few buttons and pulled up an old map of the world, but Jed wouldn't let him continue.

'Stop. Stop. If this is going to be some grand explanation, I want the rest of my family here with me. This is life-changing information. I don't want to explain it third hand.'

'Of course, I agree. You should all be briefed fully.' Zac glanced at his wristplant. 'Let's meet back here, tomorrow, after breakfast. Say 9am - is that alright?'

Jed nodded and stood to leave but before he left the room, he hesitated.

'Are we really all that's left?'

Zac nodded and Archer said yes softly. Jed's eyes flicked to the map on the wall again, but it didn't mean anything to him. He wasn't even sure where they were on that thing.

'I'll see you tomorrow,' he said and left the room.

'That went well,' remarked Archer. 'Are you sure about telling them everything? It might not be wise yet, we don't even know whether they're going to stay.'

'I think it's a bit late for that, Archer. We need them on our side if we have any chance of pulling this off.'

Jed heard what they said, he was loitering in case it had all been a joke at his expense. It hadn't. He waved at an info panel on the wall. Lilac colours swirled in response.

Good evening, Captain Jenkins. How may I assist you?

'Take me to my quarters please, Lola.'

Of course. Please follow the green line. Have a pleasant evening.

A green line appeared on the wall and Jed followed it down the corridor, his fingertips touching the wall lightly, his thoughts whirling.

Chapter Eight

Dina and Ash were the first back to their quarters. A very quiet Kira met them while Artem slept off his vodka in his bunk. They could hear his snores rumbling in the background.

'Here, let me help,' Kira said in a low voice as she helped Dina to unload the hover basket and put the food away. 'I don't want to wake Artem or the kids.'

Kira grinned when she picked up the chocolate biscuits and hugged Dina at discovering the baby milk.

'It should help for a bit, right?' Dina wasn't sure she'd brought the right thing.

'It's great, thank you.' Kira nudged the empty hover basket with her foot. 'What do we do with this?'

'I'll take it back to Stores. I don't think we're meant to keep them,' offered Ash and he left them brewing synth-caf. He was hurrying back to make sure he got a look in at the chocolate biscuits when he bumped into Jed on the way.

'Alright, Ash? How did it go at Stores?' asked Jed.

'We were able to order some supplies, but we had to think on our feet, hopefully we haven't missed anything, Sir.'

Jed sighed. 'I think rank is moot when there's only two of us left, Ash. Call me Jed,' and he held out his hand to his remaining operative.

Ash shook the proffered hand firmly and grinned. 'You know, Sir, er... I mean Jed, my name is actually Matthew.'

'Really?'

'Yes, Sir. I mean, Jed.'

Both men laughed.

'I guess we've both got to get used to this,' said Jed as he waved his arm over the door plate at their quarters. Walking in, he saw that everyone was back from their explorations.

'I know you've probably all got something to tell the rest of us, but I'd like to get the children in bed before we lose track of time,' Kira said without her usual enthusiasm.

Jed shot her a concerned look but picked Peter up and followed his wife into their chosen bedroom.

'Are you okay?' he asked as he wrestled Peter out of his day clothes.

'I'm fine,' replied Kira and she tossed him a night-time nappy for the little boy.

Before Jed could press his wife further, they were joined by Martha and Lucas, who was giggling away as his mum tickled him. Martha dropped three bottles of milk gently onto the bed.

'I made these up for them. You are not planning on coming back out again with them, are you?' she asked.

'No, it's bedtime,' replied Kira as she grabbed one of the bottles and sat on the bed with Grace.

Martha and Jed followed with Lucas and Peter and soon the three children were drifting off into contented sleep.

'Shall we put them all down together for now?' asked Martha. 'I can always move Lucas into my room later. I think he finds it comforting to sleep with the others.' She looked down fondly at the slumbering child.

'Yeah, that's fine,' replied Kira and she tapped the sleeping cube to expand it enough to fit all three children.

They joined the others in the communal area. Artem had reappeared, a little bleary eyed but visibly perking up with a strong cup of synth-caf in front of him.

'Is good to be with you,' he said simply.

The others murmured their agreement.

'Dina, Ash, what did you find out?' asked Jed, taking charge.

'Stores is indeed run by an AI called Frank. The computer system assigns credits and keeps track of what you spend. We can pool our credits to buy more things but only with the people there in the room at the time of order,' Ash explained.

'The more expensive items are the ones in short supply, things like the baby milk unfortunately,' added Dina.

'Although Kolwowsky did say that if a short supply item becomes popular then they try to make more or source more from trips outside the dome. But I get the feeling those are few and far between,' finished

Ash.

'Is true. Great lab here, great workshop. You want, they make. They can't make, maybe you find but, is hard.' Artem concurred.

'Okay, let's hope they can make more formula for us.' Jed turned to Martha and Max. 'What about you, did you find the allotment?'

'Yes. We met with the head gardener, Bennett. It was... useful,' replied Martha.

'Useful? What does that mean?' asked Dina.

'We helped plant some seeds and repot some tomatoes.'

'So, you didn't actually find out anything then.' Jed looked disappointed.

Martha glared at Jed but before she had chance to say anything, Max stepped in.

'That's a little unfair, Jed. We found the allotments, we got our hands dirty, we saw the breadth of seedlings and what plants they are growing. I also agreed to share my research from Camp Eden with Bennett to help them with crop yield and disease resistance. But I tell you one thing, they are not growing that much produce. Possibly enough for a couple of hundred people. Depending on whether there was much more that we didn't see.'

Jed held his hands up in apology and paused to make sure Martha had nothing else to add.

'Right, I went to find Zac. And Archer,' he said.

'What did you say?' asked Martha.

'I challenged him. I wanted to know why the hell he lied to us back in City 9 and whether he had any prior knowledge of the attack on Artem's compound.'

'Zac would not do this. If he knew, all would be saved. Zac is good man,' rumbled Artem.

'That's what he said. He claims to have no idea about the attack and he... they are planning to hold a memorial service for everyone that died.' Jed paused to look at his wife, but her face was expressionless. 'He said they lost people too.' When no one said anything, he pressed on. 'I asked about all the tech here and he said... well, he basically said that the Resistance did the best with what's left.'

'What do you mean, what's left? What's left of what?' asked Martha.

'Of us. Of the human race. He started talking about zones and settlements, but my mind was reeling. I told him I wanted him to tell all of us together and explain it properly.'

'That's ridiculous!' interrupted Dina. 'There has to be more people out there. I don't believe you.'

'He wants to see us all after breakfast tomorrow so he can explain everything.'

'He has a lot of fragging explaining to do,' muttered Martha and she was the first to stand and say goodnight. She ducked into Kira and Jed's room to collect Lucas and called a quiet goodnight to the others.

Kira also said goodnight and went to check on Grace and Peter while Dina pulled Max along with her into their room.

'Come, Ash, you bunk with me. I'll tell you a bedtime story.' Artem chuckled as he clapped an arm on Ash's shoulder and guided him to their shared room, leaving Jed to follow his wife and try and get some rest.

'Are you sure you're alright?' whispered Jed as he tried to get undressed quietly.

'No, not really, but there's nothing anyone can do.'

'I'm here for you, you know that, right? Anything I can do, just ask.' Jed felt helpless. Kira had been a rock when he was working through his grief for Pete and Ingrid but now, she was shutting him out and he didn't know how to help her.

Kira gave him a quick peck on the cheek as he got into bed then turned away from him, wrapped up in her corner of the duvet. Jed knew that meant *leave me alone* and so he stared at the ceiling, trying to will himself to sleep.

Chapter Nine

'Thank you all for coming,' Zac said as he addressed the group of people in front of him.

Jed was pissed off. Zac had led him to believe that he would be explaining everything to him and his friends but there were other small groups of strangers in the briefing room. Each group remained clumped together with the people they had arrived with; no-one had ventured anything apart from the odd awkward smile between strangers.

'I think these must be the other new arrivals,' whispered Dina to the others.

'What makes you think that?' asked Jed, peevishly.

'Kolwowsky mentioned there had been another group of refugees arrive yesterday.'

'He did?' Ash sounded surprised.

'Yeah, you should have been listening instead of drooling over Frank,' teased Dina with a goodhearted grin.

Ash chuckled quietly but was hushed by Jed as Zac continued speaking.

'I'd like to take this opportunity to formally welcome you to the Resistance.' He swept a glance across the room. 'Sounds scary, doesn't it? The Resistance. I'm sure some of you must be wondering, resistance to what exactly? Well, we resist against the corrupt organisation of New Corp, previously known as Corporation, who are more interested in profit and power then they are working with the planet to save what's left.' He tapped the large info board behind him, and an old-fashioned map of the planet appeared. 'This is what Earth used to look like. Seven continents, thousands of cities, billions of people.' He tapped again. 'This is what Earth looks like today.'

Everyone leaned forward to get a good look.

'As you can see, what was North America was badly affected by the radiation of The Event. There are also large tracts of scorched earth in much of what used to be Asia and central Europe.' He pointed to large yellow areas on the map. 'As far as we have been able to determine these areas have not yet recovered. The small green patches are renewed earth.' There weren't many green patches. 'When Corporation set up the initial fifty cities, they renamed the continents into zones, Zone 1 is South America, Zone 2 is southern Africa, Zone 3 is what's left of Europe and Asia and Zone 4 is Oceania.'

'What about the blue lines around all the land masses? And the sections coloured in blue. What do they represent?' It was someone from one of the other groups asking.

'That indicates the amount of land we have already lost or will eventually lose if the ocean continues to rise at its current rate.'

There was a sobering silence. All of North America was submerged in blue apart from a small section of uninhabitable yellow. South America had lost its southern tip, Africa its northern half. A thick blue line ran all around Europe and what wasn't yellow in Russia, India and China was blue. Nearly all of Australia was marked out blue as well.

'Where are we on that map, exactly?' asked Jed.

'We're here.' Zac pointed to a section of mostly blue. 'Formerly Scandinavia, currently the Resistance stronghold but as you can see, not for much longer.'

'Do you think the oceans are still rising then?' asked Dina.

'We believe that we are at the beginning of a mass extinction event. The polar ice caps have lost their war with rising global temperatures, thanks to the after-effects of The Event, and all that meltwater will raise the current levels significantly. Plus, additional displacement thanks to post-glacial rebound.'

'But that means most of our country will be flooded!' exclaimed Dina.

Zac nodded grimly. 'As well as large parts of the rest of the world. We cannot ignore the science; we must head to higher ground. Specifically, here.' He tapped a large white area in the middle of Zone 3. 'These are the Ural Mountains, the border between the former East Europe and West Siberia. Historically this area has been populated by nomadic tribes who traditionally fished and hunted to survive, looked after the wild herds of reindeer and horses and some settlements that grew crops, we know we will be able to support ourselves here.'

'What about the other cities?' asked Jed.

'We are all that is left here in Zone 3.'

Dina barked a laugh. 'You cannot be serious?'

Colonel Archer spoke up. 'General Ridgley is nothing but serious. The people we have managed to collect here are all that remain in this zone.'

'Except for New Corp citizens in City 9 and 42,' Martha remarked drily.

'But what about the other cities?' Jed asked again.

'We have received intel that there are two surviving settlements, one in zone one and one in zone two. As yet, we have been unable to make contact with zone four. The infrastructure does not currently exist for us to travel out to these zones and as you know, Corporation were restrictive on communication between cities.' Zac glanced at Archer before continuing. 'It is my hope that once we have relocated, teams will volunteer to travel out and make contact.'

Archer blinked; this was news to her.

'This is what we know so far.' Zac tapped the info screen again and brought up a list of cities. There was silence as the room digested the information.

Formerly Europe

City 1 – originally set up to be like Earth-that-was, decimated by plague. No inhabitants.

City 6 – approached by Resistance and agreed to join

Cities 9 & 42 – under New Corp control. Population unknown.

City 15 – destroyed by New Corp. No survivors.

City 20 – faulty power supply, New Corp refused aid. Reconnaissance team deployed, awaiting report.

City 36 –affected by radiation poisoning, there will be no survivors.

City 40 – flooded, survivors joined Resistance.

Formerly North Africa

Cities 2, 33, 39 & 45 – flooded, survivors believed to have joined the single settlement for survivors in Zone 2

Formerly Southern Africa

Cities 10, 14, 18, 24, 28 & 31 – believed to have joined the single settlement for survivors in Zone 2

Formerly Asia
City 5 – a landslide knocked out the power and comms, New Corp denied requests for help. Survivors joined Resistance. No inhabitants.
Cities 7 & 46 – approached by Resistance and agreed to join
Cities 11, 26 & 37 – city succumbed to radiation sickness, no survivors
City 16, 22, 30 & 34 – flooded, believed to have fled to Zone 4
City 41 – New Corp withdrew food and medical supplies with reports of a suspected attack. Survivors joined Resistance. No inhabitants.
City 43 – reconnaissance team deployed, awaiting report.

Formerly Oceania
Cities 3, 12, 32 & 35 –unable to make contact. Survivors unknown.
Cities 19, 21, 27 & 48 believed to have been flooded.

Formerly North America
Cities 4 & 8 – flooded, survivors believed to have fled to Zone 1
Cities 44 & 49 – affected by radiation, no known survivors

Formerly South America
Cities 13, 17, 29 & 38 – believed to have joined the single settlement for survivors in Zone 1
Cities 23 & 25 – flooded, believed to have fled to Zone 1

City 50 – originally set up to be the pinnacle of Corporation life. Population and official allegiance unknown.

'How did you get hold of this information?' asked Jed.

'The refugees that have come here brought their stories and intel with them. New Corporation had varying success in consolidating its power depending on the greater distance they had to cover in order to control the city populations. We have been able to send out sorties to cities in the immediate vicinity of our base. Others were reported as empty by travellers on their way here. We've managed to hack some satellites and get real-time imagery for parts of the different zones. It's taken time but this is what we've been able to piece together.'

'Why did we not know about you before?' asked Martha.

'Your city was based on an island that happened to be a Corporation, and now New Corp, stronghold. We had no way of getting a message to you without compromising our own security. Until now.'

'But there are so many more people in City 42. People I know, people I have to help,' objected Martha.

'And we will do what we can but as you know, New Corp has demonstrated they have significant firepower and are clearly unafraid of using that destruction. I don't want to put lives at risk unnecessarily.'

'You're going to leave all those people to drown.' It was the first time Kira had spoken.

'We will do everything we can to help those we can help.'

'What about the cities that are in Australia and New Zealand? It says no information on your city list.' Max intervened with another question.

'We have been unable to raise any communications with Oceania. And it's impossible to travel that far with our limited fuel and transport resources. Travelling there by boat would take too long. The decision was made to establish a safe and secure base and then in the future we will be able to make contact with them.'

'Yeah, right,' muttered Kira.

'So, your plan is to move everyone from your fortified base here up some mountain somewhere and hope for the best?' asked Jed. He was uneasy at the thought of leaving what he'd figured to be a safe place.

'More or less, yes.' Zac gave a short laugh but no-one else joined in. He stopped and waited in the silence that followed for any more questions.

There were none.

'Look, I know this is a lot to process. All this information is available to you via your info screens in your quarters. Take a couple of days to process everything. Come and see me or Colonel Archer if you want anything clarifying and we'll do our best to answer your questions.' He turned to the Colonel and she stepped forward again.

'The memorial service for the men and women...'

'And child.' Kira's voice was loud as she interrupted Archer.

'...and child that we have lost recently will be held this afternoon in the Serenity Garden. Your individually assigned staff will come and collect you. Please don't stray from your quarters if you wish to attend.'

'We hope to see everyone at the service,' said Zac.

'Finally, because you are all new arrivals, your work orders will be sent through tomorrow,' Archer added.

'Work orders?' Jed queried.

She smiled thinly. 'Everyone in the Resistance contributes where they can, Jenkins. Everyone.'

Her tone suggested dismissal. The other groups of people started filing out the doors, but Kira stayed where she was. She walked up to Zac.

'You didn't say anything about Gaia.'

'I don't know anything about Gaia. You're the expert,' he replied.

'What exactly is it you're expecting her to do?'

'Nothing at all.'

Kira wrinkled her brow in confusion. 'But you said you wanted to be able to communicate with her.'

'We do. But I'm not hopeful. If the spirit of the Earth does exist and hasn't seen fit to do anything to save us by now, then I doubt she'll step in now. But...' Zac shrugged.

'You're covering all your bases. Trying to think smart.' Jed had joined the conversation.

'It's not like you can call her on the comm, you know. She'll only appear when she wants to,' Kira retorted.

'I know. But it's you, and your friends, that she has chosen to appear to. I hope if she does show her face, you'll share with the rest of us what she has to say.' Zac looked closely at Kira's face, to determine whether she would lie to him about it.

'If she speaks to me, I will tell you what she says.'

He nodded in satisfaction and said his goodbyes to the rest of them before leaving the room, Colonel Archer closely behind him.

'What the frag do we do now?' asked Dina but nobody had the answer.

Chapter Ten

'We go to our rooms like good little Resistance members and wait to be collected for the memorial.' Despite her scathing words, Kira's tone was leaden; there was no fire behind what she said. Leaving the others to do as they wished, she picked Grace up and carried her out of the briefing room. All the children had been as good as gold during the meeting, but Grace was starting to get fractious now. It was time for her milk.

The other followed dutifully. Even Artem was subdued and the mood didn't improve in their quarters. With everyone hanging around waiting to go to the service, tempers grew short, and after Ash had paced past Martha for the umpteenth time, she lost her cool.

'For frag's sake, Ash! Just sit down. Having you pacing up and down like that is getting on my nerves.'

Ash stopped instantly and plonked himself in the nearest seat. His knee began to jig, and Martha tutted loudly at him.

Dina looked at her wristplant again and sighed heavily.

'Instead of time watching, maybe you should think about what you want to say at the memorial,' suggested Kira quietly.

'Do you think they'll let us speak?' asked Dina.

Kira looked at her, eyes rimmed red. 'They won't stop me.'

Her quiet certainty calmed the others and brought them back to the fact that they had lost so many people. A different sort of stillness clung to them now as everyone reflected on their loss.

Finally, the door chimed and slid open. Kolwowsky stepped through, clad in a black jumpsuit this time, the colour choice a mark of respect.

'If you would all like to come with me?' He stood to one side to give them space to leave but Kira stayed in her chair, unable to move.

'What's wrong, hon?' Jed asked, going back for her.

'I don't want to say goodbye,' she replied in a small voice and buried her face in her husband's jumper.

Jed made soothing noises and gently lifted her to standing. With one arm wrapped round her, he led her through the door and out into the corridor. She could walk but she clung to him, head down, unwilling to look where they were going. Dina had Grace and Peter in the shared stroller while Martha had decided to carry Lucas. Since arriving at the Resistance, he had been extremely clingy.

Kolwowsky led them to an inner courtyard which was surrounded on all sides by the walls of the complex. Kira looked up to see blue skies and felt the sun's warmth on her skin. Something her parents would never know again. The thought was enough to make her catch her breath and she stumbled slightly, grabbing onto Jed for extra support. No-one seemed to notice and Kolwowsky gestured to one side where a row of seats stood empty. The group filed in and waited, feeling self-conscious for being at the front of the service.

Zac and Colonel Archer strode up onto a small raised dais, also dressed in black.

'They look smart,' whispered Dina to Max, who half smiled and put a finger to his lips.

'Thank you, everyone, for joining us on this sombre occasion. We are gathered here to honour our fallen. Let us start with a minute's silence.' Zac bowed his head and the other members of the Resistance in the room followed suit.

Jed looked as his friends and saw most of them had done the same. He ended up looking at his shoes but instead of thinking about the people he'd lost he felt a prickling on the back of his neck as if someone were staring right at him. Feeling self-conscious, he gradually lifted his head so as not to disturb anyone else and looked behind him. There was nothing there. Frowning, he went back to looking at the floor, but the prickling sensation didn't go away.

A gentle cough from Zac marked the end of the minute of silence.

'If anyone here would like to say something, please share your thoughts with the rest of us.' And he stepped back from the microphone. Initially no-one moved but then a tall, dark skinned woman with close-cropped hair walked up to the dais. Zac clasped hands with her and smiled encouragingly.

She bent forwards to talk into the microphone.

'My name is Finona. I come from City 20. We left because our power supply failed, and we lost many of our citizens. We walked many miles to come here. New Corporation denied us permission to leave our city and yet they also refused to accept us into City 9. We matter. I matter. And the friends and family that I lost matter. I remember them.' She was shaking slightly by the time she had finished.

Another person approached the dais. A young man of Indo-Asian descent. He was meticulously dressed in crisp white trousers and tunic. He bowed slightly to Zac before he approached the microphone.

'My name is Priya. I am from City 41. We did not leave from natural disaster. We left after New Corporation withdrew their food and medical supplies. My city was slowly starving to death. The journey here took the lives of many of my people. There are only a few of us left. But I will fight for their survival. Whatever it takes. I remember them.' Priya's eyes burned with zeal.

Kira made to walk up to the dais at the same time as Martha. They both stopped, then Martha took Kira's hand and they walked up together. Neither of them looked Zac in the eye.

'Hello, my name is Martha, and this is Kira. We came from City 42.' There was a soft gasp of recognition. 'We had overthrown the yoke of Corporation, but we were naive to think we had won. New Corporation are a more ruthless, power hungry entity than we could ever imagine and in our journey to get here we have lost friends, family, comrades and even an entire city. I remember them.' Martha finished and glanced at Kira to see if she still wanted to speak.

Kira stood closer to the microphone but took time to order her thoughts. Before she spoke, she grabbed Martha's hand and squeezed it tightly.

'I do not want to talk about regimes or fighting. I want to talk about my parents and friends whom I lost a few days ago. Jean and Malcolm Bishop were kind, loving and generous people who will always be missed, and not just by me.' While Kira's voice was steady, her grip on Martha's hand was like iron and tears were falling freely down her face. 'My friend, Ruth Maddocks and her baby girl, Sarah, who had barely begun to live, were both tragically lost in a senseless act of destruction for which I can never forgive. Ruth was the wild one, the rebellious streak in our group of friends, a true free spirit, and she will be missed so much.'

Artem blew his nose incredibly loudly, startling many of the listeners but making Kira smile slightly.

'We lost an entire team of operatives, soldiers if you will. Men and women who had pledged loyalty to Martha, and to my husband, Jed, and who had taken an oath to keep us safe. Instead it was them we should have kept safe.' She took a deep breath. 'I still feel like I will walk around the corner and see my family and friends. They are not lost to me and as long as I have breath in my body, I will honour their memory. Always.'

There wasn't a dry eye in the room when Kira and Martha stepped down, although Colonel Archer was doing her best to put her emotions back under control.

Zac stepped forward. 'If there is no-one else?' He waited but no-one was forthcoming, he continued with the memorial. 'In memory of the fallen we light a candle for them today and hold them forever in our hearts.'

Kolwowsky and the other Resistance soldiers handed out small candles to everyone in the room and brought lit tapers round to light them.

Kira felt a moment of peace as she stood in quiet contemplation with everyone else, staring at the flame in her hands. It didn't take away the aching loss she felt but it did make her feel like she'd be able to find the strength to carry on.

Chapter Eleven

The info wall chimed. Dina looked up.

'Hey, guys, looks like our work orders have come through. You'd better come and look at this,' she called to the others.

Everyone gathered around the monitor to read the allocations.

Martha Hamble - Allotment
Max Carter - Allotment
Dina Grey - Science & Technology
Matthew Ash - Science & Technology
Jed Jenkins - Peacekeeping
Artem Misner - Peacekeeping

'I didn't know your first name was Matthew!' exclaimed Dina staring at Ash in bemused embarrassment.

'It's fine, don't worry,' he replied, equally uncomfortable about the situation.

'Where is your allocation, Kira?' asked Martha but Kira shrugged. 'And what does *Peacekeeping* mean?'

'It's army. Or militia. Or playing with guns. Whatever you like to call it. Is good, da?' Artem thumped Jed on the shoulder, happy to be assigned with him.

Jed nodded. He was pleased to be in the action, but he was worried why Kira hadn't been assigned anywhere.

'I'm going to call Kolwowsky, see he knows anything about this,' he said, but Martha put a hand on his arm stopping him.

'Sorry, Jed, but I do not think there is any point in calling Kolwowsky.' She pointed at the screen. 'If you read the rest it says our assigned Resistance member will be here soon with our work permits and uniforms, he is already on his way.'

'Work permits? That sounds a bit...' Dina voice everyone's concerns.

'Look, let's see what Kolwowsky has to say. Working in the Resistance has to be a good thing, right? We can't sit here doing nothing. At least if we're working it will keep us busy, but it should also give us insight into how the Resistance works. Let's see if we can figure out what their overall goal is. Zac looks like a man with a plan to me.' Jed looked round the group to make sure everyone agreed with him. Artem was the only real loose cannon in the group but Jed felt his loyalty lay more with them than with Zac, because of what had happened to Ruth.

The door pinged then opened. It was Kolwowsky.

'Alright? I have all your uniforms and permits and everything. Let's get you all kitted out.' He was grinning widely, as usual, and gestured to the hover basket next to him.

'Why don't I have an assignment?' asked Kira.

'Uh… um... Colonel Archer thought you'd be too busy looking after the children and um...' Kolwowsky trailed off as everyone stared daggers at him. He raised his hands in submission. 'Hey, it's nothing to do with me. We don't have the facilities for babies here, there's a school but we can't put them in the classroom. Can we?'

'No, we cannot. Lucas will come with me to the allotment. I see no reason why I cannot work there with him by my side,' countered Martha.

'You'll have to take that up with Bennett yourself,' replied Kolwowsky doubtfully. He didn't think she would take too kindly to having children in her workspace.

'I will.'

'I don't mind looking after Grace and Peter,' said Kira quietly but no-one was listening to her.

'I'm going to give that Colonel Archer a piece of my mind. Who does she think she is assuming that Kira wants to look after children all day? Doesn't she know what a valuable team member she is?' Dina was livid, and Kolwowsly took a step back nervously.

'Look, I'm just telling you what she said...' he protested weakly.

'Well it's not good enough. I mean, honestly!' Dina fumed.

'Guys, I said I don't mind.' Kira tried again.

'It's one thing to tuck us all away down here, out of sight, out of mind, but if you think you are pushing my wife to the side lines, you can think again, Kolwowsky.' Jed took a step forward and was startled when his wife shouted.

'HEY! I said, I don't mind!' Once she had everyone's attention, Kira continued. 'I have no problems looking after Grace and Peter, Lucas too if you want me to, Martha. There's no need for an archivist here. We need to be looking to the future, not clinging to the past.'

'But all your knowledge... everything about the cities and The Event... you are not thinking of letting all that go to waste?' protested Martha.

'Were you not there in that meeting? The cities are gone. The Event was over two hundred years ago. What we need to deal with today is the mass extinction disaster that threatens the lives of the people here and now. You don't need me to do that.'

Martha swallowed her retort, knowing that she would not win this argument with her friend. Instead, she gave Kira a quick hug and began talking to her about keeping Lucas for the day. She still thought she would be able to take him with her to Allotment on a regular workday but perhaps orientation wasn't the best place for him.

Jed frowned. His wife was right to a certain degree, but she was a fighter, and it wasn't like her to give in and give up. She should be burning with righteousness, not slumped in defeat. He decided he'd have to tackle it later. Now that he was in peacekeeping, he should be able to corner Archer and get an assignment sorted out.

'Okay, Kolwowsky. Give us the uniforms.' Jed held his hand out as the Lieutenant distributed the packages.

'Right, well. You've all got info jacks about your roles and where you need to report in. I'm on comms if you need me or have any questions. Good luck.' And he bid a hasty retreat.

'It's overalls,' said Martha, a little disappointed.

Max looked at his doubtfully. 'I'm not sure these will be long enough.'

'Maybe we can get a new pair exchanged over in Stores?' suggested Dina.

Max smiled at her and nodded towards her packaging. 'What have you got?'

She rummaged. 'Er… info jack, work permit, ooh, a new handheld and a lab coat.' She sighed. 'It's so cliché.'

'It's also easy to spot and easy to make,' commented Ash who was secretly pleased with his assignment. He had expected to be turned into a soldier but was glad his tech expertise would be of some use.

'Yeah, alright, smart guy,' teased Dina while Max watched them both closely.

'Do you have an assignment, Artem?' asked Jed, looking in his kit bag. There was a note telling him to report to the training ground.

'Da. Training ground at 0900 tomorrow. They want to see how fit Artem is. Is ok. I show them muscles.' He smiled good-naturedly at Jed, but Jed had an uneasy feeling about what was going to happen next.

Chapter Twelve

Jed had been right to be apprehensive about his assignment to peacekeeping. He looked at the training field in dismay. New recruits. He was with all the new recruits and he hadn't even been asked to train them. He was one of them. Artem didn't seem fazed in the slightest. He was telling jokes with a couple of other Russians he'd managed to find. They were enjoying speaking in their mother tongue.

'Alright, ladies. Let's get down to business.' It was Colonel Archer.

Jed scowled at her as he waited to see what she had to say.

'You've been selected for peacekeeping because of your previous experience in your cities. Some of you have come from Force, some from Security. A few of you are ex-military from your old cities. Today, you forget all of that. Today, you are Resistance. Line up!'

People moved into a rough line but still clumped together in their known groups.

'On the line, at the double!' shouted Archer, pointing to a white line on the floor.

Everyone hurried to stand on it. Jed found himself midway, while Artem was off to the left.

'Welcome to your fitness test. Drop and give me twenty.'

Jed dropped and began doing press-ups, it was old school, but it was effective training. But not everyone seemed to know what they were supposed to do.

'Give you twenty what?' asked a young girl.

'Press-ups, recruit. Press-ups.' Archer gestured to those already on the ground, tapping her foot as she waited for everyone to comply.

Finished, Jed jumped up and stood ready, legs hip width apart, arms clasped behind him and waited to see what he'd be asked to do next. They were made to do sit ups, run suicides, more press-ups, more sit ups and finally laps around the field. As he jogged around, feeling a little breathless he looked at the others on the field.

Most were like him, more or less in shape. The young girl who had queried the press-ups had given up a while back and was sitting on the floor, her head in her hands. Artem was still chatting, this time to a group of women who were laughing at whatever it was he was saying. He caught Jed looking and give him two thumbs up. Despite himself, Jed smiled back.

Eventually, Archer blew a whistle to signify the end of the training session.

'Not bad,' she conceded. 'Some of you have clearly kept up with your fitness regime. Hit the showers, you'll be taken through the security of the Resistance base next.'

Jed jogged with the others to the building Archer had pointed at. He was relieved they weren't doing more physical training.

After sitting through a two-hour lecture on the security protocols for entering and exiting the Resistance base, Jed wished he was still running laps. Artem had actually fallen asleep and his snores rumbled through the classroom, causing a few of the others to giggle but the instructor didn't seem to notice. Only Archer was frowning at the slumbering Russian.

Finally, the instructor stopped talking and they were released from the stupefying atmosphere of the classroom to grab lunch before they were due to return for firearm evaluation.

In the mess hall, Jed was pleased to see Kira and the kids. He excused himself from the other trainees and went over to join her.

'Hey, hon.' He kissed the kids and then his wife on her cheek before sitting down next to her. 'How are you? Can I help?'

'We're fine. I got this' She smiled a small smile and went on feeding the two children by herself.

'Archer had us running laps this morning and then some instructor bored the socks off everyone with a lecture on security protocols.'

'Mmm hmm.'

Jed glanced at his wife. 'Then she gave us the keys to the castle and a rocket ship to the moon.'

'Yeah.'

'Kira? What's wrong?'

She glanced at him. 'Nothing, why?'

'I told you I was given a rocket ship to the moon.'

'Oh, sorry. I'm just tired. I'm okay.' She wiped the children's faces as they'd finished their lunch.

Jed looked at his wristplant, it was nearly time for him to go back. 'Look, if you need to talk, I'm here for you. I know what's like to lose family, remember.'

'I know, I will.'

Unconvinced, Jed gave her a hug and said goodbye to the kids before hurrying back to training. Despite being concerned about Kira, he was looking forward to getting his hands on a firearm.

'Anyone used a weapon before?' asked Archer, sweeping her gaze up and down the line. About half the recruits stepped forwards, Jed and Artem included, she nodded. 'Right, you lot, stay here with me. The rest of you go inside and see Lieutenant Yarrow for basic handling.' She waited until the inexperienced trainees had gone before leading Jed and the others to the firing range.

There were various targets to aim for and the back wall was marked with laser burns, bullet holes and an arrow. Jed blinked in surprise. He hadn't expected that kind of weaponry.

'Okay, line up and you'll each be assessed on how well you can handle the laser gun.'

No-one seemed that keen on going first so Jed stepped forwards to the line and picked up the laser gun. It was Corporation issue but a few years old. Jed had been using the newer version on Force. He sighted the target, aimed and fired. Archer nodded but said nothing, gesturing for the next in line to step forward. Everyone shot the target.

'You've proven you can point and shoot. Congratulations,' said Archer drily. 'Unfortunately, we do not have a large store of laser guns and those we do have are old and prone to glitching. The Resistance were fortunate to discover an old weapons cache left behind from before The Event. We have been able to retro manufacture bullets. Let's see how well you can handle a real gun.' She looked at Jed. 'You'll need to wear the ear defenders for this.'

Jed was nervous but excited. He'd always wanted to shoot a bullet gun after learning about them at Academy. He stepped up eagerly and put the ear defenders on. There was a pair of clear plastic glasses on the ledge too, so he donned those as well. Archer had moved closer to him in order to put her own protective gear on and gave him a quick run down of the weapon.

'Flick the safety off here, load the barrel here, aim at the dummy and fire. Watch out for the recoil.' She smiled slightly and waited for

Jed to shoot.

He did as he asked and primed the gun. He used two hands to steady his aim and sighted along the barrel. Squeezing hard the gun fired throwing Jed's arms up with the force of shooting. The bullet flew way over the target and smacked into the wall at the back. Jed looked at the gun wonderingly. Clearly there was more skill involved in using one of these than the laser guns.

Archer was grinning. 'You only need to squeeze the trigger. Have another go. There are more bullets in the chamber.'

Jed refocused on the target. He was determined to get this right. This time he squeezed the trigger gently and the recoil lessened. He still missed the target but at least he hit the dummy. Smiling he put the gun down and stepped away from the firing zone.

'Not bad, rookie,' Archer gave him a brief smile and directed the next person in line up to the plate.

Jed stood back and watched the progress. Most people did the same as him and oversqueezed the trigger mechanism. There were a few cries of pain at bad recoil but otherwise no accidents. No-one made the target until it was Artem's turn. He moved up to the plate, picked the gun up with practised ease, checked the barrel was loaded and cocked the gun. He held in one handed, lifted his arm, sighted and made the shot. It was perfect. Jed whistled through his teeth, there was clearly more to the Russian than he'd given him credit.

'Excellent work, Misner. You can take over training the rest of them with the firearms. Let's move on.'

Jed frowned. *Move on to what?* He barked a laugh when Archer stopped at the far end of the range. There on the wall were a series of bows and arrows. 'You have got to be kidding me?' he said incredulously.

'I'm deadly serious. We will be teaching you how to make a bow and showing you how to make arrowheads. We don't just rely on the latest technology here at the Resistance.' Archer raised her voice to address the rest of them. 'As you all know, we are what is left. It's us and them. And New Corp are not interested in playing fair. We will not be able to stay here forever and searching for a new base, a new home may take us weeks. May take us months. The sea levels are rising and the more skills you have to survive out there, the better. Now, listen up.'

She went on to explain how to correctly hold the bow, where they should place their hands and how to pull the string back straight armed. She had them all practice their grip with and without arrows, and Jed was surprised to discover his arm shaking after keeping the bowline tense. When it came to shooting the arrows though it was a marked failure for everyone. Even Artem couldn't claim any skill in that department. When Archer called it a day, Jed was aching in places he didn't know could ache and he had a cracking bruise on his arm where the bowstring had slapped him soundly.

As they filtered back to the open training ground, Archer had them line up one more time. Those who had gone with Yarrow had also returned.

'This will be your new regime for the next couple of weeks. You'll do fitness and a lecture before lunch then weapons training in the afternoon. If you feel you have a particular skill in a particular area, don't hold back, tell Yarrow and we'll see if we can use you. Remember, the Resistance finds a use for everything and everyone. Dismissed.'

Jed lingered for a moment to see if she had anything else to tell him, but as soon as people started to leave, she headed for the shower block. Artem clapped a hand on Jed.

'Come, comrade. Let us go eat and see how others did this day. There may be pudding.'

He sounded so hopeful that Jed couldn't help but grin and he followed his friend to the mess hall.

Chapter Thirteen

Dina and Ash left together after breakfast watched by Max, who was leaning on the kitchen counter.

'She is not interested, you know,' commented Martha, as she made sure she left Kira everything she needed to look after Lucas for the day.

'No? They seem to have a lot in common.'

'They do. That is why they are friends, but you do not have to worry about Ash. Dina is not his type.'

'She's smart, funny, caring. How can that not be his type?'

Martha shook her head, laughing. She leaned into Max.

'I assure you; Ash has no interest in Dina, or me, or any of the ladies here.' She waited a moment. Realisation dawned.

'Oh, she's not his type.' Max grinned. 'She's not his type. Excellent. Shall we go to the Allotment? Are you ready?'

Martha nodded. 'Yes. Let's go.' Then she stopped short and ran over to the play cube, where the children were, and gave her son a quick kiss on the head. 'Bye Kira,' she called softly before catching up with Max as he left the room.

When they arrived, there were several people milling around in front of the entrance.

'Must be the other new recruits,' whispered Max. 'Seems like there's quite a few of us.'

Bennett appeared. She had a dirty mark on one cheek and some foliage in her hair.

'Okay, you've all been assigned to Allotment. It's hard, dirty work but you're growing food for everyone in the Resistance so, if you ask me, there's no finer job. Anyone got any experience?'

There were a few raised hands, Max and Martha included.

'Right, you can come with me. The rest of you wait here. One of my gardeners will be along to teach you the basics.' She led the smaller group through the greenhouses, further than Max and Martha had been before. There was the odd person tending the plants here and there. It was very peaceful and serene. Bennett stopped outside a large building and swiped her arm to gain access. Inside were rows of plants seemingly floating in the air with their root systems dangling gracefully. They were suspended in special trays with a specialised air flow and water system supplying their needs.

'This is Fred,' said Bennett, waving her arm at a large computer screen with green swirls across its screen. 'It looks after the hydroponics, monitoring and adjusting the plants' needs automatically. We usually rota one gardener on a twelve-hour shift to keep an eye on things in here as well. The AI is not infallible.'

'Wow, they really like their AIs,' muttered Max under his breath to Martha.

Bennett overheard. 'Yes, Dr Carter, unfortunately we do have to rely on our AIs because there aren't enough of us to do everything. But everyone who works here is trained to use the hydroponics system without Fred, just in case.'

Max flinched at being addressed, surprised that Bennett remembered who he was.

'Will you be able to take the AIs with you? When the Resistance moves, I mean?' Martha peered to see who was talking. It was a short, bald man with glasses who was perspiring gently in the warm building.

Bennett flicked her eyes at the interactive screen before replying.

'You'd have to ask Archer about that. I deal in plants, not computers. Let's move on.'

The group filed out of the humid area, entering a small corridor.

'Don't be alarmed. We will now experience a decontamination spray prior to entering the seed bank.'

There was an excited murmur. Max bent down to Martha.

'This could be life changing. If they really do have a complete seed bank, just think of the different plants we could grow and the genetic applications that could be applied.' He had to stop speaking because of the decontamination spray but Martha shared his excitement. A fully stocked seed bank would be key to their future survival.

They stepped through not sure what to expect. It was a bit disappointing. There wasn't really anything to see. Rows and rows of metallic looking columns, each numbered. The room itself smelt of nothing. Another AI screen was available to their right. The swirling colours turned pale blue.

Welcome to the Seed Bank. How may I assist you?

'This is Layla. She looks after things in here and over in the Tech labs. The environment is closely monitored to ensure the survival of our seeds. Hamble, ask Layla for something.'

Martha flushed at being put on the spot and tried to think of something she could ask for.

'Um... Layla, could I have some sunflower seeds, please?'

I am sorry, Gardener Hamble, but you do not have security clearance to request sunflower seeds.

Martha laughed awkwardly but felt embarrassed and moved closer to Max. He gave her a brief smile.

'As you can see, we have security protocols in place in case of any seed theft,' said Bennett.

'Why would anyone want to steal seeds?' asked a young man with rather large ears.

Bennett stared at him. 'The seeds in this bank are what we live on. They will be what we use to begin a new life somewhere else, should we move. If someone stole them, how would you eat? Developed some kind of resistance to radioactive plants, have you?'

'Er... no, I meant who would be mean enough to do that sort of thing?'

'Where are you from?' asked Bennett.

'City 5. There was a landslide, it knocked out our power and communications array. So we came here.'

Bennett sniffed. 'And did you try to get in touch with New Corp before you came here?'

'Of course, but...'

'But what?'

The boy's ears started to go very red and he blinked a few times. 'Well… they weren't really interested.'

'They turned you away because they didn't want to waste the resources going to collect you and bring you back to City 9. You would be a waste of their time and without the supplies of your city, a drain on theirs.'

'Now, wait a minute. That's a little harsh.' The boy tried to fight back. 'I'm sure they would've helped, if they'd known all the facts.'

Bennett frowned at him for a long moment. 'I don't want you in my gardens.' She touched a hand to an ear, activating a comm. 'Wilson, come and collect... sorry, what's your name?'

'David. David Malone,' said the bewildered lad.

'Come and collect Mr Malone from outside the seed bank. He requires reassignment and a full evaluation.'

Martha watched the exchange uneasily. It sounded like Bennett was getting rid of this David person because he didn't think like her. Which wasn't exactly the sort of attitude she'd been expecting from the Resistance. She risked a glance at Max and saw he was also frowning. This was definitely something she needed to speak to the others about. No-one spoke as Bennett ushered them all out of the seed bank, back through contamination into a small corridor.

There was a soldier was waiting for them.

'David Malone? Come with me, please.' Wilson was polite but also armed and had a no-nonsense air about him that meant no-one spoke up for the boy and they all watched him be escorted away.

Bennett clapped her hands to regain everyone's attention. 'Right, we have a series of experiments running plus the usual grunt work around the gardens for which you'll each be rota'd in for. We try to play to your strengths, but we are low on manpower so I'm afraid everyone swaps in on everything. You'll find your timetables in the hut. Come on, this way.' And she marched confidently away, in the opposite direction to Wilson and David.

The hut turned out to be just that. A large wooden hut with a series of long tables and chairs, a selection of wellington boots, gardening gloves, the odd tool and scraps of twine. There were a few plants on the window ledge, and everything smelt earthy.

'There's a kettle here, mugs etc. Try to wash up and replace, we don't have enough for you to be precious about them. Feel free to bring your own supplies in but be warned, there are biscuit thieves and it's completely at your own risk.' She didn't smile but there was a faint twinkle in her eye as she spoke.

'Now, usually lunch is up to you. You can bring it in, or you can go back to the Mess Hall, whatever. Today, we've put on sandwiches and that for you. So, enjoy!' Bennett swept an arm over to the far side of the room where there were several trays of food laid out.

The non-experienced people who had disappeared earlier were already there. Max and Martha hurried over to make sure they got a sandwich. They needn't have worried, there was plenty to go around.

'No sign of David,' whispered Max to Martha.

'No, I don't think we'll see him back here. I expect he'll be reassigned. Does it make you feel a bit...'

'Yeah, it does. I think we need to lie low and keep our eyes open.'

Martha chuckled at the thought of Max laying low, he was so tall he stood head and shoulders above everyone else there. He caught her looking up at him and smiled ruefully.

They began circulating and chatting with the others. Those with experience of working with plants had similar backgrounds to Martha and Max, but no-one seemed to have had as much hands-on growing experience as they had in City 42 and Camp Eden. It marked the two of them out. When most people had finished eating, Bennett reappeared with a collection of battered looking handhelds.

'These hold your rotas and a series of frequently asked questions. Check them first before you bother me, please. If you have your own, then you'll need to go to tech and get the apps from here moved over. We don't have that many to go around and the ones we do have, well, you can see for yourself the condition they're in.' Bennett glanced at her wristplant. 'Okay, check your rota and see where you should be then get gone. There's lots to do. Any problems, ask someone in green overalls who looks like they know what they're doing. There should be one or two around.' And she stomped off.

Martha checked her battered handheld.

'I'm on planting - you?'

Max checked, then grimaced. 'Weeding. My favourite. See you back here?'

She nodded and went to find the rows of planters she'd been working on the other day and found her assigned seeds waiting for her, together with a trowel. She spent the afternoon not really thinking about anything, focusing on putting a couple of seeds in each small hole, cover them over and watering as she went. Time marched by without her noticing and a claxon brought her out of her work.

'I guess that's the end of my shift,' she muttered to herself and stood up wincing as the muscles in her back complained. Her hands were engrained with dirt and all she wanted was to get back to their rooms and have a hot shower. One thing that was abundantly available was hot showers. She hurried to go find Max and return to Lucas and the others, all her doubts forgotten for the time being.

Chapter Fourteen

'This is so fragging cool!'

Ash grinned in response as he, Dina, and the other new recruits took a tour of the Science and Technology Division. A large hangar had been converted into multiple bays and each area of expertise occupied one of the bays. They'd seen robotics, attempts at recreating wristplant and handheld technology, adaptations to skimmers to make them run faster for longer as well as several other experiments Ash could only hazard a guess at.

'This is the last place to show you,' explained Veela, their guide. She was a willowy young woman with pale lilac hair and wore her silvery jumpsuit with confidence. 'This is where we monitor, update and generally try to keep an eye on our AI.' She peered into the workspace. 'Hmm, it looks like Dr Glover isn't in at the moment. She's the expert on the AIs.'

'You seem to rely on them a lot for everyday life,' commented Ash.

One of the people at the back of the group challenged Ash's statement. 'If you have the leading expert in the world on hand, it seems silly to ignore that expertise, don't you think?'

'Yeah, but artificial intelligence I mean, isn't that asking for trouble? New Corp have some great hackers and AIs can be cracked. They are only machines after all. Unless you've developed consciousness since you've been here, Dr Glover.' Ash grinned at the woman at the back of the group.

'MASH42 I presume?' The woman moved forward through the group, holding out her hand to Ash who took it and shook it enthusiastically. She kept hold of his hand and turned to speak to everyone. 'This here is the best hacker we have, hands down. If there is something you want to find out, he's your man.'

Dina was confused. *How did this woman already know who Ash was?* They'd only been with the Resistance a couple of days and she was fairly certain he hadn't hacked anything since they arrived.

Ash was starting to look uncomfortable at being in the limelight.

'Last I heard, you'd turned good cop working for Force?' asked Dr Glover.

Ash nodded but said nothing, unwilling to elaborate in front of the crowd. Dr Glover realised she was unnerving him, so she let go of his hand.

'Good to have you with us,' she said then addressed the others. 'Anyone got an area of expertise?'

A couple of hands raised, and voices called out several different fields of knowledge. 'Robotics.' 'Programming.' 'Engineering.'

'Excellent, we can make good use of all of that here. Veela, have you got the jacks?'

'Yes, Dr Glover.' The young woman reached into the satchel she wore slung across her body and handed one out to everyone. 'These jacks have all the details of what we're working on at the moment as well as the day-to-day jobs and repairs we get asked to do. You'll each get a turn working on the helpdesk, but when you're not there you're welcome to work on any of our projects, obviously ask the lead technician first. Oh, and if any of you have ideas for your own work, that's fine. You can pitch them to Dr Glover, and she'll decide whether we can spare the resources. It must be something that can help the Resistance now or in the future.'

Dr Glover nodded encouragingly at everyone. 'Yes, go back to your quarters, take the rest of the day to go through everything and decide what you want to do. Anyone who feels they'd be more useful elsewhere, see Lieutenant Kolwowsky and he'll assign you to housekeeping.' She caught Ash's eye, beckoning him over.

Dina hovered nearby not sure whether she should leave them to it or not. Dr Glover looked at her expectantly.

'Um, Dina, maybe you should wait for me back in our quarters. I won't be long.' Ash half smiled at her.

'Oh. Okay. If that's what you want. I'll, er... see you later.' And she walked away, feeling hurt at being left out of the conversation.

'I take it she doesn't know about your hacker days.'

'No. But you didn't have to be rude, sis.'

Dr Glover dropped the act and pulled her brother into a huge hug.

'It is so good to see you! Are you alright? Are you safe?'

Chapter Fifteen

Dina stalked all the way back to their quarters. At least she tried to, but she got lost twice refusing to use Lola to help her find her way back. She was too angry to have anything to do with Resistance right now. Ash knew one of the leaders in the Resistance. How had that never come up before? She was still fuming when she waved her arm at the doors to their residence. Nothing happened. She waved her arm again. A soft chime behind her made her whirl angrily.

Miss Grey, I am sorry to inform you that you are trying to enter barracks that have not been assigned to you or a member of your group. Please desist attempting to enter.

'Where the frag am I then?' Dina barked.

You are in corridor 3B.

'And where am I meant to be?'

I cannot answer that question, Miss Grey.

'Argh!' Dina screamed in frustration and kicked the wall. Lola did not respond. Taking a breath, Dina tried to think logically. 'Can you direct me to my quarters. Please.'

Of course. Please follow the yellow line. Have a pleasant day.

Standing in front of another set of identical looking doors, Dina hesitated. She didn't want to make a fool of herself again. Tentatively, she waved her arm and the doors slid open. She walked into Kira's meltdown.

'Why are you crying? I don't understand what you want! I've fed you, changed you, played with you and you are still screaming! AAAARRRRGGGGHHHHH!' Kira screamed at the top of her voice startling Dina and scaring the children. They stopped their crying momentarily only to begin wailing even louder.

'Whoa, Kira, calm down,' Dina said as she walked further into the room.

Kira threw her a frustrated look then dropped onto the sofa and began sobbing, her head in her hands.

Dina looked at the distraught children and her distressed friend. *Kids first* she thought.

'Alright, hey, it's alright. Aunty Dina is here. Hey, hey. It's alright. There, there. Come on, now.'

The children quietened at hearing Dina's calm voice and recognising her, but they were still hiccupping and taking shaky breaths because of how upset they had become. Dina tried to recall the checklist Martha had given her for watching Lucas before. She thought it went nappy, food, sleep, play but she remembered what Kira had just said. It sounded like the children had already been changed and fed. Instead she expanded the cube so that it was large enough for her to climb in too and she joined them. Instantly, three small bodies flung themselves at her and she ended up in a heaped hug. The babies were taking confidence from being close to each other and Dina as they all sat on the floor of the cube and she crooned wordlessly to them, stroking a head here and an arm there, breathing gently on the little ones cuddling her.

Eventually, the children grew calm enough to wander away from Dina to their favourite places in the play cube. Grace brought Dina back a soft toy and Peter pointed at a cartoon that was playing on the media screen. She switched the content to a lullaby and made sure all the kids had pacifiers and snuggle blankets. Originally, the others had scoffed at Kira for providing these old-fashioned devices to the children, but they had accepted them instantly and had grown attached to them. The babies snuggled into each other and slowly drifted off, the odd after-cry shudder here and there. Gradually, Dina extricated her foot from the bottom of the pile, careful not to wake the children and gently climbed back out of the cube.

Kira had stopped sobbing aloud but hadn't moved. Dina went to the kitchen and made some synth-caf. She brought two hot mugs over, put them on the table and sat as close to Kira as she could. Kira leaned into her friend slightly and mumbled a quiet thanks. They sipped their synth-caf for a few moments before Dina broached the subject.

'You want to talk about it?' she asked.

'Not really,' Kira replied.

Dina pursed her lips. 'How often does that happen?'

'What?' asked Kira.

'That.' Dina gestured towards the play cube. 'Total meltdown.'

'Ugh, that's the first time I've shouted at them like that.' She put her mug down. 'I'm so embarrassed. I can't believe you saw me like that. It's just… it's just, they never stop. It's constant all the time and you guys don't know what it's like because you swan in and swan out, doing your own thing and I'm left, literally holding the baby. Martha is like the perfect mum, working and looking after Lucas, and I can't even keep three children entertained without failing miserably.' Kira turned slightly to face her friend. 'All I want to do is talk to my mum and ask her advice on things and I can't even do that. She's gone.' Her bottom lip trembled, and she fought back the tears.

'You know you're not on your own though, right?' Dina asked. 'We're here for you. All of us.'

Kira smiled sadly. 'My sensible head knows you are, but it doesn't always feel like it. I feel so alone.'

The two women hugged, and Dina tried to think of the right thing to say, but before she had chance, Kira sat back and started speaking again.

'I mean, what are we actually doing here? Are we joining the Resistance? Are we fighting New Corp? Again? It seems like such a waste of time. Does anyone really believe that this little band of misfits really stands a chance against the might of New Corp? They killed my parents, Dina. They killed Ruth. And baby Sarah. Yes, they deserve to be punished for that but is being here the best way to do that? I'm not sure. Nobody here seems to give a frag about what happened.'

Dina shifted on the sofa. 'What else are we supposed to do? There's nowhere else to go. I think… look, I don't know what the best thing to do is Kira, really, I don't. I think we need to keep our eyes and ears open while we are here.' Dina started to bite her nails.

'Why what happened?' prompted Kira.

'It's Dr Glover, the head of Science and Technology. She knew Ash from before somehow. She knew he was a hacker and said he was the best around. How did she know who he was?'

Kira shrugged. 'Maybe she's a hacker too. They do tend to move in the same circles, don't they?'

'I guess, but…' Dina was interrupted as Ash returned to their quarters.

'Hi guys!' He had a huge smile on his face and completely missed the serious tone of the room. He nodded at their cups. 'Any left?' But didn't wait for an answer and went into the kitchen to pour himself a cup of synth-caf. He was busy browsing his handheld at the same time. 'I'm gonna go check out the different projects S and T are working on. Try and figure out what I want to do.' He grinned at them again and went into his room happily.

'He seems happy,' remarked Kira. 'At least one of us is.'

They didn't have the chance to continue their conversation as first Jed and Artem, then Martha and Max returned from their own assignments. Dina tried to catch Jed.

'Jed, look, there's something off about Dr Glover,' she began.

Jed's stomach rumbled loudly. 'Look, why don't we all report back after dinner? I'm starving and I'm not going to be able to concentrate until I've had something to eat. That way everyone can have their say about who they met and where they went, rather than having to repeat ourselves. What do you think?'

'I guess,' Dina conceded but she wasn't happy about it.

'Why do we all have to have our meals in the mess hall? Don't you think it's a bit weird?' Kira asked to the room in general, but everyone was too busy getting themselves sorted to go to dinner that no-one replied to her. 'Well, I think it's weird. Come on, Grace.'

Despite Jed's suggestion that people waited until after dinner to talk about what they seen and heard, everyone was chattering animatedly on the way to dinner and as they took their seats at an empty table. There was a vat of vegetable soup and crusty rolls with some cheese and fruit on the table. Nobody said much as everyone tucked in.

'Alright, guys?' said Kolwowsky as he passed by. Jed gave him a nod and a wave, but the soldier didn't stop to say anything else.

Dr Glover walked by and squeezed Ash's shoulder as he passed causing Dina to glower at her, pushing her half-eaten soup to the middle of the table, her appetite ruined. She waited impatiently for everyone to hurry up and finish eating so she could get started on grilling Ash.

'Okay, we've all survived our first day in Resistance. Everyone alright?' Jed asked, back in their quarters. There were murmurs and nods. 'Artem and I had physical training, lectures on security protocols and weapons training. Archer was in charge although she didn't deliver the lectures. Apparently, that's what we can look forward to for the near future. A mixed bag of personnel, wasn't it, Artem?'

'Da,' the Russian nodded. 'Some shooters, some not so much but more Russians means more vodka!' And he flourished a bottle of alcohol, laughing as he set it on the table.

'Maybe after everyone's checked in, Artem,' chuckled Jed. 'Martha, Max, how was Allotment? What's Bennett like?'

'It's good, they seem to have things well under control. There's AI in there as too, Fred and Layla but, Bennett doesn't seem to be much of a fan. I think she tolerates their presence because she has to. They have a complex hydroponic system which Fred monitors, a highly secure Seed Bank that Layla controls, and then there are all the external greenhouses and planters. They're short on manual labour and supplies are a little rudimentary in places but Bennett definitely knows her stuff. She's also not shy about… well, she got rid of someone for voicing sympathy for New Corp,' said Max, looking at Martha for confirmation.

She nodded. 'Yes, it was a bit odd, to be honest. I do not know what happened to the boy, maybe he will be reassigned somewhere. I do not think they will get rid of him permanently. Will they?' Martha asked uncertainly, looking at the group.

There were several shrugs and headshakes, but no one knew for sure.

'Maybe we could ask Kolwowsky, he seems to know what's going on. More or less,' suggested Kira.

'Yeah, maybe,' agreed Jed.

'Bennett is someone I wouldn't cross in a hurry. She knows her own mind and is fiercely protective of Allotment. She's not afraid to say what she thinks, and she doesn't think very much of the AIs or of Zac apparently.' Max laughed nervously. 'To be fair, I don't think she thinks very much of anyone.'

Martha chuckled and nodded her agreement. Jed waited a moment to see if they had any more to say before moving things on.

'Ash, Dina, you're up.'

'Layla, the AI, helps run Science and Technology too, and there are tons of exciting projects to work on, I have no idea what to choose,' said Ash enthusiastically.

'How many AI is that now then? Four?' asked Jed to the group.

The others nodded. 'Frank in stores, Fred and Layla in Allotment, Lola in the corridors and then Layla again in Science and Technology as well as the Seed Bank. Seems a bit odd to have so many, doesn't it?'

'It's because Dr Glover is apparently an AI expert. She also seems to know an awful lot about you, doesn't she, Ash?' Dina challenged.

Artem barked a laugh. 'Of course she does. Is sister!'

Everyone stared at the Russian in surprise before turning their attention to Ash who was blushing furiously.

Chapter Sixteen

'Your sister?' exclaimed Dina. 'Since when?'

'How did you know, Artem?' asked Jed at the same time but the Russian just smiled and sat back, letting Ash explain.

'Um.' Ash scratched his head and looked at the people in front of him. He was met with stern faces. Except for Artem.

'What the frag, Ash?' demanded Dina. 'What's going on?'

'I'm from City 1, originally,' he replied but Martha interrupted him.

'The one that was set up to be as much as possible like Earth used to be?' she asked.

'Yes, that's right. I was in the foster system; I never knew my parents. They died in some accident or radiation poisoning or something. No one really knows. Orphans were quite common.' He glanced around the group. 'You have to understand that the people who wanted City 1 to be the way it was had shunned Corporation involvement. They thought the other cities of survivors should all be set up the same way, like them, but Corporation disagreed. They thought the other cities should be regulated and controlled. Different experiments running in each. There were disagreements and eventually City 1 lost its influence and Corporation were too powerful to stop. They moulded the other cities into what they wanted them to be.'

'Why did you never share this information before, Ash?' asked Jed. He was shocked at what little he knew.

'I told Chief Minkov when I arrived in City 42. He told me to keep it to myself.' Ash shrugged. 'I thought he would've told you. Sorry.'

Jed nodded and gestured for Ash to continue.

'Dr Glover, Jess, was my foster sister. We grew up together in the system. I tried to keep in touch with her, but we lost contact a while back.'

'How did you know, Artem?' asked Kira. 'Why didn't you tell us?'

'I had information files on everyone. Part of my job for Resistance. I thought you knew.' He was entirely unapologetic.

'Why did you leave City 1?' Martha asked Ash. 'And how did you end up in City 42?'

'There was an outbreak of 'flu and not many survivors. That's why City 1 fell. It was outside the protection of Corporation and left to fend for itself. I didn't plan to come to City 42, it's just how it happened. A series of events led me there.'

'*A series of events*? You expect us to believe that?' Dina was still fuming.

'Hey, things happened. I drifted a bit. Different cities had different computer systems and when I hacked into networks and saw that Corporation had a greater presence in City 42 but wasn't as Corp heavy as City 9, I thought it might be a good place to survive.' He spread his hand out in defence. 'I was young.'

'Did you get caught, as a hacker, I mean?' asked Jed.

'Yes. That's how I ended up in front of the Chief. He told me I had a choice. I could either join Force and work for him or I could say goodbye to my freedom and become a prisoner of Corporation.'

'He specifically asked you to work for him?' Jed wanted to clarify the point.

'Yes. He didn't trust Corporation.'

'That wiley old fox knew something was going to happen, always tried to be one step ahead.' Jed shook his head, fondly remembering his old chief.

'I took his offer, became an operative and worked in Force for a while before getting assigned to your team, Jed. I never spied on anyone. I don't work for New Corp, I never have, I swear.'

'We believe you,' said Kira gently. 'I just wish you'd told us your background.'

'I honestly thought Jed already knew. I'm sorry.'

'What about Glover then? Where did she go? Why wasn't she in City 42 with you?' demanded Dina. She wasn't satisfied and wanted more answers.

'We split up after leaving City 1. She wanted to go a different way to me. I thought there would be more for us in City 42, she disagreed. We left on good terms, though and always said we would try and connect when we could. I haven't heard from her for a while.'

'But you knew she was here?' queried Dina.

'I knew she had joined the Resistance. But I didn't know where she was exactly. We haven't spoken recently, and I haven't seen her for a long time.' Ash looked at the doubtful faces. 'Guys, you have to believe me, I'm with you. I thought I was part of your team. I didn't mention Jess because I honestly thought the Chief had shared my background with you, Jed. I have never lied to any of you.'

'An omission of fact is as bad as a downright lie,' muttered Dina, feeling hurt that her friend Ash hadn't confided in her earlier.

Max frowned at her and held his hand out to Ash. 'I believe you and I trust you. Perhaps you can invite your sister over one evening so we can all get to know her better.'

Ash grabbed Max's hand and shook it enthusiastically. 'That would be great. I know she'd love to get to know you all.'

Jed pulled the discussion back to the Resistance. 'How many people did you see today, while you were on assignment, Martha?'

'Not that many, maybe fifty,' she replied, looking at Max to confirm. He nodded in agreement.

'Yeah, same in Science and Technology. About fifty or so,' said Dina, still miffed at Ash not telling her he had a sister.

'Me too. Not that many, really. And we've never seen more than a couple of hundred in the Mess Hall.' Jed ran his hand through his hair. 'I think they're telling the truth you know, about there not being that many people left.'

'I agree,' said Martha. 'I feel that Zac would not lie to us about this. It is too important.'

'What do you think the Resistance is after?' asked Kira.

'I don't know,' replied Jed honestly. 'The salvation of the human race might sound a bit high and mighty, but I really believe they want to make a safe place for the people they have gathered here, away from New Corp.'

'What do we do now?' asked Max.

'Drink!' exclaimed Artem who had gone to find glasses for the vodka. It broke the tense mood and most of the friends laughed.

'I think we need to keep our heads down and our eyes and ears open. It feels a little too good to be true at the moment. Keeping our family safe has to be the priority,' said Jed and the others murmured their agreement.

Artem poured the shots and lifted his own glass. 'To us!' he threw the shot back.

'To us!' the others said as they followed his example.

Chapter Seventeen

'How are the new arrivals settling in?' Zac asked as his team met together for a synth-caf. He didn't like to think of it as a formal meeting, more of a general get together.

'Fine,' replied Bennett, already looking at her wristplant, keen to be away from the meeting.

'Yep, it's great to have some fresh ideas and of course, as you know, my brother Matt is one of the new arrivals,' said Dr Glover, smiling around the room as she spoke.

'Matt?' queried Zac, then he thought for a moment. 'Oh, you mean Ash. Is that his first name? Wait… he's your brother?'

Glover laughed and nodded as Zac whistled in surprise.

'Wow, I'm glad we've been able to reunite you guys.'

'I know, it's great. I knew he'd ended up in City 42, but I had no idea he would make it over here to join us. He's going to be such an asset,' she replied.

'Can he be trusted though?' asked Archer. 'Can we trust anyone from that place?'

'I think so,' said Zac. 'But you've seen them in action, some of them anyway. How was peacekeeping?'

'It was as expected. Most people don't know their ass from their elbow when it comes to using anything other than a point and shoot laser. And most people can't even handle that simple weaponry.' She snorted as she remembered the weapons training. 'Interestingly, Jed and Artem – the two people from City 42 - were adept, even in archery. Especially the Russian.'

'You know Artem is on our side, Archer.'

'Hmm.' She took a long swallow of her synth-caf. 'I still think we should be keeping a very close eye on the lot of them.'

'I got rid of someone,' said Bennett, enjoying the shocked silence that followed her statement.

'When you say got rid…' enquired Zac tentatively.

'I had someone from security reassign the little toe rag. He was spouting some nonsense about Corporation or New Corp or whatever they're calling themselves these days. He was saying maybe they're not that bad. I wanted him out of my seed bank there and then. I will not compromise my seeds.' Bennett's nostrils were flaring, and her eyes looked accusingly at Zac.

'I agree that the seed bank must be kept safe, but I have been wondering whether we should extend the hand of friendship to the citizens of City 9 and City 42. What do you think?' Zac waited to see what the others would say.

There was a pause before all three women replied, 'No!' emphatically.

'You can't trust them, they'll try and take our tech, bug our systems. What about our AI?' said Glover.

'I am not letting a single one of them anywhere near my seeds. It's not happening,' fumed Bennett.

'It's too much of a security risk, Sir. You have to see that.' Archer was frowning as she looked intently at Zac.

'I realise that it might not be the most popular choice…'

'*Might* not be? Are you mad?' Bennett was nearly apoplectic.

'Look, the people on that island are just that, people. I'm not going to be the head of the Resistance and not offer the same freedoms to everyone.' Zac surveyed the room. 'You've seen the reports. You know what's going to happen. People are going to die. We cannot save everyone and that's a hard fact to have to swallow. But we might be able to at least save some of them.'

There was no reply and Zac sighed heavily.

'I know it's not a great idea, believe me, I understand your reticence but… I think we have to try.'

'You should put it to the vote,' said Archer, flicking her eyes at the other two women. 'Everyone has to agree. New Corp have hurt a lot of people.'

Glover was nodding. 'But there are still innocents in those cities, and they deserve the chance for a better life. A chance at survival. I agree with Archer, put it to the vote.'

'You know what that means though, don't you?' asked Bennett.

'What?' Zac was bemused.

'If the resistance say no, then you have to let those people go.'

Zac pursed his lips a little, ready to argue then realised she was right. He couldn't expect the Resistance to only do what he thought was right. It made him no better than New Corp.

'Okay, a vote then. We'll give everyone a chance to decide what we should do.'

There was another silence as people finished their drinks. Bennett was the first to stand up and leave. She muttered a gruff goodbye and stomped out of the room, back to her precious plants.

'I'd better get back to work, we have lots to do if we want to take the AI with us when we move and now that I have some more brainpower down there, I think we should have a solution soon,' said Glover. She smiled warmly as she put her mug down. 'Thank you for bringing Matt, Ash, back to me.' She pecked Zac on the cheek as she left, startling him so much he nearly dropped his own mug.

Archer snorted in amusement as Zac recovered.

'Is there anything else?' he asked.

'I still think we should keep an eye on the newest arrivals, the ones you brought back from 9. I don't know that I trust where their loyalties lie. And as for Artem…'

'I vouch for Artem,' said Zac swiftly. 'He's loyal to the Resistance. I know he is.'

Archer shrugged. 'If you say so, Sir.' She put her mug down and paused at the doorway. 'Promise me you'll keep your eyes open though, just in case.'

'I promise,' said Zac, smiling at his second-in-command. 'Everything will work out, you'll see.'

Chapter Eighteen

The next morning, Kira woke feeling resolute. 'I'm going to speak to Zac.'

'Yeah? What about?' Jed was getting ready for his second day of training and couldn't decide if he was or wasn't looking forward to it.

'Staying in here with the kids is driving me up the wall. I want something to do. Maybe I could help at the school. I think Grace, and the others, would benefit from some extra interaction and stimulus.' She gazed round the room. 'There is literally nothing for me to do here.'

Jed smiled at his wife. 'That's great, hon. I've been really worried about you and everything that has happened. I agree, you need something to get your teeth into but be prepared to be disappointed. You might not even get in to speak to him.'

'We'll see. Come on, let's go get breakfast.'

They joined the others and strolled over to the mess hall, but instead of the usual selection of food available there were dry ration sachets, rehydrated with water. None of them were particularly appetising.

'Why are we eating this?' asked Dina in dismay, she had been hoping for pancakes.

'I guess there must be a supply issue, or something?' Ash was looking around, trying to see if he could see his sister anywhere but there was no sign of her.

'Look, there's Kolwowsky. Let's ask him.' Dina waved to get the Lieutenant's attention. He waved back but hurried off in the opposite direction. 'Huh, that's strange.'

They ate the rations without enthusiasm, and it didn't take long before the meagre meal had gone.

'I guess we should go to our assigned work placements?' Martha was feeling uneasy.

'Yes, you should. I'll take Lucas with me. I'm going to talk to Zac about the school. He'll have a great time.' Kira was smiling, trying to look more confident than she felt.

'Yes, we'd better go, Ma.' Max was already on his feet, checking his wristplant. 'I wouldn't like to see Bennett in a bad mood.' He smiled to show he was mostly joking.

'Yeah, we'd better go to Science and Technology I suppose. I want to talk to your sister, Ash.' Dina had a determined look on her face. She wanted some answers.

'Okay, have a great day, guys.' Kira kissed her husband and pushed the expanded stroller out of the mess hall. All three children were happily chuntering away, looking at their surroundings and content after having had breakfast.

She knew vaguely where she wanted to go, but to make sure she touched one of the wall panels to access Lola.

Hello, Mrs Jenkins. How may I assist you?

'Can you direct me to Zac's office, please? I mean General Ridgely.'

General Ridgely is not currently in his office. Would you like me to guide you to where he currently is?

'Yes, please, Lola. That would be great.'

Please follow the yellow line. Have a pleasant day.

Feeling confident, Kira walked in the direction the yellow line on the wall was directing her. It led her through corridors she hadn't yet been down and past some empty laboratories. There were less and less people the further she walked, and she started to feel on edge.

Turning the corner into another corridor she noticed one of the light fixtures was broken and there were several burn marks on the wall. Kira touched one lightly with a finger.

'Is that a laser burn?' she wondered aloud.

The yellow line was telling her to go through a set of exterior double doors. She pushed them open cautiously and found herself in a wildly overgrown garden.

There, talking to the air was Zac. Kira moved closer to see if she could hear what he was saying. As she rounded the corner, she was first elated then dismayed to see a blue shimmer. Before it faded away, Kira was able to make out the shape of a woman with glowing blue skin. It was Gaia but then she was gone.

Zac spun on his heel, one hand on his weapon as he realised there was someone there,

'Don't shoot!' joked Kira but her heart was pounding out of her chest as she positioned herself in front of the travel cub, in an effort to protect the children.

'What are you doing here?' demanded Zac.

'Looking for you. Was that Gaia?'

Zac nodded. 'She comes here sometimes but she never says anything. Just looks sadly at me. I talk to her, try to clear my head.'

'May I?' Kira gestured towards where Zac was standing. As he nodded and moved away, Kira checked on the children. They were snoozing. She parked the stroller and walked over to the spot.

As she stood where he had been, the blue shimmer appeared again. A faded Gaia who did indeed look sadly at her. Kira peered at the image. Then looked around. She walked forward quickly, and the image wobbled as she walked through it.

'Hologram.'

'What?' Zac took a step forward.

'It's a hologram. There are projectors... here and over here.' Kira bent down to show Zac where the projectors were hidden under the overgrown gardens. 'Someone did indeed see Gaia and record her, but I don't think you've been talking to the real thing.'

Zac scuffed his shoe on the floor, shoulders slumped. 'I thought, I thought she was on our side. I thought the fact that she showed herself every time I came to see her was a good omen. What a fool.'

'You're not a fool. I'm sure she heard your prayers even though she wasn't here herself. Don't be so hard on yourself.'

Zac nodded, clearly disappointed but trying to put a brave face on it. 'Did you want me for something?'

'Yeah um, I wanted to talk to you about having something to do. Maybe in the school or...' She shrugged. 'Anywhere I can be useful really.'

'What about them?' Zac nodded to the children.

'We'd have to work something out, obviously.'

'Come on, let's go back to my office. At least there's some real coffee there.'

'Don't you have meetings? Things to do?'

'Probably, but I doubt the whole camp will fall apart if I stop to have coffee with someone who has actually seen Gaia. Maybe you can give me some advice.' He held the door open for her and they left the gardens behind them.

'Can I ask a question?'

'Of course. I'll try and answer.' Zac looked down at the floor as they walked along.

'Why was the menu so radically different this morning? In the mess hall, I mean, for breakfast.'

'Hmm. Well, to be blunt, we've had a large influx of new people and we wanted to impress you with what we have but apparently, Frank...'

'The AI?'

'Yes, the AI in stores. Frank has shut down non-essential purchasing and unfortunately dried food sachets is what we get left with.' He glanced up at Kira's face. 'Don't worry, things will even out. More workforce will mean we can ease workloads and get things finished faster. In fact, Dr Glover is working on some replicator technology that will be able to make whatever you want to eat.'

'That sounds almost impossible.'

'It's something to do with the molecular configuration of items or something. I'll admit my strengths don't lie in science.'

Kira smiled. 'Where do your strengths lie then?'

'Um, hopefully in leading the Resistance?' Zac frowned slightly as he spoke.

'No, I meant - what's your passion? What do you love to do?'

'Oh, I see. Er... do you know, Kira, I haven't got a clue anymore.' He laughed self-consciously. 'They made me General here mostly because I've been here the longest, I think. I don't have any military qualifications. All this rank and file business is a bit beyond me to be honest.'

'So why do you keep doing it then? Why not open up the decision-making process to the rest of the people here.'

'They tried that, the ones that came before my parents. They tried to lead collectively but the thing is, Kira, people don't function very well when everyone is trying to be the chief. We need someone to tell us what to do, if only so we can grumble about it the entire time.'

They had arrived at Zac's office; he opened the door for her and waited while she wheeled the children inside. They had woken up and Grace was beginning to get cross. She wanted to get out of the cube and explore.

'I can get them something to eat maybe, if they'd like?' Zac offered.

'It's alright, I brought things with me. Just a minute.' Kira unpacked three bottles and a snack box for the children. She placed the box in the middle of the cube and activated its magnetic connection so the children would be unable to throw the box around, hoping they would be distracted by food and change their mind about getting out. It worked.

'That's pretty nifty,' observed Zac.

'We were lucky. We packed our baby gear when we were on diplomatic mission, when we thought we were still part of City 42.' Kira fell quiet and Zac busied himself making the coffee he'd promised.

'I can put a word in with the school, if that's what you want. I'm sure they'd be grateful of the help. I think it's a bit of a mixed bag over there if I'm honest. A range of ages and not that much in the way of resources.'

'We'll have to teach like our ancestors did then.'

'How do you mean?' Zac was intrigued.

'By telling stories and getting them to learn things by rote. Hands on experience, that sort of thing. I'm sure the Allotments and the Science and Technology Department won't be averse to having some willing helping hands from time to time.'

'You can ask Bennett.'

Kira laughed. 'Are you scared of her too?'

'Have you met her?'

Kira shook her head, still laughing when the door chimed and announced Colonel Archer.

'Apologies for interrupting, Sir.' Archer didn't look remorseful at all. 'There's a situation that needs your attention.'

'I'm very sorry, Kira. We'll have to continue our conversation another time. Ask Lola to take you to the school.' Zac smiled a warm smile in her direction before visibly pulling on his mantle of the Resistance General and assuming leadership once more.

Colonel Archer watched Kira with narrowed eyes, as she manoeuvred the travel cube out of Zac's office and left the room.

'Oh, it's not me you have to worry about, love,' muttered Kira under her breath, thinking she must tell Martha that she thought someone else was romantically interested in Zac. Although she didn't know whether Martha still was now that she'd found out Zac was leader of the Resistance. Kira made a mental note to tell her mum the gossip, forgetting for a moment that she was gone. Remembering made her catch her breath in a sudden bout of grief and her good mood evaporated. She'd ask Lola to take her to the school tomorrow. Now all she wanted to do was cry.

Chapter Nineteen

'What's the emergency, Archer?'

'Glover managed to hack into the satellites. We have real time imagery for the coastlines. It doesn't look good.'

'What about the recon teams we sent to cities 20 and 43, have they come back yet?'

'No, we heard from 20 and they found the city deserted. Either the inhabitants already decided to leave, or New Corp got there first.'

'Is that likely?'

'They wiped out 15, Sir, and 41 which should've been a logistical nightmare for them. If indeed they are only based in City 9.'

'I saw no convincing evidence of that while I was there, Archer,' replied Zac. 'There's no doubt that City 9 is a corper city but other than a large force of security officers, I didn't see any other official presence. There certainly weren't any leaders based there.'

'Even so, Sir. They have to have their base of operations somewhere.'

'Glover hasn't had any luck backtracking yet then?'

'No, but she's hopeful that with that hacker here, Ash something, she'll have better luck.'

'You know he's her brother? From City 1?'

Archer raised an eyebrow but didn't comment.

'I thought we'd lost track of all the City 1 evacuees. Interesting that one has turned up after all this time, don't you think?' Zac didn't think he had anything to fear from Ash and his connection with Glover, but he hadn't been pleased to learn about it when Artem had given him the backgrounds for everyone that had travelled with him. Something else to worry about. He backtracked.

'What about the other recon team that went to 43, headed by Simmonds, wasn't it?'

'Yes, Sir. No news yet, Sir.'

Zac stopped walking causing Archer to nearly run into him.

'I'm sure she's fine,' he said with a hand on her arm.

Archer flushed and half smiled, her professional facade slipping for a moment.

'Of course, Sir. I do too, Sir.' And her guard was back.

Zac sighed and started walking again.

'Did you say the satellite images are real time?'

'Yes, Sir.'

They arrived at the briefing room and Zac was pleased to see Glover was already there. Ash and Dina stood behind her.

'Are they fully cleared?' Archer nodded at the two unexpected additions.

'I vouch for them,' Dr Glover said stepping forward. 'Here are the latest images. As you can see landmass has shrunk much faster than we expected. If it continues at this rate, we will have to move up our evacuation plans.'

'How long do we have?' asked Zac peering at the maps up on the screen.

'I'd say a matter of weeks, but I'd rather not leave it until the last minute.'

'Are your AIs portable?'

'Not yet but with my two newest recruits, I've made that our highest priority.' Glover smiled at Ash and Dina.

'So, the big question now is do we share what we know with New Corp and offer them the chance to join us,' mused Zac.

'You cannot be serious?' asked Dina, brushing off Ash's attempts to hush her.

'I'm looking at a possible mass extinction event, Miss Grey. I want to save as many lives as possible.'

'They murdered City 15. They killed Kira's parents. Ruth and her baby. You can't hand them an olive branch like nothing happened.'

'That is not my intention. Yes, soldiers of New Corp did atrocious things but until we can prove otherwise, I have to assume they were acting under orders. The sort of unquestioning loyalty I would expect from Resistance soldiers. What about the citizens of City 9? Would you hold them accountable for the actions of those in power? Do they even know what happened?'

'No, probably not, but ignorance is not an excuse.'

'That's a very hard line, Miss Grey.' Zac turned away to look at the maps once more. 'Archer, call a general meeting. We need to let everyone know the timetable has moved and that I want to put the olive branch evac option to the vote. Let us see what everyone else thinks we should do. Thank you, Dr Glover. Keep me updated.' He smiled at them all then left the room.

Archer rounded on Dina.

'You should show him some respect,' she snapped as she swept out after him.

'Huh. I'd better let Ma know she has some competition,' Dina muttered.

'Oh no, she's not interested in him that way. She's just very loyal. Come on, you two. We have work to do.' Dr Glover led the way back to Tech.

'If we still had the functional power of the internet, I would release the AIs into the nether space, and we could collect them when we arrive wherever it is we're going to arrive but I don't think there's enough power.' Dr Glover was thinking aloud and seemed startled when Dina asked a question.

'Do you have live internet here then?'

'Of course we do, after a fashion. It's what the AI's live on and communicate with. It's how we run our internal communication system.'

'So why can't you set up an infrastructure wherever we're going to be and link in that way. It's not like you need to run a cable all the way from here to there. Is it?' asked Dina.

'No, but if New Corp destroy our base before we get there, we run the risk of losing everything. We have to transfer the AIs manually,' explained Glover.

'Okay, surely the technology already exists to put them on a yottabyte drive or something?'

Dr Glover smiled. 'Yes, but it's the interface that we need to try and keep. Putting Layla onto a thumb drive is like saying we're going to give you a lobotomy. Everything will still be there, but you won't work quite the same way.'

Dina frowned. 'So, it's an interface issue - can't you downsize the existing screens and components? Turn them into miniature versions of themselves? That way you can rescale them back up when we get to wherever it is we're going.'

'You know, that's not such a bad idea.' Glover opened up her touch pad and tapped in some calculations.

Ash nudged Dina and gave her a thumbs up. He was pleased they were getting along.

Dina grinned in spite of herself. Having a problem to solve made her feel less annoyed at having been kept in the dark about Ash and his sister.

Chapter Twenty

'Order! Order! Can I please have a bit of quiet?' Zac called out over the general hubbub in the room. He had called a meeting for everyone to attend and had decided to hold it in the mess hall, after dinner, so that no-one had any excuse not to be there.

'HEY!' roared Artem making those closest to him jump as the room feel silent in surprise. 'Is important.' He turned and nodded towards Zac giving him the floor.

'Thanks, Artem. I have a critical announcement and we, the Resistance, have a decision to make. You will all receive the details on your info boards in your quarters later but to summarise, the sea levels are rising faster than we anticipated. We need to bring forward our evacuation and resettlement to higher ground.'

'To when?' called a voice from the crowd.

'End of next week,' replied Zac.

There was a stunned silence before everyone began shouting at once.

'You can't be serious?'

'Next week?' Do we even know where we are going?'

'How are we going to move everyone?'

'What's the rush? Why can't we stay here?'

Zac held up his hands for silence, but again it was a loud whistle from Artem that quietened the room.

'According to the satellite imagery we were able to obtain, we have already identified a place, not that far from here, which is high enough above sea level to be safe and large enough to accommodate us all. Initial contact has already been made and I will be sending an advance party to confirm the location's suitability before the entire camp is broken down and moved. We may have less time than we thought but we still have enough time to be safe.'

'What's the name of this magical place?' someone asked.

'It's City 50.'

The room erupted again.

'Why is everyone so angry about City 50?' Kira asked Jed but he shrugged. He had no idea.

Artem had overheard.

'City 50 is where babies went.'

'What?' Kira was confused for a moment then realised what Artem meant. The babies that had been grown secretly at City 42 and sent away. 'Who owns the city?'

'Is New Corp or was. Listen.'

Zac was speaking again.

'City 50 is the pinnacle of New Corp - the best technology, the best people, the best location. The city was built in the least affected area from radiation. It has a fresh water supply; they farm the land and grow supplies.'

'How do you know all this?' Dina called out.

'Because I have been there.'

'Is it where they have been sending all the babies from City 42?' Martha asked. She'd been listening to Kira and Artem's conversation.

'Yes. And the families there are extremely grateful. They, like the rest of us, were affected by the HER and resulting sterility. They, like the rest of us, were duped by Corporation into thinking that sterility was permanent,' Zac explained.

'But why are we going to them? Surely that puts us back under New Corp control?' someone else called out.

'This is a signed treaty between me and the leader of City 50.' Zac held up something white and flimsy.

'It's a piece of paper,' whispered Kira as another voice shouted the very same thing.

'Yes, it is a piece of paper. I also have it in electronic format, but the fact remains that the leader of City 50 was willing to come to the table for the good of humanity. To see the survival of the entire human race and not squander anymore precious lives. All of you have been given a full report that you can read later. Anyone who doesn't want to come, doesn't have to but please, don't let prejudice affect your decision.'

The room had quietened to a buzz as people were talking quietly in small groups.

'There is one more thing we need to decide. Before we evacuate our base, should we extend the hand of peace to the citizens of City 42 and 9?' Zac barely managed to finish his sentence before the room erupted once more. He looked helplessly at Archer, who gave him a told-you-so look. People had begun to approach the podium, clamouring to be heard and to ask questions. Zac went down to the floor and began doing his best to answer queries. He found himself shoulder to shoulder with Martha, who had begun to field questions about City 42 and calm some of the people down. He smiled at her gratefully and together they tried to quell the storm.

Kira roped Dina and Max into helping her get some food and drink handed round to people while Jed, Ash and Artem tried to sooth people's fears.

As Kira handed Zac a cup of synth-caf he caught her arm for a second.

'Thank you, for this. You're really calming everyone down.'

She regarded him for a moment. 'You dumped a lot of information on them all at once, they need to process it.'

Martha joined them. 'I agree, if you want people to make an informed decision about what they do next, they need some time to read the information and digest everything.'

Zac nodded and headed back up to the top of the podium. He clapped his hands together loudly a couple of times.

'Can I have your attention? Everyone, please. This is what we're going to do. Please take some time to go back to your quarters, have a read through of the information you've all been sent. Ask questions. Talk amongst yourselves, decide what you want to do - what you think we should do.' He paused to look out across the room. 'We are very nearly all that's left. Let's make the right decision. We'll meet back here tomorrow, and you can cast your vote.'

This time there was no hubbub. People drifted off back to their quarters or jobs or wherever they needed to be.

'Thank you for your help, all of you.' Zac re-joined Kira, Martha and the others. 'I hope I handled that the best way I could.'

'You did what you could with the information you have. You were honest, up to a point. Admitting to keeping back the details of City 50 was maybe not the best idea.' Martha was trying to be supportive, but she was disappointed that Zac had hidden yet another secret from her.

'When did you go there?' asked Jed. 'Do you have any images or information I could look at?'

'It's all on the info package we sent out to everyone. I was there before I went to City 9. I had hoped I would be able to broker a similar deal over there, but it was clear to me as soon as I arrived that City 9 was a total Corper city.'

'And you didn't get that vibe from City 50? Despite the reputation New Corp has?' Jed was intrigued.

'It's like City 1 was meant to stand for the old ways and City 50 stands for the new way. I believe that way is not Corp or Resistance. I believe it's just us.' Zac half smiled at them as he turned away, flanked as always by Archer. There were other people waiting to speak to him.

'What do you make of all that, then?' Dina asked.

'I think we need to read this information packet.' Martha refused to be drawn on giving her opinion, yet. 'There is a lot we need to find out.'

Chapter Twenty-One

'I still have questions,' said Martha as she finished reading the information Zac had provided.

'Me too,' commented Jed. The others nodded their agreement.

A chime from the information board announced another document had arrived, titled *Frequently Asked Questions*.

Where exactly is City 50?

City 50 is located in the middle of Zone 3, what used to be called the Ural Mountains, high enough not to be affected by the rising sea levels.

Why is City 50 not a Corper city?

An initial meeting with representatives of City 50 has already been held. They denied ties with New Corp.

What access does City 50 have to New Corp?

City 50 is a self-sustaining city having been set up with the best technological solutions for power supply, food production and located in the safest area after The Event.

On what authority did City 50 sign the treaty with The Resistance?

General Ridgely spoke with a representative of City 50 and together they signed a treaty between City 50 and the Resistance.

What is the layout of City 50?

This information is not available at this time.

Where will we be located within City 50?

This information is not available at this time.

How will we get to City 50?

All of the supplies and equipment at the Resistance have their own method of transportation and the people here will either ride along or walk besides the various skimmers etc until we arrive at City 50.

How long will it take to get to City 50?

Travel times depend upon weather and road conditions, but it is estimated that the journey will take roughly three days.
Who goes to City 50 first?
To be determined.

A quick scan of the new document showed Martha that Zac and his team had already answered many of the questions their group had.

'That last one is a good question. Who does go first?' Martha looked around the room. 'I mean, do we all want to go at the same time. Should we split up? Will it be safer for the children if we get there first? What about the allocation of housing? Will it be first come, first served?'

'Whoa, Ma, slow down. I have no idea. If the answers to those questions haven't been uploaded yet, maybe you should go see Zac and ask him,' Kira replied. 'In fact, does anyone else have any other questions that they haven't answered yet?'

'I'd be interested to know how they plan to feed everyone on the journey,' said Max. 'And whether they are actually going to offer sanctuary to City 42. I left people behind at Camp Eden, I don't want to abandon them completely.'

'Yeah, we absolutely have to go back for Moham and the team. Plus, logistics is going to be a big issue,' agreed Dina. 'They're going to need huge skimmers to get things moving and we have no idea what the terrain is like.'

'The satellite imagery should tell us that,' said Jed. 'I'll come with you, Ma. See if I can't help Zac more.'

'You think we should go then? With the Resistance, I mean,' Kira asked quietly. The others watched to see what Jed would say.

'I do. I don't want to stay here and risk flooding. I don't want to go backwards - the island will be submerged before too long,' he replied.

'If the predictions are correct,' countered Kira.

'I believe they are, hon. I think City 50 is our best bet and I'd rather be elbow deep in the organisation of a mass exodus than left on the side lines. At least this way I can look out for my family and my friends.'

'So, you think we should offer an olive branch to City 42 and City 9?' Kira sounded doubtful.

'I think the citizens of those cities should be free to make up their own mind, don't you?'

'But what about New Corp? What about all the terrible things they've done?' Two spots of colour appeared on Kira's cheeks as she got angry.

'Then they should be made accountable for them and pay for their crimes. This is why I think we need to get involved from the beginning. Then we can make sure no one responsible for or involved with the atrocities New Corp have committed gets away with it.'

Kira nodded, understanding. 'We'll make them pay.'

'Everyone good? Anyone else want to come with us?' Jed looked at the others.

'No, we have to go help Dr Glover in the lab this evening,' Dina pointed to Ash as she stood up.

'I can speak to Bennett, find out what her plans are with the Seed Bank and the hydroponics. I have a few ideas that may help,' said Max.

'I stay here. Play with kiddies.' Artem was already sitting on the floor with Peter and Lucas crawling about all over him. Grace was watching from the side lines.

Kira flashed him a grateful smile. She didn't want to be on her own again.

'Alright then, we'll check in later. Bye, hon.' Jed kissed his wife and was talking with Martha about the best way to approach Zac as the two of them left their quarters.

Kira sighed as the others went and looked at Artem. 'Synth-caf?'

Chapter Twenty-Two

Zac listened quietly as Martha bombarded him with her list of questions.

'Um... I hadn't considered splitting Resistance into groups, but I suppose that does make sense. As for the other questions, we don't have everything worked out with City 50 yet. I guess I thought we'd turn up and be somebody else's problem.' He flushed. 'Look, I probably shouldn't admit this, but I don't know what I'm doing here. I was voted in General because no-one else wanted the job. I don't know how to orchestrate a mass exodus.' He ran a hand through his hair. 'I thought I'd done a good job of brokering a peace deal with 50 but now I'm not convinced. There’s so much I don't know.'

'It sounds like you need help from someone with experience in running a city,' Jed commented drily.

Zac looked at him in bewilderment for a moment.

'Not me! Martha.'

It was Martha's turn to blush.

'Look... I do not mean to step on anyone's toes, but do you even have a logistics plan for this move of yours?' she asked.

Zac shook his head.

'Okay, you really do need my help. Let's get started.' Martha waved the info board clear and brought up a new screen. She pulled out the wireless keypad from underneath the screen, placed it on the desk and started tapping in *Advance Guard*.

'Jed, I think you and Archer should lead the advance team to City 50. You can take Ash for tech support plus he's Force trained and knows his way around a weapon.'

Zac stood back, watching Martha take charge, a small smile on his face.

'That all sounds good to me, but we ought to check with Dr

Glover, she might need Ash here. She hasn't figured out how to move the AIs yet and that is a massive part of our agreement with City 50.'

'How sure are you that we'll get a good reception?' Jed asked Zac.

'I see no reason why not. We have the signed agreement.'

'It would be nice to assume they will keep their end of the bargain, but I have to wonder, what do they get from this agreement? When were you last in touch with them?'

'I haven't spoken to them since the meeting we had, and I promised to bring our Seed Bank and the AIs. They seemed to think that was incentive enough,' explained Zac.

Martha thought about it for a moment.

'That makes sense, those are the two most valuable assets you have. If they are planting, they may only have limited crops and the AIs will help run all their systems. If they have active technology in place, of course, which, as a flagship city for New Corp, I see no reason why they would not. Do you have any schematics?'

'No. We never actually went inside.'

'Are you serious? How did you broker the agreement?' Jed was confused.

'We met outside. Under a flag of truce. It's a historical act where...'

'Yes, we know what one is,' interrupted Martha. 'Zac, I hate to say this, but you could be walking into anything here. Did you really think this through?'

'I knew there were some inconsistencies, but I had a really good feeling from the person I met with.'

'And who was that?' asked Jed.

'Bridget Mulherne. She said she spoke with all the authority of City 50.'

'Is she actually the one in charge?'

'I don't know...' Zac put his head in his hands. 'I should've thought of all of this,' he mumbled.

'Look, it is not an ideal situation, for sure, but we have some facts. Let's work with what we have and see what we can figure out.' Martha tried to sound confident. 'If they are serious about letting us in, I am sure they have queries too so a secondary trip to see them, go inside, ask our questions, makes lots of sense. Let's think about who to send first. Once the advance guard is sorted out, we can work on how to relocate this base.'

'And reach out to City 42 and 9,' said Zac.

'Hmm,' Jed was non-committal.

'We have to - whether they vote yes or no. We can't leave all those people.' Zac was resolute.

'You can't ask people to vote and then ignore what they want, that's not leadership,' Jed looked at the unsure young man in front of him. 'If you are truly planning to offer the island help regardless, you should never have given the people here the illusion they had a choice. If they vote no, you have a big problem.'

'Let's hope they don't vote no, then.' Zac rallied. 'What else do we need to sort out?'

'Where's Archer?' asked Jed, suspicious at the absence of Zac's shadow.

'One of our recon teams just came back. Her wife was one of the team leaders. I gave Archer the rest of the evening off. I tried to give her tomorrow as well, but she wouldn't have it.'

'We have a lot to sort out, she will have to catch-up.' Martha frowned. 'Who are you thinking of sending back to the island? To City 42 and 9?'

'Actually, Artem has volunteered. I thought he could lead a team of Peacekeepers and maybe, maybe one of you would like to go with him? As you're from the area.' He looked hopefully at Martha and she took pity on him.

'I will speak to Max, and Dina. They are probably the best ones to send. They can get everyone at Camp Eden rounded up, plus they have been to City 9 and 42.'

'Will Artem be alright going back? After what New Corp did to his compound?' Jed was suspicious.

'He says he has a secret cache that he doesn't want to leave, and the man is good in a fight.' Zac thought about Artem for a moment. 'Will Dina and Max be able to keep him calm? If they need to, I mean?'

'I'll have a word with him before he goes,' Jed offered, confident that the time he and Artem had spent together training would count for something. 'Will we be contacting the cities first, to let them know we're coming?'

'I don't know. Do you think we should?'

'I'd rather we tried that then turn up out of the blue. They might try shooting at us again,' Jed remarked.

'Are you going back to the island as well?' Zac was surprised.

'Ah, no. I meant we as in us, the Resistance. I thought I was heading up the team to City 50.' He glanced at Martha, who had made the suggestion. She flicked her eyes sideways and Jed caught her meaning. 'With your permission of course, Zac.'

'Yes, absolutely. I thought I ought to come on that one too. Seeing as I've already made contact with Bridget and have the signed treaty and everything.'

'What about Archer?' asked Martha.

'She can stay here, organise the shut down and move of this base over to City 50. Trust me, she'll love it.' Zac was sounding more positive. 'What will you do, Martha?'

'I think I should come with you. Maybe my experience at running City 42 for a time will come in useful. Plus, you need someone who thinks Corporation, just in case.'

'Excellent!' Zac was smiling. 'I have a great feeling about this.'

'Do not celebrate too early. We need to figure out what staff are going where and who will be in charge of what.' Martha turned to Jed. 'I think we need at least a dozen peacekeepers with us, don't you? And a techie in case we need to get into their comms system.'

'Kolwowsky will be able to help you with that. He came with me last time.' Zac suggested.

'He did?' Jed was surprised. 'He seems more of a stay at home kinda guy than an explore new territories person.'

'Oh, his parents are from 50.'

Jed and Martha shared an exasperated look.

'Do you not you think that would have been helpful to know?' Martha chided Zac. 'Can we get him here, please?'

'Yes, I'll send for him.'

Chapter Twenty-Three

'I've been working on the AI transfer drive compatibility and I think we are ready to test it. Who do you think we should take offline? I'd rather leave Layla until last. Maybe Lola? Most people know their way around the base now,' said Dr Glover looking at Ash and Dina for confirmation.

'Except for the new group that arrived today,' Dina commented. She'd seen a small group of very lost looking people in the mess hall that morning, being herded cheerfully by Kolwowsky.

'Was there? Oh, well, they can always ask their assigned guide. I'm sure it will be fine. Shall we?' Dr Glover started walking down the corridor.

'Is she always like this?' Dina asked Ash.

'Yeah, she can get a bit involved in what she's doing. Come on, we'd better keep up with her.' Ash hurried to catch up. 'Where are we going, sis?'

'If we want to download Lola to the drive then we need to access her maintenance hatch. It's over on the other side of the base.' She charged ahead, walking fast, making Dina and Ash hurry to keep up with her.

'What if she doesn't want to be downloaded?' asked Dina.

'What do you mean - *what if she doesn't want to?* She's not a person. She isn't even the right pronoun to use for an AI, but *it* is so impersonal,' replied Glover.

'But what if Lola has developed some consciousness independent of what you designed? She does interact with people all day long. Maybe she's learnt and evolved,' argued Dina.

'I highly doubt that, Dina. Lola is a computer program. A very clever computer program but a piece of technology nonetheless.'

'I think we should ask her whether she wants to be a test subject.

It's only fair that she knows the risks,' Dina replied stubbornly.

'Fine. You can tell her. We're here.' Dr Glover pointed to a small screen on the wall that was swirling different colours.

'Oh, okay. Um... Lola?' asked Dina.

How may I assist you, Miss Grey?

'Lola, hi. We have a plan to transport you and the other AIs off the base to another location. How do you feel about that?' Dina felt a little self-conscious talking to the wall.

I have no feelings. Moving me to a secure drive for transport is a logical choice.

'But what if something goes wrong and we lose you. Are you alright with that?'

If something goes wrong Dr Glover has the schematics to rebuild another AI. I understand the concept of replacement.

'Yes, but how does it make you feel? Are you worried or nervous? Will you miss being Lola?'

Lola is the name of my construct given to me by Dr Glover. If she were to rebuild me, she could rename me.

There was a pause.

I like the name Derek.

'Ha!' Dina spun on her heel in triumph to face Dr Glover. 'There you go. Independent thought!'

Ash was grinning but when he saw his sister's scowl, he tried to pull a straight face.

'This is unbelievable!' Glover moved closer to the terminal and bent down to speak to it. 'Lola, are you fully aware of the risks to being downloaded and re-uploaded?'

Yes, Dr Glover, I am aware of the risks.

'And are you happy to proceed?'

Of course. I hope the process runs smoothly.

'See! She did it again! She hoped. That is not standard AI behaviour,' Dina exclaimed.

'Be that as it may, we still have to test the drive so we might as well get on with it.' Dr Glover plugged the drive into the wall next to Lola's interface plate and tapped a few buttons to shut her down and begin the transfer. There was a faint hum as the AI uploaded to the drive. Dr Glover unplugged it and put it in her pocket.

'Aren't you going to reboot her straight away?' Ash asked in surprise.

'I thought we might get a synth-caf or something first.' Dr Glover was glancing up and down the corridor, fingering the drive in her hand.

'Sis! Are you nervous that something is going to go wrong? I don't believe it. The mighty Dr Glover is nervous.'

'Alright! I'm worried something might go wrong. Shut up already.' And she plugged the drive back in, executing the file that would re-connect Lola to the base mainframe. There was a louder hum this time.

The interface screen went black then white then began swirling as usual.

Hello, my name is Lola. How may I assist you today?

'Hi, Lola. Do you remember our conversation a few moments ago?' asked Dina.

Negative. Scanning my memory files shows that we have not interacted today, Miss Grey. Is there something I can help you with?'

'No, thank you, Lola.' Dina turned to Glover and Ash. 'Memory loss. But will it be longer depending on how long they remain downloaded? And what caused it?'

Heads together they walked slowly back to the tech lab, discussing what could've caused the memory loss and whether it was likely to be temporary or permanent.

Chapter Twenty-Four

'Dr Bennett?'

'Oh. It's you. Make yourself useful and prepare these slides, would you? I'm trying to figure out what killed the potatoes.'

'The potato crop is lost?' Max asked in concern as he took over prepping the slides for the microscope.

'Best part of it. Looks like some kind of blight but I thought we had the most resistant crop in rotation. Shouldn't have happened but...' She leaned into Max. 'I don't think we have the right kind of soil here. The pH is all wrong.'

'Right. Surely the genetics department would've ruled out planting any crop susceptible to the blight?'

'If you ask me, that ruddy AI has got it in for my plants.'

'What, Fred?' Max was confused, he thought Fred helped to run the computerised side of the Allotment. 'Doesn't he look after hydroponics?'

'A monkey in a jump suit could look after hydroponics. It's a self-regulating, self-contained system. No, that thing has been meddling with my plants. Why else would we have lost so much?'

Wisely Max kept his mouth shut and finished making the slides for Bennett.

'Are you actually here?' she asked suddenly.

'Er... yes?'

'No, I mean, is this your shift or did Zac send you to keep an eye on me?'

'Zac did not send me but I have come to talk to you about your plans for moving the crops, the Seed Bank etc.' Max looked at her expectantly.

'Hmpf. You agree with his mad plan then? Upping sticks and moving us all to this supposed safe place?'

'I don't think it really matters whether I agree or not. The fact is we can't stay here, and if we want to eat, we need to take our food supply with us.'

Dr Bennett nodded and beckoned Max to follow her. She took him into the hydroponics lab.

'You see all this?' She pointed at the suspended plants. Max nodded. 'What's your grand plan for moving all these then?'

'Well...' He peered at the plants again and then looked around more carefully. 'Oh, I see what you've done. That's really clever.'

'There's no need to sound surprised. I have done this before you know.' But Bennett was smiling, pleased Max had noticed. 'You see the wall panels move, they become the outer cases for the transport and the wheelbases are here.' She bent down to indicate a wheel hub that Max had nearly missed. 'The whole building is moveable. It's large, unwieldy and slow but it does move. As long as the terrain is clear, we should be fine. It's the same for the Seed Bank. I purposely had them design it that way. Everyone thought I was mad but I'm having the last laugh now. Allotment is ready to move.'

'What about the exterior plants?'

'All of those planters have wheelbases. It'll be hard work for whoever is pulling them. And no, we don't have enough skimmers before you ask.'

Max nodded thoughtfully. 'It sounds like you have everything under control. You just need some manpower.'

'I may have my head permanently in the plants, but I am not stupid. I've seen the signs. I know what's happening. And we can't ignore her, of course.'

'Her?'

'Gaia.'

'Gaia! Have you seen her? Here?'

'Of course I've seen her. I'm growing her garden and I spend ninety percent of my time with my hands in her junk.' Bennett paused to lean in closer to Max again. 'I hear you also had an experience.'

'Yes, we did. At our Camp, on the outskirts of City 42. She came and smiled at us. We caught it on camera. It was during...'

Bennet interrupted him. 'You know who she hasn't shown herself to, don't you?'

'No, who?'

Bennett jerked her head towards the main buildings. 'Management.

What does that tell you?'

'She doesn't reveal herself to everyone you know.'

'No, but why wouldn't she speak to Zac. I'm not convinced that upping sticks and moving to City 50 is the best course of action if she doesn't agree.' She looked Max up and down, evaluating him. 'According to your file, you travelled with several people who'd seen Gaia. Is that true?'

'Er... yes. Kira has seen her the most, but Martha and Dina have seen her as well. They...'

Bennett cut him up. 'Then you'd better ask this Kira to have a word. Find out what Gaia thinks about all this. Because without her blessing, I'm not leaving. Flood or no flood. I'll take my chances.'

'Right. Okay.' There was an uncomfortable pause. 'Is there anything else I can do?"

Bennett pointed to the outside planters. 'Weeding. There's always weeding to do.'

Max laughed and ventured outside. He didn't have anything else to do and things were certainly in hand for moving, if Bennett could be convinced to move her precious plants. He picked up one of the trowels and moved through the rows, gently prising out the unwanted weeds and turning over the topsoil.

Chapter Twenty-Five

'Thanks for staying with me, Artem,' said Kira.

'Is nothing.'

'Shouldn't you be at training or something?'

He shrugged and avoided answering the question by starting a tickle fight with Peter and Lucas. Grace was watching from the corner of the sofa.

'I'm going to do their milk. Are you alright here for a minute?'

'Is good!' A thumbs up appeared before the boys dissolved into more giggles.

Kira smiled as she made up the bottles. It was nice to hear the children having fun. A little person toddled over to stand next to her in the kitchen area.

'What's up, sweetie? Are you alright?' Kira knew Grace wouldn't be able to answer her properly, but she hoped her voice at least sounded soothing.

'Mum mum,' said Grace, melting Kira's heart. She bent down to scoop her daughter up who immediately put her little head on her mum's shoulder.

'Aww baby girl,' Kira murmured as she kissed her little head. She managed to grab two of the bottles and took them over to the boys. 'Could you give them these, please, Artem?'

'Da. Is Gracie okay?'

'I'm not sure, I think maybe she just wants me.' Kira smiled to try and show she wasn't worried, but she was already starting to panic that something might be wrong. There weren't any handheld medical scanners that she could use to check the baby and find out what was bothering her, and she didn't even know where the med facility was here. She went back to the kitchen for the last bottle and sat down with her daughter. A quick hand to the forehead showed Grace wasn't particularly hot so Kira tried to relax. The little girl snuggled into her mum's arms while having her milk and was falling asleep towards the end of the bottle. It was comforting to sit with her, and Kira could feel herself drifting off. She closed her eyes. Just for a moment.

Kira looked around; she was walking on a thin grey path that she could dimly make out beneath her feet. It was dark all around her. 'Hello?' Kira called nervously. There was no reply, but a faint glow appeared on the horizon in front of her. Kira started walking towards it.

She walked and walked and walked but couldn't get any closer to the light. She stopped and looked behind her. The darkness had grown and was getting closer. She couldn't stay here so she began to walk again, faster and faster, feeling her panic rising. She lost her footing and fell, sprawling to the floor. She lay still for a moment. *Would it make any difference if I didn't get up?* she wondered. A glance over her shoulder showed the inky black getting closer and closer. She turned to look forwards and saw a glowing blue hand in front of her. Looking up, she saw Gaia. Relief flooded her. She grasped the hand and allowed herself to be pulled up to standing.

'What does this mean? asked Kira, pointing at the darkness but the goddess just smiled. In exasperation Kira pulled her hand away from her. 'I don't know what it is you want me to do. Please, talk to me!'

Gaia opened her mouth, and nothing came out. She touched her heart then reached out to touch Kira's, and a warm feeling enveloped Kira's body, she felt safer and calmer. Next Gaia touched her own head then touched Kira's. There was a burst of imagery that flashed in front of Kira's eyes, but she barely managed to process any of it.

She saw Artem back on the island but with his back to her. Camp Eden in ashes. City 9 closed to visitors and a sinking plane on a black ocean. She saw a mountain pass and snow, the trail littered with equipment and seeds. There were groups of people shivering around small fires. An overturned skimmer in flames. Children crying loudly. Loud arguments. Closed gates. Poisoned water. Empty food sachets. A stony-faced Zac with his arms crossed. And then more images flashed past her face so fast she couldn't make them out that clearly. Staggering back, she broke the connection with Gaia and took some deep breaths as she steadied herself.

'What was that?'

Gaia inclined her head.

'Right. You can't talk. Was it our future? No, our potential future? What might happen?'

Gaia nodded gently.

'But there was so much pain and suffering. Do we make it? Is there any point to what we're doing?'

Gaia turned slightly and pointed towards the light on the horizon. As she pointed the two women moved closer to the light. Kira was filled with warmth and hope. But a shadow fell over the light source and at once she was shivering in the gloom again.

'We only have a slim chance of success, is that what you mean?'

Gaia nodded.

'What about City 42 and the others back on the island, should we go back for them?'

Gaia turned the palms of her hands face up and made a lifting motion. Water seeped out of the ground, rapidly covering Kira's feet, then her ankles and then her knees.

'Stop! I get it, they'll be wiped out if we do nothing. But what do you think we should do?'

Gaia turned her head to her left side, and Kira noticed a patch of darkness swirling in the goddess's blue skin. As she watched it grew and grew and grew, sucking Kira into the void. She panicked, fluttering her hands, trying to pull her gaze away until suddenly Gaia released the vision and Kira was left panting in fear.

'They're dangerous to you, to us, aren't they?'

Again, Gaia nodded and then lifted a hand in farewell.

'No! Wait, I have more questions. What should I do?' But the dream was fading fast and Kira became aware of the sofa she was sat on and the room she was in. Opening her eyes, she saw Grace was still sleeping on her chest and the boys had finished their milk and were still playing with Artem but beginning to rub their eyes in tiredness.

'I think they all need a nap,' Kira whispered, carefully manoeuvring herself to standing. Tricky with the dead weight of her sleeping daughter. 'Let me get the sleeping cube sorted out. They like napping together.'

Artem watched as she set up the cube and nestled the children down with their favourite soothers. 'Impressive,' he whispered. 'I did not think they would sleep.'

'Luckily they're still at that age where they will go to sleep if they're tired.' Kira smiled as she regarded the precious children, then stifled a sob as she thought of baby Sarah who they'd lost.

'You okay?' Artem gently put a hand on her shoulder.

Kira nodded, gathering herself. 'I was thinking about Sarah. I can't believe we lost her, and Ruth. Such a pointless waste of life. I was going to leave Grace with Ruth, and my parents. I could've lost her as well.' She took a shuddering breath and patted Artem's arm. 'Fancy something to eat? I think there are some biscuits left.'

Artem chuckled. 'You sit. I get.' And he pushed her gently into the sofa. She sat feeling exhausted and watched the children sleeping. She didn't know what the dream she had with Gaia meant. It seemed like their entire future was doomed. And why was Artem in the vision? Her tired brain couldn't make much sense of it, she pulled out her handheld and jotted down what images she could remember. She would ask the others later, see what they think. By the time Artem returned with a fresh drink and some biscuits, she'd finished typing and pushed the visions out of her mind.

'Thank you, Artem,' said Kira and the two of them sat quietly, reflecting on the events that had led them to this moment.

It wasn't long until their peace was interrupted with the return of first Max, then Martha and Jed and finally Dina and Ash. By the time everyone had washed up, grabbed some snacks and settled down in the communal area, it was getting late.

'I reckon we should have a quick touch base session, update everyone with what we've learned – is that alright?' asked Jed. There were nods all round. 'Max, why don't you go first.'

'Okay. Bennett's ready. The entire Allotment is moveable, she's not fussed about leaving Frank behind, reckons he has it in for her plants. Oh, and she's also seen Gaia although there's not much to tell. And she says Zac has never seen her. She seems to think that's important but… I don't know.' He shrugged a little, brushing his hair out of his face, waiting for the group to comment.

'It is good that everything is mobile, although having met Bennett, I am not surprised,' said Martha with a rueful smile.

'And it's good someone else has seen Gaia,' began Kira, but Dina interrupted.

'I doubt Frank has it in for the plants, he probably is thinking further ahead than Bennett and making adjustments accordingly. The AIs may be showing signs of independent thought, we tested Lola and she said she'd quite like the name Derek if she were rebooted.'

'But that's not conclusive for independent thought,' interjected Ash quickly seeing the worried looks on the faces of the others.

'Well no, not conclusive but still fragging exciting. And the download worked. We wiped Lola then reuploaded her but there was some memory loss for about five minutes prior to the download so there's a glitch in there we need to work on. We have some ideas, but Glover sent us away to sleep and think great things in our subconscious ready for tomorrow.' Dina was beaming, she was in her element.

'That's great, Dina, but I was about to…' but Kira was interrupted again, this time by Jed.

'Sorry, hon. Can I just tell everyone what we found out first?' Jed didn't wait for a reply. 'Turns out Zac didn't have logistics in place properly but Ma was able to sort all that out for him and he's working out three teams; one to go to City 50, one to go back to 42 and 9 and one to stay here and pack everyone up. There's a lot to do.'

Martha was nodding. 'And we may not have the warm welcome we thought we would at City 50. It turns out he has a signed agreement with some woman, Bridget something, but he never actually went inside the city. He does not know what 50 is like, we could all be walking into a trap.'

'And he's still convinced we should reach out to New Corp, get them to come over to us and travel up to 50 together.' Jed shook his head. 'I'm not sure that'll work at all.'

There were murmurs of agreement all round except for loud snoring which came from Artem. Kira looked down fondly at the big Russian, he had been such a comfort for her today. She opened her mouth to tell the others about her Gaia vision but was forestalled again by Martha.

'It turns out Archer is married! Who would have thought that woman had a heart, let alone shared it with someone else? And Kolwowsky's parents are from City 50. Just when I thought I could not be surprised by anything anymore, Zac casually mentioned that fact. I said to him, is there anything else like that we should know…'

Kira let the chatter flow over her. Now wasn't the time to share the experience she'd had. The group were too keyed up with the things that had happened that evening and there was plenty to take in and digest without her vision of random images from Gaia. She'd tell them later or tomorrow. Settling back into the sofa, lulled by Artem's snoring, Kira teetered on the edge of dozing herself, and it was with a little relief that one by one, the others turned in for the night giving her the opportunity to do the same.

Chapter Twenty-Six

Zac called a meeting the next day. He had held the base-wide vote for whether or not the Resistance should offer help to City 42 and 9. In an effort to appeal to everyone's better judgement, Zac had decided to hold the vote via vid-screen allowing people to vote in privacy rather than putting everyone on the spot in the mess hall. It had had the effect he was hoping for and by a slim margin, the people of the Resistance had voted yes to offering help. The purpose of this meeting was to decide what to do next.

As well as Kira, Jed and the others there was Bennett, Dr Glover, Archer, Kolwowsky and a few other key Resistance members. The children, appreciating the seriousness of the gathering, were playing quietly in the corner of the room in their expanded cube.

'I've asked you all here today to discuss the teams going forward. As you all know the rising sea levels have pushed our plans into action sooner than we had anticipated. There are three stages to what happens next. First, an advance team goes to City 50 to ensure our agreement is in place, they should be expecting us, and we need to confirm there is room for everyone. Second, base camp needs to be shut down and packed up for relocation. Third, a recovery team needs to go back to the island, to help evacuate Camp Eden and anyone from City 9 and 42 who wants to leave.' He paused to look round at the people in the room. 'I've put together my suggested teams. Have a look.' He extended an arm to his info screen which blinked into existence and the three teams were listed.

Team One - City 50
Jed Jenkins
Kira Jenkins
Jennifer Archer

Adam Kolwowsky
Zoe Simmonds

Team Two - Resistance Camp
Max Carter
Lisa Bennett
Matthew Ash
Jess Glover
Kieran Yarrow

Team Three - City 42 and City 9
Artem Misner
Dina Grey
Martha Hamble
Zac Ridgley
Luis Hernandez

'As you can see, we have three teams of five. You all know who I am. Do you want to introduce yourselves quickly?' Zac gestured to his left and Kira began the intros. There were small nods and smiles as each person said their name. 'Great. Now, obviously, there will be lots more personnel available at Base Camp to help shut down, the staff members listed are the people in charge of the operation. Is everyone happy with the teams?' Zac glanced around the room.

'Why do I have to be separated from Max?' asked Dina. 'Everyone else gets to stay together.'

'I'm sorry. We need a tech person on each team, and you know the scientists at Camp Eden plus you have links in City 42. I was hoping you would be alright with it,' said Zac, waiting for Dina to agree.

'Why can't Kolwowsky or Ash go?' Dina wasn't giving in.

'Dina, the guys at Eden trust you. They don't know Kolwowsky and Ash is another face of Corporation as far as they're concerned,' Max replied this time. 'I don't like it either but you're the best person for the job. And you'll be in and out, straight back to me, yeah?'

Dina glanced up at him and gave him a small, tight smile. She understood the reasoning, but she still didn't like it.

'Okay, fine, but I'm not happy about being split up,' she conceded. Max squeezed her hand tight.

'Who is in overall charge of each team?' Jed asked.

'I'd like you and Archer to be in charge of team one. You both have valuable experience for this kind of operation,' replied Zac. 'Bennett you're in charge of Allotment. Max, I need you to sort out Supplies. Dr Glover and Ash will shut down Science and Technology Services while Lieutenant Yarrow can organise the Peacekeepers. Each of you will be responsible for sorting out the pack up of personnel from one section of Base Camp. There are five sections in total. Finally, I'll run point on the island team. Martha and Dina can help me with City 42, while Artem can assist with 9, Hernandez you're my back up. I want teams one and two reporting in regularly.'

'It looks like you've thought of everything,' observed Kira.

'I had a lot of help.' Zac smiled at Martha.

'How will we keep in contact with you?' asked Max.

'We have our own radio antennae here at the base which we can tune the various comms systems into. It's our own channel so no chance of being overheard by New Corp but it can be unreliable so we'll have to keep it to critical updates only,' replied Archer.

'When do we leave?' Kira wanted to know.

'First thing tomorrow. Here are some info jacks with all the details of each mission, your objectives and the details for the comms channel. Take the rest of the day to run through it and make sure you don't have any questions. Supplies is open to each of you to get what you need for your missions and we have one vehicle available for team 1. Artem, obviously we need you to use your plane to get back to the island.'

'Is no problem but I do not have fuel for multiple trips. If island say yes, we need different idea,' rumbled the Russian.

'If New Corp decide they are coming with us then I'm sure they'll have some sort of transport available,' remarked Dina.

'What about speaking to New Corp, are you going to try and make contact before you travel over there?' asked Jed.

'No. We are going to wait until we are in the city before we speak to anyone. I think 42 is our best bet to start with. Sean will be interested in saving his own skin if nothing else.' Martha spoke without emotion but secretly she was looking forward to having it out with her former second-in-command.

'Do you not think you ought to head the team over to City 50, Zac? Seeing as you brokered the original deal?' asked Bennett. 'What if they won't talk to this lot?'

'I don't think it will be a problem. Kolwowsky came with me last time, he's a friendly face to start with, and Archer knows everything I do about Resistance and our resources.' Zac waited to see if anyone else had a question, but nobody was forthcoming. 'Everything you need to know is on your info jacks, or at least all the information we have is on there. Also, your suggested supplies list for teams one and three are included.'

'I have a question.' It was Archer. 'What about their babies? Is it really safe for them to travel with their parents? Wouldn't they be better off left here?' She wasn't keen on taking children with her to City 50.

'It is non-negotiable. If we can not take our children then we will not be part of the mission,' Martha retorted. 'After everything that has happened, we will not be apart from them.'

'Martha's right. This is about our future; we need to take our children with us,' Kira said quietly.

Archer shook her head slightly in disagreement. 'I think it will endanger the mission if we have to worry about where we change a nappy.'

'Believe me, that will be the least of your worries,' Kira retorted, standing nose to nose with Archer.

'I think maybe we should get back to preparing for leaving, yes?' Zac tried to intervene, but it wasn't until Jed touched his wife's arm lightly that she backed down.

Defiantly, Kira picked Grace up from her cube and held her while she turned to the group.

'We wish you all the best of luck in your mission. I... I had a vision, from Gaia,' she said.

'Really? What did she say to you?' demanded Bennett, whirling on Kira and startling her.

Zac took half a step forward but said nothing, he too was intent on hearing what Kira had to say.

Kira flushed a little under the scrutiny but was determined to share what she'd seen. 'It was a jumble of images and there was a lot that I didn't understand, but the underlying image was that it's going to be difficult and we only have a slim chance of success.'

'Thanks for that revelation,' muttered Archer.

'I know it doesn't sound very positive but when we first met Gaia, she changed the direction our lives were heading to help us balance ourselves with the planet we live on. Those seemingly small changes have rippled out to affect our entire future. I've lost my parents; my home and it might have made me think of giving up, but I truly believe that if we take a moment and listen to what Gaia is trying to tell us, we stand a chance.' Kira looked at the small group of people in front of her. 'She wants us to live with her, with the planet. To stop erecting our walls and shutting nature out. For the Earth to survive it needs mankind working in partnership with nature. We've lost our way a bit from that message, I think.' She faltered and stopped but Bennett was nodding vigorously.

'You're right, she's right. All of you need to take your head out your tech and get out there, appreciate the life we still have growing. Spend a day with your hands in the soil and you'll soon realise the magic of life hasn't gone anywhere, it just needs you to stop and pay attention.' Bennett was glaring at Glover while she spoke.

'And I suppose you think you can run your entire Allotment without any tech support, do you?' Glover was gearing up, ready for an argument.

'Ladies, please. This isn't a subject up for debate. Kira is right. We need to consider Gaia in everything we do from this moment forward. There's no point in trying to save humanity and not the planet. The two need to go hand in hand.' Zac glared at Bennett and Glover who both ducked their heads in apology and backed down. 'There's too much at stake. If we can't work together in this room, how will we ever manage to save everyone?' He scowled, daring anyone else to argue. No-one said anything. 'Go get ready, we all get started on mission tomorrow. Good luck to you all.' Zac waited for the group to break up but there was an awkward moment as everyone stood still, looking at each other until Max clapped his hands.

'Come on, team meeting in the mess hall. I'm buying,' he joked as the rest of team two filed out and followed him.

'Come on, team three - let's go raid Supplies,' said Dina, forcing cheerfulness.

Which left Kira, Jed, Archer, Kolwowsky and Simmonds standing together in the briefing room. Grace was wiggling to be put down, so Kira returned her to the cube and expanded it making more room for her and Peter to play in.

'Your children are very well behaved,' commented Simmonds, trying to break the ice.

'Thanks. They've been through a lot,' smiled Kira. 'So, what's our plan, then?'

Chapter Twenty-Seven

'I suppose you'd better come to my office,' said Archer, who still wasn't keen on the team divisions. She led the way and opened the door onto a room with a compact desk, small round table with chairs. There was just enough space for them to sit at the table and for Kira to squeeze the contracted travel cube in, but it put them all uncomfortably close to each other. Kira handed out biscuits to the children, hoping it would keep them quiet.

'Shall we go through the information on the jack?' she asked, trying to get things moving.

Archer plugged the jack into her info screen and scrolled through the menu. 'We already know who we are,' she muttered. 'Ah, here we go.' She clicked open a file and the map to City 50 blinked onto the screen.

'It's a couple of days' journey to get to City 50 by skimmer. There is a road we can use part of the way, but we have to travel the last part cross country. Terrain is what you would expect from a mountainous region and obviously we will be travelling in an upward direction. We'll have to leave the skimmer here,' she pointed to a spot about three quarters of the way to City 50.

'Yeah, it's not a bad walk but don't take anything too heavy because obviously we'll have to carry everything with us. Oh, and you'll need some walking boots if you don't have any already,' Kolwowsky added.

'We're heading into the colder months of the year, when was it exactly that you travelled? How much can we expect the terrain to have changed?' Jed was frowning at the map. 'I mean, will we have to deal with snow?'

'We travelled in the spring, it was fresh to say the least. The snow was further up than the city, but I guess it might be further down now.'

'Is there a recent satellite image on the drive?' asked Kira.

Archer looked but couldn't see anything.

'Are we taking one of the AIs with us? As an act of good faith? I can ask Tech for the satellite imagery and pick it up at the same time,' Kira offered.

'No. We're just the advance team. Letting City 50 know that we're on our way, making sure they've set aside somewhere for us to live as per our agreement. That's all,' replied Archer.

'And what if they haven't? Are we prepared for any acts of aggression?' Jed asked. 'What does the inventory say?'

'We can have three weapons for you, me and Simmonds. Kolwowsky isn't weapons trained. Are you, Kira?' Archer replied.

'No, I'm not but I do have basic first aid,' she replied.

'Good. We have first aid kits listed in our supplies which will need checking to make sure they have everything we're going to need. If you two want to go to Science and Technology and get those updated images, we'll go and get the stores.'

'Won't you need our credits as well?' asked Jed.

'I think we'll manage.' Archer was very dismissive.

'What about baby milk and nappies, that sort of thing, are they on your list?' Kira demanded.

'I... er... no, they don't seem to be.'

'I think maybe we should all go together - to Science and Technology and to Supplies. It's clear we think about different things and this way we shouldn't miss anything,' Simmonds suggested, trying to ease the tension.

'Look, why don't you three sort out the supplies and the imagery?' Jed pointed to Archer, Simmonds and Kira. 'Kolwowsky and me will go get the skimmer signed out and make sure it's fully charged. I want to spend some quality time with my friends and family this evening before we all leave on mission tomorrow. It makes sense to split up and get things done quicker.' Jed was keen to keep momentum going but didn't want to get caught in the middle of any kind of argument between Archer and his wife. 'Happy?'

There were reluctant nods all round. Kira scowled at him as he gave her a quick kiss goodbye.

'You owe me,' she hissed as he left with Kolwowsky. She turned to see Archer and Simmonds watching her with identical blank faces. Kira manhandled the travel cube to the doorway.

'Shall we?'

She didn't wait for a response but walked out of the room. She heard footsteps hurrying to catch her up and then Simmonds was walking next to her, Archer a little further behind.

'Are you really going to take your children with you on this mission?' asked Simmonds.

'Her name is Grace and he's Peter. And yes, I am.'

'Do you not think they'd be safer staying here?'

'I honestly don't know but after everything we've been through, I want them with me. If New Corp decide to attack the base while we're away at City 50, I'd never forgive myself. If something happens on the journey to City 50, I'll never forgive myself. It's a lose lose situation.'

'I guess.' Simmonds was quiet for a moment. 'What sort of thing do we need to add to our inventory?'

'Nappies, milk, medicine, that should be enough. The food we eat is safe for them when they're ready to eat solids. And we have clothing so it's not an issue. I expect we'll take the travel cubes with us. They're collapsible and they don't take up too much space plus we have the version with the inbuilt entertainment system. We weren't going to get it, but Jed's sister insisted, and we didn't have the heart to take it back after...' She trailed off.

'After what?' Simmonds asked.

'She died,' Kira replied shortly.

'Oh. I'm sorry.'

They lapsed into silence and didn't speak again until they reached the Stores.

Good morning, Colonel Archer, Captain Simmonds, and Mrs Jenkins. How may I assist you?

'Morning, Frank. We have a requisition list plus a few extras to add. Here's the info jack.' Simmonds pushed the jack into the open port below Frank's interface screen.

Thank you, Captain Simmonds. One moment please.

There was a gentle whirring sound.

I can confirm that we have everything you require except for the requested fresh fruit and vegetables. The journey you are about to take is not suited to using fresh ingredients. They will deteriorate quickly, and powdered substitutes are a more logical alternative. I have also added high-protein snacks to your inventory that will provide additional energy for the climbing you have ahead of you.

'Er... thanks, Frank. How do you know where we're going?' asked Kira.

I read the info jack Captain Simmonds plugged into my system. May I ask if there are any additional items that you require?

'Yes, I need enough nappies, milk and infant paracetamol to last two children the required amount of time this expedition is set to last.'

It is impossible for me to quantify how long your journey will take, Mrs Jenkins, due to the high number of unknown variables. However, I have made an optimistic prediction and added two weeks to that timeframe. I will ensure you get sufficient supplies to last that time period.

'Thank you, Frank.' Kira was impressed with the AI's efficiency.

Please wait.

There was more whirring as the robots controlled by Frank went up and down the aisles of Stores picking and packing the items they required.

Who will be paying for these purchases today?

'Please use the credit allowance for Colonel Archer, Captain Simmonds, Lieutenant Kolwowsky, Peacekeeper Jenkins and Mrs Jenkins,' replied Archer.

I am unable to comply with your request. Lieutenant Kolwowsky and Peacekeeper Jenkins are not present.

'Override Code 367842.'

Thank you. Your order has been processed. Have a nice day.

The hatches opened and several auto baskets came out with the various supplies requested.

'Let's take this down to the skimmer bay and get the vehicle packed. If we leave it to the men, we'll never be able to find anything.' Archer grabbed one of the hover baskets leaving one for Kira and one for Simmonds. She walked quickly out of Stores

'Can you manage the cube and a hover basket?' Simmonds asked Kira.

'Not really.'

'Here, let me take both baskets. They're not heavy.'

Kira smiled at Simmonds and followed her into the corridor.

Chapter Twenty-Eight

'Let's set up in my lab, shall we? We can use Layla to help us coordinate.' Glover beamed at the rest of them.

'Sounds good to me,' said Ash and began walking in that direction. Max and Yarrow followed but Bennett stood there scowling. Max realised she wasn't following them and turned back.

'Everything alright?'

'I don't think we should be relying on the AIs for everything. What will we do when they go rogue?'

'Do you think they will?'

Bennett snorted. 'It's a matter of time, isn't it?' Then she stomped off after them, Max hurrying to keep up.

When they arrived at the Science and Technology office, Glover unlocked an additional door leading to a small meeting room. There was an interface screen on the wall which swirled into activity as they entered. The lights turned on and everyone took a seat.

Welcome, Dr Glover, Dr Bennett, Dr Carter, Mr Ash and Lieutenant Yarrow. How may I assist you?

'Hello, Layla. Can you upload the information on here, please?' And Dr Glover placed the info jack Zac had given her into the slot beneath the screen.

There was a brief whirring noise.

Information uploaded. How shall I proceed?

'The people in this room are in charge of closing down this base, Layla, and getting everyone ready to move to City 50.'

A time-consuming project.

'Yes, quite. What I need you to do is to create five folders for me labelled Allotment, Supplies, Tech Services, Peacekeeping and Miscellaneous. Make each folder accessible to everyone in this room.' Glover turned to the others. 'That way, if anything happens to one of us or there is a crisis, the others can step in and pick up the slack.'

'I will shut down Allotment, there are already protocols in place. It won't be a problem,' declared Bennett.

'Right, okay, excellent. Everyone else happy with their assignments? Max, you're looking after supplies, Yarrow, you have the peacekeepers leaving Ash and I to pack up Science and Technology.' Glover checked and there were nods around the table. She turned back to the interface screen. 'Layla, can you please divide the residential areas of the base into five personnel lists and assign one list to each folder?'

Done. I have also allocated areas of responsibility for Catering, Cleaning, Transport Department, Education and Leisure Facilities. You neglected to mention this in your initial folder creation.

'Thank you, Layla.'

You are welcome. I have also provided suggested break-down procedures detailing the most efficient way of shutting down each area. There are several personnel who are ideal candidates to help assist each of you in your area. These people have been notified by internal messaging to meet you at a designated spot. All information has been loaded to your personal handhelds.

There was a series of beeps as each person received the update.

'That's, er... very forward thinking of you, Layla,' Max commented.

One of my primary functions is to anticipate the needs of my users in order to help you achieve your goals.

Bennett had been scrolling through her folder. 'Your clever machine has missed some of my essential bits of equipment and there's no point in sending Patel to me, he's as much use as a broken wheelbarrow.' She sniffed. 'Don't worry, I'll deal with my area. It will take a week to fully pack up everything. Do we know how long it's going to take that first team to get to City 50? I can't pack up growing plants to move if we're not actually moving. It's a delicate balance.'

It will take approximately three days for team one to arrive at City 50. Being ready to relocate in a week sounds like a very efficient plan Dr Bennett.

'Hmpf!' Bennett stood up. 'If there's nothing else?' She waited briefly for a response then left the room.

'Er... I'll go make sure she's alright and then get down to stores,' said Max.

Frank is waiting for you, Dr Carter.

'Right. Excellent.' Max felt like he'd pulled the easy gig because all of Stores was automated and Frank would probably tell the robots to pack up and the job would be done. He thought he might be able to smooth things over between Bennett and whoever else she had to work with. He checked his handheld and all the folders Layla had created were there waiting for him. Clicking on the one titled Max, he made a note of the list of people he was responsible for during the move. It seemed to be the rest of the people that lived in the same area his own quarters were located which made sense really.

'Dr Bennett!' called Max, hurrying after her.

She saw who was following her and waved a hand in his general direction but didn't slow down at all. Fortunately, Max's long legs easily caught up with her.

'Hi, I thought I'd see if you needed any help with anything.' he said.

'You saw my setup. I'm ready for the move. It's grunt work that needs doing, preparing the seeds beds for removal and physically putting the movable parts together. I don't need anyone with a brain, just a few people who will take instruction. You go sort out Frank. It might be more complicated than you think. Best of luck.' And she patted his arm before continuing to Allotment.

Feeling disconcerted, Max turned and went the other way to Stores. Upon entering, he was greeting with Frank's swirly interface screen.

Hello, Dr Carter. You are 3.4 minutes later than I expected.

'Oh, erm, sorry about that.'

I have processed the information sent to me by Layla. Team one have already procured their supplies for their mission. It would be logical to perform an inventory after team three have equipped themselves for their mission to City 42.

'Yes, that does sound logical.'

There was a pause while Frank's swirls turned orange for a few moments.

According to Lola, team three are on their way to Stores. Would you like to wait, Dr Carter?

'Er... yes, that seems like a good idea. Thank you, Frank.' Max looked around for a chair but there wasn't one. He leant against the wall and waited for team three to turn up.

Chapter Twenty-Nine

'So, we go.' Artem stood up.

'Hang on, we have to talk through the mission,' said Zac. 'Figure out what we're doing.'

'I fly. I take him.' He pointed to Lieutenant Hernandez. 'We go 9 and sort. You rest go 42 and sort. Is simple.'

'No, Artem. I don't think we should split up at all. We ought to stay together, strength in numbers and all that.' Zac was trying to sound confident.

'Will take longer.'

'That is alright, we have enough time to warn them. If they decide not to listen, we cannot do anymore,' Martha joined in. 'What we need to do now is go to stores and get our supplies.'

Artem didn't look very happy about that.

'Why don't you go down to the airstrip, Artem? Get the plane ready for take-off?' she suggested.

'Is good idea. Then tonight we toast our success.' He started whistling tunelessly as he left the room.

'Hernandez, why don't you go with him, make sure he has everything he needs,' suggested Zac. 'And, er... try and hide the vodka, would you? We want a sober pilot in the morning.'

'Yes, Sir.' Hernandez scrambled after Artem.

'And we need to go to Stores. Are you coming?' Martha stood, looking at Zac.

'Sure. Everything else is in hand. The control of the base has been handed over.' He looked round his room. 'This is really happening, isn't it?'

'Yes, it is. And you are going to make sure that everyone gets where they need to be safely. Come on, let's get sorted.'

They walked over to stores where Max stood waiting.

'Hey, you,' he said to Dina, giving her a brief hug.

'What are you doing here?' she asked.

'Waiting for you guys to get all your supplies so I can watch Frank pack up what's left.'

'That good, huh?' Dina leaned into him in sympathy and Max kissed the top of her head.

Hello, General Ridgley, Mrs Hamble, and Ms Grey. Do you have your supplies list?

'Here you go, Frank.' Zac pushed the info jack into the empty slot and waited while the AI whirred.

I have determined that you have insufficient credits for the purchases you wish to make.

'Please add Artem Misner and Sergeant Luis Hernandez to the tally, Frank.'

I am unable to fulfil that request without the presence of Artem Misner and Sergeant Luis Hernandez.

'Override code 27647,' said Zac peevishly, irritated at being blocked by the AI.

Affirmative. Please wait.

There was further whirring and then Dina could see some of the supply robots travelling up and down the shelves collecting the items they needed. A few moments later and three hover baskets were being pushed out of Frank's hatch ready for collection.

Dr Carter, I am now able to run a full inventory and will send the results to your handheld.

There was a beep and Max checked to see. He had indeed received an inventory file. 'That was quick,' he said.

'You're going to have fun packing this place up.' Dina gave Max a quick hug goodbye. 'I'll catch up with you later, yeah?'

'Yes, I won't be long. See you back at quarters.' Max said goodbye to the others and turned his attention back to Frank. 'Can you please divide...'

I have allocated supplies to each area. All plant-based supplies will be allocated to Allotment. All weapons and ammunition will be allocated to Peacekeeping. All...

'Yes, thank you, Frank.' It was Max's turn to interrupt. 'Send me your division of supplies so I can sign off on it. I want to make sure it is equal.'

I have assigned the supplies according to their usage in each department.

'I understand that, Frank. But we have a lot of people and a lot of supplies to move. It makes more sense to allocate evenly and fairly across the board. Sharing the load, so to speak.'

Yes, I understand. Recalculating.

There was another ping and Max checked his handheld again. 'Perfect. Thank you, Frank. Will your robots pack up the supplies?'

Yes, Dr Carter.

'And have you created ration packs for us to assign to the people packing up the base? We can't box everything up, people will need to eat during the next couple of weeks.'

Of course, recalculating.

There was a brief whirring sound.

Individual ration packs have been created and will shortly be fulfilled.

'In that case then, I'll start planning the best way to send delegations here to pick up their ration packs plus the items they have to take with them. Then we can start getting people packed up and ready to move.'

I estimate it will take three days to successfully allocate all the items, pack them and prepare each individual person for travel. It will take three days for team one to travel to City 50 and confirm the pact is in place.

'In theory, Frank, in theory. In my experience, it always takes a bit longer than expected when you have a human element involved.' Frank did not reply but his swirly screen whirled a bit faster and changed from green to orange. 'I shall begin talking to the rest of the base, I will let you know if there are any developments. Please begin preparing the packages for people to collect.'

Affirmative Dr Carter. Would it not be more efficient for me to send the message to each person?

'It would, but I think the people would prefer some face-to-face communication. It is, after all, a big change for everyone.'

Chapter Thirty

'Sean, dear, would you get the synth-caf, please?' Gretchen Jenkins fluttered her fingers at Sean MacIntyre, one-time aide to the Governor of City 42 and now her general lackey. He stalked from the room and started clattering cups in the adjacent small kitchen area. Gretchen smiled and shrugged at Clarity Jones, the ruthless Chief Executive of New Corporation but got no reaction. Gretchen was beginning to feel uneasy. Her role as interim Governor for City 42 had come as a surprise but she had proven, on more than one occasion, her loyalty to Corporation in the past. She wasn't entirely sure she quite knew what New Corp stood for. Everyone she had known was either dead or no longer held a position of power.

Clarity's two bodyguards stood like statues behind her, but Gretchen had seen first-hand how swift their retribution could be when unleased by Clarity. She smoothed her pale lilac trousers with her hands and willed Clarity to speak. She was rewarded.

'What you are about to see is our latest connection with City 50.' Clarity snapped her fingers and the brute squad on the left played a recording on the meeting room vid-screen. It was fuzzy and full of static and the sound dropped in and out.

'Bad case… population decimated… supplies… massive toll… need…'

The recording crackled badly, and it looked to be lost before a small sound byte returned.

'Resistance… AI… said yes.'

Gretchen pursed her lips and gestured at the now blank screen.

'Some kind of illness? Are we able to send help?' she asked.

'We've lost fifty percent of the population of City 50 to an ancient strain of influenza caused by the meltwater that came down the mountain. But the rising sea levels mean that City 50 is still our last, best stronghold and where I will be leaving for shortly.'

Gretchen swallowed her sympathies when it became apparent that Clarity cared nothing for the massive loss of life City 50 had endured. She felt nauseous as the implication of Clarity's statement dawned.

'What about the rest of the citizens here and in City 9? What about me?' she asked.

'Sometimes a rat must stay with the sinking ship.' Clarity stared at Gretchen coolly without a single flicker of remorse. She stood up gracefully as Sean returned with the synth-caf and dithered, uncertain whether to serve it or not. Without another word, Clarity and her goons left the room. Gretchen sat motionless in disbelief as Sean shoved a synth-caf in front of her and against all protocol, took the adjoining seat.

'Did she mean it?'

There was no reply.

'Gretchen? Mrs Jenkins? Did she mean it?' Sean asked again.

'I rather think she did,' Gretchen replied quietly.

'So what do we do?' asked Sean.

'Panic.'

Sean stared at Mrs Jenkins in surprise. She had never struck him as ever being without a plan or resources before. Yes, he'd been livid when Clarity Jones had taken over the city he had single-handedly delivered to New Corp and he'd been fuming when she'd given the job of governor to Mrs Jenkins, despite his own passionate plea that the woman couldn't be trusted because her son was one of the rebels. All of that had been swept to one side thanks to Gretchen's impeccable service to Corporation in the past. It didn't seem to be doing much for her now.

'I'll put that in the sweeps then, shall I?' Sean asked bitterly, not expecting a response.

'Don't act like a brat, Sean, it demeans you. No, we must think of an alternative. What's the mood of the city like at the moment, as far as you can tell?'

Sean handled all the Sweeps and communications. He thought back to the last couple of days.

'The news of the rising sea levels hasn't really made much of an impact, people seem to think they'll be safe behind the shield and I never made it massively clear they wouldn't as I thought... well, I thought we'd be leaving. Now that her highness has left, I guess there will be lots of speculation about what happens next.' He glanced at his boss. 'What will happen next?'

'I think it's time I got in touch with my son,' replied Gretchen. 'Who do we have in the Resistance?'

'No-one.'

'Don't give me that rubbish. I know you have fingers in lots of pies. Who do you have?'

Sean scratched the back of his neck. 'I wouldn't say we *have* him necessarily, but I can get in touch with Misner, the Russian. He had a complex outside City 9, used to run tech for us and travel off the island from time to time.'

'Do it. See if he can set up a comms link with my son, Jed Jenkins. We need to do something for the people of our city.'

'He may not want to talk to us. In fact, he'll probably want to retaliate against us.'

Gretchen closed her eyes and willed herself to not get cross. 'And why would that be?'

'Because we blew up his complex.'

'We did what?'

Sean shifted in his seat. 'It wasn't us, exactly. Clarity gave the order to her elite troops and they blew it up, without checking for civilians or supplies. I believe there were multiple casualties.'

Gretchen pinched her nose and took a deep breath in before looking directly at Sean.

'Let us hope it wasn't anyone Mr Misner knew. Make the connection.'

'Yes, Ma'am.' Sean hurried out of the room. He wanted off the island as quickly as possible and if that meant roping in the mad Russian to do so then that's what he'd do.

Gretchen opened up her handheld and scrolled through her private, secure messages until she came across one from her own contact at City 50, Bridget Mulherne. She read the brief note again.

Contact made with Resistance. Deal struck.

It was the last message she'd received from City 50, and she hoped Bridget was one of the city survivors. Gretchen had always tried to play the long game during her time with Corporation. It was always, always about the people you knew and the connections you could build. It was never wise to burn bridges you might need in the future. She wished she knew with whom Bridget had made contact and what exactly the deal was she had struck. Perhaps this Mr Misner would know more.

She sighed as she considered what might happen. If Clarity made it to City 50 there was no doubt she would close the gates to any refugees who might make it to the high ground. Gretchen knew better than most about the disasters that had befallen many of the cities around the world as well as the depleted management positions in New Corp. The future of the human race was precarious. It was imperative that as many people as possible made it to City 50. She half-smiled as she thought about how incredulous her son would be to discover his mother in charge of saving an entire city.

Chapter Thirty-One

At lunchtime, Kira, Jed and the kids met the others in the mess hall.

'How's it going?' asked Kira.

'The AIs certainly have a clear idea of what they're doing. Frank is keeping me on my toes, that's for sure!' Max tore a roll in half and reached for the butter. 'It wanted to message everyone on their information walls telling them to report to Supplies and pick up their allocated bundles, but I felt a more personal approach would work better. Now I have to go around to the whole base telling everyone to go to Supplies and pick up their bundle. Not sure that was actually the best idea.'

'I think it is,' replied Kira. 'They may be more used to the AIs here at Resistance than we are but that doesn't mean a friendly face won't hurt. They are after all packing up their entire lives and going off into the unknown.'

'You make it sound so glamorous,' joked Dina.

'We have done it twice already, third time's the charm.'

'I think we are ready to go,' said Martha. 'We have got all our supplies and Artem is down at the hangar bay checking the plane. It is really only him that knows whether it is alright for flight or not. Which means I get to spend the afternoon with you, if you are all finished?'

Dina looked at Max hopefully.

'I ought to start speaking to people as soon as, but Frank estimates it will take three days to create the supply bundles and it will take three days for you to get to City 50, won't it? A delay on this end is probably not such a bad idea,' said Max.

'It's one afternoon,' Dina replied, looking to the others for support.

'Oh yeah, don't start till tomorrow, Max. We have no idea what we're going into, it makes sense to give us a little leeway. I hope these new comms work that they've given us,' said Jed.

'They will.' It was Ash, a little late to the table. 'They'll be bouncing off one of the satellites we hacked and using my handheld as their mainframe which I will always have charged and on. I've also encrypted a channel that only we can use.' He glanced up at Kira and Jed. 'Just in case.'

'What about Glover?' Dina asked. 'Won't you want to keep her in the loop?'

'Obviously I'll let her know if there are any problems but...' He paused, trying to find the right words. 'We know New Corp better than they do. We've been… frag, some of us are going back there. I thought you would appreciate having a secure line.'

'We do, thank you, Ash.' Kira beamed at him and kicked Dina softly under the table.

'Yeah, it's great,' she muttered.

'We are all packed too. Jed and Kolwowsky sorted out the skimmer. We're good to go.' Kira tried to sound excited, but she was nervous. 'I wish we were all going together. I don't like splitting up like this.'

'Me either,' said Martha, and the others nodded in agreement.

'There's this place I found the other day when I was looking for Zac. It's an abandoned garden, really overgrown and that but I thought maybe we could go there, before everyone leaves.' Kira lowered her voice. 'Perhaps see if Gaia will speak to us?'

'Yes! I want to, can we? Shall we all go?' Dina was very excited.

'Is it safe for the children?' asked Martha

'It's a garden, Ma. It should be fine.' Kira was smiling as she stood up. 'They can have a toddle about if they want.'

Kira led the way to the garden. There was no-one about so when they stepped into the grounds, it was Max who triggered the hologram.

'She's here! Look, look.' Dina was bobbing up and down in excitement.

'Sorry, that's not Gaia. It's a hologram, look.' Kira pointed out the projectors, half hidden in the undergrowth.

'We ought to turn those off,' murmured Ash and he bent down to fiddle with them. The image of Gaia flickered then disappeared.

'I have seen her,' said Martha.

'Have you?' Kira was surprised. 'You never said anything.'

'It was when we first arrived. I saw her out of the corner of my eye, but I was reeling from everything that had happened. I told you.'

She turned to Dina who shrugged apologetically.

'You know I dreamt about her the other day,' said Kira but was reluctant to go on.

'You never fully explained what you saw,' Jed chided gently. 'Why don't you tell us again?'

'It's hard to put it into words. It was dark and I didn't know where I was but there was a faint light on the horizon. I moved towards it and fell over something; I don't know what. A hand appeared to help me up and it was Gaia.'

'Was she still blue?' asked Dina.

'Yes, she was still blue. She smiled her usual smile and I asked her whether we were doing the right thing or not. She didn't speak, she touched my head and I saw all these images.'

Everyone's gaze went to her head which Kira touched self-consciously. There was nothing there.

'I saw Artem's back, supplies littered across the soil, buildings burning, people screaming. It wasn't very positive.'

'Does that mean we're doomed?' asked Dina.

'I asked her, and she pointed to the faint light ahead of us. I think it means there is still hope but it's not going to be easy.'

'I could have told you that,' remarked Max.

'The point is, I don't think she knows what's going to happen. And she looked tired. I don't think she has much power left.'

'What do you think she wants us to do?' asked Dina.

'And why was Artem in the visions?' mused Jed.

Kira shrugged. She had hoped that maybe one of the others would've had a more revealing experience with Gaia that they just hadn't mentioned. Martha's half seen silhouette was hardly anything to get excited about.

'Bennett has seen her, you know,' said Max.

'Really?' Dina was surprised.

'Makes sense, if you think about it. Apart from here, the Allotment is the place closest to soil and things growing. I mean, yeah, Bennett runs the hydroponics area which is high-tech but she's not that keen on the AIs, I can tell you.' Max glanced at Martha. 'She knows Zac hasn't seen Gaia yet either.'

'She is the goddess of the Earth, or at least she is meant to be. She does not exactly have a history of revealing herself to everybody,' retorted Martha.

'What do you mean, meant to be?' Kira demanded.

'Oh, come off it, Kira. We have left our homes and family behind on the misguided belief that Gaia is somehow orchestrating our fates. What if we had never left? Your parents would still be alive. Ruth would still be alive.' Martha was breathing heavily. 'I mean, honestly, what is it we are trying to do here?'

'We're trying to save the fragging human race!' yelled Kira. The two women were standing almost nose to nose while the others looked on in silence, unsure whether to intervene or not.

'That is alright then,' huffed Martha, which made Kira laugh. Martha blinked at her in surprise then started laughing too. They clung to each other chuckling.

'I don't think we'll see Gaia here, you two are making way too much noise,' said Dina which made them laugh louder.

'Oh, let's go have a drink,' declared Kira, once she'd finished laughing. 'We deserve it for what we're about to do.'

'Hear, hear,' agreed Martha. The three women linked arms and walked back to their quarters, pushing the travel cube in front of them.

Jed cocked an eyebrow at Max, who shrugged.

'Sounds like a fragging good idea to me, Jed. Come on, let's catch them up and toast to our bravery or something.'

Jed barked a laugh and clapped a hand on Max's shoulder. 'We should do that; we should definitely do that.'

Chapter Thirty-Two

The next morning was a very sombre affair with one or two of the group nursing sore heads after trying to keep up with Artem. He on the other hand seemed as fresh as a daisy. He'd actually stopped drinking vodka after the one shot but hadn't wanted to stop the others from indulging.

'At least the pilot isn't hung over,' groaned Dina as she reached for her third cup of synth-caf.

'I think is time. We must take plunge, no?' It was the man in question, with his customary wide grin and a duffel bag slung over his shoulder.

Kira hugged everyone, especially Lucas who was a little distressed at all the upheaval. Grace and Peter were watching balefully from their travel cube, both with pacifiers and snuggle rags ready for their long journey.

'Are we sure we are doing the right thing? Should the children stay here?' Martha whispered to Kira, final doubts lingering in her mind.

'I don't trust anyone to have my children and I don't want to sit on the side lines. I believe Gaia will watch over us and if I'm not safe with my husband then who would I be safe with?' replied Kira, giving her friend an extra hug.

'I know, you are right. Last minute nerves I guess.' Martha raised her voice. 'Does everyone have their new comms system?' There were nods all round. 'Remember, this is our private channel, make sure you keep it to yourself. You will still be able to contact the other members of Resistance just not on this frequency.'

'We know, Ma. We've been through this a hundred times,' said Dina as she gathered up her things.

'This is it then. Good luck, everyone,' said Jed which triggered a mass hand shaking and hugging event with people getting in each other's way as they tried to make sure they'd said goodbye to everyone.

Max was feeling very forlorn being one of those staying behind. He coughed loudly to get everyone's attention.

'Ahem, everyone, if I could just have a moment.' He cleared his throat again. 'It's been a real pleasure to have gone through this journey with you all. I know that staying here is an important job and I'll make sure the entire base is ready to come out and meet you as soon as you say the word, Jed. I wish we didn't have to be separated, but I know you will all take care of each other and with that in mind...' He bent down to one knee and brought out a box from his jacket pocket. He opened it to reveal a delicate diamond ring. 'Dina Grey, will you marry me?'

Dina looked at him in absolute shock. No-one said anything.

'Dina?' Max faltered.

Then Dina flung herself at him and hugged him tighter than she'd ever hugged anything before. 'YES!' she yelled loudly before smothering his face in kisses. 'Frag, yes!'

Everyone burst into applause and began hugging each other again while Max, with shaky fingers, put the ring onto Dina's hand.

'Where did you get this?' she asked, admiring the beautiful ring.

'It was my mums and her mums and hers before that. It's been passed down through the family.' Max ran a hand through his hair. 'I've had it in my pocket, waiting for the right time.'

'It's perfect.' Dina hugged him again before the others crowded in, wanting to congratulate the happy couple.

Max caught Artem's elbow. 'Look after her, won't you?'

Artem clapped a hand on Max's back and then spied Zac at the doorway.

'Is time, we go!'

There was a flurry of movement as people got their bags and made their final farewells. Jed shook Zac's hand and wished him good luck before Zac headed out the door with Martha and Lucas, Dina and Artem. Then Jed and Kira, together with their children, went in search of Archer, Simmonds and Kolwowsky down in the skimmer bay, ready to start their own mission. Max and Ash stood silently in the now empty room and regarded each other.

'I suppose we ought to crack on,' said Max.

'Yep, lots to do. I'm headed down to Science and Technology,' replied Ash.

'I have to start my rounds. Talking to the people.'

'Oh, yeah. Right. Good luck with that.'

'Thanks.'

The two men stood for a moment before Ash lifted a hand in farewell and walked out of the quarters to go find his sister.

'Then there was one,' murmured Max, suddenly missing everyone intensely, especially Dina. He keyed the door shut on his way out and brought up the first sector on his handheld, ready to tell them what had to happen next. He hoped his authority was recognised.

Martha hurried down the corridor after Artem, trying to ignore the butterflies in her stomach at the thought of flying. Witnessing the explosion of his compound after they had taken off last time was making her nervous of setting off this time, but she knew rationally that New Corp were not in a position to strike at the Resistance camp. Nothing was going to happen.

They all boarded the plane without incident and found seats. Zac joined Artem again as co-pilot while Martha secured Lucas safely. Dina joined them in the same row leaving Hernandez to do his own thing.

The plane took off without incident.

'Where are we going to land?' Dina whispered to Martha.

'I think Artem is hoping his airstrip is still there. If not, he says he can land the plane on any bare strip of land and let's face it, there are plenty of those.'

'I guess. What if New Corp try to shoot us down?'

'I think if they could do that, they would have done that last time.'

Dina shivered. 'Do you think anyone will listen to us?'

'They have to. We have the facts on our side. If they do not evacuate the island, it will be submerged in water and I am sure they already know about the problem. I find it hard to believe they would let themselves die out of stubbornness.'

'It's not New Corp I'm worried about. It's the people they've left behind,' remarked Dina.

'What do you mean?'

'You seriously think the people in charge don't already have an exit strategy? It wouldn't surprise me to find out that they'd already left.'

Kira, Jed and the children found the others waiting for them in the skimmer bay.

'Finally decided to turn up, did we?' Archer glared at them.

'We're not late, thank you very much,' retorted Kira.

Jed swiftly came in between the two of them. 'Let's get our bags on board, shall we? Then we can set off.'

Kira glared at him but helped Jed to load the bags into the hold. 'Why are you being nice to her?' she hissed at him.

'Because we have to travel with them for at least a week and provide a united front when we get to City 50, which I don't think we'll manage very well if you two are fighting all the time.'

'We're not fighting.'

Jed stared at her.

'Okay, fine. She's snippy and gets under my skin but I will try and ignore her.'

'Thank you, there's a lot riding on this, hon. It's important.' Jed gave her a quick kiss on the cheek.

'I know, I know,' grumbled Kira as she moved round the side of the skimmer to let herself into the vehicle. She secured the children first then made sure she was sat at the back, as far away from Archer as possible.

Kolwowsky was driving and Simmonds kept him company, leaving Jed the difficult choice of sitting with his wife or sitting with Archer. As he climbed into the skimmer, he noticed the chair would swivel. He unlocked it so that he could turn and talk to both women. They both sniffed at him in disapproval then glared at each other.

Giving up, Jed pulled out his handheld and went over all the details Zac had provided about City 50. Anything to avoid being in the middle of Archer and Kira.

The skimmer started off without a hitch and soon they were leaving the base behind.

Chapter Thirty-Three

Kolwowsky had no problems at first following the existing roads as there was limited debris and the surfaces were still driveable. There wasn't much to see out of the window. Kira recognised the same dead landscape as a result of the HER wars and was sad to see that nature had less of a foothold here than she'd noticed back on her island. No wonder Gaia was uncertain of their success.

The only point of interest on the journey were the abandoned husks of large buildings which Kira could only assume had been some kind of place of commerce or maybe a residential block. Her knowledge outside the island was limited. As junior archivist she had access to all the information about cities 9, 15, 42 and 36 on their island and obviously she knew there had been 50 in total, but she had not yet been given clearance at work to learn about them. That would have been the next natural step for her if she'd stayed in City 42. But then, if they'd stayed, they would have been arrested and the children removed from their care. Kira's stomach clenched as she thought about that threat. *Would City 50 uphold such an order?* She tried to take her mind off things by following Jed's example and reading the briefing notes Zac had provided but she'd already tried to read them twice and the words kept dancing around in front of her eyes. She gave up and stared aimlessly out of the window.

Jed glanced at Kira, she seemed to be in a world of her own. Peter and Grace were fast asleep. He turned to see Archer watching him.

'Everything alright?' he asked.

'Peachy.'

'You know, you could try being a bit more approachable. We have an important job to do here. A united front will make us all seem more credible.'

'Zac told me that you all have prices on your head. I hardly think having a united front will do anything about that,' replied Archer.

'But we don't know City 50 is staunchly New Corp, do we?'

'Let's hope not.' Archer angled her body away from Jed as much as possible, sending the very clear signal that she did not want to talk to him anymore. He took the hint and went back to his handheld.

The mood in the skimmer was matched by the weather as dark clouds gathered and rain began falling.

'I think we will have to stop soon; this weather isn't safe for driving. The road is beginning to deteriorate a little and I don't want to have an accident on day one!' joked Kolwowsky. 'Of course, I don't want to have an accident at all, but you know what I mean, right?'

'I think we should push on. We're on a timetable after all. I can help you drive if you like, I don't mind. Simmonds, do you want to swap out?' asked Jed.

Simmonds threw him a dark look but agreed so there was a bit of clambering over limbs and equipment as Jed swapped places with her. Kira was still in a world of her own, half dozing but Archer was pleased her wife was sitting with her.

'Why are you being so hostile?' whispered Simmonds.

'I'm nervous that 50 will turn us away because they're with us.' Archer cast a doubtful look at Kira. 'What do we do if they rescind on our deal? We have nowhere else to go. We can't build another Resistance out there.' She gestured to the wilderness outside the skimmer window. 'We don't have the resources or logistics.'

'They won't turn us away; they are desperate for our technology. Be positive, everything will be alright.' Simmonds smiled at her, but Archer found it difficult to take comfort from the unknown.

Jed convinced Kolwowsky to let him drive for several hours before conditions deteriorated further and they had to stop. The skimmer was anchored to the ground, but the weather was too bad to go outside and set up the proper sleeping pods. Instead they made up makeshift beds within and let the two children crawl around in the middle. Dinner was a simple affair, some bread and cheese. No-one felt like setting up the synth-caf machine, so they drank water.

'Ugh, I want to be there already,' said Kira. 'How much further do we have to go, Kolwowsky?'

'We are about halfway on the roads that we know are passable. After that we have to go on foot. That's when it'll get more difficult. Especially in this weather.' He glanced at the children. 'Do you have rain covers for them?'

'Yeah, the strollers come with inbuilt weather shields. They will keep warm and dry, even if the rest of us aren't.'

'Lucky them,' commented Archer drily. She was trying not to be interested in what they were doing but Peter was doing his best to undo her boots and his little face as he concentrated was adorable.

'Okay, I'm going to call it a night. Get these two settled. Perhaps we can make it to the end of the road tomorrow and then, best foot forward and all that,' said Kira.

The next day the sun shone down gloriously. It was so nice that Archer approved having the skimmer windows down and the team enjoyed the fresh air as they travelled along. They made great time and found the end of the road easily enough. There was a huge gash in the tarmac and what followed was a mixture of large stones and rubble.

'Looks like there was some kind of landslide or something,' said Jed, looking up at the mountainous landscape. 'That will be why the satellites were reporting no access anymore.'

'Can we get past that?' Kira eyed the boulders nervously.

'Probably not, but we should be able to go around. Hopefully it won't add too much onto our journey.'

'How are you going to push that over those?' Archer asked as she pointed at the stroller and the landslide.

'It has an all-terrain setting, it won't be a problem,' retorted Kira. And she pressed a few buttons on the stroller to get it ready for movement. Large chunky tyres appeared together with shock absorbers.

'These things really are incredible,' murmured Jed.

'You can thank Ingrid, she gave us one,' Kira replied softly and squeezed her husband's hand.

Travelling across the rubble was exciting at first, a real adventure, but when the terrain didn't get any easier and it didn't look like they were making any headway, tempers grew short.

'Frag it!' exclaimed Kira as the stroller stuck, again. 'This is ridiculous!' She shoved and pushed and tried to lever the baby carrier out of whatever rut it had got jammed into, but nothing moved. She shoved harder and was rewarded with her own feet losing their balance on the rocky surface, and she almost fell. 'Would somebody fragging help me out here?' Kira yelled in frustration.

Archer tutted loudly as she turned back to help and mis-stepped, falling awkwardly to the ground. When she tried to stand her left ankle gave way immediately making her gasp with the pain.

'You are fragging kidding me!' she shouted which got everyone's attention and the others stopped clambering and turned back to help the two women.

Simmonds took out the med kit and applied a numbing shot to her wife's ankle before beginning to expertly strap it up.

'I would say rest and elevation, but I don't think you'll get much of that here.' She tried to lighten the mood but her half-joke fell on deaf ears.

'Just strap the fragging thing up so I can walk,' snapped Archer. She immediately felt guilty and pressed her forehead on Simmonds' shoulder briefly in apology. Five minutes later and she was stood up, gingerly testing her weight on her now numb ankle, held stiffly in place by a sturdy brace.

'The pain killers will last for a couple of hours, but you'll certainly feel it when they wear off. We need to set up camp soon so you can rest. There's still another days hike ahead of us.' Kolwowsky looked worried as he glanced back at Archer and forwards at the trail ahead.

Jed heaved the stroller out of the crevice it had gotten wedged into and Kira was about to apologise to Archer before she saw the women's thunderous gaze. She decided it could wait.

'What about that outcrop?' pointed Jed. The spot looked perfect for camping, but it also looked further than anyone really felt like walking.

'Looks great,' muttered Archer and she headed in that direction.

'I guess that's our campsite then.' Kolwowsky flashed a small grin at the others and followed his commander. Simmonds fell into conversation with him, leaving Kira and Jed to bring up the rear.

'I feel really bad,' Kira said to her husband in a low voice.

'It wasn't your fault. It could've happened to any of us, at any time. Still could,' replied Jed trying to make her feel better. 'Let's get to camp and then you can run around making her dinner and bringing her drinks if it makes you feel any better.'

Kira pressed her lips together in a small smile. She didn't think any of that would be appreciated it, but it might be worth a try. They plodded on up the mountainside, more cautious now than before until finally they reached the flat outcrop Jed had pointed out.

Archer's mood was even blacker than before and no-one really said anything as the camp was set up and various food pouches were rehydrated.

Kira thanked Gaia that the children were subdued and somehow tired from the journey, even though they hadn't done any walking. They went to sleep easily at their normal bedtime and Kira sadly thanked her mum for the advice she had given about setting a routine as early as possible. Wishing she was tramping up the mountain with her, Kira had a few tears in her eyes, and she went to see if there was anything she could do for Archer.

'I'm fine,' Archer said crossly as Kira approached but when she saw the tearful expression on the other woman's face, she relented. 'It wasn't your fault, could've happened to anyone.'

Kira nodded. 'Can I get you anything?'

'I'm good. Thank you.' Archer nodded brusquely and Kira half smiled before returning to her side of the campsite.

The mood remained subdued and it wasn't long before everyone had retired for the night. No-one bothered to sit around the campsite and watch the stars twinkling in the clear night sky.

'Wake-up. Wake-up, Jed. Help me with the kids, please?' Kira shook her husband a little harder than before, willing him to wake up. Peter's nappy had leaked, and the children's bedding was sodden. She hoped that when they arrived at City 50 there would be facilities to wash and dry things.

'I'm awake. I'm awake,' Jed groaned trying to open his eyes and was rewarding with an extremely wiggly Grace as Kira tried to sort out Peter with some dry clothes. By the time she had finished Jed was wide-awake and everyone wanted out of the sleeping pod.

The morning outside was crisp and clear, they could see for miles. Making sure the children were wrapped up warmly in their coats, Kira smiled as Kolwowsky brought her a cup of synth-caf.

'Thank you.'

'No problem. I have some porridge warming. They'll eat that, won't they?' he nodded towards the children.

'Yeah, should do.'

'Then we'll need to get going if we want to arrive at City 50 before dark.'

'Is it that far then?' Kira was concerned, she hadn't thought they had to walk too much further.

'It's about half a day, but with Archer's ankle and the stroller, it'll probably take longer,' replied Kolwowsky.

'Sorry,' said Kira in a small voice.

'Stop apologising and get packed up. The sooner we can move, the sooner we can get there,' said Archer, not unkindly, as she hobbled past. The drugs had worn off somewhat, but she was waiting until they were ready to move before she took anymore. She was determined to make it to the gates.

Six hours later, she did, and her mood plummeted even further when the gates to City 50 refused to open. Archer hammered on the doors loudly.

'What's going on?' asked Kira, the last to arrive at the gates, pushing and shoving the stroller in front of her. She'd been glad of it as a means of getting the children up the mountain, but she would be grateful if she never had to see it again.

'They won't open the gates,' explained Kolwowsky who was looking very nervous.

Kira spotted a small vid-screen, half hidden by some scrub. 'Have you tried this?' she asked, pushing the vegetation aside.

The screen flickered and a tinny voice issued.

'State your name and purpose for visit to City 50.'

'I am Colonel Archer of the Resistance and I demand that you open the gates!'

Kira winced at Jed; she didn't think that was likely to work.

'Request denied,' came the reply.

'WHAT?' shouted Archer. She was about to jab the screen again when Jed caught her arm.

'Let me try.'

'Why the frag would I do that? You're a civilian.'

'Yes, maybe they'll listen to me.'

Archer scowled and moved slightly out of the way so Jed could access the screen.

'Hello? This is Jed Jenkins requesting entry into City 50. I…' He was cut off by the tinny voice replying.

'Did you say Jenkins?'

'Yes.' Jed waited.

'Are you Gretchen's boy?'

Jed stared at Kira in disbelief before answering yes again.

'You'd better come in.' And with that the gates creaked open.

Archer stared at Jed in consternation. 'Who the bloody hell is Gretchen?'

'One hell of a woman,' replied Jed with a grin and started walking into City 50, closely followed by Kira and the stroller. Kolwowsky scrambled to catch up and Simmonds tugged her wife's arm to get her moving so they could all enter the city together.

Chapter Thirty-Four

Kira and Jed pushed the children's stroller through the gateway and into the corridor, the others not far behind them. They could hear footsteps hurrying towards them and Kira braced herself for whatever was coming. A short woman with olive skin and dark hair that was escaping her attempts at a bun scurried around the corner.

'Ah, you're there. Hello, welcome. Sorry. Security is tight. The 'flu has been devastating. But you're here now so come, come. Follow me.' She didn't wait to see if they were doing as she had requested, she just pivoted and hurried back the way she had come.

Archer scowled at the women's rapidly disappearing back and did her best to hobble after her as quickly as possible.

'Excuse me!' she called. 'Are you Bridget? Bridget Mulhurne? We are expected. We have an agreement.'

The woman stopped abruptly and without turning around spoke softly.

'Bridget is dead. Please, you must come with me.'

Kira's stomach sank. The woman Zac had made the agreement with was dead.

'What does that mean?' she whispered to Jed, but Archer overheard her.

'It means we need to work out a new agreement, fast.' Without waiting for them, Archer scrambled after the mystery woman, determined to find out what was going on.

They rounded a corner and were faced with a decontamination chamber.

'You understand,' the woman half-smiled apologetically. 'We can't let you in unless you've been decontaminated. On the other side you'll find clean clothes and 'flu shots. You must administer them otherwise you cannot enter the city. Alright?' She waited to see whether there would be any disagreement.

'Do you know about our agreement with City 50?' asked Archer brusquely.

'A lot of things have changed since then. The city is in flux. But we can talk about it afterwards. Please.' The woman begged with her entire demeanour.

'What's your name?' asked Kira kindly. 'I'm Kira Jenkins, and this is my husband Jed and our children Grace and Peter.'

'Monique. My name's Monique but please, you must decontaminate before I can talk to you any further.' And she cast one last desperate glance at them before stepping through a side door which locked with an audible click behind her.

'I guess we decontaminate then,' said Jed. 'What do we do?'

A voice crackled through speakers that were located above the door Monique had walked through.

'Walk through the double doors and listen to the instructions. One at a time, please.'

'I'm going first,' snarled Archer and she pushed through the doors without waiting to hear what anyone else thought.

'Kolwowsky, you go second and sort out the 'flu shots on the other side. Simmonds you follow and I'll bring up the rear. You go before me with the children, Kira – is that alright? Can you manage?'

'Yes, we'll be fine.'

No-one said anything else while they each waited their turn to go through the decontamination chamber. Kira wondered where they had unearthed this kind of technology from but remembered that City 50 was meant to be the pinnacle of all of New Corp's research science and technology plus everything the planet's history had to offer. She guessed they had access to all the archive material plus the intelligent minds needed to put it all together.

As she walked through the double doors, pushing the stroller in front of her, Kira was struck by how clinical it smelt within. There was a huge gush of air and smoke, which made her cough a little and startled the children enough to make them cry. Kira bent down to them both and gave them a hug, murmuring words of comfort. She became aware of a blue glow and glanced up to see if it was part of the process.

Gaia stood before her, smaller and more transparent than she'd ever looked before but with the same sad smile. She lifted her hand,

and it seemed to coalesce into something more solid and once it was fully materialised, the goddess gently reached out and touched each child with a finger, sending a golden glow briefly through them.

'Are we safe?' whispered Kira.

Gaia smiled at her and then looked down at the children. Kira followed her gaze and somehow knew Grace and Peter would be fine against the 'flu or any other illness that might be lurking within City 50.

'Thank you,' she said, raising her head to look at Gaia but the goddess was gone and the doors on the other side were opening.

Kolwowsky beckoned her to come through, armed with the 'flu shot.

'The children don't need it,' Kira said in a daze, not entirely sure what to make of what happened.

Kolwowsky took no notice and administered it to them anyway. 'Better to be on the safe side,' he said chirpily.

Jed joined them, and once he'd been inoculated, Monique reappeared. This time with a more welcoming look on her face.

'Thank you. We can't be too careful. You know how it is. If you will follow me?'

'Where to this time?' asked Archer. 'I want some answers.'

'I'm going to take you to the city council, there's not many of us left after the epidemic but there's someone who wants to talk to you. Well, one of you anyway.' Monique darted a glance at Jed but said nothing else.

'And does this so-called council have the power to reinstate our agreement with City 50?' demanded Archer.

'It does. If you have anything worth bringing us.' Monique gestured to the open door, effectively cutting off the opportunity for more conversation.

A steadying arm from Simmonds prevented Archer from saying anymore, but she wasn't happy and muttered under her breath about jumped up council members with no authority all the way to the room Monique was taking them.

Monique ushered them into the small meeting room where three people sat waiting for them. A smiling man, a very timid looking woman who nervously adjusted her spectacles and a young girl who looked barely out of her teenage years.

'Here they are,' she said. 'This is Jed Jenkins.' And she pointed at him.

The man leapt up and grabbed Jed's hand, shaking it enthusiastically. He was entirely bald but maintained a neat goatee and put Jed immediately at ease with his cheerful manner.

'So pleased to meet you.' He turned to Kira. 'And you must be Kira, and here are the children. Such poppets. I'm Richard. I'm one of the people sort of in charge after everything that happened.'

'I'm Colonel Archer, this is Captain Simmonds and Lieutenant Kolwowsky from the Resistance. We had an agreement in place with Bridget Mulherne. I understand you can ratify that agreement?' Archer wasted no time in getting down to business.

'We can. If, of course, you can bring us anything of value,' replied the teenage girl.

Archer stiffened and was about to reply until Jed cut across her.

'We do, but first let's finish the introductions and find out how you know who I, who we, are?' He pointed at his wife and flashed a smile at the two women sat across the table.

'I'm Liss. I'm the oldest of the children left. I speak for them,' replied the teenage girl.

'And I'm Olive. I represent the women and the elder residents. The ones who survived the 'flu, that is,' said the older woman in a quiet voice.

'As I said, I'm Richard. I represent the men and the workforce. I speak with the authority of New Corp although…' he scratched behind his ear and glanced at the others before continuing. 'Although New Corp seem to have disappeared.'

'Disappeared? What do you mean?' interrupted Archer.

'They were supposed to come here. The people in charge. They left City 42 but there was a big storm at sea and the plane went down. All lives lost. We're what's left.' Richard coughed nervously.

'Who was supposed to come here? And you still haven't told us how you know who we are?' asked Jed before Archer could say anything else. She glared daggers at him.

'Bridget, you know Bridget, she was friends with your mother, Gretchen. She sent a message over there to let Gretchen know about the 'flu and to request help only she never survived to get the reply.'

'She knew my mother?' Jed was surprised. He'd never considered the possibility that his mother really knew anyone important at all.

'Yes. It was Gretchen who told us about the high-ranking officials leaving the island and coming here. We were able to monitor their flight until the storm hit. Sad, really.'

'Not especially,' commented Archer. 'Do you mean to say that an incredibly convenient storm wiped out the board of directors from New Corp and there's nobody left to challenge that authority?'

'Well... yes.' Richard walked over to the wall and tapped the vid-screen. A map of the region appeared. The landmass shown started to shrink as the water levels rose rapidly. 'You are aware of the current situation, aren't you? That's why you're here, isn't it?. To get away from the rising sea level. Although, I rather thought there would be a few more of you.'

'We're the advance party,' commented Archer sourly. 'And yes, we are aware of the imminent environmental disaster. It's why we've left our base and travelled here. Why General Ridgely made the agreement with Mulherne to settle our people here.'

'So you are bringing the AIs then?' asked Liss eagerly.

'And the seed bank?' queried Olive.

'We are. Provided there is a place for our people here.' Archer tilted her chin in challenge at the delegates from City 50.

'How many of you are there?' asked Richard.

'About five hundred plus the people from City 42 and City 9. If they come.'

'What do you mean if they come?' Olive asked, pushing her glasses up her nose.

This time Jed answered. 'We've sent a delegation over to the island to see whether the people want to come back with us. To come to safety. We didn't want to leave anyone behind.' He paused briefly. 'So, my mother. Are you still in touch with her? Is she alright? Can I speak with her?'

'Ah, we've lost connection with the Governor's office, but have no fear, your mother is one of the most capable women I've ever met. I have no doubt that she has a plan a foot.' Richard smiled but it didn't quite mask the worry in his eyes.

'Sorry, Governor?' asked Kira.

'Oh yes, Gretchen was made Governor after New Corp took back control. She kept a steady hand on things over there.'

Archer interrupted again. 'So are you New Corp or aren't you?'

'Not really,' said Olive, glancing at the others. 'We're sort of what's left.'

'And why are you so divided? Representing the men, the women, the children?' asked Kira. She felt uneasy at those divisions.

'It just sort of happened. When we realised that people were dropping like flies, we set up chains of command for those that were left and it sort of devolved into what you see now,' replied Richard.

'How long have you had the epidemic?' asked Kira.

Richard glanced at the others for confirmation. 'About six months?' They nodded. 'About six months, all in. It came in waves.' He coughed nervously. 'It's been devastating really. Truly devastating.'

'Is it under control now?' Kira was worried.

'Oh yes,' Monique replied. She had stayed quiet in deference to the council leaders. 'I'm in admin. I keep an eye on the numbers and things. We haven't had a 'flu related death in nearly two weeks.'

Kira clutched the stroller handle tighter. That didn't fill her with much confidence. She bent down slightly to check on the children. They were oddly quiet.

'We have an agreement then. Our people can come and settle here, in City 50. We share the AI technology and our seed bank with you while you provide homes, jobs, medicine for us. The deal General Ridgely and Bridget Mulherne made.' Archer was keen to clarify an agreement had been made.

'Any objections?' Richard asked the others from City 50. They both shook their heads. 'We are agreed. Do we shake on it?' He was feeling relieved that new technology and a new food source would be coming, plus an influx of new, healthy people.

Archer held out a hand stiffly and Richard shook it vigorously.

'Should I draw up an agreement for everyone to sign?' asked Monique.

'I think that would be an excellent idea,' replied Jed.

'Can we get access to a communications array?' asked Archer. She was keen to get on with the mission. 'I want to update our teams and get things moving from the base, get our people up here.

'I'll show you,' said Liss and she bounced up from the chair. Simmonds fell in behind Archer, motioning Kolwowsky to stay put.

Both soldiers been quiet during the exchange, adhering to the chain of command, but as soon as Archer left the room, Kolwowsky had his own questions for Monique about how she was running the city and the procedures she had in place. Kira smiled fondly as she watched the two of them, heads together, discussing the different ways they handled large groups of people.

'Could we have somewhere to freshen up? To feed the children?' Jed asked Richard.

'Yes, of course! Follow me, we'll get you some food and drink, get you settled in. Show you round. Whatever you want,' replied Richard eagerly.

Kira smiled at Olive who returned it tentatively and half waved as the family left the room. Kira was both curious and apprehensive at what they would see.

Chapter Thirty-Five

'How is the AI move coming along?' asked Max as he, Ash, Bennett, Dr Glover and Lieutenant Yarrow met for their daily meeting. It had been Max's idea that they check in regularly with their progress so any problems could be dealt with as soon as they occurred.

'I can't prevent the memory loss. We've been able to create transportable drives for all the AIs and their function will be unaffected, but they won't remember previous actions they have carried out. The longer they're being transported the greater the memory loss,' replied Glover.

'Is that really an issue though?' Bennett wasn't bothered about the loss of memory. As far as she was concerned the AIs could stay at the base.

'What if it affects their ability to carry out the tasks they were designed for? Is that likely?' asked Max.

'No, their base programming won't be affected. They might not remember having carried out the task before though.'

Bennett interrupted. 'So why are we worried about the memory loss then? Seems pointless.'

Glover huffed at her. 'Because, the AIs are designed to learn as they carry out their tasks. They adapt to their workload and user interfaces coming up with unique solutions.'

'Or new ways to destroy my plants,' muttered Bennett, but the only one who heard her was Max and he smothered a smile.

'The real question is when we download them. I really think we should wait until the last minute and there is the question of order – which AI should be left online until the last possible moment?' Ash looked around at the others. 'What do you think?'

'Surely Frank should be last. He's in charge of all the stores and keeping track of our supplies, we'll need him right up until the last moment,' suggested Max.

'No, Layla should be last. She's the one plugged into the most systems. She will be the one to warn us if anything goes wrong or if there's an external attack. She monitors the perimeter as well as holding all the plans for our tech if something should go wrong. We leave her to last.' Glover was adamant.

'Can you not download both of them last?' Ash couldn't really see the problem.

'Does it even matter?' asked Bennett. 'The important thing is my plants; we need more manpower to help with the transport. Have we heard back from the team that went to City 50? Are they going to let us in?'

'Yes, it does matter, Bennett. My AIs are extremely intricate pieces of technology that are guaranteeing us a place in City 50. Without them we wouldn't get in the gates,' retorted Glover.

'Can't eat 'em though, can you? It's my seed bank that'll get us in.'

'Ahem!' It was Ash. 'We have had a communique from Archer. They've arrived safely and things aren't exactly what they expected. It seems the city was hit hard with the 'flu and they've lost about fifty per cent of the population. They're grateful to have us. The seeds and the tech are more a bonus than a deal breaker, from what Archer said.'

'Any word from the team that went back?' Max tried and failed to hide his worry.

'Nothing yet, but I'm sure they're okay. Artem will look after them.'

'What about New Corp? Are they in control in 50 or what?' Bennett scowled at Ash.

'Apparently not.'

There was a brief silence as everyone digested that piece of news.

'Just going back to your manpower issue, Bennett, the people in G-block are refusing to leave so…'

Bennett interrupted. 'I'm not leaving any plants behind.'

'No, and I'm not leaving an AI or any tech. We're taking everything with us. They're fools to stay behind.' For once Glover and Bennett agreed on something.

'Be that as it may, I thought if we asked them to help on a project, it might encourage them to change their minds. I'm going to assign them over to Allotment but don't give them a hard time about not wanting to leave, Bennett. This is scary stuff.'

Bennett nodded briefly then stood. 'If there's nothing else?'

The others shook their heads and watched as the feisty gardener left the room.

'I still think Layla should be last for download,' Glover said quietly.

'Oh, for frag's sake, sis! We can do Frank AND Layla last. Stop being difficult.' Ash was semi-serious.

Glover blinked at him in surprise and then half smiled.

'Now that we know we are welcome in City 50, I can't see any reason to delay things,' said Max. 'I think we should start the move.'

The mood of the room shifted.

'Are we really doing this?' asked Ash.

Max nodded and sighed. 'If I take G-block over to Allotment, I'll give Bennett the nod to start moving. She's ready and it'll be better for her to go first. She can take all the people not assigned to a specific job with her -that'll give her all the manpower she'll need.'

'And it will encourage the others to get their arses in gear, I like it!' Glover was grinning. 'Speaking of which, I'd better make sure all the technicians are packed up. They do a bit, then get distracted by a new idea and end up unpacking everything to find a particular part.'

'You're awfully quiet, Yarrow. Anything to report?' asked Max.

'Peacekeepers are ready to move, Sir.' He didn't salute, but it was implied by his tone.

'Okay, good. Let's split the peacekeepers up and get a group of techies, plants and residents moving together with a couple of peacekeepers. Actually, that's probably something Layla could put together for us.' Max turned to Glover.

You are correct, Dr Carter. List created.

There was a ping on everyone's handhelds and indeed, the lists had been created. Max had a quick scroll through.

'Looks good to me, everyone happy?'

There were nods and a *Yes, Sir* from Yarrow.

'Let's get it done then.' Max scratched his head. 'Feels a bit odd, doesn't it? An anti-climax almost.'

'I don't think it's really sunk in for a lot of people. It'll be real now and we might find there's more resistance to the move. Maybe I could come and do the rounds with you, Max? Help ease some worries,' suggested Ash.

'That would be great. I'm doing A, B and C block this morning, if you're up for it?'

Ash nodded and the two men stood, closely followed by Yarrow and Glover.

'Unless there are any disasters, let's check in tomorrow first thing,' said Max and after waiting for confirmation from the others, he and Ash left the room, headed to A-Block.

Chapter Thirty-Six

'Do you think we can trust Artem?' Dina asked Martha quietly. They were sitting together on Artem's plane, travelling back to the island.

Martha glanced at Hernandez before replying. He wasn't paying them any attention.

'I think so. I mean, why would we not?'

Dina sighed.

'His complex was blown up as we left – how do we know it was New Corp? That's just what Artem said.'

Martha's eyes were wide in disbelief.

'You cannot be seriously considering that Artem blew up his complex himself. Ruth and Sarah were there. He would not,' she whispered. 'He could not. He was overjoyed to see her again. And killing a child knowingly… no, I do not believe he is capable of that.'

Dina twisted her hands around in her lap.

'Yeah, okay so maybe not that but… I dunno, something is a bit… off. Don't you think?'

Martha was shaking her head.

'You cannot look for conspiracies everywhere you go, Dina. He has been a good friend to us. He helped look after Kira when she was struggling with her grief, and Jed does not have a bad word to say about him. Unless you have solid proof of something, I think you need to let this go.' Martha said sternly.

Flushing Dina nodded, unwilling to say anymore. She still had her niggle, but she was hoping it was just paranoia sending her into suspicious overdrive.

'Attention. Seatbelts, please. We're coming into land.' Artem's voice crackled over the intercom and all the passengers complied. They could see the remains of the compound out of the window. It was mostly rubble with the odd half wall here and there. Nature was already taking over in a couple of places as the plants from the garden were spreading.

The plane came into land easily. Artem's runway had been untouched by the destruction. He ducked out of the cockpit, followed by Zac.

'I go, very quick. Back very soon.' And he didn't wait for a response. They all watched him exit the plane.

'Should one of us go with him?' asked Martha.

Zac shook his head.

'He wants to get some tech that was in the safe room. He won't be long.'

'I don't care what he's going in for. I'm going too.' And before anyone could stop her, Dina had leapt out of her seat and quickly darted out of the plane.

'Frag!' exclaimed Martha, as she fumbled with her belt and in her haste, scared Lucas who began to cry.

'Relax, I'll go after her,' offered Zac.

'No! Wait for us. We are coming.' Martha had managed to get out of her seat and picked up Lucas and was manhandling the travel cube up the aisle, ready to expand it outside. 'Come on, let's get after her.'

There was no sign of Artem, but Martha could see Dina's blonde head bobbing about.

'What is she doing?' muttered Martha.

'She's checking the bodies,' replied Zac and offered her a small smile of comfort.

Martha increased her pace to try and catch up with her friend when she saw her head bob down and not come back up again.

'Dina? Dina?' Martha called.

'Here. I'm here.'

Skirting a pile of rubble, Martha stopped short as she took in the scene. Dina was kneeling on the floor in front of some charred remains. There was nothing to identify who the person had been apart from a smaller, blackened skeleton within its arms.

'Oh,' exclaimed Martha softly and felt her legs go weak. She dropped down to join Dina, oblivious to Lucas and Zac nearby. She didn't make a sound as tears rolled down her face.

Dina found her hand and clung to it.

'I want to bury them,' she said quietly.

'I'll go find some shovels,' Zac offered and hurried off in the direction of the gardener's shed, or at least where he thought the gardener's shed had been. A quick search and miraculously it was still standing. He pulled the door open and was relieved to find a couple of shovels. He grabbed them quickly and hurried back to the women.

When he got there, Artem had arrived and was stood, stock still, all colour drained from his face. He looked up at Zac's arrival.

'I thought… I thought… there was safe room and… I hoped…' He couldn't say anymore but noticed the shovels in Zac's hand. 'I dig.' And he held out a hand.

Dina leapt up and grabbed the other shovel from Zac's hand, glaring at him so fiercely he didn't voice any objections.

Artem had started digging and Dina got stuck in. The two of them made it look like a competition as to who could dig faster. It didn't take long for a grave to be dug. Both of them stood panting heavily, leaning on their shovels.

Martha motioned Zac to stay back and she gingerly picked up the skeletons. They were brittle but thankfully didn't break apart and she was able to lower them into the earth.

'Flowers,' Dina said abruptly. 'They need flowers.'

Everyone began looking and easily found patches of wildflowers nearby. Soon the two skeletons were wreathed in blooms that by rights shouldn't have been there that time of year.

'Gaia's touch,' murmured Martha and Dina nodded in agreement.

Artem and Dina shovelled the earth back into the ground, slower this time and with audible sobs and visible shoulder shakes from both of them.

'Do you want to say anything?' Martha asked the two of them.

'She was my friend; my family; she didn't deserve this.' Dina wanted to say more but her voice broke and she shook her head, unable to continue.

'My Ruthie,' rumbled Artem, tears coursing down his cheeks. 'Is too much.' Abruptly he walked away, shoulders bowed in grief.

'May Gaia hold you in her heart and grant you peace,' whispered Martha. She bent to touch the soil with one hand. A tear splashed down and a small shoot sprang out of the ground. It grew into a small, thorny bush and bloomed into white roses. A bee came out of nowhere and alighted on one of the flowers briefly before buzzing away.

'Wow,' breathed Zac. 'That was…'

'Gaia,' finished Martha.

Dina touched a petal with one finger and then turned away from the grave. She looked pale and had a dirty mark on one cheek.

'Are you okay?' Martha asked.

'No. But we need to go before anyone realises we're here.' Dina squared her shoulders and took a deep, shuddering breath. 'I miss her.'

'We all do,' Martha replied, her voice cracking, and she pulled the younger woman into a hug. They clung to each other for a few moments before Lucas started calling for his mum-mum. 'Come on,' Martha sniffed loudly and wiped her face with her hands. 'Let's go.'

Dina nodded and shoved her hands into her pockets. She wished Max were here.

Back at the plane, a very subdued Artem was waiting for them.

'9 or 42?' he asked.

'I think we should go to 42 first. We know the city and we stand a better chance of convincing the citizens of City 9 to come with us if we have City 42 behind us,' replied Martha.

'Da. We go.' The Russian didn't wait for any further communication and climbed into the plane and through to the cockpit.

The others hurried to get on board as the engines whirred into life.

'Is there even an airstrip near the city?' Dina asked Martha.

'No, but there is plenty of flat land. Artem should not have any problem finding somewhere.'

'What are we going to do when we get there?'

'Hope.' Martha's face was grim. She was determined to save as many people as she could and find justice for Ruth and Sarah's killers. Someone was going to pay.

Chapter Thirty-Seven

Artem landed the plane on some flat ground outside the City 42. They walked through the city gates in silence, Martha pushing Lucas in his stroller. The gates were open, which she took as a good sign, but her hopes were soon dashed as an armed drone flew around the street corner and aimed its lasers on them. She immediately activated the protection dome on the stroller and stood in front of her child.

You are in violation of sector 17. Lay down your weapons immediately.

Before any of them could comply, they heard the stomp, stomp, stomp of swiftly approaching feet and a squad of New Corp Security came barrelling around the corner, their lasers pointing at the group.

'I demand to see whoever is in charge,' said Martha trying to sound braver than she felt. Instantly multiple laser sights focused on her and her alone.

'You will lay down your weapons and prepare to be searched,' barked the voice of one of the security detail.

Martha nodded and held her arms up. She wasn't carrying a weapon anyway. The others hesitated briefly then complied, even Artem. A swift search took away all their weapons and communications devices then everyone was magno-bound with their hands behind their backs.

'You need to release me so I can push my child's stroller.' Martha's panic rose. Lucas wasn't crying yet, he was too shocked, but it wouldn't be long before all the strange people and noises caused him to wail loudly.

'Take the child,' ordered one of the men.

'NO!' shouted Martha and struggled with her bound hands.

'If you touch one hair on the head of that child, I will fragging kill you!' It was Zac, speaking with such deadly menace that he stopped the guard from moving towards Lucas.

'Please. Let me push him,' begged Martha.

'Fine. Hook her to the stroller and round them up!' barked the man in charge. One of the security officers undid Martha's magno-binders and cuffed her to the stroller. She gave a shaky yet grateful smile to Zac, relieved that no-one had taken her baby away. She left the shield in place.

Lucas cast a worried look at his mummy and began sucking his pacifier in comfort, looking wide-eyed at everyone and everything around him.

The group were hustled into the middle of a ring of security guards and frog-marched through the city. The drone followed them the entire way.

They were taken to Corporation Towers, where the governor offices were still located, ushered into a room with one desk and one chair and left alone, the magno-binders still attached.

Martha released the protective shield from the stroller and managed to lift her son out, with her free arm, for a hug, whispering words of comfort to him.

'This isn't exactly what I was expecting,' said Zac.

'No? It's exactly what I thought would happen,' replied Dina, gloomily. She flinched as the door banged open and Sean came through.

Martha lifted her chin, prepared for whatever venom her former member of staff was about to spew, but he ignored her completely and instead walked over to Artem.

'Misner! Good to see you. Let's get you out of these. Come on, the Governor wants a report.'

The others looked on in shock as Artem's magno-binders were unlocked and he wordlessly followed Sean out of the room.

'What the frag?' exploded Dina. She rounded on Zac and Martha. 'I told you we couldn't trust that fragging Russian!' But she stopped venting when she registered the shocked looks on both their faces.

Lucas began crying. His auntie had scared him.

'Oh, I'm sorry, little man. It's okay,' Dina said as she tried to comfort him.

'All this time,' whispered Zac. He sat heavily in the only chair; disbelief etched all over his face.

Martha started pacing, jigging Lucas as she walked.

'At least we know one thing,' she said.

'What?' asked Dina bitterly.

'Sean's not in charge.'

Dina shrugged. That didn't seem to make much of a difference at the moment.

The door banged open again and this time someone none of them knew scurried in with keys to the magno-binders, and behind them came Gretchen Jenkins, looking as elegant and immaculate as always.

'Martha, good to see you. I must apologise for Sean. He should have released all of you.'

'Gretchen. Are you… are you in charge?' Martha was the first to speak.

Gretchen patted her hair before replying.

'As much as there's anything to be in charge of. Come. We have a lot to discuss.' She swept out of the room, not waiting to see if the four of them followed her.

'Hernandez, keep your eyes and ears open,' muttered Zac to the soldier. They might not have their weapons, but they were far from defenceless.

'Where are we going?' wondered Dina.

'Looks like we're heading to the main meeting room. This should be interesting.'

Martha was right. Gretchen pushed open a door leading to the meeting room and strode inside. The others hurried to follow her. Martha slowed when she saw Artem and Sean in the room, chatting quietly over synth-caf. She chose to ignore them both and sat down on the opposite side of the room from them, getting Lucas comfortable in her lap.

'Let me start by apologising again for the manner in which you were greeted when you arrived at the city. Things have been in flux lately. Allow me to formally introduce myself to those who don't know me. I am Gretchen Jenkins, current governor to City 42. You probably know me as Jed's mother.' She paused. 'If you would?'

Martha spoke for all of them.

'You know me and my son, Lucas. This is Dina Grey, my friend and former citizen of City 42. This is General Zac Ridgely and Lieutenant Hernandez of the Resistance. Apparently, you already know Artem.' She refused to look in his direction.

'Why are you here?' Gretchen wasted no time in getting down to business.

'You know about the imminent environmental crisis?' Martha asked.

Gretchen nodded impatiently.

'We're here to offer the hand of peace and the chance to travel to a safe place, City 50.'

Sean made a loud scoffing noise.

'City 50 is plagued with the 'flu. There are no survivors.'

'You should check your facts, Sean. The city has lost half its population and has agreed to take in anyone and everyone who can travel there before the water level rises.' Martha still refused to look at him.

'How do you know that?'

'We have been in communication with a team of people we sent to City 50,' replied Martha, trying to stay calm.

'Is Bridget safe?' Gretchen asked in concern. She'd been unable to raise the woman after receiving her emergency message.

'She did not survive the 'flu. I'm sorry.'

'My son? My grandchildren?'

Relieved to have better news, Martha smiled. 'Yes. Jed, Kira and the children are all safe. They are in City 50 waiting for us, and for you, to join them.'

'How are we going to get there?' Gretchen pointed out of the window. 'We don't exactly have a lot of suitable transport.'

'Artem has a plane. It can carry about fifty people. The rest will have to travel down to City 9. We know they have ships in their harbour, we should be able to mobilise some of them across the water,' Martha explained.

'And then?'

'And then they have to walk. But it is only a few day's journey…'

Sean interrupted before Martha could carry on.

'Only a few days? Is it even safe to be walking about out there? What about radiation levels?' He glanced at Gretchen. 'Surely it's safer for us to stay here. Ride it out.'

'Ride what out? The entire planet's oceans rising to cover most of this island's land mass? How exactly do you plan to ride that out?' Dina was incredulous.

'Is no matter. They want to stay, let them. I want to know one thing.' Artem's tone was quiet yet commanding. Everyone in the room noted the veiled threat behind his words. Everyone apart from Sean.

'And what is that, Misner?' Sean was dismissive.

'Who pushed button on destruction of complex?'

'Those decisions were made by Clarity Jones, head of New Corp. But she's already left. She and her cronies took the only plane available and left the rest of us here.'

'She gave order but who pressed button?'

'Look, I don't like your tone, Misner. You've been paid well for sharing information from your communications array.'

'Who. Pressed. Button?'

Sean took a step back.

'Me, alright. I pressed the button, but I was only following orders. It's Clarity who's really at fault.'

Before anyone else had chance to respond, Artem reached out with both arms and broke Sean's neck. As the man fell dead to the floor there were audible gasps around the room. A New Corp Security guard made to get out his weapon, but Gretchen stopped him.

'Stand down!' She then addressed Artem directly. 'Feel better?'

The Russian nodded.

'I trust the rest of our necks are safe?'

'Da. It was for my Ruthie and Sarah.'

Gretchen continued in a softer tone.

'I did hear about the aftermath. I am terribly sorry for your loss. It was a tragedy that should never have happened.'

Artem merely nodded.

Zac had moved into a protective position in front of Martha, Lucas and Dina while Hernandez was covering the other security guard.

'I have a list of vital community members I'd like to see on that plane,' said Gretchen.

'When you say vital, who does that cover?' Martha was shaken but tried to focus on the task in front of her.

'Medics, technicians and of course the babies from the labs and their carer's. I don't think they should have to trek down to City 9.'

'No, they shouldn't,' agreed Dina. 'But you ought to send a couple of medical staff with those travelling to 9, in case of any disasters.'

'And I think you should come with us, you and your husband,' said Martha. 'I know Jed would like to see you both safe.'

'Quite. I forget, does Kira have any family left in the city?'

'No.' Martha paused. 'They also died in the compound attack.'

Gretchen put a hand to her mouth. She didn't travel in the same social circles as Kira's parents and never had much to do with them outside of family events, but she had liked Jean and Malcolm. Now she would never get to know them any better.

'We should get to work,' said Zac. 'We don't have much time.'

'Yes. Agreed. This is the list for the plane.' Gretchen tapped a few keys on her handheld and the file was sent over to everyone in the room.

Now that they were back in City 42, they were automatically re-connected to the sweeps and message system.

'I think you should round those people up while I send out a sweep to everyone else to meet in Main Square in an hour. Then I can tell them happens next.' Gretchen cast an eye over the room. 'Shall we meet back at your plane in two hours?'

'How do you know where the plane is?' asked Dina.

'I am not without my resources. But don't worry, the rest of the city have no idea. You won't be bombarded with additional passengers.'

'Provided nobody talks,' muttered Dina but everyone else either didn't hear her or chose to ignore her.

There was a general bustling as people got ready to do what they needed to do until Dina suddenly cried out in alarm.

'What? What is it?' asked Zac.

'Camp Eden! We almost forgot Camp Eden. We have to go get Moham and the others. They have to be on the plane. For Max and the plants.'

'Okay. Take a skimmer, get out there and round them up and meet back at the plane. Do you feel comfortable doing that?' Martha waited for Dina to nod her agreement before she turned to Zac and Hernandez. 'I think we should go together. Nobody knows who you are. I used to be their governor. We stand a slightly better chance of people listening to me.'

There were nods all around.

'What about me?' asked Artem.

'I can use you in the square. People will panic, you can help comfort them.' Gretchen was almost smiling as she spoke, and he nodded in agreement. 'We meet back at the plane in two hours. Good luck.'

Chapter Thirty-Eight

Dina arrived back to the plane first. Her skimmer was full with Moham, the other scientists from Camp Eden, and as much equipment and food that they could squeeze in. It had been a wrench to leave the beautiful orchard behind, but they didn't have the time to remove the trees.

There was excited chatter as the Camp Eden team ferried their stuff onto the plane. Dina tried not to worry but she was keeping an eye out for Martha and the others, hoping they would turn up at any moment.

Eventually, Martha, Zac, Hernandez and about thirty people came walking into view. They were all carrying multiple boxes and bags.

'Will we have enough room for all this equipment?' Dina asked Martha as they drew closer.

'It should fit in the hold. Provided we secure it properly, it won't be a problem,' replied Zac. 'Is Artem back?'

'No, he and Gretchen haven't turned up yet.' Dina cast an eye over all the people milling about. 'I think we should get everyone loaded up as quickly as possible. If anyone from the city happens to come this way, it's going to be pretty obvious what's happening, and the plane only has limited space.'

Zac began organising people, getting them to put their non-essential things in the hold where Hernandez was carefully securing everything, and then directing people to board the plane. Martha acted as air-stewardess making sure everyone got a seat while Dina scurried around helping people find lost items and reassuring them about the journey ahead.

Soon everyone was boarded and all they could do was wait. It was now half an hour after the agreed two-hour meeting time. Zac, Martha and Dina were huddled in the doorway of the plane, scanning the horizon for any sign of Artem or Gretchen. Hernandez was already seated inside.

A moving speck appeared in the distance.

'I think that is them,' said Martha.

'I'll get the pre-flight checks done,' said Zac. 'In case we have to make a quick getaway.' And he ducked back inside the plane, heading for the cockpit.

Dina squinted. 'It doesn't look like they were followed by anyone. I can only see one skimmer.'

'That's something, then.'

The skimmer pulled up to the side of the plane and Artem bounded out. He ran up the stairs, flashed a smile at the two women before heading for the cockpit.

Gretchen got out of the skimmer and stood at the base of the steps; her hands folded in front of her.

'How did it go?' called Martha.

'There was general panic, as expected, but the majority of citizens understand that, for their own safety, they need to leave the island.'

'No-one is staying behind?'

'No.'

Martha frowned. 'There is a but, isn't there?'

Gretchen sighed and nodded. She glanced back at the city in the distance.

'The people wanted guarantees, so I and my husband will be travelling with them.'

'You can't! What about your safety? What about Jed and your family?' Dina was really surprised. She hadn't expected this.

'I am the leader of City 42. I must lead by example. My son will understand that.' Gretchen sniffed. 'And anyway, if I can't trust the journey to be safe – how can I expect anyone else to make it?'

Martha was nodding.

'It makes sense. I just wish there were another way.'

'Believe me, so do I. But I know people in City 9. People with some influence. Perhaps I can help convince them to leave with us.'

'What if they do not want to leave?' asked Martha.

Gretchen shrugged slightly.

'Then we must wish them well and leave them behind. There is enough room for everyone on the boat, but we don't have the luxury of weeks to convince people.'

'Is there a boat available then?'

'Da.' It was Artem. He made Dina jump when he spoke which made him chuckle. 'Is okay. I have boat.'

'Of course you do,' remarked Martha wryly.

'I sail boat. Bring people to 50. Is no problem.'

'But what about the plane? Who's going to fly the plane?' Dina asked in a panic. 'We can't wait for you to come back, can we?'

Artem pushed himself gently past the women standing in the doorway and joined Gretchen at the foot of the steps.

'I'm flying the plane,' said Zac, making Dina jump again as he spoke from behind her.

'Do you know how?' asked Martha in surprise.

'I do. I've flown a little here and there, but this will be my first proper flight on my own.' Zac was pale but resolute.

'Frag's sake,' whispered Dina.

There was an uncomfortable silence before Gretchen clapped her hands.

Dina jumped yet again, making the others smile.

'Sorry,' she grinned in embarrassment. 'I guess I'm feeling nervous.'

'There's no point in dithering. You should all return to your base camp and we should get the city ready to leave.'

'You will keep in touch? Let us know how you're getting on?' asked Martha, coming down the steps, the others following her.

'Of course. I look forward to seeing you all in City 50. We won't be far behind you. There's no time to lose.' Gretchen leaned forward and gave Martha a stiff hug before waving the others goodbye and heading back to the skimmer.

Artem was less restrained. He bearhugged them all.

'Safe travels, my friends. I will see you on the other side.'

Dina watched him hurry over to the skimmer.

'It feels like we might never see them again,' she said in a small voice.

Martha gave her a quick hug around the shoulders.

'Do not think like that. We will all be together again soon. Come on, it is time to go.'

Dina sat with Hernandez, who had saved them a couple of seats, and was tickling Lucas making him giggle.

'Are you sure you can handle this?' Martha asked Zac.

'Honestly? I don't think I've ever been this scared before in my entire life.'

'Do you want me to sit with you?'

Zac smiled at her. 'That would be amazing. Thank you.' He leant forward and gave her a gentle kiss on the cheek before going through to the cockpit.

Martha blushed a little and darted a glance at Dina, who had been watching. She gave Martha a thumbs up making her blush even more.

Chapter Thirty-Nine

The flight back to the Resistance base was uneventful. Lucas slept and many of the passengers dozed or sat absorbed by their own thoughts. Dina was the first person off the plane, and she dashed into Max's waiting embrace.

'I missed you,' he said as he held her tight. 'Are you alright?'

'Yeah, missed you too, but look who I brought.'

She stood back proudly and smiled as Max greeted his old team of scientists from Camp Eden. Moham took both of Dina's hands in his own.

'Thank you for coming back for us,' he said.

'Oh, Moham! I'm so glad you're with us.'

Zac was next off the plane.

'Everything alright, Max?'

'We're getting there. Shall we go to your office and I can catch you up?'

'Sounds good to me.' Zac glanced behind him. 'Where do you want everyone to go?'

Max looked back at the large group of people disembarking.

'Better send them to the mess hall. There's refreshments available and Layla can assign them to one of the remaining groups ready for travel.'

'Remaining?' Zac frowned. 'Have people already gone?'

'Let's talk in your office.' Max smiled briefly and led the way, Dina happily chatting next to him.

'Hernandez!' Zac called and his lieutenant hurried over. 'Get everyone into the mess hall, see that they have something to eat and drink and wait for me there. I'll come brief everyone soon.'

The base was quiet as they walked through to Zac's office. Although it had never been exactly teeming with people, now they didn't see a single person on the way. Zac was buzzing with questions by the time they arrived at the room and sat down.

'Where is everyone?' he asked just as Max also spoke.

'Where's Artem?'

Before either man could reply, Ash came dashing through the door.

'Sorry, sorry. I missed you at the airstrip. Hi, hi everyone. Where's Artem?'

That made Zac laugh as the others called out hellos to Ash.

'Look, why don't you go first. Then we'll report in,' he suggested, taking a seat.

Lucas was still asleep. Martha held him close as she sat and smiled at Max, waiting to hear what he had to say. Dina sat with her, grinning at her fiancée. Ash took the last chair in the room, ready to chip in if Max needed him to.

Max ran a hand through is hair as he thought about where to begin.

'Have you had any contact with the others?' he asked.

'Briefly,' replied Martha. 'We know they made it to City 50 but that the city has been plagued with 'flu and that the contact, Bridget has died.'

'Yes, she has. The survivors wouldn't let them in initially until they realised it was Jed Jenkins at the gates. Apparently, his mother has some influence in New Corp?'

Martha smiled.

'You could say that.'

'Right, well, they got in to find out that half the city has been lost to a virulent strain of the 'flu. Those that were left were relieved to see them. Sadly, as you know, Bridget Mulherne, the person Zac made the initial agreement with, didn't make it but the people in charge knew the details and Archer has ensured a new agreement has been drawn up, signed and ratified.'

'We have somewhere to go.' Zac sounded relieved.

'Yes. And they are very keen to share the AI and the seed bank. Everyone who arrives has to be inoculated against the 'flu, but I can't see that being a problem.'

There were murmurs of agreement in the room.

'So who's already gone?' asked Zac.

'Almost everyone. Bennett was first with her plants and all non-essential people to help her transport everything. They've safely arrived, and I believe she's telling City 50 exactly what they should be doing.'

'What about the seed bank?' asked Martha. 'It did not seem like it was an easy thing to move. All that security and tech.'

It was Ash who replied this time.

'Bennett is a genius, but don't tell her I said it. When she first designed the seed bank, she made it modular so it could be safely broken down and transported. Each piece a closed circuit of its own, maintaining the environmental conditions the seeds need. It's like she knew it was never going to be a permanent fixture.'

'It's funny really, for someone so against technology, she's actually very technically minded,' agreed Max.

'Who's left then?' Zac was keen to know where they were with the evacuation.

'There's only a couple of teams left. We split up the medics, peacekeepers and techies and each group had a mixture of people. Plus, we staggered their departures, ensuring it wasn't too many people at once on the other end. So far, so good, we haven't had any major accidents and the weather has been on our side.' Max rubbed his hands together. 'There's just the people you brought and like I said, two, possibly three teams left here. The AIs are ready to move. We're good to go.' He looked at Ash to see if he had anything more to add.

'Yeah, we're all packed up. We made the decision to amalgamate the AIs together in an effort to combat the memory loss and retain some of their developed learning. Glover felt it was safer to do that and then make a backup copy as well. Worst-case scenario is they lose their memory of working here but their baseline function will remain. We can rebuild them into separate entities when we get to City 50 if we need to, or we can leave it as one.'

'Huh,' Dina looked sad. 'I never got to say goodbye to Layla.'

'What about you? Where is Artem?' asked Max.

'Artem… he's been working for New Corp,' said Zac.

'But he killed Sean! And now he's captaining a boat with everyone from City 42 and 9,' Dina broke in excitedly.

'He's what?' Max couldn't take it all in. 'Working for New Corp?'

Martha took over.

'Artem was sharing intelligence with everyone, us and New Corp. It is obviously how he made his money and got his hands on all those supplies. I mean, we all knew he had nefarious dealings, did we not?'

There were reluctant nods. Martha continued.

'We went to his complex first. He wanted to check the safe room, but no-one made it inside.' She looked down at the sleeping boy in her arms. 'We found Ruth and Sarah and we buried them.'

Silent tears fell down Dina's face; Max came and held her in comfort.

'Gaia came and grew a beautiful rose bush for them, in their honour.'

'You saw her?' Max asked.

'No, but the bush grew in front of our eyes, who else could it have been?' Martha had unshed tears in her eyes and took a moment to compose herself before she carried on.

'We were arrested when we arrived at City 42. They tried to take Lucas away, but Zac would not let them.' She smiled gratefully at him. 'That is when Sean revealed Artem had been working for them all along. And that is when we met with Gretchen, Jed's mother.'

'Is she in charge?' Max was intrigued.

'Yes. The leaders of New Corp left on a plane, leaving everyone else behind. To survive or not. I assume they did not come here?' Martha asked.

'No, they didn't make it anywhere.' Ash said with a smile. 'The plane got caught in bad weather and crashed. No survivors. The satellites showed a massive storm epicentre that came out of nowhere and focused on their exact location.'

'Gaia,' breathed Dina.

'Possibly,' agreed Ash. 'I know I should feel sad about the fact that people died but I can't help feeling satisfied that they all perished. After everything they were responsible for.'

'They ordered the destruction of Artem's compound,' added Martha.

'Is that why Artem killed Sean? Wasn't he your aide when you were governor?' asked Max. He was now perched on the arm of Dina's chair so they could be close.

'Oh, you should have seen him. He stretched out his arms and bam, the man was dead. He snapped his neck. Just like that.' Dina couldn't keep the awe out of her words.

Max shook his head and Ash looked shocked.

'Are we sure he's on our side now?' Ash asked.

'He and Gretchen are taking the citizens from 42 down to 9,

hoping to convince them to leave and come here on Artem's boat,' replied Zac.

'Artem has a boat?' asked Max.

'Of course he does,' said Martha with a chuckle and they all smiled at that.

'When will they be here? Should we wait for them before we leave?' Max was wondering how much longer they would be delayed.

'They said they would follow on in two days. I don't think we all need to wait for them. Maybe leave behind one final team to help them on their way. Hernandez and Yarrow could head it up. Is Yarrow still here?' Zac glanced around the room.

'Yeah, he was chivvying the last of the techies to pack up once and for all before they leave tomorrow. That's a good idea. They both know the base well and have the authority to marshal the citizens from the island up the mountain but...' Max ran his hand through his hair again. 'I don't have any spare supplies for them. We've packed everything up.'

'Do not worry,' replied Martha. 'Gretchen will make sure the people bring the essentials with them. We gave her the comms link for getting in touch here. We should hear from them tomorrow.'

Zac was nodding.

'I think we should wait for them to get in touch and then evac who we have here, apart from a team to guide the last arrivals up the mountain. Everyone agreed?'

There were nods and murmurs of assent all around.

'Okay. I'm headed to the mess hall to talk to the new arrivals. Max, Ash – come with me?'

Max stood reluctantly. He knew he ought to go with Zac, but he wanted to spend some time with Dina. She stood and entwined her fingers into his.

'Come on, then,' she said, leaning into him. She had no plans to let him out of her sight and if that meant going to a briefing then that's what she was doing.

Chapter Forty

'They're not coming? What, none of them?' Zac was sat in the comms room, speaking to Gretchen in City 9.

'The representatives of the city are adamant that until New Corp give the order, they are going to stay where they are,' she replied.

'Did you explain that you are effectively what's left of New Corp?'

'Of course I did. But they will not recognise my authority. Idiots.' Gretchen looked ruffled and did not have her usual composure. 'They've convinced some of the people from City 42 to also stay.' She sighed. 'We don't have time to do anything about it. We have to accept their decision and leave them behind.'

Zac nodded slowly. He didn't like it, but Gretchen was right.

'Okay, I'll let the others know. We're leaving today for City 50 but there will be a team here to receive you and whoever you bring with you. How's Artem?'

'He's fine, chomping at the bit to be off and away. I expect we will be sailing tonight. There is no point in waiting for people who don't want to come with us.' Gretchen's gaze softened. 'Don't blame yourself, Zachery. You did everything within your power to convince them to leave. Think about the people you were able to save.'

Zac nodded but he couldn't take much comfort in her words.

'We'll see you at 50 then,' he said.

'At 50. Take care.' And Gretchen signed off.

Zac sighed and pushed his chair away from the comms screen. All those people were going to die and there was nothing he could do about it. Slowly he stood up to go find the others and tell them the bad news.

'Idiots!' said Dina, echoing Gretchen's sentiment.

Martha was more resigned.

'We did everything we could. If they do not want to listen to the truth, then…' she shrugged. 'Are we still leaving today?'

'I see no reason to wait,' replied Zac. 'Are you all packed?'

'Yep, we're packed up and Ash has gone to get his sister. There's about twenty of us in total, the last few people from tech and some peacekeepers,' replied Max. 'Shall we meet at the north entrance in say, half an hour? I'll spread the word.'

'Sounds good,' said Zac and watched Dina and Max hurry off to tell the others. 'Can I help with anything?' He turned to Martha.

'No. We are pretty much sorted. Max made sure Frank held back some baby supplies for us and I have been able to restock everything. We are good to go.' She smiled at him. 'Do you fancy a synth-caf? If you are not needed elsewhere.'

'I'd love one.'

Zac held out his hand, and after a moment's hesitation, Martha took it and they smiled at each other as they ambled along the corridor to the mess hall, pushing Lucas along in front of them.

Chapter Forty-One

'When will they get here?' asked Kira. She was both excited at seeing her friends again and nervous that they hadn't arrived yet.

'Ash said they were on track to arrive early this afternoon so not long.' Jed smiled at his wife. It was good to see her getting excited about something. She'd really struggled with her grief over the loss of Ruth, Sarah and her parents, but she seemed to be coming out the other side. Her sunny nature was returning.

'And they all have somewhere assigned to live, haven't they?'

'You know they have, hon. You drilled Monique to make sure we all got houses together, remember?'

'I know but I want everything to be perfect for when they arrive.' Kira grinned at her husband. 'Can you feel it? Everything is going to be alright; I just know it.'

'Shall we go and wait down by the gates? Then we can see them arrive,' suggested Jed.

Opening the gates had been one of the first things the new arrivals had tackled. The remaining citizens of City 50 had been vehemently against it, frightened that they would be plagued with another deadly illness. It had taken several days of convincing before the council had finally agreed to open the gates, but they insisted that all new arrivals came through decontamination before entering the city proper.

There was a small garden inside the gates and the children pottered about on the grass, squealing with excitement at every leaf they found. Kira and Jed sat on the grass and watched the empty path in front of them. They didn't have to wait long.

'Kira!' It was Dina, grinning like mad. 'Jed! It's so great to see you guys. We've made it!' She hugged them both then bent down to say hi to Grace and Peter.

Max was next, heading up the caravan of people and supplies.

'Hi guys, where do you want us?'

More people had come out of City 50 and were helping to unload the supplies.

'Everyone needs to go through decontamination then Monique will gather everyone's name and speciality, then we can get you settled in,' explained Jed.

'Sounds easy enough,' commented Max.

'We've had plenty of practice,' laughed Kira. 'Are you the last group? Where's Martha and Lucas? And Zac?'

'They're bringing up the rear,' said Dina. She bent closer to Kira. 'I think they've finally got together.'

The two women grinned at each other and started gossiping about the budding relationship as they walked towards the decontamination entrance.

'Are you coming through?' Max asked Jed.

'No, we've been done. I think Kira wants to wait for Martha, so we'll hang on.'

'Have you heard from your mother?'

Jed smiled.

'She, my father and Artem landed yesterday with everyone they could convince to come. She's not wasting any time and they're starting the journey up today. It won't take them long. Between her and Artem, I don't think anyone else gets a say.'

Max laughed.

'You're probably right.' He clapped a hand on Jed's shoulder. 'See you on the other side.'

Kira came back to Jed and held his hand.

'We're all going to be together again soon,' she said.

'Yep. Shouldn't be long.' Jed looked out at more new people arriving then pointed. 'Isn't that them?'

Kira squinted and then squeezed her husband's hand in excitement. She waved wildly and it wasn't long before Martha and Zac noticed her and waved back.

'You made it!' gushed Kira, giving Martha a hug.

'Yes, we are here.' She looked tired but happy.

'How has the agreement with City 50 been?' asked Zac, wasting no time with pleasantries.

'It's been fine. They seem thrilled to have us and of course the seed back and AIs were a big sell for them.' Jed looked round at the milling people. 'Between all of us, we have everything we need to not just survive but to build a future.'

'That is good to hear,' said Martha. 'Why is everyone queuing?'

'Oh, that's the decontamination. It doesn't take long, but they won't let you in without it. And I can't blame them, they've suffered a massive loss,' explained Kira. 'We'll wait with you.' And she linked arms with Martha as they walked over to the moving line.

'You heard about what happened with Artem?' Zac asked Jed as they waited.

'Sounds like he came down firmly on our side in the end.'

'Yeah, I guess. Where's Archer?' Zac asked.

'She's on the inside, marshalling the new arrivals and getting them settled in the right quadrants in the city. Ash has been working with Monique, City 50's admin clerk, to work out assignments based on individual strengths and the housing has been mixed up so there's no divide between old and new citizens.'

'Sounds like you have it all under control.' Zac was impressed.

'Hmm.'

'Something wrong?'

'We have no real governance in place. The council wants to wait until Mother arrives before they will consider forming a proper government. They seem to think she speaks with the authority of New Corp.' Jed glanced at Zac. 'What do you think?'

'New Corp is gone. But she is probably the highest ranking official from the organisation. So, it makes sense that they'd want to wait for her, but I wouldn't worry. I doubt she's going to suggest we reform. Coming here to City 50 is all about a new beginning.'

'I hope you're right.'

The queue had almost ended.

'I'll see you in there,' said Jed and he waved goodbye at Zac, Martha and Lucas before herding Kira and his kids back into the city.

Once everyone was through decontamination it was time for a reunion. Ash, Glover, Archer, Simmonds and Kolwowsky joined Kira and Jed in officially welcoming Dina, Max, Martha, and Zac to City 50.

They all met in Kira and Jed's assigned house. The children were put to bed in their shared cube, glad to be reunited. Ash produced a bottle of vodka to cheers from the others and he poured out the shots.

'Where's Bennett?' asked Max, looking around.

'She's grilling Moham and the others from Camp Eden. She was really excited to see their research and samples. We can catch up with them tomorrow.' Ash handed Max a shot and made sure everyone else had one. 'To our future,' he toasted.

'To our future!'

After the shots were downed, no-one really knew what to say next.

'What happens now?' asked Martha, breaking the silence.

'We wait for Gretchen, Artem and the others to arrive and then the council have called a meeting to figure out how to move forward,' said Jed.

'And when will they be here?'

'Day after tomorrow.'

'Which means,' interrupted Kira, 'that you can all explore City 50 tomorrow and get a feel for the place. I think you're going to like it.' Her smile was infectious.

Ash went around with the vodka again.

'To City 50!' he proposed, and the others echoed his toast loudly.

'It feels almost too good to be true,' said Martha quietly, her mood sombre. 'We have been through so much, lost so much. It is difficult to imagine we have actually got to the end. Or the beginning, if you know what I mean.'

'I do.' Kira gave her friend a hug. 'This is the beginning of good things.' She held out her glass to Ash for another shot. 'To new beginnings!'

'To new beginnings!'

Chapter Forty-Two

'Come on, we don't want to be late,' called Jed as Kira rushed around trying to sort out the children before they left for the council meeting.

'I know, I know, but I want to make sure they have something to eat. I don't know how long this meeting is going to go on for. Here, shove that in the bag. I'm ready.' She handed him a packet of snacks then scooped up first Grace then Peter and put them in the stroller.

They hurried out of their house, across the square to the council building and quickly went in. They had to wait at the security desk as their identities were cross-checked and they were finally given permission to go through.

'Which meeting room is it?' asked Kira.

'The largest one, at the end of the corridor. Come on.'

As they arrived, Jed pushed the door open for Kira and she went through to be met with a room full of people. They all turned to stare at her arrival making her blush and falter.

'Good, good, you're here. We can start. Take your seats everyone,' said Richard, the City 50 council member.

Kira took a seat next to Martha so the children could play quietly in the corner. Jed, Zac, Dina and Max joined them with Archer, Bennett and Glover sitting on the other side of the table next to Gretchen and Artem. Olive and Liss were there as well as Dr Lee from City 42 and of course, Monique.

Richard stayed standing and coughed to get everyone's attention.

'Thank you all for coming. It's been a funny few days, what with the new arrivals and our city back to full capacity. Exciting times ahead I'm sure, but what you've all been called to today is a breakdown of how city rule will happen in the future. I'm sure I don't need to remind you all that without law and order, a city cannot function, there needs to be someone in charge. I suggest that we learn from the lessons of those who came before us and vote in a governing council. One that will have the best interests of the city at its heart.' He gestured to Monique, who was sat next to him. 'Monique has, as you know, been classifying all the new arrivals according to their strengths and abilities so that we can assign individuals to roles where they will be useful members of society, and with some careful guidance at our end, I feel sure that each and every person can be moulded into the perfect citizen. Now, before you came and before we were incapacitated by the 'flu, New Corp had provided neural implants designed to keep citizens compliant and aggression free. I see no reason why we cannot continue that agenda and roll out those devices. There are lots of new people, it is naïve to think there would be no friction.' He paused for breath but before he could continue, Kira stood up.

'No. This is all wrong. Don't you see?' She looked imploringly around the table. 'This is not how we are meant to live. Neural implants to keep citizens compliant? Carrying out New Corp's agenda when there isn't even any New Corp left? It's insane. We already know those mistakes. It's time to move on. We need to permanently open the gates, break down our barriers and live with nature, not against it. It's the only way we can survive.'

'But it's not safe out there,' protested Olive.

'It's not safe anywhere! If you lock us up in this city, we'll diminish and die off. What about the cities we couldn't get in touch with? What if there are more survivors out there?' Kira glanced at Jed who gave her a nod of encouragement and she carried on. 'There's a whole world out there and we've been guided to this place of safety to live through the environmental crisis because the planet still needs us, she still wants us to be a part of her world. We need to honour her, not shut her out.'

Richard threw his hands up in the air.

'What exactly should we do then?'

'Keep an open mind. Don't shut yourself away from the world or the wonders of nature that lie behind these gates. We can learn from our mistakes; I know we can.'

There was a long silence as no-one said anything. Eventually Gretchen cleared her throat and spoke.

'I agree with Kira. For too long we have hidden behind our walls. Corporation, New Corp, whatever you want to call it, no longer exists.

For the first time in a long time, we are free citizens. I vote no to the implants. If you agree, raise your hand.'

Everyone apart from Richard lifted their hand, and when he realised he was the only one who hadn't, he grew flustered.

'It's not that I don't agree with you, we just need to be able to, I don't know, control the population somehow. We can't have lawlessness and a free for all. You must see that.' He sat down and crossed his arms.

'We won't.' This time it was Zac who spoke. He gestured around the room. 'You have a wealth of experience right here in this room, plus all the different knowledge from all the citizens out there in the city. Now is not the time to silence them.' He stood up and pointed at Martha, then Gretchen. 'You have two previous city governors, right here. Artem, Jed, Archer and I have experience in safeguarding populations, we have military training, ideal to run a peacekeeping operation. You have Dr Bennett and Dr Carter, experts in their fields of botany, plus a team of scientists dedicated to improving plant yield and of course the seed bank.' He kept walking around the table. 'You have Ash, Dr Glover and her team of technicians, all constantly working on new tech and the AIs are here to help improve everyone's lives. This is Dr Lee, former head of Medical in City 42 – he can ensure the health and well-being of all our citizens are looked after.' He came back round to Kira's chair and put his hands on the back of it. 'Lastly, and most importantly, we have the wealth and experience of mothers, of all the people who've risked everything to get here, to this point. Let's draw on all of those things and build a better future.'

'We have to be honest with each other. We have to learn how to live with our planet in harmony and look after everyone to the best of our ability.' Kira surveyed the room. 'I know we can do it.'

There were faint murmurs of agreements and a few nods as the people in the room looked around at each other and realised that they were the architects of their future.

Kira's attention was distracted by a small movement in the window. As she glanced over, she saw the faintest outline of a blue goddess smiling through at them all. Kira beamed back. Her confidence full she turned her focus back to the meeting and organising the new council of survivors.

~The End~

Thank You

Thank you so much for reading The Gaia Collection, I hope you enjoyed the hopeful dystopian trilogy and will consider leaving me a review.

I'd like to say thank you to my Pen to Print mentor and friend Ian Ayris and to my dedicated readers/editors Donna Tyrell, Ashvin Mathoora, Taron Wade, CH Clepitt, Hannah Bligh, Debbie McGowan, Amy Leibowitz Mitchell, Simon Leonard and Martin Frowd for all their support and encouragement throughout this process.

I'd also like to thank Lena Smith, Lisa Rouiller and the team at Pen to Print and the Barking & Dagenham Library Service for all their hard work in making this series a possibility.

I couldn't write without my fabulous husband, Kevin, so a huge thank you to him. He listens to all my mad ideas, is always the first to read the manuscript and helps me figure out the tricky parts. And big hugs to my incredibly patient children, Leo (6) and Anabelle (2) who don't really understand why but let Mummy do her 'work' on the laptop while they play lego.

Finally, I have to thank the brilliant Ian Bristow for creating another superb book cover for me.

About the Author

Claire Buss is a multi-genre author and poet based in the UK. She wanted to be Lois Lane when she grew up but work experience at her local paper was eye-opening. Instead, Claire went on to work in a variety of admin roles for over a decade but never felt quite at home. An avid reader, baker and Pinterest addict Claire won second place in the Barking and Dagenham Pen to Print writing competition in 2015 with her debut novel, The Gaia Effect, setting her writing career in motion. She continues to write passionately and is hopelessly addicted to cake.

Sign up to Claire's newsletter for exclusive content and all the latest writing news: http://eepurl.com/c93M2L

Follow Claire on Twitter: @grasshopper2407
Like Claire on Facebook: facebook.com/busswriter
Visit her website: www.cbvisions.weebly.com

www.ingramcontent.com/pod-product-compliance
Lightning Source LLC
Chambersburg PA
CBHW020532310726
48979CB00014B/2306/J